Also available

The Mammoth Book of Arthurian Legends
The Mammoth Book of Awesome Comic Fantasy
The Mammoth Book of Battles
The Mammoth Book of Best New Erotica
The Mammoth Book of Best New Horror 2000
The Mammoth Book of Best New Science Fiction 14
The Mammoth Book of Bridge
The Mammoth Book of British Kings & Queens
The Mammoth Book of Cats
The Mammoth Book of Chess
The Mammoth Book of Comic Fantasy
The Mammoth Book of Dogs
The Mammoth Book of Endurance and Adventure
The Mammoth Book of Erotica (New Edition)
The Mammoth Book of Erotic Photography
The Mammoth Book of Fantasy
The Mammoth Book of Gay Erotica
The Mammoth Book of Great Detective Stories
The Mammoth Book of Gay Short Stories
The Mammoth Book of Haunted House Stories
The Mammoth Book of Hearts of Oak
The Mammoth Book of Historical Erotica
The Mammoth Book of Historical Whodunnits
The Mammoth Book of How It Happened
The Mammoth Book of How It Happened in Britain
The Mammoth Book of International Erotica
The Mammoth Book of Jack the Ripper
The Mammoth Book of Jokes
The Mammoth Book of Legal Thrillers
The Mammoth Book of Lesbian Erotica
The Mammoth Book of Lesbian Short Stories
The Mammoth Book of Life Before the Mast
The Mammoth Book of Locked-Room Mysteries and Impossible Crimes
The Mammoth Book of Men O'War
The Mammoth Book of Murder
The Mammoth Book of Murder and Science
The Mammoth Book of New Erotica
The Mammoth Book of New Sherlock Holmes Adventures
The Mammoth Book of Private Lives
The Mammoth Book of Pulp Action
The Mammoth Book of Puzzles
The Mammoth Book of SAS & Elite Forces
The Mammoth Book of Seriously Comic Fantasy
The Mammoth Book of Sex, Drugs & Rock 'n' Roll
The Mammoth Book of Short Erotic Novels
The Mammoth Book of Soldiers at War
The Mammoth Book of Sword & Honour
The Mammoth Book of the Edge
The Mammoth Book of The West
The Mammoth Book of True Crime (New Edition)
The Mammoth Book of True War Stories
The Mammoth Book of UFOs
The Mammoth Book of Unsolved Crimes
The Mammoth Book of Vampire Stories by Women
The Mammoth Book of War Correspondents
The Mammoth Book of Women Who Kill
The Mammoth Book of the World's Greatest Chess Games
The Mammoth Encyclopedia of Science Fiction
The Mammoth Encyclopedia of Unsolved Mysteries

The Mammoth Book of
Comic Crime

Edited by Maxim Jakubowski

CARROLL & GRAF PUBLISHERS
New York

Carroll & Graf Publishers
An imprint of Avalon Publishing Group, Inc.
161 William Street
New York
NY 10038 2607
www.carrollandgraf.com

First published in the UK by Robinson,
an imprint of Constable & Robinson Ltd, 2002

First Carroll & Graf edition 2002

Collection and edited material
copyright © 2002 Maxim Jakubowski

ISBN 0–7867–1002–0

Printed and bound in the EU

Library of Congress Cataloging-in-Publication Data
is available on file.

CONTENTS

ACKNOWLEDGMENTS

2001 by Peter Guttridge. First appeared in SHERLOCK MAGA-ZINE. Reprinted by permission of the author. SMELTDOWN by Mike Ripley, © 1990 by Mike Ripley. First appeared in A SUIT OF DIAMONDS. Reprinted by permission of the author. TAKING CARE OF FRANK by Antony Mann, © 1999 by Antony Mann. First appeared in CRIME WAVE. Reprinted by permission of the author. AND THE BUTTOCKS GLEAMED BY NIGHT by Mat Coward, © 2002 by Mat Coward. Printed by permission of the author. THE LAST SNOW-FLAKE IN TEXAS by Liz Evans, © 2002 by Liz Evans. Printed by permission of the author. A SORT OF MISS MARPLE? by H R F Keating, © 1994 by H R F Keating. First appeared in ROYAL CRIMES, edited by Maxim Jakubowski & Martin H Greenberg. Reprinted by permission of the author and his agents Peters, Fraser & Dunlop. THE STORY-BAG by Philip Gooden, © 1997 by Philip Gooden. First appeared in JELLYFISH CUPFUL. Reprinted by permission of the author. SLAUGHTER IN THE STRAND by Keith Miles, © 2002 by Keith Miles. Printed by permission of the author. THE CHICKEN by Jürgen Ehlers, © 1995 by Jürgen Ehlers. First appeared as "Das Huhn" in DER MORDER KOMMT AUF SANFTEN PFOTEN. Reprinted by permission of the author. THE POSTMAN ONLY RINGS WHEN HE CAN BE BOTHERED by Peter Guttridge, © 1999 by Peter Guttridge. First appeared in FRESH BLOOD 3, edited by Mike Ripley & Maxim Jakubowski. Reprinted by permission of the author. FATHER BROWN IN MUNCIE, INDIANA by Ruth Dudley Edwards, © 2000 by Ruth Dudley Edwards. First appeared in THE OXFORD BOOK OF DETECTIVE STORIES edited by Patricia Craig. Reprinted by permission of the author. TICKLED TO DEATH by Simon Brett, © 1982 by Simon Brett. First appeared in WINTER'S CRIMES 14, edited by Hilary Hale. Reprinted by permission of the author and his agent, Michael Motley. THE DETTWEILER SOLUTION by Lawrence Block, © 1975 by Lawrence Block. First appeared in ALFRED HITCH-COCK'S MYSTERY MAGAZINE. Reprinted by permission of the author. BIG SURVIVOR by Peter T Garratt, © 2002 by Peter T Garratt. Printed by permission of the author. DR BUD, CA by Michael Z Lewin, © 1994 by Michael Z Lewin. First appeared in CRIME YELLOW, edited by Maxim Jakubowski. Reprinted by permission of the author. FRIDAY NIGHT by Graeme Gordon, ©

1996 by Graeme Gordon. First appeared in FRESH BLOOD, edited by Mike Ripley & Maxim Jakubowski. Printed by permission of the author. MALICE IN BLUNDERLAND by Kevin Goldstein-Jackson, © 1977 by Kevin Goldstein-Jackson. First appeared in ELLERY QUEEN'S MYSTERY MAGAZINE. Reprinted by permission of the author. DRIVING FORCES by Carol Anne Davis, © 2000 by Carol Anne Davis. First appeared in SHOTS. Reprinted by permission of the author. HOPPER AND PINK by Barry Fantoni, © 1989 by Barry Fantoni. First appeared in NEW CRIMES, edited by Maxim Jakubowski. Reprinted by permission of the author. WHERE DO YOU FIND YOUR IDEAS? by Martin Edwards, © 1996 by Martin Edwards. First appeared in CRIME WRITERS' ASSOCIATION ANTHOLOGY. Reprinted by permission of the author. DEATH BY A THOUSAND CUTS by Rebecca Tope, © 2002 by Rebecca Tope. Printed by permission of the author. THE TROUBLE AND STRIFE by Catherine Aird, © 2002 by Catherine Aird. Printed by permission of the author. BROTHERLY LOVE by Mike Ripley, © 1994 by Mike Ripley. First appeared in ROYAL CRIMES, edited by Maxim Jakubowski & Martin H Greenberg. Reprinted by permission of the author. AN ACQUAINTANCE WITH MR COLLINS by Sarah Caudwell, © 1990 by Estate of Sarah Caudwell. First appeared in A SUIT OF DIAMONDS. Reprinted by permission of the Karpfinger Literary Agency. COME AGAIN? by Donald E Westlake, © 2001 by Donald E Westlake. First appeared in THE MYSTERIOUS PRESS ANNIVERSARY ANTHOLOGY. Reprinted by permission of the author. CRY WOLF by Hilary Bonner, © 2001 by Hilary Bonner. First appeared in SUNDAY EXPRESS MAGAZINE. Reprinted by permission of the author. "IT'S CLEVER, BUT IS IT ART?" by M J Trow, © 1989 by M J Trow. First appeared in NEW CRIMES, edited by Maxim Jakubowski. Reprinted by permission of the author. ONE FOR THE MONET by David Stuart Davies, © 2002 by David Stuart Davies. Printed by permission of the author. WHO KILLED PYRAMUS? by Amy Myers, © 2002 by Amy Myers. Printed by permission of the author. THE HAMPSTEAD VEGETABLE HEIST by Mat Coward, © 1994 by Mat Coward. First appeared in THIRD CULPRIT edited by Liza Cody, Michael Z Lewin & Peter Lovesey. Reprinted by permission of the author. THE ELEVENTH LABOUR by David Wishart, © 2002 by David Wishart.

INTRODUCTION

The killing bone and the funny bone have been an integral part of human nature from time immemorial.

Granted, they prove uncomfortable neighbours in the best of situations, but writers have always enjoyed a challenge and those we have selected in this bumper anthology have come up trumps.

Comic crime has long been a tradition of the crime and mystery field with authors from all times and origins attempting the balancing act of making evil and transgression somehow humorous, if not harmless. From the cipher- and cartoon-like characters of the game of Cluedo to the often grotesque figures of over-the-top evil in, say, the caper novels of Carl Hiaasen, Christopher Brookmyre or Donald E Westlake, or the bumbling and often involuntary detectives of the novels of Simon Brett, Mike Ripley and many others as well as the tongue-in-cheek heroines and acolytes of the adventures of Elizabeth Peters, Sarah Caudwell, Lawrence Block's Bernie Rhodenbarr series and countless other masters and mistresses of the genre, a modicum of laughter and wit has always proven a salutary release valve for the scares and horrors of criminality.

Television and newspapers daily reveal tales of burglaries or heists gone badly wrong, if only by reasons of fate or coincidence, or more likely bad planning or sheer ineptitude, and crime and mystery fiction is heavily populated by figures of fun, sidekicks who never get anything right and whose only function is to act as a foil for the valiant sleuth and hero. Just like life really!

So, even if your initial thought when you came across the title of this collection was to ponder about the uneasy relationship between crime and comedy, and you wondered about the morality of bedding both subjects under the same cover, I urge you to keep an open mind and enjoy the ironies, the belly laughs, the subtle satire and the sheer sense of fun many of these stories convey. You'll never think of crime-that-goes-wrong in the same way again!

Putting together a barrel of laughs of this kind has been a righteous, if guilty pleasure, and I must thank all the authors who contributed stories or penned new ones and recommended tales which I was blissfully ignorant of. So, an additional smile for Mike Ripley, Ed Gorman, Basil Copper, Jürgen Ehlers along the way, and a grimace for anyone I might have forgotten, as we all know how much laughter cleanses the memory cells!

Maxim Jakubowski

MY MOTHER WAS A BANK ROBBER

NICHOLAS BLINCOE

I

She knelt on the pavement outside the Spar Superstore on Finchley Road, struggling with the hood-catch of my old push-chair. Mum was twenty-two then; a young mother with her hands full, trying to unpack a child and a box of groceries into the back of her Cortina estate. The engine was running, the car was nose-out towards the oncoming traffic. When two armed men came running out of the bank, she jumped for the car and ditched every-thing else: the box, the baby, the pram. The men dived in the open back, scrabbling to hold the door closed as she swerved across the traffic. The car's rear-end swiped my pushchair as she hauled to the left. The eyewitness said she was heading north towards the A1. They were no more help: too concerned looking for the remains of the baby she'd hit as she zoomed away. The pram was empty. I was at home with my Grandma.

They dumped the Cortina in a side-street off Child's Hill. Mum had another car waiting for them there, a Morris Minor. They looped back to town at a crawl, through Hampstead and down into Chalk Farm. That weekend, one of the men started mouthing-off in a pub but it was another five weeks before the police caught Mum. A photograph taken outside the Old Bailey shows a blond woman in a thigh-high dress, smiling towards the camera. The same photo appeared in most of the papers, especially the Sundays. It was only two years since the film *Bonnie and Clyde* so everyone was hyped for her story. When I was older, I read the clippings and found out the rest. I've played the scene-of-the-crime reconstructions through in my head. I didn't need to be there.

My memory kicks in around 1970, soon after Mum was sent to Holloway. She got three years, I was eighteen months old. Back then, Holloway was red-brick and solid Victorian. When I visited I'd come on the overland from Willesden, badly slowed by my Gran. Mum would be waiting in the big hall. The room was unbelievably noisy. The whole of the prison stank of shit and cabbage. Most people grow to hate that smell but I never have. From the stone floors to the high ceiling, the place rang with laughter. It's the only way I can remember it, each week in seamless continuity so I don't know if I'm remembering her first day or another day. She always looked the same: her hair scraped back, no make-up, skinny, big-eyed, smiling, hands in front of her on the table.

She lifted a hand and waved with her fingers as I came charging down the steps. I was on a pure high, bouncing through the hall like a space-hopper in my one-piece padded baby suit.

Mum stayed in her chair throughout, keeping watch as I ran around. I was out of control, tripping over chairs and running like crazy. A friend of Mum's caught me and started tickling through the quilted material. I was screaming with laughter and kicking my legs around. From the far side of the room, I heard my Mum shout, "Have you got him, Jo?"

"Yeah."

"Then spank his arse and send him back."

I was laughing, screaming *No No No* as Aunty Jo turned me upside down. She started chanting "Who's a naughty boy, then?", scoring alternate syllables with a fat slap on my padded bottom. Three spanks and I was turned upright, totally hysterical with the giggles. Aunty Jo ruffled through my hair and wet-kissed my forehead. She shouted, "He's a good kid really. Can I keep him?"

My Mum said, "Sure. You keep him, Jo."

But no one would let her. There was always someone else ready to grab for me. The second my feet touched the stone, I was off again, straight into another pair of arms. That's how it was. Aunty Jo, Aunty Maureen, Aunty Frankie and the rest, they couldn't get enough of me. They were my friends, families, neighbours. I grew up knowing their names and their stories, just like I knew the stories of the lezzas who guarded the doors.

I spent my childhood wondering what a boy had to do to get sent to a woman's prison. It was years before I realised I wasn't seeing the whole picture; like maybe the girls didn't spend every second of the day laughing their heads off.

Something my Mother said brought it home. She told me, watching me grow up was like playing with a flicker book. She flipped the corners of the pages and my picture changed. Except she did it so slowly, one page a week, she always lost track. The way her voice cracked, it tore me up. I even remember when she said it: Cookham Wood, June 1987, when she was eight years into her twenty for armed robbery and grievous assault.

But she had it wrong. She imagined I had another life in the pauses between my visits. I didn't. I was eighteen and the whole of my life could be boiled down to one long, fixed shot of an endless visiting hour. The shot established my Mum was in prison but told me nothing else because nothing ever happened when I was in the frame. For the bigger picture, I relied on Women's Prison films.

The titles are the giveaway: *Woman Hunt*, *Women in Chains*, *Women Without Names*, *Women Without Men*, *House of Women*, *Love in A Women's Prison*, *Prison Without Bars*, *Bare Behind Bars*, *Girl Behind Bars*. I bought anything with "Girl" in the title: *Jailhouse Girls* and *Delinquent Schoolgirls* were obvious selections, *Girl On Approval* and *A Nice Girl Like Me* were lucky finds. But films like *So Evil So Young* or *Sunday Daughters* came down to pure intuition. I swear I could smell the prison, the shit, the cabbage and the hot cat-fights.

II

Mum began hitting banks again the day her first stretch ended. Her new partners were called Charlie Warren and Derek Pease but she tagged them the Karamazovs. Charlie was the driver, Mum had graduated to shotgun. She would walk into the bank ahead of Derek, dressed in kitchen sink drag and a waterproof headscarf. She needed to cover up if she was going to play the part of a hopeless old cow, waiting in line with two heavy bags. When Derek came charging through the doors, waving his shotgun and shouting like a loony, everyone would freeze. They never noticed Mum haul out her sawn-off. She would hammer on the nearest cash window, one time only, hard enough to shake the glass. It rarely broke but sounded so loud everyone was sure a shot had been fired. By the time the counter-girls caught their breath, they were looking down the barrel of her gun.

In seventy-seven jobs, Mum only ever had to shoot two people. In total, she shot a few more before she was caught but her tactics were psychologically sound. When adrenaline kicks in, the only buttons are fight and flight. There is no middle route, it's not a multiple choice scenario. Once the bystanders copped Mad Derek, it was down to the law of averages: half would swing one way, the rest would swing the other. But the shock of seeing Mum brandishing a double-ought sent them all into paralysis. They'd know, whichever way they'd swung, they were cooked. Mum bagged the swag and sailed out of their lives. Derek held the rear, following her to the pavement where Charlie was waiting in the Karamazov sledge. Then off they'd go, sleigh-bells jingling in the snow. It was her life, until it all went wrong at a road block, three hundred yards the wrong side of a job in Hornsey.

They were dragged out of the car by armed cops and driven in chains and gaffa-tape to police central. Charlie cracked after three seconds' hard questioning. The trial was a wash-out. The only drama happened outside court when Derek Pease slipped custody. He was free for six months. The papers said he was caught climbing aboard a Russian boat in Ipswich. When Mum read it, she said her Karamazov gag must have stoked his taste for romance. Maybe it had, but her jokes went down less well with the judge.

She went back to Holloway in 1979, sentenced to twenty years modelling prison pinnies and share-wear lingerie. The black eye and broken nose she got in her first month completed the full ensemble.

The sight of her there, her face half-beaten and swollen, sent my Grandma into a freak. Her twitching hand grazed my shoulder, as though she hoped she could brush me away and ask the serious questions mother-to-daughter. She wished I'd start running like I used to when Mum was last inside. I didn't move. I fixed on the bruising and I stared. I was ten years old and nothing like the same skittering satellite of energy and emotion I was as a toddler. There was a buzz about the place and I was tuned to it. I knew that no one, least of all Mum, cared about the black eye.

Over the months even Gran gave up waiting for an explanation. By the time the bruises disappeared, Gran had accumulated a whole stack of new questions and an hour a week is not enough time for an openly Oprah exchange. Mum was fine. She was still joking and still shouting to her friends. I had a new set of Aunties, just as good as the first. My Aunty Jackie would always go on about how pale I was, didn't I ever go out? Aunty Ruth would ask what I'd been doing, hitting puberty a bit too hard? Jackie and Ruth were both toms, but Aunty Ben was more innocent. She was a Nigerian lady who got twelve years after she was caught at Heathrow with a wodge of smack up her privates.

I remember Aunty Ben asking me what I did all week. I told her I'd been watching the telly.

She said, "What do you like, love?"

My favourite programme was *Within These Walls*. She'd never heard of it but it got a big laugh off everyone else. We were still laughing when the cripple came hobbling down the steps into the visiting hall.

The room went quiet for a second, then erupted into a sneer. There is no other way of putting it. The cripple kept her eyes on the floor and carried on limping to her chair.

The moment I saw her, everything clicked. She used to sit at the far end of the hall, outside the circle of my Mum and her friends, among her own people. She'd been a kind of off-screen presence, a heavy-duty shadow that I knew to avoid. And despite only having a dark image of her, I knew she had never limped. Now, her left leg was three inches shorter than the other and she needed two sticks to get around on her own.

I said, "What's up with her?"

Mum said, "She's been up the infirmary."

"What happened? She done her leg?"

"Just the one, but she shattered every bone. The only way that slag's ever going to get back on top is to sleep her way there."

That's how my Mum came to be a boss. From then on, she ran every wing she was ever put in. It made things easier, especially for Gran. She continued to ship in chunks of dope and bags of pills but the amounts became larger and she no longer had to worry about being discreet. At the end of the visiting hour, a rough lezza called Winifred would hand my Gran a wad of money, minus twenty per cent. My Mother always gave the screws their cut directly, it made for good working relations.

III

The Seventies began and ended in prison, that's the frame for my decade, my Mother's Holloway Sandwich Trick. In the middle years, the Karamazov boys saw more of her than I did. She was too busy chasing money with a smoking sawn-off to topple into domesticity. I lived with Gran and shaped my weeks round the Sunday episodes of *Within These Walls*. When Mum went down for the second time, I took it well. I pictured her as the star of her own long-running show, another weekly serial for me to look forward to. My appetite for prison drama was getting more intense. Now, it's out of control.

This is my Top Ten:

1. *Yield To The Night* (Diana Dors playing Ruth Ellis)
2. *The Weak And The Wicked* (Dors again, re-teamed with the same director, J Lee-Thompson)
3. *Caged Heat* (*Charlie's Angels* on amphetamines)
4. *Jackson County Jail* (Redneck rape classic)
=5. *Bare Behind Bars* (Hi-speed Spic flick with all the ingredients: cat-fight, fire-hoses, naked-in-solitary)

=5. *Second Chance* (Catherine Deneuve as crazed jail nymph slut)
7. *And God Created Woman* (Not that good actually, but Rebecca de Mornay strips)
8. *High Heels* (Would have been a Top Three if the prison sequence wasn't so short)
9. *Dyke Island* (Hell-cats in knotted blouses, spoilt by poor production values)
10. *Human Experiments* (Another redneck pic, not to be confused with the *SS Experiment Camp* series)

It's amazing how often the same type recurs, the particular Blonde. Outside of films, prison life soon washes the blonde away. Mum was a semi-natural who kept the colour cold and bright with regular tint jobs and a string of personal stylists. Women's prisons are packed with trainee hairdressers. Any one of them would scratch out an eye for the chance to work on Mum's roots. Though after she transferred to Cookham Wood, scratching wouldn't have done them any good. Mum found her soul mate out there.

Aunty Jess was twenty-one when they met. She was an ex-tom from up Bradford way who turned round and killed a punter. No one ever found out why she'd done it, least of all the jury at her trial. She'd been through rapes and beatings but there was no evidence the guy she choked was a psycho. I guess he was just in the wrong place at the wrong time. Aunty Jess was dumb enough to use his credit cards and the prosecution argued her only motive was robbery. She was sixteen when she was given life. All long-term and lifers eventually end up in Cookham Wood so it was a cert that her and Mum would meet, but that doesn't mean it wasn't also fate.

Mum was transferred from Holloway in '80. She was lucky, there. The old prison was being refurbished so a quarter of Holloway went with her. She swept into Cookham Wood with a ready-built reputation and could have had any woman she wanted. But Aunty Jess meant more to her than a tint and a squeeze. They were inseparable for the six years they were together.

Mum's hair turned straw-dirty in the summer of '87, soon

after Aunty Jess got out on licence. This was the same year Mum told me how much she regretted the time we spent apart. I didn't want to hear her talk like that. Like some stranded old slag, hauled into life by weekly visits and a drip-feed of sentiment. I couldn't stomach the sentimentality and, really, I never believed her. She was a hopeless junkie by then, wrapped in self-pity and ready to say anything. It was even worse after Gran had a stroke because I was the one who brought Mum the drugs. I would have stopped if I could but it was a business so I had no choice.

With Aunty Jess on the outside, Mum started taking as much smack as she was dealing. It was a real touch-and-go scene for more than a year. Mum could never have dried out on her own but the long pleading letters Aunty Jess wrote did more harm than good. In the end, it was the Aunties inside who pulled her through. I owe them all but especially Aunty Myra. She never left Mum's side through the worst of her withdrawal.

I was scared to tell Gran just how much we owed Aunty Myra. I thought the news would kill her. Gran had been down on her from the moment she saw her in Cookham Wood. I remember asking why she was so freaked. She had said, "You just keep away from her. Myra's done really nasty things to little kids."

It didn't worry me then. I'd done plenty of nasty things to little kids, that's what I did at school. By 1987 I knew more about it but I still say Aunt Myra is okay. She did a lot for Mum and anyone who's ever been around Cookham Wood will say the same. I don't know what Gran says, I never understood a word she said since the stroke.

IV

Gran doesn't come up to Cookham Wood at all any more. It's a haul for her, all the way to Rochester, even with me doing the driving. Aunty Jess has moved to Walthamstow now, which is handy. I pick her up at her flat and we go see Mum together. We keep the conversation light, I talk about films and she promises to re-do my roots.

Mum's in her mid-forties. Considering where she is, she

doesn't look bad. She still won't wear make-up, even founda-
tion, so her skin's a weird colour but everything else is as sharp
and bright as it ever was. The first thing she says is, How's your
Gran? I tell her the home news and the conversation trips on.

"Are you looking after her?"

"Course I am. I left her a ton inside the gonk on the mantelpiece and there's a bloke coming round later to wheel her round
the shops."

"Where's she going this week?"

"I don't know. Whiteleys I think. The cinema's showing a
reissue of *The Sound Of Music* and she always liked that."

Mum said, "Have you got anything for me?"

I picked up a re-issue of *Scrubbers* the other week but didn't
get around to copying it. I gave Mum a video of *Shock Corridor*
instead. It's set in a nut farm, not a prison, but it's a good laugh
and she's not as bothered about prison flicks as me. I thought
she'd go for the scene in the nympho ward and gave it ten
minutes worth of scholarly introduction before I left her and
Aunty Jess alone to catch up.

I spent maybe twenty minutes with Aunty Myra. When I got
back, Mum had last Sunday's copy of *The People* spread out on
the table in front of her. She was biting it back as she said, "You
didn't tell me about Derek and Charlie."

I gave Aunty Jess a look but she only shrugged. I said, "Yeah,
well, it's only just got in the papers. I was chewing it over before
I said anything."

I was lying. The story hit the papers a month back. It started
out as a page three filler. When it reached the centre spread, it
was decked out with fuzzy surveillance pictures and an artist's
impressions of the robbers. Mum had read the whole thing.

She said, "It's them. Who else is it going to be? It's the exact
same style and everything."

I said, "It's not both of them. Charlie Warren's got asbestosis.
He's bought himself a council house and retired to Leeds."

"Then it's Derek. He's out."

I said, "Do you know how long Derek Pease got?"

She shook her head, "He was on the run so he didn't go to
trial until after I was sent down. After a stunt like that, I
assumed he'd get at least as long as me."

"He got less than three years. He was out in eighteen months."

She sat there with her mouth open, stunned. I said, "You didn't know that, did you? Ain't it a shocker?"

I dropped Aunty Jess off on my way back to Willesden. We waved bye close to Walthamstow Market and I told her I'd see her later. I got to the bank at 3.30pm and joined the queue. There were four people ahead of me, including a retired type who was trying to fill in a deposit form without his spectacles. As the line got shorter, he told me to take his place, "I'm not ready yet, dear."

I clicked past him with a thanks, the high heels were chafing and the carrier bag never got any lighter. As I stepped up to the window, Derek came charging through the door with a shotgun in his hand and a stocking over his face. The stockings were mine. He'd broken his nose sometime in the past fifteen years and the tight nylon mesh squeezed it flat. He would have frightened anyone, even without the gun. The whole bank froze.

It takes less than ten seconds for a counter-girl to get it together and reach for the panic button. I never give them the chance. I pulled my shotgun out of my bag and rammed it up against the window. Using my high, sweet voice I told her to keep still, "The glass is no protection."

There was a woman standing shaking behind the security door at the far end of the counter. I shouted down to her and told her to buzz my partner through. Derek took up his position in the doorway, swinging his shotgun between the customers and the staff at their desks.

There were three girls working the counter, including the one at my window. I pointed at two of them and said, "Get away from the tills. Marcia, here . . ." I'd read her name tag by this time ". . . she's going to open them up and pass me the money."

I filled my carrier bag with notes. At a glance, I'd say there was no more than five thousand pounds. As I finished, I smoothed down my skirt and coat and prepared to walk out. It's a habit I picked up from nowhere but it's always helped me to stay calm. I left holding the money in one hand and my shotgun in the other. Derek followed on behind, backing out to make sure no one moved.

He only turned around once he was safely out of the door. He was a professional, leaving it to the last moment before he looked to see if Aunty Jess was ready with the car. He expected to see me climbing inside. I wasn't. I was stood right behind him with the shotgun levelled at his head. I didn't really catch his expression before I blew him away.

As I trotted over to Jess's Sierra, she fired a smoke grenade over my head. I heard it whistle and explode behind me. We would drive out of a storm of smoke and blood. No one would ever follow us and there would never be a road block waiting ahead. Derek was the grass, so he got smoked.

LIZ PETERS, PI

ELIZABETH PETERS

I did not have a hangover. Those rumors about me aren't true; they are spread by people who are jealous of my ability to handle the hard stuff. The truth is, I can polish off three giant-sized Hershey bars before bedtime and wake clear-eyed as a baby.

All the same, I wasn't at my best that morning. When I put my pants on, one leg at a time (I always do it that way), my heel caught in the hem, and then the zipper jammed and I broke a fingernail trying to free it. The weather was lousy – gray and bleak and dripping cold rain that didn't have the guts to turn into snow. On Christmas Eve, yet. You'd think that the Big Gal Up There would have the decency to provide a white Christmas. I didn't count on it. I don't count on much.

My office was pretty depressing too. The velvety bloom on the flat surfaces wasn't the winter light. It was dust. My cleaning woman hadn't shown up that week.

I work out of my house because it's more convenient; I mean, hauling a word processor and printer around with you gets to be a drag. I'm a mystery writer. It's a dirty job, and nobody really has to do it. I do it because it's preferable to jobs like embalming and mucking out stables. They say a writer's life is a lonely one. That's a crock of doo-doo. I've got enough of a rep so that people come to me. Too darned many of them, but then that's the way it goes in my business. Too darned many people. You could say the same thing about the world in general, if you were philosophically inclined. Which I am.

You might ask why, if my profession is that of writer, I call myself a PI. (You might ask, but you might not get an answer. It's nobody's business what I call myself.) The truth is, I don't know how I got myself into this private-investigating sideline. It sure as heck wasn't for the money. Everybody knows PIs can't make a living; look at their clothes, their scrungy living quarters, their beat-up cars. Some of the gals can't even afford to buy a hat. So why did I do it? Simple. Because it was there – the dirt, the filth, the injustice, the pain. All of suffering humanity, bleeding and hurting and crying for help. When one of them bled on my rug, I had to do something. I mean, what the heck, that rug set me back a bundle. It's an antique Bokhara. I should let people bleed all over it?

I have to admit it wasn't a pretty sight that morning. Dust, dog hairs, cigarette ashes, and a few other disgusting objects (including the dogs themselves) dulled its deep-crimson sheen. After a cup of the brew, with all the trimmings – that's how I drink it, and if people want to make something of it, let them – my eyeballs felt a little less like hard-boiled eggs. I lit a cigarette. What the heck, you only die once. My desk squatted there like an archaeological mound, layers deep in the accumulated garbage of living. I had to step over a couple of bodies to get to it. There was another limp carcass on my chair. When I moved it, it bit me. So what was one more scar? I'm covered with them. That's the way it goes in my business. Cats are only one of the hazards. The dogs are no picnic either. They don't bite, but I keep falling over them.

I sat down on the chair and lit a cigarette. The blank screen of the word processor stared at me like the eye of a dead Cyclops. My stomach twisted like a hanged man spinning on the end of a rope. Shucks, I thought. Here we go again. I forced my fingers onto the keyboard. It was like that every morning. It never got easier, it never would. There are no words. That was the trouble – no words. At least not in what passes for my brain. But somehow I had to come up with a few thousand of them, spell them right, put them into the guts of the machine and hope they came out making sense. That's my job. There are worse ones –

performing autopsies and cleaning litter boxes, for example. But at 9 A.M. on a dreary winter morning on a mean street in Maryland, with dust and cat hairs clogging my sinuses and a couple of dogs scratching fleas, and my head as empty as Dan Quayle's, I couldn't think of one. I lit a cigarette.

The coffee cup was scummed with cold froth and the ashtray was a reeking heap of butts when I came out of my stupor to see that there were words on the screen in front of me. They seemed to be spelled right, too. I wondered, vaguely, what had interrupted the creative flow – and then I heard the footsteps. Heavy, halting steps, coming nearer and nearer, down the dim hallways of the house, inexorably approaching. . . . I looked at the dogs. They're supposed to bark when somebody comes to the door. They never do. If I hadn't heard them snoring I'd have thought they were dead.

Closer and closer came the footsteps. Slower and slower. He was deliberately prolonging the suspense, making me wait. I took one hand off the keyboard and pushed the shining waves of thick bronze hair away from my brow.

The lamp on the desk beside me cast a bright pool of light across the keyboard, but the rest of the room was dark with winter shadows. He was a darker shadow, bulky and silent. I lit a cigarette.

"Hey, Jaz," I said. "Got time for some—"

He didn't. He was a big man. When he hit the floor he raised a cloud of dust that fogged the lamplight and my sinuses. Got to call that cleaning woman, I mused between sneezes. She was Jaz's cousin, or grandmother, or something. He'd found her for me. He was always doing things like that for me. He always had time for some . . .

I got to my feet and looked over the desk. He lay face down, unmoving. A film of gray covered his thick black hair. I know what death looks like. I've dealt with it . . . how many times? Forty, fifty times, maybe more. I can handle it. But I found myself thinking I was glad he'd fallen forward, so I couldn't see his face – the strong white teeth bared, not in his friendly grin but in a final grimace of pain, the soft brown eyes fixed and staring and filmed with dog hairs . . . Call me sentimental, if you want, but dusty eyeballs still get to me.

As I stood there, fighting those softer feelings that hide deep inside all us mystery writers who moonlight as private investigators, despite our efforts to build a tough shell so we can deal with the sick, disgusting, hideous realities of life without losing our integrity or our nerve and go on with our jobs of removing an occasional small piece of filthy slime from the world so it's a better place, if only infinitesimally so . . . Anyhow, after I had wiped my eyes on my sleeve, a little spark of light winked at me from the center of his broad back.

I had to push the dogs away before I could kneel beside him. They're so doggone stupid. They couldn't even tell he was dead. They were nudging him, wanting him to get up and play, as he always did.

It could have been a jeweled decoration or medal, if it had been on his chest instead of his back. The colorless stones glimmered palely in the dusky room. They weren't diamonds or even rhinestones. They were glass. I should know. I had only paid ten bucks for the hatpin. I collect hatpins. Just one of my little weaknesses. The last time I'd seen this particular specimen . . . I couldn't remember when it was. Had it been in the procelain holder with the others, the last time I looked? Trouble was, I hadn't really looked. You don't look at familiar objects, things that have been in their places for weeks or months or years. You just assume they're there, the way they always have been. I recognized it, though – the head of it, I mean – and I knew only too well what the rest of it was like. Ten inches of polished metal, rigid and deadly. In Victorian days they passed laws limiting the length of the pins women used to hold those enormous hats in place. Ironic, I thought, lighting another cigarette. Men turn purple with outrage when some legislator tries to keep them from stockpiling Uzis, but a woman couldn't even own a lousy hatpin . . .

The mind plays funny tricks on you when a friend drops dead on your floor. I was wondering whether there were still laws on the books banning hatpins when I heard something that woke me up like a dash of icy water in the face. Mine is the last house on a dead-end road, out in the country, so when I hear a car I know it's heading for me. This one was coming too fast, tires screeching around the steep downhill curve. I got to the window in time to see it slow for the sharp turn into my driveway. Amazing. He'd had sense enough not to use the siren. He can never resist the flasher, though; it spun like a dying sun, sending red beams through the rain.

It was like a thick curtain had been yanked away, clearing my head; I saw it all, clear as a printed warrant. I'd been set up. But good. A dead man in my study, my hatpin through his heart, and the fuzz tipped off in time to catch me red-handed. (A figure of speech we PIs use; there wasn't much blood, and I hadn't been stupid enough to touch the body.) I was in deep doo-doo, though. That wasn't generalized fuzz, it was my nemesis, Sheriff Bludger. We had tangled before, on issues like gun control, and he wasn't awfully crazy about little me. A thickheaded red-necked male chauvinist, he would be drooling at the prospect of catching me with my hatpin in somebody's back.

The cruiser swung into the driveway and accelerated, sending the gravel flying. One of the cats growled. I looked at him. "Hold 'em off, Diesel," I snapped. He jumped off the window-sill and headed for the back door. The dogs were already there, stupid tails wagging. They could hardly wait to jump all over the nice cops and lick their hands and bring them balls to throw. The dogs were about as much use as fuzzy bunnies, but as I grabbed my purse I saw that Diesel had rallied the rest of the cats, six of them in all. They were all inside that day on account of the rain. Diesel himself weighs almost twenty pounds, and Bludger suffers from terminal ailurophobia. I figured I had maybe three minutes.

I went out the front door while Bludger and Company were trying to get in the back. Unfortunately the Caddy was also in the back. I circled carefully around the house, shivering as the cold rain stung my face, and crept through the shrubbery till I reached the garage. Peering around the corner, I saw the cruiser parked by the back steps. The back door was open, and from inside I could hear a lot of noise – dogs barking and men cursing. There was no sound from the cats. Unlike dogs and rattlesnakes, they don't warn you before they strike. They aren't gentlemen. That's one of the reasons why I like them.

The Caddy purrs like a kitten and turns on a dime. I was out of the garage and heading down the drive before Bludger got wind of what was happening. Darned fool – if he'd left the cruiser blocking the gate I'd have been in big trouble, but no, he had to come right up to the door. That big beer belly of his makes him reluctant to walk farther than he has to, I guess. It was wobbling like a bowl of custard when he came barreling out of the back door, waving his stupid little gun and yelling. I waved back as I sent the Caddy shooting through the gate.

I pushed a lock of shining bronze hair out of my eyes and shoved my foot down hard on the gas. The car roared up the hill like a rocket, taking the curves like the sweet lady she is. You can have your Porsches and Ferraris; I always say there's nothing like a Cadillac brougham for eluding the cops. Not that I was up for a high-speed chase across the county. Excessive speed is socially irresponsible, and besides, Bludger could cut me off at the pass; he knew the back roads as well as I did and he had plenty of manpower. I had to get out of sight, but fast – within the next thirty seconds – and I knew just how to do it.

I'm not given to praying, but I sent a passionate petition to the patron saint of private eyes as I thundered toward the stop sign at the top of the hill. She came through for me; the main road was clear. Instead of turning right or left, I hit the brake and sent the Caddy slithering across the road and up the bank on the opposite shoulder. A big green-and-white construction trailer stood there; the bridge across the creek had been finished three months earlier, but they hadn't got around to removing the trailer. Typical. And lucky for me. I barely made it, though. A couple of inches of my back fender were still visible when the cruiser appeared, but Bludger didn't notice. He was too busy trying to figure out which way I had turned. The decision was easy, even for his limited brain; a right turn would have taken me onto the bridge and a mile-long stretch of straight road. To the left the road rises and curves. He went left.

I waited till he was out of sight. Fastening my seat belt, which I hadn't had time to do before, I backed out of my hiding place and headed across the bridge. I have to admit my pulse was pretty fast; this was the tricky part, if Bludger got smart and turned back too soon, he'd see me. I couldn't stay where I was for the same reason, the Caddy would have been visible to a car coming down the hill.

Saint Kinsey was still with me. Across the bridge and over the hill, to Grandmother's house we go . . . The driveway was a rutted track, with only a few grains of gravel remaining, the house looked like an abandoned ruin. She came out on the sagging porch, her shotgun over her arm, squinting through the rain. When she recognized me, a toothless grin split the wrinkled face under the faded sunbonnet.

"Hey, Liz. Got time for—"

"No, Grannie." I slung my purse over my shoulder. "I need to borrow the pickup. If Bludger finds the Caddy, tell him I stole your truck, okay?"

Grannie spat neatly into the weeds beside the steps. "Keys are in the ignition. Leave yours; I'll pull the Caddy into the shed after you go."

Movement at the window caught my eye. Something fluttered against the pane, like a trapped moth. A hand – too small and thin, too pale . . . I swallowed hard and waved back. "How's Danny doing?"

"Okay. That wheelchair you got him was a big help. Don't s'pose you've got time to come in and say hello? He don't see many folks, and he's crazy about you . . ."

"That's 'cause he don't see many folks." I forced a smile, directed it at the window, where Danny's small pale face was pressed to the glass. The wheelchair might have been a help, but it was a heck of a Christmas present for a kid. I'd tied a big red bow across the seat and then ripped it off – too much of a contrast between holiday cheer and sad reality – one of those ironic contrasts we PIs keep seeing all around us . . .

I swallowed harder, stuck my cold hands in the pockets of my jeans. My fingers touched something soft. I pulled it out. It was a little squashed, but Danny and I had agreed we liked chocolate that way. "Give him this, Grannie. As a token of better things to come. Tell him – tell him I'll be back to spend Christmas Eve with him."

Grannie's rheumy eyes opened as wide as her wrinkled lids allowed – not much. "But, Liz, it's your spare. What'll you do without—"

"I'll manage," I said gruffly. "No big deal. See you later, Grannie – unless I'm in the slammer."

She offered me the shotgun, the sunbonnet, and the dirt-colored sweater she had thrown over her shoulders. I took the last two, winked at her, and headed for the truck.

Heading south on 75 I met two cruisers heading north. I smiled without humor. The county crooks would have a field day today, beating up their wives and dealing drugs and driving drunk unmolested; Bludger would have every available cop out looking for harmless little old me.

I'd had my eye on Bludger for months. I couldn't believe he was as stupid as he looked; but if he wasn't up to his thick neck in the drug traffic, why did he keep getting in my face very time I tried to nail a local dealer? Over the past years, drug traffic in the county had increased a hundredfold. It wasn't just kids and adult delinquents growing marijuana in woodland clearings, it was crack and coke brought in by big-city dealers who found lucrative markets and safer operations out in the boonies. Every now and then Bludger would round up some kids from the Projects, and there'd be a big hurrah in the local paper. But I knew, and Bludger should have known, that that wasn't going to solve the problem. The people who lived in the Projects weren't supporting a million-dollar industry. The buyers had to be people with money, and they weren't buying off the streets.

I had a personal interest in the drug biz. It lost me a darned good cleaning woman – Danny's mom. She was sixteen when she had Danny, after a hasty marriage to a scuzzball who beat her up with monotonous regularity before he got bored with the entertainment and walked out on her. Three kids (two of them died, don't ask how), no education, no skills – it's a wonder she stuck it out as long as she did. It was after the second baby died that she started doing drugs. Eventually, inevitably, they killed her. So now Grannie was trying to raise a seven-year-old on nothing a month and I was stuck with a lazy incompetent for a cleaning woman. You understand, it was the inconvenience that ticked me off. Not sentimentality. We tough female writer-PIs aren't sentimental.

Grannie's pickup made a noise like a tractor. I encouraged it onto the freeway ramp and headed east toward Baltimore. A couple of miles and I'd be over the county line. Not that that would do me much good; Bludger would certainly have alerted the state cops as well as his counterparts next door. I drove at about forty, not because I was trying to avoid traffic cops but because that was as fast as the pickup would go.

There had to be some connection between Jaz's murder and my recent investigations. Could it be Bludger himself who had set me up? I'd talked to Jaz about my suspicions, after he told me about a friend of his who'd been arrested for dealing dope down in D.C. (These days it's hard to find someone who doesn't know someone who's been arrested for dealing dope down in D.C.) Would Bludger commit murder just to get me off the trail? Not unless I was sniffing right at his heels. If I was, I sure as heck didn't know it.

The sleety rain was falling harder and the windshield wipers seemed to be suffering from mechanical arthritis. I decided I'd better get off the road. Pulling into a McDonald's, I ordered coffee and a Big Mac with everything (what the heck, you can only die once) and parked.

I always get my best ideas when I'm eating. Don't know why that is. Maybe cholesterol stimulates the brain cells. After finishing my Big Mac I lit a cigarette and drove on to the shopping center. It was all decorated for Christmas – had been since mid-October – and it was the most depressing darned sight I had ever seen. The plastic wreaths and garlands had faded to a sickly chartreuse; they hung like dead parrots from lampposts and storefronts. Rain dripped drearily off the shiny red plastic bows. Strategically spotted speakers blared out that lovely classic carol, "I Saw Mommy Kissing Santa Claus." Next on the agenda, no doubt, would be "All I Want for Christmas Is My Two Front Teeth," or "I Don't Care Who You Are, Fatty, Get Those Reindeer off My Roof." I swallowed the tide of sickness rising in my throat and reminded myself to replenish my supply of Di-Gel. We PIs buy a lot of antacids. Especially around Christmas.

I miss the old-fashioned telephone booths, with doors you can close, but Grannie's sunbonnet was a big help; it kept the rain off my face and kept passersby from hearing my end of the conversation.

First I called Jaz's office. Mary Jo was on that day. She wanted to talk, but I cut her short. I sure as heck didn't want to be the one to tell her about Jaz. I asked her where he was due to be that morning, before he came to me. Some of the names I knew, some I didn't. But they made a pattern. After I hung up I called Rick. He wanted to talk too. Everybody wants to talk. I told him what I wanted. He gasped. "G—d d—n it, Liz—"

"Watch your mouth, Rick. You know my readers don't like dirty words."

"Oh – oh, yeah. Sorry. But what—"

"Never mind what. Just be there. I've cracked the case. You can make the arrest. I don't want the credit. I never do."

"But—"

I hung up.

Rick already owed me a couple. This would make three – no, four. You could call our relationship a social one – at least you'd better call it that. We'd met at a party, one of those boring Washington affairs writers get sucked into; I was sulking in a corner, nursing my drink and wondering how soon I could cut out, when I saw him. And he saw me. Our eyes met, across the room . . . Later, we got to talking. He asked me what I did for a living, I politely reciprocated – and that's how it began. He'd been promoted a couple of times since I started helping him out and he was man enough to give me credit – privately, if not to his boss at the Agency – so I knew he'd respond this time.

It would take him an hour or more to get there, though. I dawdled in the drugstore, picked up a package of Di-Gel and a few other odds and ends I figured I would need, and then headed back to town at a leisurely thirty miles per hour. The rain slid like tears down the cracked facade of the windshield. Tears for a good man gone bad, for a sick world that teaches kids to get high and cop out. I felt sick myself. I chewed a Di-Gel and lit a cigarette.

I had to circle the block three times before I found the parking spot I wanted, right across from the sheriff's office. No hurry. Rick wouldn't be there for another half hour, and I sure as heck wasn't walking into the lion's den without him. I'm tough, and I'm smart, but I'm not stupid. I ate a couple of Hershey bars while I thumbed through the latest issue of

Victorian Homes. Then I lit a cigarette. I had smoked three of them before Rick showed up. I watched him as he trotted up the stairs. He was a big man. (I like big men.) I waited till he'd gone in, then pulled my sunbonnet over my head and followed.

A fresh kid in a trooper's uniform tried to stop me when I headed for Bludger's office. I straight-armed him out of the way and went on in. Rick was sitting on the edge of the desk and Bludger was yelling at him. He hates having people sit on the edge of his desk. When he saw me, his face turned purple. "D—n it, Grannie, how'd you get past—"

"I don't allow talk like that," I told him, whipping off my sunbonnet. "And I'm not Grannie."

His eyes bulged till they looked like they'd roll out of the sockets. Rick was grinning, but he looked a little anxious. The third man started to stand up, and fell back into his chair with a groan. I sat down on the other corner of Bludger's desk.

"Hi, Jaz," I said. "Feeling better?"

Bludger got his voice back. "You're under arrest," he bellowed.

I raised one eyebrow. "What's the charge?"

"Attempted murder!"

"With this?" I picked up the plasticine envelope. The hatpin had been cut down from ten inches to about two. "Darn it," I said. "I paid ten bucks for this. It's ruined."

"You shoved that thing into him—" Bludger began.

"Is that what he says?" I looked at Jaz.

He ran his fingers through his thick dark hair. "I don't . . . I can't remember . . ."

I lit a cigarette. "Oh, yeah? Well, let me refresh your memory. You stuck that pin into your own back just before you walked into my house. It's three and a half miles from the previous stop on your schedule; you couldn't possibly have driven that far without noticing that you had a sharp object in your back. My cleaning woman is a friend of yours; she stole that hatpin for you, several days ago. I was getting too close, wasn't I, Jaz? And I made the mistake of discussing my ideas with you – my questions about how drugs were being delivered in the county. What better delivery system than good old reliable National Express? You're on the road every day, covering the same territory. You've got your own private delivery schedule, haven't you?"

His eyes narrowed. I wondered why I'd never noticed before how empty they were, like pale marbles in the head of a wax dummy. "You're bluffing," he snarled. "You can't prove—"

"I never bluff," I told him, brushing a lock of shining auburn hair away from my forehead. "The truck will be clean, but you had to package the garbage somewhere. Your own apartment probably. I'd try the kitchen first, Bludger. There'll be traces left. Men don't know how to clean a kitchen properly. And, as I have reason to know, neither does Jaz's 'cousin.'"

I didn't expect him to break so fast. He got to his feet and started toward me. Rick moved to intercept him, but I shook my head. "Don't dirty your hands, Rick. Come any closer, Jaz, and you get this cigarette right in the face."

"You don't understand," he groaned. "It was her idea. She made me do it."

"Sure," I said bitterly. "Blame the dame. You and that MCP Adam."

"Adam?" He looked like a dead fish, eyes bulging, mouth ajar. "How many guys do you have dropping by for some—"

"Never mind." It was all clear to me now. I felt a little sick. Men, I thought bitterly. You try to be nice, offer a guy some milk and cookies, listen to his troubles, and he starts getting ideas.

I lit a cigarette. "He's all yours, boys. You'll have to figure out who has jurisdiction."

"I'm sheriff of this county," Bludger blustered.

"I wouldn't be surprised if a state line got crossed," Rick drawled. "And the DEA has jurisdiction—"

"Fight it out between yourselves," I told them. "Frankly, I don't give a darn."

Jaz dropped back onto his chair, face hidden in his hands. A lock of thick black hair curled over his fingers. I headed, fast, for the door.

Rick followed me out. "What say I drop by later for some—"

"You're all alike," I said bitterly. "Wave a chocolate-chip cookie in front of you and you'll do anything, say anything."

He captured my hand. "For one of your chocolate-chip cookies I would. They're special, Liz. Like you."

"Sorry, Rick." I freed my hand so I could light another cigarette. "I've got a chapter to finish. That's what it's all about, you know. The real world. Putting words on paper, spelling them right . . . All the rest of it is just fun and games. Just . . ."

The words stuck in my throat. Rick leaned over to look into my face. "You're not crying, are you?"

"Who, me? PIs don't cry." I tossed the cigarette away. It spun in a glowing arc through the curtain of softly falling snow. Snow. Big fat flakes like fragments of foam rubber. They clung to my long lashes. I blinked. "Rick. Isn't there a reward for breaking this case?"

Rick blinked. He has long thick lashes too. (I like long thick lashes in a man.) "Yeah. Some guy whose kid died of an overdose offered it. It's yours, I guess. Enough to buy a lot of cigarettes and chocolate chips."

I took his arm. "You'll get your chocolate-chip cookies, Rick. But first we're going shopping. Toys 'R' Us, and then a breeder I know whose golden retriever has just had a litter. A tree, a great big one, with all the trimmings, the fattest turkey Safeway has left . . . Pick up your feet, Rick. We've got a lot to do. It's Christmas Eve – and it's snowing!"

I lit a cigarette. What the heck, you only live once.

A DOUBLE-BARRELED DETECTIVE STORY

MARK TWAIN

The first scene is in the country, in Virginia; the time, 1880. There has been a wedding, between a handsome young man of slender means and a rich young girl – a case of love at first sight and a precipitate marriage; a marriage bitterly opposed by the girl's widowed father.

Jacob Fuller, the bridegroom, is twenty-six years old, is of an old but unconsidered family which had by compulsion emigrated from Sedgemoor, and for King James's purse's profit, so everybody said – some maliciously, the rest merely because they believed it. The bride is nineteen and beautiful. She is intense, high-strung, romantic, immeasurably proud of her Cavalier blood, and passionate in her love for her young husband. For its sake she braved her father's displeasure, endured his reproaches, listened with loyalty unshaken to his warning predictions, and went from his house without his blessing, proud and happy in the proofs she was thus giving of the quality of the affection which had made its home in her heart.

The morning after the marriage there was a sad surprise for her. Her husband put aside her proffered caresses, and said:

"Sit down. I have something to say to you. I loved you. That was before I asked your father to give you to me. His refusal is not my grievance – I could have endured that. But the things he said of me to you – that is a different matter. There – you needn't speak; I know quite well what they were; I got them from authentic sources. Among other things he said that my character was written in my face; that I was treacherous, a dissembler, a coward, and a brute without sense of pity or compassion: the "Sedgemoor trade-mark," he called it – and "white-sleeve badge." Any other man in my place would have gone to his house and shot him down like a dog. I wanted to do it, and was minded to do it, but a better thought came to me: to put him to shame; to break his heart; to kill him by inches. How to do it? Through my treatment of you, his idol! I would marry you; and then – Have patience. You will see."

From that moment onward, for three months, the young wife suffered all the humiliations, all the insults, all the miseries that the diligent and inventive mind of the husband could contrive, save physical injuries only. Her strong pride stood by her, and she kept the secret of her troubles. Now and then the husband said, "Why don't you go to your father and tell him?" Then he invented new tortures, applied them, and asked again. She always answered, "He shall never know by my mouth," and taunted him with his origin; said she was the lawful slave of a scion of slaves, and must obey, and would – up to that point, but no further; he could kill her if he liked, but he could not break her; it was not in the Sedgemoor breed to do it. At the end of the three months he said, with a dark significance in his manner, "I have tried all things but one" – and waited for her reply. "Try that," she said, and curled her lip in mockery.

That night he rose at midnight and put on his clothes, then said to her:

"Get up and dress!"

She obeyed – as always, without a word. He led her half a mile from the house, and proceeded to lash her to a tree by the side of the public road; and succeeded, she screaming and struggling. He gagged her then, struck her across the face with his cowhide, and set his bloodhounds on her. They tore the clothes off her, and she was naked. He called the dogs off, and said:

"You will be found – by the passing public. They will be

dropping along about three hours from now, and will spread the news – do you hear? Good-bye. You have seen the last of me."

He went away then. She moaned to herself:

"I shall bear a child – to *him*! God grant it may be a boy!"

The farmers released her by and by – and spread the news, which was natural. They raised the country with lynching intentions, but the bird had flown. The young wife shut herself up in her father's house; he shut himself up with her, and thenceforth would see no one. His pride was broken, and his heart; so he wasted away, day by day, and even his daughter rejoiced when death relieved him.

Then she sold the estate and disappeared.

2

In 1886 a young woman was living in a modest house near a secluded New England village, with no company but a little boy about five years old. She did her own work, she discouraged acquaintanceships, and had none. The butcher, the baker, and the others that served her could tell the villagers nothing about her further than that her name was Stillman, and that she called the child Archy. Whence she came they had not been able to find out, but they said she talked like a Southerner. The child had no playmates and no comrade, and no teacher but the mother. She taught him diligently and intelligently, and was satisfied with the results – even a little proud of them. One day Archy said:

"Mamma, am I different from other children?"

"Well, I suppose not. Why?"

"There was a child going along out there and asked me if the postman had been by and I said yes, and she said how long since I saw him and I said I hadn't seen him at all, and she said how did I know he'd been by, then, and I said because I smelt his track on the sidewalk, and she said I was a dum fool and made a mouth at me. What did she do that for?"

The young woman turned white, and said to herself, "It's a birthmark! The gift of the bloodhound is in him." She snatched the boy to her breast and hugged him passionately, saying, "God has appointed the way!" Her eyes were burning with a fierce light, and her breath came short and quick with excitement. She said to herself: "The puzzle is solved now; many a time it has been a mystery to me, the impossible things the child has done in the dark, but it is all clear to me now."

She set him in his small chair, and said:

"Wait a little till I come, dear; then we will talk about the matter."

She went up to her room and took from her dressing-table several small articles and put them out of sight: a nail-file on the floor under the bed; a pair of nail-scissors under the bureau; a small ivory paper-knife under the wardrobe. Then she returned, and said:

"There! I have left some things which I ought to have brought down." She named them, and said, "Run up and bring them, dear."

The child hurried away on his errand and was soon back again with the things.

"Did you have any difficulty, dear?"

"No, mamma; I only went where you went."

During his absence she had stepped to the bookcase, taken several books from the bottom shelf, opened each, passed her hand over a page, noting its number in her memory, then restored them to their places. Now she said:

"I have been doing something while you have been gone, Archy. Do you think you can find out what it was?"

The boy went to the bookcase and got out the books that had been touched, and opened them at the pages which had been stroked.

The mother took him in her lap, and said:

"I will answer your questions now, dear. I have found out that in one way you are quite different from other people. You can see in the dark, you can smell what other people cannot, you have the talents of a bloodhound. They are good and valuable things to have, but you must keep the matter a secret. If people found it out, they would speak of you as an odd child, a strange child, and children would be disagreeable to you, and give you nicknames. In this world one must be like everybody else if he doesn't want to provoke scorn or envy or jealousy. It is a great and fine distinction which has been born to you, and I am glad; but you will keep it a secret for mamma's sake, won't you?"

The child promised, without understanding.

All the rest of the day the mother's brain was busy with excited thinkings; with plans, projects, schemes, each and all of them uncanny, grim, and dark. Yet they lit up her face; lit it with a fell light of their own; lit it with vague fires of hell. She was in a fever of unrest; she could not sit, stand, read, sew; there was no relief for her but in movement. She tested her boy's gift in twenty ways, and kept saying to herself all the time, with her mind in the past: "He broke my father's heart, and night and day all these years I have tried, and all in vain, to think out a way to break his. I have found it now – I have found it now."

When night fell, the demon of unrest still possessed her. She went on with her tests; with a candle she traversed the house from garret to cellar, hiding pins, needles, thimbles, spools, under pillows, under carpets, in cracks in the walls, under the coal in the bin; then sent the little fellow in the dark to find them; which he did, and was happy and proud when she praised him and smothered him with caresses.

From this time forward life took on a new complexion for her. She said, "The future is secure – I can wait, and enjoy the waiting." The most of her lost interests revived. She took up music again, and languages, drawing, painting, and the other long-discarded delights of her maidenhood. She was happy once more, and felt again the zest of life. As the years drifted by she watched the development of her boy, and was contented with it. Not altogether, but nearly that. The soft side of his heart was larger than the other side of it. It was his only defect, in her eyes. But she considered that his love for her and worship of her made up for it. He was a good hater – that was well; but it was a question if the materials of his hatreds were of as tough and enduring a quality as those of his friendships – and that was not so well.

The years drifted on. Archy was become a handsome, shapely, athletic youth, courteous, dignified, companionable, pleasant in his ways, and looking perhaps a trifle older than he was, which was sixteen. One evening his mother said she had something of grave importance to say to him, adding that he was old enough to hear it now, and old enough and possessed of character enough and stability enough to carry out a stern plan which she had been for years contriving and maturing. Then she told him her bitter story, in all its naked atrociousness. For a while the boy was paralyzed; then he said:

"I understand. We are Southerners; and by our custom and nature there is but one atonement. I will search him out and kill him."

"Kill him? No! Death is release, emancipation; death is a favor. Do I owe him favors? You must not hurt a hair of his head."

The boy was lost in thought awhile; then he said:

"You are all the world to me, and your desire is my law and my pleasure. Tell me what to do and I will do it."

The mother's eyes beamed with satisfaction, and she said:

"You will go and find him. I have known his hiding-place for eleven years; it cost me five years and more of inquiry, and much money, to locate it. He is a quartz-miner in Colorado, and well-to-do. He lives in Denver. His name is Jacob Fuller. There – it is the first time I have spoken it since that unforgettable night. Think! That name could have been yours if I had not saved you that shame and furnished you a cleaner one. You will drive him from that place; you will hunt him down and drive him again; and yet again, and again, and again, persistently, relentlessly, poisoning his life, filling it with mysterious terrors, loading it with weariness and misery, making him wish for death, and that he had a suicide's courage; you will make of him another Wandering Jew; he shall know no rest any more, no peace of mind, no placid sleep; you shall shadow him, cling to him, persecute him, till you break his heart, as he broke my father's and mine."

"I will obey, mother."

"I believe it, my child. The preparations are all made; everything is ready. Here is a letter of credit; spend freely, there is no lack of money. At times you may need disguises. I have provided them; also some other conveniences." She took from the drawer of the typewriter-table several squares of paper. They all bore these typewritten words:

$10,000 REWARD

It is believed that a certain man who is wanted in an Eastern
state is sojourning here. In 1880, in the night, he tied his young
wife to a tree by the public road, cut her across the face with a
cowhide, and made his dogs tear her clothes from her, leaving
her naked. He left her there, and fled the country. A blood-
relative of hers has searched for him for seventeen years.
Address   , Post-office. The above re-
ward will be paid in cash to the person who will furnish the
seeker, in a personal interview, the criminal's address.

"When you have found him and acquainted yourself with his
scent, you will go in the night and placard one of these upon the
building he occupies, and another one upon the post-office or in
some other prominent place. It will be the talk of the region. At
first you must give him several days in which to force a sale of
his belongings at something approaching their value. We will
ruin him by and by, but gradually; we must not impoverish him
at once, for that could bring him to despair and injure his
health, possibly kill him."

She took three or four more typewritten forms from the
drawer – duplicates – and read one:

. . . . . . , ... , 18 . . .

To Jacob Fuller:
You have . . . days in which to settle your affairs. You will
not be disturbed during that limit, which will expire at . . .
M., on the . . . of . . . You must then MOVE ON. *If you*
are still in the place after the named hour, I will placard you
on all the dead walls, detailing your crime once more, and
adding the date, also the scene of it, with all names concerned,
including your own. Have no fear of bodily injury – it will in
no circumstances ever be inflicted upon you. You brought
misery upon an old man, and ruined his life and broke his
heart. What he suffered, you are to suffer.

"You will add no signature. He must receive this before he
learns of the reward placard – before he rises in the morning –
lest he lose his head and fly the place penniless."

"I shall not forget."

"You will need to use these forms only in the beginning –
once may be enough. Afterward, when you are ready for him to
vanish out of a place, see that he gets a copy of *this* form, which
merely says:

MOVE ON. *You have* . . . . . . *days.*

"He will obey. That is sure."

3

Extracts from letters to the mother:

DENVER, *April 3, 1897*

*I have now been living several days in the same hotel with
Jacob Fuller. I have his scent; I could track him through ten
divisions of infantry and find him. I have often been near him
and heard him talk. He owns a good mine, and has a fair
income from it; but he is not rich. He learned mining in a good
way – by working at it for wages. He is a cheerful creature,
and his forty-three years sit lightly upon him; he could pass
for a younger man – say thirty-six or thirty-seven. He has
never married again – passes himself off for a widower. He
stands well, is liked, is popular, and has many friends. Even I
feel a drawing toward him – the paternal blood in me making
its claim. How blind and unreasoning and arbitrary are some
of the laws of nature – the most of them, in fact! My task is
become hard now – you realize it? you comprehend, and make
allowance? – and the fire of it has cooled, more than I like to
confess to myself. But I will carry it out. Even with the
pleasure paled, the duty remains, and I will not spare him.*

*And for my help, a sharp resentment rises in me when I
reflect that he who committed that odious crime is the only one
who has not suffered by it. The lesson of it has manifestly
reformed his character, and in the change he is happy. He, the
guilty party, is absolved from all suffering; you, the innocent,
are borne down with it. But be comforted – he shall harvest his
share.*

I placarded Form No. 1 at midnight of April 3; an hour later I slipped Form No. 2 under his chamber door, notifying him to leave Denver at or before 11.50 the night of the 14th.

Some late bird of a reporter stole one of my placards, then hunted the town over and found the other one, and stole that. In this manner he accomplished what the profession call a "scoop" — that is, he got a valuable item, and saw to it that no other paper got it. And so his paper — the principal one in the town — had it in glaring type on the editorial page in the morning, followed by a Vesuvian opinion of our wretch a column long, which wound up by adding a thousand dollars to our reward on the paper's account! The journals out here know how to do the noble thing — when there's business in it.

At breakfast I occupied my usual seat — selected because it afforded a view of papa Fuller's face, and was near enough for me to hear the talk that went on at his table. Seventy-five or a hundred people were in the room, and all discussing that item, and saying they hoped the seeker would find that rascal and remove the pollution of his presence from the town — with a rail, or a bullet, or something.

When Fuller came in he had the Notice to Leave — folded up — in one hand, and the newspaper in the other; and it gave me more than half a pang to see him. His cheerfulness was all gone, and he looked old and pinched and ashy. And then — only think of the things he had to listen to! Mamma, he heard his own unsuspecting friends describe him with epithets and characterizations drawn from the very dictionaries and phrase-books of Satan's own authorized editions down below. And more than that, he had to agree with the verdicts and applaud them. His applause tasted bitter in his mouth, though; he could not disguise that from me; and it was observable that his appetite was gone; he only nibbled; he couldn't eat. Finally a man said:

"It is quite likely that that relative is in the room and hearing what this town thinks of that unspeakable scoundrel. I hope so."

Ah, dear, it was pitiful the way Fuller winced, and glanced around scared! He couldn't endure any more, and got up and left.

During several days he gave out that he had bought a mine in Mexico, and wanted to sell out and go down there as soon as he could, and give the property his personal attention. He played his cards well; said he would take $40,000 – a quarter in cash, the rest in safe notes; but that as he greatly needed money on account of his new purchase, he would diminish his terms for cash in full. He sold out for $30,000. Then, what do you think he did? He asked for greenbacks, and took them, saying the man in Mexico was a New-Englander, with a head full of crotchets, and preferred greenbacks to gold or drafts. People thought it queer, since a draft on New York could produce greenbacks quite conveniently. There was talk of this odd thing, but only for a day; that is as long as any topic lasts in Denver.

I was watching, all the time. As soon as the sale was completed and the money paid – which was on the 11th – I began to stick to Fuller's track without dropping it for a moment. That night – no, 12th, for it was a little past midnight – I tracked him to his room, which was four doors from mine in the same hall; then I went back and put on my muddy day-laborer disguise, darkened my complexion, and sat down in my room in the gloom, with a gripsack handy, with a change in it, and my door ajar. For I suspected that the bird would take wing now. In half an hour an old woman passed by, carrying a grip: I caught the familiar whiff, and followed with my grip, for it was Fuller. He left the hotel by a side entrance, and at the corner he turned up an unfrequented street and walked three blocks in a light rain and a heavy darkness, and got into a two-horse hack, which of course was waiting for him by appointment. I took a seat (uninvited) on the trunk platform behind, and we drove briskly off. We drove ten miles, and the hack stopped at a way-station and was discharged. Fuller got out and took a seat on a barrow under the awning, as far as he could get from the light; I went inside, and watched the ticket-office. Fuller bought no ticket; I bought none. Presently the train came along, and he boarded a car; I entered the same car at the other end, and came down *the aisle and took the seat behind him. When he paid the conductor and named his objective point, I dropped back several seats, while the conductor was changing a bill, and when he came to me I paid to the same place – about a hundred miles westward.*

From that time for a week on end he led me a dance. He traveled here and there and yonder – always on a general westward trend – but he was not a woman after the first day. He was a laborer, like myself, and wore bushy false whiskers. His outfit was perfect, and he could do the character without thinking about it, for he had served the trade for wages. His nearest friend could not have recognized him. At last he located himself here, the obscurest little mountain camp in Montana; he has a shanty, and goes out prospecting daily; is gone all day, and avoids society. I am living at a miner's boardinghouse, and it is an awful place; the bunks, the food, the dirt – everything.

We have been here four weeks, and in that time I have seen him but once; but every night I go over his track and post myself. As soon as he engaged a shanty here I went to a town fifty miles away and telegraphed that Denver hotel to keep my baggage till I should send for it. I need nothing here but a change of army shirts, and I brought that with me.

SILVER GULCH, *June 12*
The Denver episode has never found its way here, I think. I know the most of the men in camp, and they have never referred to it, at least in my hearing. Fuller doubtless feels quite safe in these conditions. He has located a claim, two miles away, in an out-of-the-way place in the mountains; it promises very well, and he is working it diligently. Ah, but the change in him! He never smiles, and he keeps quite to himself, consorting with no one – he who was so fond of company and so cheery only two months ago. I have seen him passing along several times recently – drooping, forlorn, the spring gone from his step, a pathetic figure. He calls himself David Wilson.

I can trust him to remain here until we disturb him. Since you insist, I will banish him again, but I do not see how he can

*be unhappier than he already is. I will go back to Denver and
treat myself to a little season of comfort, and edible food, and
endurable beds, and bodily decency; then I will fetch my
things, and notify poor papa Wilson to move on.*

DENVER, *June 19*

*They miss him here. They all hope he is prospering in
Mexico, and they do not say it just with their mouths, but out
of their hearts. You know you can always tell. I am loitering
here overlong, I confess it. But if you were in my place you
would have charity for me. Yes, I know what you will say,
and you are right: if I were in your place, and carried your
scalding memories in my heart—*
I will take the night train back to-morrow.

DENVER, *June 20*

God forgive us, mother, we are hunting the wrong man! *I
have not slept any all night. I am now waiting, at dawn, for
the* morning *train – and how the minutes drag, how they
drag!*
*This Jacob Fuller is a cousin of the guilty one. How stupid
we have been not to reflect that the guilty one would never
again wear his own name after that fiendish deed! The
Denver Fuller is four years younger than the other one; he
came here a young widower in '79, aged twenty-one – a year
before you were married; and the documents to prove it are
innumerable. Last night I talked with familiar friends of his
who have known him from the day of his arrival. I said
nothing, but a few days from now I will land him in this town
again, with the loss upon his mine made good; and there will
be a banquet, and a torch-light procession, and there will not
be any expense on anybody but me. Do you call this "gush"? I
am only a boy, as you well know; it is my privilege. By and by
I shall not be a boy any more.*

SILVER GULCH, *July 3*

*Mother, he is gone! Gone, and left no trace. The scent was
cold when I came. To-day I am out of bed for the first time
since. I wish I were not a boy; then I could stand shocks better.*

They all think he went west. I start to-night, in a wagon – two or three hours of that, then I get a train. I don't know where I'm going, but I must go; to try to keep still would be torture.

Of course he has effaced himself with a new name and a disguise. This means that I may have to search the whole globe to find him. *Indeed it is what I expect. Do you see, mother? It is I that am the Wandering Jew. The irony of it! We arranged that for another.*

Think of the difficulties! And there would be none if I only could advertise for him. But if there is any way to do it that would not frighten him, I have not been able to think it out, and I have tried till my brains are addled. "If the gentleman who lately bought a mine in Mexico and sold one in Denver will send his address to" (to whom, mother!), "it will be explained to him that it was all a mistake; his forgiveness will be asked, and full reparation made for a loss which he sustained in a certain matter." Do you see? He would think it a trap. Well, any one would. If I should say, "It is now known that he was not the man wanted, but another man – who once bore the same name, but discarded it for good reasons" – would that answer? But the Denver people would wake up then and say "Oho!" and they would remember about the suspicious greenbacks, and say, "Why did he run away if he wasn't the right man? – it is too thin." If I failed to find him he would be ruined there – there where there is no taint upon him now. You have a better head than mine. Help me.

I have one clue, and only one. I know his handwriting. If he puts his new false name upon a hotel register and does not disguise it too much, it will be valuable to me if I ever run across it.

SAN FRANCISCO, *June 28, 1898*

You already know how well I have searched the states from Colorado to the Pacific, and how nearly I came to getting him once. Well, I have had another close miss. It was here, yesterday. I struck his trail, hot on the street, and followed it on a run to a cheap hotel. That was a costly mistake; a dog would have gone the other way. But I am only part dog, and

*can get very humanly stupid when excited. He had been
stopping in that house ten days; I almost know, now, that
he stops long nowhere, the past six or eight months, but is
restless and has to keep moving. I understand that feeling!
and I know what it is to feel it. He still uses the name he had
registered when I came so near catching him nine months ago
– "James Walker"; doubtless the same he adopted when he
fled from Silver Gulch. An unpretending man, and has small
taste for fancy names. I recognized the hand easily, through
its slight disguise. A square man, and not good at shams and
pretenses.*

*They said he was just gone, on a journey; left no address;
didn't say where he was going; looked frightened when asked
to leave his address; had no baggage but a cheap valise;
carried it off on foot – a "stingy old person, and not much loss
to the house." "Old!" I suppose he is, now. I hardly heard; I
was there but a moment. I rushed along his trail, and it led me
to a wharf. Mother, the smoke of the steamer he had taken
was just fading out on the horizon! I should have saved half
an hour if I had gone in the right direction at first. I could
have taken a fast tug, and should have stood a chance of
catching that vessel. She is bound for Melbourne.*

HOPE CAÑON, *California, October 3, 1900*
*You have a right to complain. "A letter a year" is a
paucity; I freely acknowledge it; but how can one write when
there is nothing to write about but failures? No one can keep it
up; it breaks the heart.*

*I told you – it seems ages ago, now – how I missed him at
Melbourne, and then chased him all over Australasia for
months on end.*

*Well, then, after that I followed him to India; almost saw
him in Bombay; traced him all around – to Baroda, Rawal-
Pindi, Lucknow, Lahore, Cawnpore, Allahabad, Calcutta,
Madras – oh, everywhere; week after week, month after
month, through the dust and swelter – always approximately
on his track, sometimes close upon him, yet never catching
him. And down to Ceylon, and then to – Never mind; by and
by I will write it all out.*

I chased him home to California, and down to Mexico, and back again to California. Since then I have been hunting him about the state from the first of last January down to a month ago. I feel almost sure he is not far from Hope Cañon; I traced him to a point thirty miles from here, but there I lost the trail; some one gave him a lift in a wagon, I suppose.

I am taking a rest, now – modified by searchings for the lost trail. I was tired to death, mother, and low-spirited, and sometimes coming uncomfortably near to losing hope; but the miners in this little camp are good fellows, and I am used to their sort this long time back; and their breezy ways freshen a person up and make him forget his troubles. I have been here a month. I am cabining with a young fellow named "Sammy" Hillyer, about twenty-five, the only son of his mother – like me – and loves her dearly, and writes to her every week – part of which is like me. He is a timid body, and in the matter of intellect – well, he cannot be depended upon to set a river on fire; but no matter, he is well liked; he is good and fine, and it is meat and bread and rest and luxury to sit and talk with him and have a comradeship again. I wish "James Walker" could have it. He had friends; he liked company. That brings up that picture of him, the time that I saw him last. The pathos of it! It comes before me often and often. At that very time, poor thing, I was girding up my conscience to make him move on again!

Hillyer's heart is better than mine, better than anybody's in the community, I suppose, for he is the one friend of the black sheep of the camp – Flint Buckner – and the only man Flint ever talks with or allows to talk with him. He says he knows Flint's history, and that it is trouble that has made him what he is, and so one ought to be as charitable toward him as one can. Now none but a pretty large heart could find space to accommodate a lodger like Flint Buckner, from all I hear about him outside. I think that this one detail will give you a better idea of Sammy's character than any labored-out description I could furnish you of him. In one of our talks he said something about like this: "Flint is a kinsman of mine, and he pours out all his troubles to me – empties his breast from time to time, or I reckon it would burst. There couldn't

*be any unhappier man, Archy Stillman; his life had been
made up of misery of mind – he isn't near as old as he looks.
He has lost the feel of reposefulness and peace – oh, years and
years ago! He doesn't know what good luck is – never has had
any; often says he wishes he was in the other hell, he is so tired
of this one."*

4

*No real gentleman will tell the naked truth in the presence of
ladies.*

It was a crisp and spicy morning in early October. The lilacs
and laburnums, lit with the glory-fires of autumn, hung burning and flashing in the upper air, a fairy bridge provided by kind
Nature for the wingless wild things that have their homes in the
tree-tops and would visit together; the larch and the pomegranate flung their purple and yellow flames in brilliant broad
splashes along the slanting sweep of the woodland; the sensuous
fragrance of innumerable deciduous flowers rose upon the
swooning atmosphere; far in the empty sky a solitary esophagus* slept upon motionless wing; everywhere brooded stillness,
serenity, and the peace of God.

To the Editor of the Republican:
   *One of your citizens has asked me a question about the
"esophagus," and I wish to answer him through you. This is
the hope that the answer will get around, and save me some
penmanship, for I have already replied to the same question
more than several times, and am not getting as much holiday
as I ought to have.*
   *I published a short story lately, and it was in that that I put
the esophagus. I will say privately that I expected it to bother
some people – in fact, that was the intention – but the harvest
has been larger than I was calculating upon. The esophagus
has gathered in the guilty and the innocent alike, whereas I*

* From the Springfield Republican, April 12, 1902.

*was only fishing for the innocent – the innocent and confiding.
I knew a few of these would write and ask me; that would give
me but little trouble; but I was not expecting that the wise and
the learned would call upon me for succor. However, that has
happened, and it is time for me to speak up and stop the
inquiries if I can, for letter-writing is not restful to me, and I
am not having so much fun out of this thing as I counted on.
That you may understand the situation, I will insert a couple
of sample inquiries. The first is from a public instructor in the
Philippines:*

SANTA CRUZ, *Ilocos, Sur, P.I.*
February 13, 1902

*My dear Sir, – I have just been reading the first part of
your latest story, entitled "A Double-barreled Detective
Story," and am very much delighted with it. In Part IV,
Page 264,* Harper's Magazine *for January, occurs this
passage: "far in the empty sky a solitary 'esophagus' slept
upon motionless wing; everywhere brooded stillness, serenity,
and the peace of God." Now, there is one word I do not
understand, namely, "esophagus." My only work of reference
is the* Standard Dictionary, *but that fails to explain the
meaning. If you can spare the time, I would be glad to have
the meaning cleared up, as I consider the passage a very
touching and beautiful one. It may seem foolish to you, but
consider my lack of means away out in the northern part of
Luzon.*

Yours very truly.

*Do you notice? Nothing in the paragraph disturbed him but
that one word. It shows that that paragraph was most ably
constructed for the deception it was intended to put upon the
reader. It was my intention that it should read plausibly, and
it is now plain that it does; it was my intention that it should
be emotional and touching, and you see, yourself, that it
fetched this public instructor. Alas, if I had but left that one
treacherous word out, I should have scored! scored everywhere; and the paragraph would have slidden through every
reader's sensibilities like oil, and left not a suspicion behind.*

The other sample inquiry is from a professor in a New England university. It contains one naughty word (which I cannot bear to suppress), but he is not in the theological department, so it is no harm:

Dear Mr. Clemens: "Far in the empty sky a solitary esophagus slept upon motionless wing."

It is not often I get a chance to read much periodical literature, but I have just gone through at this belated period, with much gratification and edification, your "Double-barreled Detective Story."

But what in hell is an esophagus? I keep one myself, but it never sleeps in the air or anywhere else. My profession is to deal with words, and esophagus interested me the moment I lighted upon it. But as a companion of my youth used to say, "I'll be eternally, co-eternally cussed" if I can make it out. Is it a joke, or I an ignoramus?

Between you and me, I was almost ashamed of having fooled that man, but for pride's sake I was going to say so. I wrote and told him it was a joke – and that is what I am now saying to my Springfield inquirer. And I told him to carefully read the whole paragraph, and he would find not a vestige of sense in any detail of it. This also I commend to my Springfield inquirer.

I have confessed. I am sorry – partially. I will not do so any more – for the present. Don't ask me any more questions; let the esophagus have a rest – on his same old motionless wing.

MARK TWAIN

New York City, April 10, 1902
(Editorial)
The "Double-barreled Detective Story," which appeared in Harper's Magazine *for January and February last, the most elaborate of burlesques on detective fiction, with striking melodramatic passages in which it is difficult to detect the deception, so ably is it done. But the illusion ought not to endure even the first incident in the February number. As for the paragraph which has so admirably illustrated the skill of*

Mr. Clemens's ensemble and the carelessness of readers, here it is:

"It was a crisp and spicy morning in early October. The lilacs and laburnums, lit with the glory-fires of autumn, hung burning and flashing in the upper air, a fairy bridge provided by kind nature for the wingless wild things that have their home in the tree-tops and would visit together; the larch and the pomegranate flung their purple and yellow flames in brilliant broad splashes along the slanting sweep of the woodland; the sensuous fragrance of innumerable deciduous flowers rose upon the swooning atmosphere; far in the empty sky a solitary esophagus slept upon motionless wings; everywhere brooded stillness, serenity, and the peace of God."

The success of Mark Twain's joke recalls to mind his story of the petrified man in the cavern, whom he described most punctiliously, first giving a picture of the scene, its impressive solitude, and all that; then going on to describe the majesty of the figure, casually mentioning that the thumb of his right hand rested against the side of his nose; then after further description observing that the fingers of the right hand were extended in a radiating fashion; and, recurring to the dignified attitude and position of the man, incidentally remarked that the thumb of the left hand was in contact with the little finger of the right – and so on. But was it so ingeniously written that Mark, relating the history years later in an article which appeared in that excellent magazine of the past, the Galaxy, *declared that no one ever found out the joke, and, if we remember aright, that that astonishing old mockery was actually looked for in the region where he, as a Nevada newspaper editor, had located it. It is certain that Mark Twain's jumping frog has a good many more "pints" than any other frog.*

October is the time – 1900; Hope Cañon is the place, a silver-mining camp away down in the Esmeralda region. It is a secluded spot, high and remote; recent as to discovery; thought by its occupants to be rich in metal – a year or two's prospecting will decide that matter one way or the other. For inhabitants, the camp has about two hundred miners, one white woman and child, several Chinese washermen, five squaws, and a dozen vagrant buck Indians in rabbit-skin robes, battered plug hats, and tin-can necklaces. There are no mills as yet; no church, no newspaper. The camp has existed but two years; it has made no big strike; the world is ignorant of its name and place.

On both sides of the cañon the mountains rise wall-like, three thousand feet, and the long spiral of straggling huts down in its narrow bottom gets a kiss from the sun only once a day, when he sails over at noon. The village is a couple of miles long; the cabins stand well apart from each other. The tavern is the only "frame" house – the only house, one might say. It occupies a central position, and is the evening resort of the population. They drink there, and play seven-up and dominoes; also billiards, for there is a table, crossed all over with torn places repaired with court-plaster; there are some cues, but no leathers; some chipped balls which clatter when they run, and do not slow up gradually, but stop suddenly and sit down; there is a part of a cube of chalk, with a projecting jag of flint in it; and the man who can score six on a single break can set up the drinks at the bar's expense.

Flint Buckner's cabin was the last one of the village, going south; his silver-claim was at the other end of the village, northward, and a little beyond the last hut in that direction. He was a sour creature, unsociable, and had no companionships. People who had tried to get acquainted with him had regretted it and dropped him. His history was not known. Some believed that Sammy Hillyer knew it; others said no. If asked, Hillyer said no, he was not acquainted with it. Flint had a meek English youth of sixteen or seventeen with him, whom he treated roughly, both in public and in private; and of course this lad was applied to for information, but with no success. Fetlock Jones – name of the youth – said that Flint picked him up on a prospecting tramp, and as he had neither home nor friends in America, he had found it wise to stay and take Buckner's hard usage for the sake of the salary, which was bacon and beans. Further than this he could offer no testimony.

Fetlock had been in this slavery for a month now, and under his meek exterior he was slowly consuming to a cinder with the insults and humiliations which his master had put upon him. For the meek suffer bitterly from these hurts; more bitterly, perhaps, than do the manlier sort, who can burst out and get relief with words or blows when the limit of endurance has been reached. Good-hearted people wanted to help Fetlock out of his trouble, and tried to get him to leave Buckner; but the boy showed fright at the thought, and said he "dasn't." Pat Riley urged him, and said:

"You leave the damned skunk and come with me; don't you be afraid. I'll take care of *him*."

The boy thanked him with tears in his eyes, but shuddered and said he "dasn't risk it"; he said Flint would catch him alone, some time, in the night, and then – "Oh, it makes me sick, Mr. Riley, to think of it."

Others said, "Run away from him; we'll stake you; skip out for the coast some night." But all these suggestions failed; he said Flint would hunt him down and fetch him back, just for meanness.

The people could not understand this. The boy's miseries went steadily on, week after week. It is quite likely that the people would have understood if they had known how he was employing his spare time. He slept in an out-cabin near Flint's; and there, nights, he nursed his bruises and his humiliations, and studied and studied over a single problem – how he could murder Flint Buckner and not be found out. It was the only joy he had in life; these hours were the only ones in the twenty-four which he looked forward to with eagerness and spent in happiness.

He thought of poison. No – that would not serve; the inquest would reveal where it was procured and who had procured it. He thought of a shot in the back in a lonely place when Flint would be homeward bound at midnight – his unvarying hour for the trip. No – somebody might be near, and catch him. He thought of stabbing him in his sleep. No – he might strike an inefficient blow, and Flint would seize him. He examined a hundred different ways – none of them would answer; for in even the very obscurest and secretest of them there was always the fatal defect of a *risk*, a chance, a possibility that he might be found out. He would have none of that.

But he was patient, endlessly patient. There was no hurry, he
said to himself. He would never leave Flint till he left him a
corpse; there was no hurry – he would find the way. It was
somewhere, and he would endure shame and pain and misery
until he found it. Yes, somewhere there was a way which would
leave not a trace, not even the faintest clue to the murderer –
there was no hurry – he would find that way, and then – oh,
then, it would just be good to be alive! Meantime he would
diligently keep up his reputation for meekness; and also, as
always theretofore, he would allow no one to hear him say a
resentful or offensive thing about his oppressor.

Two days before the before-mentioned October morning
Flint had bought some things, and he and Fetlock had brought
them home to Flint's cabin: a fresh box of candles, which they
put in the corner; a tin can of blasting-powder, which they
placed upon the candle-box; a keg of blasting-powder, which
they placed under Flint's bunk; a huge coil of fuse, which they
hung on a peg. Fetlock reasoned that Flint's mining operations
had outgrown the pick, and that blasting was about to begin
now. He had seen blasting done, and he had a notion of the
process, but he had never helped in it. His conjecture was right
– blasting-time had come. In the morning the pair carried fuse,
drills, and the powder-can to the shaft; it was now eight feet
deep, and to get into it and out of it a short ladder was used.
They descended, and by command Fetlock held the drill –
without any instructions as to the right way to hold it – and Flint
proceeded to strike. The sledge came down; the drill sprang out
of Fetlock's hand, almost as a matter of course.

"You mangy son of a nigger, is that any way to hold a drill?
Pick it up! Stand it up! There – hold fast. D—you! *I'll* teach
you!"

At the end of an hour the drilling was finished.

"Now, then, charge it."

The boy started to pour in the powder.

"Idiot!"

A heavy bat on the jaw laid the lad out.

"Get up! You can't lie sniveling there. Now, then, stick in the
fuse *first*. *Now* put in the powder. Hold on, hold on! Are you
going to fill the hole *all* up? Of all the sap-headed milksops I –

Put in some dirt! Put in some gravel! Tamp it down! Hold on, hold on! Oh, great Scott! get out of the way!" He snatched the iron and tamped the charge himself, meantime cursing and blaspheming like a fiend. Then he fired the fuse, climbed out of the shaft, and ran fifty yards away, Fetlock following. They stood waiting a few minutes, then a great volume of smoke and rocks burst high into the air with a thunderous explosion; after a little there was a shower of descending stones; then all was serene again.

"I wish to God you'd been in it!" remarked the master.

They went down the shaft, cleaned it out, drilled another hole, and put in another charge.

"Look here! How much fuse are you proposing to waste? Don't you know how to time a fuse?"

"No, sir."

"You *don't*! Well, if you don't beat anything *I* ever saw!"

He climbed out of the shaft and spoke down:

"Well, idiot, are you going to be all day? Cut the fuse and light it!"

The trembling creature began:

"If you please, sir, I—"

"You talk back to *me*? Cut it and light it!"

The boy cut and lit.

"Ger-reat Scott! a one-minute fuse! I wish you were in—"

In his rage he snatched the ladder out of the shaft and ran. The boy was aghast.

"Oh, my God! Help! Help! Oh, save me!" he implored. "Oh, what can I do! What *can* I do!"

He backed against the wall as tightly as he could; the sputtering fuse frightened the voice out of him; his breath stood still; he stood gazing and impotent; in two seconds, three seconds, four he would be flying toward the sky torn to fragments. Then he had an inspiration. He sprang at the fuse; severed the inch of it that was left above ground, and was saved.

He sank down limp and half lifeless with fright, his strength gone; but he muttered with a deep joy:

"He has learnt me! I knew there was a way, if I would wait."

After a matter of five minutes Buckner stole to the shaft, looking worried and uneasy, and peered down into it. He took in the situation; he saw what had happened. He lowered the ladder, and the boy dragged himself weakly up it. He was very white. His appearance added something to Buckner's uncomfortable state, and he said, with a show of regret and sympathy which sat upon him awkwardly from lack of practice:

"It was an accident, you know. Don't say anything about it to anybody; I was excited, and didn't notice what I was doing. You're not looking well; you've worked enough for to-day; go down to my cabin and eat what you want, and rest. It's just an accident, you know, on account of my being excited."

"It scared me," said the lad, as he started away; "but I learnt something, so I don't mind it."

"Damned easy to please!" muttered Buckner, following him with his eye. "I wonder if he'll tell? Mightn't he? . . . I wish it *had* killed him."

The boy took no advantage of his holiday in the matter of resting; he employed it in work, eager and feverish and happy work. A thick growth of chaparral extended down the mountainside clear to Flint's cabin; the most of Fetlock's labor was done in the dark intricacies of that stubborn growth; the rest of it was done in his own shanty. At last all was complete, and he said:

"If he's got any suspicions that I'm going to tell on him, he won't keep them long, to-morrow. He will see that I am the same milksop as I always was – all day and the next. And the day after to-morrow night there'll be an end of him; nobody will ever guess who finished him up nor how it was done. He dropped me the idea his own self, and that's odd."

5

The next day came and went.

It is now almost midnight, and in five minutes the new morning will begin. The scene is in the tavern billiard-room. Rough men in rough clothing, slouch-hats, breeches stuffed into boot-tops, some with vests, none with coats, are grouped about the boiler-iron stove, which has ruddy cheeks and is distributing a grateful warmth; the billiard-balls are clacking; there is no other sound – that is, within; the wind is fitfully moaning without. The men look bored; also expectant. A hulking broad-shouldered miner, of middle age, with grizzled whiskers, and an unfriendly eye set in an unsociable face, rises, slips a coil of fuse upon his arm, gathers up some other personal properties, and departs without word or greeting to anybody. It is Flint Buckner. As the door closes behind him a buzz of talk breaks out.

"The regularest man that ever was," said Jake Parker, the blacksmith: "you can tell when it's twelve just by him leaving, without looking at your Waterbury."

"And it's the only virtue he's got, as fur as I know," said Peter Hawes, miner.

"He's just a blight on this society," said Wells-Fargo's man, Ferguson. "If I was running this shop I'd made him say something, *some* time or other, or vamos the ranch." This with a suggestive glance at the barkeeper, who did not choose to see it, since the man under discussion was a good customer, and went home pretty well set up, every night, with refreshments furnished from the bar.

"Say," said Ham Sandwich, miner, "does any of you boys ever recollect of him asking you to take a drink?"

"*Him*? Flint *Buckner*? Oh, Laura!"

This sarcastic rejoinder came in a spontaneous general outburst in one form of words or another from the crowd. After a brief silence, Pat Riley, miner, said:

"He's the 15-puzzle, that cuss. And his boy's another one. *I* can't make them out."

"Nor anybody else," said Ham Sandwich; "and if they are 15-puzzles, how are you going to rank up that other one? When it comes to A1 right-down solid mysteriousness, he lays over both of them. *Easy* – don't he?"

"You bet!"

Everybody said it. Every man but one. He was the newcomer – Peterson. He ordered the drinks all round, and asked who No. 3 might be. All answered at once, "Archy Stillman!"

"Is he a mystery?" asked Peterson.

"Is *he* a mystery? Is Archy *Stillman* a mystery?" said Wells-Fargo's man, Ferguson. "Why, the fourth dimension's foolishness to *him*."

For Ferguson was learned.

Peterson wanted to hear all about him; everybody wanted to tell him; everybody began. But Billy Stevens, the barkeeper, called the house to order, and said one at a time was best. He distributed the drinks, and appointed Ferguson to lead. Ferguson said:

"Well, he's a boy. And that is just about all we know about him. You can pump him till you are tired; it ain't any use; you won't get anything. At least about his intentions, or line of business, or where he's from, and such things as that. And as for getting at the nature and get-up of his main big chief mystery, why, he'll just change the subject, that's all. You can *guess* till you're black in the face – it's your privilege – but suppose you do, where do you arrive at? Nowhere, as near as I can make out."

"What *is* his big chief one?"

"Sight, maybe. Hearing, maybe. Instinct, maybe. Magic, maybe. Take your choice – grownups, twenty-five; children and servants, half price. Now I'll tell you what he can do. You can start here, and just disappear; you can go and hide wherever you want to, I don't care where it is, nor how far – and he'll go straight and put his finger on you."

"You don't mean it!"

"I just do, though. Weather's nothing to him – elemental conditions is nothing to him – he don't even take notice of them."

"Oh, come! Dark? Rain? Snow? Hey?"

"It's all the same to *him*. He don't give a damn."

"Oh, *say* – including *fog*, per'aps?"

"*Fog*! he's got an eye't can plunk through it like a bullet."

"Now, boys, honor bright, what's he giving me?"

"It's a fact!" they all shouted. "Go on, Wells-Fargo."

"Well, sir, you can leave him here, chatting with the boys, and you can slip out and go to any cabin in this camp and open a book – yes, sir, a dozen of them – and take the page in your memory, and he'll start out and go straight to that cabin and open every one of them books at the right page, and call it off, and never make a mistake."

"He must be the devil!"

"More than one has thought it. Now I'll tell you a perfectly wonderful thing that he done. The other night he—"

There was a sudden great murmur of sounds outside, the door flew open, and an excited crowd burst in, with the camp's one white woman in the lead and crying:

"My child! my child! she's lost and gone! For the love of God help me to find Archy Stillman; we've hunted everywhere!"

Said the barkeeper:

"Sit down, sit down, Mrs. Hogan, and don't worry. He asked for a bed three hours ago, tuckered out tramping the trails the way he's always doing, and went upstairs. Ham Sandwich, run up and roust him out; he's in No. 14."

The youth was soon downstairs and ready. He asked Mrs. Hogan for particulars.

"Bless you, dear, there ain't any; I wish there was. I put her to sleep at seven in the evening, and when I went in there an hour ago to go to bed myself, she was gone. I rushed for your cabin, dear, and you wasn't there, and I've hunted for you ever since, at every cabin down the gulch, and now I've come up again, and I'm that distracted and scared and heartbroke; but, thanks to God, I've found you at last, dear heart, and you'll find my child. Come on! come quick!"

"Move right along; I'm with you, madam. Go to your cabin first."

The whole company streamed out to join the hunt. All the southern half of the village was up, a hundred men strong, and waiting outside, a vague dark mass sprinkled with twinkling lanterns. The mass fell into columns by threes and fours to accommodate itself to the narrow road, and strode briskly along southward in the wake of the leaders. In a few minutes the Hogan cabin was reached.

"There's the bunk," said Mrs. Hogan; "there's where she was; it's where I laid her at seven o'clock; but where she is now, God only knows."

"Hand me a lantern," said Archy. He set it on the hard earth floor and knelt by it, pretending to examine the ground closely. "Here's her track," he said, touching the ground here and there and yonder with his finger. "Do you see?"

Several of the company dropped upon their knees and did

their best to see. One or two thought they discerned something like a track; the others shook their heads and confessed that the smooth hard surface had no marks upon it which their eyes were sharp enough to discover. One said, "Maybe a child's foot could make a mark on it, but *I* don't see how."

Young Stillman stepped outside, held the light to the ground, turned leftward, and moved three steps, closely examining; then said, "I've got the direction – come along; take the lantern, somebody."

He strode off swiftly southward, the files following, swaying and bending in and out with the deep curves of the gorge. Thus a mile, and the mouth of the gorge was reached, before them stretched the sage-brush plain, dim, vast, and vague. Stillman called a halt, saying, "We mustn't start wrong, now; we must take the direction again."

He took a lantern and examined the ground for a matter of twenty yards; then said, "Come on; it's all right," and gave up the lantern. In and out among the sage-bushes he marched, a quarter of a mile, bearing gradually to the right; then took a new direction and made another great semicircle; then changed again and moved due west nearly half a mile – and stopped.

"She gave it up, here, poor little chap. Hold the lantern. You can see where she sat."

But this was in a slick alkali flat which was surfaced like steel, and no person in the party was quite hardy enough to claim an eyesight that could detect the track of a cushion on a veneer like that. The bereaved mother fell upon her knees and kissed the spot, lamenting.

"But where is she, then?" some one said. "She didn't stay here. We can see *that* much, anyway."

Stillman moved about in a circle around the place, with the lantern, pretending to hunt for tracks.

"Well!" he said presently, in an annoyed tone, "I don't understand it." He examined again. "No use. She was here – that's certain; she never *walked* away from here – and that's certain. It's a puzzle; I can't make it out."

The mother lost heart then.

"Oh, my God! oh, blessed Virgin! some flying beast has got her. I'll never see her again!"

"Ah, *don't* give up," said Archy. "We'll find her – don't give up."

"God bless you for the words, Archy Stillman!" and she seized his hand and kissed it fervently.

Peterson, the new-comer, whispered satirically in Ferguson's ear:

"Wonderful performance to find this place, wasn't it? Hardly worth while to come so far, though; any other supposititious place would have answered just as well – hey?"

Ferguson was not pleased with the innuendo. He said, with some warmth:

"Do you mean to insinuate that the child hasn't been here? I tell you the child *has* been here! Now if you want to get yourself into as tidy a little fuss as—"

"All right!" sang out Stillman. "Come, everybody, and look at this! It was right under our noses all the time, and we didn't see it."

There was a general plunge for the ground at the place where the child was alleged to have rested, and many eyes tried hard and hopefully to see the thing that Archy's finger was resting upon. There was a pause, then a several-barreled sigh of disappointment. Pat Riley and Ham Sandwich said, in the one breath:

"What is it, Archy? There's nothing here."

"Nothing? Do you call *that* nothing?" and he swiftly traced upon the ground a form with his finger. "There – don't you recognize it now? It's Injun Billy's track. He's got the child."

"God be praised!" from the mother.

"Take away the lantern. I've got the direction. Follow!"

He started on a run, racing in and out among the sage-bushes a matter of three hundred yards, and disappeared over a sand-wave; the others struggled after him, caught him up, and found him waiting. Ten steps away was a little wickiup, a dim and formless shelter of rags and old horseblankets, a dull light showing through its chinks.

"You lead, Mrs. Hogan," said the lad. "It's your privilege to be first."

All followed the sprint she made for the wickiup, and saw, with her, the picture its interior afforded. Injun Billy was sitting on the ground; the child was asleep beside him. The mother hugged it with a wild embrace, which included Archy Stillman, the grateful tears running down her face, and in a choked and broken voice she poured out a golden stream of that wealth of worshiping endearments which has its home in full richness nowhere but in the Irish heart.

"I find her bymeby it is ten o'clock," Billy explained. "She 'sleep out yonder, ve'y tired – face wet, been cryin', 'spose; fetch her home, feed her, she heap much hungry – go 'sleep 'gin."

In her limitless gratitude the happy mother waived rank and hugged him too, calling him "the angel of God in disguise." And he probably was in disguise if he was that kind of an official. He was dressed for the character.

At half past one in the morning the procession burst into the village singing, "When Johnny Comes Marching Home," waving its lanterns, and swallowing the drinks that were brought out all along its course. It concentrated at the tavern, and made a night of what was left of the morning.

6

The next afternoon the village was electrified with an immense sensation. A grave and dignified foreigner of distinguished bearing and appearance had arrived at the tavern, and entered this formidable name upon the register:

SHERLOCK HOLMES

The news buzzed from cabin to cabin, from claim to claim; tools were dropped, and the town swarmed toward the center of interest. A man passing out at the northern end of the village shouted it to Pat Riley, whose claim was the next one to Flint Buckner's. At that time Fetlock Jones seemed to turn sick. He muttered to himself:

"Uncle *Sherlock*! the mean luck of it! – that *he* should come just when . . ." He dropped into a reverie, and presently said to himself: "But what's the use of being afraid of *him*? Anybody that knows him the way I do knows he can't detect a crime except where he plans it all out beforehand and arranges the

clues and hires some fellow to commit it according to instructions. . . . Now there ain't going to *be* any clues this time – so,
what show has he got? None at all. No, sir; everything's ready.
If I was to risk putting it off – . . . No, I won't run any risk like
that. Flint Buckner goes out of this world to-night, for sure."
Then another trouble presented itself. "Uncle Sherlock'll be
wanting to talk home matters with me this evening, and how am
I going to get rid of him? for I've *got* to be at my cabin a minute
or two about eight o'clock." This was an awkward matter, and
cost him much thought. But he found a way to beat the
difficulty. "We'll go for a walk, and I'll leave him in the road
a minute, so that he won't see what it is I do: the best way to
throw a detective off the track, anyway, is to have him along
when you are preparing the thing. Yes, that's the safest – I'll
take him with me."

Meantime the road in front of the tavern was blocked with
villagers waiting and hoping for a glimpse of the great man. But
he kept his room, and did not appear. None but Ferguson, Jake
Parker the blacksmith, and Ham Sandwich had any luck. These
enthusiastic admirers of the great scientific detective hired the
tavern's detained-baggage lockup, which looked into the detective's room across a little alleyway ten or twelve feet wide,
ambushed themselves in it, and cut some peep-holes in the
window-blind. Mr. Holmes's blinds were down; but by and by
he raised them. It gave the spies a hair-lifting but pleasurable
thrill to find themselves face to face with the Extraordinary
Man who had filled the world with the fame of his more human
ingenuities. There he sat – not a myth, not a shadow, but real,
alive, compact of substance, and almost within touching distance with the hand.

"Look at that head!" said Ferguson, in an awed voice. "By
gracious! *That's* a head!"

"You bet!" said the blacksmith, with deep reverence. "Look
at his nose! look at his eyes! Intellect? Just a battery of it!"

"And that paleness," said Ham Sandwich. "Comes from
thought – that's what it comes from. Hell! duffers like us don't
know what real thought *is*."

"No more we don't," said Ferguson. "What we take for
thinking is just blubber-and-slush."

"Right you are, Wells-Fargo. And look at that frown – that's *deep* thinking – away down, down, forty fathoms into the bowels of things. He's on the track of something."

"Well, he is, and don't you forget it. Say – look at that awful gravity – look at that pallid solemnness – there ain't any corpse can lay over it."

"No, sir, not for dollars! And it's his'n by hereditary rights, too; he's been dead four times a'ready, and there's history for it. Three times natural, once by accident. I've heard say he smells damp and cold, like a grave. And he—"

" 'Sh! Watch him! There – he's got his thumb on the bump on the near corner of his forehead, and his forefinger on the off one. His think-works is just a-*grinding* now, you bet your other shirt."

"That's so. And now he's gazing up toward heaven and stroking his mustache slow, and—"

"Now he has rose up standing, and is putting his clues together on his left fingers with his right finger. See? he touches the forefinger – now middle finger – now ring-finger—"

"Stuck!"

"Look at him scowl! He can't seem to make out *that* clue. So he—"

"See him smile! – like a tiger – and tally off the other fingers like nothing! He's got it, boys; he's got it sure!"

"Well, I should *say*! I'd hate to be in that man's place that he's after."

Mr. Holmes drew a table to the window, sat down with his back to the spies, and proceeded to write. The spies withdrew their eyes from the peep-holes, lit their pipes, and settled themselves for a comfortable smoke and talk. Ferguson said, with conviction:

"Boys, it's no use talking, he's a wonder! He's got the signs of it all over him."

"You hain't ever said a truer word than that, Wells-Fargo," said Jake Parker. "Say, wouldn't it 'a' been nuts if he'd a-been here last night?"

"Oh, by George, but wouldn't it!" said Ferguson. "Then we'd have seen *scientific* work. Intellect – just pure intellect – away up on the upper levels, dontchuknow. Archy is all right, and it don't become anybody to belittle *him*, I can tell you. But his gift is only just eyesight, sharp as an owl's, as near as I can make it out just a grand natural animal talent, no more, no less, and prime as far as it goes, but no intellect in it, and for awfulness and marvelousness no more to be compared to what this man does than – than – Why, let me tell you what *he'd* have done. He'd have stepped over to Hogan's and glanced – just *glanced*, that's all – at the premises, and that's enough. See everything? Yes, sir, to the last little *de*tail; and he'd know more about that place than the Hogans would know in seven years. Next, he would sit down on the bunk, just as ca'm, and say to Mrs. Hogan – *Say*, Ham, consider that you are Mrs. Hogan. I'll ask the questions; you answer them."

"All right; go on."

" 'Madam, if you please – attention – do not let your mind wander. Now, then – sex of the child?'

" 'Female, your Honor.'

" 'Um – female. Very good, very good. Age?'

" 'Turned six, your Honor.'

" 'Um – young, weak – two miles. Weariness will overtake it then. It will sink down and sleep. We shall find it two miles away, or less. Teeth?'

" 'Five, your Honor, and one a-coming.'

" 'Very good, very good, *very* good, indeed.' You see, boys, *he* knows a clue when he sees it, when it wouldn't mean a dern thing to anybody else. 'Stockings, madam? Shoes?'

" 'Yes, your Honor – both.'

" 'Yarn, perhaps? Morocco?'

" 'Yarn, your Honor. And kip.'

" 'Um – kip. This complicates the matter. However, let it go – we shall manage. Religion?'

" 'Catholic, your Honor.'

" 'Very good. Snip me a bit from the bed blanket, please. Ah, thanks. Part wool – foreign make. Very well. A snip from some garment of the child's, please. Thanks. Cotton. Shows wear. An excellent clue, excellent. Pass me a pallet of the floor dirt, if you'll be so kind. Thanks, many thanks. Ah, admirable, admirable! *Now* we know where we are, I think,' You see, boys, he's got all the clues he wants now; he don't need

anything more. Now, then, what does this Extraordinary Man
do? He lays those snips and that dirt out on the table and leans
over them on his elbows, and puts them together side by side
and studies them – mumbles to himself, 'Female'; changes
them around – mumbles, 'Six years old'; changes them this
way and that – again mumbles: 'Five teeth – one a-coming –
Catholic – yarn – cotton – kip – damn that kip.' Then he
straightens up and gazes toward heaven, and plows his hands
through his hair – plows and plows, muttering, 'Damn that
kip!' Then he stands up and frowns, and begins to tally off his
clues on his fingers – and gets stuck at the ring-finger. But
only just a minute – then his face glares all up in a smile like a
house afire, and he straightens up stately and majestic, and
says to the crowd, 'Take a lantern, a couple of you, and go
down to Injun Billy's and fetch the child – the rest of you go
'long home to bed; good-night, madam; good-night, gents.'
And he bows like the Matterhorn, and pulls out for the tavern.
That's *his* style, and the *Only* – scientific, intellectual – all over
in fifteen minutes – no poking around all over the sage-brush
range an hour and a half in a mass-meeting crowd for *him*,
boys – you hear *me*!"

"By Jackson, it's grand!" said Ham Sandwich. "Wells-
Fargo, you've got him down to a dot. He ain't painted up
any exacter to the life in the books. By George, I can juse *see* him
– can't you, boys?"

"You bet you! It's just a photograft, that's what it is."

Ferguson was profoundly pleased with his success, and grateful. He sat silently enjoying his happiness a little while, then he
murmured, with a deep awe in his voice,

"I wonder if God made him?"

There was no response for a moment; then Ham Sandwich
said, reverently:

"Not all at one time, I reckon."

7

At eight o'clock that evening two persons were groping their
way past Flint Buckner's cabin in the frosty gloom. They were
Sherlock Holmes and his nephew.

"Stop here in the road a moment, uncle," said Fetlock, "while I run to my cabin; I won't be gone a minute."

He asked for something – the uncle furnished it – then he disappeared in the darkness, but soon returned, and the talking-walk was resumed. By nine o'clock they had wandered back to the tavern. They worked their way through the billiard-room, where a crowd had gathered in the hope of getting a glimpse of the Extraordinary Man. A royal cheer was raised. Mr. Holmes acknowledged the compliment with a series of courtly bows, and as he was passing out his nephew said to the assemblage:

"Uncle Sherlock's got some work to do, gentlemen, that'll keep him till twelve or one; but he'll be down again then, or earlier if he can, and hopes some of you'll be left to take a drink with him."

"By George, he's just a duke, boys! Three cheers for Sherlock Holmes, the greatest man that ever lived!" shouted Ferguson. "Hip, hip, hip—"

"Hurrah! hurrah! hurrah! Tiger!"

The uproar shook the building, so hearty was the feeling the boys put into their welcome. Upstairs the uncle reproached the nephew gently, saying:

"What did you get me into that engagement for?"

"I reckon you don't want to be unpopular, do you, uncle? Well, then, don't you put on any exclusiveness in a mining-camp, that's all. The boys admire you; but if you was to leave without taking a drink with them, they'd set you down for a snob. And besides, you said you had home talk enough in stock to keep us up and at it half the night."

The boy was right, and wise – the uncle acknowledged it. The boy was wise in another detail which he did not mention – except to himself: "Uncle and the others will come handy – in the way of nailing an *alibi* where it can't be budged."

He and his uncle talked diligently about three hours. Then, about midnight, Fetlock stepped downstairs and took a position in the dark a dozen steps from the tavern, and waited. Five minutes later Flint Buckner came rocking out of the billiard-room and almost brushed him as he passed.

"I've *got* him!" muttered the boy. He continued to himself, looking after the shadowy form: "Good-bye – good-bye for good, Flint Buckner; you called my mother a – well, never mind what: it's all right, now; you're taking your last walk, friend."

He went musing back into the tavern. "From now till one is an hour. We'll spend it with the boys: it's good for the *alibi*."

He brought Sherlock Holmes to the billiard-room, which was jammed with eager and admiring miners; the guest called the drinks, and the fun began. Everybody was happy; everybody was complimentary; the ice was soon broken, songs, anecdotes, and more drinks followed, and the pregnant minutes flew. At six minutes to one, when the jollity was at its highest –

Boom!

There was silence instantly. The deep sound came rolling and rumbling from peak to peak up the gorge, then died down, and ceased. The spell broke, then, and the men made a rush for the door, saying:

"Something's blown up!"

Outside, a voice in the darkness said, "It's away down the gorge; I saw the flash."

The crowd poured down the cañon – Holmes, Fetlock, Archy Stillman, everybody. They made the mile in a few minutes. By the light of a lantern they found the smooth and solid dirt floor of Flint Buckner's cabin; of the cabin itself not a vestige remained, not a rag nor a splinter. Nor any sign of Flint. Search-parties sought here and there and yonder, and presently a cry went up.

"Here he is!"

It was true. Fifty yards down the gulch they had found him – that is, they had found a crushed and lifeless mass which represented him. Fetlock Jones hurried thither with the others and looked.

The inquest was a fifteen-minute affair. Ham Sandwich, foreman of the jury, handed up the verdict, which was phrased with a certain unstudied literary grace, and closed with this finding, to wit: that "deceased came to his death by his own act or some other person or persons unknown to this jury not leaving any family or similar effects behind but his cabin which was blown away and God have mercy on his soul amen."

Then the impatient jury rejoined the main crowd, for the storm-center of interest was there – Sherlock Holmes. The miners stood silent and reverent in a half-circle, inclosing a large vacant space which included the front exposure of the site of the late premises. In this considerable space the Extraordinary Man was moving about, attended by his nephew with a lantern. With a tape he took measurements of the cabin site; of the distance from the wall of chaparral to the road; of the height of the chaparral bushes; also various other measurements. He gathered a rag here, a splinter there, and a pinch of earth yonder, inspected them profoundly, and preserved them. He took the "lay" of the place with a pocket-compass, allowing two seconds for magnetic variation. He took the time (Pacific) by his watch, correcting it for local time. He paced off the distance from the cabin site to the corpse, and corrected that for tidal differentiation. He took the altitude with a pocket-aneroid, and the temperature with a pocket-thermometer. Finally he said, with a stately bow:

"It is finished. Shall we return, gentlemen?"

He took up the line of march for the tavern, and the crowd fell into his wake, earnestly discussing and admiring the Extraordinary Man, and interlarding guesses as to the origin of the tragedy and who the author of it might be.

"My, but it's grand luck having him here – hey, boys?" said Ferguson.

"It's the biggest thing of the century," said Ham Sandwich. "It'll go all over the world; you mark my words."

"*You* bet!" said Jake Parker, the blacksmith. "It'll boom this camp. Ain't it so, Wells-Fargo?"

"Well, as you want my opinion – if it's any sign of how *I* think about it, I can tell you this: yesterday I was holding the Straight Flush claim at two dollars a foot; I'd like to see the man that can get it at sixteen to-day."

"Right you are, Wells-Fargo! It's the grandest luck a new camp ever struck. Say, did you see him collar them little rags and dirt and things? What an eye! He just can't overlook a clue – 'tain't *in* him."

"That's so. And they wouldn't mean a thing to anybody else; but to him, why, they're just a book – large print at that."

"Sure's you're born! Them odds and ends have got their little old secret, and they think there ain't anybody can pull it; but, land! when he sets his grip there they've got to squeal, and don't you forget it."

"Boys, I ain't sorry, now, that he wasn't here to roust out the child; this is a bigger thing, by a long sight. Yes, sir, and more tangled up and scientific and intellectual."

"I reckon we're all of us glad it's turned out this way. Glad? 'George! it ain't any name for it. Dontchuknow, Archy could've *learnt* something if he'd had the nous to stand by and take notice of how that man works the system. But no; he went poking up into the chaparral and just missed the whole thing."

"It's true as gospel; I seen it myself. Well, Archy's young. He'll know better one of these days."

"Say, boys, who do you reckon done it?"

That was a difficult question, and brought out a world of unsatisfying conjecture. Various men were mentioned as possibilities, but one by one they were discarded as not being eligible. No one but young Hillyer had been intimate with Flint Buckner; no one had really had a quarrel with him; he had affronted every man who had tried to make up to him, although not quite offensively enough to require bloodshed. There was one name that was upon every tongue from the start, but it was the last to get utterance – Fetlock Jones's. It was Pat Riley that mentioned it.

"Oh, well," the boys said, "of course we've all thought of him, because he had a million rights to kill Flint Buckner, and it was just his plain duty to do it. But all the same there's two things we can't get around: for one thing, he hasn't got the sand; and for another, he wasn't anywhere near the place when it happened."

"I know it," said Pat. "He was there in the billiard-room with us when it happened."

"Yes, and was there all the time for an hour *before* it happened."

"It's so. And lucky for him, too. He'd have been suspected in a minute if it hadn't been for that."

8

The tavern dining-room had been cleared of all its furniture save one six-foot pine table and a chair. This table was against one end of the room; the chair was on it; Sherlock Holmes, stately, imposing, impressive, sat in the chair. The public stood. The room was full. The tobacco-smoke was dense, the stillness profound.

The Extraordinary Man raised his hand to command additional silence; held it in the air a few moments; then, in brief, crisp terms he put forward question after question, and noted the answers with "Um-ums," nods of the head, and so on. By this process he learned all about Flint Buckner, his character, conduct, and habits, that the people were able to tell him. It thus transpired that the Extraordinary Man's nephew was the only person in the camp who had a killing-grudge against Flint Buckner. Mr. Holmes smiled compassionately upon the witness, and asked, languidly:

"Do any of you gentlemen chance to know where the lad Fetlock Jones was at the time of the explosion?"

A thunderous response followed:

"In the billiard-room of this house!"

"Ah. And had he just come in?"

"Been there all of an hour!"

"Ah. It is about – about – well, about how far might it be to the scene of the explosion?"

"All of a mile!"

"Ah. It isn't *much* of an alibi, 'tis true, but—"

A storm-burst of laughter, mingled with shouts of "By jiminy, but he's chain-lightning!" and "Ain't you sorry you spoke, Sandy?" shut off the rest of the sentence, and the crushed witness drooped his blushing face in pathetic shame. The inquisitor resumed:

"The lad Jones's somewhat *distant* connection with the case" (*laughter*) "having been disposed of, let us now call the *eye*-witnesses of the tragedy, and listen to what they have to say."

He got out his fragmentary clues and arranged them on a sheet of cardboard on his knee. The house held its breath and watched.

"We have the longitude and the latitude, corrected for magnetic variation, and this gives us the exact location of the tragedy. We have the altitude, the temperature, and the degree of humidity prevailing – inestimably valuable, since they enable us to estimate with precision the degree of influence which they would exercise upon the mood and disposition of the assassin at that time of the night."

(*Buzz of admiration; muttered remark, "By George, but he's deep!"*) He fingered his clues. "And now let us ask these mute witnesses to speak to us.

"Here we have an empty linen shot-bag. What is its message? This: that robbery was the motive, not revenge. What is its further message? This: that the assassin was of inferior intelligence – shall we say light-witted, or perhaps approaching that? How do we know this? Because a person of sound intelligence would not have proposed to rob the man Buckner, who never had much money with him. But the assassin might have been a stranger? Let the bag speak again. I take from it this article. It is a bit of silver-bearing quartz. It is peculiar. Examine it, please – you – and you – and you. Now pass it back, please. There is but one lode on this coast which produces just that character and color of quartz; and that is a lode which crops out for nearly two miles on a stretch, and in my opinion is destined, at no distant day, to confer upon its locality a globe-girdling celebrity, and upon its two hundred owners riches beyond the dreams of avarice. Name that lode, please."

"The Consolidated Christian Science and Mary Ann!" was the prompt response.

A wild crash of hurrahs followed, and every man reached for his neighbor's hand and wrung it, with tears in his eyes; and Wells-Fargo Ferguson shouted, "The Straight Flush is on the lode, and up she goes to a hundred and fifty a foot – you hear *me*!"

When quiet fell, Mr. Holmes resumed:

"We perceive, then, that three facts are established, to wit: the assassin was approximately light-witted; he was not a stranger; his motive was robbery, not revenge. Let us proceed. I hold in my hand a small fragment of fuse, with the recent smell of fire upon it. What is its testimony? Taken with the corroborative evidence of the quartz, it reveals to us that the assassin was a miner. What does it tell us further? This, gentlemen: that the assassination was consummated by means of an explosive. What else does it say? This: that the explosive was located against the side of the cabin nearest the road – the front side – for within six feet of that spot I found it.

"I hold in my fingers a burnt Swedish match – the kind one rubs on a safety-box. I found it in the road, six hundred and twenty-two feet from the abolished cabin. What does it say? This: that the train was fired from that point. What further does it tell us? This: that the assassin was left-handed. How do I know this? I should not be able to explain to you, gentlemen, how I know it, the signs being so subtle that only long experience and deep study can enable one to detect them. But the signs are here, and they are reinforced by a fact which you must have often noticed in the great detective narratives – that *all* assassins are left-handed."

"By Jackson, *that's* so!" said Ham Sandwich, bringing his great hand down with a resounding slap upon his thigh; "blamed if I ever thought of it before."

"Nor I!" "Nor I!" cried several. "Oh, there can't anything escape *him* – look at his eye!"

"Gentlemen, distant as the murderer was from his doomed victim, he did not wholly escape injury. This fragment of wood which I now exhibit to you struck him. It drew blood. Wherever he is, he bears the telltale mark. I picked it up where he stood when he fired the fatal train." He looked out over the house from his high perch, and his countenance began to darken; he slowly raised his hand, and pointed:

"There stands the assassin!"

For a moment the house was paralyzed with amazement; then twenty voices burst out with:

"Sammy Hillyer? Oh, *hell*, no! *Him*? It's pure foolishness!"

"Take care, gentlemen – be not hasty. Observe – he has the bloodmark on his brow."

Hillyer turned white with fright. He was near to crying. He turned this way and that, appealing to every face for help and sympathy; and held out his supplicating hands toward Holmes and began to plead:

"*Don't*, oh, don't! I never did it; I give my word I never did it. The way I got this hurt on my forehead was—"

"Arrest him, constable!" cried Holmes. "I will swear out the warrant."

The constable moved reluctantly forward – hesitated – stopped.

Hillyer broke out with another appeal. "Oh, Archy, don't let them do it; it would kill mother! *You* know how I got the hurt. Tell them, and save me, Archy; save me!"

Stillman worked his way to the front, and said:

"Yes, I'll save you. Don't be afraid." Then he said to the house, "Never mind how he got the hurt; it hasn't anything to do with this case, and isn't of any consequence."

"God bless you, Archy, for a true friend!"

"Hurrah for Archy! Go in, boy, and play 'em a knockdown flush to their two pair 'n' a jack!" shouted the house, pride in their home talent and a patriotic sentiment of loyalty to it rising suddenly in the public heart and changing the whole attitude of the situation.

Young Stillman waited for the noise to cease; then he said:

"I will ask Tom Jeffries to stand by that door yonder, and Constable Harris to stand by the other one here, and not let anybody leave the room."

"Said and done. Go on, old man!"

"The criminal is present, I believe. I will show him to you before long, in case I am right in my guess. Now I will tell you all about the tragedy, from start to finish. The motive *wasn't* robbery; it was revenge. The murderer *wasn't* light-witted. He *didn't* stand six hundred and twenty-two feet away. He *didn't* get hit with a piece of wood. He *didn't* place the explosive against the cabin. He *didn't* bring a shot-bag with him, and he *wasn't* left-handed. With the exception of these errors, the distinguished guest's statement of the case is substantially correct."

A comfortable laugh rippled over the house; friend nodded to friend, as much as to say, "That's the word, with the bark *on* it. Good lad, good boy. *He* ain't lowering his flag any!"

The guest's serenity was not disturbed. Stillman resumed:

"I also have some witnesses; and I will presently tell you where you can find some more." He held up a piece of coarse wire; the crowd craned their necks to see. "It has a smooth coating of melted tallow on it. And here is a candle which is burned half-way down. The remaining half of it has marks cut upon it an inch apart. Soon I will tell you where I found these things. I will now put aside reasonings, guesses, the impressive hitchings of odds and ends of clues together, and the other showy theatricals of the detective trade, and tell you in a plain, straightforward way just how this dismal thing happened."

He paused a moment, for effect – to allow silence and suspense to intensify and concentrate the house's interest; then he went on:

"The assassin studied out his plan with a good deal of pains. It was a good plan, very ingenious, and showed an intelligent mind, not a feeble one. It was a plan which was well calculated to ward off all suspicion from its inventor. In the first place, he marked a candle into spaces an inch apart, and lit it and timed it. He found it took three hours to burn four inches of it. I tried it myself for half an hour, awhile ago, upstairs here, while the inquiry into Flint Buckner's character and ways was being conducted in this room, and I arrived in that way at the rate of a candle's consumption when sheltered from the wind. Having proved his trial candle's rate, he blew it out – I have already shown it to you – and put his inch-marks on a fresh one.

"He put the fresh one into a tin candlestick. Then at the five-hour mark he bored a hole through the candle with a red-hot wire. I have already shown you the wire, with a smooth coat of tallow on it – tallow that had been melted and had cooled.

"With labor – very hard labor, I should say – he struggled up through the stiff chaparral that clothes the steep hillside back of Flint Buckner's place, tugging an empty flour-barrel with him. He placed it in that absolutely secure hiding-place, and in the bottom of it he set the candlestick. Then he measured off about thirty-five feet of fuse – the barrel's distance from the back of the cabin. He bored a hole in the side of the barrel – here is the large gimlet he did it with. He went on and finished his work; and when it was done, one end of the fuse was in Buckner's cabin, and the other end, with a notch chipped in it to expose the powder, was in the hole in the candle – timed to blow the place up at one o'clock this morning, provided the candle was lit about eight o'clock yesterday evening – which I am betting it was – and provided there was an explosive in the cabin and connected with that end of the fuse – which I am also betting there was, though I can't prove it. Boys, the barrel is there in the chaparral, the candle's remains are in it in the tin stick; the burnt-out fuse is in the gimlet-hole, the other end is down the hill where the late cabin stood. I saw them all an hour or two ago, when the Professor here was measuring off unimplicated vacancies and collecting relics that hadn't anything to do with the case."

He paused. The house drew a long, deep breath, shook its strained cords and muscles free and burst into cheers. "Dang him!" said Ham Sandwich, "that's why he was snooping around in the chaparral, instead of picking up points out of the P'fessor's game. Looky here – *he* ain't no fool, boys."

"No, sir! Why, great Scott—"

But Stillman was resuming:

"While we were out yonder an hour or two ago, the owner of the gimlet and the trial candle took them from a place where he had concealed them – it was not a good place – and carried them to what he probably thought was a better one, two hundred yards up in the pine woods, and hid them there, covering them over with pine needles. It was there that I found them. The gimlet exactly fits the hole in the barrel. And now—"

The Extraordinary Man interrupted him. He said, sarcastically:

"We have had a very pretty fairy tale, gentlemen – very pretty indeed. Now I would like to ask this young man a question or two."

Some of the boys winced, and Ferguson said:

"I'm afraid Archy's going to catch it now."

The others lost their smiles and sobered down. Mr. Holmes said:

"Let us proceed to examine into this fairy tale in a consecutive and orderly way – by geometrical progression, so to speak – linking detail to detail in a steadily advancing and remorselessly consistent and unassailable march upon this tinsel toy fortress of error, the dream fabric of a callow imagination. To begin with, young sir, I desire to ask you but three questions at present – *at present*. Did I understand you to say it was your opinion that the supposititious candle was lighted at about eight o'clock yesterday evening?"

"Yes, sir – about eight."

"Could you say exactly eight?"

"Well, no, I couldn't be that exact."

"Um. If a person had been passing along there just about that time, he would have been almost sure to encounter that assassin, do you think?"

"Yes, I should think so."

"Thank you, that is all. For the present. I say, all *for the present*."

"Dern him! he's laying for Archy," said Ferguson.

"It's so," said Ham Sandwich. "I don't like the look of it."

Stillman said, glancing at the guest, "I was along there myself at half-past eight – no, about nine."

"Indeed? This is interesting – this is very interesting. Perhaps you encountered the assassin?"

"No, I encountered no one."

"Ah. Then – if you will excuse the remark – I do not quite see the relevancy of the information."

"It has none. At present. I say it has none – at present."

He paused. Presently he resumed: "I did not encounter the assassin, but I am on his track, I am sure, for I believe he is in this room. I will ask you all to pass one by one in front of me – here, where there is a good light – so that I can see your feet."

A buzz of excitement swept the place, and the march began, the guest looking on with an iron attempt at gravity which was not an unqualified success, Stillman stooped, shaded his eyes with his hand, and gazed down intently at each pair of feet as it passed. Fifty men tramped monotonously by – with no result. Sixty. Seventy. The thing was beginning to look absurd. The guest remarked, with suave irony:

"Assassins appear to be scarce this evening."

The house saw the humor of it, and refreshed itself with a cordial laugh. Ten or twelve more candidates tramped by – no, *danced* by, with airy and ridiculous capers which convulsed the spectators – then suddenly Stillman put out his hand and said:

"This is the assassin!"

"Fetlock Jones, by the great Sanhedrim!" roared the crowd; and at once let fly a pyrotechnic explosion and dazzle and confusion and stirring remarks inspired by the situation.

At the height of the turmoil the guest stretched out his hand, commanding peace. The authority of a great name and a great personality laid its mysterious compulsion upon the house, and it obeyed. Out of the panting calm which succeeded, the guest spoke, saying, with dignity and feeling:

"*This* is serious. It strikes at an innocent life. Innocent beyond suspicion! Innocent beyond peradventure! Hear me *prove* it; observe how simple a fact can brush out of existence this witless lie. Listen. My friends, that lad was never out of my sight yesterday evening at *any* time!"

It made a deep impression. Men turned their eyes upon Stillman with grave inquiry in them. His face brightened, and he said:

"I *knew* there was another one!" He stepped briskly to the table and glanced at the guest's feet, then up at his face, and said: "You were *with* him! You were not fifty steps from him when he lit the candle that by and by fired the powder!" (*Sensation.*) "And what is more, you furnished the matches yourself!"

Plainly the guest seemed hit; it looked so to the public. He opened his mouth to speak; the words did not come freely.

"This – er – this is insanity – this—"

Stillman pressed his evident advantage home. He held up a charred match.

"Here is one of them. I found it in the barrel – and there's *another* one there."

The guest found his voice at once.

"*Yes* – and put them there yourself!"

It was recognized a good shot. Stillman retorted.

"It is *wax* – a breed unknown to this camp. I am ready to be searched for the box. Are you?"

The guest was staggered this time – the dullest eye could see it. He fumbled with his hands; once or twice his lips moved, but the words did not come. The house waited and watched, in tense suspense, the stillness adding effect to the situation. Presently Stillman said, gently:

"We are waiting for your decision."

There was silence again during several moments; then the guest answered, in a low voice:

"I refuse to be searched."

There was no noisy demonstration, but all about the house one voice after another muttered:

"That settles it! He's Archy's meat."

What to do now? Nobody seemed to know. It was an embarrassing situation for the moment – merely, of course, because matters had taken such a sudden and unexpected turn that these unpractised minds were not prepared for it, and had come to a standstill, like a stopped clock, under the shock. But after a little the machinery began to work again, tentatively, and by twos and threes the men put their heads together and privately buzzed over this and that and the other proposition. One of these propositions met with much favor; it was, to confer upon the assassin a vote of thanks for removing Flint Buckner, and let him go. But the cooler heads opposed it, pointing out that addled brains in the Eastern states would pronounce it a scandal, and make no end of foolish noise about it. Finally the cool heads got the upper hand, and obtained general consent to a proposition of their own; their leader then called the house to order and stated it – to this effect: that Fetlock Jones be jailed and put upon trial.

The motion was carried. Apparently there was nothing further to do now, and the people were glad, for, privately, they were impatient to get out and rush to the scene of the tragedy, and see whether that barrel and the other things were really there or not.

But no – the break-up got a check. The surprises were not over yet. For a while Fetlock Jones had been silently sobbing, unnoticed in the absorbing excitements which had been following one another so persistently for some time; but when his arrest and trial were decreed, he broke out despairingly, and said:

"No! it's no use. I don't want any jail, I don't want any trial; I've had all the hard luck I want, and all the miseries. Hang me now, and let me out! It would all come out, anyway – there couldn't anything save me. He has told it all, just as if he'd been with me and seen it – I don't know how he found out; and you'll find the barrel and things, and then I wouldn't have any chance any more. I killed him; and *you'd* have done it too, if he'd treated you like a dog, and you only a boy, and weak and poor, and not a friend to help you."

"And served him damned well right!" broke in Ham Sandwich. "Looky here, boys—"

From the constable: "Order! Order, gentlemen!"

A voice: "Did your uncle know what you was up to?"

"No, he didn't."

"Did he give you the matches, sure enough?"

"Yes, he did; but he didn't know what I wanted them for."

"When you was out on such a business as that, how did you venture to risk having him along – and him a *detective*? How's that?"

The boy hesitated, fumbled with his buttons in an embarrassed way, then said, shyly:

"I know about detectives, on account of having them in the family; and if you don't want them to find out about a thing, it's best to have them around when you do it."

The cyclone of laughter which greeted his naïve discharge of wisdom did not modify the poor little waif's embarrassment in any large degree.

9

From a letter to Mrs. Stillman, dated merely "Tuesday."

Fetlock Jones was put under lock and key in an unoccupied log cabin, and left there to await his trial. Constable Harris provided him with a couple of days' rations, instructed him to keep a good guard over himself, and promised to look in on him as soon as further supplies should be due.

Next morning a score of us went with Hillyer, out of friendship, and helped him bury his late relative, the unlamented Buckner, and I acted as first assistant pall-bearer, Hillyer acting as chief. Just as we had finished our labors a ragged and melancholy stranger, carrying an old handbag, limped by with his head down, and I caught the scent I had chased around the globe! It was the odor of Paradise to my perishing hope!

In a moment I was at his side and had laid a gentle hand upon his shoulder. He slumped to the ground as if a stroke of lightning had withered him in his tracks; and as the boys came running he struggled to his knees and put up his pleading hands to me, and out of his chattering jaws he begged me to persecute him no more, and said:

"You have hunted me around the world, Sherlock Holmes, yet God is my witness I have never done any man harm!"

A glance at his wild eyes showed us that he was insane. That was my work, mother! The tidings of your death can some day repeat the misery I felt in that moment, but nothing else can ever do it. The boys lifted him up, and gathered about him, and were full of pity of him, and said the gentlest and touchingest things to him, and said cheer up and don't be troubled, he was among friends now, and they would take care of him, and protect him, and hang any man that laid a hand on him. They are just like so many mothers, the rough mining-camp boys are, when you wake up the south side of their hearts; yes, and just like so many reckless and unreasoning children when you wake up the opposite of that muscle. They did everything they could think of to comfort him, but nothing succeeded until Wells-Fargo Ferguson, who is a clever strategist, said:

"If it's only Sherlock Holmes that's troubling you, you needn't worry any more."

"Why?" asked the forlorn lunatic, eagerly.

"Because he's dead again."

"Dead! Dead! Oh, don't trifle with a poor wreck like me. *Is* he dead? On honor, now – is he telling me true, boys?"

"True as you're standing there!" said Ham Sandwich, and they all backed up the statement in a body.

"They hung him in San Bernardino last week," added Ferguson, clinching the matter, "whilst he was searching around after you. Mistook him for another man. They're sorry, but they can't help it now."

"They're a-building him a monument," said Ham Sandwich, with the air of a person who had contributed to it, and knew.

"James Walker" drew a deep sigh – evidently a sigh of relief – and said nothing; but his eyes lost something of their wildness, his countenance cleared visibly, and its drawn look relaxed a little. We all went to our cabin, and the boys cooked him the best dinner the camp could furnish the materials for, and while they were about it Hillyer and I outfitted him from hat to shoe-leather with new clothes of ours, and made a comely and presentable old gentleman of him. "Old" is the right word, and a pity, too: old by the droop of him, and the frost upon his hair, and the marks which sorrow and distress have left upon his face; though he is only in his prime in the matter of years. While he ate, we smoked and chatted; and when he was finishing he found his voice at last, and of his own accord broke out with his personal history. I cannot furnish his exact words, but I will come as near it as I can.

THE "WRONG MAN'S" STORY

It happened like this: I was in Denver. I had been there many years; sometimes I remember how many, sometimes I don't – but it isn't any matter. All of a sudden I got a notice to leave, or I would be exposed for a horrible crime committed long before – years and years before – in the East.

I knew about that crime, but I was not the criminal; it was a cousin of mine of the same name. What should I better do? My head was all disordered by fear, and I didn't know. I was allowed very little time – only one day, I think it was. I would be ruined if I was published, and the people would lynch me, and not believe what I said. It is always the way with lynchings: when they find out it is a mistake they are sorry, but it is too late – the same as it was with Mr. Holmes, you see. So I said I would sell out and get money to live on, and run away until it blew over and I could come back with my proofs. Then I escaped in the night and went a long way off in the mountains somewhere, and lived disguised and had a false name.

I got more and more troubled and worried, and my troubles made me see spirits and hear voices, and I could not think straight and clear on any subject, but got confused and involved and had to give it up, because my head hurt so. It go to be worse and worse; more spirits and more voices. They were about me all the time; at first only in the night, then in the day too. They were always whispering around my bed and plotting against me, and it broke my sleep and kept me fagged out, because I got no good rest.

And then came the worst. One night the whispers said,

"We'll never manage, because we can't see him, and so can't point him out to the people."

They sighed; then one said: "We must bring Sherlock Holmes. He can be here in twelve days."

They all agreed, and whispered and jibbered with joy. But my heart broke; for I had read about that man, and knew what it would be to have him upon my track, with his superhuman penetration and tireless energies.

The spirits went away to fetch him, and I got up at once in the middle of the night and fled away, carrying nothing but the hand-bag that had my money in it – thirty thousand dollars; two-thirds of it are in the bag there yet. It was forty days before that man caught up on my track. I just escaped. From habit he had written his real name on a tavern register, but had scratched it out and written "Dagget Barclay" in the place of it. But fear gives you a watchful eye and keen, and I read the true name through the scratches, and fled like a deer.

He has hunted me all over this world for three years and a half – the Pacific states, Australasia, India – everywhere you can think of; then back to Mexico and up to California again, giving me hardly any rest; but that name on the registers always saved me, and what is left of me is alive yet. And I am *so* tired! A cruel time he has given me, yet I give you my honor I have never harmed him nor any man.

That was the end of the story, and it stirred those boys to bloodheat, be sure of it. As for me – each word burnt a hole in me where it struck.

We voted that the old man should bunk with us, and be my guest and Hillyer's. I shall keep my own counsel, naturally; but as soon as he is well rested and nourished, I shall take him to Denver and rehabilitate his fortunes.

The boys gave the old fellow the bone-smashing good-fellowship handshake of the mines, and then scattered away to spread the news.

At dawn next morning Wells-Fargo Ferguson and Ham Sandwich called us softly out, and said, privately:

"That news about the way that old stranger has been treated has spread all around, and the camps are up. They are piling in from everywhere, and are going to lynch the P'fessor. Constable

Harris is in a dead funk, and has telephoned the sheriff. Come along!"

We started on a run. The others were privileged to feel as they chose, but in my heart's privacy I hoped the sheriff would arrive in time; for I had small desire that Sherlock Holmes should hang for my deeds, as you can easily believe. I had heard a good deal about the sheriff, but for reassurance's sake I asked:

"Can he stop a mob?"

"Can *he* stop a mob! Can Jack *Fairfax* stop a mob! Well, I should smile! Ex-desperado – nineteen scalps on his string. Can *he*! Oh, I *say*!"

As we tore up the gulch, distant cries and shouts and yells rose faintly on the still air, and grew steadily in strength as we raced along. Roar after roar burst out, stronger and stronger, nearer and nearer; and at last, when we closed up upon the multitude massed in the open area in front of the tavern, the crash of sound was deafening. Some brutal roughs from Daly's gorge had Holmes in their grip, and he was the calmest man there; a contemptuous smile played about his lips, and if any fear of death was in his British heart, his iron personality was master of it and no sign of it was allowed to appear.

"Come to a vote, men!" This from one of the Daly gang, Shadbelly Higgins. "Quick! is it hang, or shoot?"

"Neither!" shouted one of his comrades. "He'd be alive again in a week; burning's the only permanency for *him*."

The gangs from all the outlying camps burst out in a thundercrash of approval, and went struggling and surging toward the prisoner, and closed around him, shouting, "Fire! fire's the ticket!" They dragged him to the horse-post, backed him against it, chained him to it, and piled wood and pine cones around him waist-deep. Still the strong face did not blench, and still the scornful smile played about the thin lips.

"A match! fetch a match!"

Shadbelly struck it, shaded it with his hand, stooped, and held it under a pine cone. A deep silence fell upon the mob. The cone caught, a tiny flame flickered about it a moment or two. I seemed to catch the sound of distant hoofs – it grew more distinct – still more and more distinct, more and more definite, but the absorbed crowd did not appear to notice it. The match went out. The man struck another, stooped, and again the flame rose; this time it took hold and began to spread – here and there men turned away their faces. The executioner stood with the charred match in his fingers, watching his work. The hoof-beats turned a projecting crag, and now they came thundering down upon us. Almost the next moment there was a shout:

"The sheriff!"

And straightway he came tearing into the midst, stood his horse almost on his hind feet, and said:

"Fall back, you gutter-snipes!"

He was obeyed. By all but their leader. He stood his ground, and his hand went to his revolver. The sheriff covered him promptly, and said:

"Drop your hand, you parlor desperado. Kick the fire away. Now unchain the stranger."

The parlor desperado obeyed. Then the sheriff made a speech; sitting his horse at martial ease, and not warming his words with any touch of fire, but delivering them in a measured and deliberate way, and in a tone which harmonized with their character and made them impressively disrespectful.

"You're a nice lot – now ain't you? Just about eligible to travel with this bilk here – Shadbelly Higgins – this loud-mouthed sneak that shoots people in the back and calls himself a desperado. If there's anything I do particularly despise, it's a lynching mob; I've never seen one that had a man in it. It has to tally up a hundred against one before it can pump up pluck enough to tackle a sick tailor. It's made up of cowards, and so is the community that breeds it; and ninety-nine times out of a hundred the sheriff's another one." He paused – apparently to turn that last idea over in his mind and taste the juice of it – then he went on: "The sheriff that lets a mob take a prisoner away from him is the lowest-down coward there is. By the statistics there was a hundred and eighty-two of them drawing sneak pay in America last year. By the way it's going, pretty soon there'll be a new disease in the doctor-books – *sheriff complaint*." That idea pleased him – any one could see it. "People will say, 'Sheriff sick again?' 'Yes; got the same old thing' And next there'll be a new title. People won't say, 'He's running for sheriff of Rapaho County,' for instance; they'll say, 'He's running for Coward of Rapaho.' Lord, the idea of a grown-up person being afraid of a lynch mob!"

He turned an eye on the captive, and said, "Stranger, who are you, and what have you been doing?"

"My name is Sherlock Holmes, and I have not been doing anything."

It was wonderful, the impression which the sound of that name made on the sheriff, notwithstanding he must have come posted. He spoke up with feeling, and said it was a blot on the country that a man whose marvelous exploits had filled the world with their fame and their ingenuity, and whose histories of them had won every reader's heart by the brilliancy and charm of their literary setting, should be visited under the Stars and Stripes by an outrage like this. He apologized in the name of the whole nation, and made Holmes a most handsome bow, and told Constable Harris to see him to his quarters, and hold himself personally responsible if he was molested again. Then he turned to the mob and said:

"Hunt your holes, you scum!" which they did; then he said: "Follow me, Shadbelly; I'll take care of your case myself. No – keep your pop-gun; whenever I see the day that I'll be afraid to have you behind me with that thing, it'll be time for me to join last year's hundred and eighty-two"; and he rode off in a walk, Shadbelly following.

When we were on our way back to our cabin, toward breakfast-time, we ran upon the news that Fetlock Jones had escaped from his lock-up in the night and is gone! Nobody is sorry. Let his uncle track him out if he likes; it is in his line; the camp is not interested.

10

Ten days later.

"James Walker" is all right in body now, and his mind shows improvement too. I start with him for Denver to-morrow morning.

Next night. Brief note, mailed at a way-station.

As we were starting, this morning, Hillyer whispered to me: "Keep this news from Walker until you think it safe and not likely to disturb his mind and check his improvement; the ancient crime he spoke of was really committed – and by his cousin, as he said. *We buried the real criminal* the other day – the unhappiest man that has lived in a century – Flint Buckner. His real name was Jacob Fuller!" There, mother, by help of me, an unwitting mourner, your husband and my father is in his grave. Let him rest.

1902

THE POMERANIAN POISONING

PETER LOVESEY

ROSEBUD BOOKS
VOLUMES OF ROMANCE
Battersea Bridge Road
London SW11
12 May

Dearest Honeypot,

Have you gone into hiding? My telephonist has a sore finger from trying your number, and your Grizzly Bear is going spare. Can't work, can't think of anything else. Horrid fears that his Honeypot has been stolen by some other bear and taken to another part of the forest.

Put him out of his misery, won't you, and tell him it isn't true? The weekend in Brighton wasn't so disappointing as all that, was it? The trouble with this bear is that he's too excitable when he gets the chance of Honey, but he remains huggingly affectionate. He passionately wants another chance to prove it.

Do pick up the blower and comfort your fretful

Grizzly

P.S. Are you writing anything at present? A brilliant opportunity has cropped up. Couldn't possibly make Honeypot any sweeter, but could guarantee to make her infinitely richer.

310 Arch Street
Earls Court
SW5
Sunday afternoon

Dear Frank (I'd rather drop the nursery names, if you don't mind),

As you see, I've moved from Fulham. Your letter was sent on. Take a deep breath and pour yourself a double Scotch, Frank. I'm living with a guy called Tristram. He's my age and could pass for my twin brother and we have so much in common I can hardly believe it's true. We both adore Brad Pitt, Harry Potter, Chinese takeaways, Robbie Williams, Porsches, Spielberg, line dancing, goosedown duvets and so much else it would take the rest of today and next week to list it. Tristram went to public school (Radley) and Sussex University. He has a degree in American Studies and he's terribly high-powered. He knows Martin Amis and P.J.O'Rourke and masses of people who come up on the box. I know you'll understand when I say I'm totally committed to Tristram now.

Pause, for you to top up the Scotch.

Frank, I want you to know this has nothing to do with what happened, or didn't quite happen, that Saturday night in Brighton. I blame that stuff we smoked. We should have stayed on G and T. Whatever, no hard feelings, OK?

I'm not sure if you still feel the same about the business opportunity you mentioned, but I *am* quite intrigued, as a matter of fact. Yes, I've been doing some writing – tinkering away at a novel about the women's movement, the first of a five-book saga, actually – but Tristram and I are both on the Social so I wouldn't mind putting the novel on one side if there's cash on tap now. But I must make it clear that it's my writing talent, such as it is, that's up for grabs, and nothing else. Putting it another way, Frank darling, I'm open to advances in pounds sterling.

We don't have a phone yet – not even a mobile – and it gets expensive using pay-phones, so be a darling and write by return.

Be kind to me.

Luv,

Felicity

ROSEBUD BOOKS
VOLUMES OF ROMANCE
Battersea Bridge Road,
London SW11
23 May

Dear Felicity,

You may wonder why it took me so long to answer your letter; on the other hand, you may wonder that I bothered to answer it at all. I need hardly say that I am deeply hurt. For me, the age-difference between us was never an impediment, and I rashly imagined you felt the same way. You gave me no reason to suppose there was anyone else in your life. You appeared to enjoy our evenings together. True, I caught you closing your eyes at the Proms from time to time, but I took it that you were transported by the music. You always seemed to revive in time for our suppers in the Trattoria. I find myself putting a cynical construction on everything now.

I suppose I must accept that I was just a meal-ticket, or a sugar-daddy, or whatever cruel phrase is currently in vogue.

As to that literary project I happened to mention, I shall obviously look elsewhere. The work required is undemanding and I dare say I shall have no difficulty finding an author willing to make a six-figure sum for a short children's book.

You may keep my LP of the Enigma Variations. To listen to it ever again would be too distressful.

Your former friend,

Franklin.

310 Arch Street,
SW5
Wednesday morning

Grizzly Darling!

What a wild, ferocious bear you were last night! Honey-pot has never felt so stirred.

When I arrived with the Elgar and the Bacardi, I honestly meant to say sorry and a civilized goodbye. You're so masterful!

If you still mean what you said (and if you don't I shall throw myself under a train) could you come with the van some time between six-thirty and seven on Friday evening? Tristram will be at his karate class and it will avoid a scene that might otherwise be too hairy for us all. I haven't much stuff to move out, darling. One trip will be enough, I'm sure.

Hugs and kisses,

Your

Felicity

310 Arch Street,
SW5

My own dearest Tristram,

Please, darling, before you do anything else, read this to the end. It's terribly important to our relationship that you understand what I have done, and why.

I've moved out. I'm going to stay with Frank, that doddery old publisher guy I told you about. Before you blow your top, Tris, hear me out. I've agonized over this for days. Darling, you know I wouldn't walk out on you without a copper-bottomed reason. Frank means nothing to me. He's a dingbat: pathetic, ugly, flabby, but – and this is the point – he knows a way to make me fabulously rich. I mean stinking rich, Tris. We're talking telephone numbers. And for what? For some book he wants me to write. He hasn't given me all the details yet. He's boxing clever until I move in with him, which is part of the deal, but I understand it's only a children's book he wants. I can finish it in a matter of days if I pull out all the stops, and then I'll be off like a bunny, sweetheart.

He insists I go and live in his house in the backwoods of Surrey while I'm writing the thing. Isn't it a drag? I'm not giving you the address because I know what you'll do. You'll be down there kicking in the door, and who could blame you? But just pause to think.

If I pass up this opportunity, what sort of future do you and I have? I mean, I *know* it's terrific being together, but what prospect is there of ever getting out of this damp slum? I've had enough, Tris, and so have you. Admit it.

I can almost hear you say I'm selling myself, and I suppose I am if I'm honest, but let's face it, I spent a weekend with Frank in Brighton before I met you. It's not as if he's a total stranger. And if I am selling myself, what a price!

Which is why I'm asking you to keep your cool and try to understand this is the best chance we've got. Just a short interval, darling, and then we can really start to motor.

There won't be a minute when you're out of my thoughts, lover.

I'll write again soon.

Be patient, darling!

Ever your

Felicity

> This dreary pad in Surrey
> Saturday night

Dearest Tristram,

Has it been only a week? It feels like *months*. A life sentence with hard labour, and I've been doing plenty of that. Writing, I mean. Non-stop. The reason I can do so much is that I know every word, every letter, I write is worth mega-bucks. Guaranteed. It's crazy, but it's true. I'm on to a winner, Tris. You see, Frank – he's my publisher-friend – has told me exactly how this is going to work, and he's right. It can't miss. He and I are going to split – wait for it – a million US dollars!

For a kids' book?

Yes!

Scrape yourself off the floor and I'll tell you how this miracle works.

You know that Frank is the chairman of Rosebud Books, who publish romantic fiction, and before you knock it, remember that my only published work, *Desire Me Do*, paid for our new telly, among other things. Frank's outfit isn't exactly Mills & Boon, but he helps beginners like me to get started and I dare say it makes life more tolerable for a few thousand readers of the things.

One of Frank's regular writers was an eccentric old biddy called Zenobia Hatt. That was her real name, believe it or not. I'm using the past tense because she died four or five years ago, before I got to know Frank. Apparently there were hundreds of Hatts. Her books didn't sell all that well, but she kept producing them. And she expected to see them in the shops. Each time she walked into a supermarket and spotted a display of paperbacks, she checked to see if her latest was among them. If it wasn't, she made a beeline for Rosebud Books to tear a strip off Frank. She was always tearing strips off Frank. Even if the book was in the shop, something about it would upset her, like the cover, or the quality of paper they were using. I don't know why he continued to publish her, but he did. She always appeared with her two dogs in tow. They were Pomeranians. If you think I'm rabbiting on about nothing important, you're making a big mistake. The Pommies *are* important.

Do you know about Pomeranians? They're toy dogs. Funny little things with enormous ruffs, neat faces and tiny legs. They come in most colours. You know how some old ladies are with dogs? Zenobia doted on hers.

Well, like I said, she died, and this is the important bit, Tristy. In her will, she left the house and everything she had to be divided between her relatives. That is, except any future income from her books. You get royalties trickling in long after a book is published, you see. Zenobia decreed that the future profits from her writing should go into a trust fund to pay for her dogs to be kept in style in some rip-off place in Hampstead that caters for pampered pets who have come into money. The residue was to be awarded annually as a literary prize: the Zenobia Hatt prize.

Nice idea, right? The snag was that Zenobia wasn't really in the Barbara Cartland class as a best-selling writer. The royalties paid the fees at the dogs' home for a couple of years and then the Pommies got arthritis (so it was claimed) and were put down. There was no money left, so the prize was never awarded.

End of story? Not quite. Cop this, love.

A couple of months ago, Frank had a phone call from California. Some film producer was asking about the rights to a Rosebud book called *Michaela and the Mount*, by – you guessed – Zenobia Hatt! It was a cheap romance she published years ago, so long ago, in fact, that it was out of print, so Frank wouldn't make a penny out of any deal. Don't ask me why, but this book is reckoned to be the perfect vehicle for some busty starlet they reckon is the next Madonna. Tris, darling, they bought it for a million bucks! The money goes into the trust and by the terms of Zenobia's will it has to be offered as the prize for 2002. The lot. The doggies aren't on the payroll any more, so every silver dollar is up for grabs. And who do you think is going to win?

Shall I tell you how? The point is that Zenobia didn't offer her money for any common or garden novel. She had very clear ideas about the sort of book she wanted to encourage. She had it written into her will that the Zenobia Hatt prize should go to the best published work of fiction that featured a Pomeranian dog as one of the main characters. As you can imagine, that limits the competition somewhat.

When Frank cottoned on to this, he did some quick thinking. Animal stories don't usually feature on the Rosebud list, but he reckoned he could stretch a point and commission a book for kids featuring Tom the Pom that he'd rush through before the end of the year to scoop the prize. He'd go fifty-fifty with the writer, and that's me, sweetheart! I've signed an agreement and pay-day will be some time in January, when the trustees award the prize. As simple as that. No one else has time to get a book out, because the news hasn't broken yet, and won't until the film deal is finalized. You know what American lawyers are like. Well, perhaps you don't, but the trustees expect to sign the contract in October or November. *Tom the Pom* will hit the shops in time for Christmas and it doesn't matter a monkey's how many it sells, because it's certain to clean up half a million bucks.

That's the story so far, my love. Naturally I can't wait to finish *my* story and hand it over. Then there'll be nothing to keep me here. I hope to see you Friday at the latest, and what a reunion that will be . . .

Luv you,
Felicity

Same Place, Unfortunately
Thursday
Tris darling,

I'm not going to make it by tomorrow. I showed Frank what I've written so far and he wants some changes, some of them pretty drastic. I tried pointing out that it didn't really matter if the writing was sloppy in places, so long as I finished the flaming book and it got into print before the end of the year, but he came over all high and mighty and sounded off about standards and the reputation of his house. I wondered what on earth his house had to do with it until I discovered he was talking about Rosebud Books, his publishing house. He says he doesn't want an inferior book to carry his imprint, especially as *Tom the Pom* is certain to get a lot of attention when it wins. I suppose he has a point.

So it's back to the keyboard to hammer out some revisions. What a drag!

I suppose Monday or Tuesday would be a realistic estimate.

Impatiently,
Luv,
Felicity

Purgatory
Wednesday

Oh, Tris,

I'm so depressed! I've had the mother and father of a row with Frank. I finished the book yesterday, with all the changes he wanted. He read it last night. He wasn't exactly over the moon, but he agreed it couldn't wait any longer, so he would hand it over to his sub-editor. I said fine, and would he kindly drop me and my baggage at the flat on his way to the office. Tris, he looked at me as if I was crazy. He said we had an agreement. I said certainly we had, and I'd fulfilled my side of it by finishing the book. Now I was ready to go home.

Whereupon he deluged me with a load of gush about how it was much more than a publishing agreement to him. He wouldn't have asked me to write the book if he hadn't believed I was willing to move in with him. I meant more to him than all the money and if I walked out on him now he would drop the typescript in the Thames.

Tris, I'm sure he means it. He knows I need the money and he's going to keep me here like a hostage until the book is in the shops. He could cancel it at any stage up to then. I'll be here for *months*.

There's no way out that I can see. You and I are just going to have to be patient. The day the book is published, I'll be free. And ready to collect my share of the prize. Let's go skiing in February, shall we? And what sort of car shall we buy? We can have that Porsche. One each, if we want. If we both look forward to next year, we can get through. We *must* get through.

Tris, don't try and trace me here, darling. It would be too painful for us both.

I'm thinking of you constantly.

Your soon-to-be-rich, but sorry-to-be-here
Felicity

As Before
1 August

Tris, my love,

Did you wonder if I was ever going to write again? Are you starting to doubt my existence? Dear God, I hope not.

The reason it's been so long is that I get dreadfully depressed. I've written any number of letters and destroyed them when I read them through a second time. It's no good wallowing in self-pity, and it certainly won't do much for you.

So this time, I'll be positive. Another month begins today. For me, another milestone. I've endured ten weeks now, and I'm still looking at my watch all day long.

I expect you'd like to know how I pass my days. I get up around nine, after he's left for work. Breakfast (half a grapefruit, coffee and toast), then a walk if it's fine. Without giving anything away – and I won't, so don't look for clues – there are some beautiful walks through the woods here. I see squirrels every day and sometimes deer. Often I collect enough mushrooms to have on toast for lunch, or if I'm really energetic I might put them into a quiche. The rest of the morning and most of the afternoon is devoted to my writing. The novel, I mean. It's slow work, but it's good stuff, Tris, a sight better than *Tom the Pom*, which is going to make so much more money. Crazy. (*T. the P*. was in proof four weeks ago, by the way, and this is the good news: LIBERATION DAY is earlier than I dared to hope – 30 September.) Later in the afternoon I might do some reading. The bind is that the only books here are Rosebud Romances, which depress me, even if they're sufficiently well written to be readable, and boring non-fiction on hunting, shooting and fishing that he only keeps for the leather bindings.

Around 6, I get something out of the freezer for the evening meal. He comes home about 7 and that's all I'm going to say about my day. I stop living then.

Maybe you wonder why I don't slip away to London during the day to see you. Tris, I've often thought of it. I know I couldn't bear to come back here if I did. He'd stop publication of the book and you and I would have endured all this for nothing. No, I must hold out here.

Less than two months to go!

Love,

Felicity

Still doing time
19 August

Tris darling,

I have a horrid feeling Frank suspects something. It's like
this. Ever since he moved me here, he's assumed it's for
keeps. He constantly goes on about his future as if I'm part
of it. Like the two of us (him and me) taking trips to the
Bahamas when we've got our hands on the Zenobia Hatt
prize. Naturally I play along with this, letting him think I
can't imagine anything more blissful than sharing the rest of
my life with him and a million bucks.

Up to now, I'm sure he believed me. Up to last night,
anyway. Then, out of the blue, he mentioned you, Tris. I
don't think either of us have spoken your name since he
brought me here. He asked me if I'd been in touch with you,
and of course I denied it. Just to sound more convincing, I
went a bit further and said I'd dumped you and forgotten all
about you.

Frank went on to say he only happened to speak of you
because by chance he was driving along Arch Street at
lunchtime yesterday and he saw a tall, dark guy in
leathers coming out of number 310 with his arm around
a strikingly good-looking redhead. I must admit he
caught me off guard for a moment. I expect I looked
concerned, because he took me up on it at once and asked
why I'd gone so pale.

I see now that it was a shabby, underhand trick to test my
reactions. I can't fathom how he knows you go in for
leathers, because I've never told him, but I'm sure of one
thing, and that's that you wouldn't cheat on me while I'm
going through hell here.

If Frank wants a battle of wits, he'll find I'm more than a
match for him. I think last night was just a try-on, but I'm
taking no chances. I'll make sure no one sees me posting
this.

I've discovered a way of making my walks more interesting. Among those boring old books on blood sports in the
library I found an illustrated guide on the fungi of Great
Britain. I take it with me and try and identify the different

species along the paths. I'm doing quite well so far, with four different sorts of toadstools as well as the mushrooms I have for lunch.

Six weeks today and we'll be together, Tris. For keeps. I'll write when I can.

Miss you so much.

Felicity

Still Holed-Up Here
10 September

Well, Tris, my darling,

It's a day for celebration. I've actually had a copy of *Tom the Pom* in my hands! The printers delivered on time. But before you uncork the champagne, let me explain that this still isn't publication day. That remains the same, 30 September. They send the books out to the shops and book reviewers ready for the big day, but no one is supposed to sell them before then. In theory, Frank could cancel the publication, call them back and burn them all, and I actually believe he would if he knew I was planning to dump him once I've qualified for the prize.

The book strikes me as pretty abysmal now I've had a chance to read it again. However, they've dressed it up in a shiny laminated cover with cute illustrations by some artist (who won't have any claim on the prize, incidentally, because it's awarded to the writer) and I expect they'll sell a few hundred.

I'm glad to have something to give me a boost, because Frank has been driving me mad. He keeps wanting assurances that I'm committed to him for life, and he constantly paws me. I think he senses I find it disagreeable, and that makes him even more persistent. He often mentions you now, and that redhead he is supposed to have seen you with. It's as if he knows what's in my mind and wants me to break down and admit it.

Sometimes I feel so angry I'd like to stop him getting *any* of the prize, like the Poms that were put down before they could come into a fortune. You and I would be twice as well off then.

I do my best to divert myself on my walks, which I'm now taking morning and afternoon, in all weathers. I'm becoming quite an expert on fungi. I've found and identified several more species, including *Amanita Phalloides*, known commonly as the Death Cap or the Destroying Angel. Not to be confused with the mushroom, as it is fatal if eaten. There's a small crop of them under an oak only five minutes from here.

Only three weeks now, my love!
Felicity

> Here, but not for much longer
> One day to Liberation!

Darling Tristram,

By the time you get this, it will be Publication Day and I will have freed myself from Frank for ever. He has become insufferable.

I've come to a momentous decision. It's been forced on me partly because I'm desperately frightened to tell him I'm leaving him. I don't want the confrontation, and I know if I just walk out, he'll track me down. I don't ever want to see him again. He gives me the creeps. And I feel bitter that he's due to collect such a large share of the prize. It's supposed to go to the writer, Tris, and I was the one who slogged it out for days inventing a story. Frank didn't do a damn thing except hand it to the printer.

I want you to do something for me, Tris. Please, darling, burn every one of the letters I wrote you. I don't want anyone to know I was ever here. *Make sure you do this*.

Trust me, whatever happens, because I love you.
Felicity

6.30

Dear Grizzly,
Quiche in the oven.
Luv
Honeypot

Sydney, Australia
25 April

Dear Felicity,

I'm not sure whether you're permitted to receive letters in prison, particularly letters from former boyfriends. Maybe you don't want to hear from me anyway, but I think I owe you some kind of explanation. If it upsets you, well, you've got twenty years or so to get over it.

I followed your trial in the Aussie papers. They covered it quite fully in the tabloids. Apparently murder by poisoning is still a good paper-seller. They don't have Death Cap toadstools here, but there are other kinds of poisonous fungi that I suppose anyone with murder in mind could disguise in a quiche. The reports I read suggested you didn't know it would take up to a week for Frank to die. Books on fungi don't always go into that sort of detail. I wondered why they couldn't save him by washing out his stomach or something, but apparently the toxins are absorbed before the first effects appear. Looking at it from his point of view, poor sod, at least he lived long enough to tell his suspicions to the police.

You'll notice I haven't given an address above. That isn't from secrecy. It's because I'm on a cruise around the world. Some months ago I met this gorgeous redhead called Imogen. To be brutally honest, Immie moved in with me at Earls Court the week after you went to live with Frank. I got lonely, Fel, and I figured you had company, so why shouldn't I?

Imogen is one of those quiet girls who are capable of surprising you. I didn't know she found a bunch of your letters to me and secretly read them. I didn't know she had any talent as a children's writer until last January, when she was announced as the winner of the Zenobia Hatt prize. I don't suppose you had a chance to see the press reports. The trustees received only two entries. Imogen's *One Hundred and Two Pomeranians*, which she published privately at her own expense in December, was adjudged to be closest to the spirit of the award.

No hard feelings? The cash wouldn't have been much use
to you in the slammer, would it?

Cheers, love.

Tristram

THE MAN WHO SHOT KENNEDY

MARC BLAKE

It has come to light that agents or agencies unknown had doctored a number of transcripts of testimonies given during the Warren Commission investigation into the Kennedy assassination. Forensic scientists working in tandem with type and restoration experts have now painstakingly reassembled many of these documents, offering a clearer picture of the events that occurred on that fateful day. The following sheds light on a formerly marginalized witness. This testimony was taken on 22 July 1964 in the office of the US attorney, 301 Post Office Building, Bryan and Ervay Streets, Dallas, Texas, by Wesley J. Liebeler, assistant counsel of the President's Commission, and is printed here in full for the first time.

Testimony of Abraham Zapruder

Hearings before the Commission on the Assassination of President Kennedy (the Warren Commission) Volume VII.

Mr LIEBELER: Mr Zapruder, would you stand and take the oath, please? Do you solemnly swear this testimony you are about to give will be the truth, the whole truth and nothing but the truth, so help you God?

Mr ZAPRUDER: I do

Mr LIEBELER: Would you state your full name, please?

– Abraham Zapruder.

– That's spelled (spelling) Z-a-p-r-u-d-e-r? Is that correct?

– Yes.

– What is your home address?

– 3909 Marquette.

– Here in Dallas?

– In Dallas, yes.

– Are you in business here in Dallas, Mr Zapruder?

– Yes.

– What business are you in?

– Manufacturing ladies' dresses.

– I understand you took some motion pictures at the time of the assassination?

– That is correct.

– Could you tell us about the circumstances under which you did that, where you were at the time? What happened, what you saw?

– Well, what I saw you have on film.

– (No response)

Mr ZAPRUDER: It was around 11.30. I was in my office, which is right next to the building where the alleged assassin was, just across 501 Elm Street. I had my camera and I told my secretary that maybe I might take pictures from the window but I figured I would maybe go down and get better pictures down on Elm Street. And so I walked on down to the lower part, closer to the underpass. I was trying to pick a space from where to take those pictures and I tried one place. It was on a narrow ledge and I couldn't balance myself. I tried another that had some obstruction and signs. Finally I found a place near the underpass – a square of concrete about four feet high.

Mr LIEBELER: I'm showing you a picture marked Hudson exhibit No. 1. I ask if you can see yourself in that picture?

– Yes, that's me standing there.

– You are pointing out a concrete abutment immediately to the right of the sign that reads "Stemmons Freeway". Who is that behind you?

– That's the, uh, girl that works in my office.

– So, you and this girl are shown standing on top of this concrete abutment here.

– (Pause) Yes. I would say this couldn't be anybody else, unless . . . if this is an authentic photograph and it wasn't composed or changed, I would say that's me.

– Are you saying that this is a doctored photo?

– (Pause) No, sir.

– This picture is one of a series being sold here in Dallas by a fellow named Willis.

– Oh, that (inaudible).

– As you stood on this abutment with your camera the motorcade came down Houston and turned left on Elm Street, did it not?

– That's right.

– And it proceeded then toward the triple underpass: correct?

– That's correct. I started shooting when the motorcade started coming in.

(Extraneous noise. Identified as chair scraping back.)

Mr LIEBELER: You started what?

Mr ZAPRUDER: Shooting. With my camera. I wanted to get it coming in from Houston Street.

Mr LIEBELER: (Pause) Tell us what happened when you took these pictures.

– Well, as the car came in line almost, I was standing up there and I was using a telephoto lens, which is a zoom lens, and as it reached about – I imagine it was around here – I heard the first shot and I saw the President lean over and grab himself like this (holding his left chestal area).

– Grab himself on the front of his chest?

– Right. He was sitting like this and waving and then after the shot he just went like that.

– He was sitting upright in the car and you heard the shot and you saw the President slump over.

– Leaning toward the side of Mrs Kennedy. And then before I had a chance to organize my mind I heard a second shot and then I saw his head opened up and the blood and everything came out and I started – I can hardly talk about it (the witness crying).

– That's all right, Mr Zapruder, would you like a drink of water? Why don't you step out and have a drink of water?

– (Pause) I'm sorry. I'm ashamed of myself really.

– Nobody should be ashamed of feeling that way, Mr Zapruder. I feel the same way myself. It was a terrible thing . . .

– (No response)

Mr LIEBELER: Let me go back now for a moment and ask you how many shots you heard altogether?

Mr ZAPRUDER: I heard the second shot – I saw him leaning over after and then I started yelling, "They killed him, they killed him." And I just felt that somebody had ganged up on him and I was still shooting pictures until he got under the underpass. I don't even know how I did it. And then – I don't even remember how I got down from that abutment – I walked back towards my office and people that I met on the way didn't even know what happened and they kept yelling "What happened?" It seemed that they heard a shot but they didn't know exactly what happened as the car sped away. And finally I got to my office. My secretary – I told her maybe we ought to call the police or the Secret Service. I was very much upset. I couldn't imagine such a thing.

Mr LIEBELER: But she did not, at that time, call the police?

– We were very upset. As to what happened, I remember there were police running behind me, from where the shot came from.

– You were standing on this abutment facing Elm Street. You say the police ran over behind this concrete structure and down the railroad track behind?

– After the shots?

– Yes.

– (No response)

Mr LIEBELER: Do you have any impression as to the direction from which these shots came?

– I thought they could have come from back of me.

– (Pause)

Mr LIEBELER: You stood on the abutment and looked down into Elm Street, you saw the President hit on the right side of the head and you thought the shots had come from behind you?

– Well, yes.

– From the direction behind you? But at the time you didn't form an opinion, with all the yelling, as to the direction the shots came from actually? They could have come from behind or from any other direction except perhaps from the left. Or even from the front?

– Huh?

– They could as easily have come from the Book Depository.

– Well, you could hit a place from any point. I have no way of determining what direction the bullet was going.

– So (writing) from-the-Depos –

– No, wait.

– Did you form any opinion of the direction of the shots by the sound, or were you too upset by the thing you had seen?

– There was too much reverberation. There was an echo which made sound all over.

– An echo from the shots fired from the Depository?

– I meant to ask – what is a depository? People are, well you read that some people are calling it the Repository now.

– (Unidentified sound. Pause)

Mr LIEBELER: One thing I would like you to do now. We have a series – a little book here that is Commission Exhibit number 885 – and it consists of a number of frames from your motion picture. Certain numbers of them are important to our work here, and I want you to look at these and see if you recognize that these are individual frame by frame pictures of the pictures that you took?

Mr ZAPRUDER: They aren't too clear. The telephoto lens is not too good to take stills.

– Specifically, I draw your attention to No. 185.

– This is where he came in from Houston Street and turned –

– Yes, they are going down Elm Street now.

– This was before – this shouldn't be here – the shot was fired, wasn't it? You can't tell from here . . .

– (No response)

Mr ZAPRUDER: I believe it was closer down here where it happened. Of course on the film you could see better but you take 8 millimeter and enlarge it and you lose a lot of detail.

Mr LIEBELER: Does No. 185 look like one of the frames, sir?

– Yes.

– I have a list of them here that I want to ask you about – picture 207. It appears there was a sign in the picture.

– Yes, there were signs and trees.

– And the knoll.

– Knoll?

– From where you say you heard the shots?

– Oh, that grassy mound?

– (Pause), Yes. How about this one. 222? Here you see the President's car coming out from behind the sign. And you see Governor Connally right there in the center seat, I believe?

– Yes. The car was kind of low – I didn't get the full view of the shot.

– Let's turn to 225 and here the car is coming further out from behind the sign. You see the President for the first time.

– Yes, that's the President.

– He appears to have his hand up by his throat.

– Yes, it looks like he was hit it seems, there, somewhere behind the sign.

– Here in 227 his hand comes up even more and he starts to move a little to his left.

– They started speeding the car then.

– In 229 it's even more pronounced.

– It looks to me he went like this – did he go to his throat – I don't remember.

– Let's turn over here to picture 231. These appear to be the same sequence of pictures, do they not?

– Yes, you get about 16 per second and I think my camera was moving a little fast, maybe 18 frames per second.

– How about 249?

– He has his hand on his head.

– And 253?

– I used to have nightmares. I wake up and see this.

– He starts to move sharply to the left. Toward Mrs Kennedy.

– What number are you on?

– 313 – you remember that one?

– That was – that was the horrible one.

– It appears to you then that this book here, as you look through it, contains your pictures.

– Except that one. The President didn't have a mustache.

– (No response)

– And that one is back to front. And –

Mr LIEBELER: (Unidentified sound) Let's go forward a way and take a look at 326. What do you see now?

Mr ZAPRUDER: (Pause) Well, er. It's blurred.

Mr LIEBELER: I see three figures. A woman and a man with his hand held up. Up and to the right. Flip over to 329 and the movement is you see, across to the right. The man is waving.

– When you pick one of them out it's hard to break it down.

– The woman is reaching right across there. Here, go back – to a child, with something – what would you say that was?

– A napkin?

– And what do you see behind?

– A wooden. A fence.

– If you run through 334 to 366 the whole angle is lower but you see, Mr Zapruder, you near that burning metal structure?

– It's hard to tell. The blurring.

– Holding some kind of implement. It glints in the sun. Also, from the shadow cast we estimate the time as being at least one to two hours after the assassination.

– Unless the film were doctored?

– (No response)

Mr ZAPRUDER. And so many people have looked at this film, the FBI, the Secret Services, *Life* magazine . . .

– On the end of the metal implement, and for one moment I'll say nothing of the umbrella in back, do you see that object?

– In 366?

– Yes in 366.

– I don't see –

– It's a wiener, Mr Zapruder. The rest of your home movie footage shows a barbecue. A barbecue you filmed directly after the President was assassinated.

– Well, I don't.

– The waving man is your brother stood right under the umbrella or parasol here. And there if you look in 368 is the blurred image of your wife passing with a plate of chicken. See the housecoat? And there also is your brother's wife standing back and to the right by the fence.

– Back, and to the right?

– And you are the one in the hat.

– (Pause) Could I have some water?

Mr LIEBELER: How is it you come to capture the most horrific assassination in our nation's history, but fail to hand over the film to the authorities and instead throw a barbecue?

Mr ZAPRUDER: (Pause) I w-wanted to use up the film.

– To use up the roll?

– 8 millimeter is expensive.

– (Pause) Mr Sorrels from the Secret Service tells us he received your film at four ten p.m. Over three and a half hours after the President was assassinated.

– I . . . took a nap.

– You took a nap?

– My brother and his wife can be exhausting.

– The 35th President of the United States has his brains shot out over his wife and car and these two still come over to chow down at your place on Marquette?

– (Inaudible)

– Please speak up, Mr Zapruder.

– They . . . they didn't know it had happened. When I got home, Saul –

– Saul?

– My brother. He had the steaks cooking. The salad was out already. He hates to waste food. I didn't have the heart to . . .

– So when did they find out you covered up the details of the assassination?

– (Pause) Around three. Some neighbors came by. They had gone to see it downtown on TV in a store window. I guess they had been drinking a lot after that. They came home and saw my brother singing "That's Amore" which he always does when he gets drunk and that's around when the brawl broke out.

– Your wife knew you had gone to shoot the motorcade. How did that conversation go?

– I made sure the radio was turned off when I got back home. I told her the President looked nice. I got my shots. There was a little trouble.

– The President was placed in a finely calibrated kill zone and eliminated by a cabal of trained marksmen and you call that a little trouble?

– He was what?

– (Unidentified) Strike that. (Unidentified) Yeah, strike that right now. Go back to, let's talk about when you handed over the film to Mr Sorrels.

Mr ZAPRUDER: (No response)

Mr LIEBELER: You took a nap after, or maybe you didn't. Either way you then handed over the film to the Secret Service.

– Yes.

– Copies were made for the FBI and dispatched by Army plane to Washington. Did Mr Sorrels explain you would be reimbursed for the film?

– I don't recall.

– You knew that at some time you would have to hand over the film. The Commission is aware that you received a sum of money for it from *Life* magazine. Would you mind telling us how much they paid you for that film?

– For the film?

– Yes.

– Well, it involves an awful lot of things, and it's not one price, but a question of how they were going to use it. And if they were going to use it, so I really don't know how I should answer that question.

– Well, we will ask the question and if you would rather not answer that is OK, but the Commission feels it would be helpful. One thing I think we can agree on is they had no intention of printing your barbecue pictures and selling them on around the world.

Mr ZAPRUDER: (Pause) I received $25,000 as you know and I have given that to the Firemen's and Policemen's Benevolence.

Mr LIEBELER: Thank you. Will you please now turn to frame 378?

– Frame 378?

– Yes. From the angle I would say your son filmed this.

– That is correct.

– Here, by your expression I would guess a remark had been made. The pressure you put on the burger in your hand caused the catsup to squeeze out and emerge at speed.

– Where you drew in the arrow?

– Yes. The trajectory. The catsup hits your shirtfront and also your left wrist. But look here. It also landed on your brother's wife's blouse.

– I . . . I saw the catsup and everything and I started. I can hardly talk about it. (The witness crying)

– Don't be ashamed, Mr Zapruder. It's a family argument.

– I'll have that water now, if I may.

(The witness is fetched some water)

Mr LIEBELER: Now, Mr Zapruder, with your permission I want to go right back to the start of your testimony. Your business is manufacturing ladies' dresses. Is that correct?

Mr ZAPRUDER. Yes.

– I would think that in making ladies' dresses, some stock would get spoiled during the process – say by poor stitching or measuring?

– There are some that fail quality inspection. For the reasons you state, also dyeing errors.

– And what happens to these damaged dresses? Are they thrown away?

– Yes. No. What does the Commission –?

– (Interrupting) Or given away as gifts?

– No, I –

– We have pictures of your and your brother's wife wearing dresses manufactured by your company. Also your brother.

– That was a party. A dumb joke. He went as Mr Hoover.

– (Pause) Earlier, you said you had your camera in your office.

– When?

– On the morning of the assassination. Had you brought it in from home that morning?

– No, it was already there.

– In your office.

– Yes.

– And your building is right next to 501 Elm St, where the alleged assassin was. Mr Oswald.

– Yes.

– You keep your home movie camera in your office, Mr Zapruder?

– No.

– Only on days when you might like to shoot a President?

– I had left it there a couple of days.

– (Pause) Let's go on. You walked down Elm to the underpass. There were obstructions so you moved to the knoll. Hudson exhibit No. 1, you have testified, shows you stood there.

– Yes.

– And behind you is the girl that works in your office.

– Yes.

– Your secretary.

– (Inaudible)

– Will you please state for the commission, Mr Zapruder? If that was your secretary?

– Yes.

– She's wearing a pretty dress.

– Unless the photo was doctored?

– When I mentioned earlier that fellow Willis. You know he took and is selling these shots in Dallas. Mr Zapruder, please look up.

– I'm a little tired. Could I face away from the sun now? Or maybe one of you guys might close the blinds?

– In a moment. Mr Zapruder, were you aware that Phil Willis is a part-time investigator?

– (No response)

– Who tells us you bought up all the copies of that shot and the negative. Why would that be?

– I'm a keen photographer. That's why I have an expensive movie camera.

– And a suspicious wife.

– You talked to my wife?

– Not yet.

(The witness crying. Speech inaudible)

– Mr Zap –

– Please don't.

Mr LIEBELER: OK. Let's look at a theory here if you don't object? Willis had something on you and you were trying to cover that up. Also, you returned from the assassination with the roll of film. Maybe you had to make it look like you always had your camera with you, like that was a regular thing – would that be fair, Mr Zapruder?

– (No response)

– A regular thing to shoot both the arrival of the motorcade and the barbecue on the same day. So you would have many rolls of film being processed at any one time. That would appear innocent, wouldn't it?

– Yes.

– But maybe it was intended that way if you see the thing the way I do. Because you had no intention of shooting the President and maybe not even the barbecue? For the record the witness is nodding his head. The reason the camera was in the office was you intended that roll for another reason.

– Like what?

– Like who. Like the girl stood beside you on the knoll. Your secretary. You had been coozing up for some time and that is why you had to have those photographs from Willis – because your wife already hired him to get evidence.

– (No response)

– You make a lot of money from the dress business, Mr Zapruder?

– I do OK, I guess.

– And your wife knew that. And if she got the proof about Helen, then you could kiss that all goodbye.

– (The witness crying)

Mr LIEBELER: So now we have to look at this from a whole other angle. Let's have the slide of picture 378.

(Sounds. Identified as blinds being drawn, a projector)

Mr LIEBELER: Would you look at the slide please?

Mr ZAPRUDER: That one here?

– Yes. This is a blow-up of picture 378 from your pictures. Would you state for the commission this image is from your home movie pictures?

– Unless it's been doctored.

– Will you cut that out? Now, as you see, the remark has been made. From the angle of your face, we can tell your wife is off and to the right. This caused you to put pressure on the food in your hand, causing the catsup to partially explode.

– Oh, my. That is the terrible one, yes.
– Off your wrist and back there and land on your brother's wife's blouse.
– I see it.
– Your wife was real mad at you that afternoon, wasn't she?
– (No response)
– She knew you had gone to see the motorcade and she knew you would be going with your secretary and she wasn't pleased about that one bit, was she? She was left home with Abraham Jnr who also was not invited to see the President.
– (No response)
– But your staff had half the morning off – we checked. So from after ten, you and Helen had the office alone. That's a lot of time before the President got to Houston St at twelve fifteen.
– I, you're. This is through the looking glass.
– You're denying that for the Commission?
Mr ZAPRUDER (long pause): How long are these conversations going to be kept secret?
Mr LIEBELER: Maybe 50–75 years.
– But at least 50 years.
– Oh, at least. (Pause) What are you counting, Mr Zapruder?
– She's forty-nine now, so . . . OK. Yes. I was with Helen.
– Alone?
– Very.
– Let the record state that Mr Zapruder has concurred with Mr Liebeler's version of events. So you go see the President together, and you were careful that Helen was behind you and to the right so she wouldn't ever be in shot. And that's OK but for two things. First the President is assassinated and suddenly you have one hot roll of footage. And that means everyone is going to want to talk to you and ask who you were there with. So you panic. You don't tell anyone, Helen gets back to work in six minutes – we checked that out too. You, Mr Zapruder, rush home with the camera and play for time by shooting the rest of the roll during the barbecue.
– You guys are real thorough. Or paranoid.
– Thank you. During the barbecue at some point your wife makes a remark. Disparaging to you. And the catsup flies all over.

– (No response)

– You knew the film was important. You knew it would have to be handed over.

– Yes. I knew it would be a matter for the Secret Service. The neighbors got back and the big fight started with my brother; you should also know his wife somehow got hold of a baseball bat. When that turned ugly, I snuck off to my den to think.

– You felt bad about getting them into that because you didn't tell them about the President being shot?

– No. About my camera being in the office already. The actual reason I had it there was so I could film Helen without – film Helen. For my personal library. Then I figured it had to be worth something.

– The film of Helen?

– Of the President. I figured that if I made the price high enough no one would ever get to see it.

– So you valued your adultery above national security?

– You have to put it like that?

– If this is difficult for you, we can stop and begin again at another time?

– (Pause) I figure I answered your questions. Or do I have to talk more about seeing the President shot down like a dog?

– No, but we might talk about impounding your personal library.

– (No response)

– OK, swing the projector light away from Mr Zapruder's face and turn it off. Also, let's open the blinds.

– Thank you.

– The last thing, which I want to discuss with you, is the second problem you had when the President was killed. And that was this guy Willis taking photographs. Originally, it all looked innocent, like you and Helen your secretary just captured the visit of the President, but when he got shot that meant that every photograph was going to be scrutinized and maybe even put in the press.

– Yes.

– Did you think Willis was there to film you specifically?

– I could never figure that out. I knew my wife had hired

someone. She has before. I think he would have been there anyway. And because I was there, well, for him that would be like killing two birds with one stone.

– Yeah, or one President with three . . . (pause) Strike that too. But you spoke to him after? Willis?

– A few days after, yes. Some of his other work appeared in the local papers. I had to pay a lot for the shots, but I was satisfied I had, well, I hope all of them.

– And so your wife remains suspicious.

– (No response)

– But with no real proof.

– (No response)

– And she won't get it from Willis. Or from your footage.

– (No response)

Mr LIEBELER: Thank you, Mr Zapruder. I enjoyed meeting you very much and thank you for coming in. Do you have any final questions at all?

Mr ZAPRUDER: Uh, well. You spoke with Willis. Can you tell me if this guy sold any of the shots of me with Helen?

– (Inaudible) Yeah. OK. Just one I know of. I believe you were cropped out, but he sold one of Helen to that guy Jack Ruby.

– That fuck.

– You know him?

– No.

– Well, thank you a lot, Mr Zapruder.

– Thank you. Goodbye.

– Can we give you a ride?

– No, I have an errand.

– Goodbye.

(Witness has left the room)

END OF TESTIMONY

HERE COMES
SANTA CLAUS

BILL PRONZINI

Kerry sprang her little surprise on me the week before Christmas. And the worst thing about it was, I was no longer fat. The forty-pound bowlful of jelly that had once hung over my belt was long gone.

"That doesn't matter," she said. "You can wear a pillow."

"Why me?" I said.

"They made me entertainment chairperson, for one thing. And for another, you're the biggest and jolliest man I know."

"Ho, ho, ho," I said sourly.

"It's for a good cause. Lots of good causes – needy children, the homeless, three other charities. Where's your Christmas spirit?"

"I don't have any. Why don't you ask Eberhardt?"

"Are you serious? *Eberhardt*?"

"Somebody else, then. Anybody else."

"You," she said.

"Uh-uh. No. I love you madly and I'll do just about anything for you, but not this. This is where I draw the line."

"Oh, come on, quit acting like a scrooge."

"I *am* a scrooge. Bah, humbug."

"You like kids, you know you do—"

"I don't like kids. Where did you get that idea?"

"I've seen you with kids, that's where."

"An act, just an act."

"So put it on again for the Benefit. Five o'clock until nine, four hours out of your life to help the less fortunate. Is that too much to ask?"

"In this case, yes."

She looked at me. Didn't say anything, just looked at me.

"*No*," I said. "There's no way I'm going to wear a Santa Claus suit and dandle little kiddies on my knee. You hear me? Absolutely no way!"

"Ho, ho, ho," I said.

The little girl perched on my knee looked up at me out of big round eyes. It was the same sort of big round-eyed stare Kerry had given me the previous week.

"Are you really Santa Claus?" she asked.

"Yes indeedy. And who would you be?"

"Melissa."

"That's a pretty name. How old are you, Melissa?"

"Six and a half."

"Six and a half. Well, well. Tell old Santa what it is you want for Christmas."

"A dolly."

"What sort of dolly?"

"A big one."

"Just a big one? No special kind?"

"Yes. A dolly that you put water in her mouth and she wee-wees on herself."

I sighed. "Ho, ho, ho," I said.

The Gala Family Christmas Charity Benefit was being held in the Lowell High School gymnasium, out near Golden Gate Park. Half a dozen San Francisco businesses were sponsoring it, including Bates and Carpenter, the ad agency where Kerry works as a senior copywriter, so it was a pretty elaborate affair. The decoration committee had dressed the gym up to look like a cross between Santa's Village and the Dickens Christmas Fair. There was a huge gaudy tree, lots of red-and-green bunting and

seasonal decorations, big clusters of holly and mistletoe, even
fake snow; and the staff members were costumed as elves and
other creatures imaginary and real. Carols and traditional
favorites poured out of loudspeakers. Booths positioned along
the walls dispensed food – meat pies, plum pudding, ginger-
bread, and other sweets – and a variety of handmade toys and
crafts, all donated. For the adults, there were a couple of city-
sanctioned games of chance and a bar supplying wassail and
other Christmassy drinks.

For the kiddies, there was me.

I sat on a thronelike chair on a raised dais at one end, encased in
false whiskers and wig and paunch, red suit and cap, black boots
and belt. All around me were cotton snowdrifts, a toy bag over-
flowing with gaily wrapped packages, a shiny papier-mâché
version of Santa's sleigh with some cardboard reindeer. A couple
of young women dressed as elves were there, too, to act as my
helpers. Their smiles were as phony as my whiskers and paunch;
they were only slightly less miserable than I was. For snaking out
to one side and halfway across the packed enclosure was a line of
little children the Pied Piper of Hamlin would have envied, some
with their parents, most without, and all eager to clamber up onto
old St. Nick's lap and share with him their innermost desires.

Inside the Santa suit, I was sweating – and not just because it
was warm in there. I imagined that every adult eye was on me,
that snickers were lurking in every adult throat. This was
ridiculous, of course, the more so because none of the two
hundred or so adults in attendance knew Santa's true identity. I
had made Kerry swear an oath that she wouldn't tell anybody,
especially not my partner, Eberhardt, who would never let me
hear the end of it if he knew. No more than half a dozen of those
present knew me anyway, this being a somewhat ritzy crowd;
and of those who did know me, three were members of the
private security staff.

Still, I felt exposed and vulnerable and acutely uncomfortable. I felt the way you would if you suddenly found yourself
naked on a crowded city street. And I kept thinking: What if one
of the newspaper photographers recognizes me and decides to
take my picture? What if Eberhardt finds out? Or Barney Rivera
or Joe DeFalco or one of my other so-called friends?

Another kid was on his way toward my lap. I smiled automatically and sneaked a look at my watch. My God! It seemed as though I'd been here at least two hours, but only forty-five minutes had passed since the opening ceremonies. More than three hours left to go. Close to two hundred minutes. Nearly twelve thousand seconds . . .

The new kid climbed onto my knee. While he was doing that, one of those near the front of the line, overcome at the prospect of his own imminent audience with the Nabob of the North Pole, began to make a series of all-too-familiar sounds. Another kid said, "Oh, gross, he's gonna throw up!" Fortunately, however, the sick one's mother was with him; she managed to hustle him out of there in time, to the strains of "Walking in a Winter Wonderland."

I thought: What if he'd been sitting on my lap instead of standing in line?

I thought: Kerry, I'll get you for this, Kerry.

I listened to the new kid's demands, and thought about all the other little hopeful piping voices I would have to listen to, and sweated and smiled and tried not to squirm. If I squirmed, people *would* start to snicker – the kids as well as the adults. They'd think Santa had to go potty and was trying not to wee-wee on himself.

This one had cider-colored hair. He said, "You're not Santa Claus."

"Sure I am. Don't I look like Santa?"

"No. Your face isn't red and you don't have a nose like a cherry."

"What's your name, sonny?"

"Ronnie. You're not fat, either."

"Sure I'm fat. Ho, ho, ho."

"No, you're not."

"What do you want for Christmas, Ronnie?"

"I won't tell you. You're a fake. I don't need you to give me toys. I can buy my own toys."

"Good for you."

"I don't believe in Santa Claus anyway," he said. He was about nine, and in addition to being belligerent, he had mean little eyes. He was probably going to grow up to be an axe murderer. Either that, or a politician.

"If you don't want to talk to Santa," I said, feigning patience, "then how about getting off Santa's lap and letting one of the other boys and girls come up—"

"No." Without warning he punched me in the stomach. Hard.

"Hah!" he said. "A pillow. I *knew* your gut was just a pillow."

"Get off Santa's lap, Ronnie."

"No."

I leaned down close to him so only he could hear when I said, "Get off Santa's lap or Santa will take off his pillow and stuff it down your rotten little throat."

We locked gazes for about five seconds. Then, taking his time, Ronnie got down off my lap. And stuck his tongue out at me and said, "Asshole." And went scampering away into the crowd.

I put on yet another false smile behind my false beard. Said grimly to one of the elves, "Next."

While I was listening to an eight-year-old with braces and a homicidal gleam in his eye tell me he wanted "a tank that has this neat missile in it and you shoot the missile and it blows everything up when it lands," Kerry appeared with a cup in her hand. She motioned for me to join her at the far side of the dais, behind Santa's sleigh. I got rid of the budding warmonger, told the nearest elf I was taking a short break, stood up creakily and with as much dignity as I could muster, and made my way through the cotton snowdrifts to where Kerry stood.

She looked far better in her costume than I did in mine; in fact, she looked so innocent and fetching I forgot for a moment that I was angry with her. She was dressed as an angel – all in white, with a coat-hanger halo wrapped in tinfoil. If real angels looked like her, I couldn't wait to get to heaven.

She handed me the cup. It was full of some sort of punch with a funny-looking skinny brown thing floating on top. "I thought you could use a little Christmas cheer," she said.

"I can use a lot of Christmas cheer. Is this stuff spiked?"

"Of course not. Since when do you drink hard liquor?"

"Since I sat down on that throne over there."

"Oh, now, it can't be that bad."

"No? Let's see. A five-year-old screamed so loud in my left ear that I'm still partially deaf. A fat kid stepped on my foot and nearly broke a toe. Another kid accidentally kneed me in the crotch and nearly broke something else. Not three minutes ago, a mugger-in-training named Ronnie punched me in the stomach and called me an asshole. And those are just the low lights."

"Poor baby."

". . . That didn't sound very sincere."

"The fact is," she said, "most of the kids love you. I overheard a couple of them telling their parents what a nice old Santa you are."

"Yeah." I tried some of the punch. It wasn't too bad, considering the suspicious brown thing floating in it. Must be a deformed clove, I decided; the only other alternative – something that had come out of the back end of a mouse – was unthinkable. "How much more of this does the nice old Santa have to endure?"

"Two and a half hours."

"God! I'll never make it."

"Don't be such a curmudgeon," she said. "It's two days before Christmas, we're taking in lots of money for the needy, and everybody's having a grand time except you. Well, you and Mrs. Simmons."

"Who's Mrs. Simmons?"

"Randolph Simmons's wife. You know, the corporate attorney. She lost her wallet somehow – all her credit cards and two hundred dollars in cash."

"That's too bad. Tell her I'll replace the two hundred if she'll agree to trade places with me right now."

Kerry gave me her sometimes-you're-exasperating look. "Just hang in there, Santa," she said and started away.

"Don't use that phrase around the kid named Ronnie," I called after her. "It's liable to give him ideas."

I had been back on the throne less than ten seconds when who should reappear but the little thug himself. Ronnie wasn't alone this time; he had a bushy-mustached, gray-suited, scowling man with him. The two of them clumped up onto the dais, shouldered past an elf with a cherubic little girl in hand, and confronted me.

The mustached guy said in a low, angry voice, "What the hell's the idea threatening my kid?"

Fine, dandy. This was all I needed – an irate father.

"Answer me, pal. What's the idea telling Ronnie you'd shove a pillow down his throat?"

"He punched me in the stomach."

"So? That don't give you the right to threaten him. Hell, *I* ought to punch you in the stomach."

"Do it, Dad," Ronnie said, "punch the old fake."

Nearby, the cherub started to cry. Loudly.

We all looked at her. Ronnie's dad said, "What'd you do? Threaten her too?"

"Wanna see Santa! It's my turn, it's my turn!"

The elf said, "Don't worry, honey, you'll get your turn."

Ronnie's dad said, "Apologize to my kid and we'll let it go."

Ronnie said, "Nah, sock him one!"

I said, "Mind telling me your name?"

It was Ronnie's dad I spoke to. He looked blank for two or three seconds, after which he said, "Huh?"

"Your name. What is it?"

"What do you want to know for?"

"You look familiar. Very familiar, in fact. I think maybe we've met before."

He stiffened. Then he took a good long wary look at me, as if trying to see past my whiskers. Then he blinked, and all of a sudden his righteous indignation vanished and was replaced by a nervousness that bordered on the furtive. He wet his lips, backed off a step.

"Come on, Dad," the little thug said, "punch his lights out."

His dad told him to shut up. To me he said, "Let's just forget the whole thing, okay?" and then he turned in a hurry and dragged a protesting Ronnie down off the dais and back into the crowd.

I stared after them. And there was a little click in my mind and I was seeing a photograph of Ronnie's dad as a younger man without the big bushy mustache – and with a name and number across his chest.

Ronnie's dad and I knew each other, all right. I had once had a hand in having him arrested and sent to San Quentin on a grand larceny rap.

Ronnie's dad was Markey Waters, a professional pickpocket and jack-of-all-thievery who in his entire life had never gone anywhere or done anything to benefit anyone except Markey Waters. So what was he doing at the Gala Family Christmas Charity Benefit?

She lost her wallet somehow – all her credit cards and two hundred dollars in cash.

Right.

Practicing his trade, of course.

I should have stayed on the dais. I should have sent one of the elves to notify Security, while I perched on the throne and continued to act as a listening post for the kiddies.

But I didn't. Like a damned fool, I decided to handle the matter myself. Like a dammed fool, I went charging off into the throng with the cherub's cries of "Wanna see Santa, *my* turn to see Santa!" rising to a crescendo behind me.

The milling crush of celebrants had closed around Markey Waters and his son and I could no longer see them. But they had been heading at an angle toward the far eastside entrance, so that was the direction I took. The rubber boots I wore were a size too small and pinched my feet, forcing me to walk in a kind of mincing step; and as if that wasn't bad enough, the boots were new and made squeaking sounds like a pair of rusty hinges. I also had to do some jostling to get through and around little knots of people, and some of the looks my maneuvers elicited were not of the peace-on-earth, goodwill-to-men variety. One elegantly dressed guy said, "Watch the hands, Claus," which might have been funny if I were not in such a dark and stormy frame of mind.

I was almost to the line of food booths along the east wall when I spotted Waters again, stopped near the second-to-last booth. One of his hands was clutching Ronnie's wrist and the other was plucking at an obese woman in a red-and-green, diagonally striped dress.that made her look like a gigantic candy cane. Markey had evidently collided with her in his haste and caused her to spill a cup of punch on herself; she was loudly berating him for being a clumsy oaf, and refusing to let go of a big handful of his jacket until she'd had her say.

I minced and squeaked through another cluster of adults, all of whom were singing in accompaniment to the song now playing over the loudspeakers. The song, of all damn things, was "Here Comes Santa Claus."

Waters may not have heard the song, but its message got through to him just the same. He saw me bearing down on him from thirty feet away and understood immediately what my intentions were. His expression turned panicky; he tried to tear loose from the obese woman's grip. She hung on with all the tenacity of a bulldog.

I was ten feet from getting *my* bulldog hands on him when he proceeded to transform the Gala Family Christmas Charity Benefit from fun and frolic into chaos.

He let go of Ronnie's wrist, shouted, "Run, kid!" and then with his free hand he sucker-punched the obese woman on the uppermost of her chins. She not only released his jacket, she backpedaled into a lurching swoon that upset three other merrymakers and sent all four of them to the floor in a wild tangle of arms and legs. Voices rose in sudden alarm; somebody screamed like a fire siren going off. Bodies scattered out of harm's way. And Markey Waters went racing toward freedom.

I gave chase, dodging and juking and squeaking. I wouldn't have caught him except that while he was looking back over his shoulder to see how close I was, he tripped over something – his own feet maybe – and down he went in a sprawl. I reached him just as he scrambled up again. I laid both hands on him and growled, "This is as far as you go, Waters," whereupon he kicked me in the shin and yanked free.

I yelled, he staggered off, I limped after him. Shouts and shrieks echoed through the gym; so did the thunder of running feet and thudding bodies as more of the party animals stampeded. A woman came rushing out from inside the farthest of the food booths, got in Markey's path, and caused him to veer sideways to keep from plowing into her. That in turn allowed me to catch up to him in front of the booth. I clapped a hand on his shoulder this time, spun him around – and he smacked me in the chops with something warm and soggy that had been sitting on the booth's serving counter.

A meat pie.

He hit me in the face with a *pie*.

That was the last indignity in a night of indignities. Playing Santa Claus was bad enough; playing Lou Costello to a thief's Bud Abbott was intolerable. I roared; I pawed at my eyes and scraped off beef gravy and false whiskers and white wig; I lunged and caught Waters again before he could escape; I wrapped my arms around him. It was my intention to twist him around and get him into a crippling hammerlock, but he was stronger than he looked. So instead we performed a kind of crazy, lurching bear-hug dance for a few seconds. That came to an end – predictably – when we banged into one of the booth supports and the whole front framework collapsed in a welter of wood and bunting and pie and paper plates and plastic utensils, with us in the middle of it all.

Markey squirmed out from underneath me, feebly, and tried to crawl away through the wreckage. I disentangled myself from some of the bunting, lunged at his legs, hung on when he tried to kick loose. And then crawled on top of him, flipped him over on his back, fended off a couple of ineffectual blows, and did some effectual things to his head until he stopped struggling and decided to become unconscious.

I sat astraddle him, panting and puffing and wiping gravy out of my eyes and nose. The tumult, I realized then, had subsided somewhat behind me. I could hear the loudspeakers again – the song playing now was "Rudolph, the Red-Nosed Reindeer" – and I could hear voices lifted tentatively nearby. Just before a newspaper photographer came hurrying up and snapped a picture of me and my catch, just before a horrified Kerry and a couple of tardy security guards arrived, I heard two voices in particular speaking in awed tones.

"My God," one of them said, "what *happened*?"

"I dunno," the other one said. "But it sure looks like Santa Claus went berserk."

*　　　*　　　*

There were three of us in the football coach's office at the rear of the gym: Markey Waters and me and one of the security guards. It was fifteen minutes later and we were waiting for the arrival of San Francisco's finest. Waters was dejected and resigned, the guard was pretending not to be amused, and I was in a foul humor thanks to a combination of acute embarrassment, some bruises and contusions, and the fact that I had no choice but to keep on wearing the gravy-stained remnants of the Santa Claus suit. It was what I'd come here in; my own clothes were in Kerry's apartment.

On the desk between Waters and me was a diamond-and-sapphire brooch, a fancy platinum cigarette case, and a gold money clip containing three crisp fifty-dollar bills. We had found all three items nestled companionably inside Markey's jacket pocket. I prodded the brooch with a finger, which prompted the guard to say, "Nice haul. The brooch alone must be worth a couple of grand."

I didn't say anything. Neither did Markey.

The owner of the gold clip and the three fifties had reported them missing to Security just before Waters and I staged our minor riot; the owners of the brooch and cigarette case hadn't made themselves known yet, which was something of a tribute to Markey's light-fingered talents – talents that would soon land him back in the slammer on another grand larceny rap.

He had had his chin resting on his chest; now he raised it and looked at me. "My kid," he said, as if he'd just remembered he had one. "He get away?"

"No. One of the other guards nabbed him out front."

"Just as well. Where is he?"

"Being held close by. He's okay."

Markey let out a heavy breath. "I shouldn't of brought him along," he said.

"So why did you?"

"It's Christmas and the papers said this shindig was for kids, too. Ronnie and me don't get out together much since his mother ran out on us two years ago."

"Uh-huh," I said. "And besides, you figured it would be easier to make your scores if you had a kid along as camouflage."

He shrugged. "You, though – I sure didn't figure on some-body like you being here. What in hell's a private dick doing dressed up in a Santa Claus suit?"

"I've been asking myself that question all night."

"I mean, how can you figure a thing like that?" Markey said. "Ronnie comes running up, he says it's not really Santa up there and the guy pretending to be Santa threatened him, said he'd shove a pillow down the kid's throat. What am I supposed to do? I'd done a good night's work, I wanted to get out of here while the getting was good, but I couldn't let some jerk get away with threatening my kid, could I? I mean, I'm a father, too, right?" He let out another heavy breath. "I wish I wasn't a father," he said.

I said, "What about the wallet, Markey?"

"Huh?"

"The wallet and the two hundred in cash that was in it."

"Huh?"

"This stuff here isn't all you swiped tonight. You also got a wallet belonging to a Mrs. Randolph Simmons. It wasn't on you and neither was the two hundred. What'd you do with them?"

"I never scored a wallet," he said. "Not tonight."

"Markey . . ."

"I swear it. The other stuff, sure, you got me on that. But I'm telling you, I didn't score a wallet tonight."

I scowled at him. But his denial had the ring of truth; he had no reason to lie about the wallet. Well, then? Had Mrs. Simmons lost it after all? If that was the case, then I'd gone chasing after Waters for no good reason except that he was a convicted felon. I felt the embarrassment warming my face again. What if he *hadn't* dipped anybody tonight? I'd have looked like an even bigger fool than I did right now . . .

Something tickled my memory and set me to pursuing a different and more productive line of thought. Oh, hell – of course. I'd been right in the first place; Mrs. Randolph Simmons's wallet had been stolen, not lost. And I knew now who had done the stealing.

But the knowledge didn't make me feel any better. If anything, it made me feel worse.

*   *   *

"Empty your pockets," I said.

"What for?"

"Because I told you to, that's what for."

"I don't have to do what you tell me."

"If you don't, I'll empty them for you."

"I want a lawyer," he said.

"You're too young to need a lawyer. Now empty your pockets before I smack you one."

Ronnie glared at me. I glared back at him. "If you smack me," he said, "it's police brutality." Nine years old going on forty.

"I'm not the police, remember? This is your last chance, kid: empty the pockets or else."

"Ahhh," he said, but he emptied the pockets.

He didn't have Mrs. Randolph Simmons's wallet, but he did have her two hundred dollars. Two hundred and four dollars to be exact. *I don't need you to give me toys. I can buy my own toys.* Sure. Two hundred and four bucks can buy a lot of toys, not to mention a lot of grief.

"What'd you do with the wallet, Ronnie?"

"What wallet?"

"Dumped it somewhere nearby, right?"

"I dunno what you're talking about."

"No? Then where'd you get the money?"

"I found it."

"Uh-huh. In Mrs. Randolph Simmons's purse."

"Who's she?"

"Your old man put you up to it, or was it your own idea?"

He favored me with a cocky little grin. "I'm smart," he said. "I'm gonna be just like my dad when I grow up."

"Yeah," I said sadly. "A chip off the old block if ever there was one."

Midnight.

Kerry and I were sitting on the couch in her living room. I sat with my head tipped back and my eyes closed; I had a thundering headache and a brain clogged with gloom. It had been a long, long night, full of all sorts of humiliations; and the sight of a nine-year-old kid, even a thuggish nine-year-old kid, being carted off to the Youth Authority at the same time his father was being carted off to the Hall of Justice was a pretty unfestive one.

I hadn't seen the last of the humiliations, either. Tonight's fiasco would get plenty of tongue-in-cheek treatment in the morning papers, complete with photographs – half a dozen reporters and photographers had arrived at the gym in tandem with the police and so there was no way Eberhardt and my other friends could help but find out. I was in for weeks of sly and merciless ribbing.

Kerry must have intuited my headache because she moved over close beside me and began to massage my temples. She's good at massage; some of the pain began to ease almost immediately. None of the gloom, though. You can't massage away gloom.

After a while she said, "I guess you blame me."

"Why should I blame you?"

"Well, if I hadn't talked you into playing Santa . . ."

"You didn't talk me into anything; I did it because I wanted to help you and the Benefit. No, I blame myself for what happened. I should have handled Markey Waters better. If I had, the Benefit wouldn't have come to such a bad end and you'd have made a lot more money for the charities."

"We made quite a bit as it is," Kerry said. "And you caught a professional thief and saved four good citizens from losing valuable personal property."

"And put a kid in the Youth Authority for Christmas."

"You're not responsible for that. His father is."

"Sure, I know. But it doesn't make me feel any better."

She was silent for a time. At the end of which she leaned down and kissed me, warmly.

I opened my eyes. "What was that for?"

"For being who and what you are. You grump and grumble and act the curmudgeon, but that's just a facade. Underneath you're a nice caring man with a big heart."

"Yeah. Me and St. Nick."

"Exactly." She looked at her watch. "It is now officially the twenty-fourth – Christmas Eve. How would you like one of your presents a little early?"

"Depends on which one."

"Oh, I think you'll like it." She stood up. "I'll go get it ready for you. Give me five minutes."

I gave her three minutes, which – miraculously enough – was all the time it took for my pall of gloom to lift. Then I got to my feet and went down the hall.

"Ready or not," I said as I opened the bedroom door, "here comes Santa Claus!"

THE STRANGE TALE
OF HECTOR'S ANGEL

MIKE PHILLIPS

One night Hector was lying on his bed thinking about nothing very much when an angel appeared in the corner of his cell.

The first thing that occurred to Hector was that someone had got in without his noticing, and instinctively he reached under his pillow for something with which to defend himself. He was already up and crouching against the wall before he realized that the figure opposite him had not moved, and this time he got a good look. What he saw startled him so much that he almost dropped the knife, but Hector hadn't got where he was by being an idiot, so, even though he was so shocked that he could feel the sweat breaking out on his forehead and his bowels straining until he was a hair's breadth away from shitting his pants, he still held on to the blade.

"So wha appen bra?" the angel asked.

Hector heard him, but at that moment he couldn't reply, because he was actually incapable of speech, and in any case he was too busy taking in the thing in front of him. Oddly enough, he had known what it was from the moment he saw it, although the truth was that it didn't look all that much like his idea of an angel.

For a start it was totally substantial, just like an ordinary person. In fact it looked a lot like Hector's Uncle C – a black man going bald in the front and with a sort of sarky smile on his face. He was also dressed in a sort of stripey robe, which, when Hector looked more closely, exactly resembled the long night-shirts that his Uncle C used to buy out of Marks & Spencer's at Christmas time. If that was all, Hector would have been safe, but towering above the black man's shoulders there were the tops of a pair of giant wings. The strange thing was that the wings were jet black, something that Hector certainly didn't expect, because every picture of an angel he'd ever seen showed them with white wings and feathers. He could have coped with the angel being a black man – no problem, if the wings had been kind of normal, but black wings! There was definitely some-thing funny going on, and as it happened, the black wings gave the angel a dark, hooded look which was extremely sinister, so that the impression in Hector's mind was of being face to face with a very large and vicious-looking vulture.

A multitude of thoughts flitted through Hector's mind. He dismissed the idea that this was a practical joke without thinking about it, because life was too serious inside for practical jokes, and there were nutters lying only a few feet away who would cut your balls off for making an irritating remark, never mind practical jokes. If anything it would have to be some kind of con, but in that case it was such an elaborate and convincing con that he couldn't think of any reason that anyone would go to so much trouble. Suddenly the solution hit him. He was dreaming. He knew how real dreams could seem and on more than one occasion he had woken up to some horror, only to find that the sensation of waking up had actually been part of a dream and he was still asleep.

Hector smiled, lay down on the bed and composed himself but, instead of drifting off as he expected, he stayed awake. He could feel the lumpy bits in the mattress where he'd stashed a few things. He could hear his own breathing. He opened his eyes and saw that the angel was still there, hovering now about a foot off the floor, the wings slightly raised and trembling. It was no use. He swung his legs off the bed, sat up, reached under the pillow, took out the knife and pressed it into his thumb. When he pulled it away he saw the beads of blood rushing out.

"Jesus," Hector said to the angel, "I'm awake."

"Don't take the Lord's name in vain," the angel said, "and as a matter of fact I don't have all night. I have to leave before the cock crows."

"There's no cocks in here," Hector said.

"You've got to be kidding," the angel replied with a straight face.

"Blood," Hector said. "Are you the Angel Gabriel? Me never knew you was black."

Gabriel was the only angel's name he could remember, and he used it because now he knew he was awake he was in a hurry to identify the angel, if only to bury the nasty suspicion which had rushed into his mind – that perhaps this angel was one of the bad ones – that this was the real meaning of the black wings.

The angel started laughing, a great booming sound which seemed to echo all over the landing and along the corridors.

For a moment Hector almost told him to hush before he woke up the whole prison, then it hit him that he would be very glad to see a few screws rush through the door and grab this creature, so he kept quiet.

"Don't worry," the angel said, apparently reading his mind. "Only you can hear me, and I'm not the Angel Gabriel. What's wrong with you, boy? You think Gabriel have time to piss about with a little convict like you? Gabriel only do important stuff, like personally serving the Lord, taking messages to the Virgin Mary, directing the hosts and the dominions and ting. Gabriel is big time, man. More than a century I been up there and I don't even see Gabriel yet."

"So you come from up that side," Hector said, pointing.

"That's right," the angel replied. "I had to leave my angel spa dem, singing and praising the Lord, cool, cool, come and look after you."

"So how come you wings black so?"

"Well," the angel said, "I and I hear you favour Rasta, so we make everything like black you no see?"

"Well aright," Hector said, "but why me? Why did you come?"

"Jesus," the angel exploded.

"Don't take the Lord name in vain," Hector cut in quickly.

"Blood," the angel shouted. "When I say it, is different. I worship the Lord name, not like you – you dam blasphemer, and don't make I vex now. Otherwise me might have to humble you."

When he said this the angel levitated a couple of feet, spread his wings a little, and lightning seemed to shoot from his eyes. Terrified, Hector hastened to apologize.

"Sorry. Sorry," he mumbled quickly, and this seemed to mollify the angel because he settled back towards the floor.

"So what can I do for you?" he asked Hector.

Hector considered it, in something of a quandary. That fact was that he wasn't the kind of man who normally ever thought about angels, much less seeing one, and if you had suggested as much to him before this event, he would probably have punched you to the ground and kicked you until his feet hurt or he got bored. In other words he was hard. So, although the angel had shaken him at the beginning, during their conversation he had begun to grasp the explanation for what was happening, and it was now clear to him that he had gone stark, raving mad. So he decided to concentrate, closing his eyes and focusing for a few minutes on the task of regaining his mind. But when he opened his eyes again, the angel was still there, with a look on his face which suggested that although he had been waiting patiently, it wouldn't be long before he lost his cool and did some serious humbling. So at long last Hector decided to give in, accept the situation and take the angel at face value.

"Excuse me sah," Hector said politely, "but what? I get three wishes or what?"

The angel laughed.

"Three wishes to blood," he said. "You ah joker. This nah fairy story. I come to help you out with your spiritual needs and to be your companion in your journey. As a matter of fact I want to save your soul."

Hector's face creased up in sheer bewilderment. Spiritual needs didn't interest him at all, and there was nothing about the angel to suggest that he'd be a desirable companion.

"That's it?" Hector asked.

"That's it," the angel said.

"Well I don' know," Hector told him, "if you was a woman now, I would feel better. The way you look now, me cyaan listen to you. You depressing."

"A woman?" the angel asked. "Dat no problem. We could be male or female. Don' matter."

"Yeah, man," Hector said. "I know dat, but you see you don' look female." A thought struck him. "If you could look black to suit me, you could look like a woman too. Right?"

"Yeah, sure. Dat make sense," the angel said in a businesslike way. "What you want? Your favourite female?"

Hector nodded, and in a flash, the angel disappeared and his mother stood in his place. Hector started back abruptly.

"Cut that out," he shouted. "Cut that out right now."

The angel reappeared.

"I thought you loved your mother," he said.

"Yes," Hector explained, "but I want a different sort of companionship." He thought for a bit, figuring out how to explain. "You see you been dead a long time, and things different now." He pointed to the wall behind his bunk where he had a picture of Destiny's Child pinned up. "See that now dat is what I call angels."

The angel took a look and frowned.

"I never see no angel look like this. These kinda people usually go to the other place."

"Dat's not the point," Hector said. "The point is dat you suppose to save my soul, and I cyaan respond unless you look my idea of an angel. You see wha happen nowadays is that everything is image. If you want to convince people you have to look the part." The angel looked hesitant and confused for the first time, and Hector nodded encouragingly at him. "Try again."

The angel shrugged, vanished, and was immediately replaced by a six-foot beauty with a large bosom and long legs, wearing high heels, a tight sweater and a tight micro skirt.

"Oh, Jesus," Hector said. "Oh, Jesus Lord." Then he saw the look on the angel's face and he dropped to his knees immediately. "I'm praying," he cried out. "I'm praying."

"Well. At least that is progress," the angel said.

"You see," Hector said. "This is unfair and it's messing my

mind up. You have all this power and I just cyaan relate to that. Mek I tell you something. I would feel better if you just laid aside your superpowers for half an hour. Let we rap human to human. Jesus did that all the time, man."

"That's true," the angel said. "But just for half an hour."

He took a deep breath, and Hector watched in wonder and amazement, praying for real this time, as the sweater rose up and down and the angel spread his incredible human legs and stretched.

"Oh, my God," Hector said, "you are an angel."

"That's what I've been trying to tell you," the angel said.

"You're human now?" Hector asked.

"For half an hour," the angel said.

"So let's do the wrestling," Hector said.

"Wait," the angel said. "What wrestling?"

"Like Jacob and the angel," Hector said. "It's in the Bible when the angel came to convert Jacob. He wrestled with him. All night."

"You don't have to tell me," the angel said. "I know the Bible inside out."

"So let's do it," Hector said.

This is how Hector and the angel ended up in bed together, and it was only a few minutes before Hector was crying out for Jesus again, but this time the angel didn't say a word.

That was the strange tale of the seduction of Hector's angel, who oddly enough, didn't change after half an hour, but stayed wrestling with Hector until the cock began to crow in the morning, metaphorically speaking that is, and although Hector sat up every night for a year after that, watching and waiting and praying for the angel to return he never saw him again. But when you come to consider that Hector had never in his life spent so much time on his knees muttering the Lord's name, you could say that the angel had managed to convert him good and proper.

CHAPTER THE LAST

ALEX ATKINSON

Merriman Explains

It must have been a full twelve and a half seconds before anybody broke the stunned silence that followed Merriman's calm announcement. As I look back, I can still see the half-humorous smile playing about his satyr's face in the flickering firelight. I can hear again the hearty cracks he made as he pulled his fingers one by one. I couldn't help feeling that the old fox was holding something back. What lay behind the quizzical look he fired at Eleanor? Did I detect a flutter of fear on her pasty (but somehow curiously attractive) face? What was the significance of the third onion? *Was there a third onion at all*? If so, *who had it*? These and eight other questions chased themselves around in my brain as I watched Merriman pick up his Chartreuse and look round at us with quiet amusement.

It was Humphrey who spoke first, his voice echoing strangely through the quiet room, with its crossed swords, Rembrandts, and jade. "But – great Scott! – if Alastair Tripp *wasn't* there . . .!"

"Alastair Tripp," said Merriman, breathing on his monocle (the only time I ever saw him do such a thing in all the years I knew him), "wasn't, as you say, there. *And yet, in a way, he was.*"

Humphrey gave a snort of disgust, and drained his crème-dementhe noisily. Even Chief Inspector Rodd gave vent to a half-stifled groan of bewilderment.

Merriman frowned. "You really are the dumbest crew I ever struck," he snarled. His gay wit was so infectious that the tension eased at once. He pointed at Humphrey with an olive on the end of an ebony-handled poniard. "Take your mind back," he said, "to a week last Wednesday, at sixteen minutes past seven p.m., in the hall of Mossburn Manor. Haven't you realized yet that the Mrs. Ogilvie who flung the grand-father clock over the banisters was in reality her own step-mother – Eleanor's sister's aunt by marriage? Even by the light of a single candle you should have noticed the blonde wig, the false hands, or the papier-mâché mask – *the very mask which was found later up the chimney in Simon's bedroom*! Don't you see?"

Eleanor gasped. I could see Humphrey's knuckles whiten as his bony hands tightened their grip on the handle of the lawnmower. I felt that the pieces were beginning to drop into place like bits of an enormous, sinister jigsaw puzzle. The trouble was, they didn't seem to fit.

"A left shoe, my half-wits," rumbled Merriman. "A left shoe with the lace missing. One onion where there should have been three. A half-chewed sweet in an otherwise deserted goldfish-bowl. By thunder, surely you *see*?" He rose to his feet and began to pace the room, with his head bent to avoid the oak beams. Sometimes as he walked he trod on the Chief Inspector, and once as he stood upright to emphasize a point, he brought down the chandelier with a crash. "It was a chance remark from Lady Powder that tipped me off," he bellowed, pounding a huge fist on the top of Eleanor's head. Eleanor's eyes widened, and on her face there was a look I hadn't seen before. "We were on the roof, you remember, trying to find a croquet ball, and all of a sudden she said 'It hasn't rained since Monday.'" He stood in the middle of the room, with one hand on the picture-rail and the other in his trousers pocket, and surveyed us. "From that moment," he said quietly, "I knew I was on the wrong track." He started to walk about again, and some of the floor-boards didn't seem any too safe down at my end of the room.

"But – great Scott! – if Alastair Tripp *wasn't there* . . ." Humphrey began again.

"I'm coming to that." Merriman fixed me with his eccentric glare. "I believe I have told you more than once, my foolish ape," he said, "that there are a hundred and four ways of getting into a room with no doors on the inside and no windows on the outside. But that's beside the point. Consider, if you will, the night of the murder. Here we have John Smith taking a nap in the pantry. The door is locked. The window is locked. The cupboard is bare. The carpet – and mark this – the carpet is *rolled up in a corner*, tied round with ordinary common or garden string. Now then, in the first place, as you will have guessed, the lightly sleeping figure on the camp bed was not John Smith at all." Merriman fixed Eleanor with a penetrating stare. "You know who it was, don't you, *Mrs. Anstruther?*"

"Mrs. *what!*" The question left my lips before I could stop it. Eleanor turned deathly pale, and tore her cambric handkerchief in two with a convulsive movement. Chief Inspector Rodd stirred slightly in his sleep. A frown of impatience played fitfully over the chiselled features of Humphrey Beeton. Outside the rain whispered eerily against the panes.

"Good Kensington Gore!" swore Merriman, wrenching a handful of stops from his treasured organ and hurling them at the Chief Inspector: "it was so *easy!*" He sat suddenly in the wicker armchair, and all but flattened Professor Meak, whom we had somehow forgotten. "Let me take you through it step by step. A bootlace is fastened to one end of the blow-pipe, which has previously been filled with sugar. This whole deadly contraption is lowered down the chimney – oh, there was plenty of time, I assure you: remember that Mercia Foxglove had been concealed in the shrubbery since dawn, and in any case at that time nobody knew that Paul's father was really Janet's uncle from Belfast."

"But if Alastair Tripp *wasn't there* . . ." Humphrey's voice was desperate with curiosity. The lawnmower trembled in his hands.

"I'm coming to that," said Merriman, filling his pipe with herbs. "Three onions," he went on steadily, "have already been placed midway between the door and the golf-club – which, you will observe, is leaning unnoticed against the wall. Very well, then. Recall, if you will, the evidence of the so-called Alfred Harp – actually, of course, as I will show you, he is none other than our friend the mysterious "milkman": but more of that anon. Where did he find the decanter after – I repeat, *after* – the gardener's cottage had been burnt to the ground? He found it, my pretty dumbbells, in the pocket of Sir Herbert's dressing-gown – *which was nowhere to be found*." He beamed expansively. "Now do you understand?"

Humphrey rose unsteadily. His face was working, and I thought I detected a fleck of foam on his tie. I reached unobtrusively for my hat. "But if Alastair Tripp – *wasn't there –*" Humphrey almost shouted.

"I'm coming to that."

It was too much. With a mighty roar of rage and impatience, Humphrey swung the lawnmower over his head in a flashing arc.

As I groped my way down the back stairs I reflected sadly that this would probably go down in history as Merriman's Last Case.

THE LION OF DRAKSVILLE

JULIAN RATHBONE

"It has come to my notice," said Baz, "that you have published accounts of three of my cases. Under the guise of fiction."

Her tone was cool but not unfriendly. She fixed me over the gold-framed half-lenses she affected – no, that's quite wrong. In public she uses flexible contact lenses, severally tinted to change the colour of her eyes if she feels the need to assume a disguise. She fixed me over the gold-framed half-lenses she wears at home and which none but I and "Roc" Hudson, the six-foot gay Afro who is her housekeeper, has ever seen. Baz Holmes does not wear spectacles in public. Though she has been known to use a magnifying glass. I was of course immediately defensive.

"I have changed names, altered locales. As you say, they are under the guise of fiction. You have . . ."

"I am not entirely unhappy that you should be doing this. There is, after all, a precedent."

She returned to her PC, tapped through a quite long sequence, and then leant back with some satisfaction as the screen exploded in fireworks and congratulatory music. For the eighth time in a row she had gone out on Mah-Jong.

"But I should suggest that occasionally you go too far in fictionalizing. For instance the reader of *Jack the Lad-Ripper* could get the impression that I was a touch surprised at the outcome. In fact of course I was quite aware that Mrs Finlay-Camden was impersonating herself from a very early stage. Proof was what I required . . ."

You fooled me, I thought. OK. It was not just the eighth time in a row she'd gone out in Mah-Jong, so far she has never failed. Nevertheless.

"And certainly your little *racontes* do have the effect of drumming up business that might not otherwise have come our way. But I do think you have been a touch careless with the pseudonym you have adopted."

"You do? Why?"

But of course on cue the buzzer sounded and after checking him out on the discreet video that surveyed her front door, she indicated to Roc that he should show our caller into her Barbican apartment. No more was said there and then about these little *fictionalizations*.

He was tall, quite well-built, wore a long-skirted leather coat which I have to say I instantly coveted and a motor-bike leather helmet (c. 1930) with round goggles hoisted on to his forehead. He had a big bushy brown moustache set between the deep lines that ran from his cheekbones to his jowls. His pale eyes were moist beneath drooped eyelids. He was, I supposed, in his late forties, but a touch gone over, if you know what I mean. Baz motioned him to sit in the deep white hide armchair and without being asked Roc placed a small tumbler half-filled with whisky at his elbow and a small bottle of fizzy Malvern. This is now routine – men get Scotch, ladies G and T.

From her eminence perched on the straight-backed chair she uses when playing her Strad guitar, Baz knitted her long fingers, the balls of her index fingers touching to make a pointer in front of her, and thus stabbed the air in front of her guest's nose.

"I know nothing about you," she said, "except that you are Sir Hugo Draks, that you live in the West Country in a Palladian mansion known as Draksville Hall, you are used to luxurious living but you are at present strapped for ready cash.

You are gay . . ." At this Roc came back to the door that led to the dining room and the kitchen and leered for a moment over Baz's shoulder. Baz then sniffed, her huge bony nose questing towards her subject and concluded: "And you work with lions."

"Just the one," said our guest.

"Goodness, Holmes," I said, anxious to do my traditional bit, "however did you work all that out?"

But it was her guest who filled in the answer.

"*Mail on Sunday*, I should think," he said. "They did me over a couple of weeks ago."

Well, of course I don't read the *Mail on Sunday*, or on any other day for that matter, but I was not in the least surprised to learn that Baz does. Baz, undisconcerted, continued:

"What the *Mail* omitted to mention was the problem that has brought you here. I take it there have been accidents that have nearly cost you your life and you believe that someone somewhere has designs on it. Your life, that is."

Sir Hugo raised his glass.

"This time, Holmes, you do surprise me. We thought we'd hushed it up. How did you know?"

"I have my methods. Watson here will tell you. I do have my methods."

Smug bitch.

"So you know what's been happening?"

"Usual sort of thing, I suppose," Baz drawled. "An urn fell off the pediment of Draksville Hall, narrowly missing your head as you passed beneath. A salmon left as a gift by an unknown donor poisoned the cat . . ."

"Tibetan snow leopard, actually. Philip brought her back from somewhere north of K2, damn distressing actually, lovely brute . . ."

"Philip? That would be your cousin?"

"Just so." Sir Hugo . . . you know it sticks in my craw to call posing mincers of his sort "Sir". Actually I don't readily call anyone "sir" but there you go . . . "Sir" leant forwards over his tumbler, already almost empty, and leered up at Baz. "And the last attempt dashed nearly had me. Routine inspection of the spread, do it every Monday, check out the damage the oiks and yobbos did over the weekend, you know? Coming out of Long

Acre and just before I turned into the Beech Avenue, heading
for the Lion's Den—"

"You were on . . .?"

"The Norton with sidecar—"

"The 1938 model? With Plexi shock-absorbers and chrome
hubs?"

"That's the chap . . . and the fucking sidecar blew up. Pardon
my French."

"Feel free."

"Fortunately there was a passing haystack . . ."

"Which you fell in. And the Norton?"

"Write-off. Total."

"How awful. So that's why you came here on the '52
Triumph . . . I heard you as you arrived. Unmistakable."

The upshot was that after haggling for a moment over Baz's fee,
always a stupid thing to do and this time it nearly led to Roc
showing Sir H. prematurely to the door, Baz agreed to investigate these bizarre happenings.

"Unfortunately," she said, "due to publicity resulting from
my friend's publications, my, um, order book is full for the next
ten days." She consulted an electronic notebook no bigger than
a credit-card and only twice as thick. "Shall we say Friday
week? Julia, can you manage that?"

I hauled out my fat Filofax, made a show of consulting it,
pursed the lips, jotted with a pencil.

"Yes, I can manage that." Of course I bloody could, but I
don't like her to see just how eager I am to share her adventures.

"Good. Friday week, then." She smiled sweetly at Sir. "Let's
hope you survive until then."

He scowled.

"Ta!" he said. "Ta very much."

When I left half an hour later (I had an appointment coun-
selling a Lloyd's name's wife following hubby's suicide: the
session consisted of convincing her that relief is not necessarily
an inappropriate emotion at such times), Holmes already had
her guitar across her knees. She was working out her own
arrangement of a Bach allemande for solo cello. She reckons
Segovia's version doesn't capture the spirit of the original as

well as it might. It was a good sign, a sign that she was intrigued by what had turned up, was already mulling it over.

Paddington is the dreariest of stations, is it not? And not enlivened by a pretty lad with an exaggerated step-haircut and a tight arse squeezed into white jeans who plucked my sleeve as I walked on to the concourse. I am large, I am fat, and I do dress as a professional businessman except when I am at home when I wear kaftans, so I suppose I ought not to be surprised to be propositioned if I dawdle outside gents' toilets at railway termini. However, though he revealed himself indeed to be a rent boy, he also turned out to be one of Kagan's rent boys, the Dean Street Deviants, whom Holmes uses as spies, messengers and so forth.

"Message for you, darling," he piped up, in a nauseating contralto. "Like Baz Holmes begs leave to inform you she's been unavoidably detained and won't be able to make it to Draksville Hall for a coupla days at least. But she wants you to go on down, get the lay of the land like, snoop about, see what gives, OK, darling?" He did not wait for an answer since he had spotted a bishop in full purple fig, skirts down to his big black boots, well-hung gold cross bouncing on his navel, all this coming through the barrier off the Bristol and Bath Inter-City. His white rump twinkled away from me as he swooped like a hawk on his prey.

I was livid. I hate travelling by train on my own, and I certainly did not fancy turning up at Draksville Hall on my own account – I presumed Holmes had squared my lone arrival with Sir, but even so . . . Naturally I headed straight for the so-called buffet car. Well, you know what they're like on the Inter-City. Dreadful. And nowhere to sit, just a counter with a surly menial or two behind it, dispensing microwaved horrid food and drink at appalling prices. I ordered a veggie burger, a tonic (we're fresh outa slimline, ducks) and two gin miniatures. I felt that if I was to survive the next three hours I needed to be part smashed. I took them into the nearest first-class carriage, no compartments now of course, just a touch more legroom and an antimacassar, and found, across the gangway, two old chums.

Well, that's a relief, I thought.

Now, what does one do? Describe them. Not too long-winded, but give the picture. Sam and Doug. Problem is they are really very much alike, not as two peas in the proverbial pod, but . . . alike. They are both very fat, which of course I find immediately endearing, and both are in their mid-forties. They wore check shirts beneath sleeveless denim jackets, loads of pockets which professionally they need, combat trousers, also for the pockets, and of course DMs. Sam has very close-cropped hair where he isn't bald and is rather florid in countenance with a nose that droops, Concorde-style, at the tip. Doug has a broader face, and not much nose at all since some mean guy he fell out with in a pub razored off most of it leaving open nostrils, nastily deformed. He has long hair worn in a pony tail.

Professionally? They are a freelance film unit, real film or video, they do both, and they do it on their own, or, as they would put it, on their tod. Anything. Their first real break, they say, though I don't know of anyone who claims to have seen their footage, was Saigon when Charlie took over. I did see thirty seconds of a shootout in Medellín, Colombia, which won them an award but later proved to be faked. But mostly they fill in for better-known freelances when someone catches a cold or has double-booked.

They were playing three-card brag and the price I had to pay for moving across the aisle and joining them was fifteen oncers and the next round at the bar. Par for the course. Never, never move into a card-game that's already running on a train.

"Gin rummy?" I suggested, unloading the miniatures of Glenfiddich and another veggie burger.

"You're joking."

"So where are you guys heading?"

Now this is so stupid when you're telling this sort of story. Every punter out there who picks up these pages knows sodding well where they're heading. The surprise element is not there for you. But I was surprised.

Chipping Snodsbury?

No, actually, what Sam said, giving the tip of his droopy nose a swipe as if to indicate one over you here mate, was what you dear reader expect and I did not:

"Queen's Draksville and on to Draksville Hall."

"Des res of Sir Hugo Draks, actually."

"On a job?" Pretty obvious, really. The luggage racks were filled with the soft black leather cases they carry their gear in, and they had had to clear the seats on the other side of the table so I could sit with them.

"Yeah. Filming Professor Coningsby-Doulton, actually." It was Doug who kept shoving in the "actually". "You know, the old geezer what goes round country houses talking about their history and architechural feechers."

"Thinking man's Lucy Lambton. His usual crew got nicked by the poli doing hard porn."

They were both being a bit laid-back about it all. I decided a little deflation was in order.

"Never heard of him," I said briskly.

They looked a touch put out, as I hoped they would. Then . . .

"Well, tell the truth, nor had we," said Doug. "The agency said it's mostly Open University stuff, actually. Anyway, better than Sooty and Sweep, which is what we might have been doin' if this 'adn't turned up. Where are you goin', then, Jules?"

"Same place, Draksville Hall. But, actually, I shall be on the right side of the green baize door – not the hired help, but a house guest."

That shut them up for a bit. I looked out the window as Wiltshire rolled by and in the foreground the telegraph poles. I recalled reading somewhere that you can calculate the speed of a train by timing how quickly they pass if you know the regular distance they are spaced at. What a stupid way of passing time on a train.

"Another hand or two, then?" I suggested.

It turned out that they weren't staying at the hall at all, not even as servants, but at the Draks Arms in Queen's Draksville. I let them share my taxi from the station and then drove on into the countryside: mostly rolling meadowland with some timber, though presently the bleaker hills of Dartmoor showed up on the left. However, before we could climb into them we arrived at Draksville Hall which, as we cruised up a tarmacked drive through a park dotted with cedars, turned out to be as boringly typical of stately homes as I expected.

From the air it's a square, each outer wall the same length. Looked at vertically these outer walls divide into three squares, the middle one with a pediment for a lid. The main entrance is a jutting pediment supported by four pillars in the Doric mode to make a portico of it. The corners of this pediment were marked by giant urns – except that one of them was missing. It looked down over manicured lawns to a brook that widens at this point into a pond (the inhabitants call it "the lake"). Beyond this, rolling hillocks with occasional deer are framed on one side by a stand of cedars and on the other, not by the traditional folly but a genuine ruin on a hill, a Norman keep with outer walls.

The fold-out brochure I picked up at the Queen's Draksville station stated that Montagu Draks started it in 1077. What it did not say, but I had found out through looking at *History Workshop* back numbers, was that he arrived in 1067 with a suit of chain-mail, a horse, and about thirty bully-boys recruited from the Norman village where he had been a steward; he achieved blue-blooded nobility by murdering and raping the Saxon population for twenty miles in every direction over the next decade or so. Once the local population had been properly subdued (or to use yesterday's buzz word "ethnically cleansed") a grateful monarch made him an earl, and granted him hereditary rights over the land.

The present incumbent, Sir Hugo, was no relation at all. His ancestors had been slave traders and sugar plantation owners from 1680 onwards, achieving huge wealth in the next century. Their surname was Tanner, and they came from Manchester. In 1780 Bob Tanner bought the property, pulled down the Tudor mansion, built the hall, changed his name to Draks; next he raised a company of infantry who were wiped out in the American War of Independence – a loyal gesture for which George III conferred on him a baronetcy.

I paid off the cabbie, rang the bell, and while I waited cast my eye around for clues or at any rate significant features which might be of some use to my friend. Presently the door opened.

"Dr Julia Watson?"

"The same."

"Welcome to Draksville Hall."

He was a young thin wispy man who looked like an undertaker, black suit, dark tie, black-framed specs, big bony nose. He offered to carry my carpet bag up the main stairs to a room on the first floor, but looked a touch frail about it so I took it back.

"You're the butler, then," I asked, as he opened the door.

"Sir Hugo does not have a butler in his employ. I am Sir Hugo's personal assistant."

"Goodie. That means I don't have to tip you."

"As madame pleases. We dine at eight. Drinks in the blue drawing room at half seven. We do not dress for dinner."

"I bloody do. The sight of me starkers would ruin anyone's appetite."

Not even for that did he crack his face.

"Informal, but not too informal." He glanced at my baggy man's suit and at my bag, obviously weighing up the chances of my having something halfway decent in it for the evening. At that point a lion roared. Rather loud and quite close. I rushed to the window, almost expecting to see it pawing at the casement even though we were on the first floor.

I found I was looking down into a space hollowed out of the landscape with a semicircular auditorium or spectators' area directly beneath me. There were about fifty tourists scattered across tiered concrete seating with a capacity of a thousand at least. Beyond them there was an unfenced area of worn tired grass, grey boulders and plastic trees representing the sort of thorn bushes or whatever one sees in travel posters for Kenyan safaris. Finally in the background was an artificial-looking hump of possibly plastic rock with a cage in it. The cage door was open. The foreground was patrolled by one large, black-maned lion who was obviously in need of something – one suspected food.

"There's no fence," I said. "Why doesn't he just go into the audience and snack off some poor kid?"

"An invisible barrier of electro-magnetically generated sound on a frequency that is extremely painful to felines separates him from the customers. It is as impassable for him as electrified razor wire fifteen feet high would be."

"Oh, very hi-tech," I exclaimed, then thought for a moment. "And that really quite frightening roar?"

"We have implanted a voice enhancer. Sophie was actually purring."

"Sophie?"

"Sophie. When he was born, on the day of the Wessex wedding, the vet made a gender mistake but the name stuck. Otherwise he would have been Edward. If you require anything before dinner, use the telephone, pressing the button marked R. Nine will get you an outside line should you require one."

He was about to dematerialize like a ghost.

"Hang on," I cried.

"Yes?"

"Tell cook, would you, that I'm strict vegan."

"The catering staff will be informed."

And he was gone, and left not a wrack behind. I returned to the window. Presently a Jenkinson's Gazelle was released into Sophie's compound. The gazelle made a quick dash across Sophie's field of vision, and, in a rather bored way, Sophie lumbered after him, made a circus animal's leap, falling four feet short. The gazelle posed in front of him, all elegant and cocky, but Sophie knew better. Gazelle was now on the other side of the sound barrier. A tannoy boomed with the knowing jokiness of a professional commentator, a hireling tossed Sophie a haunch of Dartmoor pony, which he toyed with for a moment and then walked away. Galvanized by the commentator the audience put their hands together. It was all as tacky as a provincial re-run of *Hair*. No. Tackier. I unpacked the cashmere kaftan with real gold thread I keep for posh evenings, and hung it in the wardrobe.

The young undertaker rematerialized in the blue drawing room which really was blue: dark blue silk on the walls, paler blue upholstery on the twirly furniture, white mouldings, heavy grape-coloured drapes. He poured South African sherry – sickly and tart – and indicated where Twiglets or salted peanuts could be browsed; for the rest he remained in the background.

Very much in the foreground were the following. Sir Hugo, whom I've already done so I don't need to do again, apart from saying that he was no longer in leather but was wearing a crimson silk smoking jacket, a large buttercup-yellow bow-tie and black evening trousers. His shoes though were not patent leather but pointed, shin-high tasselled boots. His thinning hair was swept up and back, suggesting the Lion in the Wizard of Oz rather than the real thing outside.

He welcomed me, muttered something about how it was deuced odd Holmes had elected to send me on ahead (like luggage not wanted on the voyage, I thought) and introduced me to his Inamoratus.

Seven at first sight was gorgeous. Then one realized he was perfect which meant he was an artefact and therefore a touch unappealing. He was a curly blond Swede who had worked hard to have all his muscles in the right places and his vowels and manners too.

Do you react badly to continentals who speak English with a studied perfection (and one means studied – they must spend decades listening to John Gielgud records to get it that right)? Yes? Well, so do I.

"Doc-tor Julia Wat-son? I believe you wrote a most interesting monograph on the interaction between siblings of mixed race, with each other and their peer groups. You must tell me where I can get hold of it."

That told me two things. He'd looked me up in *Debrett's People of Today* (I haven't yet made it to *Who's Who*) and that he was flannelling. The reference clearly states that the paper in question was published by Lawrence and Wishart.

Next came . . . oh, how to describe her? Do you remember Rita Hayworth? A very young Rita Hayworth? With that pert used but unblemished sexiness, the cascade of red hair, the blue eyes lit with mischief, the marble shoulders cased in jade tulle, the plunging neckline? Used sexiness indeed, because this version, this vision was, to my not untutored eye, well on through the seventh month – and the rag she was wearing had been couturier-designed to accommodate the shape of things to come. Zara. That was all. Just Zara. As if I'd know.

But, as I have said, I do not read the popular sheets, so Zara meant nothing to me.

And finally Philip, Philip Draks. He was short, more or less grey-haired, broad sort of face, colour of faded Cordoban leather, lots of lines that said sun maybe, certainly too much booze. A face like a pair of shoes you've had for far too long but which for vaguely sentimental reasons you don't quite dare to throw out. Does it need to be said? All right. He was wearing the sort of safari suit a certain sort of poser used to wear six years ago, but he got away with it. This one said: actually, I courier real safaris for very well-heeled punters.

During the twenty minutes or so with the Cape sherry and the Twiglets the main subject of conversation was Prof Coningsby-Doulton. Apparently he had written in a week or so before, asking if he could do one of his programmes on the hall and the keep. A substantial fee would be paid by the Open University and in the meantime here was an advance of a thousand pounds. Sir was hard-up enough to find an offer of a grand irresistible, which caused me to wonder whether or not he would be able to meet Holmes's fee which was far in excess of that sum. The Prof had arrived the next day and since then had been an infernal nuisance, prying into every nook and cranny all over the estate, writing up the script he would use. Sir thanked his lucky stars that he had not invited him to stay at the hall but had suggested the pub instead – the man was a truly dreadful bore.

"Well," I chipped in at the end, "you won't be bothered for much longer. His film crew travelled down from town on the train with me. By the way," I added, "I take it there have been no more attempts on your life?"

"None at all, old girl. In fact I'm beginning to wonder whether Holmes's dashed expensive presence is as called for as I thought. Especially as it seems as it were to be marked by her absence."

The awkwardness of that moment was saved by a roll on a gong at the end of which we drifted into a baronial hall, absolutely out of keeping with the neo-classicism of most of the building: candelabra, suits of armour, shields and claymores on the walls, moth-eaten banners, the lot.

Ensconced, the word is prompted by recollection of the milieu, in a high-backed carved black chair, I unfolded my napkin and thought to myself: this is going to be an awful evening. Just the five of us. Well, six, if you include the undertaker's lad, but he remained firmly in the background, though he did actually eat with us. They did not speak to him much but enough for me to gather his first name was Norris. We were served by a buxom girl with bright red hair, piercing blue eyes, wearing a black sweatshirt emblazoned in white with the Draks armorial bearing, well-filled black jeans and black trainers. Her voice, when she had occasion to speak, was like Devon cream, all warm, rounded vowels and rrr's that went on for ever. Sir Hugo called her Donna and said she was new to the establishment, straight from the agency.

The food was imperial and jolly good: Anglo-Indian curries, wide variety, plenty of them vegan enough. I don't mind dairy products if I can be reasonably well assured that the animals have been properly cared for and in this case the butter that made the ghee came, so Sir said, from his own Jerseys which were the most pampered cattle this side of the subcontinent. And there was plenty to drink: iced Black Velvet – Guinness Original with Möet et Chandon, one of my favourite tipples.

I did my best to probe and pry. I gathered Philip looked after the animals; Hugo mounted the historical dramas which were a feature at the weekends when the admission price went up; Zara expected Philip to marry her before their sprog arrived and was a touch peeved that he had not already made an honest woman of her; and that there was no love lost between her and Sven who at one point blurted out that the sooner she had the brat the better, advanced pregnancy was so damned ugly.

However, in the absence of Baz herself, all were agog to hear all I could tell them about a personality, who, despite the down-to-earth accounts I have published, still has mythical status especially in the haute monde. Was she genuinely a woman, or some sort of hermaphrodite, did she really design her own drugs, was it true she had studied guitar in her adolescence with Segovia, and had she really rewritten a crap programme for the Bank of England thereby saving them billions of pounds and a lot of egg on their faces? And so on. When I am with her in such a setting she tends to be the star attraction, which is entirely as it should be; nevertheless it was quite gratifying for me to be centre-stage for once, even if Baz herself remained the subject everyone was interested in.

Tropical fruit salads, followed by walnuts and a port that was sound if a touch immature followed the curries. At this point Zara touched her swelling tum, muttered apologies and departed. Philip followed her not much later.

After a couple of ports more I declined coffee and cognac in the Blue Room: it was already nearly eleven o'clock and I felt that if I was to fulfil my friend's commission to "find out the lay of the land" I should have a reasonably early night. I was rewarded as I turned the corner of the staircase to hear Sven murmur to Sir: "Is she not just absolutely the weirdest thing you ever came across?" followed by laughter suppressed but expressing assent. Clearly my descriptions and accounts of Baz had struck a chord, though I'm not sure "weird" is the word I should have chosen. Perhaps Sven's mastery of English was not quite as boringly complete as his accent suggested.

I got lost of course, the fourth Black Velvet had perhaps been a mistake, took a left for a right at the top of the stairs. At just about the point when a turned corner revealed a wholly unfamiliar corridor and I was about to retrace my steps I heard a crash of glass or china from a nearby room . . . No. I must not fib. I deliberately took the wrong turning in the hope of stumbling on some clue that might prove useful to Holmes.

The crash was followed by the usual sort of abuse that follows such incidents.

"Get out, get out, you silly old man. I'm fed up with you, fed up with the mess you've got us into, fed up with being skint, fed up with being preggers . . ." And Zara, it must I thought be Zara, burst into sobs. These quickly modulated to an even more hysterical pitch than before: "No, don't touch me, I don't want to be touched. Just fucking well get out of my sight—"

The door handle which was now only a few inches from my ear began to turn and I turned too, scuttled away as fast as I could. Yes, even someone as fat as I can scuttle if the occasion warrants it. I turned the corner as the door opened and ran straight into a suit of armour, you know the sort of thing. It wobbled and toppled, but did not crash. It sort of thunked onto the carpet. I held my breath. But it was all right. Philip, banished from his mistress's bedroom, stayed at the door.

"All right," he bellowed, "I will marry you. Anyway. But

first get a scan. I want to know what the fucking sprog is. You owe me that much."

"If it's a boy I want to be married straight away. As quickly as possible. Yes?"

"Oh, all right."

The door lock clicked and he was allowed back in.

I picked up the suit of armour: it was surprisingly light and clearly all in one piece, not an assembly of parts. It short, it was made out of fibreglass.

II

"Get the lay of the land." As I say it had already occurred to me that if that was what I was about, early rising might be useful. I suspected that my four principal companions would not be up with the dewy morn but that if I was I might with impunity be able to explore the main rooms if not the private ones. I therefore set my alarm for seven-thirty and turned in. But sleep evaded me. First it was Sophie whose lugubrious groans and howls, voice-enhanced so they seemed to be coming from beneath my very window-sill, suggested an attack of colic. Then I too was ambushed, towards dawn just when I felt at last I might sleep by . . . well, by a colic induced by a slightly over-spiced, undercooked chick-pea dhal. Fortunately my room had an en suite with an outside wall so I imagine my elephantine trumpetings caused no nuisance to anyone but myself and possibly Sophie.

Nevertheless I stuck to it, rose at seven-thirty, encased myself not in the voluminous black suit, cut like a man's, which I usually wear during the day-time, but the equally capacious tweeds I use in the country, and pottered down to the ground floor.

I have not always been a vegetarian. Who has? And I have to confess I swing about a bit according to what is available. Indeed on a recent visit to Spain with Baz I found that my principles could accommodate large helpings of fish and crustaceans. The odours of grilled bacon and devilled kidney drew me to a breakfast room on the south-east side of Draksville Hall. Just as I arrived, Philip Draks scraped the last of his scrambled egg on to a piece of toast and rose.

"Dashed menagerie," he stuttered through it all. "Have to be supervising the feeding or they tear the place apart." And off he went.

There was a vast hotplate laden with breakfast comestibles, and, thankfully, continuing the Anglo-Indian theme of the cuisine, a very sound kedgeree: flaked fish white and smoked in a saffron rice base. Thinking of the chick-pea dhal I was put in mind of the Bard: drive in one nail to drive out another . . . something like that. Baz would know. I helped myself, took my plate to the table and tucked in.

Presently I was aware of a presence and the Rustle of Spring. The presence was Norris, the undertaker's lad, the Rustle of Spring was the noise made by the cornflakes he tipped into a small bowl. He doused them with more sugar and Jersey full-cream milk than I should have recommended, sat beside me, and began to munch his way through them. It sounded like a forest fire.

Politeness indicated I should make an effort.

"Norris, isn't it?"

"Norris Claypole."

"Do you like working here, Mr Claypole?" I asked.

"Yes and no." Shards of cereal gusted towards me but fell short. "Mostly no."

"Oh. What's wrong?" I felt this was a useful line to take if I was to get the lie or lay of the land. Something was rotten in Draksville Hall, that was already clear. However peripheral to the main current of its existence the undertaker's lad might be, what was wrong for him might very well provide a clue to more central evils.

"Mainly it's the way they treat me."

Now I am a trained counsellor and I know when to shut up. Baz, in a prelim interview situation, I have to say does not. I waited. He munched on.

"I'm sure they treat you very well," I offered at last.

"They despise me."

"Oh, surely not!"

"I am a graduate in Tourist and Related Industries, University of Tulse Hill, where I also wrote a dissertation titled 'Theming the Park'. But they treat me like, like as if I were, well. Look. For instance." He blew more cornflakes my way, then tipped the packet into his nearly empty bowl, made again with the sugar and gold top. "I have to have breakfast early to get the letters sorted and so on before Sir Hugo comes into the office. And the second day I was here, I helped myself to a cooked breakfast, I mean it was all laid out just as it is now, and then got a terrible bollocking because I'd eaten whatever it is Sir Hugo normally has. Since then I've only ever felt safe taking the cornflakes . . ."

You know, this sort of snobbery really gets on my tits. I'll not put up with it. I snatched up a warm plate, and a couple of silver servers.

"Have what you want. Anything."

"But . . ."

"No buts. If there's any comeback I'll say it was me, I, who scoffed the goodies."

"Really?"

"Really."

Looking over my shoulder he chose two fried eggs, mushrooms, tomatoes, three slices of black pudding and two of fried bread. I piled them on to the plate then went back to my own place where I finished my kedgeree. He was still tucking in when I left.

I spent the next three hours or so fulfilling my commission. First I wandered through the state rooms. These were entirely what one expected: roped-off threadbare matting marked out the route the trippers trudged from the Drawing Room with its late Sheraton, its Landseer Stag attacked by Wolves over the monumental fireplace; through the Music Room with its Victorian Broadway and the drum-kit Sir Hugo had practised on during holidays from Harrow; the Library with thousands of leather-bound tomes locked behind solid grills and its ceiling said to be by Nash; to the Billiard Room whose walls were a mausoleum made up of the dead heads of now endangered species.

None of this made any impression on me that I felt would be useful to Holmes. Occasionally I came across a skivvy or two operating electrical cleaners or polishers, not dressed in the black the serving girl had worn the night before but blue jeans and white sweatshirts with a picture of a lion's head above a representation of the Hall, with the slogan: *I did it for real at Draksville.*

I arrived back in the entrance hall just as the buxom girl from the night before took in the post at the front door. She left the quite considerable pile, perhaps forty or fifty letters and packets, on a table and went back to her polisher. Naturally I began to glance through what was there. It was a pretty heterogeneous haul, much of it junk, but there were many that were obviously invoices and many of them showing red through the windows of their envelopes. One, from the Dartmoor District Council, bore the legend: *Open immediately: failure to take instant action will result in legal proceedings.* A cough at my elbow, the undertaker's lad, covered me with confusion.

"Just going out for a stroll," I stammered, and pushed my way through the big double doors out onto the gravelled parterre on which I had been deposited the previous evening.

Again the sense of déjà vu was overwhelming: been here, done that were the words I muttered to myself as my bored eye wandered over terraces and urns, flat water with lily-pads, close-cropped meadow with deer and sheep. But over at the Norman keep there was a small buzz of activity that looked interesting and I made my way towards it. Filming was in progress, and as it always does had attracted a small group of sightseers, early arrivals on the estate.

Sam and Doug had their gear out, shoulder-mounted 16 mm film camera, sound thing that looked like Dougal from the *Magic Roundabout* or a long-haired dachshund, cables and so forth and even a polystyrene reflector board directing the watery sunlight on to a short podgy man dressed in a baggy cheap pinstripe grey suit, a cravat and a black beret. He wore gold-rimmed spectacles perched on a high nose between podgy pink cheeks, had prominent teeth which were the possible cause for a speech impediment compounded by a Glasgow Kelvinside accent – the one the professional classes of Glasgow use. To combat this he spoke slowly with dreadfully careful enunciation but in a high-pitched whine.

"It was, of course, the less than conventional design of the curtain wall, or *mur d'enceinte*, as the Norman's themselves called it, coupled with the unconventional use of mullions, that caused Cromwell's artillery some problems when he arrived in 1647 . . . Eh say, are you not going to show the features I am talking about?"

"Cut," said Sam.

"Actually," said Doug, "we film that later, and edit it into your commentary."

"That is not the method my usual crew uses . . ."

"They must be wankers if they don't. Come on, Prof, keep it going, don't stop. Norman Keeps, take three, sound."

"Live," said Sam.

"Action," cried Doug.

"Cromwell overcame this wee deefficul-ty by lining up his pieces on the crenel or embrasure you will see to my left . . . Really, you know, should you not now pan, that is the corrrect worrrd I believe, to the feature I am describing?"

"Cut! . . ."

"There's no mullions there. Those aren't mullions." A high-pitched voice, cockney but authoritative, piped up from behind my left elbow.

I looked down. At my side was a small boy of about eight in grey shorts, grey shirt, grey blazer and grey schoolboy cap with a red badge.

"Shush, dear. I'm sure the gentleman knows what he's talking about." Mum, in floral with white cardigan and tam o'shanter, sensible shoes.

"No, he doesn't. Mullions are—"

"Quiet, please," Doug bellowed. "Always nice to have an audience but we must also request perfect hush."

"Pillars separating—" the brat was persistent.

"Absolute hush, if you please . . ."

This filming business palls quickly, does it not? Presently I took a signed pathway between clipped cypress hedges to *The Draksville Hall Coffee-shop and Restaurant, The Boutique, and The Shop* all done neatly in gold lettering on black. As always these were situated in the converted stables and as always if you want a coffee and Danish, which was what I had in mind, you had to go through the money-traps to get to it. The Boutique was "Harris-Style" tweeds, silk scarves printed with Dartmoor pony designs, "Celtic" jewellery, and waxed leather jackets as worn for centuries by Dartmoor poachers and now retailing for a cool hundred sheets – £99.99, actually. The Shop was downmarket of all this: it offered six tiny honey tubs with Winnie the Pooh labels for a tenner, Tudor Fragranced pot-pourris, pop-up and cut-out Norman castles, key-rings, car-stickers and baseball caps all carrying the message again: *I did it for real at Draksville*.

I was not tempted: the smell of Keith Spiller coffee (as advertised) lured me on into a short stone-flagged passage but just as the part-glazed door into the bingeing area came into sight I was pulled up by a sudden terrible moaning, almost a bellowing, followed by the sound of a rush of liquid sludge which could only be caused by someone being violently and copiously sick. It came from behind a stout but modern door set in an alcove and labelled *Private Office*.

I pushed it open. In contrast to the twee ageing that had been inflicted on everywhere else I had been, this room was bright, functional, modern with white filing cabinets, telephones, a fax machine, two PCs, good chrome and leather chairs. The under-taker's lad was lying in the one space open enough to accom-modate him, with the side of his face, which was a quite ghastly colour, in a pool made by the only partially processed breakfast I had given him earlier. In spite of the stench I leant over him.

He murmured: "Bastard, you poisoned me."

He moaned again but more quietly, shifted a little as if to get comfortable, passed out.

III

Passed out but not snuffed. I picked up a telephone, dialled 999, and got the kitchen. It was an internal phone, dial 9 for kitchen. I tried another.

"Police, Ambulance, but not Fire. Yet," I shouted. An insultingly cool voice asked me to give the address, the phone number, blah-di-blah.

"I'm only a visitor here," I yelled back, "but I'll do my best." And did it.

I calculated: Draksville Hall was fifteen miles from anywhere of any consequence, Norris Claypole was a very nasty colour and breathing stertorously. Clearly he needed help sooner than the emergency services were likely to be able to provide it. In post-Thatcher Britain maybe up to three hours sooner. Sometimes one thinks this government believes a guy dead before he's sixty-five is a guy who will never claim the fuel allowance in the winter. I poked my head out through the door.

"Is there a doctor in the ah, er, actually anywhere near here? Um? Or someone who has rudimentary knowledge of first aid?"

The punters coming down the corridors with their plastic bags from the shops eyed me with emotions ranging from suspicion to horror and pushed by. There weren't many: it was still too early even on a Saturday morning. But somewhere in the background the hum of an electric cleaner or polisher cut out and the buxom, fresh-cheeked girl who had been polishing in the hall when I was looking at the mail poked her head round the door.

"Oh, dear," she said. "Ang on a tick."

It was a long tick. Claypole writhed a bit, vomited some more, suddenly sat up, looked at me.

"You made me eat that junk. Who are you? You can't be working for him . . ."

Then he subsided again.

It was a good ten minutes before the girl was back but this time she had a zinc tray with a zinc teapot on it and a Draksville Hall mug. The hot liquid she poured from the teapot into the mug was a sort of sick yellowish brown. A vegetable bitterness filled the air.

"Come on, zurrr, drink this," she murmured in her Devon cream accent, "you'll feel rrroigh as rrrain in no toime a'all."

And so he did. So he did. The vomiting and retching ceased, the colour came back to his cheeks. But he was seriously mussed up, and said he still felt weak. We got him up on to a chair.

"I still think he should see a doctor. Or go with the ambulance that's on its way to a hospital and have himself checked out."

"Ambulance, zurrr? On its wa-ay! Oh dear me, we don' be wannin' nun o' that zort o' bother . . ." and to my amazement she went to the phone, dialled 999 and cancelled the ambulance I had ordered.

"Are you sure about this?" I turned to Claypole. "I really do advise a proper medical examination. These rural remedies are all very well up to a point, but if they were really effective the nineteenth-century population explosion that followed on proper sewage, vaccination and pasteurization would have occurred twenty centuries earlier . . ."

"Oi don' know abou' tha-a. There don' be no rural cure for the Bla-ack Death . . . But lookee, 'e's zo much be-er already."

Was there no limit to the impudence of this huzzy . . . I mean hussy? Nevertheless Claypole did continue to improve and he insisted that all he needed was the opportunity to clean himself up, change his clothes and maybe have a short rest.

"Oi'll go ge'a bucket an' mop an' clear up in 'ere," said the buxom wench.

Well, at that moment I felt it really was too much that Holmes had still failed to put in an appearance. The lie or lay of the land was changing as fast as I got a toe-hold on it. I felt it was time I gave the whole business some serious thought, contrived to do for my friend what she had apparently decided not to do at all.

Meanwhile and without really thinking about it I found I had paid my fifty pence and wandered through a turn-stile and into the Draksville Hall Maze. The largest in Europe was the claim. Not a bad place, with its narrow alleys and high yew hedges, in which to put in some deep thinking.

Who would want to kill Norris Claypole . . . and why? I spent a good twenty minutes on that one before I finally rumbled the fact that the answer was – no one. The poisoned food was destined for Sir Hugo – who was last in to breakfast and expected to find the bacon, the eggs, the black pudding and so on waiting for him on the hot plates. The murderer, or attempted murderer (can one say that?), had known I was vegetarian, and that Claypole had been frightened off touching the stuff.

And who had been at breakfast when I arrived? Why, Cousin Philip, of course. He with the luscious but pregnant Zara in tow, whom he was to marry pretty damn soon. If he stood to inherit on Sir Hugo's death, then clearly he must be chief suspect. What I now needed to know was the terms of the entailment on the title and the Hall with all its assets. Somewhere in the house, in the library perhaps or even in Claypole's office, there would be a document that laid it all out. These things vary a lot, according to the whim of the original founder.

And so I decided to head back to the entrance as quickly as I could. Hopeless. I wandered around for forty minutes. Every route brought me back to the same point – three hedges and ten yards from the entrance. Back I went, further and further out into the wilderness each time before circling back to that same infuriating point. Worse still I was now more and more urgently in need of a loo. The day had turned hot too and I was roasting in the stupid tweeds I had put on.

God, men are so lucky in this sort of situation. They do at least have something to hang on to. And if they finally have to give in they have the means to direct it where they want – a woman's apparatus is about as guidable as a lawn sprinkler . . . I heard a voice.

"At least this maze is real enough though its system is pretty cinchy. Everything else we've seen is fake. The armour is fibreglass, the Grinling Gibbon wood carving plastic, that Coningsby-Doulton doesn't know what he's talking about. Hallo. What's that noise? Oh. It's the fat lady. She's having a pee in the middle of the path."

It was the nasty small boy who had been watching, and interrupting, the filming. With his mother behind him.

"Young man," I asked, hoisting my plus fours, "could you please tell me how to get out of here?"

"First right, first left to get to the middle, first left, first right to get out. It's dead easy really."

Bastard!

I hurried back indoors and went straight to the library where I found the buxom maid was polishing an already gleaming table. I didn't let her put me off though. It was surprisingly easy to find what I wanted. It was almost as if someone had been there ahead of me, checking out the same details, for there, on the very table she had been polishing, was a large leather-bound tome entitled *A History of Draksville Hall*. And right there in chapter one was a resumé of the Deed of Entailment.

Apparently the estate could only be passed on down the male line. Par for the course in those ignorant times. If the incumbent had no male children then it went to the oldest brother and failing that the oldest male cousin, but neither of these could inherit unless they already had a legitimate male child. If none of these conditions could be fulfilled then, and only then, the incumbent could will the lot where he wanted or even sell it and the Deed of Entailment became null and void.

So. If Philip was the father of Zara's child, and the child was male, and born in wedlock, then clearly Philip would inherit on Sir Hugo's death. QED.

All I needed now was some really concrete evidence. Which possibly I might find in Philip's room. Like a bottle labelled "Little-known Asiatic Poison"? Well, you never know. But first I felt I had to go and change into something a little cooler and looser.

Back in my room I pulled off the sticky, not to say damp, tweeds. The choice was now between the worsted pin-stripe which would be almost as hot as the tweeds, or the cashmere and gold thread (real gold thread) kaftan I had worn in the evening. Not really a choice. I look absurd anyway and if I cruised about the place looking like Montserrat Caballé as the Queen of Sheba most of the punters would probably just take me for part of the show.

Just as I was about ready to sally forth again Sophie did his voice-enhanced purr which drew me to the window. The arena below was deserted apart from two or three park attendants with brooms sweeping up yesterday's scant litter and three other recognizable figures – Prof Coningsby-Doulton, Sven, and Sir Hugo, all in what looked like earnest confabulation. And then suddenly it dawned on me, like a bolt from the blue, and I realized I had made the most perfect ass of myself.

Readers of my memoirs will recall how Holmes often uses the most impenetrable disguises to keep herself in the middle of things with no fear of being discovered. She does, however, whether out of vanity or what I do not know, always give herself names that are anagrams or close anagrams of "Conan Doyle". You will recall Conran Dial the Irish computer whizz, and Conrad Lee Doy the Thai male prostitute.

And there, walking away now from Sven and Sir Hugo and up the hill towards the Keep, was Professor Coningsby-Doulton, the academic and TV personality no one had heard of. Surely my friend and accomplice in an even more impenetrable disguise than usual. Clearly I had to devise some means of communicating with her without betraying her. There was stationery on the small desk – not headed with the Draksville Hall address but that of a small hotel in the Cromwell Road – clearly Sir Hugo nicked such hotel stationery just as most of us do. They expect it and it gets their name spread about.

"Dear Holmes," I wrote. "How silly of me not to spot you earlier. But I have not been idle. I have discovered much while fulfilling your commission . . ." and I went on to say how Claypole had been poisoned by Philip in error for Sir Hugo, about the Deed of Entailment, and finally how Philip and Zara were to marry as soon as possible and how it seemed to me that this put Sir Hugo in even greater danger than before. I stuffed it all in an envelope and rushed out.

The crowds were thickening now and for the most part moving purposefully towards the Keep. I recalled that the main attractions on a Saturday afternoon were The Storming of the Keep at half-past two, followed at half-past three by Sophie's attempt to kill an antelope followed by a lion-taming act performed by Sir Hugo. On this particular weekend this would be followed by a mass ascent of hot-air balloons. I also realized, as the fumes from various kebab, burger and hot-dog stalls breathed over me, that enthusiasm for the task in hand coupled with the unfortunate affair of the maze had led me to miss lunch. Really things in this area have moved on in the last few years and I was able to pick up a pitta filled with salad and spiced beans instead of kebab, with a passable chilli sauce. Actually two pittas.

With one in each hand and my envelope tucked under my arm, I puffed on up the hill to where the crowd were being herded into enclosures in front of the Keep. On the other side of the ropes Coningsby-Doulton, aka Basilia Holmes, was now talking to Sam and Doug. I ducked under the rope and immediately brought on my head the ire of a little Hitler in Draksville T-shirt.

"Can't you read?" he bellowed. "No audience beyond this point, it says . . ." and so on.

I gave him my pittas since I needed free hands, rushed up to the "Prof" and thrust my envelope at "him", for a moment our eyes met – "his" dark brown which did not for a moment faze me since Holmes often wears tinted lenses when incognita to conceal her remarkable violet eyes. What I did find a touch unnerving was the look of scornful hostility that lay behind those half-moon specs, but I quickly put this down to my friend's professional desire to remain in character.

Feeling elated by the skill with which I had managed all this, I reclaimed my pittas and ducked back behind the ropes but remained at the front – much to the annoyance of the small boy behind me, *the* small boy, who had thought he was set up with a prime viewing position.

"Mu-um, I can't see a thing now, tell her to move."

"Certainly not, dear. You can squeeze in beside the lady."

"Well, she'd better not wee on me, that's all."

I resisted the temptation to clout him round the ear, and gave him one of my pittas to hold while I got my teeth into the other. Then I cast my eye over the scene in front of me.

Preparations were in hand for the reconstruction of the siege of Draksville Keep, 1476. It was in the hands of the wicked Lancastrian, Philip of Malieu (pronounced "mawlee"), Constable of the Keep, and was about to be recaptured by the gallant Hugo Draks, Yorkist and rightful Earl of Draksville in the Marches of Devon. Or some such rubbish, put out over on the tannoy by the usual Mr Voiceover Man – he who always sounds as if he had been to a very minor public school before being cashiered from the Pay Corps for misappropriation of funds.

Sundry yokels clad in chain knit cord which we were invited to believe was chain mail, and clutching broad-swords, long-bows, emblazoned shields, banners and pennants began to assemble on the green sward to my right, and ditto others in the shadow of the Keep to my left. Presently an amplified fanfare announced the arrival of Philip in black armour on a black horse, with a posse of likewise black-clad ruffians sporting the red-rose of Lancashire. Mr VoM invited us to boo if we wished. Philip slid quite gracefully from the saddle, handed the bridle to a ruffian, drew his sword and waved it in the air. Boo – Booo. Then he vanished round the back of the Keep with his ruffians behind him. Presently he appeared high above us in a big arched window. More boos. At this point Sam and Doug went scampering past me, also heading towards the Keep.

Well, not actually scampering. Considering both were fat and heavily encumbered with the impedimenta of their trade, they were showing a reasonable rate of knots but not so fast that I couldn't call out.

"What's up, Doug?"

"The prof wants us to film what happens. Christ knows why." He mopped his honest brow and pressed on.

More trumpets, hautboys and sackbuts – according to Mr VoM, but played in the major and without discords, announced Sir Hugo – in silver armour and on a white horse . . . of course. And his train. Well, I don't need to go into it, do I? There was a lot of pre-recorded noise, deafening, arrows flew, primitive cannon cracked, Philip and his men made a sortie and were beaten back, a battering ram was brought up . . . and all, as Mr VoM insisted, to no avail. Escalation was what was needed. This brought titters from the crowd. Any word in the English language that rhymes with "masturbation" gets a titter from an English crowd, and Mr VoM coyly corrected himself – what he had meant to say was "escalade".

Long ladders were now brought in and placed against the wall of the Keep. Sir Hugo flourished his sword, then since he needed both his hands handed it to a lackey. To the cheers of us all he began to climb the ladder. When he was halfway up he paused. Small boy, squeezed up to me and, already halfway through my second pitta, damn him, began to jump up and down and shout.

"What's the matter?" I asked.

"The man in the tower should push the ladder over now. If he goes any further he'll be hurt . . ."

"You've seen all this before?" I asked, incredulously. I couldn't imagine anyone would want to see it twice.

"No . . . but it's obvious, isn't it?"

My God, I thought, this is it, he's right. I ducked under the rope, chucked what was left of my pitta, and headed up the hill. Assorted Hitlers closed in in pursuit, but I had a start.

"Stop, stop," I shouted. "Don't go any higher . . ."

But I was too late. As Sir Hugo's fingers reached the sill of the embrasure where Philip was stationed, Philip gave the ladder a push and sent him hurtling to the floor. He landed on his back, from forty feet, with a sort of squashy thud.

Whoops. The crowd cheered; most of them thought it was part of the show. And those that sensed an accident, or worse, also cheered – something real had happened at last, maybe they'd get themselves on South-West News as a result, or in the papers. Mr VoM urged us all to keep back, turning up the amplification with every appeal. Finally, in desperation, he put on a tape of "Greensleeves".

Meanwhile Philip (and I was just behind him so I could hear it all, in spite of the general racket) was already leaning over his cousin's inert body and wringing his hands.

"Good God, Hugo, what have I done?" he asked in manly tones.

Hugo raised himself on his elbows and shook his head. Then he tried to get up and fell back with a groan.

"Done me back in, Phil. I'm afraid you'll have to do the lion act. Mustn't disappoint the punters."

And he fell back again, closing his eyes.

Sir Hugo was stretchered back into the house to the sound of drums and trumpets while Mr VoM announced that, though hurt, he'd live, so let's put our hands together for him. Meanwhile the Lion Hunt would take place as scheduled with Mr Philip Draks, the well-known traveller and safari expert, taking Sir Hugo's place. So if we'd all like to move down the hill to the lion arena he was sure we would not be disappointed at the climax to the day's entertainments. And, oh yes, the mass hot-air balloon ascent was already in a state of full preparation.

The "accident" had cheered everybody up no end. The people in the crowd that gathered in the terraced seats of the lion arena gossiped with total strangers, a general buzz of excitement spread over the whole throng, children pestered their parents with questions – was he really hurt, will anyone else get really hurt, will we have to pay extra? and so on.

Again I managed to find a place near the front from which I could see Sophie, still caged conventionally behind bars. He was pacing up and down, big head swinging, tufted tail swishing, big clawed paws padding in that bandy-legged way lions have. He looked much livelier than he had the day before – I suspected someone had fed him up on vitamin pills or maybe popped something even more stimulating in his water bowl.

And as I sat there and the crowd built up around me I cogitated. Certainly everything did seem to be falling into place. Holmes, aka Coningsby-Doulton, had cunningly lured Philip into a trap. He had pushed the ladder too late thus ensuring Sir Hugo took a fatal tumble. But it hadn't been fatal at all and no doubt Holmes had ensured that would be the case – presumably by making sure Sir Hugo wore suitable padding beneath his armour. She had, however, got incontrovertible evidence against Philip by making making sure Doug and Sam had filmed the whole incident. Neat – if a touch over-elaborate. But if Holmes has a fault it is a tendency to over-elaboration.

And Sir Hugo's manful acceptance of what Philip had done to him? Well, as he had said, the show must go on, and Sir Hugo was nothing if not a showman. The punters came first. Once they had gone home then no doubt he and Holmes would confront Philip with his heinous attempts on Sir Hugo's life and the former would be sent packing.

At this point my meditations were interrupted. Philip, now garbed in Big White Hunter gear, appeared on one side of the semicircular performance area in front of Sophie's cage. And as he did a figure rose from the back of the terraced seating and yelled at him. It was Zara, dressed in orange and yellow silks with a large wide-brimmed black velvet hat. She had taken this off and was waving it above her head to get his attention.

"Phil, Phil," she shouted, "it's all right, it really is. I've been to Plymouth, had the scan and your sprout's a boy. I've also got a special licence – we can be married this afternoon."

Well, bully for you, I thought and settled back to enjoy what would surely be Philip's last appearance at Draksville Hall.

IV

Philip disappeared backstage, presumably to congratulate his wife-to-be, and there now followed a quite long and tedious pause. The crowd became restive but amused themselves with the Mexican Wave and chanting "Why are we waiting, why-y are we waiting?" and so forth. Presently I felt a hand on my shoulder.

Doug, distressed nostrils flaring, leant over the rail that separated the open space from the seats and I caught the smell of whisky and beefburger on his breath. The whisky I did not mind, indeed by then I could have done with a nip myself, but the meat sickened me.

"Jewel," he rasped, "message from the Prof. He's got a job for you and seems to think you'll do it."

"Sure," I replied. "Anything *he* wants."

He raised his sandy eyebrows, but made no comment.

"Follow me," he said.

I looked at the rail. Over or under? I gathered my skirts, tried over, gave up, virtually had to crawl under.

He led me across the arena, past Sophie's cage. The king of the jungle stopped pacing and looked up with quite frightening interest. I caught a strong whiff of the rank smell lions give off. Beyond the cage the plastic rock had been hollowed into a narrow cave with a steel door at the back.

I found myself in what was clearly some sort of control room. It was a drab gloomy place with consoles of switches controlling lights, sound effects and so on. There was also CCTV screens monitoring the arena outside. It all smelt damp, musty. Doug took me by the elbow and pointed at a large red switch mounted on a metal box.

"Now don't ask me any questions 'cos I won't know the answers. I'm just like doing what the Prof asked me. He wants you to hide in that alcove over there and keep an eye on that switch. If anyone comes in and throws it, then you're to wait until they've gone then throw it back again. OK?"

Well, not really. I had been looking forward to the show and seeing it on black and white CCTV was not going to be the same. But I'm always ready to carry out whatever Holmes requests.

The alcove was in fact a sort of cubby-hole where a mop and bucket had been stacked and a plastic bottle of industrial-strength cleaning fluid. There was also a tap which dripped and was the likely cause of the mustiness that pervaded the room.

I squeezed into the space, and shifted the bucket and mop so I could lean against the clammy wall. Then I remembered what I was wearing, and pulled myself upright. That silk-weight cashmere costs a fortune in specialized dry cleaning.

But I did have a clear view of the CCTV screens. The terraced seating was now just about full. Beyond that I could see the hot-air balloons preparing for their ascent – gas-fired torches heating up the huge floppy envelopes, men straining at the ropes that held them down. It looked as if a big black one was likely to be the first away.

Then at last, just when it seemed the crowd would get bored with the Mexican Wave and find something more stimulating to amuse themselves like throwing empty drink cans, a tannoy crackled and Mr VoM went into his usual routine. To huge applause, Philip walked into the arena and took several bows – or rather nodded his head briskly at each sector of the audience. Then, just as I was beginning to get excited, what happened but Norris Claypole rushed breathlessly into the room, looked at the switch Doug had told me to watch, swore audibly under his breath, and threw it. He glanced over the consoles, but never behind him, and then he was gone.

It was with me the work of a moment to disentangle myself from the mop and bucket, pick myself off the floor and get back to the switch, which I now felt sure operated the sonic fence which would keep Sophie in his place and put it back where it should be. As I did, a great roar went up, two great roars actually, one from the crowd, the other from Sophie, and out of his cage he came.

He jumped on to Philip and bit his head off.

Simultaneously the big black balloon began to climb into the sky. It had one passenger. The Prof. Oh, shit, I thought. And, worst of all, at that moment who should come bursting into the control room but Donna, the Devonshire maid. Tearing off latex, a wig, and other trappings she soon stood revealed as . . . Baz. Basilia. Basilia Holmes.

"You fucking stupid moron," she said. Without a trace of West Country accent.

It's all so obvious, and silly really. Well it is now. With hind-sight. Sir Hugo and Sven wanted to sell up Draksville Hall while it was still worth anything at all, and retire to Ibiza. As long as there was a male cousin with a legitimate male son the Deed of Entailment would not allow them to. So they wanted Philip offed before he could marry Zara.

"So," I said, "if I've got this right, this is what happened. They developed this clever wheeze of making it look as if Philip was trying to kill Sir Hugo, right up to the point where Philip would be killed but in a way that made it seem he was killed by a device of his own which had been planned for Sir Hugo. If you see what I mean."

Back in Baz's Barbican apartment, we were working our way through a plate of sushi Roc had prepared for us with that delicious green Japanese horseradish. The sake was ten years old and warm, so went straight to the cranial nodes without passing "go". My head swam with it, and the revelations still to come.

"Not precisely." Baz lunged at me with her chop-sticks, so I thought she might be fancying one of my eyeballs. She really was in a foul temper. "They were incapable of that sort of finesse. They employed someone to do their thinking for them. Anna-Maria Moriarty. My arch enemy. I'll tell you about her later."

It all fell into place. Norris Claypole's simulated attack of vomiting. It was after all s/he who switched the sonic fence off, so I would switch it on again.

"Norris Claypole was really Moriarty, then," I suggested, nodding knowingly.

"No, you fathead. Professor Coningsby-Doulton."

At last I began to understand just why she was so angry. It was after all I who had told the Prof, thinking s/he was Baz, that if Zara's sprout was a bloke then Philip was contemplating instant marriage. Consequently the evil trio had pre-empted that by moving forward the successful attempt on his life. Moriarty, whose feud with Baz went back a long way, had actually asked Sir Hugo to invite my friend, hoping to use her to achieve her evil ends and thus score a humiliating victory. That is, Moriarty's evil ends. If you see what I mean. And since technically, I, Baz's friend, had actually been a major secondary cause of Philip's death, she'd done it in spades.

I felt it was time to assert some sort of justification for the awful errors I'd made.

"Listen," I said, "you nearly always use a name related to Conan Doyle when you use a disguise. Coningsby-Doulton was good enough for me. Your Devonshire lass was called Donna."

"Donna Cloye. Think about it."

I thought about it. And sighed.

"So Sir Hugo and Sven can sell up after all. They've got away with it."

"Actually, no. A year ago Philip and Zara went through a marriage ceremony conducted by Pygmies in equatorial Africa. Apparently the Pygmies would not let them cohabit unless they were married. As is usual in such cases the ceremony was videoed and I have high hopes it will be validated by the High Court Judge who is considering it. He owes me a favour or two. Moreover the police are looking at the evidence I have put in front of them and consequently Sir Hugo and Sven have already fled the country. I have to say I was much aided in this by a small boy with acute powers of observation, combined with an intelligence capable of interpreting what he saw."

Again, I was mortified. There was a long silence. I didn't want to break it. Eventually Baz did.

She pushed her plate aside.

"Why, Julia," she asked, "do you use the pseudonym you do for your fictionalizations of my cases?"

" 'Julian' because it is the male form of my name. 'Rathbone' because, as you have often said, Basil Rathbone was the greatest portrayer of your great uncle."

"You are unaware then that there is already a published author of that name."

"Oh, Lord. I suppose I'll have to change it."

"Don't bother. He's a nonentity."

Roc cleared our plates.

Baz offered me her most malicious smile.

"Enjoy the sushi, did we?"

"Fine, thanks."

"Well, there was whale meat in it. So I expect you'll be handing in your Greenpeace badge first thing in the morning."

A pretty cheap way of getting back at me, I thought. But I had to admit the tale I will call *The Lion of Draksvill*e had all been pretty much a cock-up and largely my fault.

THE ABSOLUTE AND UTTER IMPOSSIBILITY OF THE FACTS IN THE CASE OF THE VANISHING OF HENNING VOK

(A.K.A. The Amazing Blitzen) (R.N. Jack Ralph Cole)

JACK ADRIAN

The facts were these: in the bath-tub, shifting gently under eighteen inches of rust-coloured water, lay the fully clothed (even down to his overcoat and Oxfords) corpse of Herman Jediah Klauss, the Moriarty of Manhattan, a large ornamental ice-pick sunk in his skull. Never personable (especially in the matter of nasal hair) he now gave the impression of a dead dugong.

That (that he was unequivocally dead) was one fact. A second fact was that his murderer was not in the bathroom with him. A third was that he ought to have been.

There were other facts. The apartment was in a building in the low West 70s, a spit from the Park, half a spit from the Dakota. It was on the 11th floor. It was b-i-g. It had been built at a time (maybe the 1900s) when architects had grandiose dreams and clients with money to fuel them. To Commings, the bathroom looked about as spacious as a side-chapel in St. Patrick's. The bath itself was a vast boxed-in affair, fake (or maybe not) ivory with a dark mahogany trim. The toilet, next to it, could easily have doubled as a throne. You could almost certainly have bathed a Doberman in the bidet.

Over by the door, which was at least three inches thick and might well have withstood the full blast of an RPG-7 anti-personnel rocket, Trask bellowed, "*It's impossible!*"

Which, of course, it was.

Commings thought through the sequence of events for what seemed like the fiftieth time.

Klauss had entered the apartment closely followed by patrolmen O'Mahoney and Schwaab (flagged down outside the building and invited in because, in Klauss's words, "There's a guy up there wants to ice me"). They were met by an English butler (hired for the evening, it now transpired) and a black maid (idem). They were escorted up the long hallway, past shelfloads of books (mainly mystery fiction: Carolyn Wells, H.H. Holmes, Carter Dickson, Hake Talbot, Clayton Rawson, Edward D. Hoch, Joel Townsley Rogers, a raft of others), past cabinets full of rare Golden Age comicbooks (mainly from the Quality group: *Police Comics*, *Smash Comics*, *Plastic Man*, *The Spirit*, *National Comics*, *Doll Man*, many more), and past a series of framed posters featuring a preternaturally rangy man clad in, first, evening dress ("The Amazing Blitzen: Unparalleled Feats of Legerdemain and Prestidigitation!"), second, vaguely Arabian robes ("The Sultan of Stretch, the Emir of Elongation – see the many-jointed Blitzen zip himself into a carpet-bag!"), and, third, a skin-tight black costume akin to what bathers wore two generations back ("Blitzen! Illusionist *extraordinaire*!"). Smaller bills showed him peering out from a cannon's mouth ("The Shell Man!"), being lowered into a swimming-pool by a gantry with what looked to be a half-ton of

ship's cable cocooning him ("The Man With the Iron Lungs!"),
and chained spread-eagle to a vast target ("Can he escape before
the crossbow bolt pierces his heart?!").

Henning Vok (or, as his real name now seemed to be, J.R.
Cole) had emerged from a doorway at the far end ("skinny as a
beanpole," as Schwaab said later, "but looking kind of flushed
. . . like he'd been running") and welcomed, in open-armed
fashion, his visitor, who'd turned to the two cops and warned,
"Don't trust the sucker an inch."

Vok/Cole had laughed distractedly and said, "You want the
cards or not, dammit?", gesturing at the half-open door. Klauss
had walked in and said, "This is a bathroom." Vok/Cole said,
"You catch on fast", and then, reaching behind the door, had
produced the ice-pick, with which, to the consternation of the
witnesses, he had proceeded to poleaxe Klauss, Klauss toppling
into the tub (full) and sending a tidal-wave of displaced water
spraying over Vok/Cole, the toilet, the oxygen-machine next to
the bidet and the floor. Vok/Cole had then jumped for the door,
slamming it shut and locking it.

It took the two patrolmen (not having an RPG-7 launcher)
twenty minutes to break down the door. When they finally
entered, the room was empty. Apart, of course, from the now
defunct Herman Jediah Klauss.

"Im-poss-i-*bul*!" said Trask now, through clenched teeth.
"And bull's the operative word." He clutched at a straw. "What
if they were all in it?"

Commings said, "The butler and the maid, maybe. And
could be Schwaab's on the take. But hell, Lieutenant," his
voice rose a notch or two, "O'Mahoney?"

"The Prize Prepuce of the Precinct House," groaned Trask.
"The only totally honest man on the roster. *God*!"

This last profanity was spat out not only on account of
O'Mahoney's notorious incorruptibility, which hinted at stupidity on a serious scale, but because, at that moment, a figure
of surpassing bulk, clad in a fur-coat and brandishing an
unsheathed swordstick in a hamhock-sized fist, came barrelling
into the apartment.

"Trask!" bawled the newcomer. "The Commissioner called
me! It's a demented dwarf, depend on it!"

Trask shot him a look that could have split an atom.

"Now see here . . ."

"Don't interrupt! Show Professor Stanislaus Befz an Impossible Crime and he'll show you a deranged midget with an ice-pick. They never alter their *modus operandi*, the little devils." He surged through the hall like a resuscitated Golem, cutting a swathe through cops, photogs, morgue-men in white coats, and only coming to a halt at the bathroom door. Here he yelped triumphantly. "William Howard Taft! An ice-pick! What did I say!" He jabbed the swordstick at the corpse, the blade parting Comming's hair as the detective ducked to the floor. "You've already snapped the gyves on the hunchback, I take it?"

"Professor, there *is* no hunchback . . ."

"Balderdash! Out of the three thousand thirty-three Miracle Problems I've investigated, analysed and catalogued over the past quarter-century, crazed mannikins hidden in the false humps of ersatz hunchbacks account for well over half." He glanced down at Commings. "What are you doing down there?"

Trask was snapping his fingers urgently as the behemoth-esque Befz, not waiting for a reply, strode towards the tub. Commings scrambled to his feet and handed to his chief the packet of antacid tablets kept for times like this. He wondered miserably why amateur detectives specialising in Miracle Problems were invariably fat. And loud. And . . . and *eccentric*.

"Aaron Burr!" oathed the man-mountain, jowls quivering like a turkey's wattles. "Herman Jediah Klauss, the Moriarty of Manhattan!" He spun – or, rather, lurched – round, the sword-stick scattering various detectives. "So where's the hunchie?"

Trask was holding his stomach and wincing.

He muttered, "Tell him."

Commings explained about the lack of counterfeit hunch-backs in this particular case. This took some time owing to Befz's innumerable interruptions. Commings finished, "In any case, there were four witnesses who saw Vok, or Cole, do it."

"Mass-hypnosis!" thundered Befz. "The oldest trick in the book! I have three hundred forty-eight cases in my records, of which probably the most illuminating was the Great Hollywood Bowl Pickpocket Scam. This Vok, or Cole, undoubtedly flap-doodled the witnesses into thinking he was skinny then flipped open his false hump and let the demoniacal pixie out to do its fell business. The man was clearly a master-mesmerist."

"The butler and the maid, sure," agreed Commings. "And Schwaab, too. But," his voice pitched up, "O'Mahoney?"

Befz glanced at the patrolman. "You may have a point there," he grudged. "Well, there are plenty of other Impossible Murder Methods to choose from . . ."

"Sweet galloping Jesus!" screeched Trask. "The murder method is not in question! We know how he did it! The guy even admits to it himself!" He gulped down three or four more antacid tablets. "Show him the note, Commings."

The note read:

Dear guys,

I have decided to retire on my well-gotten gains, which over the years (due to judicious investment) have made me a millionaire many times over.

Before I go, however, I believe I can do you a couple of favours.

Primus: *Attached is a list of robberies which should feature heavily in your "Unsolved" files. Strike 'em. I plead guilty on all counts;*

Secundus: *I also plead guilty to the expunging of Herman Jediah Klauss, murderer, shylock, fence (who invariably paid bottom-dollar: hence my hatred of him) extortioner, blackmailer, procurer, rabid collector and generally worthless scoundrel. Having inveigled him here on the pretence of selling him a rare set of "Woozy Winks" bubble-gum cards (circa 1948), I split his head with an ice-pick.*

I mourn the fact that I leave behind my vast collection of interesting artefacts.

That's a lie. Where I'm going, I have duplicate copies of everything.

Hasta la vista!

Henning Vok, a.k.a. The Great Blitzen

(r.n. Jack Ralph Cole)

P.S. There are plenty clues.

*   *   *

"Hmmm," larynxed Befz. "So the problem is how he escaped from the bathroom. That shouldn't prove too tricky. As you probably know if you've read my *magnum opus* on the subject, there are precisely one thousand three hundred fifty-two ways of getting out of a locked room, only seven hundred eighty-six of which depend on a reel of cotton. And out of that, only one hundred thirty-five need a new pin and split paper-match. Walls?"

"Solid brick," Trask grated.

"Ceiling?"

"Same."

"Window?"

"Hasn't been opened in fifty years."

"Floor?"

"Forget it."

"Oh."

Befz absently tapped the blade of his swordstick on the oxygen-machine next to the bidet. It made a tanging sound. His eye was caught by the large old-fashioned air-extractor fixed into the wall, high up.

"John Quincy Adams! The fan!"

"To get up there," growled Trask, "you'd need to be able to fly."

"*Precisely!*" Befz triumphantly whacked the swordstick against one of the oxygen cylinders. The blade shattered into several shards. "Damn! That's the one hundred twenty-eighth this year. The blessed things cost a fortune too. Never mind. Vok, or Cole, inflated himself with oxygen and floated up to the fan, where . . ."

"Where he'd slice himself up in the extractor blades, yeah. You're losing your touch, Befz. I might just as well ask O'Mahoney if he's got any bright ideas."

"Oh sure," said O'Mahoney. "I mean, it's transparently obvious, Lieutenant."

Numerous pairs of eyes focused on him. He hitched up his gun-belt self-consciously and began to walk around the room, slapping the tip of his nightstick into the open (gloved) palm of his left hand.

"It's an interesting problem sure enough, Professor. Uh . . .

and Lieutenant. Oh, and . . ." he glanced at Commings " . . . Sergeant. But there's really only one exit. Although, as Vok/ Cole pointed out, there are plenty clues. See, I asked myself, why the bath? But we'll get to that later. I'd like you all to follow me."

Numerous pairs of shoes and boots tramped after him into the hallway. He gestured at the posters.

"It's all there. He was a contortionist. Skinny as a rake. This is an old building. Way back, they built things bigger. Follow me."

They followed him. Back into the bathroom.

"You very nearly hit it, Professor. The oxygen-machine was crucial to his plan. Possibly not many of you know that in 1959 a technician in California hyperventilated on oxygen and then created a world record for remaining underwater for thirteen minutes forty-two seconds. Vok/Cole, as we know, had "iron lungs", but the oxygen gave him that extra edge. As you'll recall, my partner described him as looking flushed, as though he'd been running. Fact was, he seemed semi-hysterical. But like I said, it was the bathwater that tipped me. Way I figured it, water splashed from the tub would hide the tell-tale subsequent splashes of water from quite another source."

He used the nightstick as a pointer. Numerous pairs of eyes swivelled towards the mighty throne-like structure next to the tub.

"That's right," said O'Mahoney. "He flushed himself down the toilet."

THE GREAT DETECTIVE

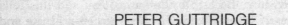

PETER GUTTRIDGE

The scene of the crime was 221b Baker Street. All the familiar objects were in place. On the mantelpiece, unanswered correspondence secured by a jack-knife. In the hearth a coal scuttle containing cigars, a Persian slipper stuffed with tobacco. Beneath the window a chemical-stained table cluttered with test-tubes.

Less familiar was the blood pooled on the leather sofa and soaking the rug laid before it.

Sherlock Holmes and Dr Watson were standing some yards to the left of the sofa. They were dressed for the outdoors in long overcoats and soft hats and were engaged in desultory conversation with an Egyptian pharaoh, a Roman centurion and an Indian chief in a feathered head-dress. A shapely slave girl in a revealing two-piece outfit – historical period indeterminate – hovered just behind this group.

Joseph – Joey – Timlin, the policeman in charge, stood by the sofa chewing his lip, his eyes fixed on the view of the London skyline through the window – the dome of St Paul's clearly visible and, behind it, Buckingham Palace, Big Ben and the Houses of Parliament.

His wife would go ape when she heard what job he'd pulled down. She thought Sherlock and his sidekick were just the cat's pyjamas. Timlin looked across at the so-called Great Detective and Dr Watson. Both were tall men, one aquiline, one stout. He called out:

"Hey, Sherlock, suppose you're going to solve this for me."

The Indian chief, the pharaoh and the Roman centurion were already walking away when the man Timlin had addressed turned a weary look on him.

"I can assure you I have no interest in usurping your role," he called back, his voice slightly nasal but strong and well modulated. "I am, after all, only—"

"I know who you are well enough," Timlin said, walking over to him. He gestured at Dr Watson. "You and this fella both." He stopped before them. "You're Basil Rathbone and Nigel Bruce."

"And who might you be, my good man?" Bruce tilted his chin at the policeman as he spoke.

Timlin introduced himself, watching the slave girl wiggle her ass across the vast gloomy hangar of a soundstage towards the exit door. There was blue sky and bright sunlight beyond. He sighed.

"Should be on my boat, day like today," he said, almost to himself.

"It's hardly our fault that you're not," Rathbone protested mildly.

Timlin looked at him.

"'S okay. I don't have a boat. Just my pipedream."

"Strange fellow," Bruce mumbled.

"My wife's nuts about you and –" Timlin tipped his head towards Bruce "– especially you, Mr Bruce. Can't get enough of you. Even got us drinking that Petri wine."

"Petri wine. Really?" Bruce guffawed and gurgled a little. "Damned fine wine, you know."

Timlin scowled. He remembered the night she'd first brought it home. He was in the kitchen when she got it out of the cupboard.

"Jesus, Bette, we're only having burgers," he said, thumbs hooked into the front of his belt, Bogart style. Apron on, she put her hands on her hips, Joan Crawford style.

"That nice Bill Forman on the Sherlock Holmes Radio Show says Petri burgundy makes any meal taste great whether it's steak or spaghetti or burgers."

No messing with her when she's got that voice on.

"You're more of a beer man, I take it," Rathbone said, a pleasant smile on his face.

"Nothing to beat an American beer." Timlin stood a little straighter, puffed out his chest, sucked in the gut. "Best in the world from the best country in the world."

"Quite so," Rathbone said. "Patriotism is an admirable thing – indeed, it is essential in these dark days. I would hazard then that you're more inclined to, shall we say, Sam Spade than Sherlock Holmes, perhaps?"

Timlin, still puffed up, nodded. He read Chandler too and thought he had the look of Philip Marlowe. Some hope. He was medium height, pasty-faced, a stone overweight, wearing a cheap suit and black, scuffed brogues that were half a size too small – either that or his feet had decided to start growing again.

"I see nothing wrong with home-grown, now that you mention it. I read these Sherlock Holmes movies you're doing are the most popular B movies ever and your radio show does pretty good too. But seems to me it's this fondness for all things British that has got us into a war in Europe that has nothing to do with us."

"I quite understand," Rathbone said soothingly.

"'Fraid I don't," Bruce grumbled. "Man's talking bunkum."

"No, no, Willy, Sergeant Timlin has a perfect right to hold that view, mistaken though we may think it. Especially as we are merely guests of his country here in Los Angeles."

"Mistaken?" Bruce harumphed. "Total balderdash."

Timlin controlled himself. His views on the war weren't exactly *pertinent* to the investigation at hand.

"Man's entitled to his opinion," he said quietly.

"Quite so," Rathbone soothed. "Quite so."

"Thought Bogie made a damned fine Sam Spade," Timlin said in a crude attempt to salvage the conversation as Bruce tutted and glowered. "You know him? Decent guy, is he?"

Rathbone nodded.

"Bogart's fine – until he's been drinking and thinks he's Bogart."

Bruce barked a quick laugh. Timlin looked from one to the other of them.

"Well, that's Irish," he said.

Rathbone gestured into the set of 221b Baker Street.

"Perhaps you can tell us what's happening? This isn't the way our Tuesday morning would usually start. Someone said there had been a murder . . ."

"Double murder," Timlin said. "Man and woman shot to death on the sofa there last night."

"Shot to death," Bruce murmured. "Terrible thing. Do you know who they were?"

"Fella by the name of Neame. Charles Neame. He's a bit-part player on your picture here. You know him?"

"Charlie Neame?" Rathbone said, dismay in his voice. "Of course we know him. Strapping fellow, good-looking. Had an eye for the ladies—"

"And a very forgiving wife," Bruce added, his eyes twinkling for a moment.

"That's the one," Timlin said. "And this particular lady was another bit-part player. Name of Lisabeth James. Lisabeth, what kind of a name is that? Who drops the first letter off a perfectly decent name—"

"Studios do," Rathbone said. "Lisabeth is their idea of a film star's name. Her real name is Doris. She's been part of our little company for several pictures, as indeed has Charlie." He shook his head. "Poor devils. They were together, you say?"

" 'Bout as together as a couple can be, if you get my meaning." Timlin smirked. "Doc who examined them sez to me it's the worst case of *coitus interruptus* he's ever seen."

"You're aware that Miss James was also married?" Rathbone said. "So you have your motive—"

"Yeah, yeah," Timlin said, pulling a piece of gum from his jacket pocket and starting to unwrap it. "I'm aware. She's married to a guy called Cohen, Arthur Cohen, big in the trucking business. And I know the statistics about murder victims knowing their murderers too." He popped the gum in his mouth and dropped the wrapper on the floor of the set. Rathbone watched it fall and frowned. "Only it just so happens both Mrs Neame and Mr Cohen have alibis."

"Alibis," Bruce said absently. He was gazing pop-eyed at the sofa, presumably imagining the scene. "Alibis, indeed."

"Murder happened sometime between eight and eight fifteen last night. We got witnesses saw the victims together just before eight sneaking in here and their bodies were discovered around eight seventeen. Mrs Neame was having dinner at the Brown Derby with a bunch of other broads from seven until ten. It was a hen night. Never left the restaurant."

"And Lisabeth's husband?"

Timlin chewed his gum.

"Oh his alibi's a dilly. You'll love it."

"Indeed?" Rathbone said.

"Sez he was at home listening to the Sherlock Holmes Show on the radio."

Timlin blew on his coffee and took a sip.

"My wife sez that's what Monday night is for," he said. "Just think, she sez, you know pretty much what everyone in America with a radio is doing come eight o'clock on a Monday evening. All over America everyone is listening to that Bill Forman announce, 'Petri wine brings you' – sappy organ riff – 'Basil Rathbone and Nigel Bruce' – more sappy organ – 'in the new adventures of Sherlock Holmes' – the organist goes nuts. D'ya ever want to clobber that guy on the organ?"

Bruce chuckled and took another sip of his coffee. Rathbone smiled.

"You're clearly a regular listener to our little entertainment, Sergeant Timlin, for you to know the opening so well."

Timlin grimaced.

"My wife, believe me, I got no choice."

He glanced around the room. They were in the cafeteria on the lot of Universal Studios, where Rathbone and Bruce were making their series of Sherlock Holmes films. Although the first two films the actors had made as Holmes and Watson had the correct period setting, once war broke out they'd begun a series set in contemporary times with the Nazis as villains.

"Isn't that . . . ?" Timlin said.

Rathbone followed his glance.

"It is, Sergeant. Would you like Willy to introduce you to her? They're great pals. She's most delightful."

"What's with the Willy business?" Timlin said as Bruce gave a little smile and waved his pipe at the beautiful blonde sitting by the window. She blew a kiss.

"It's my name," Bruce said, adding a mumbled, "stupid fellow." He looked at Timlin. "Look here, aren't you taking your investigation of these dreadful murders rather casually. I don't see how we can help you. We weren't here after lunchtime yesterday until you saw us this morning."

"Now that's the difference between your American and your Limey detective. You chaps go off like bloodhounds searching for clues –" Timlin put on a dreadful English accent "–'Quick, Watson, not a moment to lose' – whereas we approach things a little more sideways on. Besides, I already know who did it."

"Very interesting, Sergeant. Perhaps you would enlighten us."

"All in good time," Timlin said, taking a big swig of his own coffee. "First tell me about the radio show. It's live, isn't it?"

"Indubitably," Rathbone said. "Which can occasionally require a certain talent for improvisation."

Bruce leaned forwards.

"Yesterday evening, for example, the soundman made a blunder. Wilson the notorious canary trainer shot himself and the listener was supposed to hear the sound of the shot and of the body falling into water. Instead, the soundman did a shot and the sound of a glass breaking."

"And Willy saved the day by declaring 'Great Scott, his shot smashed that glass of Petri wine'," Rathbone added.

"That happened, did it?" Timlin said. He shook his head and looked glumly at the table.

"Sergeant," Rathbone said with a smile. "Could it be that you actually do need the help of Sherlock Holmes to unravel this? If so, let me reiterate, we are merely actors—"

"I'll get it out of him," Timlin said. "It's just a matter of time."

Rathbone steepled his hands in front of his face.

"I take it you're referring to Mr Cohen. You doubt his alibi."

"I doubt him," Timlin said, slapping his hand down on the table. "I'm sure the Bronx brute did it."

"Bronx brute?" Bruce said.

"Big bruiser, speaks with a *Noo Yawk* accent. Done well for himself. Smart house, fancy car, phones in every room. Think he'd rather be back on the East Coast. He's here because of his wife. She wants to be a movie star. He seems to spend all his time calling his brother Maurice back in New York. Was on the phone to him for a good half an hour yesterday, phone records show. Trunk call like that costs a small fortune."

"He suspected his wife's affair?" Rathbone said.

"He admitted that right off. Know how he figured it out?" Timlin chuckled. "Your radio show again."

"Dear me," Rathbone said. "We do seem to have quite a lot to answer for, don't we?"

"Your show is live, right? I mean, you just go in and read it right off."

"It isn't quite so simple," Bruce said, making strange noises in the back of his throat.

"Universal give us Monday afternoons off from filming to rehearse over in the radio studios and we do the show in the evening," Rathbone explained.

"See, Cohen is obviously a pretty jealous guy. Kept a close watch on his wife, never let her go out on her own. Guy never listened to the radio. That's what his wife was counting on. She'd say she was filming with you late on Mondays and that's when she'd spend a little time with Neame."

Timlin shook his head. "Problem was, Cohen's brother listens to your show. Coupla Mondays ago Cohen phones him when his wife's *working late at the studios with you* – brother Morry is listening to you on the radio. Live at eight o'clock. So last week when she said she was working late filming the latest Sherlock Holmes he said: 'He's on the radio Mondays. He ain't filming. Even Sherlock Holmes can't be in two places at one time.' Mrs Cohen had been quick, I'll give her that. According to Cohen she told him they tape the show. 'Says it's live,' he sez. 'It's taped,' she sez. That's why I asked you it was live."

"Very definitely live," Rathbone said. "And you're sure he listened to it last night?"

"Had the storyline down pat. Could even tell us about the mistake your soundman made, which nobody else seems to have picked up on."

Bruce frowned. "But why couldn't someone else have told him the story?"

"No time. We got a call from a payphone at 8.20 saying there's been a double murder on the lot and we should get around to Cohen's house quick because he did it. We send one car here and another to Cohen's house. We're knocking on Cohen's door around 8.27 before the show has even finished. And he's at home, in the kitchen. Sez he's been there all afternoon and evening, using the phone mainly then listening to your show on the radio. That's when we check the phone records."

"How far is his house from the studios?"

"Ten minutes drive. Oh he could have been there and got back sure enough. You know how security is around here – easy enough to get out of the studios without being seen and his house isn't overlooked. But how could he know the story so well – down to the last detail – if he was driving down and back to the studios and murdering his wife and her lover?"

"Car radio?" Bruce said, frowning.

"Doesn't have one."

Rathbone thought for a moment.

"Knew the story even down to the gaffe with the glass . . ." Suddenly he straightened in his chair, his face alert. "By George, I've got it!"

Bruce cocked his head.

"Got what, Mr Rathbone?" Timlin said.

"It's all as clear as mud to me," Bruce grumbled.

Rathbone chuckled and patted Timlin on the back.

"Come now, Sergeant, all it needs is a little bit of that deductive reasoning the English detective is known for and that you dislike so much."

Rathbone sat back in his chair smiling. Timlin frowned and shook his head.

"Very well, let me suggest a few apposite facts," Rathbone said. "First your wife's remarks about our show, Sergeant Timlin. Then the phone call Cohen made to New York yesterday. I would hazard this was at about 5 p.m.?"

"Perfectly correct – how did you guess?"

"It was a deduction rather than a guess, Sergeant Timlin, and it was quite elementary, as you shall see. Willy, don't look so bewildered. You know Holmes's methods. It's reasonable that Sergeant Timlin hasn't worked it out, but there's no excuse for you, as your ad-lib is the key to the whole business."

"Don't know what you're talking about," Bruce huffed. "As usual."

Rathbone laughed and patted him affectionately on the shoulder.

"Dear old Willy. Sergeant, tell us again what your wife said about our show, will you?"

"I don't much care for being cast in the Inspector Lestrade role, Mr Rathbone, and that's a goddamned fact."

"Humour me, I beg of you, Sergeant."

Timlin eased his neck in his collar.

"She sez come eight o'clock on a Monday evening you know pretty much that everyone in America is listening to the Sherlock Holmes Radio Show."

"Precisely," Rathbone said.

"Precisely what?" Timlin and Bruce said together.

"You know that the show is live. So how is it possible that listeners in New York can hear our show at exactly the same time as listeners in Los Angeles – *when New York is three hours ahead of Los Angeles time*?"

Timlin looked from one to the other and Bruce threw back his head and laughed.

"Amazing, Baz, quite amazing," he said, chuckling. "The thing was staring me right in the face."

"Well, I wish it was looking at me," Timlin said sourly.

"We do the show twice, Sergeant," Bruce said, chortling. "We do a show at 5 p.m. which goes out live on the east coast, at 8 p.m. their time. Then we go off for a spot of dinner, come back and do the show for the west coast at 8 p.m."

"Well, how was I supposed to guess that?" Timlin looked miffed. "In your candy-assed English detective shows you're supposed to have all the clues in front of you so you have a fair break."

"True, this doesn't meet the requirements of our classic

detective stories, but it's a pretty little problem all the same. Can you fill in the rest?"

Timlin nodded.

"When Arty calls Morry in New York yesterday at 5 p.m. LA time, it's to listen to the show down the phone line on his brother's radio, 8 p.m. New York time. Then that gives him space to kill his wife and lover when the show's airing here on the west coast and get home for when we come round to check on him."

"Exactly so. And I'll wager he made the call to the police about his own culpability because his alibi wouldn't work if you didn't get to him before the end of the show. Any later and you could always say somebody else told him the story."

"Still got to get him to admit it, though."

"Willy knows how you can start demolishing his alibi."

Bruce looked startled. He darted a glance from side to side. "I do? I mean, of course I do. Now, let me see. I – I –"

"The shot that broke the wine glass," Rathbone said. "It only happened in the first transmission, the one for New York and the east coast."

"By George you're right! The soundman did it correctly the second time."

Timlin got to his feet.

"I'm obliged to you gentlemen. I'm going to have a long talk with Arty Cohen and his brother Morry. It won't be pretty but I guarantee I'll get it out of them. What is it, Mr Rathbone? Why're you smiling?"

"Something has just occurred to me. Tell me again the names of the Cohen brothers, I beg you."

"Morris and Arthur. Or, for short, Morry and Arty. Why are you both laughing?"

SMELTDOWN

MIKE RIPLEY

This all started because Taffy Duck couldn't keep his mouth shut after a few drinks even if he topped his lager with super-glue, and Armstrong got belted up the backside by a diesel tanker so recently half-inched the steering-wheel was still warm.

The truck thing happened first.

I had left Armstrong parked under a street lamp in a re-spectable, middle-class street in Barking. (Who am I kidding? But that's what would have gone on the insurance claim form.) Now it's none of anybody's business what I was doing in that particular street at 5 a.m. that morning, except to say I was in the process of leaving. The lady in question has a husband who works very anti-social shifts (you're telling me – 5 a.m.!) in the London Fire Brigade and I'm not about to cross anyone who knows all there is to know about how things catch fire.

Armstrong is an Austin black cab – the London taxi you find on postcards and biscuit tins – and although I and the Hackney Carriage licensing authorities know he isn't actually a licensed cab any more, you have to look close to tell. Which is why I can usually park with impunity on a variety of yellow lines and, in this case, probably closer to a road junction than I should.

But I'm not making excuses for the tanker-driver, whoever it was, because he simply came round the corner far too fast, lost control and over-corrected, so that while the cab unit missed by a mile, the tanker unit belted Armstrong over the rear offside wheel, lifting him a couple of inches into the air with a scrunch of buckling metal.

My first reaction was to stand where I was about twenty yards away and yell, "You stupid son of a bitch!" as the tanker slowed to a stop at an angle across the street. But then, and I must have had the Fire Brigade on my mind, I thought: Petrol tanker – collision – fuel tank – fire. And I did the most sensible thing: I threw myself face down on the pavement and put my hands over my head.

Nothing happened, except it went very quiet.

I uncovered an ear and opened an eye. The tanker blocked the street, but it was still in one piece. So was I and so, almost, was Armstrong. So was the pair of feet doing a nifty four-minute mile round the corner. He could run, which is good, as everybody has to have *one* thing in life they're good at (Rule of Life No. 10) and he certainly couldn't drive.

There was no way I was driving Armstrong anywhere, not with the rear wheel arch caved in like that, and probably the wheel itself bent. This was a job for my old mate Duncan the Drunken; probably the best car mechanic in the world. But first I had to find a phone and generally get out of sight before an off-duty fire-engine drew up.

I also thought it might be an idea to move the tanker. People notice these things, especially when they are casually parked at right-angles to the road.

The tanker itself was decked out in the colours of an international oil company. It also contained diesel, not petrol, around 33,000 litres, which I calculated to be about £12,000 retail value. I wondered if I could claim salvage.

The driver had left his cab door open and the keys in the ignition, so I climbed up and settled myself behind the wheel. I felt quite at home as one of my driving licences is actually for Heavy Goods Vehicles, even though I'd never actually moved a tanker before.

I started her up and spun the wheel so the cab came back in line with the bowser, and began to climb though the gears trying to think of a suitable place to park the damn thing in what was after all a residential area.

It hadn't crossed my mind then to ask what it had been doing in the area in the first place. But that's what I was asked in the next street when I stood on the brakes to avoid the police Rover and two traffic cops got out.

They had to let me go eventually, although they took my fingerprints so they could eliminate them from those in the tanker's cab, promising – I don't think – to destroy them afterwards.

I could prove that Armstrong was mine and that I was really an innocent victim in all this. In fact, I told them the complete truth, missing out only the reason for being in that particular street at 5 a.m. Instead, I said I'd been to a party, had too much to drink and slept in the back of the cab and even had my sleeping-bag (called Hemingway) in the boot if they'd like to check – if they could get the boot open, that was. In fact, I was the one being the responsible citizen in not drinking and driving, I pointed out, claiming the moral high ground.

So they breathalysed me, but didn't get a result and had to believe me. There were a lot of questions before I was allowed to walk. Like had I ever nicked 33,000 litres of diesel before? (Armstrong ran on diesel so I was fair game.) Did I know anybody who would? Did I know a driver called Gwyn Vivian, sometimes called Taffy Duck? Where had I been the previous afternoon? Had I ever been to a transport café called Spaniard's Corner near Harwich out in Essex?

They weren't happy with all those negatives and were miffed enough not to let me use the phone on the way out, so I hoofed it to Barking station and took a tube into the City, then bus-hopped to Hackney and the house I share with assorted weirdos.

By the time I'd rung Duncan and told him where to collect Armstrong, it was early afternoon. I cooked myself some lunch, popped a can of beer and put my head down for a much-needed kip.

Duncan rang back around five and told me that it would cost up to two grand to fix Armstrong but surely the insurance would cover it. It would have, if I'd remembered to pay the last premium three weeks before. But Duncan needn't know that. I told him to go ahead and asked if he had a vehicle I could borrow in the meantime, and he said he would drop something round and put it on the bill.

I had a shower and changed into my shabbiest jeans and second-best leather jacket, having removed Springsteen from it with only a modicum of violence. He was going through a mid-life crisis (say, life number five) where he thought he was possibly not a cat at all, but some furry nesting creature.

Then it was another bus ride and another tube down to Whitechapel and, in an alley just behind the tube station, the Centre Pocket, a snooker club of ill repute where I knew I'd find Taffy Duck.

Oh yes, I'd sort of glossed over the fact that I knew him when the cops asked. In fact, I'd worked with Taffy in the past, roadying for various minor pop groups, although Taffy's heart had never been in it. He was your basic tobacconist/pub/betting-shop/back-to-the-pub man who could take two days to read the *Daily Mirror* and looked on snooker as his version of jogging. One-nighter gigs in Birmingham and then Newcastle weren't his scene.

Taffy wasn't playing on any of the tables in the Centre Pocket, he was sitting nervously on a bar stool at the corner of the bar, which had been fitted out by a carpenter who'd had bits left over from the last undertaker's he'd remodelled.

He was watching the door and was obviously relieved when he saw it was only me. He brightened when I offered to buy him another lager, but with typical Welsh foresight he said: "I can't get you one back, you know, I'm out of work."

"I know, Taffy, as of yesterday when you let those two lads walk off with your tanker."

While Taffy did a double-take, the barman gave me my pint and took a fiver from me. He didn't offer any change, but as I wasn't actually a member of the snooker club, I didn't complain too loudly.

"You've picked an expensive place to be unemployed," I said, smiling.

"Orders. I'm waiting for the boss," said Taffy and once he

was started he was difficult to stop. "How did you know about my spot of trouble?"

Before I could answer he told me the whole story. Hired as a relief driver, he'd hitched his way to Harwich with a pair of false delivery plates under his arm, which is like a free ticket in a car belonging to anyone in the motor trade. He'd collected the tanker and stopped at the Spaniard's Corner café (pronounced "caff" and, as one of the very few establishments remaining which wasn't a Little Chef, likely to get listed building status soon) for lunch, or "dinner" as Taffy put it.

On his way to the toilets, in a separate block outside, he'd been tackled – yes, tackled, just like a Welsh fly-half going over the line to score – behind the knees and gone down like a sack of coal. The coal was probably Welsh too. He'd had his hands and feet tied with electrical tape, the keys of the tanker lifted from his pocket and then he'd been dumped behind the rubbish bins, to be found by one of the cooks an hour later. There had been two attackers, both in full motorbiker kit including helmets with dark visors. They hadn't said a word to him or each other, and just after he heard the tanker leave, a bike revved up.

"What could I do, Roy? I was powerless." He said it like it was a word he'd been rehearsing. "Anyway, how did you hear about it?"

"The Boys in Blue told me, Taffy."

Then I told Taffy most of what had happened to me and he rolled his eyes and tut-tutted until I'd finished, but he made no move to buy another round.

"Now, one thing bugs me, Taffy," I said, rolling my empty glass on the bar.

"Oh, yeah. What's that, Roy?"

"How much do you reckon that tanker rig was worth?"

"Dunno." He shrugged his shoulders. "Ninety grand? It was almost new."

"And the diesel inside was maybe twelve grand. And when I found your truck this morning, it was empty. Now who do we know who has a central heating system that requires 33,000 litres of diesel? Or a fleet of about 600 black cabs? Or how about a garage which retails diesel? Or maybe a very thirsty cigarette-lighter for a chain-smoker?"

"What are you getting at?" asked Taffy.

"Who wants that much diesel? Who goes to the trouble of pinching your tanker, draining it and then dumping it?"

"You've got me there, Roy. But the funny thing is it happened two weeks ago to Ferdy Kyle. I was talking to him about it in here the other night. And he works for Mr McCandy as well. Good evening, Mr McCandy."

He said it over my shoulder and I turned slightly to find most of the light blocked out by an exhibit from the *Guinness Book of Records*. (Largest dinner jacket ever made category.)

"Who's he?"

"Name's Roy Angel, Mr McCandy," said Taffy. "You listen to what he has to say and it'll bear me out, honest it will."

"Sit. Over there."

The one who'd asked who I was wasn't quite as big as the one in the dinner jacket, but it was close. He was fiftyish and dressed in a light brown suit. He had rings made out of half-sovereigns on both hands. (Rule of Life No. 85: Never trust anyone who has rings made from coins. If they do it because they think it's fashionable, then they have appalling taste. If they do it because they're good as knuckle-dusters, keep clear of them anyway.)

"I'm Donald McCandy," said the suit. "They call me Big Mac McCandy, but not to my face."

I wasn't about to break the habit.

"And this –" he waved a ring at the huge dinner jacket "– is Domestos."

He waited for a reaction but didn't get one from me.

"That's right," said McCandy, tempting us to laugh, "Domestos, like the lavatory cleaner, because he's—"

"Thick and strong?" offered Taffy and I winced and closed my eyes, so I didn't see exactly where Domestos hit him, but I heard it.

"Good. Now that's out of the way, the rest of the evening's your own," said Big Mac pleasantly. "Let's have a drink."

We sat down, Taffy scraping his chair across the floor and staggering slightly, his eyes full of tears. I noticed that the few snooker players there were in the club had moved to the table furthest away.

The barman came to take our order. We were honoured.

"Good evening, Justin," said McCandy. "My usual, a Perrier for my colleague and whatever these gentlemen are drinking."

"Large brandy," said Taffy. He was game, I'll give him that.

"Whatever these gentlemen were drinking last," smiled Big Mac.

"It's Julian," said the barman and we all looked at him.

He was about nineteen, his hair fashionably short and there was a faint sneer on his lips.

"Julian," he said again, "not Justin."

"Whatever," said McCandy and let it go at that. The kid had either loadsa nerve or no brains at all.

"Now let's talk shop, gentlemen."

Big Mac had obviously got the outline of Taffy's tale already but he was very interested in what I had to tell him. At the end of it, McCandy said: "So where does that leave us?"

I didn't like the "us" one bit, so I kept quiet.

Taffy, of course, couldn't do that to save his life, or in this case, mine.

"Roy's got a theory, Mr McCandy."

"Then let's hear it, son. What did you say your name was?"

"Angel, and it's not much of a theory."

"Angel, eh. I don't think Domestos here has ever met an angel before."

"But I bet he's helped create a few," I risked, and McCandy grinned.

"Nice one, son. Now, in your own time . . ."

"Can I just get one thing clear? What exactly is this to do with you, Mr McCandy?" I was as polite as pie. "And I'm not being chopsy, I just don't get the whole picture."

McCandy raised an eyebrow which I hoped wasn't code for Domestos to stomach-punch me from the inside.

"Well, Mr Angel, the picture is this." He sipped on his "usual", which looked like *crème de menthe frappé*, but I bet nobody ever said anything about it. "I run an integrated business. Garages are my core business, but also a few pubs, this club and a couple of others. The secret is to have cash-flow and channel it properly.

"Now, just at the moment, my garages, like most others, are having a big push on unleaded petrol. It's the in thing. At the same time, there's a rising demand for diesel due to the increase in private cars with diesel engines. OK? Right. What this means is the small operator like me buys fuel on the spot market, but because the oil companies are running around like headless chickens supplying unleaded, there's a shortage of tankers and drivers. I have to use what talent is available." He looked scathingly at Taffy. "To top up my regular supplies, that is. One of my garages goes through two tankers of diesel a week, easy. Only I'm going to run short again this week and that means I lose customers 'cos those bastard black cab drivers take their business elsewhere."

If Taffy breathed a word about Armstrong, he wouldn't have to worry about Domestos.

"Taffy said this has happened before," I said sympathetically.

"This is number four in two months."

Taffy looked astonished.

"And were all the tankers recovered?"

"Yep. All bone dry. And anywhere from here to Dover, just left at the side of the road."

"Did they travel the same route?"

"No. Ferdy Kyle got done on the M1 at Northampton."

"At a café?"

"Yeah," said Taffy. "Ferdy knows all the caffs and truck stops."

McCandy and I looked at each other. Domestos looked at Taffy, judging the distance between them.

"Ferdy's not the villain," said Big Mac. "He got badly hurt in the kidneys."

"During the hijack?" I asked.

"No," said McCandy, all matter-of-fact. "Afterwards."

"He wasn't too chipper the other night when he was in here," said Taffy, thinking he was helping.

"And I suppose you discussed your route for your tanker," I said.

"Sure. I've been out of the game for a bit, Roy. Ferdy suggested the Spaniard's Corner place as having good nosh, as well as giving me a coupla short cuts."

"Who else was here when you and Ferdy were rabbiting?" I asked.

"Nobody. It was early on. Just me and Ferdy. No customers. Young Justin said it had been quiet all morning."

"Julian," McCandy corrected him softly.

"Do you find all your drivers in here, Mr McCandy?"

"Most. If not here, then in the Jubilee down the road."

"One of your pubs?" He nodded at me. "And do your bar staff do relief work in all your establishments?"

I thought he'd like that – "establishments" – but he just nodded silently again and then said, even quieter than before: "Julian."

Which is how I came to be following young Julian for the next three days. Big Mac had thought it a good idea as I was on hand and Taffy was a known face. And I had an incentive. Do it right and I'd never see Domestos again.

Duncan had supplied us with relief wheels while Armstrong was laid up, an ancient Ford Transit van which had been so badly resprayed you could still read WILLHIRE down the side. The clock said it had only done 8,000 miles and, charitably, I assumed it had only gone round once.

Big Mac had convinced himself that the spate of diesel thefts had been engineered by a rival to sabotage the legitimate parts of his business empire. To me, that seemed like putting a toothless flea on a Rottweiler but I did as I was told. Mr McCandy has that effect on people.

For two nights running he had pairs of his drivers meet in the Centre Pocket and discuss their tanker routes for the next day in earshot of Julian. I was to wait outside in my Transit until closing time and then see where Julian went and who he met. Nothing happened except I managed to get halfway through Paul Kennedy's *Rise and Fall of the Great Powers*, a paperback big enough to use as a weapon in case of trouble.

Julian would usher out the last snooker players, lock the front doors, presumably wash the last of the glasses, then emerge from a side door, put three or four empty beer kegs out on the pavement, lock up and walk home. In his case, and I followed on foot twice to make sure, that was the Jubilee, one of

McCandy's pubs, where he lived in the staff accommodation above the bar. Most big pubs in London have to offer rooms to their staff nowadays in order to keep them longer than a week. McCandy had leases on a dozen pubs and, by asking around during the day, I discovered he had about fifty youngish staff, mostly Irish or Australian, living in.

On the third night, I followed Julian in the van after he'd gone through his lights off, kegs out, lock up routine. He arrived back at the Jubilee and entered through the back yard, where he chatted with one of the pub's barmen who was going through the same ritual, putting out empty kegs for the delivery dray to collect next morning. Then they disappeared inside and lights came on in the upstairs rooms followed by the faint strains of a Wet Wet Wet record.

"This is getting bloody silly," Big Mac said the next day when we met as arranged in a café/sandwich bar across the road from one of his garages in Bethnal Green. "I've now got more diesel than I can sell and this is not helping my cash-flow situation at all."

As my cash-flow tended to be all one way, I found it difficult to empathize, but I pretended.

"Maybe we're wrong about Julian," I said.

"I have a feeling in my water about him," said McCandy, turning his killer look on me. "And I told Nigel that when he hired him."

"Nigel."

"My son. He runs all my licensed properties."

Well, somebody had to. With Big Mac's record he wouldn't have got a licence.

"Bright lad. Did Business Administration at university. Likes to help out his old mates and I think that's a good sign. You know, the mark of a considerate employer."

I'd assumed that the mark of a considerate employer as far as Big Mac was concerned was leaving somebody with one good eye, but I said: "Er . . . I don't follow, Mr McCandy."

"Nigel. And Julian. They were at university together. Julian couldn't get a job so Nigel took him on until something turned up. I have to be fair, we've had three or four of his old cronies through the firm and they've done OK. Two of Nigel's buddies are managers in my pubs right now. And it gives the organization a bit of class to have all those degrees after the names on the letterheads."

"So Julian's got a degree, has he?" I sipped some milky coffee and put the brain out of neutral.

"Two, as a matter of fact," said Big Mac proudly. "ABSc and an MSc. What's that got to do with anything?"

"Probably nothing." I took a deep breath. "Look, Mr McCandy, we've got to think logically about this."

"Go on, then," he said.

"You think this is somebody getting at you. You personally."

"Yeah," he said slowly, thinking about it.

"But it's not – in itself – going to put you out of business, it it? Just filching the odd drop of diesel."

"Over a hundred thousand bloody litres to date," he snapped. "That's not chicken feed."

"No, I know," I said soothingly. "But it isn't the way to really screw you, is it?"

"So?"

"So that can't be the main reason for nicking the fuel, can it? It must be because whoever's doing it actually needs the diesel."

I licked my lips which had suddenly dried out.

"Mr McCandy, what would you use all that fuel for *apart* from putting it in engines?"

"I haven't a fucking clue."

"I have."

That afternoon I drove across town to Bloomsbury and parked in a side road off Gower Street. The place I was looking for was the rear quarter of a 1930s office block converted into a laboratory and a small lecture theatre. It was part of London University, but since the upsurge in the activities of the Animal Liberationists a few years ago it hasn't appeared on any map of university buildings and the phone number is ex-directory.

Zoë had worked there on secondment from London Zoo for five years, lecturing and demonstrating on wild animal physiology and behaviour, but we went back longer than that. She used to get away from her parents overnight by telling them she was going badger-spotting, and even though she lived in a part of Tooting where they hadn't seen a tree since George III got out of his carriage to swap small talk with it, they believed her.

I had to blag my way past an ancient security guard who would have stood no chance against a Libbers steam team, but the key to their security was that no one knew of their existence. He reluctantly got Zoë on the internal phone and she reluctantly told him to let me in.

She was sitting in an empty lab cataloguing a tray of 35 mm slides and she looked up from under huge blue-framed glasses to say: "Well, a rave from the grave. Mr Angel. What are you after?"

"Now, Zoë darling, we had a pretty steady relationship once," I said, showing the good teeth.

"Just remember," she said, pointing a pencil at me, "it was purely sexual. There was nothing Platonic about it."

"You do remember."

She pretended to think for a second, then smiled, swivelled on her bench stool and opened her knees so she could pull me in close. I pushed her glasses up into her hair and fumbled a hand inside her lab coat.

Between kisses, she murmured: "So you just happened to be in the neighbourhood, eh?"

"Sort of," I whispered into her ear, my hand trying to find the place on her lower spine which I knew was The Spot so far as she was concerned. "And I just had a thought about that experiment you ran with the squirrels in the New Forest."

"Squirrels? What are you after?" She tried to push me away but I held on and then started to gently rub the spot on her back. She gave a startled little "Oh", then sighed.

"You know how you tracked them, followed their habits, with those little radios on collars."

"Mmmmm. That's my job. Mmmm. Don't stop."

"How effective are those transmitters? What range do they have?"

"A . . . mmmm . . . mile and a half. Why?"

"Got any kicking around? Any that could conveniently go missing?"

This time she did lever me away.

"It'll cost you," she said, looking me in the eye.

"How much?"

She took off her glasses, laid them on the tray of slides and shook her hair out, then put her arms around my neck.

"Did I mention money?"

I took Domestos with me because he was better than a warrant card. Norman Reeves, the manager of the Shadwell Arms, the farthest-flung pub in the McCandy empire, was also the longest-serving employee of Big Mac. Without Domestos there he would have had me out on my ear for asking questions, let alone demanding to go into the pub's cellar.

The Shadwell was a backstreet boozer within a stone's throw of the Tower of London, but few tourists were encouraged to find it. The cellar floor was cleaner than any flat surface in the bar.

"How many kegs do you get through in a week?" I asked Reeves.

"Usually two or three kils or 22s and, say, six firkins or 11s or tubs, whatever we've been selling most of," he answered carefully.

I knew enough from my own days as a barman to decode what he'd said. Strictly speaking, beer came in casks and a pressurized keg was a type of container – not a type of beer, as many think. They were known by the size of their contents: a "kil" was a kilderkin (18 gallons) and a firkin was half that, all the imperial measures being in multiples of nine up to a barrel (36 gallons). Metric containers were measured in hectolitres but, just to confuse the foreigners, publicans referred to them by their imperial equivalents: 22 or 11 gallons. A "tub" was slang for anything which wasn't a regular imperial or metric size, say ten gallons, and you'd get low-volume beers or cider in those.

"Are they all collected when the draymen deliver?"

"Yeah, we leave them out back. I don't have room to store empties down here."

"And when do you get deliveries?"

Reeves looked at Domestos, who nodded, before he answered. "Mondays, Tuesdays, Wednesdays, whenever . . ."

I frowned at him.

"Whenever the wholesalers deliver." He shrugged.

"You don't buy direct from the breweries?"

"No, we shop around."

"And do the wholesalers charge deposits on the kegs?"

"Nah," he chuckled. "We'd get a new wholesaler if they did."

"How many do you deal with?"

"Four or five. What's this all about?"

"Mr McCandy's called me in as a sort of efficiency expert. But we don't talk about it, OK?"

"Sure, sure. Never seen you."

"Good," I beamed, enjoying my newfound sense of power. "Do you have a rota for barmen for Mr McCandy's pubs?"

"Yes. Mr Nigel sends one round every week so we can swap staff if there are any gaps."

"Just what I need. Get it, will you?"

He got the nod from Domestos and disappeared upstairs.

"I need two of those in the back of the van," I said to Domestos and pointed at a row of kegs. Then I picked my way carefully through puddles of spilt beer to have a look at the damp-rotted noticeboard tacked to the cellar wall near the hatch doors which lead on to the street.

There were regulation safety notices about carbon dioxide, no heavy lifting and electrical circuits in cellars and one other which I stole and folded into the back pocket of my jeans.

Domestos was grunting up the stairs to the bar. He had to move sideways as he had an 11-gallon keg under each arm. I could see that they still had green plastic caps on the syphon unit where you plugged in the beer pipe.

"No, Domestos," I said gently. "Empty ones."

A day and most of a night later I was sitting in the Transit again, watching the back door of the Centre Pocket club. This time I had Big Mac McCandy sitting next to me and in the back Domestos snored gently.

"You sure this thing'll work?" He prodded the radio receiving unit on the dashboard.

"Up to a mile," I said, hoping Zoë had been straight with me. "Watch."

I flicked the On switch and the centre one of the three orange lights began to flash. I'd had Duncan the Drunken solder the tiny squirrel collars to the underside lip of the two kegs I'd borrowed, and right now they were about fifty yards away on the pavement, in a stack of about a dozen, outside the Centre Pocket. It was nearly five in the morning and we'd been there since three.

They came round the corner at about half five, in a box-backed truck with no markings. It stopped outside the Centre Pocket and two guys in jeans and zipper jackets with the name of a well-known London brewery stencilled on the back got out.

"Cheeky buggers," breathed McCandy as we watched them roll up the back of the truck and start loading the kegs.

The snooker club had obviously been the last hit on their run, as they were lucky to get the Centre Pocket's kegs on board.

"How many do you think they've got there?" McCandy asked me, thinking along the same lines.

"Dunno. Forty? Fifty? They reckon you need about sixty to smelt down a ton of aluminium. Scrap value, twelve hundred notes a ton."

"You know a lot," he said suspiciously.

"I asked around." Then I saw the look in his eyes. "Discreetly," I added.

"They've left a couple," he said suddenly and loudly, but we were well away and they couldn't have heard. "They know you've bugged those two."

"Relax. The two they've left are stainless steel kegs, not aluminium. There's no smelt value in them but if you stick them in the back of an old car and put it through the wrecker, they add to the dead weight scrap content."

I wondered if I'd gone too far, showing off like that, but McCandy let it go.

The truck pulled away and turned the corner. I started the Transit and flicked on the receiver. The flashing light alternated between the centre bulb and the one on the left.

"It's crude, but effective," I said. "And we keep out of sight. With so little traffic this time in the morning, I figured that was important."

McCandy weighed the receiver in one hand.

"If we lose them," he said, looking straight ahead, "you'll need surgery to remove this."

I put the pedal to the metal.

The smelter turned out to be in no-man's-land between Barking and Little Ilford, though there are people who live in Ilford who don't know there's a Little one.

It was tucked away in the corner of an old factory site which the developers called a prospective industrial park and the local residents called waste ground. We found it when the receiver started blinking right but there was no obvious right turn. Doubling back, it was McCandy who noticed something wrong with the shabby picket fence, but he told me not to stop but see if we could get round behind.

They'd been very clever, you had to give them that.

A whole section of ten-foot-high fence had been fixed so it could be slid aside to provide access to the site. The box truck had literally driven off the road, replaced the fence, and nobody would have been any the wiser if we hadn't had the transmitter bugs. The smelter itself was a good three hundred yards from the fake fence. The giveaway was its chimney – it usually is – though these guys had given the problem some thought and had kept it to no more than ten or twelve feet high and had fitted a fan on top to disperse the smoke. There were enough other old buildings, piles of scrap iron and even broken-down caravans to screen the place from casual passers-by, not that there would have been many of them.

Right next to the smelter – a one-storey brick building with double iron doors – was a black fuel tank, perhaps the remains of some heating plant.

"That's where your diesel went," I said to McCandy.

I had parked the Transit at the south end of the site, around the corner from the hole in the fence. Big Mac and I were standing on the bonnet looking over the fence and I had given him a pair of binoculars which were no bigger than opera glasses but twenty times more powerful. I'd got them from a passing acquaintance who didn't use them for bird-spotting. Well, not in the conventional sense.

"They nicked your tankers when their tank was running low.

Drive it in there, transfer the fuel and dump the rig the next day."

McCandy grunted and handed the glasses back.

The two guys we'd followed were unloading the truck, adding their haul to a rack of kegs already there. It wasn't only McCandy's pubs getting ripped; this was a well-organized operation, probably buying kegs from freelance chancers at a couple of quid a go. To the side of the smelter, there were two cars, one a Porsche, and a motorbike parked.

"Let's get closer," said Big Mac and he put his hands on the top of the rickety fence and side-jumped over.

I hesitated just long enough for Domestos to feel the need to cough discreetly, and then I followed.

We picked our way through the mud and over the junk until we were within a hundred feet of the smelter; so close I imagined I could feel the heat. We could certainly hear voices and the clanging of empty kegs and they were so confident they even had a radio on, tuned to the World Service.

Big Mac led the way around a burnt-out caravan and then stopped short. I almost bumped into his shoulder, but halted myself. Physical contact was not advisable, I reckoned.

Then I saw why he'd stopped dead: a big, sleek, brown Doberman bitch was coming at us at Mach 2, ears back in attack mode.

I looked around frantically for a weapon, and despite the junk all around, couldn't decide on anything likely to stop the dog. McCandy still hadn't moved, except to go into a fighting crouch. I did the sensible thing and moved back to give him room to get on with it.

"Hello, Louise," he said, holding out a hand. "There's a good girl."

The dog skidded to a halt and rolled over, exposing her stomach and extending her tongue to wrap around Big Mac's hand.

"How long have you had this strange power over dogs?" I asked.

"Ever since she was a puppy and we gave her to my son Nigel," he answered without looking up. Then he said: "Louise – stay."

The dog stayed. We moved nearer the smelt.

From behind a pile of building rubble we could see at least five men working. One had what looked like a homemade wrench which undid the pressurized seal on the top of the keg. That way the steel spear which fed carbon dioxide into the beer could be removed. It had to be unsealed in that way or it would have blown up as they put it in the furnace. One of the others had the job of collecting the seals and lopping off their tubular spears with a power saw. I'd heard that most smelting operations were given away when people found hundreds of discarded steel spears. They hadn't found a way of making money out of them. Yet.

McCandy and I could see right into the crude smelting oven they had constructed. Not that you need anything fancy. If you have enough diesel to burn, once you hit the right temperature, the aluminium kegs just collapse in front of your eyes. It was almost as if a giant invisible hand crushed them. One minute they were there, shaped and intact against the flames; the next minute they'd folded and turned to liquid which the smelters ran off to cool in moulds made out of kegs cut lengthwise. That was a bit of a giveaway if you ask me, as it was a none too subtle hint as to where the aluminium had come from.

One of the smelters pulled off a pair of asbestos gloves and sauntered out of the smelt and over to the Porsche. He opened the boot and took out an insulated cold box, the sort you take on picnics. He opened it and handed out small bottles of Perrier. It was thirsty work.

"Is that Nigel?" I asked McCandy softly and he nodded.

The two guys who'd brought the truck began to load it with the half-keg-shaped ingots.

"Do you want to follow them, Mr McCandy? Find out where they're selling the stuff?"

Big Mac shook his head. He was still staring across the site at the back of his son's head.

"Griffin Scrap Dealers in Plumstead, south of the river," he said without turning round.

"Oh. Er . . . one of your . . . er . . . businesses?" I stood back a bit, just in case.

"Yep," he said grimly. "Got it in one."

* * *

"You want me to *what*!"

"I want you to grass my son Nigel."

"You want me to turn him over to the Old Bill? Your son?"

"And his mates. The whole shooting match," said Big Mac, reasonably. "Well, I can't can I? I'm not a grass."

"Neither am I," I protested.

"But everybody knows I'm not. I have my position to think of."

We were sitting back in the front of the Transit, back in the City. Domestos had been sent to pick up McCandy's Jaguar from the car park of a well-known firm of solicitors.

"They send people down for smelting nowadays, Mr McCandy. The breweries have got together and they press for prosecution. It's not just a slap on the back of the legs with a ruler any more."

"I know that," Big Mac said philosophically. "Prison was an education for me. It taught me how to manage people, how to plan ahead, watch your stock control, expand your options and diversify in a static market. I think of it like other people think of school: maybe the best days of your life. Doesn't mean you want to go back, though."

He lit a small cigar and I regretted that I'd given up smoking again.

"When I think of all the dosh I've spent on private education for Nigel, and he's still daft enough to think he can cross me . . . a spot of stir will be the making of the lad."

I had a nasty feeling he was right.

"He'll thank me for it one day, but he mustn't know it was me. That's why you've got to do it. I don't care how. I need twenty-four hours to clean out the Plumstead yard. Make sure we don't have any of his – mine, I should say – metal there."

"But . . ."

"I'm sure you'll think of something, Roy. You seem a resourceful lad to me. And that old taxi you run about in. Send me the bills for having it repaired. In fact, I'll open an account for you at one of the garages and put some credit behind the counter for you. Have a year's free diesel on me. How's that?"

"Very fair, Mr McCandy. But are you sure about this?"

"Absolutely."

"I'll need a few expenses." It was worth a shot.

He produced a wallet and dealt me ten ten-pound notes on to the dashboard.

"What about Mrs McCandy, Nigel's mum?" I tried. "Won't she be upset if he goes down?"

A slow smile lit up his face.

"Mortified. Absobloodylutely gobsmacked. She'll have to resign from about five hundred committees and stop putting on airs and graces." He opened the door of the Transit and made to climb out. "Get it done," he added.

Then, when he was standing in the road holding the door, he said: "Or you will be. Done, that is."

Later that morning, when I'd worked things out, I visited one of the few genuine ships' chandlers left in London and spent some of McCandy's money. Then, just short of opening time, I called at the Shadwell Arms and, using the McCandy name, got the landlord, Norman Reeves, to take me into his cellars again.

"I need a couple more kegs, Norman," I told him. "And I want them in the back of my van now without anyone seeing us."

"What's going on?" he asked irritably.

"Why don't you ask Big Mac himself?"

"Will these two do?" He dragged two 11-gallon lager kegs towards the hatch which led to the street.

"Fine. One more thing. What do you use to unscrew the spears?"

Reeves pretended to look stupid. He was a gifted impressionist. "Don't know what you mean. Them's sealed containers. You can't tamper with 'em."

"Not even when you want to recycle some old beer, or maybe water down some good beer? I know. Now where is it?"

To my surprise he gave in before I could invoke Big Mac's name again. He reached behind a stack of boxes containing crisps and cleaning materials in equal proportions and produced a long-handled tool adapted from an adjustable wrench.

"Just lock on to the pressure seal and turn anti-clockwise," he said.

"Thanks, Norm. Shall I get Domestos to return it when I've finished?"

"Don't bother. I've got a spare."

The balloon went up, so to speak, at ten past seven the next morning.

It wasn't a balloon, of course. It was a large cloud of noxious orange smoke which even the fan they'd fitted to the smelter chimney couldn't cope with. It blew back and out of the oven itself, the smelters on duty running blindly out on to the waste ground, one of them, blinded, even tripping over the back bumper of the Porsche. I hoped it wasn't Nigel. He had enough to worry about.

Short of a big arrow coming down from heaven and pointing "Here They Are", there wasn't a better way of spotting the smelter. And the assembled hordes of policemen and brewery security men took the hint, smashing through the fake fence and surrounding the choking, crying smelters.

I was watching from the far end of the site through my binoculars, standing on the Transit as Big Mac and I had done the day before. It had all gone according to plan. McCandy had made some excuse to keep Louise the Doberman at home and the naval distress flares I'd packed into the empty kegs had worked a treat once they'd been pushed into the oven.

It had taken me a couple of dry runs in packing them with sheets of plastic so they didn't rattle or fall out when the smelters took the spear out. And they were so light, the extra weight wouldn't have been noticed. When I was satisfied, I'd called the hotline number on the notice I'd stolen from the cellar of the Shadwell Arms on my first visit. The notice had explained that keg theft was illegal and gave a phone number for anyone spotting anything suspicious.

I'd done it that way, and let the brewery guys call in the cops, so I could stay out of the action.

After all, I had my reputation to think of.

Watching people getting arrested must give you an appetite. That, and the fact that I owed her for a couple of squirrel collars and had to return her radio receiver, led me to drag Zoë out of her lab for an early lunch.

Over a bottle of Othello, a fine headbanging red wine, in a Greek restaurant off the Tottenham Court Road, I told her some of what I'd been up to. (Rule of Life No. 5: Always tell the truth, but not necessarily all of it or all at once.)

She seemed most concerned about the damage to Armstrong, but I told her not to worry, he was being well looked after. That reminded me I owed her for the transmitter collars and I reached into the back pocket of my jeans for the remains of Big Mac's folding money.

As I pulled out my depleted wad of tenners, something else came with it and fluttered to the floor under the table.

Zoë bent over and picked it up. It was the notice about keg thefts I'd pinched from the pub and it was folded so that the pay-off line, printed in red, was clearly visible. It said: KEG THEFT HOTLINE – TO CLAIM YOUR REWARD, and there was a number.

"What's this?" she asked, handing it over.

"Think of it as extra car insurance," I said. "You can never have too much."

TAKING CARE OF FRANK

ANTONY MANN

Frank Hewitt was no ordinary celebrity. For one thing, he had talent. For another, he had that indefinable quality which meant it didn't matter that he didn't have *a lot of* talent. He was a star. The camera loved him just as he loved it, so that the public, who always wanted so badly to love what the camera saw, could love him too, and feel as though he loved them back. Not only that, he had a rare cross-media appeal. His voice was average and comforting enough that his interpretations of show tunes and middle-of-the-road classics would always be big sellers, but down the years he had also appeared in a number of very successful second-rate films. He was charming, and lovable, yet with an intriguingly sordid past. He did beer adverts, too.

The only trouble with Frank Hewitt was that he was still alive, and had been for some time. It was a growing disappointment to a lot of people who mattered in the entertainment industry. Somehow, despite his hard-boozing, chain-smoking, orgiastic journey through the world of showbiz, he had managed to avoid cancer, heart failure or a stroke and arrive at the age of seventy-three looking determined to make it to eighty and beyond.

His agent (and mine), Harry Schmeltzmann, spelled it out for me on the phone.

"The trouble is," Harry was saying, "I've got the people from CBC on my back about the tribute show. Then there's the biopics. Two telemovies and a feature. *The Hewitt Story, Frank Hewitt: The Story,* and *The Story Of Frankie Hewitt.* It's a contractual thing. They can't go into full production until Frank actually kicks it. There are the exposés, too. Six unofficial biographies and two docufiction character assassinations for TV. Plus the arthouse revivals and video releases of his old movies. Not to mention the tapes and CDs of the recent Vegas shows, and the boxed sets and compilations. And guess what? There's an interactive CD-Rom lined up. Archive material and some stupid computer game and a Frank Hewitt quiz. That's without factoring in the hundred or so 'Frankie Hewitt Was A Fucking Genius' articles that the broadsheets and glossies can't run until he croaks. You know what it's about. All this crap is going to sell better when Hewitt is dead."

"But Hewitt is already old," I said. "Can't it wait until natural causes?"

"Wait? Why should it wait? A lot of people have put a lot of money into Frank's career down the years. They didn't know he was going to live this long, otherwise they might not have invested so much in the first place. Don't you think they deserve a decent return now, while *they* can enjoy it? Don't forget, Bendick, you'll be on a percentage of gross yield after Hewitt's death. If you knock him off."

"That percentage is microscopic, Harry, and you know it."

"The *percentage* might be minuscule, but the total yield adds up to quite a slice, Stan. And I'm on a percentage of *you.* So don't let me think any more that you're discouraging me from finding you gainful employment."

Not only that, but Harry must have been getting his own very special kickback from somewhere to be happy to sacrifice his 10 percent of the fortune that Frank Hewitt pulled in every year.

"Hewitt's big, Harry," I said. "Very big. Won't there be more heat than usual from outside?"

"Possibly. But the dirt stays inside the industry, no matter who, no matter what. It has to. You know that. Stop looking for excuses."

"But I *like* Frank Hewitt," I said. "My dad liked Frank Hewitt. My grandfather *raved* about him."

"Jesus, Bendick, *everyone* likes Frank Hewitt, that's the

point. Everybody *loves* him. Why do you think he's so huge? But the industry needs a boost. There hasn't been an elder statesman or Grand Dame of the entertainment world drop out of the firmament for some time now. Look, take it or leave it. I worked hard to get you this gig. I can always offer it to Grebb or Zabowski . . ."

"No, no," I said, with some reluctance. "I'll do it. Better that he gets it from a fan, eh?"

"That's the spirit, Bendick," said Schmeltzmann. "And make it look like murder. We'll get bigger press that way."

Leo Zabowski rang an hour later. I knew his ugly voice at once.

"Bendick? It's Zabowski."

"I know who it is," I said.

"So you got the Frank Hewitt job."

"How did you find out?"

"Bad news travels fast, I guess." Zabowski didn't sound jealous at all, which was all wrong for him. "You know you only got it because Schmeltzmann is your agent *and* Frank Hewitt's, don't you?"

"Perhaps so, Zabowski, but ask yourself this: *why* is Schmeltzmann one of the biggest agents in Hollywood? Because he wouldn't touch second-raters like you with a barge-pole."

Zabowski laughed. It was one of my least favourite noises.

"Are you okay, Zabowski? You sound like you're choking on your own phlegm."

"That's hilarious, Bendick. Just remember. You might have worked with the big stars for the last few years, but your time is coming to an end. This business is crying out for some new blood."

"Keep dreaming, Zabowski. The world always needs dreamers, like Frank Hewitt sings."

"Yeah, well, anyway," said Zabowski flatly, his vitriol expended.

We waited then the both of us for the other to hang up. Eventually he got bored and softly put down the phone.

Hewitt's mansion, Cedar Grove, was out in The Hills beyond The Valley. Someone – possibly Hewitt – had cut some of the cedars down a long time ago to make way for the nine-hole golf course and the tennis courts. The two-storey white house, too big for your average family but perfect for a living Hollywood legend, sat snugly against a backdrop of evergreens.

Hewitt's fourth wife Clarissa met me at the front door. I had seen her photo in the gossip sheets. She was slim and blonde, perhaps naturally. Her face was set into a careless, superior expression that reflected wealth and the boredom that went with it, but she had kept her teenage looks, possibly because she was not long in her twenties.

"Stan Bendick?"

"That's right."

"Do you have your own gun or would you like to borrow one?" She walked me through into the tiled reception hall and to the base of a wide staircase that curved up and around. We were surrounded by *objets d'art*: Monets, Epsteins, Picassos and what have you, all waiting patiently to be fought over by Clarissa and the rival ex-wives and the eight or ten children from the previous marriages.

I patted my shoulder holster through my jacket,

"As it happens, I brought my own."

"Fine. Frank should be upstairs. Third door on the left. Could you make it quick? I've got a hair appointment in forty-five minutes."

"I think your hair looks fine the way it is," I said.

She smiled sourly. "Well, thanks anyway, but what would you know?" She headed off to be rude to somebody else, but stopped in the doorway which led through to the rest of the ground floor. "Remember, third door on the left. Not second. *Third.*"

"I can count to three," I replied.

"Congratulations."

The door was unlocked. Frank was in.

He sat facing away from me, dozing in a high-backed brown leather chair in front of wide clean windows that overlooked The Valley and the winding bitumen road that led from there to here. The room was clearly Frank Hewitt's space: the soothing blue carpet was plush, the dark relief wallpaper almost three-dimensional. Frames displayed movie posters behind polished glass, and antiquated gold and platinum records. There were video tapes, photo albums and hardbacks on shelves next to the TV and VCR. Opposite the windows, beside a connecting door that was shut, sat a telephone on a small three-legged table.

Even the back of his head looked famous. I might have shot him then and there, but this was the man whose songs my grandfather had slow-danced to while courting my grandmother, whose movies my dad had sat in the back row to watch as a kid. It had been my honour to permanently retire a lot of stars in the last few years, but never one as big as Frank Hewitt. I wanted to see his face. My shoes made no sound on the thick pile.

He sat in the chair in a lemon-yellow terry towelling dressing gown and tartan slippers, the back of his skull at an angle against the headrest. His breathing was light. He had never been a handsome man and now, in his old age, his midriff was paunched and his round face wrinkled and worn. Yet even in repose he was larger than life. It's a pet theory of mine that people in the public eye are imbued with a residue of the abnormally great amount of attention that is paid them, a concentration of a kind of psychic energy if you like. This residual force is then radiated back to the public by the celebrity. It's a constant, unconscious process. It explains why, when you meet someone famous in the flesh, they always seem to be exaggerated in some way, operating in a different reality. It explains why we call them stars. I began to wish I'd brought a camera.

But there was no future in coming over all starstruck. It would only make things harder. I had to take care of Frank before he woke. I had drawn my revolver and was picking my spot when he opened his eyes and looked at me. He hadn't been asleep at all.

"Er, hello, Mr Hewitt," I said, lowering the gun sights.

"Call me Frank."

"Frank."

"Stan Bendick, isn't it?"

"Ah, that's right."

"I've heard about you, Bendick."

"You have?" Frank Hewitt had heard of *me*? I was flattered.

"We all have. You and your kind. Just because we're stars

doesn't mean we're stupid. We know what goes on. We know where you live, what you look like. Whom you've murdered."

"Wow," I said. "That's great, Mr Hewitt . . . I mean, Frank . . . I mean . . ."

"Did you meet Clarissa?"

"Who?"

"Clarissa. My wife."

"Yes, I did, she's a lovely young woman, Frank. You must be very much in love with her . . ."

"She's a bitch, even worse than the others. Don't tell her, but I've cut her out of the will. Sure, she'll contest it, maybe even win, but I like the idea of her loathsome face twisting with selfishness and anger when she hears that she doesn't get a penny." He laughed, then pointed a stubby finger at me. "Let me tell you something about fame. It's only ever an accident, and it always ends in tears. I've had four loveless marriages, I've got nine children who either hate or fear me. All the money I've earned hasn't given me an ounce of joy or contentment. Any happiness I've had – and there hasn't been much – has come from the things that I could have had anyway, *without* being a star."

I hefted the gun in my hand.

"Maybe you could look at it this way. You'll be making a lot of *other* people happy when you die."

"You mean the rich moguls?" he said bitterly. "The studio and TV bosses and the soulless parasites who buzz around them like flies on shit? The people who pollute this filthy industry more and more with every passing year?"

"Yes, them, of course, but what I meant was the ordinary people in the street, the people who look up to you without knowing what really goes on behind the scenes. Your fans will love you a lot more when you're dead."

He raised an eyebrow, "You think so?"

"Of course. Just look at Elvis. John Lennon. Look at Princess Di. After *she* croaked, there were millions of people who suddenly realized how much they loved her who didn't know more than the first thing about her!"

"That's a good point, Bendick. Not good enough to make me think that I *deserve* to die, but a good point nonetheless."

"Thanks, Mr Hewitt . . . Frank . . ."

I could hear the chutter-chutter of a helicopter in the distance, rising up out of The Valley. All else was still. I raised the gun again.

"Before you do that, you might want to take a look at the news on television," said Frank.

"If it's all the same with you, I'll buy a newspaper on the way back to town."

"It's for your sake, not mine." He shrugged. He reached down and picked up the remote from the floor, then swivelled in his chair. He pressed "on" and flicked through the channels until he found Cable News. A generic modern-style female cue-card reader with small eyes was halfway through reciting some lies about the economy, when either a mosquito got stuck in her ear or she was fed a line by the producer. She jiggled her ear piece and mustered a concerned frown, then stared into the camera.

"This just in," she said. "We're getting unconfirmed reports that singer and movie star Frank Hewitt is dead. Repeating, reports are coming in that Frank Hewitt has been shot." Then, ruining my morning, a recent photo of me flashed up on screen behind her. The newsreader continued, "Police are hunting for escaped lunatic Stan Bendick, who is wanted in connection with the shooting. Police are warning the public that Bendick is likely to be armed and dangerous, and a lunatic, and to only approach him if they can get away a clear shot with no risk to themselves. Cable News will be running a five-day Frank Hewitt retrospective, including concerts, interviews with family, friends, acquaintances and people who never knew him, and panels of experts discussing every nuance of his incredible career, as well as phone-ins, competitions and whatever else we can think of. But now let's cross to Ned Denverson in our Mobile Aerial Unit, which just happens to be in the general vicinity of Frank Hewitt's mansion in The Hills, Cedar Grove . . . can you hear me, Ned?"

"I can hear you," came Ned's voice. On screen now was an aerial view of the nine-hole golf course and the big white house. "We're approaching Cedar Grove right at this moment, Elise. All looks peaceful. Hard to imagine that only minutes ago, crazed gunman Stan Bendick allegedly shot Frank Hewitt five times in the head and left him lying in a pool of his own blood. We'll see if we can get a look at the room where we suspect Hewitt was mercilessly slain."

It was getting weird. I looked out the windows. The helicopter that I had heard was closer now. I could see it banking in towards the house. I looked at the gun in my hand. I looked at Frank. Had I *really* killed him? It didn't appear so, but then, hadn't they said so on TV?

"How did you know . . . ?"

"I heard the news crew setting up in the next room a couple of hours ago," said Frank. "Clarissa must have let them in. Just because I'm a star, doesn't make me deaf."

"There's a news crew in the *next room*?"

"You've been stitched up, Bendick. You and me both."

He was right. As he used the remote to switch off the television, the connecting door opened and Leo Zabowski walked in holding a gun. The news crew followed behind. It was a location unit comprising a female presenter, a soundman and a hand-held camera operator. There was a production assistant, too, a young man with a clipboard, and a pencil stuck behind an ear.

Zabowski was looking particularly repulsive today, I thought. Beads of sweat ran down his large bald head, adding their little bit to the stains on his shirt collar. His trousers were too baggy and, frankly, he could have done with cleaning his shoes. He was nervy and still overweight, although I'd heard he'd been trying to lose a few kilos.

"Zabowski, you're a disgrace," I said.

The presenter was a plasticky-looking brunette in her late twenties. I vaguely recognized her from the box. She glanced at Frank Hewitt sitting impassive in his leather swivel chair, then turned questioningly to Zabowski.

"He's not dead," she said.

"I'm sorry, Ms Paxton," he said meekly. But with me, Zabowski was in a snarly mood, "You see, Bendick? You see? I was right! You can't do your job properly any more! Why isn't Hewitt dead, eh? Tell me that!"

"We . . . er . . . got to chatting," I said.

"Chatting? *Chatting*? Well, come on, Bendick! Shoot him!" Zabowski gestured wildly at the window behind. "The news 'copter is almost here! It's a live feed! Do you want them to see that Hewitt is still alive? It'll ruin the broadcast!"

As far as moments in my life go, it was an odd one. I knew I'd been set up by Harry Schmeltzmann to take the fall, and also that Leo Zabowski was there to gun me down after I'd immortalized Frank Hewitt. But Zabowski could have simply shot me while he had the chance, and then finished off Frank afterwards. He made no move to. I noticed his body language. His stance indicated that he felt completely at ease. He saw no threat at all. And why should he? It was him standing next to the news crew, not me. He was on the side of the networks, caught in the illusion that the players in the world of TV and film are governed by a different set of rules from ordinary folk. I'm not saying that I didn't feel the temptation to go along with the plot, to play the part that had been written for me and slot unquestioning into prime time. I even felt the gun twitch in my hand and begin to slide across to where Frank Hewitt sat. Then I had a better idea. I shot Zabowski in the head.

The report was loud, but not surprising. It was a glancing blow that took a chunk of bone out of the top right-hand side of his skull. It all but knocked poor dumb Zabowski off his feet. With perplexed curiosity, he poked at the wound with a finger, marvelling at the blood that ran down his hand, the sudden absence of cranium which over the years he had come to take for granted.

"Bendick?" he said. "What have you done?"

"Looks like I shot you, Zabowski."

"Fucking idiot! Don't you know that you've wrecked the programme?"

"Sorry," I said. I meant it. I shot him again. This time he went down. Not even Zabowski's head was thick enough to sustain two bullets.

Now there was news, and the news crew jolted into motion reflexively. The dark-haired presenter, Ms Paxton, took control with great efficiency, I thought. She whispered something in the ear of the production assistant, who nodded, then got on the phone. She stepped over Zabowski, strode to the windows and drew the curtains moments before the helicopter made its first pass. She instructed the crew,

"Dick? Hal? Let's have one shot of the body and the gun,

another of Bendick with *his* gun, then Frank in the chair. Then we'll start setting up sight and sound for interviews with both of them."

Dick and Hal set to work as ordered. Ms Paxton sized me up.

"We'll do it this way," she said. "Turns out you're not escaped whacko Stan Bendick after all. You're actually unassuming Frank Hewitt fan Stan Bendick, who happened to be here at Cedar Grove getting Frank to sign some teddy bears for a charity auction. Lucky you carry a gun, otherwise you wouldn't have been able to thwart crazed gunman Leo Zabowski, recent escapee from the loony bin, who had broken into the house to kill Frank Hewitt and thus deprive the world of one of its greatest stars." She nodded to where the young production assistant was still talking animately into the telephone. "Mick's sorting it out now. We'll be running the correction on Cable in a few minutes." She smiled at me, almost like she meant it, "You're a hero, Bendick. How do you feel?"

"Not bad, considering."

She turned to Frank,

"Mr Hewitt? I expect we'll generate enough news and spin-offery from this incident to keep you viable. How do *you* feel?"

"I feel like I need a new agent," he said.

He wasn't the only one.

The door opened. Clarissa walked in.

"I heard the shots," she said. "Did everything go all right?" She saw Frank. "Oh. Frank. You're alive. Thank God."

"And maybe a new wife," said Frank.

"Mr Hewitt? . . . Frank?" I said. "There was something I was meaning to ask you before, but I never got the chance."

"What's that, Bendick?"

"Can I have your autograph?"

AND THE BUTTOCKS GLEAMED BY NIGHT

MAT COWARD

"Bloody hell, Charlie – you look like one of the Rolling Stones!"

"Don't exaggerate," I said. "I've had a touch of food poisoning, that's all."

"Pork pies," tutted John the Ratman, who may well be the only vegetarian Pest Control Officer in London. "Seriously, mate, you do look rough; you should be home in bed."

"Tell me the cat turned up on your watch, John, and home in bed is where I shall be."

With the help of John, my friend and occasional unpaid assistant, I was keeping nocturnal watch on a house in a north London suburb from which a cat named Tiger had disappeared. I was hoping that the cat would wander back of its own accord, and stumble into the humane trap I'd placed in its worried owner's garden, so that I could claim a finder's fee. That is what I am by profession: a finder of lost cats. If you can call cat-finding a profession, which of course you can't, not even in a world where Management Consultancy is called a profession.

"Sorry," said John. "Not a sausage. Quiet as the grave out here, all night."

I sent him home to his bed, and settled in for my shift of stray-spotting. This involves sitting in my car, smoking, listening to the radio, and above all trying not to nod off. If there was an Academy of Cat Finding (which there isn't, even though, I am told, there are schools that teach Management Consultancy), its syllabus would be dominated by lessons in How Not To Nod Off. Not nodding off is vital.

I don't think I'd been asleep for longer than a few minutes – there'd have been more drool on my collar if I had been – when the noise of a vehicle turning into the quiet street woke me. I shook my head, relit my cigarette and turned off the radio all in one movement.

A few doors up the road, a small delivery van had parked in front of a semi-detached house. There were no lights on inside the house, but there was a porch light by which I was able to watch as a tall, frizzy-haired woman in a baggy T-shirt and cheesecloth trousers got out of the driving seat and walked round to unlock the back doors. Bit late for parcel post, I thought.

I could tell that the van's cargo space was fully packed, but I couldn't make out what it was packed with until the frizzy-haired woman began, very calmly and methodically and above all quietly, to unload one hundred and one identical plastic garden gnomes.

Yes, I counted them. I think you would have too, if you'd been there.

The gnomes were moulded in such a way that they appeared to be engaging in that activity known to rugby players and Young Conservatives as "mooning". The woman carried them one by one from the van to the lawn of the semi. There she took a moment to arrange each one just so, occasionally standing back to enlist the services of perspective and then making a slight adjustment to one gnome or another. She obviously hadn't seen me, my darkened car just one among several that lined the street.

When she ran out of lawn, she started filling up the tarmac drive. It didn't take her as long to unload and meticulously arrange one hundred and one mooning gnomes as it would surely have taken me, but then she was in better shape than I was – and besides, I got the impression that she'd done this kind of thing before. There was a graceful efficiency to her work which could only have come from experience in the field, not merely from dusty lectures at the Academy of Gnome Placement.

When all the gnomes were in position she gave them one final inspection, during which one of the gnomes almost slipped from her grasp; she was wearing gloves, and there was a light drizzle falling. She removed her gloves, completed her fine-tuning, and then she got back in her van and drove off. Very quietly.

If Tiger wanted catching that night, he was out of luck. The ambient light reflecting off one hundred and one pairs of shiny plastic buttocks, all of which were pointing in my direction, was almost blinding. Frankly, even if I had been able to see properly, I wouldn't have been able to concentrate on lost Tigers. There is – and you'll probably have to take my word for this – something fundamentally distracting about the sight of two hundred and two plastic buttocks, gleaming by night in an otherwise torpid suburb. It sounds crazy, I know, but I didn't feel quite safe taking my eyes off them.

Long before dawn, I dashed out of the sanctuary of my car, scooped up my (still empty) cat trap, and drove home – one eye on the rear-view mirror until I was well clear of Buttockland.

I got about three hours sleep before a hammering on my door had me vertical again.

As I battled my way into the perforated rag that serves as my dressing-gown, I was feeling about as happy as a man whose girlfriend leaves him for someone taller two minutes before the four-minute warning. For a start, my guts were still reacting to whatever it was I'd eaten three days ago that had decided to eat me back. For a continuation, what little sleep I had managed had been punctured by nightmares involving tiny plastic men with white beards and luminous bottoms.

And for a finish, I have a doorbell, but my visitor evidently preferred to apply fist to wood rather than finger to button. In my experience, people who hammer on doors rather than ring bells do so because they consider bell-ringing insufficiently macho.

Sure enough, standing on my doorstep on that crisp autumn morn were two uniformed police constables. One short and spindly, the other short and lumpy. Both female.

We did the usual introductory dance, where the cops pretend to ask for permission to enter the citizen's premises, and the citizen pretends he'd be delighted to grant it. One day I'm going to say *No*, just to see what happens. When I get out of hospital I'll let you know.

I made us all a cup of tea because that's the sort of gent I am (the sort that sucks up to coppers, to put it bluntly), and two of us dug into the ginger biscuits (the spindly officer was on a diet, of course). I was the only one smoking. I don't usually smoke before breakfast, but then I don't usually entertain officers of the law in my kitchen before breakfast, either.

"Hibiscus Lane? Yes, I was there last night from about midnight until four, quarter past. Has there been a complaint?" I could only suppose that some insomniac resident had phoned my number plate into the police, wondering why a tubby, dishevelled man of middle years would spend four hours sitting outside a suburban house in a car that looked as if it had been bought from a scrapyard *after* it had gone through the crusher.

"Can I ask what you were doing there, sir?" said the lumpy one.

"Certainly," I said, and I told her all about it. Well, not *all* about it. I told her about being a cat-finder, and about how I'd been hired by Tiger's owner, and about how I hadn't yet found Tiger. But I didn't tell her about how it felt to be nearly fifty years old and to live in a dump and to drive a wreck and to find cats for a living. I didn't think she'd be interested, and *I* definitely wasn't.

"And I don't suppose you saw anything interesting at all, sir? Anything out of the usual?"

Plastic buttocks filled my mind.

"Is that a trick question?" I asked.

"Why would you think it might be a trick question?"

"Because of what I saw."

The lumpy one smiled. "Well, if it was a trick question, it worked, didn't it?" She had quite a pleasant smile, really, for all that her jaws were more muscular than is generally considered chic. So I told her about the gnomes.

The spindly one stopped writing in her notebook. "You actually saw them arrive?"

I shuddered. "I prefer to say I saw them *delivered*," I said. "It sounds more passive, somehow." I gave them a description of the van, and of the woman with the frizzy hair. They didn't ask for a description of the gnomes, for which I was grateful.

"You didn't get a reg number for the van?"

"Sorry. The light was poor." *And the buttocks were gleaming*, I didn't add.

That seemed to be that, so I showed the two policewomen to the door. They could have found it on their own, most likely, what with their special training and the fact that my flat only consists of one and half rooms, but manners is manners. Just as we reached the door – it was precisely where I'd left it, so no problem there – my brains began to hum a little, the way a brain will if you give it enough tea, tobacco and ginger biscuits, and I asked the obvious question.

"How come there's a police interest in this matter, anyway? Were the gnomes stolen? Does Hibiscus Lane harbour the capital's only specialist receiver of knocked-off gnomes?"

A small glance passed between the officers, accompanied on its journey by a slight shake of the head and a minor shrug. When the various tics had run their course, the lumpy cop said: "I don't know about you, sir, but some people – call them fuddy-duddy if you will – when they wake up in the morning to find one hundred and one mooning gnomes in their front garden which weren't there went they went to bed . . . well, they tend to search for answers. Thanks for the tea."

Which didn't answer the question of why the police took gnome-dumping seriously enough to send two short constables, one lumpy and one spindly, to interview a witness at breakfast-time.

Still, never mind, I thought, and went back to bed.

We were sitting in John the Ratman's car when the fire started, which was just as well since he – sensible public employee that he is – keeps a fire extinguisher in his car, whereas all I keep in my car in my ancient briefcase and all I keep in my briefcase is a notebook and a pair of socks.

John's a very big man – I used to think he was huge, but then he shaved off his beard for charity and I realized that underneath it he was merely very big – but he was out of the motor and pounding along the pavement towards the flames before the flash had faded from my eyes.

I exited the vehicle, too (albeit rather more slowly), because I discovered that I couldn't get my mobile phone out of my trouser pocket whilst in a sitting position, no matter how I wriggled. I hit the treble nine, and asked for fire brigade, ambulance and police, in that order. And then I took a moment off from my heroic labours to do some wondering about the people in Number Eleven, Hibiscus Lane – Tiger's owners.

Earlier that evening, I'd called on Mr and Mrs Perry to tell them of my progress in recovering their cat, and to tell it in such a way that they would continue to employ me. This didn't involve lying, so much as presenting failure in a favourable light. Yes, there *is* a difference; leading philosophers are agreed.

"So, in conclusion," I told them, sitting on a sofa that was covered with plastic wrap and squeaked every time I moved, "there is no specific news as yet, but I have every reason to believe that we may be approaching a breakthrough."

Mr and Mrs Perry sat opposite me on stiff armchairs. "Well," said Mr Perry, "that's all most unsatisfactory."

"Yes, it is," I agreed. Agreeing with the client is rarely a mistake. "But I am most hopeful that within a day or two—"

"Yes, we've heard all that," Mrs Perry interrupted. I smiled tightly this time, unable to force another agreement through my lips.

I didn't much take to the Perrys. They were about ten years older than me, short and round, dressed in identical dung-coloured slacks and oatmeal cardigans. You could tell them apart quite easily because he was bald, whereas she just looked like she ought to be. They struck me as the type of suburbanites who never smiled because they believed that smiling was a mark of frivolity, or low origins, or both. I pitied any cat that lived with them, and didn't blame Tiger at all for running away, if that was what he'd done. The Perrys were clearly unhappy not to know the present whereabouts of something they owned, but I doubted if they missed the cat, as a cat.

My empty pockets, however, ensured that my manners were good. I hadn't had an earning result in a fortnight, and the rent was due – by which I mean, it was so overdue that even an experienced rent-dodger like me was beginning to get embarrassed. I do occasionally charge clients up front, under very specific circumstances (specifically, when I think I can get away with it), but usually I'm paid on results. Or, of course, *not* paid on non-results.

I needed the Perrys, in short, and I needed their Tiger.

"You haven't had any further thoughts about where Tiger might have gone?" I asked, not because it was a sensible question but just because I felt like slipping the onus onto their shoulders. Imagine my surprise when the reply I received was more elaborate than the irritable denial I'd anticipated.

"We now believe the cat was stolen," said Mrs Perry.

"Oh?" I said.

"By our enemies," said Mr Perry.

"Enemies?" I said, struggling to prevent my eyebrows from cocking sceptically. *Enemies* is not a word people use much in everyday conversation. "Which enemies did you have in mind?" I asked, hoping that didn't sound as if I was suggesting that they had plenty to choose from.

"The people at Number Seventeen," said Mr Perry. It wasn't actually his turn to speak, but I was too distracted to reprimand him. Number Seventeen was the gnome house.

"And that is all we are going to say on the matter. It is a private matter," said Mrs Perry, in a tone which rebuked me for raising the sordid business in the first place.

By the time I returned to Hibiscus Lane that night, to relieve John the Ratman, I was feeling pretty sorry for myself. The way I saw it, either the "enemies" really had stolen Tiger, in which case the poor creature would be long gone; or else the Perrys were paranoid, in which case I'd got myself involved with exactly the sort of nutty, unpredictable folk that I do my best to avoid.

"My primary school teacher," said John, after I'd told him about the gnomes, the police and the Enemies, "used to tell me that when I was feeling sorry for myself, I should just remember how much worse off so many other people are."

"I never understood the logic of that," I said. "If the world's full of people who are worse off than me, all that proves is that I haven't yet reached rock bottom. The worst is yet to come."

That was as far as our Socratic debate got, because at that moment a motorbike screeched into the street, pausing outside Number Seventeen just long enough for its dark-visored, black-leathered rider to pull a beer bottle out of a saddlebag, wave a lighter over the rag sticking out of its neck, and hurl the bottle at the semi's front door.

"Molotov!" John shouted, and for a moment I thought maybe he was employing some obscure rhyming slang for "Good heavens, will you look at that!" Then I realized what he meant: someone had just firebombed Mr and Mrs Perry's Enemies.

Partly thanks to John the Ratman and his Boy Scout fire extinguisher, and largely due to the biker's poor aim, the damage to the house was minor – some scorched paintwork, and a box full of newspapers which weren't going to need recycling after all. The damage to the people who lived there was more significant: that was immediately obvious from their faces, as they stood on their charred doorstep, staring out at a world which had suddenly decided it couldn't be bothered to make sense any more.

The first thing I noticed about them was that the man was wearing a woman's dressing-gown, and the woman was wearing a man's. They looked ridiculous and traumatized in equal measures, which was no surprise to me. I long ago discovered that horror and absurdity tour the universe as a double act.

"This is Roy and Tina Walton," said John, who'd sat the Waltons down in their living room with a cup of tea, while they waited for the sirens to arrive. "This is Charlie, my mate. He's looking for a lost cat."

I shook hands with Roy. Tina's hands weren't available for shaking, as she was sitting on them. She sat on them very hard, but even so the trembling was sufficiently violent that the sofa she and Roy were perched on was steadily moving towards the kitchen at a rate of about an inch every three minutes, like one of those coastal villages they show on TV, slowly slipping into the sea.

I sat down on an astonishingly uncomfortable director's chair, and accepted a mug of tea from John. I didn't know what to say. John would already have done all the *Is everyone*

OK? stuff and the *We've phoned 999, they're on their way* bit,
and not forgetting the indispensable *Don't worry, it was probably just kids* routine. I didn't feel I could add anything. I smiled
at Roy, and sipped my tea. I sipped my tea and smiled at Tina,
but she didn't see, she was too busy trying to keep her teeth still,
so that was a smile wasted. I wondered who they thought we
were, John and I. First your house gets Molotoved, then there
are two complete strangers sitting in your front room uninvited
and asking you if you'd like a biscuit with your tea.

"Cat?" said Roy. He spoke with the abrupt randomness of a
host who realizes he's allowed a silence to mature beyond what
is considered nice.

"Sorry?"

"Your friend said you were looking for a lost cat?"

"Oh, that's right. Tiger."

"You're looking for a *tiger?*"

I don't claim to be a Professor of Tact, but somehow I
intuited that laughing in firebombed houses was not likely to
be recommended in any of the leading manuals. So I didn't
laugh. I coughed. "No, the cat's name is Tiger. He's a striped
tabby. You might know him, in fact – he lives with Mr and Mrs
Perry. At Number Eleven."

Even given the distracting circumstances, it seemed to me
that Roy's uninterested shrug was not the reaction you'd get
from a full-blooded Enemy. But, just to make sure, I said: "You
don't know them? The Perrys? They're short and round and
they wear matching cardigans."

"Don't really know anyone in the street," said Roy. "We've
not been here long."

"Won't be here much longer," said Tina. It was the first
thing she'd said since I got there, and the surprise of hearing her
own voice seemed to levitate her off the sofa and into the hall. I
heard her open her front door, and at the same time I heard the
sirens turning the corner into Hibiscus Lane. I don't know
whether she had better hearing than me, and that was why she'd
got up at that precise moment, or whether it was simply that
when your world's on fire, what's the point of sitting down?
What's the point of staying indoors?

⋆   ⋆   ⋆

We gave our statements, and then John took me to a place he knew, an all-night vegetarian, organic, wholemeal, ying-yang, health-food bar that sold booze illegally, under the counter, to favoured customers, where we feasted on a half bottle of Scotch and two bowls of nine-bean stew. I made the obvious crack about it being pretty expensive for a stew with only nine beans in it, and the waitress – who was either very po-faced or very tired or both – explained that the stew contained nine *varieties* of bean, and John made an "I can't take you anywhere" face at me, and I told the waitress that, thanks, that sounded fine.

And we discussed what John insisted on calling "The Case"; that is, the matter of Tiger, the cheeky gnomes, and the neighbourly feud that one set of purported feuders seemed not to know about.

"I believed Roy when he said they didn't know the Perrys."

John nodded. "Absolutely. They're definitely having trouble with someone, mind. Before you got there, Roy was babbling about *first the phone calls and now this*."

"Which explains why the police followed up the gnome-dumping episode. It wasn't an isolated incident."

John chased some beans down his throat with a gulp of naked whisky. Actually, it wasn't a bad combination, and it seemed, improbably enough, to be settling my stomach. "Yeah. But how do you have a one-sided feud?"

I put down my fork and picked up my glass. Beans may be good for the bones, but booze is best for feeding your thoughts. Well, it is for *my* thoughts, anyway.

At the beginning, I'd assumed that Tiger had been scared by a car or a mouse, and got himself slightly lost. Because that's the usual pattern in the cat-finding racket. Then, after the Perrys had told me about their Enemies, I'd thought that the Waltons had kidnapped Tiger, as a part of an ongoing war of neighbourly attrition. Now I was back to seeing the cat as a simple stray, but with the added complication of the one-sided feud.

Ah, shit – enough for one night. "Drink up, John," I said, refilling both glasses. "We'll get a taxi back."

I couldn't afford to pay John the Ratman for his help with cat-finding, except in the IOUs of long-term friendship, so I paid for the meal and the booze and the taxi. The rent could wait. I've learned depressingly few lessons in life, but I've learned this one: when paying the rent starts taking precedence over feeding your friends, you're in terminal trouble.

I managed about half an hour's sleep this time, before the banging at the door woke me. When the bangers turned out not to be rent collectors, I was almost pleased to see them.

"Come in, officers. I'll put the kettle on."

Two detectives, this time, a man and a woman. This pair weren't interested in garden gnomes, they wanted to talk about cats. So I went through the familiar humiliation yet again, of explaining to strangers what I did for a living.

"You've got all this in my previous two statements. What makes it interesting enough to hear thrice?"

"The Waltons received a threatening phone call in the early hours of this morning," the female DC said. "The anonymous female caller made reference to a missing cat, which she alleged had been killed by Mr and Mrs Walton. She implied that the firebombing incident was by way of a revenge attack – and that there was more to come."

I lit a cigarette, taking my time over it, to hide the confusion that would otherwise have been clear on my face. Detective constables tend to be emotionally dyslexic, quite capable of confusing confusion with collusion. "Well, that can't be anything to do with the cat I'm looking for. Tiger wasn't stolen, he was scared off by a kid chucking a firework." I couldn't have the cops finding Tiger before I did.

"Oh? You didn't mention that in your previous statements."

I rearranged my features to display contrition. "You're right. I should have reported it. Firework-chucking is a crime, after all. I could give a full statement now, if you'd like . . . ?"

The cops, paperwork-phobic like all their breed, left so quickly I hardly had time to ask them what had become of the gnomes.

"They've been impounded, awaiting claiming."

"Well, I hope you've got a good strong lock on that property pound," I said, which got me three funny looks – one each from the cops, and one from myself. *Get a grip, Charlie!*

*   *   *

If I had a thing about puzzles, I could get all the jigsaws I wanted, three for a quid, at the local charity shops. I prefer to spend my money on beer: I don't give a damn about puzzles.

The persecution of the Waltons, and the Perrys' belief that the Waltons were persecuting *them*, were puzzles indeed. They interested me, however, only as potential clues to the whereabouts of Tiger.

I'm pretty good at finding cats, provided they're easy to find. Which they usually are. The fact that, after several days of looking, I'd found not the vaguest sign of Tiger, suggested to me that the abduction theory – so beloved of distraught pet owners – had, for once, to be taken seriously.

I found the Waltons scrubbing ash marks from their stoop. I hadn't time for much in the way of niceties, so I asked them straight out: "You've told me that you don't know the Perrys, and you know nothing about their cat. Are you absolutely sure that's true? Because if it's not, nobody needs to know anything about it except you and me."

Roy looked puzzled, as if he was trying to place me among the many strangers he'd briefly met in the last twenty-four hours. Tina, by contrast, had done some of that pulling-herself-together that women specialize in. Her hair was tied back in a rubber band, her face was protectively made-up. Her slacks and shoes were so sensible they could have got jobs as road safety officers.

"No," she said. "We've never met them, we know nothing about their cat, and we're not likely to get to know them or their cat, as we will be moving out of here as soon as we can. That does answer your question, I trust?"

I told them I was sorry to have disturbed them, and that I wished them well for the future. I don't suppose they believed the former, or cared about the latter.

My question to the Perrys was a simple one but had to be phrased carefully to avoid raising their prickles. After silently rehearsing several options, I went with: "What first alerted you to the fact that the people at Number Seventeen had it in for you?"

"Our daughter," said Mrs Perry, in an irritated tone, as if

telling me something I should already have known. "She holds a senior position in the corporate hospitality industry."

"Ah," I said, as if I knew what that meant, or as if I gave a toss, neither of which was true.

"Our front hedge was vandalized," said Mr Perry. "With weedkiller. Jennifer, our daughter, was visiting us the following day, and she happened to see a can of weedkiller in Number Seventeen's garage. She wasn't prying, the door was open."

"And Tiger?"

"Shortly after the cat disappeared, Jennifer saw the people from Number Seventeen in Sainbury's, buying cat food," said Mrs Perry.

"And cat litter," said Mr Perry.

"Right," I said. "Cat litter. Well, yes, that's pretty conclusive. I think I'd better speak to Jennifer. May I have her phone number, please? If it's not too much trouble," I added, which would have been overdoing it with normal people, but these weren't normal people. They lived in the suburbs and wore matching cardigans.

"Hello, Jennifer's Japes, Jennifer speaking, how may I help you?"

Sometimes I am *so* slow. But I don't torture myself about it: I'm a middle-aged, somewhat tubby, balding cat-finder with no trade to fall back on, no education to speak of, and more old blues LPs in my bedsit than I've got pounds in the bank. Why wouldn't I be slow? Besides, where did being fast ever get anyone, except first in line when they're calling for volunteers?

Jennifer's Japes: a senior position in the corporate hospitality industry. Right, yeah, I see. OK, now: gently does it.

"Hi, Jennifer, great to connect with you. Here's the thing – my name's Charlie, I heard about you from a guy I got talking to in a wine bar in the City a while back, and right now I'm looking to put the finishing touches to a bit of a corporate hospitality bash type of thingy we're throwing. Or holding, or whatever."

"Charlie, great, that's cool. Terrific to link up with you too!" She didn't sound like she knew how to do the jargon any better than I did. "So, what kind of sector exactly are you in?"

"Oh, you know, it's the . . . you know, corporate sector."

She laughed, without comprehension. "OK, sure. Well, prices start with, say, a garage full of helium balloons at fifty pounds plus VAT, but my guess is you're looking for something a bit more special, right?"

"Special," I said. "Definitely. Look – how about this? Can we get together, run the options through my wetware? Maybe over a glass of red?"

She turned up at the wine bar ten minutes late, and then spent another couple of minutes studying all the faces in the place trying to figure out which one she was supposed to be meeting. Eventually I put her out of her misery; it's a fair bet she'd never have picked me out unaided.

"Hi, I'm Charlie."

"Oh," she said. "Really?"

"Yes, for sure," I said. "Let me put that somewhere for you." I took her crash helmet and stowed it under a spare chair. We shook hands, we sat, we ordered.

"I was thinking maybe garden gnomes," I said.

Jennifer nodded. "Gnomes we can do."

"I saw some just recently, in a place called Hibiscus Lane. I don't suppose they were yours, by any chance?"

She put her glass down carefully. "I'm afraid I can't discuss that. Client confidentiality, you understand."

I made a mental note to look up the word "client" in a good dictionary and find out whether it could conceivably be stretched to include a customer who pays you to put gnomes on someone's garden. Then I mentally scrumpled up the note and chucked it in my mental waste paper basket because I'd got enough to think about without making more work for myself.

"Of course, in that particular case, the client was yourself, wasn't it?"

She got up to leave. "The police have some of it," I said. "They don't have all of it." She sat down again. She ruffled her frizzy hair with long, nervous fingers.

"Drink your wine," I said. "And tell me about it."

It all came down to money, naturally; it usually does. Jennifer's Japes – supplier of customized practical jokes to people with more money than sense of humour – needed an injection of capital. The banks weren't sympathetic, so Jennifer Perry

turned to Mum and Dad. They weren't particularly sympathetic either, but more to the point they didn't have the funds:
not in liquid form, anyway.

"But if they sell the house in Hibiscus Lane, and move out of
London to somewhere cheaper, the way they're always saying
they'd like to – well, with their bank account sloshing with
liquidated assets, I don't think they'd have the nerve to turn me
down again."

I could believe it. That frizzy hair was enough to intimidate
anyone, with or without the motorbike leathers. But if she
wanted to drive the Perrys out, why not persecute them, instead
of Roy and Tina?

"Easier," she shrugged. "Safer. I've never lived in Hibiscus
Lane, I don't visit that often. None of the neighbours would
know who I was, even if they saw me. I chose the people at
Number Seventeen because they were new to the area. My
parents are predisposed to mistrust anyone they haven't known
for at least ten years." She chewed a mouthful of wine. "And
anyone they *have* known for ten years, come to that."

"Even so, mightn't your parents wonder why a pair of
complete strangers had suddenly become their deadly enemies?"

"No chance! All I had to do was sow the seed, and let middle-
class suburban paranoia do the rest."

I knew what she meant. Through no choice of my own, I've
spent half my adult life in the suburbs. Emphasis on *spent*, not
on *life*. But surely the people most likely to sell up and move on
were the Waltons, not the Perrys?

"Doesn't matter," she said, casually. "The point about my
parents is that they would rather die than risk a fuss. Either
they'd move, or the neighbours would move, and everyone
would know it was because of a feud with the Perrys . . ."

"In which case they'd have to move anyway, to avoid being
shown up. Nice plan." It was, too, in its way. A fireman once
told me that the main avoidable cause of death during fires in
public places was a lack of panic, caused by fear of "making a
fuss". Statistics show that crass people like me have the longest
life expectancy. And if you don't like that, you can shove it up
your arse.

"So, Charlie – or whatever your name is—"

"It's Charlie," I said.

"Well, whatever it is—"

"It's Charlie!"

"OK, Jesus! *Charlie* – what is your interest in all this? You're not a cop."

"You're facing some pretty heavy charges here, Jennifer. Vandalism, issuing threats, using a firebomb—"

"Firebomb!" she sneered. "A beer bottle with a splash of petrol in it. Hardly Hiroshima, was it?"

"But none of that matters to me," I continued. "My concern is Tiger."

"The cat? What are you, some kind of cat lover?"

"Some kind," I agreed. "Tiger's still alive, right?"

"Yeah, unfortunately. I couldn't think of a way of killing it that wasn't yucky."

"My car's in the car park here. We'll drive to your place, I'll collect the cat, and return it your parents."

"And then you forget all about me? How do I know I can trust you?"

I ignored that with the contempt it deserved. She couldn't trust me, and we both knew it. But she had nothing to lose by playing it this way, and her freedom to gain. Potentially.

But that which is potential is not necessarily actual. A potential fee for cat-finding, for instance, would, I felt, be unlikely to become concrete, if the cat-finder in question were to attempt its collection after, rather than before, shopping the cat's owners' daughter to the law.

Call me an old sentimentalist, but I do love a happy ending. I returned Tiger to the Perrys, graciously accepted an ungraciously presented cheque, and then drove straight to the local cop shop to make a statement detailing everything I knew about Jennifer and her Japes. Including a detail which they found particularly interesting: that I'd seen her take her gloves off when she was making final adjustments to the gnomes on the Waltons' lawn. One print on its own wouldn't be enough to convict her, but it was enough to warrant a forensic examination of Jennifer's home, van, bike and clothes.

Tiger didn't stay home for long. The first time the Perrys let him out of the house again, he ran straight into a humane trap being monitored by my friend, the vegetarian rat-catcher.

"What an amazing coincidence," I said, when John came round to tell me about his newly acquired pet.

"Amazing," he agreed. "I only had the trap out for five nights before the coincidence amazingly happened."

"Going to be a bit embarrassing if the Perrys hire me to find him again."

"They won't," said John, prophetically. "They'll be glad to be shot of the poor, unloved little sod."

I never did find out what happened to the gnomes. I hoped their horrible little shiny bottoms were incinerated or buried in an environmentally unfriendly landfill. I couldn't bear to think they might still be out there somewhere, mooning, looming, buttocks gleaming, shambling across the front lawns of suburbia like tiny zombie-vampires in search of prey.

And then I had a comforting thought: they wouldn't get very far, the shape they were in – kneeling over like that, with their trousers round their ankles. Apart from anything, they wouldn't be able to see where they were going.

Phew, I thought. In this world of worries, at least that's *one* less thing to worry about.

THE LAST SNOW-FLAKE
IN TEXAS

LIZ EVANS

"These."

Carole hooked the single strand of pearls from the velvet pad with one finger. The gesture was almost arrogant. But that was in character. Money, she'd discovered, meant never having to say "please" or "thank you". And at present, the less she said, the better.

The jeweller smiled. "An excellent choice, madam."

She knew he'd have used the same compliment whatever she'd chosen. Money also meant you had perfect taste – no matter how bizarre it was. But in this case he was quite right, she thought complacently. The length of perfectly matched creamy orbs were superb. She'd always had a feel for stylish living, but not the money to fund it – until now.

She extended her platinum credit card. The jeweller held it up, placed it in the card swipe, and started sorting out a case for the necklace, making a meal of finding the right holder for it. Carole watched the pantomime calmly. She was well aware that the security camera had fed the details of the card to another assistant in the back who would even now be phoning the credit company to confirm the amount of the transaction. This wasn't the kind of shop where they queried their clients' creditworthiness openly.

She examined her own reflection in the mirrored wall behind the counter. Everything she had on, from the suit to the accessories, was this year's designer chic. Even the smoked glasses that hid half her face were Armani. How could anyone doubt she could afford the five thousand plus on the pearl's price tag?

The phone at the assistant's elbow buzzed three times. He swiped her card, laying the payment slip on a leather blotter and presenting her with a pen. Shaking her head, Carole removed a Mont Blanc pen from her bag. The calf leather gloves made holding it slightly awkward, but she signed with a confident flourish: *Dallie Eisenberg-Mansotti.* Forgery had always come easily to her.

Slipping the package, in the jeweller's famous trademark packaging, into her handbag, Carole glanced at her – or rather Dallie's – gold watch. It was only three o'clock – plenty of time for a little refreshment and relaxation.

On the Continent she generally ended these expeditions with a coffee or cocktail at the sleekest pavement café in the district. It wasn't simply greed – there was also the need to stay in character. Dallie wouldn't be seen dead in a back-street workman's bar, so neither could Carole. Since they were in London, it seemed appropriate to go with the local customs and treat herself to an over-priced afternoon tea.

Selecting the most expensive hotel in the area – and one that the Mansottis had never chosen to stay in – she sank into a chair and gave her order to the waiter. Leaning back with a sigh of satisfaction, she savoured the soothing unobtrusive service that high prices and the promise of large tips invariably brought. Dallie's session at the beauty salon was scheduled to last until five o'clock; that meant she had at least another hour before she needed to return the clothes and accessories to her employer's hotel suite.

Probably more, she thought, wriggling back into the comfortable seating and slipping off the tinted glasses. If there was one thing Dallie loved it was pampering; she must have got through every massage technique, body oil, skin treatment, wonder-cream and supposedly sure-fire slimming fad known to woman. Dallie's body had, Carole reflected, seen more shrink-wrapping than the meat counter at Sainsburys. She'd be lost for hours, coming back with armfuls of products she'd only use once and bagfuls of expensive make-up that would be tossed into the garbage because it looked different now she'd got it back to the hotel suite.

Previously Carole's jobs had only provided the opportunities for a little petty pilfering: purses left in unguarded bags and wallets in discarded jackets. However, this position, as the social secretary to a young American couple touring Europe, was an absolute joy.

The Mansottis had been impressed by her references. And so they should be; she'd put some of her best work into them. She'd trawled up-market magazines and newspapers, selecting former "employers" who were travelling themselves, gambling that when they proved difficult to contact, the Mansottis wouldn't bother to check her references too thoroughly. As it turned out, they hadn't bothered to check them at all. Dallie had engaged her on the spot when it became clear Carole had the two qualities she required in an employee – the ability to pick up endlessly after Dallie and the willingness to sympathize with the real and imagined problems in Dallie's pampered existence.

"I'm all alone in the world," she'd informed Carole. "Except for my darling Jack, of course." She'd exchanged a blown kiss with the young man lounging at the far side of the luxury hotel suite.

Carole had made the right sympathetic noises. Needlessly probably. Dallie rarely heard any voice but her own.

"My family all died in two years of each other," she continued. "Great Uncle Toby started it. Why, he just keeled right over one fine morning in Galveston. It was like he started off one of those snowballs rolling down a mountain."

"They have snow in Texas?" Carole had asked, thinking she must have misheard.

Dallie squealed with laughter. "No! I mean it was like his dying nudged a little pile of snow down the slope and it just kept right on going, getting bigger and bigger, and rolling clean over my whole darn family, sucking 'em in as it went. It was no more than six months later my granddaddy died. He was cold before he hit the floor, they reckon. After that it was Uncle Cole,

Auntie Jacqueline-May, Auntie Ruth-Ellen, Auntie Beatrix, Uncle Bo, my daddy and my mama . . ."

When the Texan snowball had rolled to a standstill, it had gathered up the whole of the Eisenberg clan inside its icy interior and deposited the family's collective fortunes in a Trust Fund marked for the sole use of the last little snow-flake in the family: Dallie.

"But, heck, eighty million dollars ain't that much these days, is it?" Dallie shrugged.

Carole had nodded wordlessly, stunned into silence partly by the idea of anyone dismissing eighty million dollars, but mostly by Dallie's voice. The woman had the ugliest, harshest, voice she had ever heard.

Carole had taken the job with the idea of luxury living coupled with the chance for a little light thieving in the five-star hotels that the Mansottis would undoubtedly be travelling between. It wasn't until Rome that the idea for bigger prizes had dawned on her.

Dallie had bought an evening dress. A distinctive model in red with gold trimming. It made her look like a tawdry Christmas cracker.

"Why, isn't it just unforgettable?" she trilled, twirling in front of the hotel mirror.

It was indeed. But it seemed Dallie had managed to forget the identical model that she'd bought in Milan two weeks earlier.

Jack had made the mistake of pointing out the oversight.

"It's my money and I'll spend it on anything I darn well please," Dallie had snapped.

"Sure, honey. But if you've already got the damn dress . . ."

"I haven't. I *haven't*." Dallie stamped her foot. A pout Carole had rapidly become familiar with turned down the corners of her mouth. "Tell him, Carole. Just tell him right now, that I have not bought this *exclusive* gown before."

Carole had told him. Dallie signed her pay cheques.

By then she'd had plenty of time to experience Dallie's casual attitude to accounting. Dallie spent cash like she'd heard it was going out of fashion next week. The price tag was never a consideration. After three months Carole had already arranged for a dozen crates of clothes, furniture, antiques, paintings, silverwear, jewellery and ceramics to be shipped back into storage in the States. Better still, Dallie had no idea of keeping check of her expenditure. She threw the flimsy copies of credit slips into the rubbish bins; left receipts carelessly strewn around hotel suites, and ripped bank statements up after a casual glance. A few items had already gone "missing" en-route, but unfortunately Dallie's taste tended to match her voice – it was unremittingly ghastly. Which meant the resale value of the diverted goods wasn't as high as it might be.

Now Carole started to notice how often Dallie bought near-identical articles: thirty pairs of gold earrings; half a dozen watches by the same Swiss designer; a painting she'd admired in Paris . . . and Vienna . . . and Berlin. The Mansottis were due to go home in a few months. If she was going to take full advantage of this once in a lifetime opportunity she had to act fast.

She was the same build and height as Dallie. And with the aid of a blonde wig cut into the straight bob favoured by the American woman and a close study of Dallie's walk and mannerisms, she found that she could do a very fair impersonation of her employer.

After a couple of weeks, she'd got the act to near perfect, apart from two details that she simply couldn't do anything about. One was that damn voice. Try as she might, she couldn't get anywhere near that harsh, unflattering screech. The first time she'd walked out of the hotel dressed as Dallie, it hadn't mattered. Her heart was hammering so loudly in her ears and her throat was so dry, that she couldn't have answered the doorman's "Bonjour, Madame Mansotti" to save her life.

She'd kept the talking to a minimum in the jeweller's shop in Montmartre, pointing and arrogantly snapping her fingers as she'd indicated the rings she wanted to be shown. It had gone like a dream. Twenty minutes later she was on the pavement with a two-carat diamond mounted in white gold.

After that she'd developed a regular routine; shopping for small, easily carried jewellery and antiques that would be easy to resell when this goldmine of a job came to an end. And always ensuring that they were the sort – if not the style – of items that Dallie herself had been buying recently. If anyone checked up all they'd find was a description and a security film of

Dallie-the-ditzhead – who couldn't remember what the hell she'd bought from one town to the next.

Fortunately Dallie loved London, which meant they made regular trips through Heathrow, enabling Carole to visit her cousin Marty's bungalow in Slough and add to the growing stash in the concealed hole under his garage floor. She was sure Marty wouldn't have minded if he'd known. But since Marty was currently doing a three-stretch in one of Her Majesty's B & Bs, it didn't seem worth bothering him with the details.

The waiter slid a tray loaded with silver pots and bone china on to a small table at her elbow. "Will there be anything else, madam?"

She shook her head and waved him away before peeling off her gloves. This was the other flaw in her impersonation. Nature had given Dallie beautiful hands – perhaps it was compensation for that dreadful voice. Carole's, on the other hand – on both hands in fact – had large red knuckles, dry skin and nails chewed to the quick. Initially she'd tried to disguise them with stick-on nails during her shopping trips, but it hadn't helped. There was no way her knobbly, large-boned fingers could ever pass for Dallie's model-girl hands. In the end, she'd taken care to keep her gloves on during these impersonations unless it was absolutely necessary to remove them, like now. She reached out for the delicate bone china milk jug.

Suddenly someone spoke in her ear. "Hi, honey. Finished at the beauty parlour already?"

Carole froze. Jack Mansotti was supposed to be on a golf course in Berkshire all day. What on earth was he doing in this hotel?

"Just dropped my partner off here; he had to come back for an urgent meeting," Jack continued, answering her unspoken question.

Carole remained leaning over the table, the blonde wig concealing her face.

Puzzled by her lack of reaction, Jack reached forward and lifted a strand of hair. "Hey, anybody in there?" he joked, then he whistled. "Well, I'll be damned, Carole!"

Her bag was wide open on the table, the jeweller's distinctive package in clear view. Jack drew it out. The credit card receipt was caught in the folds of paper. He examined them both wordlessly.

Finally he looked up. "Pretty good forgery. I'm impressed." He put the slip in his pocket and handed the pearls to her. "Suppose you keep these and you and me have a little talk. I think we could do a lot for each other."

Carole hesitated. She'd written him off months ago as a gold-digging himbo – prepared to shake his ass in return for Dallie picking up the bills. But he really wasn't a bad-looking bloke – and if that's what it took to keep this scam going until Dallie flew home . . . He must have read what she was thinking in her eyes.

"No, honey. Not that. I have something else in mind. We'll discuss it later. Let's have tea, shall we? Mr and Mrs Mansotti enjoying the local hospitality."

He'd made her play the whole charade – pouring tea, nibbling at the sandwich and cake selection that the hotel provided, calling over the waiter for more hot water. And all the time watching her like a cat that had spotted a mouse with a compound fracture in its back leg. Eventually he'd paid the bill with the sort of casual charm that had hooked him a walking expense account and seen her to the door.

They'd returned to their own hotel separately. Carole had barely managed to get Dallie's outfit back into the wardrobe before the woman herself burst into the suite with a member of the beauty salon in tow.

"Carole!" she screeched. "Meet Rosita."

Carole smiled at the olive-skinned girl, who was looking around the suite with wide, assessing brown eyes.

"Rosita is the most *divine* nail technician *ever*. Will you just look at these?" Dallie flashed long silver nails, each decorated with a tiny gold palm tree. "Isn't that just the cutest thing you ever saw? And you'll just never guess? Rosita has folks in the States and she's going visiting. Now where's my address book?" Drawers and cupboards were turned carelessly on to the carpet in a jumble that someone else would have to clear up. "I've just gotta jot down all the places she has got to shop . . . I mean, these places, they've got clothes you will just *kill* for, Rosita . . ."

Killing was what Jack had in mind too. His suggestion was simple. He'd kill Dallie, Carole could impersonate her, and they'd split her fortune between them.

"You're mad. We'll never get away with it," gasped Carole.

"Why not? Dallie has no relatives and no close friends. No one is really going to miss her. And your impersonation is nearly damn perfect. All we have to do is lie low for a few years until people start to forget what the real Dallie was like. It needn't be a hardship. You and me, we could be good together, Carole." He rubbed the back of his fingers down her cheek. "I'm not suggesting burying ourselves in some backwoods dump. I hear Buenos Aires is a very sophisticated city, for instance. Or Caracas. And frankly, if I have to listen to that voice for another year, I think I'll end up strangling her anyway."

She'd turned him down, shocked at the idea. Theft was one thing . . . but murder!

"Think about it," he said quietly. "And remember." He tapped his jacket pocket. The credit card receipt crackled.

He hadn't referred to the matter again, but she'd sensed him watching her. And she *had* thought about it. If the police got their hands on that forged receipt and started to trace back all those other pieces stashed under Marty's garage, she'd probably end up joining him at the Government B & B. And even if they didn't, how long would the cash from the stolen items last? She'd grown used to the millionaire lifestyle . . . did she really want to give it up . . . ?

Disposing of Dallie in such a way that there was no chance of the body ever being found proved difficult. In the end Dallie solved the problem herself by deciding to visit Western Ireland.

"Easy access to the Atlantic," Jack remarked calmly. "Deep water. The English Channel is too shallow I read. Bodies have a habit of washing up along the coast. I'll hire a motor cruiser for the weekend. Or, rather, Dallie will. Won't you, honey?" He grinned at Carole.

She'd had to stay in the cabin, gulping down large vodka and tonics, whilst Jack cut off the head and hands on deck before dropping well-weighted packages containing the remains and the blood-soaked oil-skins and tarpaulin over the side and swabbing down every inch of paintwork.

"Now it's just you and me," he'd laughed, kissing Carole triumphantly. "And eighty million dollars! I've made an appointment with the lawyers in Houston two weeks from now. That gives us time to work on the voice."

But no matter how hard she practised, Carole found it impossible to reproduce those loud, intrusive, grating tones. Her own voice was naturally soft and when she tried to raise it, it came out as a high-pitched breathy squeak.

"Do we have to go?" she asked. "Couldn't I write to them?"

Jack shook his head. "If you want to make me a joint signatory, then we both have to sign the papers in the presence of the Trustees."

"But is that necessary? I could just draw it out and give you half?"

"You can't draw on the capital, just the income. And, no offence, honey, but I'd feel better if my name's on that cheque account too. Otherwise I could just end up with you dishing out the pocket money instead of Dallie. Equal risks, equal shares: that was the deal. Don't worry, you'll be fine. They've got a hundred lawyers in that place and this one has never met Dallie. They've only spoken on the phone." He forestalled her next objection with, "I'll tell him you've got bad laryngitis. Just keep your mouth shut and we'll sail through this one."

Jack was right. The young lawyer oozed charm as he produced papers for Carole's inspection. He sympathized with her illness, even recommending his own doctor.

Jack said hastily: "That won't be necessary. We've got it in hand. Seeing a specialist. Ready, honey?"

She'd had to take her gloves off, aware of how odd it would look if she'd failed to do so before scrawling her signature. They'd dropped through to the bottom of her handbag. She was scrambling for them when Jack took her arm and steered her firmly towards the door.

"Leave it," he whispered. "Just relax. We're nearly home free."

Trying to control her shaking, Carole sauntered towards the office door. They'd nearly reached it, when the lawyer called: "Just a minute!"

Carole tensed as he hurried across to her. "They're forecasting thunderstorms. It can really come down these fall months. Take this. You don't want to get soaked. It will make your laryngitis worse." He thrust a small black folding umbrella into her hands.

She was still trembling when they reached the George Bush Intercontinental Airport.

"Hang in there," Jack urged. "We've nearly made it."

An armed policeman loomed in front of her. Carole whimpered. She looked round. There were two more ahead – cradling automatic weapons. And more across the lobby. Through the large plate glass windows there was what looked like a small army of armed officers wandering over the tarmac and between the waiting planes. There were uniforms and guns everywhere.

The icy blast of the air conditioning hit her sweating skin. She started shivering. "They know," she hissed at Jack, barely able to keep her teeth from chattering. "They're waiting for us."

"Balls," he murmured. "Don't fall apart on me now." Leaving her standing there, he walked across and spoke to one of the check-in staff. "There's a security alert on. Some terrorist threatening to spring their boss or something," he said, striding back and pulling her case from her nerveless fingers. "But it's okay. They've got it covered. And they're still flying. Come on."

He hustled her into the line for check-in.

"This isn't the First Class desk," Carole objected.

"Hey, you've really got the hang of this high living," Jack mocked her under his breath. "First is fully booked. Unless you want to wait for the next flight?"

Carole shook her head. What was twelve inches of leg-room against a lifetime in jail? They'd been issued with their boarding cards when Carole became aware of someone waving. She moaned.

"What the hell is it now?" Jack said irritably.

"That woman. It's Rosita."

"Who?"

"Dallie's flaming nail technician. From the London hotel. Oh, God, there's no way I can fool her."

Jack thrust a pass in her hand. "Ignore her. They're boarding the flight. Get on. I'll follow as soon as I've arranged for a car to collect us in Caracas. Go."

Carole obeyed, scuttling desperately through check-in and

security and into the warm safe interior of the aircraft. Struggling to get her flight bag into the overhead locker she glanced towards the door and, to her horror, saw Rosita coming down the aisle towards her. The damn woman was on this flight.

Panic-stricken, she looked for a means of escape. The aisle was full of people finding seats and stowing luggage. If she tried to push past them to the rear door she'd just draw more attention to herself. Her mind was racing. Did they have the death penalty in this state? Or would they send her back to England to spend a lifetime in jail?

The brunette advanced with a welcoming smile. If she could just get through the nice-to-see-you routine, Rosita would, no doubt, return to her own seat. Carole prepared to brazen it out.

Slipping on her tinted glasses, she picked up the safety card ready to scrawl an explanation for her lack of conversation. And saw her hands. Her gloves, she'd forgotten to put them back on. She up-ended her handbag on to the aircraft seat. A jumble of possessions fell out. The gloves, where were the damn gloves?

Rosita had nearly reached her seat. She had to speak. To divert the woman's attention from her hands to her face.

Carole licked her lips and prayed that just once she could achieve Dallie's lung-power.

Jack appeared in the aircraft doorway. Breathing deeply, Carole raised her hand and yelled a greeting. Her voice rolled around the cabin in a screech that was several decibels louder than anything Dallie had ever achieved. The last thing she saw was Jack's horrified expression as the bullet caught her in the chest.

As the aircraft security guard later explained at the inquiry: "That little black umbrella looked like a gun. Hell, what was I supposed to think when this crazy female leaps to her feet and yells at the top of her voice: HIJACK!"

A SORT OF MISS MARPLE?

H R F KEATING

The enjoyment afforded to Her Most Excellent Majesty Elizabeth the Second, by the Grace of God, of the United Kingdom of Great Britain and Northern Ireland and of Her Other Realms and Territories, Queen, Head of the Commonwealth, Defender of the Faith, Sovereign of the British Orders of Knighthood, Captain General of the Royal Regiment of Artillery, etc., etc., by the works of the writer Agatha Christie has been often recorded.

Her grandmother, indeed, the late Queen Mary, had a standing order for each new Christie title and passed on her partiality to, in turn, her daughter-in-law and her granddaughter. A younger Queen Elizabeth has been photographed extending a white-gloved hand to the author's white-gloved hand at the premiere of the film *Murder on the Orient Express*, smiling down with look of something very like complicity. While the author once said the two most exciting events of her long life were her acquiring her first car, a bottle-nosed Morris from the advance on her fourth book, and being invited to dine at Buckingham Palace.

What is not so well known – possibly because it may never have happened – is the occasion when Her Majesty took on for a

short time the very mantle of Miss Marple. It all began one late
night in the private apartments of the Palace . . .

Something over an hour after Her Majesty had gone to bed, she
woke. An intruder? Once again? Bloody revolution at the palace
gates? A usurper armed to the teeth? None of these things.
Simply the need for a pee. Even monarchs' urinary systems can
behave oddly on occasion.

A few quick steps from her at-this-time lonely bed, across the
dressing-room and into her bathroom. And there, by what
chance she never knew, her eye happened to fall on the miniature Meissen bowl into which she was accustomed as soon as
she considered herself "off duty" to put her rings, delighted in
these latter days to be able to slip them off and relieve certain
mildly arthritic twinges. And at once something about the little
bowl struck her as being wrong.

For several moments, still sleep bemused, she stood looking
at the glitter of gold and diamonds in the tiny piece of Meissen.
Then she realized. Her wedding ring was not there among the
others.

She glanced at her hand. No, quite unadorned. She looked all
round the bathroom. Could she, in a moment of forgetfulness,
have put that ring down somewhere else? She found nothing.
She went back into the dressing-room. No gold ring glinting in
any obvious places. She felt down the sides of the armchair
facing the television set in which she sat last thing in quiet and
comfort when no duties of hospitality kept her up late into the
night. Nothing.

Back into the bedroom. Was it possible she had failed to take
the ring off with her others? And it had then slipped from her
finger to be lost among the bedclothes? Hardly. But nevertheless she rolled back the blankets – she had never had had any
truck with newfangled duvets – and searched assiduously.
Nothing. Peer under the bed. Nothing.

She sat down on the bed's edge and tried to reconstruct all her
actions from the first moment she had taken off her rings. It had
been – she could pinpoint it almost to the minute – at just a little
before ten-thirty. That was when *Newsnight* began on BBC2,
and, if she could, she watched that, always just before it began

allowing herself the luxury of slipping off her rings. And, yes, she could distinctly remember doing that last night.

So the wedding ring must have been there at ten-thirty, and the door of her bathroom had been under her own eyes up till eleven-fifteen when the programme ended. Then Meadowcroft, her personal maid, had come in and asked if she was ready to go to bed. She had undressed, taken off her make-up, and brushed her teeth. Meadowcroft and her assistant, little Smithers, had taken her clothes and left, and she had gone into the bedroom. By, say, eleven-thirty or a few minutes after. So between then and – she glanced at the pretty little Louis Seize clock on the mantelpiece – a quarter to one the wedding ring had vanished. What had happened? What could have happened?

She reviewed the situation. Could some unauthorized person have got into the dressing-room while she was asleep and on into her bathroom? There had been, of course, some years ago that funny man she had woken to find sitting on the end of her bed. On that occasion, she remembered with a smile, she had invoked almost at once old Miss Marple. What would Miss Marple have done? She would have remained calm. So she in her turn had remained calm. And the whole business had had a satisfactory outcome.

But since that night there had always been a police officer stationed where he could see the whole corridor leading to her bedroom suite.

Right.

She slipped on her dressing-gown, went to the door of the dressing-room, opened it cautiously, looked out. And, yes, there on his little gilt chair was a reassuringly large police officer.

He saw her. Scrambled to his feet. Looked as if he was not sure if he was meant to be seeing her. Actually turned a dusky red under the light of the chandelier above him.

She beckoned.

He came up, managed a duck of the head that stood in for a bow. Had he seen anyone enter her rooms after her maids had left?

"No, ma'am. I've seen no one at all. Only the two maids coming out, as per usual."

"Thank you."

Back to bed. But not to sleep. Not even to lie down again. Altogether too much on her mind. Suspicions. Nasty suspicions. Very nasty suspicions.

She looked at the little Louis Seize clock again. Five to one. Not really all that late. She reached over to the house telephone on the table beside her and pressed the single number for the duty equerry's rooms.

"Pastonbury-Quirk here."

"Ah, Robin. Were you asleep?"

"Oh, ma'am. It's you. No. No, I wasn't asleep. Er – No. No, I was just sort of finishing off the *Times* crossword. Is there something I can do?"

"Well, yes, there is. Or there may be. Could you come along to my dressing-room?"

"Of course, ma'am."

Two minutes later there came Sir Robin Pastonbury-Quirk's discreet knock on the outer door and he came in, looking, for all the fact that he must be almost forty, like a schoolboy who somehow had got into rather too grown-up clothes. Hair seeming to be kept in control by a lavish dousing of water. Face changing moment by moment from white to a rosy pink and back again. Overlarge hands with an air of having only just been scrubbed free of inkstains with pumice stone. Arms and legs never quite where they ought to be.

But underneath the awkwardness and a tendency to blather there lay, as Her Majesty knew well, a first-class mind, logical, observant, and equipped with a ferocious memory for detail. In short – she smiled to herself inwardly – Hercule Poirot made English. Or, since for all his intelligence Robin Pastonbury-Quirk was not a genius – genius something hardly needed in an equerry – perhaps he was more dear old Superintendent Battle, Agatha's other occasional sleuth. Unfoolable, undeviating Superintendent Battle, made a lot less fatherly.

So without hesitation she explained in detail what had happened. And then she went on to confess to her Battle-sleuth-alike the suspicions, the nasty, inescapable suspicions that had come crowding into her mind.

"You see, Robin, this is the awful thing. I was where I could see my bathroom from the moment I had put that ring into the little bowl where I keep them in right up until my maids left, and from then onward the police officer on duty outside had my door under his eye."

Nice Sir Robin blushed his quickly come, quickly gone blush.

"Are you beginning to think one of your two maids must have taken it?"

"But that can't be. It can't be. I mean, Meadowcroft has been with me for more than twenty years. I'd trust her with anything. And, all right, little Smithers hasn't been on the domestic staff very long. But you know what care we take about anybody new. Well, you've summarized the inquiries yourself often enough. As far as is humanly possible all newcomers are guaranteed honest, and besides I like the girl. She's obviously so proud to be doing what she does, and she's so willing. And, what's more, I flatter myself I'm not so easily deceived."

"I should say you're not, ma'am."

Sir Robin was fervent. No other word.

"So, well, what are we to do? I hate the thought even that one of those two may be guilty. I've tried telling myself it just can't be. And yet, I know, I shan't be able to see either of them ever again without a tiny niggling thought at the back of my mind that somehow she may have stolen that ring. And it will be tremendously valuable, of course, simply because it belonged to us."

She frowned.

"But I'm not going to put it all into the hands of the police," she said. "I couldn't do that. Not to either of them."

"Well, ma'am, it strikes me that there's one thing that must be done straightaway. That is – Well, that is, if you don't mind not going to – That is, if you don't mind sort of staying up a bit longer."

"Of course not, Robin. You want to make a search yourself. Quite right. And I want you to. If the ring does turn up somewhere, no one will be more delighted than myself. So off you go. Look everywhere."

"Well, yes. I mean . . . Well, I would have to go into your bedroom. Sort of heave up the bedclothes . . ."

"Of course you will, Robin, though perhaps you'd better wash your hands first if you've been doing the crossword. Mine get perfectly black after reading *The Times* in the morning. Do use my bathroom. And look everywhere in there, too, while you're about it. Don't stand on ceremony."

Blushing pink and yet pinker, Sir Robin Pastonbury-Quirk plunged into the bathroom to begin his search. But in the end, even after he had rummaged from top to bottom of the royal bed, he had to admit complete failure. Her Majesty's wedding ring, which she had taken off just before ten-thirty the evening before and to which it seemed only her two maids had had access, was beyond doubt nowhere in her own suite.

"I really think, ma'am, I've exhausted every last possibility," her slimmed-down Superintendent Battle said eventually.

"I'm sure you have, Robin. And to tell the truth, I've been aching to get back to bed for the past half-hour."

"Oh, good gracious, I've kept you – But I sort of felt I had to, well, be thorough."

"Of course you did, and of course you had to be. But let's leave it now for tonight. We'll think what's to be done in the morning. You are still on duty then?"

"Oh, yes, ma'am. My tour runs from noon today – or actually yesterday now, I suppose – till noon tomorrow. So in any case I'd be coming to discuss the Programme straight after breakfast. But even if I wasn't I'd – Well, I'd jolly well want to try and put it all right . . . It's really too bad that you feel you can't . . . Well, it's just a beastly bad show."

"Thank you, Robin. It's nice to feel I can always count on you. Good night now."

"Oh, yes. Yes. Good night. Good night. I'll leave you to get back to – Well, yes."

But in the morning, after Sir Robin had outlined the day's Programme and drawn attention to the possible snags – "I'm afraid you'll sort of have to cut the managing director there short, apparently he's a terrible gasbag and he'll make you late for the Motor Manufacturers' luncheon" "No problem" – they had come to discuss the extraordinary event of the night before. And still there seemed to be no way out. The wedding ring had disappeared. Only the two maids, Meadowcroft and Smithers, were suspects.

"Look, Robin, this is what we'll do. Who takes over from you as duty equerry?"

"It's Henry Fairmile, ma'am. But—"

"No, listen. As soon as Henry comes on duty, I want you to make enquiries – no need to say: be discreet – about both Meadowcroft and little Smithers. Find out if for some reason either of them has a sudden need for money. I know Meadow-croft has a nephew she's very fond of. Perhaps he's got himself into some sort of a scrape. Or Smithers may have a young man who's not all he might be. I'm sure you'll be able to manage that."

Robin Pastonbury-Quirk was opening his mouth to assure Her Majesty, with perhaps rather more fulsomeness than was strictly necessary, that he would do as he had been asked when the door behind them opened.

"Good morning, Mama."

She turned.

"Oh, good morning, dear. Is there anything you want? I was just asking Robin to do something for me."

"No, no. No hurry. Finish off what you were saying and then I'll have a word."

"Right, Robin. Are you all clear now?"

"Oh, yes, ma'am. I'm sure I'll manage. Be sort of discreet, but—"

"Sort of!"

It was an explosion from behind them.

"Golly, I've done my best to cure my own staff of using expressions like that, but it's a bit much to find yours doing the same thing. *Sort of, sort of*, what an appalling way of using the English language. Such sloppiness. Intolerable."

"I'm awfully sorry, Your Royal Highness. I'll really make sure I don't say it again."

"Well, I should bally well hope not."

She looked at her son with carefully concealed ruefulness.

Really, she thought, I do sometimes wonder how he'll turn out when I pop off. Such a black and white way of looking at things. Still, it won't be my worry . . .

"All right then, Robin. Come and see me just after Henry's paid his final call tonight. I'm sure I can rely on you."

"Oh, yes. Yes, indeed. You know, I'd sort – I mean, if I ever let you down I'd – Well, I'd feel terrible."

Exit of abashed equerry.

That night, after Sir Henry Fairmile had paid the duty equerry's customary brief visit to see if Her Majesty had had any last-minute thoughts, Superintendent Battle (as she had come increasingly to think of him) arrived in his turn. But he brought no new evidence.

"No, honestly, ma'am, I've made jolly stringent enquiries, and neither of them, neither Meadowcroft nor that little Smithers girl, has anything against them. Meadowcroft's nephew is in a regular job and getting good pay, and there's no hint of any gambling or anything like that. And, no, young Smithers hasn't got a boyfriend. Apparently she's always deploring the fact to her fellow maids, though actually, to be brutally frank, one can well see why. Not the most prepossessing of young women."

"Oh, Robin, what a thing to say. I know she's no beauty, but that doesn't stop a young girl acquiring followers. Though, I must say, looking at things the other way round as it were, I've often wondered why you haven't acquired a wife. All those flirtations with the ladies-in-waiting, and nothing ever coming of them."

Robin Pastonbury-Quirk blushed.

"Well, yes, ma'am, there is that. But – But, well, I really did make the most tremendous enquiries about little Marilyn Smithers, and she absolutely doesn't have anybody who might want money from her."

"Marilyn. Is that her name? Do you know I had no idea. You are a good detective, Robin."

Further blushes.

Well, she thought, I hope I've managed to put that right. I really oughtn't to have teased poor Robin like that, only he does in some ways ask for it.

"Yes," she went on, with some haste, "it's extraordinary really how easy it is to forget that one's maids are anything else than one's maids, that they have another existence outside the household that's just as real as their lives in it."

"Oh, yes, ma'am, perfectly true, perfectly true. Jolly acute of you to see it."

He looked at her, shining-eyed.

My Miss Marple persona, I suppose, seeing what's really what. It does pop up every now and again. And sometimes at quite the wrong moment. I remember at the Coronation, sitting with that fearfully heavy crown on one's head, and suddenly thinking about her, thinking like her. Miss Marple, of all people. When I was meant to be having solemn thoughts about the task I was inheriting. And most of the time I was doing that too, of course.

And, damn it, both sets of thoughts in my mind were equally proper. Tremendous hypocrisy, really, to pretend the me that, just sometimes, is Miss Marple is somehow less than the me who is the monarch. When I'm her, I'm not a sort of, to borrow that useful expression, Miss Marple. Any more than I'm a sort of monarch when I'm opening Parliament. I'm really fully both.

And, what's more, I'm sure everybody can be two things at once, both equal. Wherever they seem to come in the social scale. Whoops. Back to Meadowcroft and little Smithers – Marilyn, what a name – and I suppose the only thing left now is for me to find an opportunity of having a word with each of them. See if the Meadowcroft or the Smithers who's something else besides one of my personal maids had any other reason to take my wedding ring, which young Superintendent Battle didn't find out about.

Only . . . Exactly what kind of a word am I going to have? I can't even suggest to either of them that they took the ring. It's just that sort of suspicion about an innocent person that I must try to rid myself of. It would be too unfair to say anything, to Meadowcroft or to Smithers. Certainly, that's what Miss Marple would have insisted on. She was always absolutely firm about that.

Miss Marple. Yes, that's what I've go to do. I've got to be my Miss Marple self.

So how would she approach the subject? Oh, and I know. I know at once. Shrewd old Miss Marple would have just one question to ask. It would seem to be a question about something entirely irrelevant, and yet it would be the key to the whole mystery.

But what on earth can my Miss Marple question be?

Late that evening, while Meadowcroft was gathering together the clothes worn for the day's final engagement and Smithers had gone to fetch a new tablet of soap after Meadowcroft, the eagle-eyed, had spotted that the one on the bathroom basin was almost used up, Miss Marple got a chance to put the question she had at last hit on.

"Oh, Meadowcroft, I've been meaning to ask you . . ."

"Yes, ma'am?"

"I was wondering if you might care to have a photograph that we have signed, as a memento of your time with us and an expression of our gratitude for all you've done?"

Meadowcroft was at once overcome with embarrassment.

"Oh, ma'am, that is good of you. And there's nothing I'd like more."

Then her face resumed its habitual expression, a faint suspicion that something somewhere was out of place.

"But I hope there won't be no question of mementos for many a year yet, ma'am. I'm not near retirement. Not by a long way."

"No, no, Meadowcroft. I trust you'll be with us for a good many years still. It's just that something put the idea into my head, and I thought I'd ask you while it was in my mind."

"I'm sure it's very good of you, ma'am."

So, Superintendent Battle, when you next come to chat with Miss Marple, I think I'll be able to assure you that Meadowcroft had no more idea of secreting away my ring as a memento than she had of paying off her nephew's non-existent debts by selling it.

And a few minutes later, when Meadowcroft had gone, leaving little Smithers to perform the important task of replacing the soap, it was no more than a variant of Miss Marple's seemingly trivial question that was needed.

"Oh, Smithers, I have been thinking. You have been with us almost a year now, have you not?"

"Oh, yes, ma'am."

"And you're happy with your work?"

"Oh, ma'am, yes. It's – It's just great, ma'am."

"Great, is it? So you're not thinking of moving on to somewhere perhaps less demanding? Or to where you have more responsible tasks than replacing our soap?"

"No, no, ma'am. I – Well, I'd like to end up being with you as long as Alice – as long as Meadowcroft, that is, ma'am. Truly."

"Well, I hope you will be, Smithers. I hope you will be. Good night then."

"Oh, good night, ma'am. Good night."

But, she thought, that leaves things almost more mysterious than they were before. I'm certain now neither of those two took my ring. But if they didn't, who did? Who on earth did?

And then the answer came to Miss Marple.

"Yes," she murmured to herself. "Yes. Soap. That's the important thing."

"Soap, Super – I mean, Robin. I'm afraid it came to me later than it should have done. But the soap in my basin is what really told me the truth."

"The soap, ma'am?

Sir Robin Pastonbury-Quirk looked utterly baffled.

"Yes. You see, Robin, when you searched this room and my bedroom and my bathroom just after I'd found the ring was missing, I suggested you should wash your hands because you said you had been doing the crossword, and one always nowadays gets one's hands filthy reading *The Times*."

"Yes. Quite so, ma'am. And I did wash them. I didn't want to get your – er – your, well, sheets all covered in black ink."

"Very thoughtful, Robin. Only your hands weren't dirty. I noticed them when you came in. They looked as they always somehow do, as if you'd only just scrubbed them with pumice stone."

Sir Robin looked down at the ground.

"Perhaps – Perhaps I—"

"No, Robin."

He brought his gaze slowly up to face hers.

"Ma'am, you're perfectly right, of course. I wasn't doing the crossword. I was . . . I was . . ."

"Robin, it's better that we should have out the whole truth once and for all. You've allowed yourself to fall in love with me, isn't that it? I suppose I've been half aware of it for a long time, though I hadn't realized it. But your devotion – yes, that's the only word – your devotion to us is so excessive that there's no other explanation. You're in this state, and when you were in here the night before last, as is the equerry's duty whether it's you or Sir Henry or any of the others, to come in for last-minute changes, you yielded to sudden temptation. Of course, I never took you into account. You were like the postman in the murder stories that nobody ever thinks of as a suspect. But you slipped into the bathroom while I was still watching television and seized on the first – what? – keepsake you saw. And you were gazing at it – Oh, Robin, like a lovesick youth – instead of doing the crossword as you usually do. That is it, isn't it?"

"Oh, ma'am, how could I have—"

"Well, we won't go into that. But perhaps you should just hand it back."

Sir Robin dipped two fingers behind his schoolboyishly askew grey silk tie and drew out a little leather pouch hanging from a fine silver chain round his neck. He pulled it open and turned it over. Onto his outstretched palm there dropped a thin circlet of gold.

THE STORY-BAG

PHILIP GOODEN

Mustafa the story-maker lived in one of those old streets near the Ibn Tulun mosque in Cairo. Unlike other story-makers, who sold by weight or set a price according to the quality of their goods, Mustafa had an invariable and simple system of selling what he produced. He charged 10 piastres for every item in his range. The stories were lined up in bags on his counter and, despite the manifest differences between these bags, they went, each and every one, for 10 piastres. It made no difference that some bags were tiny, with tight-drawn strings closing up their mouths, while others were baggy with loosely secured cords around the top. No difference that some bags were made of cotton, while others were gunny, or silk, or velvet, or even paper. It was immaterial that the contents of the story-bags varied enormously, as one would expect. Each cost just 10 piastres.

The wisdom of Mustafa's pricing policy was apparent in this: by charging the same price for every item, irrespective of contents or the wrapping, Mustafa paradoxically ensured his customers' goodwill. If they bought a pig in a poke one day they knew that they were more than likely to gain a jewel on the next – because the jewels outnumbered the pigs. And since Mustafa had always pitched his price slightly below his Cairene rivals', people came to him because they believed they would get a bargain, and he prospered in his steady way.

No genre man, Mustafa produced assorted stories: pithy, epic, romantic, grotesque, poignant. Occasionally his stories failed, although less often than those of his rivals. But Mustafa never refunded the purchase price. Not even when the fault lay not in the story but in the bag containing it. Sometimes a purchaser would discover on returning home that his bag had a small tear and that the story had dribbled out as he walked past the long white walls of the mosque. Or the knot at the top was tied a little casually and the contents had eased themselves out even as the bag maintained its deceptively inflated shape on Mustafa's counter. No matter. Mustafa closed his ears to the few customers who complained. "Go to so-and-so," he would say, "if you want another story. I don't want to be dealing with you."

Like a baker, Mustafa rose early to wrap up his stories. He didn't produce his full range every day – a random morning might throw up two epic, five fabulous and three pathetic – but of course the stories did not go stale like bread (or not so quickly) and he usually had a residue of the previous days' work on the wooden counter. In addition Mustafa's habit of wrapping the stories indiscriminately in whatever bag was nearest to hand meant that the shop display gave a greater impression of variety than might have been warranted by the actual contents of the bags. In this way, the tragic story of King Tut's attempt to build a stone roof over his entire kingdom might be wrapped, incongruously, in brown paper, while the lightweight tale of how Al-Rashid ultimately cheated himself when he cheated his brother could be found lurking in the bottom of a velvet bag.

Now, Mustafa was growing old. He had trained up his oldest son in the business of making stories, and was confident that Ragab would carry on the tradition, although at the same time he was pleased that the young man, who had set up shop on the far side of the city in Heliopolis, hadn't yet gathered the custom which Mustafa had attracted over the years. By careful hoarding of his 10-piastre coins Mustafa had accumulated a tidy sum. Each day he added that day's takings to a box which he kept near the base of the old white mulberry tree in his yard. This mulberry tree was so old that its longest branches were kept up by a scaffolding of blocks and crutches. More wood sustained that tree than was to be found in it.

When young Ali moved in five doors down Quatby Street, Mustafa's decision to retire, a decision which he had been postponing for several years, was confirmed. For Ali too was a story-producer, of a new kind. For one thing, he priced his products highly, thinking that an expensive bag meant valuable contents. Or thinking that his customers would think so. But Ali's real novelty consisted in this: with his stories, he made pictures too. Out of the bags, along with the words, flew images, evanescent but highly coloured, of what was happening in those stories. Just as the words flowed into and out of a customer's ears, so the pictures unfurled in front of that customer's eyes, before a passing breeze whisked them away altogether, down alleys, around minarets and through the carved wooden mashrabiyyah that stand in windows and allow women to peer out in the cool of the evening.

Ali's illuminations were a nine-day wonder. They appealed to the childish among his customers, and even those who reckoned themselves sophisticated bought one or two story-bags from the spanking new shop on Quatby Street. But their appeal faded because underneath the colour and the newness there was almost nothing. Once Ali's stories had flown out they were forgotten. Ali did not make good stories, his material was at once fanciful and thin, and so he tried to conceal this with bright images and fresh paint. But he could not conceal it from himself. After a time, after he had seen the steady, contented return of Mustafa's customers week by week, Ali realized how foolish he had been, how ostentatious, to set up shop a few doors away from the traditional old story-maker. Ali's customers went away temporarily pleased, but ultimately dissatisfied with their colourful sacks. He didn't make the quick fortune he had hoped for; he felt that his powers of invention, unlike Mustafa's, wouldn't even see him into middle age; he grew deeply envious of the old man's skill, and of his reputed fortune. One spring day, wandering at nightfall in the alley that borders the backs of the houses in Quatby Street, Ali saw his rival open the box which he kept in the ground near the old mulberry tree and tip into it the coins of the day. Through a gap in the fencing Ali saw past the kneeling old man, and into the shop. There on the counter lay the varied story-bags, the few unsold ones. Ali was overcome with a great urge to take the money – or the bags – or the money and the bags – from his rival. He was only able to tear himself away from the scene of the frail, crouching old man, with his coins trickling into the box and fat stories sitting on the counter, when he saw Mustafa gazing directly at him through the hole in the fence.

Mustafa, perhaps using the appearance of an inferior rival down the street as a pretext, was now ready to stop. He was tired of his more extravagant or ill-disciplined stock, irrational tales of magic lamps, of worms, parchments and pyramids. He settled to making his last batches. And instead of looking out over fantastical seas or impassable deserts, Mustafa turned inwards. He turned to Quatby Street. He began to make stories about the widow and the young man (you know the ones I mean), the Greek merchant who was not as prosperous as he appeared, the Syrian who made backgammon sets, the old men in the café who smoked their pipes and played on those same sets. In this story, or rather set of stories, to which he gave in his own mind the name of "Quatby Street", Mustafa even included a portrait of himself, cunningly disguised as a baker.

Ali waited for his chance, loitering at dusk in the alley behind the yard of Mustafa's house. Inside, he had built a real hatred of the old man whose steady income, plain skill and retiring way of life were a continual insult. As the old man bent over the box concealed at the base of the mulberry tree, Ali forced his way through the gap in the fence and, in the twilight, rapidly covered the distance between himself and Mustafa. Ali held a piece of planking in his hand.

He hit the old man over the head, then rushed inside, into the shop, grabbed a cotton story-sack from the counter and stuffed it into Mustafa's mouth to stop the awful gurgling. He scooped up the money-box and as many of the story-bags as he could carry. Before squeezing his way out of Mustafa's yard, he tore the white story-bag from Mustafa's gaping, unbreathing mouth. Then he tugged at the wooden props supporting two of the most elongated branches of the mulberry. He heaved at the branches, applying his full weight, until the old things descended on Mustafa's prone form. In this way he naively hoped that Mustafa's death might be taken as an accident.

Ali returned home. He tried to sleep, and could not. As dawn came he finally fell into a state that was more like unconsciousness. He woke late the next day. On his table were Mustafa's story-bags and money-box. Instantly Ali was reminded of what he had done. He intended to pass off the stories as his own product, but one of the bags – the one he had used to stifle Mustafa – was flecked and discoloured, and Ali knew he could not sell it. He unpicked the knot that fastened the bag at the top. Out flew the story, and at first Ali was both pleased and disappointed. He was pleased because Mustafa's tale was so dull, so ordinary. But somehow this also disappointed him.

Mustafa's story was about a street. Some nonsense about competing tradesmen. Bakers. After a few moments, however, Ali's pleasure and disappointment were succeeded by something more intense as he recognized Mustafa in the person of the old baker. A few moments more, and Ali saw who the other, younger baker was. So brilliant, precise, and yet oblique, was Mustafa's characterization of him – Ali – that the murderer felt his real self was in danger of being usurped by the imaginary one. And all this achieved without pictures. Mustafa, with his old man's aloof tiredness, hadn't even bothered finding another name for Ali. Ali knew what was coming. The rivalry between the bakers turned murderous. The treacherous, younger one did what treacherous young ones are apt to do. The crude accident devised in a back yard . . . the seizing of the baker's savings . . . "Ali, your loaves will not rise . . ." floating from the mouth of the dying baker in the story and out of the bag.

"Ali . . . your loaves will not rise . . .". The same phrase repeated and repeated (inartistically, it might be said), and floating for everyone to hear – for the word once released, who can recall it? "Ali . . . your loaves will not rise . . .", going down alleys, around minarets and through the carved wooden mashrabiyyah that stand in windows and allow women to peer out in the cool of the evening.

SLAUGHTER IN THE STRAND

KEITH MILES

England, 1912

Herbert Syme had never travelled in a First Class carriage before but nothing else would suffice. It was, in a sense, the most important day of his life and it deserved to be marked by the unaccustomed display of extravagance. Impecunious librarians like Herbert were never allowed to pose as First Class passengers on a train to London. Indeed, they could hardly afford to travel by rail at all on a regular basis. Herbert always rode the six miles to work on his ancient bicycle, weaving past the countless potholes, cursing his way up steep hills, hoping that the rain would hold off and that no fierce dogs would give chase. Today, it was different. Instead of arriving at the library, breathless, soaked to the skin and, not infrequently, with the legs of his trousers expertly shredded by canine teeth, he was sitting in a luxurious compartment among the elite of society.

The fact that he was an outsider made it even more exhilarating. Habitual denizens of the privileged area were less than welcoming. They saw Herbert Syme for what he really was, a tall, slim, stooping man in his forties with a shabby suit and a self-effacing manner. The whiff of failure was unmistakable.

What was this interloper doing in their midst? Murmurs of resentment buzzed in Herbert's ears. The rustling of newspapers was another audible display of class warfare. They were professional men and he was trespassing on their territory. They wanted him out. The elderly lady in the compartment was more vocal in her criticism. After repeatedly clicking her tongue in disapproval, she had the temerity to ask Herbert if he possessed the appropriate ticket.

The librarian withstood it all without a tremor. While his companions took refuge behind their copies of *The Times*, Herbert took out the letter that had transformed his dull existence. It was short and businesslike but that did not lessen its impact. He read the words again, fired anew by their implication.

> *Dear Mr Syme,*
>
> *Thank you for submitting your novel to us. It has found favour with all who have read the book. Subject to certain changes, we will consider publishing it. To that end, we request that you come to this office on Wednesday, 16 May at 3 p.m. precisely to discuss the matter with Mr Roehampton. Please confirm that you are able to attend at this time.*
>
> *Yours sincerely,*
> *Miss Lavinia Finch (Secretary)*

There it was – his passport to fame and fortune. Other passengers might be going on routine visits to the capital but Herbert Syme was most certainly not. Thanks to the letter from Roehampton and Buckley Ltd, he was in transit between misery and joy. Long years of toil and derision lay behind him. Success had at last beckoned. Putting the magical missive into his pocket, he reflected on its contents. His novel had found favour at a prestigious publishing house. Instead of spending his days stacking the work of other writers on the shelves of his branch library, he would take his place alongside them as an equal. Herbert Syme would be read, admired and envied. Everyone's perception of him would alter dramatically. Publication was truly a form of rebirth.

"May I see your ticket, please, sir?"

"What?" Herbert came out of his reverie to find the uni-formed ticket inspector standing over him. "Oh, yes. Of course."

Newspapers were lowered and each pair of eyes was trained on Herbert as he extracted his ticket and offered it to the inspector. Everyone in the compartment wanted him to be forcibly ejected. They longed for his humiliation. To their utter disgust, the inspector clipped the ticket and handed it back politely to its owner.

"Thank you, sir," he said.

Herbert was elated by the man's deference. It was something to which he would swiftly adjust. From now on, it would be a case of First Class all the way.

The sheer size, noise and bustle of London were overwhelming at first. Herbert had never seen so many people or so much traffic. Garish advertisements competed for his attention on walls, passing vehicles and in shop windows. It was bewilder-ing. Crossing the Strand was an ordeal in itself, the long thoroughfare positively swarming with automobiles, omni-buses, lorries, horses and carts, mounted policemen, rattling handcarts, stray dogs, hurtling cyclists and darting pedestrians. When he eventually got to the correct side of the road, Herbert took a deep breath to compose himself. He needed to be at his most assured for the critical interview with Edmund T. Roe-hampton. The fact that he would be dealing with one of the partners in the firm, and not with a mere underling, augured well. His novel would finally see the light of day – *subject to a certain changes*. Whatever those changes might be, Herbert vowed that he would willingly agree to them. A publisher was entitled to make minor adjustments and add refinements.

When he located the premises of Roehampton and Buckley, Ltd, he met with his first disappointment. Such a leading publishing house, he assumed, would have palatial offices that signalled its lofty position. Instead, it appeared to operate out of three rooms above a shoe shop. Mindful of the request for punctuality, Herbert checked his pocket watch, cleared his throat, rehearsed his greeting to Mr Roehampton and climbed the stairs. When he entered the outer office, he heard Big Ben booming in the distance. A second disappointment awaited.

The middle-aged woman seated at the desk looked over her pince-nez at him.

"May I help you, sir?" she said.

"Er, yes," he replied, finding that his collar was suddenly too tight for him. "I have an appointment with Mr Roehampton at three o'clock."

"What name might that be, sir?"

"Syme. Herbert Syme." His confidence returned. "I'm an author."

"Ah, yes," she said, her tone softening. "Mr Syme. I remember now. I'm Miss Finch. It was I who wrote to you to arrange the appointment. Welcome to London, Mr Syme. Mr Roehampton will deal with you as soon as he returns from his luncheon."

"Luncheon?"

"He and Mr Buckley always eat at their club on a Wednesday."

"I see."

"Do take a seat. Mr Roehampton will be back within the hour."

Within the hour! So much for punctuality. It had taken Herbert all morning simply to reach London. To arrive in the Strand at the stipulated time had required a huge effort on the part of the provincial author. During the wayward journey from the station to the offices of Roehampton and Buckley, Ltd, his provincialism had been cruelly exposed. His instincts were blunted, his accent jarred, his lack of sophistication was excruciating. He was made to feel like a country mouse in a metropolitan jungle. All that would soon vanish, he reminded himself. He was going to be a published author. As he sank down on the chair beside the door, he consoled himself with the fact that that he had made it to the top of Mount Olympus, albeit situated above a shoe shop in the Strand. It was only right that a mortal should await the arrival of Zeus from his luncheon.

Miss Lavinia Finch offered little decorative interest to the observer. A spare, severe woman of almost exotic ugliness, she busied herself at her typewriter, striking the keys with a random brutality that made the machine groan in pain. She ignored the visitor completely. Herbert did not mind. His gaze was fixed on the oak bookcase that ran from floor to ceiling behind the secretary. The firm's output was stacked with a neatness that gladdened the heart of a librarian. He feasted his eyes on the impressive array of volumes, thrilled that he would be joining them in time and deciding that he, too, when funds permitted, would acquire just such a bookcase in which to exhibit his work. Herbert was so caught up in his contemplation of literature that he did not notice how swiftly an hour passed. The chimes of Big Ben were still reverberating when Edmund T. Roehampton breezed in through the door.

A third disappointment jerked Herbert to his feet. Expecting the Zeus of the publishing world to be a huge man with a commanding presence, he was surprised to see a dapper figure strutting into the room. Roehampton was a self-appointed dandy but the fashionable attire, the dazzling waistcoat and the gleaming shoes could not disguise the fact that he was a small man with a large paunch and a face like a whiskered donkey. Seeing his visitor, he doffed his top hat, pulled the cigar from between his teeth and manufactured a cold smile.

"Ah!" he declared. "You must be Syme."

"That's right, sir. Herbert Syme. The author of—"

"Well, don't just stand there, man," continued Roehampton, interrupting him. "Come into my office. We must talk. Crucial decisions have to be made." He opened the door to his inner sanctum and paused. "Any calls, Miss Finch?"

"None, Mr Roehampton," she said.

"Good."

"But you do have an appointment at four-thirty with Mr Agnew."

"Syme and I will be through by then."

He went into his office and Herbert followed him, uncertain whether to be reassured or alarmed by the news that a bare half an hour had been allotted to him. Had he come so far to be given such short shrift? Roehampton waved him to a seat, put his top hat on a peg then took the leather-backed chair behind the desk. Raised up on a dais, it made him seem much bigger than he was. Herbert relaxed. The office was much more like the place he had envisaged. Large and well appointed, it had serried ranks of books on display as well as framed sepia photographs of the firm's major authors. Herbert wondered how long it would be before his own portrait graced the William Morris wallpaper.

Roehampton drew on his cigar and studied Herbert carefully.

"How is Yorkshire?" he asked abruptly.

Herbert was thrown. "Yorkshire, sir?"

"That's where you come from, isn't it?"

"No, Mr Roehampton. Derbyshire. I come from Derbyshire."

"I knew it up was up there somewhere," said the other dismissively, opening a drawer to take out a manuscript. He slapped it down on the desk. "Well, Syme, here it is. Your novel."

"I'm so grateful that you are prepared to publish it, Mr Roehampton."

"Subject to a certain changes."

"Yes, yes. Of course," agreed Herbert. "Anything you say."

"Then let's get down to brass tacks," said the publisher, exhaling a cloud of acrid smoke. "Interesting plot. Well-drawn characters. Good dialogue. A novel with pace." He gave a complimentary nod. "You're a born writer, Syme."

Herbert swelled with pride. "Thank you, sir."

"But you still need to be weaned."

"I await your suggestions, Mr Roehampton."

"Oh, they're not suggestions," warned the other. "They're essential improvements. Mr Buckley and I could never put our names on a book with which we were not entirely and unreservedly satisfied."

"And what does Mr Buckley think of *Murder in Matlock*?" wondered Herbert. "Your letter said that it had found favour with all who had read it."

"Yes. With Miss Finch and with myself. We are your audience." He heaved a sigh. "Mr Buckley, alas, is not a reader. The perusal of the luncheon menu at our club is all that he can manage in the way of sustained reading. What he brings to the firm is money and business acumen. What I bring," he added, thrusting a thumb into his waistcoat pocket, "is true literary expertise and a knack of unearthing new talent."

"I'm delighted to be included in that new talent, Mr Roehampton."

"We shall see, Syme. We shall see. Now, to business." He consulted the notes written on the title page of the manuscript. "Omissions," he announced. "Let us first deal with your omissions."

Herbert was baffled. "I was not aware that I'd omitted anything."

"Yours, sir, is a novel of sensation."

"I see it more as a searching exploration of the nature of evil."

"It amounts to the same thing, man. *Murder in Matlock* inhabits the world of crime and that imposes certain demands upon an author."

"Such as?"

"To begin with, you must have a Sinister Oriental. A murder story is untrue to its nature if it does not have at least one – and preferably more than one – Sinister Oriental."

"But there are no orientals, sinister or otherwise, in Matlock."

"Invent some, man," said Roehampton with exasperation. "Import some. Bring in a Chinese army of occupation, if need be."

"That would upset the balance of the narrative."

"It will help to sell the book and that is all that concerns me." Herbert was deflated. "If you say so, Mr Roehampton."

"As to your villain, his name must be changed."

"Why? What's wrong with Lionel Jagg?"

"Far too English," explained the publisher. "We need a wicked foreigner. Do you know why Wilkie Collins chose to christen the villain of *The Woman in White* with an Italian name? It was because he felt no Englishman capable of the skulduggery to which Count Fosco sank. I applaud the thinking behind that decision, Syme. Follow suit. Lionel Jagg commits crimes far too horrible for any true-born Englishman even to contemplate. Henceforth, he will be Count Orsini."

"An Italian count in Matlock?" wailed Herbert. "It's unheard of."

"Anything can happen in Yorkshire."

"Derbyshire, Mr Roehampton. Derbyshire."

"Yorkshire or Derbyshire. Both are equally barbarous places."

"That's unjust."

"Let us move on. Criminals must be exposed early on to the reader. Lionel Jagg concealed his villainy too well. Count Orsini must be more blatant. Equip him with a limp and one eye. They are clear indications of villainy. A hare lip is also useful in this context. And he needs an accomplice, just as evil as himself."

"Not another Sinister Oriental, surely?"

"No, no. Don't overplay that hand. A Wily Pathan will fit the bill here."

Herbert was aghast. "Wily Pathans in *Derbyshire*?"

"Metaphorically speaking, they are everywhere. They are the bane of the British Empire and we must remind our readers of that fact. Now, sir, to the most frightful omission of all. A hero. Your novel must have a Great Detective."

"But it has one, Mr Roehampton. Inspector Ned Lubbock."

"Wrong name, wrong character, wrong nationality," insisted the publisher, stubbing out his cigar in the ashtray with decisive force. "Lubbock is nothing but a country bumpkin from Derbyshire."

"Yorkshire," corrected the other.

"There — I *knew* the novel was set in Yorkshire!"

"In Derbyshire. Inspector Lubbock is a Yorkshireman, working in Matlock. I thought I made that abundantly clear."

"What's abundantly clear to me, Syme, is that you need to be more aware of the market you are hoping to reach. The common reader does not want a bumbling detective from a remote northern fastness. He expects style, charm and intellectual brilliance. In short, sir, the Great Detective must be French."

"Why?" groaned Herbert.

"Because there is a tradition to maintain," asserted the other. "Vidocq, Eugene Sue, Gaboriau. They all had French detectives and not simply because they themselves hailed from France. Consider the case of Edgar Allan Poe, the American author. What is the name of his sleuth? Chevalier Auguste Dupin. It's inconceivable that someone called Ned Lubbock should solve *The Murders in the Rue Morgue*."

"It's just as ludicrous to have a French detective hailing from Yorkshire."

"Change his birthplace to Paris."

Herbert descended to sarcasm. "The Rue Morgue, perhaps?"

"And give the fellow more substance," said Roehampton, sweeping his protest aside. "This is the age of the Scientific Detective, the man with a supreme intelligence. Think of Sherlock Holmes. Think of Monsieur Lecoq. Think of The Thinking Machine."

All that Herbert Syme had thought about for years was publication. Elevation to the ranks of those he idolized most would solve everything. It would rescue him from a humdrum life in a small provincial library where he was mocked, undervalued and taken for granted. Five years had gone into the creation of the novel that would be his salvation. In that time, he had grown to love Inspector Ned Lubbock, to marvel at his invention of the dastardly Lionel Jagg and to take a special delight in the meticulous evocation of his native Derbyshire. His hopes were dashed. Edmund T. Roehampton was mangling his novel out of all recognition. He felt the grief of a mother whose only child is being slowly strangled in front of her. Anger began to take root.

"Inspector Jacques Legrand," decreed Roehampton. "That name has more of a ring to it. He uses scientific methods of detection and outwits the villains with his superior brainpower. Needless to say – and I must repair another omission of yours – he must be a Master of Disguise. Just like Hamilton Cleek – the Man of the Forty Faces."

Herbert struck back. "And what does this preposterous French detective disguise himself *as*?" he asked, his Derbyshire vowels thickening in the process. "An Italian Count or a Wily Pathan? Or maybe he can pretend to be the commander of an invading Chinese army. And where do his changes of apparel come from? I should warn you that there are no costume hire shops in the Peak District."

"I'm glad that you mentioned that, Syme."

"Does that mean I've got *something* right at last?"

"Far from it. Your location is a disaster."

"You're going to take Derbyshire away from me as well?" cried Herbert.

"I have to, man. Shift the story to London and we enlarge its possibilities."

Heavier sarcasm. "In which part of the capital is Matlock to be found?"

"Nowhere, fortunately," said Roehampton with a complacent chuckle. "Unlike your home town, we do have more than our share of Sinister Orientals here so that's one problem solved. My shirts are washed at a Chinese laundry and they are obsequiously polite to me but there's still something ineradicably *sinister* about them."

"They're foreigners, that's all. In Peking, you would appear sinister to them."

"That's beside the point. Your novel is not set in China."

"No," said Herbert, desperation taking hold. "It's firmly rooted in Derbyshire. How can a book called *Murder in Matlock* be set in the city of London?"

"By a simple slash of the pen. Here," said the publisher grandly, indicating the title page of the manuscript. "I crossed out your effort and inserted my own. I venture to suggest that it will have more purchase on the reader's curiosity."

Herbert was shaking with fury. "You've stolen my title as well?"

"Improved upon it, Syme. That is all."

"In what way?"

"See for yourself," advised the other, pushing the manuscript across to him. "Ignore the blots. My pen always leaks. Just imagine those words emblazoned across the title-page of your novel. *Slaughter in the Strand*."

"But there's no mention of the Strand in the book."

"There is now, Syme. I've also included some other elements you failed to include. As well as being a killer, Count Orsini must be a Prince of Thieves just like Arsene Lupin. You see?" he said, eyes glinting. "The Franco-Italian touch once more. Inspector Legrand must solve the crime by playing with a piece of string while sitting in the corner of a restaurant. Notice the hint of Baroness Orczy there? The Old Man in the Corner. It adds to the international flavour of the novel. On which subject, I must point out another fatal omission."

Herbert gritted his teeth. "Go on," he growled.

"There are no German spies in the book. We must have spies for the Kaiser. Remember le Queux, a true English patriot as well as a brilliant writer. He's warned us time and again about the menace of the Prussian eagle. Yes, Syme," he concluded, sitting back with a grin, "those are the few changes I require. Make them and your book may stand a chance in a busy marketplace."

"Except that it won't be *my* book," snarled Herbert.

"What do you mean?"

"I mean, Mr Roehampton, that you have been hurling names at me that I neither like nor strive to emulate. Vidocq, Sue, Gaboriau, Baroness Orczy, William le Queux. They merely skate on the surface of crime. I tried to deal with the subject in depth," argued Herbert, rising to his feet. "If you want an international flavour, listen to the names of those who inspired me to write *Murder in Matlock*. Dostoevsky gave me my villain. Balzac supplied me with my insight into the lower depths of society. Maupassant taught me subtlety. Goethe schooled my style. You wave Wilkie Collins at me but a far greater English writer suggested the infanticide with which my novel begins – George Eliot, the author of *Adam Bede*. My debt to them is there for all to see. I'll not have it obliterated."

Roehampton blinked. "Am I to understand that you reject my emendations?"

"I refuse to put my name to the rubbish you've concocted."

"Ah, yes," said the publisher, rubbing his hands. "That brings me to my final point. Whatever form the novel finally takes, we cannot possibly put your name on it."

"Why not?"

"Be realistic, man. Syme rhymes with Slime. The critics would seize on that like vultures. Herbert Syme sounds like, well, what, in all honesty, you are, a struggling librarian from a Yorkshire backwater."

"Derbyshire!" roared Herbert. "Matlock is in Derbyshire!"

"That point is immaterial in a novel called *Slaughter in the Strand*."

"I loathe the title."

"It will grow on you in time," said Roehampton persuasively.

"So will your new pseudonym. Out goes Herbert Syme and in comes – wait for it – Marcus van Dorn. It has a bewitching sense of mystery about it. Marcus van Dorn. Come now. Isn't that a name to sow excitement in the breast of every reader?"

Herbert exloded. "But it's not *my* name!"

"It is now, Syme."

"You can't do this to me, Mr Roehampton."

"I'm a publisher. I can do anything."

It was horribly true. Herbert's great expectations withered before his eyes. He was not, after all, going to be an author. If this was how publishers behaved, he was doomed. Life would become intolerable. All the people to whom he had boasted of his success would ridicule him unmercifully. He would have to return to the library with his tail between his legs. Every time he put one of Roehampton and Buckley's books on a shelf, the wound would be reopened. It was galling. Publication was not rebirth at all. It was akin to the infanticide with which his novel had so sensitively dealt.

The villain of the piece was none other than a man whom he had revered from afar. Edmund T. Roehampton had not only hacked his book to pieces, he had altered its title and deprived the author of his identity. It was the ultimate blow to Herbert's pride. His gaze fell on his precious manuscript, disfigured by ink blots and scribbled notes, then it shifted slowly to the gleaming paper knife. A wild thought came into his mind.

"Well," said Roehampton, "do you want the book published or not?"

"Only if it's my novel."

"Make the changes I want or it will never get into print."

Herbert stood firm. "I'll not alter a single word."

"Then take this useless manuscript and go back to York-shire."

"Derbyshire!"

It was the final insult. As Roehampton reached for the manuscript, Herbert grabbed the paper knife and stabbed his hand. The publisher yelled in pain but there was worse to come. Pushed to the limit, Herbert dived across the desk and stabbed him repeatedly in the chest, avenging the murder of his novel with a vigour he did not know he possessed. Alerted by her employer's yell, Miss Finch came bustling into the office. When she saw the blood gushing down Roehampton's flashy waist-coat, she had a fit of hysteria and screamed madly. Herbert was on her within seconds. Lavinia Finch was an accomplice. She had not only typed out the guileful letter to him, she had read the finest novel ever to come out of Matlock and pretended to admire it. She had deceived Herbert just as much as her employer and deserved to die beside him. He stabbed away until her screams turned to a hideous gurgling. Both victims were soon dead. They had been comprehensively remaindered.

Herbert Syme had travelled in a First Class carriage on the most significant journey of his life but his return ticket would not be used. A horse-drawn police van was his mode of transport now. As he sat in handcuffs behind iron bars, he reflected that he had, after all, achieved one ambition. His name would certainly be seen in print now. Every newspaper in Britain would carry the banner headline – *Slaughter in the Strand*. A treacherous pub-lisher may have provided the title but its author would not be Marcus van Dorn. It would be Herbert Syme, the most notori-ous criminal ever to come out of Matlock in Derbyshire. He liked that. It was a form of poetic justice.

THE CHICKEN

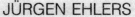

JÜRGEN EHLERS

You like reading crime stories? While you're having your breakfast and enjoying your egg, I might as well tell you what occurred to me recently. It all started with an old hen. Gero had flattened it, when speeding into our driveway. Ignoring the sign saying: "No threw road. Dead slow!" The "threw" had been corrected, of course. Knut did that. He's the one with the high school certificate, he is always fussy about such matters.

And me? I am a knife-thrower. Or rather: was a knife-thrower. At the circus. I took early retirement because of my fading eyesight, and also my hand had become a bit unsteady. No, not what you may be thinking. I have never thrown a knife in anger. Least of all at Gero.

There are five of us here at our little farm. None of us is a proper farmer. We are into alternative farming. Knut had once studied some forestry. He is our plant expert. Bernd-Otto drives the tractor, and Mireille, his wife, milks the cows. By hand, naturally, because of the "alternative". That means no machinery. At least, that is how Bernd-Otto defines it.

Bernd-Otto is our boss. He owns the farm. The old farm house, the cow shed, the barn, and a piece of land. All inherited from his uncle. That uncle also knew nothing about farming, so he had to sell more and more of his land until he died two years ago. Fortunately the remaining five acres are still just big enough for us. The cows give more milk than we need, the land yields grain and the chickens lay eggs. Except the one that was run over by Gero. But we pot-roasted it all the same. It was rather difficult to eat though with all the tiny bone splinters. But since we find it hard to make ends meet most of the time, we have to use whatever we can.

But I wanted to tell you about Gero. Well, Gero is a crook. Or, to be more exact, he was a crook. He's dead now. When you think about it, he was never really one of us. He was more of a townie with his posh car and his tailor-made suits. He had been a businessman, or so he said. That the police were after him we only learnt much later. He had traded in second-hand cars, and had cheated more than most of the others. Faked car papers. In the end he had to do a runner.

He had told us that the town was getting on his nerves. He urgently needed some peace and quiet. Life in the country was exactly what he needed, and he was alternative-minded anyway. He did not explain what exactly he meant by that. But he never lent us a hand with our work. We had our doubts about Gero from the very beginning, but we allowed him to stay, social-minded, as we are.

He caused trouble pretty soon, making eyes at Hannelore. Hannelore is Knut's girl. With her plaits she looks like eighteen, at least from the back, but really she is twenty-eight and thus two years older than Knut. Knut was furious about this flirting. He called Gero a "pig", which I think was not entirely wrong. But he only told us. In front of Gero he always pulled himself together.

Hannelore didn't really care. But there were always times when Knut was busy in the field or in the cow shed, so that they could meet for some undisturbed little tête-à-tête. I cared a lot more. After all, Gero was doing now what I used to do before his arrival, but, of course, he didn't know that. And neither did Knut.

If he had caught them in the hay or in his bed, he might have simply killed Gero, but it happened differently. One day Hannelore realized that her golden brooch was missing, the one she'd inherited from her grandmother. And although no-body directly said that Gero had taken it, it seemed somewhat strange that it had simply disappeared. Everybody had their suspicions. And relations between Hannelore and Gero cooled down considerably after that.

And then came the incident with the chicken. Gero had been into town to fetch some beer, had in the process sampled rather a lot of it, and eventually drove into our farmyard far too fast. Perhaps everything would still have been all right had he only been sober. But after he saw our baffled faces, especially that of Hannelore – for her our animals are all proper members of the family – he burst into laughter.

"It is not funny, Gero!" Knut remarked. Hannelore had tears in her eyes. She did not even look at Gero. "Such a pig," she said over and over again.

"All right, all right! I'll make up for it, I promise. I'll go straight away and get something nice. And afterwards we'll all have a nice party!"

Well, after about an hour he was back with a young sow. God knows where he got hold of it. He'd certainly not bought it and, since our neighbours don't keep animals, we assumed he must have driven quite a distance. It had taken him long enough anyway, so there was no need to worry. He imagined that the poor creature could simply be spit-roasted. We looked at each other. We understood each other even without words.

So we slaughtered the pig, using one of my large knives. It turned out to be far from easy. We had to hold tight very firmly with four people, and Bernd-Otto was not all that convincing as a butcher. He had been a baker originally, but cutting bread apparently was a good deal easier. The event turned into some kind of bloodbath. Afterwards we had to put all our clothes straight into the wash, and Mireille had to add twice the usual amount of washing-powder to get everything clean again.

Later, in the evening, we all sat around a big bonfire in the yard and drank the beer that Gero had bought. All at once we had peace and quiet again. We did not eat the pig, of course. And the young sow that Gero had brought went into the pigsty with the other three sows we had already. The four became friends straight away. I think the animals have a good time at our farm. In the autumn we will all go and gather acorns and chestnuts for them.

Mireille has a driving licence; she drove Gero's car back into town the next morning, to where he used to work. Mireille is very brave. But in town usually nobody pays attention to what is going on and they all mind their own business.

Yesterday we were visited by a policeman who enquired about Gero and whether he still lived with us or not. "No," Mireille had said, and she added that he would be welcome to come in and have a look around. And then she gave him a big piece of our sponge cake. It is very good, made with ten eggs. Hardly anybody makes something like that nowadays.

Eventually the reason for his visit became evident. Something strange had happened, he said. Some person had simply parked Gero's car in front of his old company in Marcellus Street. And then he had taken a bike from the boot and cycled off. So Mireille had been mistaken for a man. It happens time and again since she has had her hair cut. But, of course, we did not let the policeman in on that.

After the cake he wanted to stretch his legs a bit, or so he said. He pretended that he was interested in our farming and we had to explain one thing or another. In the course of this he scrutinized the whole farm and looked into every nook and cranny. But he did not find Gero. He had long since been eaten by the sows. Our four delightful sows, Bernd-Otto's whole pride and joy. Sows are known to be omnivores. They eat everything. Almost, that is.

"What about the bones?" you might ask. No, they would not eat the bones. We fed them to our chickens. Because of the lime. Or the carbonate, as Knut would call it. They need it for the eggshells. Chicken food has the same effect but is much more expensive and not the least alternative. Of course, you have to crush the bones first, with a hammer, and then the chickens eat them all up. So, if you are having a boiled egg for breakfast now, the shell may contain a minute little piece of Gero. Of course, only if your eggs are from free-range chickens. You should always go for those!

THE POSTMAN ONLY RINGS WHEN HE CAN BE BOTHERED

PETER GUTTRIDGE

Mrs Spring was floating face down in the pool when her gardener found her. She hung there, half submerged, tangled in a length of filtration pipe. It was Tuesday, 10.30 a.m. Each morning in the warm months Mrs Spring came into the garden at seven, disrobed and gingerly lowered herself into the chilly waters. The pool, installed for status not swimming, was circular. For 15 minutes Mrs Spring laboriously circumnavigated it.

From my study on the first floor of our cottage I occasionally had the misfortune to see this ritual. It was a terrible spectacle. Her body had known better days. At least for her sake I hope it had. If my window was open, I would hear her gargled gasps as she breathed with her head sometimes above, sometimes below the water.

On that Tuesday morning, I didn't know anything was wrong until I heard a commotion around eleven. I was having my ear bent, as usual, by my cleaner Donald about Roger Moore (as usual).

Rural unemployment being what it is round here, you can virtually enslave the yokels and they're poor enough to be grateful. Donald does us twice a week for less than the cost of my daily Scotch bill. And I certainly don't intend to do it myself – I'd given up my job to write, not to take on domestic duties, despite what my lovely wife Ruth might sometimes hope.

Unfortunately, he has several drawbacks, one of them being that he can – and does – turn any conversation round to Roger Moore within moments of it starting. He'd been telling me of another driver coming to grief on Century Lane, an accident blackspot two or three miles away. A 2CV had skidded off the road and been totalled against a tree. He'd immediately segued to a car chase in a Bond film in which 007 had been driving such a vehicle. And, voila, there he was on Roger Moore.

"See, Mr Stewart, people don't realize what a range he has," he was saying as he pushed a duster in a desultory way along my bookshelves. "Some bloke down the pub said he was just a pair of raised eyebrows. But I told him he's played in a lot of different movies, more than you'd think. He was a German officer in one."

"Did he do the accent?" I said wearily, scrolling through the text on my computer screen.

"Well, no, but that's not my point. My point is—"

"Leave the desk please, Donald."

"Sorry, Mr Stewart," he said, riffling quickly through the papers he'd picked up before putting them back on my desk. "See you got another letter for The Forge. That postman should be shot, then I could do his job. I'd—"

"Thanks Donald," I said sharply, though he was right about the postman. We lived in The Old Forge whilst just down the road the Parkers lived in The Forge. The postman regularly mixed up our mail, though in fairness that was also because Ruth still went by her maiden name of Parkin, which provided an additional complication for the short-sighted old gent.

Aside from being an anorak about Roger Moore – a little perverse these days, wouldn't you say? – the other drawback to Donald is that he is incurably nosy. He has a habit of rooting through the things on my desk if I'm not around to stop him.

Donald droned on then interrupted himself.

"Lummy," he said (he has a fondness for fifties Ealing films too). "Come and look at this, Mr Stewart."

I joined him at the window and looked down at two stocky men standing in Mrs Spring's pool. Stripped to their underwear, they were manhandling her body through the water towards a stretcher at the side of the pool.

Beside the stretcher were two neat piles of clothes, topped by police helmets, truncheons and other crime-busting paraphernalia. There was also a set of false teeth. Mrs Spring wore ill-fitting dentures that whistled when she was agitated. She took them out before swimming since underwater they produced a kind of death rattle. Aptly enough, it now seemed.

The body is a temple, Mrs Spring used to declare to those people who still had anything to do with her. Hers was devoted to excess. When she rolled out of the policemen's exasperated grasp just as they had her feet hoisted onto the bank, the consequent displacement of water more than proved Archimedes Principle. It soaked a third man in a smart suit who was taking down notes as he listened to the white-faced gardener.

I sent Donald away, telling him to finish off the next day, then phoned Ruth with the news. It took five minutes to tell her, given that she put me on hold every couple of syllables.

A heart attack, we supposed, my neighbours, the Westwoods, and I, an hour or so later. We had congregated with virtually all the rest of the hamlet on the grassy track that runs from the church between our adjacent gardens and Mrs Spring's. Word spreads quickly in a place like ours, cut off as it is from neighbouring villages. We occupiers of these houses huddled round the Saxon church and Jacobean manor house may be solidly middle class but we gossip like fishwives.

Murder, Mr Deacon the newspaperman announced the next morning. I met him at the post-box just after seven. He saw me crossing the lane from the track and clanked to a halt on his decrepit three-gear bike, the basket of newspapers swaying drunkenly before his handlebars.

A bike with three gears is all you need, Mr Deacon insisted, even though everyone else in the Western Hemisphere was whizzing past him on multi-gear mountain bikes. Only after many years of nagging had his wife persuaded him some months before to invest in a car, a second-hand Fiat Panda. He bought it, reluctantly, but refused ever to drive it.

The road into Novington from his shop at the base of the Downs was steep; he was as usual red-faced and panting. He was a short man, rather too short for his bike. As he sucked in air, his body rose and fell awkwardly on the crossbar lodged perilously between his thighs.

"The police phoned last night," he gasped. "Whilst I was out at darts. Mrs Deacon took the message. They want a statement from me this morning. Tell them if I saw anything yesterday morning."

"And did you?"

"Well, I saw you, Mr Stewart, with that parcel in your hand. I thought to myself, he'll never get that in the post-box." He looked at me as if I must be mad even to try. "You didn't, did you?"

I shook my head, hiding my surprise behind a smile. Although my wife, Ruth, and I had moved down here two years before I was still unused to the fact that in such a small community it was impossible to do anything unobserved, even at seven in the morning. I had seen Mr Deacon from a distance when I took the parcel to the post-box on the other side of the lane but he had given no indication that he had seen me.

I wasn't mad, however. I had discovered by chance that the door to our local post-box had a faulty catch. It didn't always lock when the postman closed it after emptying the box. Parcels that wouldn't fit in the narrow slit at the top would easily fit through the door. Inconveniently for me the box had been shut tight the previous day.

Mr Deacon, inhibited by his crossbar, made a token effort to lean conspiratorially towards me. "And I saw that Edith Macrell loitering by the church. She'll be the *prime suspect*."

With that Mr Deacon straightened his basket of newspapers and set off down the lane to the houses on the far side of Novington Place. I watched him go.

The third policeman in his smart suit came to see me on the Thursday. He introduced himself as Sergeant Pratt and watched closely to see my reaction.

"Would you like a glass of champagne?" I said, remaining deadpan and waving the half-empty bottle vaguely in his direction.

"Celebrating, are we, sir?" he said, frowning.

"Something like that," I said, sneaking a guilty glance at the huge pile of branches the tree surgeon had left by my garden shed about ten minutes before.

The timing of Pratt's visit was a bit of an embarrassment to me. As we stood on the terrace looking across Mrs Spring's vast, well-tended gardens to the sparkling waters of the English Channel I was uncomfortably aware that until this morning I had not had this view.

I should really capitalize the word "view". Novington is famous locally for its unparalleled vistas. The View of the dramatic chalk cliffs and the vast expanse of the foam-flecked sea beyond is a constant subject of conversation with those who have the misfortune not to live here but who come humbly and enviously at weekends to see it.

Novington itself is pretty enough, with its jumble of Tudor cottages and grander Georgian villas, but it is the view that both nourishes the spirit and enhances the house prices.

Mrs Spring had access to The View from every part of her exceedingly large garden. We house-owners in the four cottages on the ridge behind her garden were less fortunate. Mrs Spring, a staunch Christian, passed over the Love Thy Neighbour bit of her religion. She did not wish to be overlooked anywhere in her acreage, even in areas where she never ventured. Some years before, therefore, she had planted fast-growing firs, forsythias and rhododendrons to screen us from her sight. In consequence we lost The View.

The Westwoods had been the most affected. Two years before they had resorted to copper nails in the bases of the trees but the killing process was a slow one and the Westwoods were not in the first flush of youth. The day after Mrs Spring's death they sneaked into her garden to lop three feet off the forsythia and rhododendrons that had grown wild and high, then celebrated this partial reappearance of their view with dry martinis on the terrace.

When the tree surgeon the Westwoods had ordered came on Thursday morning to lop down the fir trees entirely, I called him over. I thought he might as well also raise the skirts of the huge chestnut tree whose lower branches obliterated the view from our garden as convincingly as its upper obscured the sun. Job completed, he got the first glass of fizz.

Cynical? Frankly, nobody cared for Mrs Spring. (It was only in the newspaper report I learned that she had a first name – Dorothy. I'd never met anyone who had the temerity to call her anything other than Mrs Spring.) She was cantankerous, vindictive, spiteful, malicious, snobbish and bullying. On a good day.

Sergeant Pratt accepted my offer of champagne then walked slowly from one end of the terrace to the other, looking thoughtfully down at the grassy track, a public right of way that separated Mrs Spring's garden from the cottages on the ridge. He sniffed the champagne, more suspiciously than appreciatively, as he looked at The View.

"Lovely view of the sea," he observed, narrowing his eyes and finally taking a drink.

"We like it," I said nonchalantly. "Can you tell me how Mrs Spring died?"

"It will be in the coroner's report next week so I think I may confide in you, sir. We thought at first it was a heart attack but Mrs Spring's heart was in good repair. Except that is for the fact it had stopped beating for ever. Nor had she drowned. A suspicious pathologist, noticing slight bruising on her neck, found evidence that she had been strangled."

"What kind of evidence?"

"It's rather technical, sir. Suffice it to say we estimate the time of death at between seven and seven-thirty on Tuesday morning. Can you tell me anything of interest about that period of time?"

"Not really. I'm sure Mr Deacon is a better bet," I said. "When I spoke to him yesterday he said he was going to make a statement. What has he got to say?"

Sergeant Pratt tilted his wine glass thoughtfully. "He hasn't got very much to say at all, sir. Unfortunately, Mr Deacon was knocked off his bicycle by a hit and run driver early yesterday morning at the bottom of Novington Lane. Mr Deacon is dead."

"What time?" I asked weakly.

"Between seven fifteen and seven forty-five. Do I understand that you saw him yesterday morning?"

"I spoke to Mr Deacon at the post-box around seven. A hit and run driver? But the road to Novington doesn't go anywhere – we never have any traffic."

"Precisely, sir." Pratt gave me another searching look. "Did you see or hear the noise of any kind of motor vehicle around the time you were talking to Mr Deacon?"

"I think I may have heard something afterwards, when I was having my breakfast in our garden. You know, Mr Deacon told me he had seen Mrs Macrell out and about on the morning of Mrs Spring's death."

Pratt cast a baleful glance on me.

"Did he indeed? Thank you, Mr Stewart. Tell me now, do you happen to own a red car?"

I shook my head.

"Not any more. I sold Edith Macrell my Golf last year. That's red. Lots of other red cars in the village. Wing Commander Westwood, Patrick Ferguson at Novington Place. My wife's car is red too."

"Would your wife mind if my men came to take paint samples?"

"It would be unwise for me to speak for her but I can't see she'd object."

When he'd gone I phoned Mrs Deacon to offer my condolences. She was tearful but hard at work. "Nobody else will do it if I don't. As Wing Commander Westwood made clear. He's the limit, he is. He phones me up yesterday to say he hasn't got his newspapers. I say 'I'm ever so sorry Wing Commander but I've just heard that Eric – Mr Deacon – has been run over.' The Wing Commander's quiet for a moment then he says: 'So who's going to deliver my paper today?'"

Sitting on the terrace I thought about Mrs Macrell. She'd been very close to Mrs Spring at one time – they were both widows. Then Mrs Spring had Mrs Macrell's chimpanzee put down. The chimp lived in a foetid room of its own in Mrs Macrell's ramshackle Georgian farmhouse. It cavorted there day and night, swinging off the central light fitting, relieving itself on the furniture below.

The chimp was playful and loved to nip. One day it mistook Mrs Spring's earlobe for some tasty titbit. The amount of blood an earlobe can produce is disproportionate either to its size or its usefulness. And that amount of blood on a silk blouse, of however overbearing a pattern, is difficult to disguise.

So Mrs Spring, one hand holding a lump of Mrs Macrell's hastily proffered kitchen towel to her ear, the other clutching her handbag to her extravagant bosom, insisted Mrs Macrell pay for the cost of a replacement blouse. Mrs Macrell – a wealthy woman who in common with many wealthy women didn't like spending her money on anything but herself – refused.

Mrs Spring, dentures clacking, threatened to have the chimp put down. Mrs Macrell threatened to set the chimp on more than Mrs Spring's ear. Mrs Spring thought it wise to withdraw. The very next day her solicitors went into action. A long legal battle was expected. Then suddenly Mrs Macrell backed down. Paid up and acquiesced when Mrs Spring vindictively insisted she have the chimp put down.

This was particularly strange as Mrs Macrell had often declared that the chimp was like a son to her – a worrying thought, especially for her actual son, Jonathan, a good-natured non-achiever in his early forties.

"She probably had an unhappy life," my wife remarked when we discussed Mrs Spring's policy of always kicking opponents when they were down. Ruth always looks for the best in people – she'd qualify for sainthood if saintliness allowed for an active sex life.

I finished the champagne thinking about the police setting a Pratt to catch a Macrell. I can't help thinking in newspaper headlines. After 25 years as a sub-editor – during which time my main functions were making the illiterate scrawlings of our celebrity columnists readable and finding puns for headlines – it's in my blood.

I enjoyed subbing – I've always liked to be thorough about details – but I was happy to throw it in when we came down here in favour of the writing I had always intended to do. I had a commission to write what I assured my publishers would be a domestic version of that old bestseller *A Year In Provence*.

The parish of Novington, some three miles long and half a mile wide, contains more millionaires than you can shake a stick at if, as Groucho Marx once said, that's your idea of a good time. There are retired racing drivers and jockeys, celebrated chefs, former actresses and a world famous artist. There are also a great many weirdos.

I'd outlined the idea of writing about this peculiar congeries, over a boozy Soho lunch, to a friend who had recently started an editing job at one of the new publishing conglomerates. My pitch was that I, Metropolitan Man *par excellence*, would live among country folk who would be as alien to me as Parisians were to Amazonian Indians. Of course, that was before I discovered just how alien they really were.

I was reminded at Mrs Spring's funeral. For someone who was so unpopular she got a very good turnout. Ruth and I could scarcely find a seat. "They've all come to make sure she's really dead," I whispered to Ruth. She looked very fetching in black seamed stockings and a short black linen dress – the only black dress she had. She shushed me, then tugged ineffectually at the skirt when she saw me leering at her thighs.

During the service I looked from one to the other of my neighbours. They were all glancing at Mrs Macrell, clearly convinced she had killed Mrs Spring. Mrs Westwood also had her down for Mr Deacon. "Maybe not deliberately," she'd said to me the previous day. "But she is a terrible driver."

The pall-bearers, buckling under the weight of Mrs Spring's coffin, led the way out of the church. Two chubby men I assumed were Mrs Spring's sons comforted a bowed old lady. She shuffled on spindly legs, clutching her handbag. If Mrs Spring had lived to be a shadow of her former self, this is who she would have been. It was Winifred, her sister. I met her at the house later.

"Dorothy was never the same after her husband died," Winifred confided to me. "She loved Frederick so. They'd been married 35 years when she was told he had cancer. He was dead a week later. She mourned him for two years. She was under the doctor with depression. When she came out of it her personality had changed. She resented everyone else's happiness."

There were tears in Winifred's eyes. "She made herself very unpopular, I know. But that was because she was so unhappy herself." She looked me straight in the eye. "Do you know who killed her?" I shook my head slowly, looking beyond her to Mrs Macrell, flushed with sherry, over by the mantelpiece.

Although she lived three houses away along the track, I'd met Mrs Macrell only about six months after we moved in. I'd put an ad in the local paper to sell my car and she'd phoned me. She wanted to buy it for her son. No, not the chimp, the other one.

I'd gone round to Mrs Macrell's house to deliver the car at nine in the morning. Mrs Macrell came to the door in a rumpled nightdress. A thin stick of a woman in her early sixties, she had in one hand a small cigar, in the other a glass of red wine.

"Is this a bad time?" I said.

"Any time's a bad time," she said, taking a swig of her wine. "I'm a manic depressive."

"That's nice," I said, momentarily nonplussed. She looked at me. I stumbled on: "Are you having a bad week?"

She sniffed.

"Bad year."

We stood in her doorway as she haggled about the price because I could only find one set of car keys. I promised I'd bring her the other set when I found it – I'm hopelessly untidy – and made good my escape. "Would you like a glass of wine?" she called after me. I shouted back my thanks but declined the invitation. It was a bit early in the day, even for me.

Janet, my first wife, always used to say drink would be the death of me. If your cooking doesn't get me first, I used to snarl back. She was a vegetarian so every meal was pulses or beans, pulses or beans. A dinner party at our house could be a hazardous affair. Our guests were discouraged from going anywhere near a naked flame for at least an hour after the main course.

Our attitude to drink – I drank, she didn't – was one of many areas of disagreement between us. But her death affected me more than I thought it would – I suppose because we had been together 15 years. The Years of Struggle we used to call them. I used to call them. I was in genuine mourning when I met Ruth. I was fifty and then this beautiful brunette, 18 years my junior, came into my life.

We got on well, even though we had little in common. She

was an MBA and had the work ethic very badly. An ambitious East End girl, still trying to earn her father's approval. He was a scrap metal millionaire and very dominant in her life.

However, I soon discovered there were two Ruths. One was a tense, driven senior executive, the other was a soft, sentimental woman who loved nothing more than cuddling up in bed for hours on end. For years she had been struggling to merge the two.

This second Ruth was hopelessly impractical in other endearing ways. She was a living rebuttal to Pavlov's theory of conditioned response. No matter that she must have used a seat belt thousands of times, when she sat in the passenger seat of a car she never, ever remembered to put the seat belt on unprompted. At home she had been using a computer for four years now but still had to ask me how to send email attachments.

Our first months in Sussex were blissful. Candle-lit dinners on the terrace, Chopin and Satie drifting through the French windows into the night. Walks at dusk through the fields, arm in arm.

It was only later that friction developed because of her gung-ho attitude to work. I have my own simple rules for life. They work for me. I sleep at night. But there was no way I could advise Ruth. She read California-speak self-help manuals about excellence, being a complete person and getting in touch with the universe within but she scorned my advice as offering simplistic post-hippy placebos.

She was after all living in the real world. She commuted each day to London from Chiltington and some evenings, fraught from work, she drove home far too quickly in her Renault turbo to find me sitting with a bottle of wine in the garden after a creative day writing in the sunshine. She didn't always conceal her irritation.

We didn't go to Mr Deacon's funeral on the following Wednesday, though we sent a wreath. The day after the funeral Mrs Deacon turned up to deliver the newspapers in a gleaming new car, a shiny blue Japanese job. I tried to remember what colour the Fiat Panda had been. Surely it had been red?

"Have the police managed to find anything out about the motorist who knocked over poor Mr Deacon?" I said when she came to the door.

"Not a thing," she sniffed, handing me the newspaper. She didn't seem overly concerned.

"New car?" I said politely. "Nice colour."

"Brand new, Mister Stewart, thanks. It's not all that's going to be new either. Mr Deacon was so mean he'd skin a flea and tan its hide. For twenty years he had me believing we were one step away from the bankruptcy court. When he died I found out how much he'd really got saved up in the building society. Now I intend to spend some of it." She walked over to the car, calling back over her shoulder. "And if he's watching from wherever he ended up, I hope it drives him mad, the miserable old sod."

The Westwoods threw a drinks party that Sunday lunchtime to show off the magnificence of their view. Mrs Spring's death had given them a new lease of life – they looked ten years younger. Their house was one of those that made me want to take a bin bag and fill it with every junky knick-knack in sight so Ruth and I stayed out on the terrace watching the seagulls wheeling above the cliffs.

I got involved in the usual fatuous conversation with Mrs Westwood, who always felt she had to talk to me about literature. From the other end of the terrace she honked, in great excitement: "Donald, do you think Shakespeare wrote the plays?"

"Frankly, Mrs Westwood, I don't give a flying fuck." Well, no, I didn't say that, but I wanted to. I was cheesed off because we were stuck with David Parker, the blacksmith with artistic pretensions who lived at The Forge. He was a big man with powerful hands. He had one of those silly beards that don't have moustaches and in his black roll-neck sweater he must have looked just the thing in 1959. Shame it was forty-odd years later.

He was married to Lucy, a sparky woman in her early fifties, who we always thought was so *together*. Yoga, pottery, herbal tea and the *Guardian*. Clearly, however, a panic had set in about an imagined lonely old age and she had married this oik. We saw them casually almost every week because of the regular mix-up over mail.

"We've got a letter for you," Lucy said now, rummaging in her handbag and producing a square brown envelope. "It came about a week ago but I put it somewhere safe then couldn't find it. Sorry."

Ruth took it from her outstretched hand, glanced at the handwriting on the envelope and quietly stuffed it into her own bag. I thought I saw her colour slightly.

As I was trying to extricate us from the Parkers, the Wing Commander bore down. "Phone," he said. "Jonathan Macrell. He and that woman can't make it. Taken in by the police for questioning. Deacon's death. Maybe Spring's too. Police have the car. Paint samples. Looks bad. Allowed one telephone call. Used it to send apologies about drinks. Ass."

When we got back to our house Ruth, looking distracted, excused herself and went up to the bathroom, taking her handbag with her. When she eventually came back down, she avoided my eyes and went out into the garden. I found her bag upstairs. There was no sign of the letter Mrs Parker had handed to her.

I watched Ruth in the garden from our bedroom window. She looked like she was settling in for an afternoon's work. I made a phone call then went over to the local stables for my regular Sunday hack. It was a hobby I'd taken up when we first moved here. I used to do a lot of things then.

When I was made redundant – excuse me, when I was *downsized* – I sold the house in London and bought a cheaper one down here – that's to say, I *downshifted*. I got the minimum pay-off might I add so I lived on the profit from the house for a while. It didn't go far.

I couldn't get an advance on my book – first-time author – so I borrowed money from Ruth's father to live on whilst I wrote it. He thought the loan was for an extension to the house. He could well afford it, but he set it against Ruth's eventual massive inheritance.

Ruth was very good about it, but the situation caused strain between us. After all, why do women go for older men if not to be taken care of, financially and emotionally? She didn't expect to be keeping me. I think she respected me less.

Maybe that's why the affair began. About three months before Mrs Spring's death Ruth began coming home late. If I asked, she'd say she'd been working. If I said I'd phoned her and there had been no answer she'd say her secretary had forgotten to switch the calls through when she left for the night.

A few times at home the phone rang on the answering machine but there was no message. We got a lot of wrong numbers. The phone had rung at six-thirty on the morning of Mrs Spring's death. Ruth had just been going out the door – she usually leaves for work about six but she was late that morning. She said the caller had hung up when she answered it.

The police let Jonathan go on Monday, although they still held his mother. The same day, Donald the cleaner delivered some hot news. He had his own key to the house, so as usual I had retreated to my study in advance of his arrival.

First he asked me if he could do the study and the other rooms upstairs the following morning as he was running late.

"Sure," I said, pleased to postpone the inevitable monologues about Roger Moore. Even then, he wasn't quite ready to go.

"Crikey, Mr Stewart, a woman in Chiltington has died in suspicious circumstances," he said, hovering in the study doorway. "That makes three."

My fingers stopped clacking on the keyboard of my computer. "I'm sorry to hear that. How did she die?"

"Riding accident. Fell off her horse and broke her neck."

"How ghastly," I said, with feeling. Unpleasant memories stirred.

"You might have known her," he said. "Valerie James. She used to keep her horse at the stables you go to."

I said nothing. He sniffed. "How's your riding coming along?"

"Fine, thanks," I said absently. I was thinking about my first wife, Janet. She had been a keen horsewoman. She used to ride in Richmond Park when we lived in Twickenham. Every Tuesday and Thursday, rain or shine. You could set your clock by her. She too had died in a riding accident. The coroner had concluded that her horse had refused a low jump, she had toppled over his head and broken her neck.

I had begun to learn to ride as a way of exorcizing my first wife's death. I'd taken it up when we first moved down here, in what Ruth called my period of second infantilism. But then she didn't know about Janet and I didn't feel I could explain to her.

Ruth had been remarkably incurious about my life before her. She had never even asked how Janet had died. But then, if I'm honest, Ruth was always too self-absorbed to bother much about anyone else.

I picked her up from the station that evening. It was close, with black clouds massing and thunder growling ominously. We were going to dinner with some friends in Chiltington. Ruth had been acting oddly towards me since the Westwood drinks party but tonight she seemed particularly subdued. "Seat belt," I said, as we waited at a set of lights. She reached for the belt but didn't speak.

We drove home in silence. Ruth went straight upstairs for a bath. When she came out of the bathroom, wearing only a towel, she came into my study, dropped an envelope on the desk without speaking and went to our bedroom.

It was the envelope Lucy Parker had given her at the West-woods' drinks party. I'd been expecting it. I flipped it over, lifted the flap and took out a second envelope. White, good quality. I looked at the familiar handwriting on the front.

There was a card inside. I began to withdraw it then stopped. I knew what it was. I dropped it back on the desk and went into our bedroom. "Do you want an explanation?" I said.

"There isn't time," she said, fiddling with the zip of her dress. "We've got to be at Tony and Ellen's by eight." She brushed past me. "I just want you to know that I know."

I guessed she wouldn't leave it at that. In the car, sitting stiffly, she said:

"So where did you meet her?"

"Seat belt," I said, glancing across. "Look, I sent her a birthday card, I admit. But that doesn't mean anything. Certainly not what you're thinking."

"Don't demean us by denying anything," she snapped at me. "What about those wrong numbers, those abruptly ended phone calls whenever I came into the room, those guilty looks? I've suspected for a long time. I pressed the redial button on the phone once after you'd been having a whispered conversation. I got through to a woman."

I didn't say anything. I was thinking furiously.

"What I don't understand is why she sent your birthday card

back to me," she went on. "What did she hope to achieve? Did she think I'd leave you because of her? Or was she being spiteful because you had finished with her? Had you?"

She fumbled in her bag for a cigarette. Her occasional cigarettes were a habit that annoyed me, but now didn't seem the time to make a fuss.

"Are you still seeing her?" she said, exhaling smoke.

Okay, okay. Time to come clean. I'd been having an affair, not Ruth. It didn't mean I didn't love Ruth. It just meant that I was bored. Bored senseless.

Have you ever tried living in the country? Oh, it sounds wonderful when you're living in the city. And at first it is. Every daybreak is magical as you wake to the birds singing in the trees, the sun burning the mist away over the sea.

You look forward to the long peaceful day stretching ahead of you. But, God, do those days *stretch*. They are interminable. After a month I was praying for the pitch black nights to fall. Some mornings, at the thought of another slow, empty day ahead I wanted to strangle those bloody birds for being so cheerful.

I was a city person. Always would be. I loved the buzz of city life, loved working on a daily paper, always up against the clock. When those bastards sacked me and I had to move down here, it was as if they passed a life sentence on me. So I started an affair. And just as easily ended it.

"No," I said truthfully. "I'm not seeing her."

The dinner went well, considering Ruth drank too much, laughed too loudly and was too nervously exuberant – but then she was always like that. I drank only mineral water. I observed Ruth distantly. I was sorry that I had hurt her but I was not distraught. I didn't care enough about her.

Don't get me wrong. I loved her – in my way. But my way isn't other people's way. There's always been a coldness in me, a chilly core. I can be gregarious, I can be concerned. But it's all pretence. At a fundamental level, I just don't care.

Tony had a friend who was a policeman. He had the latest news about the murder inquiry. The paint found on Mr Deacon's bike matched samples taken from Mrs Macrell's car. She was going to be charged.

As we were leaving, Ellen said: "You know we had our own gory death here last Sunday."

"I heard," I said, guiding Ruth towards the car.

"A woman broke her neck falling off her horse," Ellen continued. "You might have known her, Donald, she used your stables."

"I heard," I repeated. I opened the passenger door and helped Ruth get in.

"Valerie James," Ellen said as I hurried round to the driver's side and opened that door.

"Who – ?" Ruth said, leaning across towards Helen, as I closed the driver's door behind me.

"I heard," I said as I turned on the engine and the lights, put the car into gear and set it in motion.

Ruth was quiet for the first hundred yards. Then she laughed and said: "Not the Valerie James who had a birthday recently. Not the Valerie James who was my husband's mistress. The one he said he wasn't seeing any more."

I automatically glanced down. She hadn't put her seat belt on. I started to say something but she continued talking drunkenly.

"No wonder you're not seeing her." She stifled a laugh. "It would be a bit difficult. And probably illegal."

It remained an oppressive evening. Storm clouds were massed in the sky above us. I had opened the sun roof and now drove slowly through the winding lanes, pleased to feel the breeze on my face.

"Did you love her very much?"

"Don't be absurd," I said, after a moment.

Ruth leant her head against the side window and tucked her feet beneath her. Without looking at me she said dully: "Janet rode, didn't she?"

Ever since Ruth dropped the card on my desk, I'd been trying to work out what to do. Ruth was huddled on her seat, gazing blankly at the scenery rushing by. I looked fondly at her. How I loved her, in my way.

And how little that meant. I signalled a left turn.

"That damned birthday card!" I said. "Everything followed from the fact that the postman doesn't always lock the post-box properly. I thought I was the only one who knew this. But Mrs Spring knew it too. She regularly stole letters from the post-box to discover her neighbour's secrets. That must be how she got something on Edith Macrell, to make her destroy the chimp. Anyway, Mrs Spring stole my birthday card to Valerie, ten minutes after I'd put it in the box."

Ruth stirred in her seat. I could tell she was looking at the side of my face.

"Mrs Spring?" she said cautiously. I glanced at her. Suddenly she looked sober.

"Yes, Mrs Spring, darling. Do keep up. When Valerie complained she hadn't got a card from me I thought it had been lost in the post. Frankly I was relieved – never put anything in writing if you want to avoid getting caught. Then, at the summer fete, whilst I was on the bookstall selling 20-year-old Readers Digests to an old buffer from Elam, Mrs Spring flourished it in front of me."

Ruth began to breathe shallowly but said nothing. I think she was beginning to feel frightened. I took the next right turn. "She was a nasty old woman, you know. She sent it to you, not Valerie James. Sent it out of sheer malice. I couldn't have that. I love you. I don't want to lose you."

A car passed on the other side of the road, its headlights dazzling. I looked away. "Or your inheritance."

I took the third exit off a small roundabout onto Century Lane. I slowed down and reached up to close the sun roof. It had started to rain.

"So you . . ." Ruth's voice trailed off.

I smiled. "You can say it, darling. I won't be upset. Yes, I killed Mrs Spring."

Ruth laughed. Rather harshly, I thought. "You won't be upset. Now I've heard everything."

I smiled again.

"No, you haven't. You haven't heard the half of it."

The rain fell in earnest now, hammering on the roof and windscreen. "Valerie phoned me that morning to warn me. Remember the six-thirty call? She'd had a call from Mrs Spring the night before. Mrs Spring was gloating. She'd just posted Valerie's card to you.

"I went round to the post-box to retrieve it before the postman arrived but the post-box was locked. So I went to see Mrs Spring as she was about to go for her swim. If I'd known I was going to spend a fruitless week trying to intercept the bloody card maybe I wouldn't have bothered."

Ruth was looking at the road ahead again. She was wringing her hands. She still hadn't put her seat belt on but now didn't seem the time to say.

"I didn't necessarily mean to do it, darling. But she was so awful to me. I thought she was going to start shouting about it. And then the Westwoods would hear. I tried to stop her shouting. That's all I was trying to do."

"And on Sunday when you went for a drive – you went to see your mistress?" Ruth whispered. "Why did you kill her? Had she threatened to tell me about your affair?"

"Not exactly, no," I said. The rain was falling so hard, the wipers could scarcely cope. I slowed down to twenty. "Some storm, eh? Valerie thought Mrs Spring's death was fishy and she threatened to go to the police unless I left you for her. Well, I ask you, have you met her? Oh, no, of course you haven't. Well, she's attractive enough but she's also a crashing bore about horses. Always rambling on about gymkhanas. I swear I usually had sex with her to shut her up." I glanced at Ruth. "Sorry, darling, that was insensitive of me."

"But why did Edith Macrell kill Mr Deacon if she hadn't killed Mrs Spring?" Ruth looked at me. I heard her gasp of realization and felt her shrink against the passenger door. "You did it."

"Clever girl," I said.

"But how? Oh, God – you found the other set of keys to the Golf you'd sold Mrs Macrell and drove into Mr Deacon in that."

We'd reached a straight stretch of road. I steadied myself and put my foot on the accelerator. The windscreen wipers pumped rapidly.

"I regretted Mr Deacon. But when I went down the next day to intercept the postman and retrieve that damned birthday card he told me he'd seen me the previous day. I couldn't take the risk, you see. I thought I'd have to pop Mrs Macrell, too, just in case, until I had the idea of using her car to kill him."

"You killed three people so you wouldn't lose the chance to get at my father's money," Ruth said flatly.

"Well, your father's money is one of your most attractive features," I said cheerfully. "But I hear what you're saying. Thing is, it gets easier every time. And the irony is, I'm not going to get the dosh after all."

It took a few moments for that to sink in, then Ruth grappled with the handle to the passenger door.

"Child-proof lock, love."

She looked at me fiercely then subsided into her seat. "How did your first wife die?"

"I know, I know. I've no imagination. Riding accident again. But it's terribly easy to mock up, you see. Much better than other methods. I felt such a fool when the police spotted the clumsy way I killed Mrs Spring. I hoped they'd think she'd got tangled in the filtration pipe."

The rain showed no sign of slackening. The lane began to wind again. We were approaching the accident black spot.

With Ruth dead there would be no way to link me to the other deaths because nobody else knew about my affair with Valerie. Nobody alive anyway.

It was going to be dicey for me when we came off the road and hit a tree but for the sake of verisimilitude I was prepared to spend a week or so in hospital. I figured that at thirty miles an hour I would easily survive the impact, given the driver's airbag and my seatbelt. Ruth, sadly, wouldn't be so lucky.

It was a shame I wouldn't be able to get at Ruth's inheritance. But at least there was the insurance money. I'd test negative for alcohol in my blood so the insurance company would have to pay up. And I'd learned from the meagre pay-off I'd got after my first wife's death not to under-insure my second one.

I slowed, spun the wheel and took the car off the road. I was trying to think of a headline. Author Writes Second Wife Off, perhaps. Time moved very slowly. I heard Ruth scream. I think I felt her hand clutch my arm. I braced myself as the thick trunk of a tree rushed towards us. A split second before we hit I thought of Donald the cleaner. Coming back to do my office in the morning. Nosing around. Reading the birthday card for Valerie James lying open on my desk.

FATHER BROWN IN MUNCIE, INDIANA

RUTH DUDLEY EDWARDS

"Can it be Father Brown?"

The little black-clad figure sitting in the hotel foyer nodded.

"My God," said the Magna Cum Murder fan. "What are you doing here?"

"I don't quite know," said Father Brown. "It is a mystery or a miracle. Two very different ideas, but they are of course in their spiritual essence and simplicity essentially the same."

"I can see you haven't changed," said the fan. "I never did understand what you were driving at."

"That is because the truth so often makes little sense."

"Yes, yes," said the fan hastily. "But metaphysics apart, is there a rational reason for you being in Muncie?"

"Metaphysics and reason are supremely rational."

The fan was beginning to shift restlessly, when a whirlwind arrived, scooped the little priest into her arms and cried, "Kathryn Kennison, Father, I just knew you wouldn't let me down."

The fan nodded. "Now I understand. I have heard of this from other guests. You find yourself in Muncie without having any real idea why you're here except that Kathryn Kennison seduced you over the phone."

"Perhaps seduction is a concept which . . ." began Father Brown as Kathryn Kennison replaced him tenderly in his chair and bounded away to embrace another arrival.

". . . is inappropriate when applied to a priest," said the fan.

"Alas, my son, that is not the case. Are priests gods that they cannot be seduced?"

"Yes, but I had thought such talk distasteful to a priest of your generation. You knew nothing of sexual scandals of the kind that grip the ecclesiastical world these days."

The little head shook. "You never understood, did you? Spending so much of my life in the confessional box, I knew all the sins of the world. Who better than a priest knows the secrets of the human soul?"

"So you're not shockable?"

"No. I am not. That delightful young woman understood that, which is why she asked me to come here to solve the Bobbit case."

The fan clutched his head. "The Bobbit case?" he asked wildly. "The John Wayne Bobbit case? What is there to solve about the Bobbit case?"

"Everything in the world and nothing in the world," said Father Brown simply, as he picked up his umbrella and glided away towards the lift. "But the good God may help me to reveal the truth at lunchtime on Saturday."

"So what happened?" asked the fan's wife when he rang her on Saturday evening to report. "What did he say?"

"That Lorena didn't do it."

"Who did?"

"He did."

"Father Brown did it?"

"No, silly. Bobbit did it."

The fan's wife's incredulity rendered her momentarily incapable of speech. "Why would he cut off his own . . .?"

"Because he wanted to be rich and famous."

"So why didn't he admit he'd done it?"

"Because he would have got a bad press. It isn't something with which one should collude."

The fan paused to consult his notes. "Remember

Deuteronomy? 'He that is wounded in the stones, or hath his privy member cut off, shall not enter into the congregation of the Lord.' Even in this secular age, Father Brown points out, men think emasculation renders them outcasts. Therefore they can't admit to outcasting themselves, as it were."

The fan's wife, who had little patience with her husband's hobby, raised her voice. "You've bought this crazy idea, you schmuck? Why did Lorena admit to it, then? Not to speak of driving wildly round the country with the missing part."

"She thought she'd done it, you see. Apparently, she's very very absent-minded, she'd had a few drinks and when Bobbit shouted "Look what you did. Call the hospital," she panicked and made off with the evidence."

"I cannot believe," said his wife grimly, "that even you, whose brains are addled with mystery stories, should have been taken in like this by a man of 140 in a dog-collar."

"It must be true," said the fan simply. "Fictional detectives are always right."

The fan's wife spoke very slowly and through gritted teeth. "You mean that because Father Brown doesn't really exist, his explanation is correct?"

"Exactly," said the fan. "That's metaphysics."

TICKLED TO DEATH

SIMON BRETT

If a dead body could ever be funny, this one was. Only intimations of his own mortality prevented Inspector Walsh from smiling at the sight.

The corpse in the greenhouse was dressed in a clown's costume. Bald plastic cranium with side-tufts of ropey orange hair. Red jacket, too long. Black and white check trousers suspended from elastic braces to a hooped waistband. Shoes three foot long pointing upwards in strange semaphore.

"Boy, he's really turned his toes up," said Sergeant Trooper, who was prone to such witticisms even when the corpse was less obviously humorous.

The clown's face could not be seen. The back of a plate supplied a moonlike substitute which fitted well with the overall image.

"Going to look good on the report," Sergeant Trooper continued. "Cause of death – suffocation. Murder weapon – a custard pie."

"I suppose that *was* the cause . . . Let the photographers and fingerprint boys do their bit and we'll have a look."

These formalities concluded, Inspector Walsh donned rubber gloves and cautiously prised the plate away. Over its make-up, the face was covered with pink goo. It was clogged in the nostrils and in the slack, painted mouth.

"Yes, Sergeant Trooper, it looks like suffocation."

"Course it does. What's your alternative? Poisoned custard in the pie?"

"Well, it's certainly not custard." The Inspector poked at the congealed mess. It was hard and crumbly. "Even school custard wasn't this bad. No, it's plaster of Paris or something. They don't usually use that for slapstick, do they?"

Sergeant Trooper shook his head. "Nope. Foam, flour and water, dough . . . not plaster of Paris."

"Hmm. Which probably means the crime was premeditated."

The Sergeant thought this too obvious to merit a response. Inspector Walsh bent down and felt in the capacious pockets of the red jacket.

"What are you looking for? I don't think clowns carry credit cards or passports."

"No," Inspector Walsh agreed, producing a string of cloth sausages and a jointless rubber fish.

"Wonder if there's anything else." He felt again in the pockets. His rubber-gloved hand closed round a soft oval object. He squeezed it gently.

"Bloody hell," said Sergeant Trooper.

Thin jets of water found their way through the caked white beneath the clown's eyes. Inspector Walsh drew out a rubber bulb attached to a plastic tube.

"Old clown's prop – squirting eyes."

He reached into the other pocket and found what felt like a switch. He pressed it.

The two tufts of orange hair shot out at right angles from the clown's bald head. As they did so, the noise of a klaxon escaped from somewhere inside the jacket.

Inspector Walsh stood up. "I don't know," he said. "It's a funny business."

"The fact is," objected the Teapot, "it's damnably inconvenient. These people are our guests. We can't just keep them here against their will."

"No, we can't," the Pillar-box agreed shrilly. "What will they think of our hospitality?"

The Yorkshire terrier, scampering around the study, barked its endorsement of their anger.

"I'm sorry." Inspector Walsh leant coolly back against the leather-topped desk. "But a murder has been committed and we cannot allow anyone to leave the building until we have taken their statements."

"Well, I may be forced to speak to your superior," snapped the Teapot. "I am not without influence in this area."

"I'm sure you're not," the Inspector soothed. "Now why don't you take your lid off and sit down?"

The Teapot flounced angrily, but did remove its hatlike lid and, hitching up its wired body, perched on a low stool.

"You may as well sit down too, madam." The Inspector pointed to a second stool and the Pillar-box, with equally bad grace, folded on to it. Pale blue eyes flashed resentment through the posting slit.

"And can we get rid of that bloody dog?" A uniformed policeman ushered the reluctant Yorkshire terrier out of the study. "Oh, and get us some tea while you're at it, could you, Constable?" The Inspector smiled perfunctorily. "Now let's just get a few facts straight. You are Mr and Mrs Alcott?"

The two heads nodded curt agreement.

"And this is your house?"

Two more nods.

"And, Mr Alcott, you have no doubt that the dead man is your business partner, Mr Cruikshank?"

Alcott's head, rising tortoise-like from the top of the Teapot, twitched from side to side. "No doubt at all."

"He had been wearing the clown costume all evening?"

"Yes. It's one of our most popular lines. As partners, we always try to demonstrate both the traditional and the new. Mr Cruikshank was wearing one of Festifunn's oldest designs, while I –" unconsciously, he smoothed down the Teapot frame with his spout "– chose one of the most recent." He gestured proudly to the Pillar-box. "My wife's is also a new design."

Some response seemed to be required. The Inspector murmured, "Very nice too," which he hoped was appropriate.

"And your guests?"

"They're all dressed in our lines too."

"Yes. That wasn't actually what I was going to ask. I wished to enquire about your guest list. Are all the people here personal friends?"

"Not so much friends as professional associates," replied the Teapot tartly.

"So they would all have known Mr Cruikshank?"

"Oh, certainly. Mr Cruikshank always made a point of getting to know our staff and clients personally." The Teapot's tone implied disapproval of this familiarity.

"So I would be correct in assuming that this Fancy Dress Party is a business function?"

The Teapot was vehement in its agreement with this statement. The party was very definitely part of Festifunn's promotional campaign, and as such (though this was implied rather than stated) tax-deductible.

"You don't think we do this for fun, do you?" asked the crumpled Pillar-box.

"No, of course we don't." The Teapot assumed an accent of self-denying righteousness. "It's just an opportunity to demonstrate the full range of our stock to potential customers. And also it's a kind of thank-you to the staff. Something that I wouldn't do voluntarily, I hasten to add, but something they demand these days as a right. And one daren't cross them. Even the novelty industry," he concluded darkly, "is not immune to the destructive influence of the trade unions."

"But presumably everyone has a good time?"

Mr Alcott winced at the Inspector's suggestion. "The Fancy Dress Party was not originally my idea," he said in further self-justification.

"Mr Cruikshank's," Walsh deduced smoothly.

"Yes."

"Then why is it held in your house?"

"Have you recently examined the cost of hiring outside premises?"

"I meant why not in Mr Cruikshank's house?"

The Pillar-box tutted at the idea. "Mr Cruikshank's house would be totally unsuitable for a function of this nature. It's a terrible mess, full of odd machinery and designs he's working

on . . . most unsalubrious. I'm afraid his style of living, too, is –
was – most irregular. He drank, you know."

The Inspector let that go for the moment. "Mr Alcott, would
you say Mr Cruickshank had any enemies?"

"Well . . ."

"I mean, did he tend to annoy people?"

"Certainly."

"In what way?"

"Well, I have no wish to speak ill of the dead . . ."

"But?"

"But Mr Cruikshank was . . ." the Teapot formed the words
with distaste, ". . . a practical joker."

"Ah." The Inspector smiled. "Good thing to be in your line
of business."

"By no means," the Teapot contradicted. "Most unsuitable."

Again Walsh didn't pursue it. Time enough for that. "Right
now, I would like from you a list of your guests before I start
interviewing them." He took a notebook from his pocket, then
turned round to the desk and picked up a pencil that lay beside
an old-fashioned biscuit-barrel.

"Well, there's Mr Brickett, our Sales Manager . . ."

Inspector Walsh bent to write the name down. The pencil
squashed softly against the paper. It was made of rubber.

"I'm sorry. That's one of our BJ153s. Joke Pencil – Many
Minutes of Mirth."

"Ah."

At that moment the uniformed constable arrived with the tea-
tray. The three helped themselves and then, when the Inspector
again looked round for something to write with, the Teapot
said, "There's a ball-point pen just the other side of the biscuit-
barrel."

"Thank you." The Inspector picked it up to continue his list.

"Sugar?" the Pillar-box offered, adding righteously, "We
don't."

"Well, I do." He took two lumps, put them in the tea, and
reached for a spoon. When he looked back, the lumps of sugar
were floating in the top of his cup.

"I'm sorry, Inspector," said the Teapot. "You've got some of our GW34s. Silly Sugar – Your Friends Will Be Tickled To Death."

The young man looked sheepish. Since he was dressed as a sheep, this wasn't difficult.

"Might I ask, Mr O'Brien . . ." Despite the request for permission, Inspector Walsh was clearly going to ask anyway, ". . . why you went out to the greenhouse at the time that you discovered the body?"

"Well, I . . . er . . . well, um . . ." the young man bleated.

"I think you'd do better to tell me," Walsh advised portentously.

"Yes. Well, the fact was, I was . . . um, there was a young lady involved."

"You mean a young lady was with you when you found Mr Cruikshank?"

"No. No, no, she was still in the house, but I was . . . er . . . sort of scouting out the . . . er . . . lie of the land. Do I make myself clear?"

"No."

"Oh. Am I going to have to spell it out?"

"Yes."

"Well, you see, this young lady and I are . . . er . . . rather good friends. I'm at Festifunn in Indoor Firework Testing and she's in Fancy Dress Design, so we see quite a lot of each other and . . . er . . . you know how it is . . ."

The Inspector nodded indulgently, awaiting further information.

"Unfortunately, her father doesn't approve of our . . . er, er . . . friendship. He thinks, as a profession, Indoor Fireworks is too . . . er . . . volatile. And my landlady's a bit old-fashioned, so we can only really meet at work, or in secret . . ."

"Yes?"

"Which, I mean, is okay. It works all right, but it sometimes leads to complications. Like tonight."

"What happened tonight?"

"Well, um . . ." Insofar as it is possible for a sheep to blush, the Sheep blushed. "You see, it comes down to . . . sex."

"It often does," Walsh observed sagely.

"Yes. Well, um . . . do I really have to tell you this?"

"Yes."

"Right. Well, normally we . . . um . . . go into my car for . . . um . . ."

"I understand."

"Thank you. But you see, this is where feminine vanity raises problems. At least it did tonight. You see, my friend, as any woman would, was anxious to look her best for the party and, since she works in Fancy Dress Design, nothing would stop her from coming in her latest creation. No woman could resist such an opportunity to show off her skills."

"No," Walsh agreed with a worldly shake of his head. "And may I ask what your friend is dressed as?"

"An Orange," the Sheep replied miserably.

"Ah."

"And I've only got a Mini."

"I begin to understand why you were checking out the greenhouse, Mr O'Brien."

The Sheep looked, if it were possible, even more sheepish.

"And what happened to the trifle?"

"The top flipped off, there was a loud squeak, and I saw the mouse in the bottom of the dish."

"Would that be a real mouse?" Inspector Walsh asked cautiously.

Joan of Arc was so surprised at the question that she removed the cigarette which drooped from her generously lipsticked mouth. "No, a rubber one. It's just the basic BT3, Squeaking Mouse, incorporated into the HM200, Tricky Trifle."

"Oh, I see. And Mr Cruikshank offered it to you?"

"Yes. I shouldn't have fallen for it. Good Lord, I handle half a dozen HM200s a day in the shop. But it was a party, you know, I wasn't concentrating – perhaps even a bit tiddly." She simpered. "Honestly, me – a couple of Babychams and I'm anybody's."

She moved her body in a manner calculated to display her bosom (a wasted effort for someone dressed in complete armour).

"I see," said Inspector Walsh again, more to change the

subject than for any other reason. "Why I'm asking about the incident, Mrs Dancer, is because we believe you may have been the last person – except, of course, for his murderer – to see Mr Cruikshank alive."

"Oh, fancy that."

"And handing you the Tricky Trifle may have been his last action before his death."

"Good Lord." Joan of Arc paused, then set her painted face in an expression of piety, as if prepared to hear voices. "Oh well, I'm glad I fell for it then. It's how he'd have wanted to go."

"I'm sorry?"

She elaborated. "He loved his jokes, Mr Cruikshank did. He designed almost all the novelties at Festifunn. Always working on something new. His latest idea was a customized Jack-in-a-Box. Really novel. Clown pops out when the box opens and a personal recorded message starts up. You know, you get different ones – jolly for kids' parties, fruity for stag nights, and so on.

"Full of ideas, Mr Cruikshank always was. Really loved jokes. So, you see, I'm glad about the Tricky Trifle. Because if he had to die, he'd have been really chuffed to die after catching someone out with one of his own novelties."

The Inspector was tempted to ask how anyone could be "chuffed" while being suffocated by a custard pie, but contented himself with another "I see." (In his early days as a detective, Walsh had worried about how often he said "I see" during interrogations, but long since he had come to accept it as just an occupational hazard.) "And before this evening, Mrs Dancer, when did you last see Mr Cruikshank?"

"Well, funnily enough, I saw him this afternoon."

"Ah."

"Yes, he came into the shop."

"Was that unusual?"

"Not unusual for him to come in, no – he liked to keep in touch with what was happening in the business – but unusual for him to come in two days running."

"I see. What did he come in for?"

"Oh, a chat. See how the stock was going. He was particularly worried about the Noses. Always get a run on Noses this time of year. We're very low on Red Drunken and Warty Witch's – and completely out of Long Rubbery."

"Oh dear," the Inspector commiserated. "And this afternoon, when Mr Cruikshank came into the shop, did you notice anything unusual about him?"

"No." Joan of Arc stubbed her cigarette out on her cuirass as she reconsidered this answer. But she didn't change her mind. "No. Well, he had a knife through his head, but—"

"I beg your pardon?"

"Knife-Through-Head – JL417. As opposed to Tomahawk-Through-Head – JL418 – and Nail-Through-Head – JL419."

"Uhuh." Curiosity overcame Inspector Walsh's customary reserve. "Which one of those is the most popular?"

"Oh, 417," Joan of Arc replied without hesitation. "Sell a few Nails, but very little call for Tomahawks these days. It's because they're not making so many Westerns – all these space films instead. Mr Cruikshank was trying to come up with a Laser-Beam-Through-Head, but it's not as easy as it sounds."

"No, I suppose not." Walsh digested this gobbet of marketing information before continuing. "And did Mr Cruikshank often come into the shop with a knife through his head?"

"Yes. Well, that or some other novelty. Boil-On-Face, Vampire Teeth, Safety-Pin-Through-Nose, that sort of thing. Lived for his work, Mr Cruikshank."

"And he didn't say anything strange that afternoon?"

"No." She pondered. "Well, yes, I suppose he did, in a way."

"Ah."

"He said he'd come to say goodbye."

"Goodbye?"

"Yes, he said someone was out to kill him, and he didn't think he'd live more than twenty-four hours."

Walsh sat bolt upright. "What! Did he say who was out to kill him?"

"Oh yes." Joan of Arc reached casually into her habergeon and brought out a packet of Players Number Six. She put one in her mouth, reached past the biscuit-barrel and picked up a box of matches. She opened it and a green snake jumped out. "BK351," she said dismissively.

"Mrs Dancer, who? *Who* did he say was out to kill him?"

"Oh, Mr Alcott."

"But that's terribly important. Why on earth didn't you mention it before?"

"Oh, I thought it was just another of Mr Cruikshank's jokes."

"So what did you do when he told you?"

"Oh, I just offered him some Squirting Chocolate and went back to stock-taking the Severed Fingers."

"You have to understand that I'm a professional accountant . . ." The Baby self-importantly hitched up his nappy and adjusted the dummy-string around his neck. ". . . and I am bound by a code of discretion in relation to the affairs of my clients."

"This *is* a police investigation, Mr McCabe . . ."

"I am aware of that, Inspector Walsh."

". . . into the most serious crime one human being can commit against another."

"Yes."

"So I suggest you save time and answer all my questions as fully as possible."

"Oh, very well." With bad grace, the Baby threw his rattle on to the desk and sat down.

"I'm going to ask you a direct question, Mr McCabe, and I require you to give me a direct answer."

The Baby's bald head wrinkled with disapproval at this proposal. But he said nothing, just stared pointedly upwards at the ornate ceiling-rose over the desk.

"Right, Mr McCabe, was there any cause for dissension between the two partners in Festifunn?"

"Well . . . As you have probably gathered, Inspector, Mr Alcott and Mr Cruikshank were men of very different personalities . . ."

"I had gathered that, yes."

"And so, inevitably, they did not always see eye to eye on the daily minutiae of the business."

"There were arguments?"

"Yes, there were."

"Threats?"

"Occasionally."

"What form did the threats take?"

"Well, they –" The Baby stopped short and coloured. The flush spread from his head to just above the navel. "Inspector, are you suggesting that *Mr Alcott* . . ."

"We have to consider every possibility, Mr McCabe. In our experience, people are most commonly murdered by their loved ones. Since, in this case, Mr Cruikshank had no immediate family, we are forced to consider those who worked closely with him."

"If you're making accusations against Mr Alcott, I don't think I can answer any further questions without a solicitor present."

The Baby sat back complacently after this repetition of something he'd heard on television. Then Inspector Walsh spoiled it by asking, "Whose solicitor?"

"I beg your pardon?"

"Whose? Yours? Mr Alcott's?"

"Oh. Um . . ."

"Anyway, I'm not making accusations at the moment, so just answer the questions!"

The Baby was suitably cowed.

"Right, was there any recent cause for more serious disagreement between the two partners of Festifunn?"

"Well . . ."

"Answer!"

"Yes, right, fine." The words came out quickly. "There has recently been an offer to take over the firm. An offer from the Jollijests Corporation."

"And the partners disagreed about the advisability of accepting the offer?"

"Precisely. Mr Alcott recognized it for the good business proposition it was. Mr Cruikshank opposed it on the somewhat whimsical grounds that he didn't want Festifunn's output limited to the manufacture of party hats and squeakers."

"Sounds a reasonable objection."

The Baby gave a patronizing smile. "When you've been in the novelty business as long as I have, Inspector, you will understand that it is not an area where sentiment should be allowed to overrule common sense."

"I see. So the argument about the proposed take-over was quite violent?"

"Certainly. At the last board meeting, Mr Cruikshank's behaviour was most unseemly. He used language that was distinctly unparliamentary." Then, after a pause, "He drank, you know."

"Yes, I did know. But he wouldn't accept the deal?"

"Under no circumstances. In fact he said, if it were to take place, it would be *over his dead body*."

The words were out before the Baby realized their significance and coloured again.

At first, Walsh restricted himself to another "I see." Then, piecing his question together slowly, he asked, "So, from the point of view of Mr Alcott's plans for the future of Festifunn, Mr Cruikshank's death couldn't have come at a more convenient time?"

Mr McCabe rose with all the dignity that a fifty-year-old accountant in a nappy can muster. "I don't see that I have to answer any further questions, Inspector. You can't make me. I suggest that you carry on the rest of your investigation without my assistance."

"Fair enough." Walsh didn't bother to argue. "Thank you, anyway, for all the invaluable help you've already given me."

The Baby, moving away, turned his head to flash a venomous look at his interrogator.

"Hey, watch out! That Yorkshire terrier's misbehaved." The Inspector pointed to where the Baby's knobbly-veined foot was about to land. Neatly on the carpet, like a pointed cottage loaf, lay the brown, glistening lump of a dog's mess.

The Baby sneered openly. "When you've been in the novelty business as long as I have, Inspector, you will learn to recognize the product. That, if I'm not very much mistaken, is an AR88 – Naughty Puppy – All Plastic, Made In Taiwan." He bent down to pick it up. "Oh."

He was very much mistaken.

Sergeant Trooper broke into Mr Brickett, the Sales Manager's, disquisition on the boom in Revolving Bow-ties in the Tyneside area. "I put it down to unemployment," he was saying. "People got time on their hands, that's when they need a laugh and we—"

"Sorry to butt in, sir, but it's important. Got the preliminary medical report, Inspector." The Sergeant handed over a buff envelope.

"Oh, thank you. Mr Brickett, if you'd mind just stepping outside, and we'll continue when . . ."

"Fine, fine." Mr Brickett, who was dressed as the Tin Man from *The Wizard of Oz*, obligingly squeaked his way out of the door.

"This is very interesting," commented Inspector Walsh, as he scanned the report.

"Yes. Looks like he would have died of the overdose of sleeping pills without the custard pie. Mogadon, they reckon."

The Inspector looked sternly at his underling. "You aren't meant to read this."

"No, well, I –" Trooper tried to get off the hook by changing the subject. "I've checked. Mrs Alcott uses Mogadon. What's more, there are twenty-five tablets missing from her supply. She knows, because she started a new bottle last night."

"Hmm. That's very good, Trooper, but it doesn't change the fact that you shouldn't have looked at—"

"And, on top of that, the boys were looking round Mr Alcott's workshop and, shoved under a couple of old sacks, they found – this."

On the word, the Sergeant dramatically produced an old paint-pot lid, to which clung the powdery traces of a thick pinkish substance.

"Polyfilla, sir," he announced with a dramatic efficiency which he then weakened by lapsing into another of his jokes. "What they stuff dead parrots with."

Receiving not the slightest encouragement to further humour, he hurried on. "And exactly, according to the forensic boys, what the custard pie was made of."

"Hmm. Prospect doesn't look too promising for Mr Alcott, does it, Trooper?"

"No, sir. Interesting thing is, though, this bit of the report suggests he needn't have gone to all that trouble."

Inspector Walsh didn't even bother to remonstrate as he followed his Sergeant's stubby finger to the relevant paragraph.

"My investigation," the Inspector began, "is now nearly complete and I have gathered you all here because I wish to piece together the murder, and some of you may be able to conform as facts details which at the moment are mere supposition."

He paused impressively, and looked around the crowded study. Towering over the assembly were the built-up shoulders of Charles I, whose head dangled nonchalantly from its owner's fingers. The Teapot, which had resumed its lid, sat primly behind its desk, with the Pillar-box, equally prim, at its side. A Salt Cellar and a Pepper Mill leant sleepily against each other. A Nun had her hand inside Julius Caesar's toga. A large cigar protruded from the Gorilla's bared teeth. A Rolling Pin, whose year at secretarial college hadn't prepared her for the effects of gin on an empty stomach, swayed gently. The Front Half of the Pantomime Horse had collapsed in a heap on the floor, while the Back Half had its arm lasciviously round The-Princess-Of-Wales-On-Her-Wedding-Day. Hereward the Wake snored contentedly in the corner, and Attila the Hun ate a jelly with a plastic spoon.

There was little movement, except from the Orange, which kept slipping off the Sheep's knee, and from the Baby, who kept sniffing his hands apprehensively.

"Right, now," the Inspector continued, "what has happened here this evening has been a crime of vicious premeditation. There is one person in this room who has always borne a grudge against the deceased, Mr Cruikshank, and seen him as an obstacle to the advance of his own career.

"That person planned this crime with great – but, alas, insufficient – care. That person appropriated some of Mrs Alcott's sleeping pills and, probably by crushing them into his drinks, forced Mr Cruikshank to take a fatal overdose.

"Then, not content to let the old man slip quietly away to oblivion, that person made assurance doubly sure by mixing a cruel custard pie of Polyfilla – and with that he asphyxiated his already incapable victim."

The Inspector allowed another impressive pause. This time

there was no movement. The Orange defied gravity on the Sheep's knee. The Baby ceased momentarily to worry about the smell of his hands. Even the Rolling Pin stopped swaying.

"There is only one person in this room who had the motivation and the opportunity to commit this despicable crime. And that person is . . ."

Long experience of denouements had taught him how to extend this pause almost interminably.

It had also taught him how suddenly to swing round, point his finger at the Teapot and boom in the voice of the Avenging Angel, "Mr Alcott!"

All colour drained from the face framed by pot and lid. The pale mouth twitched, unable to form sounds. You could have heard a pin drop. The Rolling Pin, deserted by all faculties but a sense of timing, dropped.

"What? It's not true!" the Teapot finally managed to gasp.

"But it is, Mr Alcott," Inspector Walsh continued implacably. "All the evidence points to you. There is no question about it."

"No!"

"Yes. And the sad irony of the whole crime, Mr Alcott, is that it was unnecessary. Our medical report reveals that Mr Cruikshank was suffering from terminal cancer. Had you only waited a couple of months, nature would have removed the obstacle to your plans."

"What?" the Teapot hissed.

"I am afraid I am obliged to put you under arrest, Mr Alcott. And I would advise you not to make any trouble."

"No!" the Teapot screamed. "You will not arrest me!" And its handle shot out to a desk drawer, only to reappear holding a small, black automatic.

Inspector Walsh checked his advance for a second, but then continued forward. "You're being very foolish, Mr Alcott. Threatening a police officer is a very serious—"

"Stop or I'll shoot!"

"*Shooting* a police officer is an even more serious—"

"I'll fire!"

The room was silent. Except that she hadn't recovered from the last time, you could have heard a Pin drop again.

And still the Inspector advanced on the Teapot behind the desk.

"I will fire! One – two – three. Right, you've asked for it!"

The entire room winced as the Teapot pulled the trigger.

There was a click and a flash of movement at the end of the gun.

When they opened their eyes, they all saw the little banner hanging from the barrel. BANG! it said in red letters.

The Orange began to giggle. Others would have followed her example but for the sudden movement behind the desk. The Teapot's spout had reached into the other drawer and emerged with a gleaming knife appended.

"Out of my way, Inspector!"

Walsh stood his ground. The Teapot came lunging at him, knife upraised.

Suddenly, Joan of Arc interposed her body between the Inspector and certain death. The knife plunged up to its hilt into her chest.

The room winced again, waiting for the spurt of blood and her collapse.

But neither came. Joan of Arc pulled the knife from the Teapot's nerveless spout. "NH257," she said contemptuously. "Retractable-Blade-Dagger. Recognize it anywhere."

This second failure (and the accompanying laugh) was too much for the Teapot. Clasping its handle to its lid, it collapsed backwards into the chair behind the desk. Then it slumped forward and, with cries of "Damn! Damn! Damn!" began to beat clenched handle and spout against the desk-top.

It must have been this which animated the biscuit-barrel. With a shrieking whistle, the lid flew off and a model clown on a long spring leapt into the air.

Then, over the screams and giggles, a disembodied voice sounded. It was an old voice, a tired voice, but a voice warmed by a sense of mischief.

"Hello, everyone," it said, and the reaction showed that everyone recognized it. "If all's gone according to plan, Rodney Alcott should by now have been arrested for my murder. And I will have pulled off the greatest practical joke of my career.

"The fact is, I'm afraid, that Rodney didn't kill me. I, Hamish Cruikshank, killed myself. I heard from my doctor last week that my body is riddled with cancer. I had at best three months to live and, rather than waste away, I decided it was better to choose my own manner of departure. About which you all, I'm sure, will now know. I have prepared the custard pie, will shortly take the overdose of Mogadon and, as I feel drowsiness creep over me, will bury my face in the soft blanket of Polyfilla. Oh, Mr Cruikshank, I heard you all saying – plastered again.

"But, by my death, I will take my revenge on Rodney Alcott for what I have always regarded as his unpardonable crime. No, not his meanness. Nor his selfishness. What I refer to is his total lack of sense of humour, his inability ever to laugh at any joke – whether mine or someone else's – and the fact that he has never in his life provided anyone with that most precious of worldly commodities – laughter.

"Well, it may have taken my death to do it, but let me tell you – Rodney Alcott's going to give you a good laugh now!"

The recorded voice stopped with a click. Whether it was that or some other invention of the old man's fertile mind that triggered the device, Hamish Cruickshank's timing, to the end, remained perfect.

The ceiling-rose above the swivel chair opened, and a deluge of bilious yellow custard descended on the Teapot below.

And the staff and clients of Festifunn laughed and laughed and laughed. And Inspector Walsh and Sergeant Trooper couldn't help joining in.

"And you're not even going to charge him with threatening behaviour?" asked the Sergeant.

"No. He's paid his dues. Gone to bed now with one of the Pillar-box's remaining Mogadon. No, case is finished now. Just have another cup of tea, and we'll be on our way. Mrs Dancer, do you think tea's possible?"

Joan of Arc, who had lingered after the others had left, smiled a motherly acquiescence. "Don't see why not."

"All I want to do is put my feet up for ten minutes."

The Inspector sank heavily into an armchair. As he did so, a loud flubbering fart broke the silence of the room.

At the door, Joan of Arc, without even turning round, said, "KT47. Whoopee Cushion. Hours of Fun. Your Friends Will Roar."

THE DETTWEILER
SOLUTION

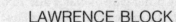

LAWRENCE BLOCK

Sometimes you just can't win for losing. Business was so bad over at Dettweiler Bros. Fine Fashions for Men that Seth Dettweiler went on back to the store one Thursday night and poured out a five-gallon can of lead-free gasoline where he figured as it would do the most good. He lit a fresh Philip Morris King Size and balanced it on the edge of the counter so as it would burn for a couple of minutes and then get unbalanced enough to drop into the pool of gasoline. Then he got into an Oldsmobile that was about five days clear of a repossession notice and drove on home.

You couldn't have had a better fire dropping napalm on a paper mill. Time it was done you could sift those ashes and not find so much as a collar button. It was far and away the most spectacularly total fire Schuyler County had ever seen, so much so that Maybrook Fidelity Insurance would have been a little tentative about settling a claim under ordinary circumstances. But the way things stood there wasn't the slightest suspicion of arson, because what kind of a dimwitted hulk goes and burns down his business establishment a full week after his fire insurance has lapsed?

No fooling.

See, it was Seth's brother Porter who took care of paying bills and such, and a little over a month ago the fire-insurance payment had been due, and Porter looked at the bill and at the bank balance and back and forth for a while and then he put the bill in a drawer. Two weeks later there was a reminder notice, and two weeks after that there was a notice that the grace period had expired and the insurance was no longer in force, and then a week after that there was one pluperfect hell of a bonfire.

Seth and Porter had always got on pretty good. (They took after each other quite a bit, folks said. Especially Porter.) Seth was forty-two years of age, and he had that long Dettweiler face topping a jutting Van Dine jaw. (Their mother was a Van Dine hailing from just the other side of Oak Falls.) Porter was thirty-nine, equipped with the same style face and jaw. They both had black hair that lay flat on their heads like shoe polish put on in slapdash fashion. Seth had more hair left than Porter, in spite of being the older brother by three years. I could describe them in greater detail, right down to scars and warts and sundry distinguishing marks, but it's my guess that you'd enjoy reading all that about as much as I'd enjoy writing it, which is to say less than somewhat. So let's get on with it.

I was saying they got on pretty good, rarely raising their voices one to the other, rarely disagreeing seriously about anything much. Now the fire didn't entirely change the habits of a lifetime but you couldn't honestly say that it did anything to improve their relationship. You'd have to allow that it caused a definite strain.

"What I can't understand," Seth said, "is how anybody who is fool enough to let fire insurance lapse can be an even greater fool by not telling his brother about it. That in a nutshell is what I can't understand."

"What beats *me*," Porter said, "is how the same person who has the nerve to fire a place of business for the insurance also does so without consulting his partner, especially when his partner just happens to be his brother."

"Allus I was trying to do," said Seth, "was save you from the criminal culpability of being an accessory before, to and after the fact, plus figuring you might be too chickenhearted to go along with it."

"Allus *I* was trying to do," said Porter, "was save you from worrying about financial matters you would be powerless to contend with, plus figuring it would just be an occasion for me to hear further from you on the subject of those bow ties."

"Well, you did buy one powerful lot of bow ties."

"I knew it."

"Something like a Pullman car full of bow ties, and it's not like every man and boy in Schuyler County's been getting this mad passion for bow ties of late."

"I just knew it."

"I wasn't the one brought up the subject, but since you went and mentioned those bow ties—"

"Maybe I should of mentioned the spats," Porter said.

"Oh, I don't want to hear about spats."

"No more than I wanted to hear about bow ties. Did we sell one single damn pair of spats?"

"We did."

"We did?"

"Feller bought one about fifteen months back. Had Maryland plates on his car, as I recall. Said he always wanted spats and didn't know they still made 'em."

"Well, selling one pair out of a gross isn't too bad."

"Now you leave off," Seth said.

"And you leave off of bow ties?"

"I guess."

"Anyway, the bow ties and the spats all burned up in the same damn fire," Porter said.

"You know what they say about ill winds," Seth said. "I guess there's a particle of truth in it, what they say."

While it didn't do the Dettweiler brothers much good to discuss spats and bow ties, it didn't solve their problems to leave off mentioning spats and bow ties. By the time they finished their conversation all they were back to was square one, and the view from that spot wasn't the world's best.

The only solution was bankruptcy, and it didn't look to be all that much of a solution.

"I don't mind going bankrupt," one of the brothers said. (I think it was Seth. Makes no nevermind, actually. Seth, Porter, it's all the same who said it.) "I don't mind going bankrupt, but I sure do hate the thought of being broke."

"Me too," said the other brother. (Porter, probably.)

"I've thought about bankruptcy from time to time."

"Me too."

"But there's a time and a place for bankruptcy."

"Well, the place is all right. No better place for bankruptcy than Schuyler County."

"That's true enough," said Seth. (Unless it was Porter.) "But this is surely not the time. Time to go bankrupt is in good times when you got a lot of money on hand. Only the damnedest kind of fool goes bankrupt when he's stony broke busted and there's a depression going on."

What they were both thinking on during this conversation was a fellow name of Joe Bob Rathburton who was in the construction business over to the other end of Schuyler County. I myself don't know of a man in this part of the state with enough intelligence to bail out a leaky rowboat who doesn't respect Joe Bob Rathburton to hell and back as a man with good business sense. It was about two years ago that Joe Bob went bankrupt and he did it the right way. First of all he did it coming off the best year's worth of business he'd ever done in his life. Then what he did was he paid off the car and the house and the boat and put them all in his wife's name. (His wife was Mabel Washburn, but no relation to the Washburns who have the Schuyler County First National Bank. That's another family entirely.)

Once that was done, Joe Bob took out every loan and raised every dollar he possibly could, and he turned all that capital into green folding cash and sealed it in quart Mason jars which he buried out back of an old pear tree that's sixty-plus years old and still bears fruit like crazy. And then he declared bankruptcy and sat back in his Mission rocker with a beer and a cigar and a real big-tooth smile.

"If I could think of anything worth doing," Porter Dettweiler said one night, "why, I guess I'd just go ahead and do it."

"Can't argue with that," Seth said.

"But I can't," Porter said.

"Nor I either."

"You might pass that old jug over here for a moment."

"Soon as I pour a tad for myself, if you've no objection."

"None whatsoever," said Porter.

They were over at Porter's place on the evening when this particular conversation occurred. They had taken to spending most of their evenings at Porter's on account of Seth had a wife at home, plus a daughter named Rachel who'd been working at the Ben Franklin store ever since dropping out of the junior college over at Monroe Center. Seth didn't have but the one daughter. Porter had two sons and a daughter, but they were all living with Porter's ex-wife, who had divorced him two years back and moved clear to Georgia. They were living in Valdosta now, as far as Porter knew. Least that was where he sent the check every month.

"Alimony jail," said Porter.

"How's that?"

"What I said was alimony jail. Where you go when you quit paying on your alimony."

"They got a special jug set aside for men don't pay their alimony?"

"Just an expression. I guess they put you into whatever jug's the handiest. All I got to do is quit sendin' Gert her checks and let her have them cart me away. Get my three meals a day and a roof over my head and the whole world could quit nagging me night and day for money I haven't got."

"You could never stand it. Bein' in a jail day in and day out, night in and night out."

"I know it," Porter said unhappily. "There anything left in that there jug, on the subject of jugs?"

"Some. Anyway, you haven't paid Gert a penny in how long? Three months?"

"Call it five."

"And she ain't throwed you in jail yet. Least you haven't got her close to hand so's she can talk money to you."

"Linda Mae givin' you trouble?"

"She did. Keeps a civil tongue since I beat up on her the last time."

"Lord knew what he was doin'," Porter said, "makin' men

stronger than women. You ever give any thought to what life would be like if wives could beat up on their husbands instead of the other way around?"

"Now I don't even want to think about that," Seth said.

You'll notice nobody was mentioning spats or bow ties. Even with the jug of corn getting discernibly lighter every time it passed from one set of hands to the other, these two subjects did not come up. Neither did anyone speak of the shortsightedness of failing to keep up fire insurance or the myopia of incinerating a building without ascertaining that such insurance was in force. Tempers had cooled with the ashes of Dettweiler Bros. Fine Fashions for Men, and once again Seth and Porter were on the best of terms.

Which just makes what happened thereafter all the more tragic.

"What I think I got," Porter said, "is no way to turn."

(This wasn't the same evening, but if you put the two evenings side by side under a microscope you'd be hard pressed to tell them apart each from the other. They were at Porter's little house over alongside the tracks of the old spur off the Wyandotte & Southern, which I couldn't tell you the last time there was a train on that spur, and they had their feet up and their shoes off, and there was a jug of corn in the picture. Most of their evenings had come to take on this particular shade.)

"Couldn't get work if I wanted to," Porter said, "which I don't, and if I did I couldn't make enough to matter, and my debts is up to my ears and rising steady."

"It doesn't look to be gettin' better," Seth said. "On the other hand, how can it get worse?"

"I keep thinking the same."

"And?"

"And it keeps getting worse."

"I guess you know what you're talkin' about," Seth said. He scratched his bulldog chin, which hadn't been in the same room with a razor in more than a day or two. "What I been thinkin' about," he said, "is killin' myself."

"You been thinking of that?"

"Sure have."

"I think on it from time to time myself," Porter admitted. "Mostly nights when I can't sleep. It can be a powerful comfort around about three in the morning. You think of all the different ways and the next thing you know you're asleep. Beats the stuffing out of counting sheep jumping fences. You seen one sheep you seen 'em all is always been my thoughts on the subject, whereas there's any number of ways of doing away with you yourself."

"I'd take a certain satisfaction in it," Seth said, more or less warming to the subject. "What I'd leave is this note tellin' Linda Mae how her and Rachel'll be taken care of with the insurance, just to get the bitch's hopes up, and then she can find out for her own self that I cashed in that insurance back in January to make the payment on the Oldsmobile. You know it's pure uncut hell gettin' along without an automobile now."

"You don't have to tell me."

"Just put a rope around my neck," said Seth, smothering a hiccup, "and my damn troubles'll be over."

"And mine in the bargain," Porter said.

"By you doin' your own self in?"

"Be no need," Porter said, "if you did *yourself* in."

"How you figure that?"

"What I figure is a hundred thousand dollars," Porter said. "Lord love a duck, if I had a hundred thousand dollars I could declare bankruptcy and live like a king!"

Seth looked at him, got up, walked over to him and took the jug away from him. He took a swig and socked the cork in place, but kept hold of the jug.

"Brother," he said, "I just guess you've had enough of this here."

"What makes you say that, brother?"

"Me killin' myself and you gettin' rich, you don't make sense. What you think you're talkin' about, anyhow?"

"Insurance," Porter said. "Insurance, that's what I think I'm talking about. Insurance."

Porter explained the whole thing. It seems there was this life insurance policy their father had taken out on them when they weren't but boys. Face amount of a hundred thousand dollars, double indemnity for accidental death. It was payable to him while they were alive, but upon his death the beneficiary changed. If Porter was to die the money went to Seth. And vice versa.

"And you knew about this all along?"

"Sure did," Porter said.

"And never cashed it in? Not the policy on me and not the policy on you?"

"Couldn't cash 'em in," Porter said. "I guess I woulda if I coulda, but I couldn't so I didn't."

"And you didn't let these here policies lapse?" Seth said. "On account of occasionally a person can be just the least bit absent-minded and forget about keeping a policy in force. That's been known to happen," Seth said, looking off to one side, "in matters relating to fire insurance, for example, and I just thought to mention it."

(I have the feeling he wasn't the only one to worry on that score. You may have had similar thoughts yourself, figuring you know how the story's going to end, what with the insurance not valid and all. Set your mind at rest. If that was the way it had happened I'd never be taking the trouble to write it up for you. I got to select stories with some satisfaction in them if I'm going to stand a chance of selling them to the magazine, and I hope you don't figure I'm sitting here poking away at this typewriter for the sheer physical pleasure of it. If I just want to exercise my fingers I'll send them walking through the Yellow Pages if it's all the same to you.)

"Couldn't let 'em lapse," Porter said. "They're all paid up. What you call twenty-payment life, meaning you pay it in for twenty years and then you got it free and clear. And the way pa did it, you can't borrow on it or nothing. All you can do is wait and see who dies."

"Well, I'll be."

"Except we don't have to wait to see who dies."

"Why, I guess not. I just guess a man can take matters into his own hands if he's of a mind to."

"He surely can," Porter said.

"Man wants to kill himself, that's what he can go and do."

"No law against it," Porter said.

Now you know and I know that that last is not strictly true. There's a definite no-question law against suicide in our state, and most likely in yours as well. It's harder to make it stand up than a calf with four broken legs, however, and I don't recall that anyone hereabouts was ever prosecuted for it, or likely will be. It does make you wonder some what they had in mind writing that particular law into the books.

"I'll just have another taste of that there corn," Porter said, "and why don't you have a pull on the jug your own self? You have any idea just when you might go and do it?"

"I'm studying on it," Seth said.

"There's a lot to be said for doing something soon as a man's mind's made up on the subject. Not to be hurrying you or anything of the sort, but they say that he who hesitates is last." Porter scratched his chin. "Or some such," he said.

"I just might do it tonight."

"By God," Porter said.

"Get the damn thing over with. Glory Hallelujah and my troubles is over."

"And so is mine," said Porter.

"You'll be in the money then," said Seth, "and I'll be in the boneyard, and both of us is free and clear. You can just buy me a decent funeral and then go bankrupt in style."

"Give you Johnny Millbourne's number-one funeral," Porter promised. "Brassbound casket and all. I mean, price is no object if I'm going bankrupt anyway. Let old Johnny swing for the money."

"You a damn good man, brother."

"You the best man in the world, brother."

The jug passed back and forth a couple more times. At one point Seth announced that he was ready, and he was halfway out the door before he recollected that his car had been repossessed, which interfered with his plans to drive it off a cliff. He came back in and sat down again and had another drink on the strength of it all, and then suddenly he sat forward and stared hard at Porter.

"This policy thing," he said.

"What about it?"

"It's on both of us, is what you said."

"If I said it then must be it's the truth."

"Well then," Seth said, and sat back, arms folded on his chest.

"Well then what?"

"Well then if *you* was to kill yourself, then *I'd* get the money and *you'd* get the funeral."

"I don't see what you're getting at," Porter said slowly.

"Seems to me either one of us can go and do it," Seth said. "And here's the two of us just takin' it for granted that I'm to be the one to go and do it, and I think we should think on that a little more thoroughly."

"Why, being as you're older, Seth."

"What's that to do with anything?"

"Why, you got less years to give up."

"Still be givin' up all that's left. Older or younger don't cut no ice."

Porter thought about it. "After all," he said, "it was your idea."

"That don't cut ice neither. I could mention I got a wife and child."

"I could mention I got a wife and three children."

"Ex-wife."

"All the same."

"Let's face it," Seth said. "Gert and your three don't add up to anything and neither do Linda Mae and Rachel."

"Got to agree," Porter said.

"So."

"One thing. You being the one who put us in this mess, what with firing the store, it just seems you might be the one to get us out of it."

"You bein' the one let the insurance lapse through your own stupidity, you could get us out of this mess through insurance, thus evenin' things up again."

"Now talkin' about stupidity—"

"Yes, talkin' about stupidity—"

"Spats!"

"Bow ties, damn you! *Bow ties!*"

You might have known it would come to that.

*   *   *

Now I've told you Seth and Porter generally got along pretty well and here's further evidence of it. Confronted by such a stalemate, a good many people would have wrote off the whole affair and decided not to take the suicide route at all. But not even spats and bow ties could deflect Seth and Porter from the road they'd figured out as the most logical to pursue.

So what they did, one of them tossed a coin, and the other one called it while it was in the air, and they let it hit the floor and roll, and I don't recollect whether it was heads or tails, or who tossed and who called – what's significant is that Seth won.

"Well now," Seth said. "I feel I been reprieved. Just let me have that coin. I want to keep it for a luck charm."

"Two out of three."

"We already said once is as good as a million," Seth said, "so you just forget that two-out-of-three business. You got a week like we agreed but if I was you I'd get it over soon as I could."

"I got a week," Porter said.

"You'll get the brassbound casket and everything, and you can have Minnie Lucy Boxwood sing at your funeral if you want. Expense don't matter at all. What's your favorite song?"

"I suppose 'Your Cheatin' Heart.'"

"Minnie Lucy does that real pretty."

"I guess she does."

"Now you be sure and make it accidental," Seth said. "Two hundred thousand dollars goes just about twice as far as one hundred thousand dollars. Won't cost you a thing to make it accidental, just like we talked about it. What I would do is borrow Fritz Chenoweth's half-ton pickup and go up on the old Harburton Road where it takes that curve. Have yourself a belly full of corn and just keep goin' straight when the road doesn't. Lord knows I almost did that myself enough times without tryin'. Had two wheels over the edge less'n a month ago."

"That close?"

"That close."

"I'll be doggone," Porter said.

Thing is, Seth went on home after he failed to convince Porter to do it right away, and that was when things began to fall into the muck. Because Porter started thinking things over. I have a hunch it would have worked about the same way if Porter had won the flip, with Seth thinking things over. They were a whole lot alike, those two. Like two peas in a pod.

What occurred to Porter was would Seth have gone through with it if he lost, and what Porter decided was that he wouldn't. Not that there was any way for him to prove it one way or the other, but when you can't prove something you generally tend to decide on believing in what you want to believe, and Porter Dettweiler was no exception. Seth, he decided, would not have killed himself and didn't never have no intention of killing himself, which meant that for Porter to go through with killing his own self amounted to nothing more than damned foolishness.

Now it's hard to say just when he figured out what to do, but it was in the next two days, because on the third day he went over and borrowed that pickup off Fritz Chenoweth. "I got the back all loaded down with a couple sacks of concrete mix and a keg of nails and I don't know what all," Fritz said. "You want to unload it back of my smaller barn if you need the room."

"Oh, that's all right," Porter told him. "I guess I'll just leave it loaded and be grateful for the traction."

"Well, you keep it overnight if you have a mind," Fritz said.

"I just might do that," Porter said, and he went over to Seth's house. "Let's you and me go for a ride," he told Seth. "Something we was talking about the other night, and I went and got me a new slant on it which the two of us ought to discuss before things go wrong altogether."

"Be right with you," Seth said, "soon as I finish this sandwich."

"Oh, just bring it along."

"I guess," said Seth.

No sooner was the pickup truck backed down and out of the driveway than Porter said, "Now will you just have a look over there, brother."

"How's that?" said Seth, and turned his head obligingly to the right, whereupon Porter gave him a good lick upside the head with a monkey wrench he'd brought along expressly for that purpose. He got him right where you have a soft spot if you're a little baby. (You also have a soft spot there if someone gets you just right with a monkey wrench.) Seth made a little sound which amounted to no more than letting his breath out, and then he went out like an icebox light when you have closed the door on it.

Now as to whether or not Seth was dead at this point I could not honestly tell you, unless I were to make up an answer knowing how slim is the likelihood of anyone presuming to contradict me. But the plain fact is that he might have been dead and he might not and even Seth could not have told you, being at the very least stone-unconscious at the time.

What Porter did was drive up the old Harburton Road, I guess figuring that he might as well stick to as much of the original plan as possible. There's a particular place where the road does a reasonably convincing imitation of a fishhook, and that spot's been described as Schuyler County's best natural brake on the population explosion since they stamped out the typhoid. A whole lot of folks fail to make that curve every year, most of them young ones with plenty of breeding years left in them. Now and then there's a movement to put up a guard rail, but the ecology people are against it so it never gets anywheres.

If you miss that curve, the next land you touch is a good five hundred feet closer to sea level.

So Porter pulls over to the side of the road and then he gets out of the car and maneuvers Seth (or Seth's body, whichever the case may have been) so as he's behind the wheel. Then he stands alongside the car working the gas pedal with one hand and the steering wheel with the other and putting the fool truck in gear and doing this and that and the other thing so he can run the truck up to the edge and over, and thinking hard every minute about those two hundred thousand pretty green dollars that are destined to make his bankruptcy considerably easier to contend with.

Well, I told you right off that sometimes you can't win for losing, which was the case for Porter and Seth both, and another way of putting it is to say that when everything goes wrong there's nothing goes right. Here's what happened. Porter slipped on a piece of loose gravel while he was pushing, and the truck had to go on its own, and where it went was halfway and no further, with its back wheel hung up on a hunk of tree limb or some such and its two front wheels hanging out over nothing and its motor stalled out deader'n a smoked fish.

Porter said himself a whole mess of bad words. Then he wasted considerable time shoving the back of that truck, forgetting it was in gear and not about to budge. Then he remembered and said a few more bad words and put the thing in neutral, which involved a long reach across Seth to get to the floor shift and a lot of coordination to manipulate it and the clutch pedal at the same time. Then Porter got out of the truck and gave the door a slam, and just about then a beat-up old Chevy with Indiana plates pulls up and this fellow leaps out screaming that he's got a tow rope and he'll pull the truck to safety.

You can't hardly blame Porter for the rest of it. He wasn't the type to be great at contingency planning anyhow, and who could allow for something like this? What he did, he gave this great sob and just plain hurled himself at the back of that truck, it being in neutral now, and the truck went sailing like a kite in a tornado, and Porter, well, what he did was follow right along after it. It wasn't part of his plan but he just had himself too much momentum to manage any last-minute change of direction.

According to the fellow from Indiana, who it turned out was a veterinarian from Bloomington, Porter fell far enough to get off a couple of genuinely rank words on the way down. Last words or not, you sure wouldn't go and engrave them on any tombstone.

Speaking of which, he has the last word in tombstones, Vermont granite and all, and his brother Seth has one just like it. They had a double-barreled funeral, the best Johnny Millbourne had to offer, and they each of them reposed in a brass-bound casket, the top-of-the-line model. Minnie Lucy Boxwood sang "Your Cheatin' Heart," which was Porter's favorite song, plus she sang Seth's favorite, which was "Old Buttermilk Sky," plus she also sang free gratis "My Buddy" as a testament to brotherly love.

And Linda Mae and Rachel got themselves two hundred thousand dollars from the insurance company, which is what Gert and her kids in Valdosta, Georgia, also got. And Seth and

Porter have an end to their miseries, which was all they really wanted before they got their heads turned around at the idea of all that money.

The only thing funnier than how things don't work out is how they do.

BIG SURVIVOR

PETER T GARRATT

447 BC. Building of the sodding Parthenon. Slaves built the old Greek one, and if we Big Survivor competitors get told to build one here on Valinos Island, eleven of the twelve who work on it won't get paid a thing. Unless you count the chance to go on more TV shows.

4.47 a.m.: Bloody Uncivilized Time. Nearly five, and by my reckoning, dawn's not far off in the Greek islands. I always wake at dawn. Usually I get back to sleep, but it's Day One of Big Survivor. It's time Andy Bravo was up and in training.

5 a.m., Day One. I'm Andy Bravo, bookies' favourite to be the Big Survivor. It's high time I'm up, even if the tent flap's open and it's as black as Thatcher's heart out there and rosy-fingered sodding Dawn is wearing gloves like a burglar.

I unzip the sleeping bag, quietly, don't want anyone to wake up and see my training routine, worse still copy it; vault off the camp bed, and wind up flat on my face. Or rather someone else's face.

Nature of Problem: there's a body on the ground in the Spartan Men's tent. Status of body: alive, trying to kick, struggling and shouting: "Hey! What . . . ! Oh. Oh, yes, sorry . . . really sorry!"

By the time I recognize the voice, I've got my flashlamp on, and the other sodding Spartans are starting to wake up. I'm in my boxers, sprawled on top of Archie Hollister, the last man I'd ever expect to be sprawled on, if I sprawled on men at all! He's a history teacher, failure on legs, rank outsider in the contest. I say: "You . . . you're an Athenian! What are you doing in my sodding tent?"

"I . . . I'm sorry! The other Athenians . . . well, there's not much secret that they're both gay, and there was talking . . . I couldn't sleep there!"

"Bloody hell! You mean they're . . . Just what are they up to?"

"Well, sleeping. It was all talk. But I can't sleep in that ambience."

"Well, you're not sodding sleeping in this ambient tent! You'll just have to get round the tarts! Failing that, and I should think you might, it'd do you good to kip under the stars. It's not cold!"

In fact it's colder than you'd think, but the guy's a hypochondriac. I can't understand how he got into the game. His luxury item's some sort of quack remedy, made from a plant that looks like a panda's arsehole. I figure a few nights in the open should be enough to get him off the island and save the trouble of voting him out.

By this time, I'm off Archie and back on the camp bed. The others are trying not to laugh. In fact they're trying to sound hard and angry. "What's effin' goin' on?" That's Marleyman Friday, former sprint champ. Then he remembers he's supposed to be a hard man from the Yard, and says: "You'an you goofyboys stay away from mi, or mi an'mi ain't no friends on this i'lan!"

"Cool it, Man!" I say. He hates being called Man, but there's no point in not riling him. Man's from Streatham out of Guyana, parents teachers. He's no more from the Yard than Prince Harry is. As for hard, he won a UK hundred metres once, but I never heard of him lasting through the heats on the four hundred. Distance would kill him, and this game's the hardest distance since the first Marathon.

"Why the fook are you oop anyway?" Good question, if, like Skelmer Kelly, you don't usually get up at all. Skel comes from genuine Liverpool docker stock, which means he's never done a day's work, and got into the contest as a token hard-up Scouser. Hard-up, maybe; hard I doubt. They're looking at me, so I come clean. "Training. It's nearly dawn." I still don't want them knowing my routine, so I challenge: "Anyone up to a run?"

They all accept, even Archie. Maybe they know I'm the fancied man, and want to suss me out. They'll know I was invalided out of Special Forces round the time of the Gulf. That I was injured falling off the podium of a strip joint on a stag night is Classified Info.

We kit up and get going. We're on the South Bay of Valinos Island, rosy-fingered Dawn is still fingering her boyfriend so we set off for the wide path up the West Headland with stars and a crescent moon for light. I set a good pace and tempt Man to race me, but he hangs back. They're in a knot behind my shoulder like Quasimodo's hunch, even Archie keeping up. We keep going; rosy-fingered Dawn's boyfriend is getting his money's worth; we must be nearer the tropics than I'd thought. We're well to the west before I turn back. There's light in the sky now, not rosy but turquoise. It's the only time the sea looks wine-dark. Air's clean, and I think as we head for the camp, that Valinos could be a good place for a holiday.

But that's not why we're here. I'm reminded when I see another runner coming off the far headland. From the legs, it has to be Lizzie Masters. She's got the longest legs since Velociraptor, and could be twice as dangerous. Degrees from Oxford and from Cambridge, she's been a policewoman and an anti-everything protester, mainly endangered animal protests. She's been on other gameshows. What matters is that she's been a triathlete.

I'm distracted by Lizzie; Man sprints past me and heads for the showers before I know he's got anything left. But Lizzie is more dangerous. All you need to do to run a hundred metres is be late for a bus. Triathlon's different.

I grab my towel and start a queue for the men's shower. Man's in there singing "Marleyman" to the tune of "Rasta Man". His voice is less Bob Marley than Bob Dylan. There's not much water on this side of the island, most of it comes from

Paros in a plastic tank towed by a lugger. We don't know when the next consignment's due, and what's left could become a luxury at any time. At least I'm first in the queue for when Man finishes. Skelmer wanders over, while Archie hops around looking uncomfortably from the shower to the khazi, as though he can't decide which gets priority. One of his many ailments is constipation. I feel a bit sorry for him, then get realistic. There's a half million at stake, and it won't go to a geek who can't shit and can't live without a shit.

I'm not surprised when Lizzie saunters over. She's wearing a hand towel slung round her neck, and what looks like a face flannel knotted at her waist. She says: "They don't seem to have got ours working yet."

I didn't see her check the female shower. I say: "I don't mind. Don't know about the producers. Those cameras should be getting rolling any minute now."

"Probably already are." She stretches catlike, raising her arms and dislodging her breasts from the ends of her towel. "That's what this game is about. We do the work, vote each other down to the last three, the viewers see the lot, then they get to sit in their armchairs and decide who wins. So they might as well get their money's worth." She starts a regular warm-down programme of stretches. I remember I ought do the same, and start my own programme. We carry on till Man's out of the shower, Skelmer's sneaked in past us, and Archie's hobbled off to try his luck in the khazi. She says to me in a stage whisper: "You and I need to talk."

"Do we?" The stretching has displaced her towels. She's got a model's tan, tiny white triangles from a bikini that must have been stuck on with glue. Nice, but she knows how to play this game. I wish I could remember what show she was on before. Whichever, it's wiser to not trust her.

"We do. You and I are the bookmakers' favourites for the prize, but you know how people actually vote in this sort of game."

"You think they might gang up to get us off?"

"I'm sure of it." All through this conversation she keeps up her stretches, like a cat doing yoga. "You think they're all saying, 'Andy and Lizzie are the toughest, and probably the brightest, so we want them here when the public finally get to vote?' I don't think so!"

It's a sod, but she's right. "You want some kind of alliance?"

"We need one. Ourselves, the next best if we have to, someone who thinks he's better than he is if we can find one. We need to suss them out and draw them in fast."

It makes sense. First few rounds, if we're up for exile, we're against the other four Spartans, and they're just bright enough to try and get us out while they can. If we get a good alliance, it could be handy once we're up against Athenians as well. I nod.

"Good. Get thinking about who to approach."

Skel's out of the shower and she flicks off her towels and steps in with a sort of curtsey, as if I'd made way for her.

Day 1: Breakfast – Don't Ask!

First Challenge: I don't know if hidden cameras got Lizzie's antics at the shower, but open filming starts at nine. Beastly Barry is present and correcting us. We're using too much water. Our first task is to find more on this side of the island. There's a spring the other side, but that serves the private palace of the Aristophanes family, the Greek tycoons who own Valinos down to the last snake and the last discarded snakeskin. They don't like the south side . . . too hot. If English mad dogs camp out round here, we can find our own water.

Another mad thing. The Athenian team are supposed to decide where the water is, while we then have to dig a well. Problem: most of the Athenians couldn't find water in a Perrier bottle.

Meantime we Spartans go fishing. The girls get into the water in bikinis with spears and nets. Lizzie's bikini is even smaller than the one which gave her the tan. Man rushes in to join them, but Skel and I settle down with improvised rods, saving our strength for later.

About the alliance: Skel might be able to think tactically, but I doubt he'd expect to last as long as me or Lizzie, and might not want to link up with us. Man's a bit tougher, but not very tactical. I don't know the other two girls yet.

Skel and I catch a fish each, the others one between them.

Late morning: the Athenians decide on a site for the well. It's on flat ground, stony, about fifty feet above the level of the campsite. I never do find out why they chose it.

The Spartans get digging. Man, Lizzie and I take the first shift. It's hard going, lots of stone in the soil . . . in fact there's virtually a cliff. We have to dig down beside it. Then there's a big surprise. Archie offers to help. In his own way.

He's found a dustpan and brush, and he uses them to get the dirt off the "cliff". He's not putting his back into it; but he's concentrating and working carefully. I'm starting to wonder what he's up to. We'd all be muttering that he's not actually digging, but it's hot and dusty and we can use the rest. So we rest.

I'm deciding this is a scam to show us Spartans shirking while an Athenian does our work, when he says: "Ah!" in a loud voice, as if he'd managed to get a condom on he'd thought wouldn't unroll.

The "cliff" is part of a wall. To prove it, there's a painting of a woman's head. He brushes some more, and we get to see the rest of her. Almost all of her. She's topless, hair in ringlets, holding up what look like strands of snaky hair. Then I see they are snakes.

An Athenian girl squeals. "Aaagh, holding snakes. How horrible!"

Man is saying: "That's very . . . top rankin', but are you goin' to let mi an' mi Spartans finish our well diggin' task or what?"

Archie jumps up. "No! All digging has to stop till we can get professional archaeologists involved!"

Skel looks over. "So this is soom kind of ruin, like." He looks at the wall. "What was it, soom kind of old Roman knocking shop, like them ones at Pompey, like?"

"No! It's much more important than that. If I'm right this is a Minoan Cretan Snake Priestess. This whole area could have been a Minoan palace."

Beastly Barry takes an interest. He's been smirking away while we've been sweating. He says: "What do you think, Miss Aristophanes?"

I haven't noticed her! Jackie Aristophanes! You'd think Andy Bravo would notice a billion drachmas arrive! Maybe it's because she's the only woman on the island who's dressed. Our girls are in bikinis, and Barry's production bimbos down to shorts and bras. Jackie A wears jeans that are so designer the diamanté patterns are real diamonds, a Versace top that's probably worth more, dark, dark shades. Her arms are brown as dark honey, but her face is pale as if she's looked in the mirror and seen a ghost.

Archie looks up eager as a puppy. "Miss Aristophanes, this could be the most important discovery since . . . Phillip of Macedon's tomb!"

She says, in a cut-glass voice without much Greek accent: "I wouldn't want to be party to damaging our national heritage. Do you think this would attract . . . a lot of visitors?"

"Educated ones, I suppose, if it's properly excavated."

She owns Valinos, but I don't know how much of the rest of old Stavros's billions she has. Stavros Aristophanes wouldn't have let a jerk like Barry lug water on the island, let alone rent half of it for a gameshow. I heard Jackie's half-brothers had got the supertankers, and some of those are bigger than the island. She says: "We could do with some educated visitors. A small hotel, perhaps."

Skel says: "So you want us to stop digging, like?" He sounds a bit eager, considering Skel himself hasn't done any actual digging all day, but no one disagrees, and he goes on: "So this challenge looks like a victory for us Spartans, eh?"

There's a squawk of disagreement from the Athenians and he says: "You lot were meant to find the fooking water. Do you think them Ancient Cretin builders would have put their foundations right on the only water for fooking miles? Our Challenge!"

Barry half agrees, then says he'll have to consult London. He likes surprises, but only sprung by him.

Lunch

Good. We get rice with the three fish shredded in and some bits of pepper and spices. Lizzie cooks with Imelda Girton, about the brightest of the Athenians. I remember which show Lizzie was on before: nothing athletic, ChefStars. She wasn't a finalist, but did quite well. Imelda helps, but snipes: "I thought you were a vegetarian. Animal rights type."

"No," Lizzie says carefully. "Not as such. I do conservation work for SpeciesPeace, but whales eat fish, so why shouldn't I?"

After lunch most people favour a siesta, till the well fiasco is resolved. I whisper to Lizzie: "So far I think Skel."

"So do I."

Skel has made a shelter for his angling on a small headland. I join him and start talking tactics. "Lizzie and I were thinking . . ."

"So that's why you're always whispering . . ."

"Exactly. What else could it be?" Lizzie appears beside us. "We . . ."

There's a shout from the camp: "Oh, *God*, No! *Nooo*! You Bastards! *Bastards*! *Bastards*!" We hurry over and find Archie stomping round the camp, looking angry and pathetic at the same time. He's still shouting: "They've gone! Oh, God, they're gone!"

Imelda turns up. She says: "What is it? Who's gone?"

We're all hoping some competitors have given up, but Archie howls on: "My Panda Pills! They've been stolen!"

Imelda says: "You mean the pills made from a panda's rectum?"

"They're an ancient Chinese Chop Feng remedy for constipation."

She sniffs: "Same principle as using a rhino horn for impotence?"

"No! This is serious! They come from a herbal tuber that just happens to look like a rectum. It's an outrage they were classed as a luxury. They're medicine! What am I going to do without them?"

I can think of a lot of answers to that, but just say: "What's happened to them?"

"I don't know, but they're not where they should be! It's obvious someone's stolen them!"

Skel mutters: "I can't think what fooker would!"

"Well, if no one's unlucky enough to need them, it must be someone who wants me off the island and out of the game!"

I can believe that. There's half a million in it for the Big Survivor, and the someone must want it badly.

It occurs to me that if I can work out who that someone is, there'll be two competitors less for the price of one without a vote taken.

The obvious suspects are the remaining Athenians. Archie's party piece with the snake lady has saved them all from humiliation over the hunt for water, but given him a leg up with the folks getting old at home. They need him out of the game fast.

I decide to ask Lizzie's opinion, then slap myself, realizing how near I am to trusting her. Lizzie wants an alliance, but that's because she didn't enter Big Survivor to come second. She'll have seen Archie take charge of the dig, and she'll know he's the only person who thinks his luxury item is a necessity. So, he's both a threat and a sitting target.

But then anyone could see him that way, so I can't rule out the other Spartans. But neither women nor Spartan men would have an excuse to rummage round the Athenian men's tent, so if no one was seen rummaging, Archie's tent-mates are the prime suspects.

By this time, Archie is storming off to find Beastly Barry. None of us competitors are allowed a mobile. The rest start to trail after. I step out to get near the front.

Barry and the crew aren't in the camp. They've got a lodge, halfway round the island to the west, an outpost of the Aristophanes gaff. They don't have to put up with rosy-fingered Dawn, but they can toast the sunset. It's a real hike, good training if you have to do it every day. Barry doesn't have to do it at siesta time, when the sun's hotter than Chernobyl. This blew up so fast most people haven't brought sunblock or even water. Luckily – well, it isn't luck, I've trained myself – I take a canteen everywhere. By the time we're on the approach to the lodge, we're strung out in a line, Archie storming ahead as if his arse depends on this . . . Well, it does, according to him. I'm planning this like a race: as Archie gets in hailing distance of the lodge, I move up through a chasing group which consists, predictably, of Lizzie, Man and, less predictably, Skel. When Archie tells Barry to find the thief and sling him off the island, I'll be right behind him.

It's a cute little lodge, not much bigger than the terrace of back-to-backs where Skel was dragged up, white with blue shutters like on Mykonos. They've even got a white dovecote, with the regulation small white church at the back. Barry and his bimbos are on the terrace. They're not talking to London, unless it's London Gin.

Jackie Aristophanes is reclining by the pool, a seawater job, water pumped up by windmills. Some flunkey is carrying out a drink. She wears a turquoise and silver swimsuit, technically one-piece, but consisting of long strategic strips and not covering much more than our girls' bikinis. I doubt it costs as little as all of them together.

Barry's sunbathing in Bermuda shorts. He hurries into the house when he sees us coming, and a camera starts to track us. Archie storms on, gaining momentum like a cavalry charge. I keep up my pace, but the rest slow down; I don't know why, because this'll be great TV, and that's what we're here for.

Barry comes back to the terrace, pulling on a Hawaiian shirt and a sunhat labelled "Ibiza", as if he's dressing as a thousand islands. Archie launches into his rant about the theft. Barry listens for a little, then says: "Archibald, you seem to be trying to rewrite all the rules of this contest. I don't think that's very fair to the others."

He's using a smarmy tone which means he won't concede a thing if he can help it. I say: "If there is a thief, if he's trying to put Archie out of the game, he could try again. That's not fair on anyone!"

Barry looks at me uneasily. He knows I've got a security firm, and that I've seen active service, though he doesn't know where. I don't think he knows about the strip club incident, so he probably thinks it was the Gulf. (Where it actually was, no one is allowed to know!) Maybe he's afraid that if he annoys me, I might try to kill him with my bare hands. He says: "So what should I do?"

I say: "It's simple. You've got cameras on all the time. They'll tell you if anyone went into Archie's tent who shouldn't have been there round the time the pills went missing."

"Now, Andrew, that's not in the rules. The film shot here is for the public, not the participants. Though when you get back to England, you'll be able to watch the repeats, of course!"

Archie's trying not to lose it, but he's almost lost: "I need my pills! Someone's got to find them! And find out what happened to them!"

Barry shrugs. "You've been allowed your luxury item. You've lost it. You're not much of a survivor if you expect us to find it for you."

Imelda arrives. Another teacher. She's short and dark, not bad-looking, but not fit even compared to the other Athenians. She's running with sweat, as if she's worked off half her extra weight just keeping in sight of the rest of us, and we weren't even running. She takes a deep breath, and says fairly steadily: "I thought there were rules in this contest! You've got cameras everywhere, even Liz's secret nude beach. You have to use them to establish the truth!"

We all mutter agreement, as if she'd offered free cold beer. Man shouts: "It looks like some bastard's pickin' us off one by one, and you're doin' nothin!"

There are twelve of us, all looking as angry as Manchester United fans who've accidentally gone to a live match and had to watch a nil – nil draw in the rain. Barry's got two camera men, a sound man, and three girls in shorts who run his errands. Most of them were at the campsite around the time the pills went AWOL, filming as the lunch was cooked and eaten. Barry knows all our profiles. I wouldn't put it past him to have sent someone to steal Archie's pills, to boost his TV ratings, or to punish Archie for disrupting the day's schedule.

I sense something. The others don't, but I have trained senses. Three men have appeared from the lodge. They all wear pressed white shirts and slacks. No one introduces them, but I can sense who they are . . . Jackie A's bodyguards. Man to man I could take any of them, but it's her island, and they'll be armed.

Jackie herself hasn't left her recliner. She's trying to look relaxed, but she isn't missing anything . . . in fact she's pushed up her sunglasses and is looking at us, blinking as if her eyes aren't used to the unshaded world. Her half-brothers' lawsuit for the shipping company must have been a big shock to her. For the first time, she's contemplating having to live on the small change the rest of us are competing to win. Gossip has it when Stavros was alive she lost half-mills on horses and jewel-thief boyfriends. That's stopped since he died. But she owns the island outright, and she'll lose the worry if she can plug it into the TV and tourism industries.

Great. We yomped halfway round the island with ten suspects, assuming Archie didn't simply fake the theft to cause trouble. Now we have twelve, including one with three armed guards.

The oldest of the production bimbos, the one with the permanent job, is whispering to Barry. He says: "It's a contest with fair rules. We don't interfere, but if you folk are big enough survivors to catch your own thieves and vote them off, that's part of the game!"

I say: "We can, Barry. But we need to see the film of—"

He cuts in: "Andrew, we know your backgrounds. You run a security company. Elizabeth used to be in the police, Special Branch, wasn't it, Liz? You can do it as survivors. Or can you?"

I start to say that most of my work is setting up CCTV systems, and he just ignores me, turns his back and goes into the lodge. I turn to the others and say: "We're wasting our time here! Let's get back to the camp and get on with it!"

I drink some water and storm off. The others aren't ready to give up on arguing with Barry, and that suits me. It's Barry all over to not play ball over the film, and real anger's a liability in this game. Fake anger is an asset to get away from the others without arousing suspicion. I need time to search for the missing pills and the first place I'll be looking is my own kit.

Fact: it'll be a nightmare working out who saw who go where. If anyone saw anyone acting suspiciously, they'd have said it by now.

Fact: no one is stupid enough to steal the pills and hang on to them. They might just dump them in the sea, but if I was pathetic and desperate enough to pull a stunt like that, I'd plant them in someone else's kit.

Racing certainty: if anyone's being set up, it's me, or maybe Liz.

Inconvenient fact: Archie came to my tent last night and sneaked in. If it was to avoid the two gays, it's odd he didn't leave till they were asleep and doing nothing. Maybe Archie's playing a long game, thinking his brain's sharp enough to get past the Athenians, but that he needs me out of the way before the two teams merge.

The track from the lodge to the camp is rough going. I cut corners by going over terrain which looks worse, but isn't. I'm lengthening my stride as I do this, to get over obstacles, rocks and holes, and I'm almost running as I get in sight of the camp. No one is there, and I make straight for the Spartan men's tent.

I've left my camp bed regulation neat, and I put a bit of time into a careful search of the bed and the area round and beneath it. Next, I turn the items out of my kitbag.

Everything there that should be.

Nothing there than shouldn't.

"What's goin' on?" Man and Skel are back. I explain, not forgetting to point out that Archie might have planted something that morning. I suggest that each searches his own kit, supervised by the other.

It works. At least, it shows that neither Skel nor Man has the pills, so it doesn't look like an Archie planting job.

By now the others are struggling back. It's time to learn a bit more about them. There's the two gay Athenian men, Alfie and Reggie; both are the butch, cropped, tattooed type. I remind myself that they aren't an item and won't necessarily be working together. They know there can only be one winner. All the girls but Lizzie are bringing up the rear. I saunter over, to present the search idea, and set up some system for finding out who's been into Archie's tent. Imelda says: "Barry's on his way. I think he's got his orders from London, or Miss Greek Tycoon, or whoever gives them." Then she says: "What were you trying to prove just now, dashing off like that? That you're a big macho ex-SAS hero who can set records in cross-country? It's not necessary in this heat!"

I'm wrong-footed. I'm not ashamed of trying to burn out unfit competitors like Imelda, but that wasn't why I ran back to camp. She's countering with a gameplan of her own, trying to isolate me.

Something catches my eye, distracts me. I look round. It's still pretty hot, and most people are sitting down waiting for

Barry, who isn't in sight yet, or trying to wash off some of the dust and sweat of the day. Lizzie is the exception. She's walking rapidly away from the camp towards the East Headland; the area where she was running at dawn. It's lower and gentler than the one in the west, and she starts picking her way round the lowest part. It looks as though she's found a way to another beach. I wonder if it's the one Imelda calls "Lizzie's secret nude beach", then reflect that Lizzie isn't exactly secretive about nudity. She didn't reply to Imelda's crack and, come to think of it, she's hardly said anything since the theft was discovered. That's not like her, but it makes a lot of sense if she's got something to hide. In my experience, crims may or may not return to the scene of the crime (the ones who don't usually don't get caught) but if they do they say too much and the wrong things. Lizzie hasn't made that mistake, but she may have gone too far the other way. I forget everything and follow her.

At the sea end, the East Headland is just an awkward jumble of rocks. Someone who lived on the island before Stavros made it his playground has left us the ghost of a path. I doubt if Archie or Imelda would even notice it, but Lizzie moves surefootedly up it and disappears over to the other side.

With due respect to Lizzie's Spartan skills, she has to have been this way before. If not, it would have been easier to wade or swim round the headland. What I thought was a path has more stones than an Iranian wedding where the bride's been found in bed with the best man. I don't make as good time as she has, even though near the top I'm cooled by a Meltemi from the east, from which we're sheltered in the bay.

I come to a wide gap in the path, almost a small crevasse. I check, it's just narrow enough to step across without needing to jump, and not quite deep enough to do me a serious injury if I fall. Which is just as well, because there's no room to take a run-up for a jump without making enough noise to attract attention. I stretch my right leg over, get a secure foothold on the other . . . *Shit!* I dislodge the stone I'm relying on on the far side. It rattles down the slope, creating what sounds like a small avalanche! My right foot slides down so I'm clinging to the far side by a toehold, my hands not quite in reach of either side, trying to balance over a drop which suddenly seems a lot deeper than before, while doing the biggest split since Madonna's last stage show. I assume Lizzie will hear something and investigate. Instead, the wind carries her voice to me. She can't be very far ahead, but I've no idea who she's talking to.

"Look, it doesn't matter who privatized Archie's pills. We may find out, we may not. The thing is, it'll look bad if he's made to stay in the contest without them."

I can't hear anyone reply. I just hope whoever it is talks some sense into her. I'm trying to decide whether to use my secure left foot to spring myself back, or try and use my toehold to jump-scrabble to the far side. Either way runs a risk of making a noise.

I look back to check if anyone in the camp is witnessing this. No one is looking, because Barry is approaching, surrounded by staff and of course cameras. He's talking into a mobile. Then I hear Lizzie say: "If you can't get them in Greece, how about giving him one phone call to someone on the team who's coming over soon? Tell her where to get them? Maybe Lucy the film editor? She's flying out tomorrow, isn't she? Let her buy some and bring them over."

Though my weight's in a place I don't want it to be, and I feel like I'm being stretched on the rack, I stop wondering how to get to one side or the other and try and make out what's going on. Lizzie must have hidden a mobile, which is against the rules. She's using it to tell Barry what to do, which is unprecedented. She should now be prime suspect for the theft, but she's trying to undo the effects of the theft! In the meantime, she says: "That's settled, then!" and I see Barry in the distance put his mobile away. Just afterwards I hear Lizzie's voice again: "It's actually working out. Stand by for the call."

I can't stay like this. I shift position to try and get back, and nearly overbalance into the crevasse. I manage to right myself, but wind up with my legs at full stretch and my arms out to the side, like a tightrope walker with no tightrope.

"There's an easier jump down here." Lizzie appears nearer the sea. She leaps nimbly across the gap, then hurries up. "I should really wave and let them get this on camera. It'd make great TV!"

Instead she braces her feet and stretches out a hand to grasp one of mine. With her help it's easy to get back. Her skin is soft as velvet and her muscles hard as mail. She smells of sea-salt and a blandly perfumed deodorant. She says: "We'd better get back. What were you doing? Hoping to watch me skinny-dip?"

"I'm bound to see that sooner or later! More to the point, what were you doing?"

"Oh, organizing my thoughts, thinking aloud."

"Or talking on a secret mobile. About Archie's pills."

"You think I want him out of the game that much? How can I prove I don't?" She answers herself: "I don't need to cheat. Let's think, skinny-dipping, needing Archie out. I'll show you how much!"

Barry is in a grim mood. He says abruptly as soon as Lizzie and I join the others: "Today's challenge is given to the Spartans, as the Athenians chose the wrong place for the well, but Archie gets immunity from exile at the first vote for spotting it was a ruin."

"Big deal!" shouts Archie. "It doesn't mean a thing with no pills!"

"Archie, you get one phone call to one of my staff, who'll buy the bloody Panda's bottom if she has to buy the whole bloody panda and bring it out here.

"As for investigating the thief, you have to deal with that. Be survivors, not whingers!"

It sounds like a good time to organize a search, and maybe a "who was where" session, but Lizzie gets in first. She shouts: "I've a great idea for a group bonding exercise! Should cool us down and be one in the eye for the viewers!"

Imelda sneers: "Knowing you, it'll be some kind of nude swimming contest!"

"Swimming, yes. Nude, why not?" She points to a yacht belonging to the production crew, which is anchored about three hundred yards offshore. "Once round the boat, first one back's the winner, last one nude's a prude!"

The idea takes off in every sense. The gay guys and one of the Spartan girls are undressing before Lizzie finishes speaking. It's still hot, and the sea may not be wine-dark, but it looks spritzer-cool. Lizzie herself flips off her shoes, then flicks off her bikini as though she's done that a thousand times, and gets a head-start in the charge down the beach. She looks a perfect natural athlete as she runs in the nude, like in the old Greek Olympics.

What about me? Andy Bravo's no prude. On the other hand, I've no medals for speed-stripping. Man's hopping around trying to run and get his shorts off at the same time, Archie makes such a mess of it he falls flat on his face, and I just lose my shoes and run after Lizzie in my shorts. She runs into the sea then launches herself forwards like a torpedo. I gain a little ground till I hit the water, but I can't match her speed once I'm in it. She was UK triathlon bronze and swimming was her best discipline. She keeps forging ahead till she's round the boat and can see the rest of us. I'm with a chasing pack about forty yards back, but we're not really chasing. We're trying to enjoy ourselves. She's trying to prove she's got no need to cheat. The viewers will love her, if we let her get to the final stages. I round the yacht and see that Lizzie is already going inshore past Archie, and he's still coming out. It fact he's slowing. She's onshore drying herself before he's round the yacht.

OK. Point taken. Lizzie has nothing to fear from Archie. He's here for brainpower and she's here for stamina, but she can beat him for both. And most of the others. She doesn't need to cheat.

So why's she phoning Barry? And who did steal those pills?

It's been a long afternoon. Skel caught one fish: the rest of us hardly bothered, so supper is mostly rice. There's vague gossip about the theft, but Archie's getting more pills, and it looks like no one was seen in his tent who shouldn't have been there. People are losing interest, which worries me. Someone's getting away with weakening a contestant, even if they haven't got him out of the game this time. There'll be another time.

I try for an early night, and I'm just getting to sleep when there's a commotion. Something going on on the beach over to the east, near Lizzie's path over the headland. I stagger out in my boxers: it's dark and before moonrise, so I take my flashlight.

I get near and I hear Lizzie's voice: "Turn down that light!" and then: "Get away from her! You can't touch her!"

"Touch?" This is Skel's voice. "That fooking creature's our fooking meal-ticket . . . maybe for as long as we're on this fooking dump!"

It's very dark, and I put my torch to dim. By it and starlight and the dying campfire, I see a humped shape about a yard long moving slowly up the beach. Several people are around it. None are very close till Skel goes up to it and it stops. He says: "Damn! It's gone into its shell! How are we going to kill it?"

Lizzie snaps: "You're not. All turtles in Greece are protected! You can't even touch her. We've got to keep away from her, then if she lays eggs get the hatchery marked out and protected . . ."

Skel interrupts: "I didn't get into this game to starve on rice while you play Greenpeace and get protective over a dozen eggs and a walking bowl of soup!"

"I know you didn't. You came to win. Did you know that eating an endangered species is a criminal act? That if you survive to win you could lose every penny as proceeds of crime?"

Skel flinches, but then Imelda steps forwards. She's been sulking since the swimming race. She says: "Who gave you the right to be judge and jury? I found it, so it's mine!"

Lizzie says: "If anyone owns a turtle on this island, it's Jackie A!"

Imelda jumps onto the animal's back: "I claim this turtle in the name of Queen . . ."

Lizzie jumps over the turtle. She gives Imelda a little push, and one of Lizzie's feet is behind Imelda's ankles. Imelda winds up on her arse in the sand snapping: "For Christ's sake! There are meant to be rules in this game!"

Lizzie snaps: "It was never meant to be a game! It's a fucking experiment in tricking people into degrading themselves for viewing figures! She's been in the world since the Cretaceous, since the dinosaurs, and now she's endangered because with all the beaches in the world, people can't leave her just enough to lay her eggs!"

Imelda staggers to her feet. "I want a vote!"

Man, Archie, myself, and most of the rest vote with Lizzie. Imelda and Skel drift off and, when the turtle doesn't come out of its shell, so do the rest. Lizzie says: "I'd better keep an eye on it."

I say: "Lucky turtle! It's got 'someone to watch over me!' "

"Keep watch with me?"

"I'll get my coat." While I'm fetching it, I consider everything I know of Lizzie. When I get back I say: "Pandas are endangered, right?"

"The incontinent one is the Red Panda, and that's less endangered than the Giant. But if this nonsense of cutting them up to cure constipation takes off, that could change."

"So Archie was lying about his pills coming from a plant that just looks like a panda's arse?"

"Not necessarily. There is a herbal version, and it's probably more effective. Unfortunately, that's an endangered species as well. It's a traditional remedy in Bhutan and Nepal, but it isn't farmed, and demand from other areas means it's getting very rare. But it isn't cuddly like a panda."

"It's a bit pointless taking these particular pills from Archie, isn't it?"

"No. I'm a research officer for SpeciesPeace, and Barry's film editor Lucy is one of our members. When I heard that Archie was bringing a luxury item based on an endangered species, I realized we didn't know Panda Pills were on sale in the UK. I thought that if he happened to lose his, and someone else had to get the replacements for him, we could find out who was selling them and maybe how they get into the country."

"So that's what that phone call . . . why did Barry play ball?"

"Tapes. I've got one of Barry coming on to me during ChefStars . . . unsuccessfully, for better or worse, and one of the girl who came third, whose hotel room was next to mine, doing a Meg Ryan with some help from Barry."

"Came third?"

"Yes. Barry was straight about that. He said he could get me into the final, but couldn't fix who won. It was easier with this one; the public didn't see the selection stages."

Lizzie explains that she watched Archie from Gatwick, saw he kept the pills in a flap pocket of his kitbag. It was a stroke of luck that he changed tents on the first night, making it easy to take the pills and hide them with her mobile.

The moon's coming up. Under other circumstances, I'd think it an ideal setting to be sitting with a woman like this. But it's a contest, and my main opponent is sounding more resourceful by the incident. I say: "How do you know I won't do the publicity on this?"

"I don't think you will. But if you decide to, I'll just have to blackmail you."

"With what?" I start to wonder if she's really been in the Special Branch, maybe still is.

"Your famous injury in the Gulf. In fact the Blue Pussy Club in Dean Street. You were pushed off the stage, pissed, by a stripper."

"How the hell do you know that?"

"I was the stripper." She shrugs. "It was better money than a student loan."

Across the sand, the turtle begins to move. Perhaps she's sensed a stalemate: White King, Red Queen, no danger to her, or to each other.

DR BUD, CA

MICHAEL Z LEWIN

"I can't get over what a *beautiful* residence decision you made here," Dr Bud said.

"I'm so pleased you like it," Mr Mallory said.

"It's how old?"

"Oh, only late Victorian."

"Victorian . . . Wow! That's hundreds of years old, right?"

"About a hundred, yes."

"A hundred years old," Dr Bud said. "Back home I have a patient in my rebirthing class who is ninety-two, but Victorian . . . That seems so much . . . so much older, you know?"

"A patient, sir?"

"Well, I qualified as a dermatologist," Dr Bud said, "but right from the start I had no intention of being culturally impeded by my training. I'm into quite a few redirections so now I'm only a dermatologist by day."

"And what might you be by night?" Mr Mallory asked.

"Ha ha, that's a good one," Dr Bud said. "I always heard how dry you Brits are and you sure do live up to it."

Mr Mallory redirected himself. "How long are you planning to be with us, doctor? The note I saw by your reservation indicated you were uncertain when you booked."

"The person I spoke to . . . She was very helpful and knowledgeable, by the way. Was that your significant other?"

"My . . . ah, my wife. Yes."

"Well, she said it didn't matter if I didn't make up my mind until the impulse took me."

"It's not vital, no."

"Ah, 'vital'. Not 'vital'. That was the word she used too. You must be on a very harmonious and resonant wavelength, the two of you. You've been married a long time, I bet. Am I right?"

"Thirty-two years," Mr Mallory felt forced to admit.

"Oh, well done," Dr Bud said. "Congratulations. I doubt I'll ever even dream of that. In this day and age it's nearly a record. I bet you don't have any friends who have been married longer than that, do you?"

"I'm sure there are still many, many people with long marriages."

"And modest with it. I do envy you. My own first wife took off after twenty-eight months. I say first not because I have a second one yet, but because I believe in an optimistic attitude to life and relationships."

"So you aren't yet certain about your length of stay?" Mr Mallory said.

"I'm just going to stay here as long as it takes. You have plenty of room at this time of year. That's what Ms Mallory said. Or did she keep her maiden name? Not that I'm prying about whether she was a maiden."

"We do have only one other guest at the moment," Mr Mallory said. "And it is normally a quiet season for us."

"All the Americans have gone home by now, right?"

"We do enjoy the company of many visitors from abroad, happily."

"I know. That's how I got your phone number. Friends of mine stayed here two years ago and when they heard I was looking for somewhere in England to restore my inner harmony they said they had just the place. The Rohrmanns? Do you remember them? Chuck and Sophie? Fabulous couple. Fabulous."

"I'm not sure that I do. But I don't have the best memory for names."

"Sea salt," Dr Bud said.

"Pardon?"

"For the memory. Tops up your trace elements."

"I'll try to remember that."

"*Remember*! Ha ha! You guys are a hoot."

Mr Mallory said, "Would you . . . care to see your room now?"

"Yeah, good idea," Dr Bud said. "It's going to be an important space for me. To tell you the truth, why I'm in England is that I've had a prolonged emo-psychic displacement following the non-equal cessation of a major long-term-oriented relationship."

"Oh."

"What I need to do is work as hard as I can to get in touch with myself."

"My headmaster said it makes you go blind," Mr Mallory said.

"What?"

"But he may have got it wrong, of course. Would you care to step this way?"

Dr Bud did not return to the lobby until after nine, and when he did he found Mr and Mrs Mallory watching television behind the door marked "Private".

"Oh, there you are," Dr Bud said.

Mr Mallory rose. "Is there some problem?"

But Mrs Mallory patted the cushion beside her on the settee and said, "Sit down. I've heard so much about you. Turn the television off, Geoffrey."

Mr Mallory sat down again and by remote control silenced the television sound while leaving the picture.

"I've been hunting everywhere for your other guest," Dr Bud said. "In case he or she might want someone to talk to or go for a walk with. It's such a beautiful night. When I came out of my trance I was nearly overcome just looking out the window."

"Alas," Mrs Mallory said, "Mr Baker always stays out past midnight when he's with us. He's a salesman, and he entertains. He's been with us many times and we know his routine. Then when he does return he goes straight to bed."

"Might you like a walk? Or Mr Mallory? He told me about your marriage by the way. Congratulations!"

A quick look from Mrs Mallory was answered by her husband's shrug. She said, "There's always Andrew. He loves to go out."

"Andrew?" Dr Bud said.

"But it depends how you feel about animals."

"I feel they have every right to co-exist with us in their natural state. As far as humans are concerned, might does not make right, in my opinion."

"So you don't approve of pets?"

"Animal companions?" Dr Bud said. "Oh, I try to keep an objective view about situations of inter-species relationship which can be mutually beneficial."

"What she's asking is whether you fancy walking the dog," Mr Mallory said without turning from the television screen.

The dog – Andrew – was more interested in running than in walking and controlling him – it – took more physical than psychic strength. The longer the outing went on, the more Dr Bud marvelled at Andrew's energy. He began to muse upon whether Andrew might, in fact, be morbidly hyperactive.

Dr Bud's attempts at one-on-one communication with Andrew were not well received. The dog did not bite, but neither would it remain forehead-to-forehead with Dr Bud long enough for the two creatures to share bio-electrical interaction.

Nevertheless Dr Bud began to formulate a therapeutic plan for Andrew, because the longer he remained on the restraining end of the extendable lead, the more certain he was that Andrew was not in a peaceful relationship with his environment.

"I warned you he was quite a handful," Mr Mallory said when Dr Bud returned, forehead glistening with perspiration.

"I'd like to get to know him better," Dr Bud said. "I sense his inner-caninity is out of balance, and I'd enjoy the opportunity of seeing if I can restore some of his equipoise. There'll be no charge."

Mr Mallory said, "Have a word with Betty in the morning. He's her creature."

Dr Bud felt that the casual ownership concept was a clue to

Andrew's restlessness but he felt too tired to engage Mr Mallory immediately, so he smiled and waved good night.

Dr Bud rose at six-thirty with the brain-brightness of renewed purpose. At seven-thirty, confirmed in his existence by fifty minutes meditation and ten minutes wash and shave, he descended to the guest-house dining room.

"Good morning!" Betty Mallory said. "Will you have some breakfast?"

"I will indeed," Dr Bud said. "But first will you hug me?"

"Pardon?"

"More than food I need to start each day with a good hug."

"Oh," Betty Mallory said. "All right then."

For a minute by the watch Dr Bud hugged her and cooed and chortled. She did her best.

When it was over she said, "Now, what would you like to eat?"

But as Dr Bud considered his options, his concentration was interrupted by heavy footsteps behind him.

"Mornin'," said a round middle-aged man whose shirt parted below the button and above the belt to reveal his navel. The man touched Dr Bud on the shoulder, but passed by to give Mrs Mallory a wet kiss on the lips. "How you doin' this a.m., Betty, love? Got your pan hot and ready for me?"

"Ready as ever," Mrs Mallory said as the man released her and pinched a buttock.

"Let's see. Three eggs, scrambled. Fried bread. Black pudding. Fried mushrooms. Grilled tomatoes. Make it two of those big sausages I like. And four rounds of toast, don't spare the butter. Got it?"

"Got it," Mrs Mallory said.

"I'll get it one of these days," the man said, winking and pinching Mrs Mallory's other buttock. He turned to Dr Bud. "They may hold out for a while, but nobody resists me for ever. Persistence. It's the secret of my success. Winthrop Baker. How d'you do?"

It was just then that Mr Mallory entered the kitchen from the back garden. He was obviously upset. "Andrew's dead," Mr Mallory said. "He's been strangled."

*   *   *

Saying that it was a matter of respect for Andrew's departed life-force, Dr Bud remained at the guest-house all day. But in truth he was too upset to do anything else.

His upset began to melt into anger as time passed and no policeman appeared. Cops are cops, national boundaries notwithstanding, Dr Bud thought. Now if it had been a *man* strangled, they'd have fallen over themselves to get here when they'd been rung. But because it was "only" a dog. . . However, Dr Bud knew himself well enough to know that his anger was not one of the constructive forces in the universe. With colonic irrigation not at present a practical option, Dr Bud sat – cross-legged, eyes open, and totally still – on the "private" sitting room floor.

The law did not, in fact, arrive until late in the afternoon, and even then the young constable who did appear confided that she was only able to investigate the crime because other criminal activity in the city was slack.

"Did anyone have anything against Andrew?" WPC Vanda Graff asked the Mallorys.

Mr Mallory recalled slighting comments from a neighbour up the hill, comments muttered one afternoon as he passed the neighbour, Andrew straining at his lead. "And I don't even know the man," Mr Mallory said. "He moved in about five years ago and those were the first words we ever exchanged."

"Exchanged?" WPC Graff said. "Does that mean you spoke to him as well?"

"I told him to mind his own business," Mr Mallory admitted. "It was only a week ago, only a few days after we got Andrew, and now *this*."

"It does seem quite a concidence," WPC Graff said. "I'll have a word with your neighbour."

"Good," Mr Mallory said.

"I can't think of anybody who had a grievance against Andrew," Betty Mallory said. "I've racked my brain all day long, but I can't think of a single person."

Dr Bud said, "Mmmmmmmmmmm."

"What was that?" WPC Graff said.

"Mmmmmmmmmmmm."

The constable looked at the two guest-house proprietors. "Is he a hippie or something?"

"American," Mrs Mallory said.

"Dermatologist," Mr Mallory said. "By day."

"Ah."

And just then Dr Bud rose from his cross-legged position on the floor. He blinked his eyes three times and he said, "If I were you, I'd look in the bedroom of Winthrop Baker."

"You would?" WPC Graff said.

"I would."

"And why would that be, sir?"

"To find what you seek," Dr Bud said.

Andrew's collar was discovered beneath Baker's clean underpants.

At first WPC Graff suspected that Dr Bud had put it there himself. Fortunately for Dr Bud, WPC Graff handled the collar with textbook care and the forensic laboratory found clear fingerprints on it belonging to Winthrop Baker. Confronted with the evidence Baker confessed.

His story was that from childhood he had suffered from an uncontrollable fear of dogs. His occupation as a salesman required that he treat life with bluff and bluster, but whenever confronted by a dog – especially a large one – he went weak at the knees.

Throughout his sales area he had discovered congenial guest-houses where the owners were dogless. Then, between his last visit and this, to his dismay the Mallorys had acquired Andrew.

But by the time he discovered the change in circumstances he had already checked in and, as always, he had a tight schedule and a strict routine. Besides, he liked the guest-house. He liked the Mallorys. The ancient city always provided him with good business. What *was* he to do? With so few options, he could think of only one solution. And he took it.

WPC Graff's investigation, however, revealed that Baker had committed similar crimes before. Not only was he afraid of dogs, he had an irrational compulsion to rid the world of them.

Baker was taken away in handcuffs, begging for the chance to submit to therapy.

WPC Graff would only say, "That's for the judge to decide."

*   *   *

When it was all over the Mallorys went straight to Dr Bud. "But how did you know?" they both asked.

"Life," Dr Bud said, "is all about finding a way to stay in harmony with nature. Winthrop Baker was obviously a disturbed person."

"He was?" Mr Mallory said.

"Oh yes. Obviously." Dr Bud turned to Betty. "But you knew that, didn't you, Mrs Mallory?"

But Mrs Mallory shook her head.

"Think of that breakfast he ordered! 'Three eggs, scrambled. Fried bread. Black pudding. Fried mushrooms. Grilled tomatoes. Make it two of those big sausages I like. And four rounds of toast, don't spare the butter.'"

"What about it?" Mrs Mallory said.

"All the cholesterol. All the calories. It's a clear cry for help. Virtually a suicide attempt. Where I come from if someone went to a hotel and ordered a breakfast like that the waitress would play for time while the owner phoned for the town counsellor."

Mr and Mrs Mallory stared at their guest. They looked at each other.

"Would you like to meditate with me?" Dr Bud said. "We can do it right here. Come on. Each of you, give me a hand. Close your eyes."

Despite themselves, the Mallorys each gave Dr Bud a hand.

MALICE IN BLUNDERLAND

●   ●

KEVIN GOLDSTEIN-JACKSON

Little Elica was beginning to get bored. She was named Elica because her parents had wanted a boy named Eric. When their only child turned out to be female, they took her to their local church to be christened Erica, but the clergyman was Japanese and couldn't pronounce the letter "r" – hence her present name Elica.

The fact that Elica is, as you have probably noticed, an anagram of Alice, is irrelevant but intentional.

Anyway, the reason why five-year-old Elica was bored was because she had tried to turn on a TV set, but nothing had happened. And what, thought Elica, is the use of a television set without pictures or conversations?

Soon she began to feel drowsy – until a rather fat kangaroo came bounding past her, puffing, "The weight of this skin is killing me." Then this kangaroo took out a handkerchief from its pouch and dabbed at its eyes.

There was nothing really surprising in this – after all, little Elica Higginbottom *was* in a television studio waiting for her cue to take part in a new children's TV series.

Being bored, however, Elica decided to follow the kangaroo, as she had just observed it waddle out of the studio.

"Perhaps it went to its dressing room," she murmured, entering the passageway that led to the actors' rest area. And as a man wearing only a barrel rushed past her, she wondered which of the many doors might lead to the kangaroo.

Elica opened the first door and saw a giant caterpillar puffing away at a peculiar-smelling cigarette.

"Hi, man!" called the caterpillar.

"I'm not a man, I'm a little girl," replied Elica.

"Crazy, man. Hey, want a puff of this?"

"No, thanks," said Elica hastily, and continued her walk along the corridor.

From behind various doors she could hear snatches of conversation: "You know, she's so cross-eyed that when she cries the tears run down her back." "Nature is really amazing. I mean, look where Nature placed our ears – just in the right place for the inventor of spectacles." "She sure had early American features – she looked like a buffalo." "I went out with a spiritualist last night – I wanted to try a new medium."

As she continued down the corridor she passed several more animals.

"Hello, little girl," said a lady mouse. "If a buttercup is yellow, what color is a hiccup?"

"I don't know," confessed Elica.

"Burple!" said the mouse, giggling uncontrollably. "And do you know the difference between unlawful and illegal?"

Elica shook her head, so the mouse explained, "Unlawful is against the law, illegal is a sick bird."

Elica left the giggling mouse and pushed open a large door. She found herself in one of the property storerooms. It seemed deserted, but as soon as Elica entered, someone closed the door behind her, and she could hear the key turning in the lock.

"Oh, dear!" said Elica. "I hope I'm not trapped and have to stay here all night."

Elica rattled the doorknob, but no one came to help her.

She slumped down by the door and sighed. "Oh, how I wish I were small enough to crawl through the keyhole – or perhaps be a champion limbo dancer so I could limbo under the crack at the bottom of the door."

She sat for a few minutes, then decided to explore the room.

Elica examined the shelves and found several bottles marked POISON, but she knew they were only fake bottles made out of wax so they would break easily when an actor was hit over the head with them.

One bottle, however, was *not* marked POISON, nor was it made of wax. In fact, it contained a browny-colored liquid.

Elica sipped from the bottle. The liquid was very nice – a flavor she had never tasted before.

She drank deeply from the bottle, and very soon she felt her head going fuzzy, and her body didn't do what she told it to do.

"Curiousher and curiousher," said Elica, much surprised that her words came out with a slurring sound.

Had she but known she'd been drinking beer, she would not have been so surprised when her legs decided they were incapable of supporting her and made her fall to the ground. Her head seemed to be spinning round and round. It was then that the bottle slipped from her hand and, as she groped for it, trying to find the container of wonderful brown liquid, her hand brushed against something soft and wet.

She turned and tried to focus her eyes on what she had just touched.

It was the kangaroo. It was lying on the floor beneath a large table, and its skin where Elica had touched it was wet with blood. The kangaroo was dead.

Elica began to cry, and although she tried to tell herself that big girls of five don't cry, the tears streamed from her eyes until she passed into a soothing, calming sleep.

When Elica awoke – about two hours, twenty-three minutes, and sixteen seconds later (give or take a second) – she saw a duck peering at her through the open door of the storeroom.

"Oh!" said Elica. "My head hurts terribly." As she focused her eyes she asked, "Who are you?"

But the duck did not answer. "Perhaps it's a foreign duck," murmured Elica. "Maybe it's from Bombay."

Then the duck saw the body of the kangaroo, uttered a shrill scream, and ran off to call the police.

Half an hour later (give or take two hours, twenty-three minutes, and sixteen seconds), all the animal actors and actresses – plus Elica and the man dressed only in the barrel – were assembled in the storeroom being questioned by Chief of Police, Carroll Lewis.

"Now," he said. "We know Keith the kangaroo was killed at two o'clock this afternoon." He paused, then turned and pointed a finger at a grinning gorgonzola cat. "Where were *you* at that time?"

"I was sitting in a tub of steaming poultices, strangling goldfish," replied the cat.

"Have you got a goldfish-strangling license?" demanded Carroll.

"No."

"That's all right. You don't need one. Trick question. Can anyone confirm your alibi?"

"The goldfish."

"Good. Now, does anyone want to confess? It must have been *one* of you who did it."

"But how can you say that?" protested the duck. "You've only just arrived here and haven't even had time to examine the body properly. Look at all those bruises down the front of his neck—"

"Yes, his alimentary, my dear Watson. I *did* notice that. At first I thought he might have done it himself while trying to remove a chicken bone from his throat, so I immediately suspected fowl play. Then –"

The Chief of Police moved toward a grand piano in the corner of the storeroom.

"– I discovered *this*."

He held up a dead fish which he had extracted from the instrument.

"Oh, that's all right," said the animals in unison, "that's only the piano tuna."

"It still sounds fishy to me," commented Carroll.

"I don't see why," said a large porcupine. "I've just found this box of vestas with your name on it."

He handed the box to Carroll who glanced at it and said, "Yes, at last I have met my match. But *I* didn't kill the kangaroo. I'm the Chief of Police and have only just arrived. Someone else must have dropped this box."

"Talking of fish," commented an African wildebeest, "it reminds me of the song called *Whale Meat Again*. Or even *If You Were the Only Gill in the World*."

"Oh, my cod!" exclaimed Carroll. "Speak up, I'm hard of herring – or shall I sing *Salmon Chanted Evening*?"

"I'd prefer *Mackerel the Knife* – no relation to Jack the Kipper," replied the wildebeest. "But I'll just mull over the matter or ask minnow, minnow on the wall, who is the fairest of them all?"

"Eel have to go," said Carroll. "You might be having a whale of a time, but it serves no useful porpoise, so shut up or I'll give you an electric shark."

"But *who* killed the kangaroo?" asked Elica, trying to bring the conversation back to abnormality.

"It's obvious when you think about it," said Carroll. "Everyone here is dressed as an animal except you and that man wearing only the barrel. Now, if the kangaroo had been killed by an animal, surely the victim would have ripped the animal's costume in his death struggle – yet no one here has a torn costume, and there are no costume fibers under the fingernails – paws – of the kangaroo. This means that either you, little girl, or the man in the barrel committed the murder."

The animals gasped.

Carroll continued, "Now, a barrel is also known as a butt, so a person wearing a barrel must be known as a butt-ler. It follows logically from this that the butt-ler did it."

The man in the barrel, whose name was Diogenes Dingbat, broke down and confessed to murdering the kangaroo. It turned out that the kangaroo had been blackmailing Dingbat about his forthcoming marriage to an actress named Edith, who was playing the part of the mouse. The marriage would be biga-mouse since Dingbat was already married to an actress named Kate, from whom he could not get a divorce and, as the man in the barrel wryly said, "You can't have your Kate and Edith."

Thus, as the Chief of Police led the murderer away to face a midget judge (a small thing sent to try us), Elica pictured to herself how she would tell this tale to her children when she was old; and how they would tell it to their children . . .

DRIVING FORCES

CAROL ANNE DAVIS

"I'll have me some of that," Arnie whistled as we reached the estate. For a moment I thought he meant Shenaz, the girl he was keen on. She'd only come to the shop with us to help carry the six packs, was walking on his other side. Then I saw the car parked outside the bookies and suddenly knew exactly what he desired.

A Lamborghini. Low-slung, high speed, the shade of glossy red that supermodels slick on their bee-stings. Even a non-mechanical guy like me knew that he was looking at engine class. With a car like that you could go someplace, be someone – just looking at it made my balls weak with wanting. You wouldn't have to buy overpriced cans of leg-over if you owned a vehicle like that.

A vehicle like that lasts an hour in an area like this. It takes that long to check that it doesn't belong to any of the big drug dealers. After that there's a race to see who does the breaking and driving away. But a word in a few shell-likes brought back the news that the car belonged to Bevan which meant that it was here to stay.

You didn't mess with Bevan. One student dropout had been stupid enough to welsh on a deal so Bevan had sent round some of his men to kick the door down. They'd gone in wearing Ku Klux Klan hoods and rearranged his dental work to scare the hell out of him. If the guy had had any sense, he'd just've put his teeth under the pillow and drunk Carlsberg till he was seeing fairies. But this stupid wee bampot let his fingers do the walking and phoned the police. They'd turned up after a good three days: it probably took them that long to get the reinforced patrol car from the army. "I can identify some of the men by their tattoos," the student had explained.

Even the police had been lenient enough to give the guy a second chance, not getting out the Basildon Bond too quickly. "Are you sure, sir?" He had been and had named names after which . . . Well, someone heard a muffled scream, after which Bevan had a fire burning in his flat for a full five days despite the fact that it was the hottest July on record. And rumour had it that an onyx nose-stud just like the one the student wore had been found sizzling in the grate.

Anyway, I thought Arnie would now forget all about the car. Especially as the local wags had only nicknamed him Arnie because he was thin as a beansprout and a girl-sized five foot three. With his little tan leather trousers and his wee tape recorder spouting Tammy Wynette from his pocket, he was about as hard as a Euro mountain of cream.

"I'm going to take Shenaz away in that," he told me as we brought my kitchen table into the living room and deposited all of the cans on it: full preparation for a party.

"In Bevan's car? You're going to take it round the block?"

"Christ, no."

"Thank God for that." I opened a can and drank deeply.

"No, I'm going to take it and scarper for good," Arnie said.

As I wiped the spluttered export from my shirt, I wondered if he'd been sniffing the Tippex. Either that or he was climbing the high bit of a manic depressive phase. In the six months I'd lived here Arnie had been the most legit of all my neighbours. But he'd told me all about his earlier failed life of crime.

It was a catalogue of crimes. Well, catalogue crime to be precise. He'd simply phoned one of the big mail order firms to place an order on credit. Each time he did so he gave yet another name and address, using the details of someone who lived nearby. The firm would take the order and arrange to send round the goods at a specified date and time, then they'd do so.

The householder would take the parcel and sign for it and then the courier would drive away.

Cue Arnie turning up on the householder's doorstep: "I've just phoned my mail order firm – they think that my parcel's come here to the crescent instead of the terrace." Most times the patsy handed over the parcel and Arnie waltzed away.

He got caught because the mail order firm was sending out dozens of leather jackets and trousers for men with very wee arms and legs – that, and equally wee tape recorders. They sent out a few wee blank tapes for Arnie to tape his country music from the radio, too. Arnie knew what he liked and he liked it big time – at one stage he had "Stand By Your Man" playing in every room of his squat.

Anyway, he and his *Best Of Crystal Gale* cassette did a little time then moved into the hard-to-let housing. I moved next door to him a few months later after the university kicked me out. We were never going to be soulmates, but – through a shared inability to find something to do with our lives and a complete aversion to the needles that every other male on the estate was using – we palled along all right.

Sometimes he'd get lucky with a bar whore and would leave a Two's Company sticker on his door to ensure I didn't call him. Other days I'd be doing the business and would use this Men At Work sign I'd nicked from a woefully optimistic building site. Around here it was usually cash before coitus – the girls knew that they were sitting on a copper mine. Shenaz was the first girl that Arnie fancied who he might actually have a non-paying relationship with.

She was class compared to him – her mum and dad were still together and neither of them knew their way to the pawnshop. She'd only visited our estate because the council had paid for her and some other art students to paint a big picture on the houses' gable ends.

Bevan's house had more front to it than a crooked MP. He'd bought three council houses in the names of long-dead men and persuaded some junkie architect to merge them all together. Chez Bev thus had the benefits of a regular mansion yet was still set squarely in his turf so that he could keep an eye on everyone and everything. Now he had his Lamborghini parked outside his house during the day to give his henchmen something other than their noses and his girls to aim for. At night he kept it in the garage attached to his pad.

"No way can you break into that garage without someone hearing you," I said baldly.

"No, but I can break out of it, can't I?" Arnie said. I choked on some more beer and watched regretfully as it spurted from my nostrils: this was wasteful. And at this rate I'd need my dole money for Arnie's RIP card.

"You know how the girls go round to Bevan's on a Thursday night?" Arnie asked. I knew. We all figured they came for more than their cut – especially as of three weeks ago when Bevan's wife had left him. There wasn't a breast or buttock within drug ring distance that Bevan hadn't had a close acquaintance with. "Well, I'll ask one of them to use the downstairs loo just before she leaves – and leave the window open for me. I'll crawl in, shut the window and hide in the cupboard under the stairs till Bevan's gone to his kip."

"You know what he's like. He'll probably have a girl or two in with him." Bevan's girls were legend.

"Well, if he's doing the business he'll not hear me opening the door that connects the house to the garage and opening the garage doors from the inside."

"And if he sleeps light?"

Arnie looked down at his matchstick limbs. "Hell, I'm slimmer than him. I can run faster. And I've got a half-brother in Paisley who'll put me up if I have to hide."

Arnie was a nice guy, if a mite optimistic at times. I blamed it on the country and western. If your lover left you in those songs you found solace in old mountains or new friends then had some fun on the bayou. The worst thing that ever happened was that your faithful sheepdog died.

For Arnie, the Lamborghini was to die for. I wished that I could freeze-frame time but Thursday crept determinedly round. I watched from my window as Bevan's girls traipsed in twos and threes up the path – with their ultra-short skirts and mega-low tops he knew exactly what he was getting. Then came Bevan's henchmen, as presumably even he wasn't greedy enough to keep so many apertures to himself.

A couple of hours later they left again. I'd gone to bed but heard the various car doors slam, then silence. I could picture Arnie crouching in the dark cupboard and prayed that he hadn't left a sliver of leather trouser sticking out. Bevan didn't strike me as a particularly tidy man but if he was to decide to open a certain doorway . . . I shivered as I waited for the local Horlicks, a valium, to kick in.

I slowly unpinned the towel that covered my bedroom window the next day. I half expected to see Arnie's head impaled like a pickle on the metal fencing. But there was no Arnie – and, according to the gossip in the Credit Union, no car.

Arnie and the car going missing at once: you didn't have to be Carol Vorderman to do the arithmetic. Everyone said that take-no-prisoners Bevan was out for the wee man's skin. Then a few days later they said that Bevan had sorted it out and said no one was to touch Arnie if they saw him. I figured that this was just a smoke-screen and that he wanted to castrate the wee eejit himself. But six months later someone on the estate unpeeled the newspaper from their curry sauce and chips – and found Arnie smiling up at them. Well, his wedding photo at a neighbouring town's Registrar's to be more precise. He looked exactly the same – just a bit more bright-eyed, if anything. Shenaz looked great.

Great minds think alike – but in Arnie's case he'd also become one lucky bastard. I realized that when I bumped into him at the dogs a few years later. I was serving in the stadium's restaurant at night and making music – aka busking outside the railway station – by day. Arnie was with three other guys in nice light suits: they had the best window table. He stuck to one half pint of lager tops and looked long-term clean.

"Business meeting," he said after we'd done the nod and grin that passes for a handshake or a hug around these parts, "I'm running a stall now."

"Yeah?" I tried to find a subtle way to ask what he was selling as I set down the basket of complimentary bread.

"A Country and Western stall," he continued. His dinner guests looked as relaxed as he: there was no front to them. "Y'know, the videos, the CDs, the clothes."

"I'm in the music game myself if you're ever looking for a little live entertainment . . ." The boss was giving me drop-dead looks so I hastily got out my order pad.

Arnie padded over to join me after I finished my shift. "A drink downstairs for old times' sake?"

I nodded, feeling surprisingly pleased to see him again and patted my back trouser pocket. "They tip well, your mates."

"My *suppliers*. Gave me a good deal on some imports."

I looked at him keenly. "Gear?"

"Not the kind you mean." He grinned as we walked towards the bar lights. He had dimples where hollows once had been and his matchstick legs had filled to a healthier cigar size. "Western gear – fringed calfskin jackets and leather skirt and hipsters from the American events."

"No uppers to keep you going through the all night dancing?"

"Nah, no need mate. Other than the odd toke on a Saturday with Shenaz, I'm strictly legit."

"Same here," I said, ordering two Jack Daniels from the bar whilst Arnie put "Good Year For The Roses" on the jukebox. "Haven't done much stuff since moving up here. It was that place, you know?"

He nodded, drank, then set down his glass. "Too true. Hardly a day went by without somebody doing a maddie. D'you remember when that man with the terriers held his bairn out of the window until his estranged wife came back?"

I nodded. A ten-foot drop and the bairn all of four and the police trying to get a mattress from a ground-floor flat whilst the owner held on for dear life because he had his stash underneath it. If they hadn't found the madman's wife at the Boilerman's Club or if his hand had slipped . . .

We talked and drank some more then I asked what I'd been dying to ask all night.

"Bevan's car – you got away with it?"

He nodded sagely.

"Still got it?"

"Of course not. Sold it and rented Shenaz and I a decent flat."

I looked down at the thick gold band on his finger. "I saw

your wedding photo at the time." We did a high five then grinned at each other sheepishly. "She sorted you out?"

He nodded, looking as close as the vertically challenged can get to walking tall. "It was her idea that we use most of the money we got for the car to buy the stall."

"And it's worked out fine?"

"Worked out great. I know my stuff and country is still big business. Shen and I work together half the week and let a couple of trainees do the quieter times."

"And Bevan didn't ever . . . I mean, you've moved some but you're not that far away." Bevan's long arms had been legend.

Arnie smiled to himself. "Oh sure, he could've found me any time but he decided to stay away." He resettled himself on the stool then looked over at me, the way you look at someone when you're wondering how much to tell them. I tried to look innocent – hell, I was innocent. Whatever had happened, I wasn't going to give the game away.

He obviously saw in my eyes that I was just curious, not looking to have something to use against him. So we started in on another whisky and he continued to tell what he'd done. "That night I crept into Bevan's hall cupboard. I heard the girls leave along with the dealers. Then it sounded as if someone had stayed behind to sort out a bit more business and then I heard the springs creaking as Bevan got into bed."

I nodded, thinking back to the big renovated house with its multiple wee rooms and man-sized cupboard. "I crept out and was about to make for the connecting door when I heard Bevan cry out."

"Jesus," I said.

"It's not what you think," said Arnie.

I stared across at him open-mouthed. "He hadn't heard you?"

"No, but I heard him. He was in bed with Big Tam."

In bed with Big Tam. Bevan, who'd been seen with more girls than you could fit into a Chippendales audience. Bevan, who never failed to whistle and wink at anything in a skirt. Arnie had peered through the chink in the door and from what he saw and heard Big Tam wasn't just big in the stature department. And Bevan, for all his macho posturing by day, turned out to be a passive kind of guy at night.

"So I scarpered with the car and sent him word that I'd left details of his private life with various solicitors." Arnie gave me the cheekiest of grins.

I choked on my Scotch. He'd always made me choke on beer. "Various solicitors?"

Arnie looked at me patiently. "If you live on the estate for a few years you get to know a lot of briefs."

"And Bevan accepted it?"

"I said that if anything happened to me my briefs would send proof of Bev's preferences to his less faggot-friendly friends and enemies. I suggested that for once it might be better to give than to receive."

He got up to go. I whistled through my teeth. It seemed impossible that this wee country n' western fan could have outwitted one of Glasgow's hardest dealers.

"But it was just your word against his, Arnie. You took a chance."

"Chanced nothing." Arnie patted his top pocket as he turned towards the door and for the first time I noticed he still had his miniature recorder. "It meant recording over Nashville but I got Bevan's live bed show on tape."

HOPPER AND PINK

BARRY FANTONI

The three words painted in flaking gold leaf on the sign outside my office door read, "press and wait". Above them was the dusty black silhouette of a pointing hand which directed clients to a buzzer. Most clients didn't bother with that, though; they just walked right in. Not this client. The buzzer went and that was all. I had just gone back to an article in the *Saturday Evening Post* about how much ice cream Americans ate each year when the buzzer went again. It was another short, tentative buzz, as if whoever it was standing in the corridor outside didn't really want the services of a private detective. Thinking eight million gallons was a lot of cow's milk and frozen sugar, I dropped the magazine on my desk and shouted, "Come on in, the door's open."

I had half expected no one to respond. Fooling around with my buzzer was one of the ways the janitor's kid filled his summer vacation, along with getting his head stuck in railings and giving a hot foot to any of my clients who stood around long enough. Just to see anyone walk through the door would have been enough to raise my eyebrows. The guy who materialized practically took them off my forehead. At a guess, he was well over seventy, short, weighed no more than 140 lbs, and was dressed mainly in a multi-check cotton sports jacket with colours that would make a Hawaiian sunset look forgettable.

He was wearing the full drape jacket over an electric blue sports shirt complete with a canary yellow polka-dot bow tie, and stone flannel plus-fours. A pair of two-tone golf shoes extended merrily from pale mauve clock socks. As a precaution against looking drab he had chosen a Panama hat with a band of indigo and scarlet satin and decorated it with a lime green feather tinged with crimson. But in each case, the brightness of his clothes, his jacket, his shirt, his bow tie, had faded slightly, mostly by the same degree. The result left him looking like someone who had stepped out of a coloured photograph exposed too long to the sun. Or a vase of dying flowers.

"Mike Dime?" my visitor asked, standing half in, half out of the room. "I do hope I ain't interrupting nothing." A shaft of light from the window cut across his shoes so the white tips shone like snow on a pair of sunlit peaks.

To give my dazzled eyes a rest I let them drop to the cover pic of the magazine in front of me. No change. It showed Hollywood's latest investment, a tall blonde in a two-piece bathing suit who was trying hard to look like an actress. I shook my head slowly. "Just dreaming," I sighed and looked back at the old man in the technicolour outfit. I hoped he wasn't an interior designer pitching for work. "How can I help?"

"Maybe I should have called first," he said with an apologetic smile. "It's always good manners to call before dropping in on someone."

"Wouldn't have made any difference." I waved an inviting hand at the visitor's chair. "Until twenty minutes ago I was on the other side of Philly. Been in West Philadelphia most of the day. Business."

My visitor crossed the room with short, uncertain steps. "I'm so pleased to hear that," he said and sat down as carefully as if there had been a kitten asleep on the shiny leather upholstery. "I sure wouldn't want to interrupt nothing."

I leaned back clasping my hands behind my head and took a closer look at the polite old man sitting across the desk. The top half of his face was dominated by a pair of circular spectacles the size of the big wheel on a penny farthing bike. It gave his dry old face the look of an owl thinking things over but that was as far as the resemblance went. Unlike an owl, he didn't look in the least bit wise, just sad. He didn't speak at once. New clients often find the first sentence the toughest. And it doesn't help to push. I let the heavy tick of the office clock fill in the silence and waited while the old man sat perfectly still, staring at the water cooler by the door. Then, having arranged his thoughts into something he could get his voice involved with, he turned and faced me. "To acquire your services," he asked in the way he might be ordering champagne in an expensive restaurant, "it requires a lot of capital? I mean, maybe you charge more than ten bucks an hour?"

I laughed and leaned forward. "If I charged ten bucks an hour I wouldn't be paying rental on a used auto. I'd be driving this year's Cadillac."

He smiled again, this time with more confidence. "So a ten spot would buy quite a sizeable piece of your professional experience?" He reached forward and placed the something he'd been fumbling in his breast pocket for squarely on the cover of the magazine in front of me. The blonde's two-piece changed from tiger stripes to green.

"Sizeable," I repeated, and looked at the engraved portrait of Lincoln. But I made no attempt to pick it up. "Of course, it wouldn't cover me shooting anyone or getting hit over the head," I said, "but it would certainly entitle you to bend my ear for a while." There was a packet of cigarettes on my desk. I tapped a couple loose and offered one to the old man who held up a palm.

"Thanking you just the same," he said, the remains of the punch drunk Bronx accent falling easy on the ear. "I never picked up the habit of smoking cigarettes. Sure, I smoke a cigar on stage, but that's just for show. As a matter of fact, I can make a full Corona last a couple of months."

I was getting interested. He looked too old for divorce and the mention of stage work had me guessing. I plugged a cigarette into the corner of my mouth and set light to the end. "You an actor?"

This time the smile was broad enough to show his teeth. "A comedian," he answered, but in spite of the smile there was sadness in the way he said it. "I hoped that maybe you might've recognized the face."

I blew out smoke. "Apart from watching the cops in this town chase crime," I said, "I don't get to see much in the way of comedy acts these days."

The old man nodded sympathetically. "Pity. You would have liked us. Hopper and Pink, 'laughter makes a flat world round'. Milly Pink – that was my wife's name – she thought up the tag line. To tell you the truth, Mr. Dime, Milly thought up most of the stuff we did on stage. Clever gal, a real bright spark and the sweetest woman you ever met. She passed over last December, by the way." He paused to swallow something large. "My name is Harry, Harry Hopper," he resumed, brightening a little. "A pleasure to make your acquaintance."

The surviving half of Hopper and Pink extended a small hand across the desk. I reached forward and gave the smooth skin and bird-brittle bones a gentle shake.

"And what is this ten bucks of yours expected to buy?" I asked amiably. "All my gags are old."

Harry Hopper took off his hat and placed it reverently on his lap. "Yours and mine," he said. "In my case seventy-eight years old, and married to Milly for over sixty of them. Young Milly – I still call her that, even though she's dead and gone – young Milly was my life and inspiration, and I ain't ashamed of saying so. No gag I ever cracked, no matter how worn thin ever sounded so bad when Milly Pink was standing on stage along-side me."

I had been listening carefully for a clue as to what Harry Hopper was doing in my office. There hadn't been one. "From what you have told me so far," I said, "I can't see how a private dick can earn ten bucks."

Harry Hopper put a finger to his lips, as if he had expected me to add more. "There's no mystery," the comedian said flatly. "I don't laugh anymore, Mr. Dime, and I don't make folks laugh any more either. Put plain, I lost the worst thing a funny man can lose. I lost my sense of humour, lost it the day Milly died."

I stubbed out my cigarette. "Don't tell me, Mr. Hopper, you want me to find it." I was gagging, figuring that's what an old timer from Vaudeville would go for. But Harry Hopper was serious.

"Why not?" he asked with large hopeful eyes. "Let me tell

you, without laughter I might as well be dead. And there are times when I miss Milly so much I wish I were."

I stood up, walked the two paces to the open window behind my desk and looked down at the noisy street below. A freckle-faced kid in a baseball hat was doing tricks on roller skates on the sidewalk. A Negro with short white hair thinning at his temples and a stained apron wrapped around his girth was laying mustard on a hoagie. A businessman with an out of town look on his face was mopping sweat off his brow with a handkerchief, his hat held at the end of an outstretched arm, as if he were catching rain. A nun was waiting to cross the street. A cop was staring at a high window in an apartment a block away. A hundred ordinary men and women were doing a hundred ordinary things. Once in a while I wondered what it was like to be one of them. I went back to my chair and sat down again.

"You don't want a private investigator, Mr. Hopper," I said as soothingly as I knew how. "You want a doctor, and not one who hands pills for lumbago."

The comic took off his spectacles and wiped them absently with the end of his tie. "Harry," he said softly. "Call me Harry. Everyone else does."

I crossed my arms. "Okay, Harry let me give it to you straight. A sense of humour is not one of the things a dick gets hired to find. Jewels, autos, dogs, even people – you'd be surprised just how many people lose themselves – but what you are asking . . ." I let my sentence fade.

"I already seen the kind of doctor you're recommending," Harry Hopper said heavily, replacing his spectacles. "You laughed when I asked what you charge an hour. You'd have died laughing if I told you what that guy took home."

He sounded genuine, but I was still only half convinced that the comedian wasn't shooting me a line. I decided to play him along a little, but gently and not too fast.

"This ten bucks," I said, and nodded at the bill. "Is that some kind of a down payment for hiring me?"

"I want one hour of your time, that's all, Mr. Dime."

"To do what?" I asked. "No one gets paid for sitting around doing nothing."

Harry Hopper began to rise apologetically from his chair. "Maybe there's something else you have to do, something that won't wait an hour?"

"Sit down, Harry," I said evenly. "I've got plenty of time. But if you're feeling lonesome, ten bucks buys a swell bottle of bonded."

"I already tried hiding in a bottle." There was a hint of pain in the man's voice. "Even an old campaigner like me can find solace in a drink or two." Harry Hopper shifted in his seat and recrossed his bony legs. His pants hung in loose folds, like a slack tent canvas. "But as everyone knows the effect don't last long, and soon you got to start looking deeper. You got to start looking for the answers."

I waited until he got comfortable once more. "Answers to what, Harry?"

He gave me another of his big smiles. "You know something, Mr. Dime," he said. "I was seven-years-old when I walked out in front of a house full of paying customers and told my first gag. Just think of it – a seven-year-old kid."

I knew Harry had reached the point they all reach. Every client who gets to stick around for longer than three minutes will tell a dick their story. Automatically, I picked up a pencil and examined the lead. There wasn't a lot showing but I didn't expect to be writing much down. Harry's file wouldn't need no notes, no surveillance, no loaded revolvers. Just laughs. I had finally realized why I'd been hired.

"Remember that first gag?" I asked and gave him plenty of room to answer.

"Right here in this very town. The Walnut Street Theatre. You can forget a lot of things in a life as long as mine, but your first laugh, well, that ain't one of them."

It was a humid afternoon. Even though the window was wide open and the desk fan full on, the air was still thick and clammy. Harry Hopper held his hat by the crown and began fanning his face. "Milly was with me right from the word go," he went on enthusiastically. "Her folks were Italian, a knife-throwing act mainly, with a little tumbling and juggling. Milly was the eldest daughter of five, although Pink wasn't her real name. She was originally called Emillia Pinchonetti, but we changed it to make it fit Hopper better. In those days vaudeville shows were a bit like circuses, on the road together for years sometimes. That's how I met Milly, being from a showbiz family myself. We practically grew up together."

I sucked some smoke into my lungs. "No kidding?"

"Sure. Milly and me used to fool around a lot back stage, practising all the gags we heard the big names perform and imitating the way they did things. Believe me, Mr. Dime, some of those acts we had in them days were good, and I mean good. So like I was saying, we'd be clowning all hours and I guess it must have sounded pretty professional, young as we were. We'd always have an audience of stage hands who'd be laughing tears with me acting like I'd been married fifty years already, Milly playing the part of a real scatterbrain. Then one night we got a chance to show what we could really do. For some reason the husband and wife act that closed the first half of the show didn't turn up; it later transpired she'd run off with the strongman from a show playing in the theatre across the street. My pa Eddie Hopper, who as well as being a top-class song and dance man, was also a pal of the manager, suggested that to save the show, he put us kids on. And that's just what happened." The old comedian chuckled to himself. "A couple of kids dressed as grown-ups. Ma's high heels and lipstick for Milly, a cane and gloves and pa's long pants tucked up for me."

Suddenly Harry Hopper leaped smartly off his seat and strode to the middle of the floor. He replaced his Panama and gave the crown a friendly pat on top. "Hi, folks, glad to be here," he announced and gave the ends of his bow tie an exaggerated tug. "I just flew in from Las Vegas, and boy, are my arms tired."

I'd heard it a million times – everyone had – but I laughed just the same. The comedian acknowledged my appreciation by tilting his hat. "We did a lot of those one-liners, Mr. Dime. Say, did I ever tell you about the walls of our apartment? I wouldn't say that they are thin, but last night I asked my wife the time and a guy four blocks away told me to get my watch. Did I say thin? The other day I gave the place a coat of paint and the dame next door complained that the colour clashed with her drapes. And the landlord. He's so tight-fisted. One time he paid for a round of drinks and it took major surgery to remove his wallet. It was his birthday last week. I gave him a left calf glove."

I did as Harry ordered.

"Because he never takes his right hand out of his pocket."

So it went on, one corny gag after another, his self-assurance swelling with every punchline. Then, exactly one hour after beginning his routine, he took a short bow and crossed the room to where I was sitting. "You've been a swell audience," he said. "Small, but appreciative. Let me tell you, Mr. Dime. For the first time since Milly died I feel like a human being. Strange, ain't it?"

"Not really," I said. "Laughter makes a flat world round. Remember?" I got up and walked the comedian to the door, where we shook hands. "Drop by any time you're passing, Harry," I called as the door closed. "You know where the buzzer is."

When the room had finally stopped echoing with the sound of Harry Hopper's vaudeville humour, I tried deciding what to do with his ten dollars. Clearly I hadn't earned it; if anything I should have been paying him for the laughs. For want of something better I slipped the bill into an envelope, marked it with his name and put it in the desk drawer.

During the weeks that followed I kept an ear open for the buzzer, a sign that Harry Hopper wanted to give me another chapter of his life. But he never did show. I figured that either he couldn't find ten bucks, or more probably, once was enough. Even so I often wondered what had become of him. I wasn't left wondering long.

A month after his visit I was glancing through *Variety*, while waiting to see a prospective client in the entertainment business, when my eye caught the headline, "Vaudeville Star Dies". The obituary gave a brief but warm appraisal of Harry's career with Milly, and explained that he had passed away peacefully in his sleep. It closed with details of the funeral service to be held at the Mount Miriah Cemetery the following day. I told the secretary that five minutes was too long to wait, even for a theatrical producer, and drove back to my office.

Within minutes of reading the news I was ordering a wreath over the phone.

"I want flowers," I said. "Big, happy flowers."

"You got a price in mind?"

I hadn't. But still had Harry Hopper's ten-dollar bill in my desk drawer. I took it out and turned it over between my fingers. "Ten bucks?" I offered.

"Ten bucks won't buy much," the voice came back. "Half a wreath at the most."

I thought about it for a second. "That's not such a bad idea," I said. "Send half a wreath."

The florist gave a snort. "Half a wreath? What are you, bud, some kind of a comedian?"

"Not me," I said. "I can just about crack a hard-boiled egg. But you should have heard the guy who's paying."

WHERE DO YOU FIND YOUR IDEAS?

MARTIN EDWARDS

Who would it be?

Looking down on the ground floor of the bookshop from his vantage point in the gallery, where he skulked in the aisle which divided Psychology and The Occult, Gerard Babb watched the punters drifting in from the street and asked himself which of them would put the question he had come to dread.

He checked his watch for the twentieth time. Five minutes to go. In reality, ten minutes, for the manager was sure to insist on delaying the start in the vain hope of a late surge of interest from the reading public of this drab Midlands town. Of course there would be no surge. All that was likely to happen was that two or three of the characters who now roamed the street in search of care in the community might wander in for a place to shelter and swig out of beer cans.

"Ready?"

Brian had appeared at his side. A squat and mournful fellow, Brian seemed to Gerard to be temperamentally unsuited to his job as a sales rep. He'd been made redundant eighteen months earlier from his job as marketing manager for a company which sold artificial bonsai trees and had kicked his heels in the dole queue for a year before taking a post with the firm which published Gerard. He'd confided that he regarded selling books as much the same as selling phoney miniature plants and he'd made it very clear to Gerard that he thought fiction a complete waste of time: why bother to read something that wasn't even true? Gerard couldn't help looking forward to the day when Brian, like a superannuated politician, was given another chance to spend rather more time at home with his family.

"As ready as I'll ever be."

"Not much of a crowd, I'm afraid." Brian prided himself on his realism.

"Better than Stoke-on-Trent."

Brian grimaced. They both knew that a turn-out of three would be better than Stoke-on-Trent.

Downstairs the manager was pacing up and down in the manner traditionally associated with expectant fathers. He at least had claimed enthusiasm for crime fiction of the type which Gerard wrote, although Gerard had noted his failure to have read any of the Inspector Dooley novels.

Not that he was alone in having denied himself that pleasure. Years ago Gerard had resolved that in future he would never, at parties, admit to being a crime writer. He could no longer bear the puzzled frowns of people he met as they struggled to remember if they had ever heard of him. The giveaway was that polite enquiry: "And do you write under your own name?" A civilised reminder of his lack of a public profile.

"Course," said Brian, "the weather will have kept a lot of people away."

"It's not rained all week."

"Exactly. People will be out enjoying themselves."

Gerard found himself envying them. Twenty years – even a decade – back, it had all been so different. Inspector Francis Xavier Dooley had achieved a modest following; if not in the Morse class as a puzzle-solver, at least he could claim a full complement of first names. Crime round-ups in regional newspapers usually included a mention of Gerard's books and smaller publications, whose reviewers valued a regular supply of free novels, had been known to describe them as "unputdownable". The posher Sundays, although more enigmatic, on occasion said things like "the mayhem quotient is as high as ever" and Gerard had been happy to take that as praise. In those days, he had been accompanied on book-signing tours by a young woman publicist and a couple of times the girl sent by head office had been sufficiently starry-eyed about authors to be persuaded to share his bed in the second-rate provincial hotels where they stayed. All that had changed now: he was expected to be grateful for the company of the local area rep, who was dying to dash back home at the earliest opportunity.

He gazed disconsolately down on his expectant audience. The usual crowd. A scruffy student with features cast in a permanent sneer; a bespectacled would-be writer thirsting for tips; an earnest young woman with a notepad and pencil; two old ladies who came to everything and never bought anything; and a tramp who could be relied upon to start snoring the minute Gerard began his talk. The manager had stationed his assistant next to the till while he gloomily contemplated the stacks of books which Brian had insisted on Gerard signing so as to avoid the risk of their being returned to the warehouse unsold.

How many minutes would pass before the question was asked? He was sure he would not have to wait long. How would Inspector Dooley rise to the challenge? With his customary determination, Gerard thought gloomily. Dooley was a loner, a maverick who was perhaps a little too fond of the bottle. No lover of discipline, he had a running feud with his boss, a play-it-by-the-book time-server who was always threatening to take him off the case. In his tyro days, when he had still fancied himself as a budding Graham Greene, Gerard had made Dooley a lapsed Catholic who wrestled with his own sense of original sin during each investigation. But his then editor, an unsympathetic atheist who refused to accept any novel over 180 pages in length, had urged him to concentrate on crime rather than character and although the editor had long ago found himself a better paid job in publishing computer manuals, Gerard nowadays never allowed his detective more than two paragraphs of introspection per sixty thousand words.

It was ironic, he mused, that at the point in his career where his reputation should have been secure, when his name should be cropping up with tedious regularity on the shortlists for all the genre's top awards, the kind of book he wrote should have fallen out of fashion. He regarded himself as an entertainer first and last, but it was difficult to entertain people who were unaware of his existence. Of course, he'd always suffered because of niggardly publicity budgets, but the last couple of years had been the most disastrous he'd ever known. His American publishers had ditched him and even in the UK, no paperback contract had been forthcoming for the last Dooley title. His agent was philosophical – "Trade's very difficult at present, darling" – but she could afford to be: she now acted for Mandy Deville, brightest new star in the criminal firmament (as *The New Statesman* had it), creator of Jess Valetta, the feisty Afro-Caribbean private eye who solved crimes in a tracksuit whilst jogging around Battersea Park and whose first two adventures had loped to the top of the bestseller charts.

Down below the manager was looking out of the shop's front door. With a sad shake of the head, he turned back inside and indicated to Brian that they might as well begin.

"Better get it over with, then, eh?" Brian suggested.

They went down the stairs and the manager shepherded Gerard to the front of the sparsely occupied black plastic chairs. Against the back wall stood a showcard emblazoned with Gerard's name and the jacket of *Dooley Takes A Break*. Beneath it could still be discerned faint details of the previous week's bookshop guest – an alternative comedian who had written a novel which was at one and the same time a hilarious satire and a searing indictment of government policy. The comedian had attracted a full house, naturally, and the manager hadn't omitted to mention it.

In introducing Gerard, the manager said a few words – a very few, sixteen in fact, Gerard counted them – and the desultory clap of greeting from the two old ladies and the tramp scarcely qualified as even a ripple of applause. Gerard forced a smile and opened with his customary quip about the traffic cop and the crime novelist. Even in Stoke-on-Trent it had received a better reception.

As usual, he talked about his career to date. Increasingly, he thought, it had come to sound like an obituary composed by an unsympathetic rival. The early days of struggle; the joy of achieving published status; the naive dreams of glory; the years of decline. He had come to see a sort of parallel between the fate of his literary career and his relationships with women. His wife had finally left him for good after years of mutual infidelities. She had taken up with a solicitor who specialised in matrimonial law and wrote poems about cats in his spare time.

"He has more artistic ability in his little finger than you have in your whole body," she had spat in one of their final arguments. Her invective always compensated in ferocity of delivery for its lack of originality.

"Half a dozen bits of doggerel in a magazine for wannabe writers?"

"He's a successful professional man," she had said. "He doesn't *need* to write full time."

And, it was true, the lawyer had certainly proved good at his job. Gerald had been screwed so badly on the divorce settlement that he'd been forced to move into a scruffy furnished flat in the sort of urban area where old folk burned to death in their homes because they could not break through the security barriers when a fire broke out. Money was short and to pay the rent Gerard had even had to stoop to writing five-minute mysteries for women's magazines. Under a pen-name, of course: he had his pride.

As he came to the Raymond Chandler joke which always began his peroration, he turned his mind to his audience. Who was going to torment him this time? The student was composing his sneer with some care and the aspiring writer had scribbled furiously throughout the entire talk. They were the likeliest to ask the question Gerard feared most, but neither of the old ladies could be ruled out of contention. One was fiddling with her false teeth as if making ready to put him on the spot, whilst her friend had finished the packet of humbugs she had been guzzling from the moment he first opened his mouth.

Why was he so keyed up, why bother about the reactions of a small group of people about whom he had no reason to care? Even when he was starting out, surely he had not felt as tense as this? Even though he was saying nothing he had not repeated a hundred times before, it seemed as though the words were sticking to the roof of his mouth. He paused and, giving the audience a tight smile, poured himself a glass of water.

For God's sake, pull yourself together, he instructed himself. *Soon it will be over.*

Yet even as the words echoed in his head, he realised that they applied with as much force to his writing career as to this latest unimportant talk. How could he go on, when he couldn't answer a simple question to which even a first time novelist can respond with a smug smirk?

He stumbled over the last few sentences in his notes and it was plain when he had come to the end that those present had not even realised he had finished. After an expectant pause the manager clambered awkwardly to his feet and said, "Well, thank you, Mr Babb for a most, er, interesting insight into the literary life. And now, I'm sure, everyone will be bursting with questions . . ."

His reedy voice trailed away as every hand in the audience remained resolutely on its owner's lap. This was Brian's cue. With every sign of resentment, he raised his arm and Gerard gave him the nod.

"I wonder if you could tell us what the future holds in store for Inspector Dooley?"

Dead easy. But Gerard bumbled on inconclusively in reply and Brian's expression made it clear that he wished he had kept his mouth shut. At least the ice had been broken, however, and the student had thought of something to ask.

"What do you see as the novelist's function?"

Gerard gave him a chilly look. "To make money," he replied and the sight of the student's face gave him a thrill of pleasure almost reminiscent of the days when writing THE END on the last page of his manuscript had given him a sense of achievement rather than making him tremble at the thought that he might never finish another book.

The would-be author was next. "What's your writing routine each day?"

Maybe things would not be so bad tonight after all. Gerard reeled off the standard nine-to-five answer with a fluency he had thought beyond him these days. He said nothing about the long hours spent in the cubbyhole he now dignified with the name of study, staring at damp patches on the walls and seeing in them, like ink blots, the scornful faces of people he knew. His wife; his agent; his new editor, a sweet-looking girl with a foul tongue who was already casting round for an excuse to drop him from her list.

Timidly, the old lady with the false teeth lifted an age-spotted claw. "Can I ask, please, who is your favourite detective story writer?"

Gerard didn't see it as his job to promote the competition. "Agatha Christie," he said promptly. Bloody woman, she'd been dead thirty years and she still outsold him by a hundred to one. But at least you could never describe Miss Marple as feisty.

"Why did you set your last book in Cornwall?" asked the young woman sharply. "I missed the Lancashire setting."

God, a regular reader. They were thin on the ground these days. And she had a point. In the early Dooleys, Gerard had traded on the rugged Northern background against which the Inspector carried out his investigations. On his last outing, Dooley had been suspended for cuffing a teenage yobbo round the ear and had spent the time before his case came to court touring round the South West. In the time-honoured tradition of all holidaying sleuths, he there stumbled across a mystery crying out for his special deductive gifts. Gerard was uncomfortably aware that the puzzle, which hinged on an unbreakable alibi, and Dooley's solution (the murderer conveniently had an identical twin brother) owed more to guesswork and cliché than to ratiocination. Yet it was a novel which, as authors so often say, *had* to be written. In his present straitened circumstances, Gerard could only afford a few days away if he could claim tax relief on the expense and the Inland Revenue demanded that he justify his outlay by producing a book. Besides, the homicide rate on the western slopes of the Pennines had already reached Miami standards and Gerard had been desperate for a change. But he gave the girl some flannel about pushing out the boundaries of detective fiction and she nodded sagely as if she understood what he was talking about.

"When are your books going to be on the telly?" demanded the humbug-eater, evidently one of those who believed that anything of merit would sooner or later find its way to the small screen.

Gerard grunted. Years back, an independent production company had taken out an option on the Dooley series. He'd allowed himself to be seduced by the notion for a year or two, mentally casting Anthony Hopkins as the Inspector and worrying about whether he would have a right of veto if the script editor decided to marry Dooley off to a blonde bimbo with a view to boosting the ratings. In the end he had not needed to fear that his artistic vision and integrity might be compromised by the demands of commercial television. The option had expired without being renewed.

Still, one could dream. He gave the woman an enigmatic smile and said, "These things are very delicate, you know. I do have hopes but I'm sure you'll appreciate that I can't say anything at present. I have to respect confidentiality."

At the back of the room, Brian choked back a snort of derision and checked his watch. Gerard began to breathe easier. It looked as though he would be spared the question.

And then the tramp stirred. He had seemed half asleep and he did not bother to raise his hand, perhaps assuming that life on the road entitled him to disregard the conventions. To Gerard's surprise, he spoke in a rich and resonant tone. Evidently a man of education.

"I wonder if you would enlighten us about one thing, Mr Babb?"

Gerard gave him a cautiously encouraging smile.

"You see, I have done a little writing myself over the years . . ."

Ah, Gerard reflected amiably, that would explain the long straggly beard and the unkempt appearance. He was just one more author awaiting an overdue royalty cheque.

". . . and although I fancy I have an elegant enough turn of phrase, I struggle to put together a full-length work of prose. So I wonder, can you tell me this: *where do you find your ideas*?"

Gerard banged his glass down on the table, spilling the water over his notes so that the ink began to run. The manager frowned. Brian gazed at the heavens.

"I. . . . er . . ."

It was no good. He could not form the words of his reply. For this was the question that terrified him, the familiar enquiry to which he could not bear to respond. To admit the truth would be impossible.

Quite simply, Gerard had not had an idea in years. The last

half-dozen Dooleys had recycled the plots and themes of all the early books in the series. In *Dooley Takes A Break* he had even found himself plagiarising large chunks of his own dialogue. Fortunately, the Inspector was so gruff and monosyllabic that no one – certainly not his foul-mouthed editor – had noticed. It had occurred to him that no one cared whether he repeated himself or not. And yet he cared. He, Gerard Babb, still wanted desperately to write novels. There was nothing else he could do. He could not claim to be a successful novelist, still less a success as a human being – and yet the urge to write was as strong within him as ever. The only trouble was that he could not think of a single new thing to write about.

Everyone, he realised, was looking at him. Experimentally, he opened his mouth a couple of times, but an answer would not come. *If only I knew where and how to find a few ideas*, he felt like saying, *I wouldn't need to be stuck up here in front of you lot, trying to give a civil response to your bloody stupid questions*.

Brian was shaking his head. The manager coughed nervously. The student had begun to snigger and the would-be writer still had his pen poised over a virgin page in his notebook. Gerard realised he must say something. Anything.

"I wish I knew," he croaked.

It was more than an admission, it was like a tidal wave breaking down a harbour wall. Awareness of his own desperate inadequacy began to flood through him as never before. He could no longer hide from the truth that he had for so many years suspected yet never had the courage to confront: he was finished as a writer. His fictions were as dead as last autumn's leaves. Brian had put his finger on it after all. Who in their right mind would bother with a story that he, Gerard Babb, had clumsily made up, when it had never actually happened?

And as he stared out, unseeing, beyond the puzzled faces of his audience, he forced himself to face reality. He had told lies for a living for far too long to have a hope of finding another trade. His whole existence had become as pointless as his work. So why go on?

"Why go on?" he said, his voice still hoarse.

He was vaguely aware of the manager blundering to his feet and saying. "Well, yes, perhaps we have slightly over-run our time. As a result, of course, of all the interesting questions. And perhaps we'd just like to show our appreciation to Mr Babb for sparing the time from his busy schedule to be with us this evening."

The old lady with the false teeth clapped quietly, as if she had been so programmed that she could do nothing else, but the rest of the audience appeared to be baffled that the proceedings, though never more than desultory, had finally come to an unsatisfactory end. Gerard heard the student snort and the would-be writer murmur with disapproval. Brian's emotions appeared to be mixed: he seemed annoyed by Gerard's performance, but glad that he now had the chance to escape.

"Mr Babb will be available to sign copies of his latest . . ." began the manager, but he realised he was speaking to rapidly retreating backs. Even the tramp had hauled himself to his feet with a show of disappointment, as if he were accustomed to much better fare.

Brian came over to Gerard and muttered in his ear, "What d'you think you were playing at? After I'd been to such trouble, too. I'll have to report this to Carol-Jane, you know that, don't you?"

Gerard shrugged and turned towards the manager, whose mouth was beginning to set in a petulant line.

"Well, Mr Babb, I won't pretend this has been the most successful event Porlock and Macdonald have ever hosted."

He did not offer his hand and Gerard lumbered towards the door. He was turning his mind towards death. Funny, he had written so much about it and yet he had so seldom contemplated it. How should be proceed? Whisky, aspirin and a polythene bag offered one popular escape route. He did not care if it upset his landlady: the old cow deserved a bit of a fright. Finding the wherewithal to purchase a decent bottle of whisky might prove more of a problem and doing the job with the aid of a few glasses of Sainsbury's finest somehow seemed like too much of an anticlimax.

What would it be like, death? As he stepped into the cold night air, he trembled at the prospect of the unknown. Would there be pain? He realised his pulse was racing and the ironic notion occurred to him that suddenly he felt more alive now that he was facing the end than – oh, for as long as he could remember.

Fifty yards ahead of him, the tramp was ferreting in a litter bin. Who was he? That cultivated voice had suggested a man with a past, someone who had fallen on difficult times. What was his story? A marriage gone wrong, a vengeful wife? A gambling addiction that had caused his downfall? The jealousy of work colleagues who had conspired to make sure that he lost his job?

Funny, Gerard was using his imagination again for the first time in years. And okay, it was rather like taking a huge old machine out of mothballs, cranking it up and hoping for a smooth response. But at least he was doing it.

Gerard walked towards the tramp. Might it help to approach the man, learn a little about him? It was possible the chap might make a good character in a story.

Catching his breath, Gerard realised that he had begun to think as a writer should. The creative urge had caught hold of him again. He was only a few yards behind the tramp now. The man was absorbed in an old newspaper he had fished out of the litter bin and was oblivious of Gerard's approach.

Gerard looked around. Although it was still only early evening the street was deserted apart from the two of them. The bald spot on the crown of the tramp's head glinted under a yellow street light. It fascinated Gerard, drew him on. And yet, somehow, it offended him. Must get rid of it, stop the bloody thing shining in the night. A broken bit of paving stone lay in the gutter. Gerard picked it up and raised it briefly to the heavens before dashing it down on the tramp's head. The man gave a shocked gasp and collapsed to the floor. Gerard lifted his foot and began to kick at the blood-oozing bald patch.

And as he delivered the fatal blow, the germ of a story came to him. A killer, driven to savage and motiveless murder, stalking the streets of dreary English towns. Forget about Inspector Dooley, this would be a non-series suspense novel, searing and bleak. A story about a truly perfect crime.

Gerard could not help exclaiming with joy. He was saved. He knew the secret now and he need never again run short of inspiration.

At last he had discovered where to find his ideas.

DEATH BY A THOUSAND CUTS

REBECCA TOPE

The sound of breaking glass cast an instant spell of paralysed silence on the main – well, *only* – street of the village. "Clumsy!" giggled Maggs, before noticing the trained-gundog reaction from Den at her side.

"That sounded like something big," he said. "Not just a dropped milk bottle. More like plate glass."

"Ignore it," Slocombe advised him. "You're not on duty now."

"We're always on duty," gritted Detective Sergeant Den piously. "Like you."

Den and Maggs both glanced at the undertaker's trouser pocket, where his mobile phone lurked, ready to summon him to the removal of a body, even on a sunny May Saturday in a tourist village on Devon's south coast. The threesome were escaping from the Cup Final, bonded by a loathing for football.

"We should go and see what it was," Den pressed. There were stirrings in the sparsely thronged street. People's heads were turning and cocking, voices were erupting – *What was that?* they asked each other, interrupting their desultory efforts to fly kites or race toy cars in the areas provided. The buzzing of the small motors was a constant background noise. Children

were skittering, refusing to be frightened. Nobody was screaming.

"Nobody's screaming," said Maggs. "Can't be anything
important."

"But where was it?" Den wondered. "This place only has one
street."

Slocombe had taken a few steps towards a snicket, a ginnel –
or twitten as his mother would say. "Down here I think," he
offered. Other people were peering in the same direction. Two
small boys scampered towards them, evidently excited by the
sudden drama. They carried something awkwardly between
them, catching Maggs a glancing blow with a sharp corner.

"Oi!" she shouted after them. "Mind what you're doing."

"No consideration, these days," shrilled an elderly woman,
shifting neatly out of their way.

Halfway down the narrow alleyway there was a small open
square, where a building must once have stood. A tourist
teashop fronting onto the village street had opened up a back
entrance, and set chairs and tables in the square for open-air
tea-taking. Following Den, the other two were slow to observe
the broken glass strewn amongst the furniture nearest the shop.
A woman stood wringing her hands close by, another emerged
breathlessly from the back door of the teashop's neighbour,
holding a broom.

"Quick thinker," murmured Maggs.

"Oh, my God!" the first woman wailed. "What a mess! I was
upstairs with the telly on. I thought the crash was part of the
film I was watching, at first."

"What happened?" Den asked her, neglecting to flash his
identity card at her. He stood tall and responsible, even in
sleeveless shirt and shorts.

"The window just blew out," she told him shakily. "With no
warning."

"Blew out?" he repeated. "How could it do that?" He
scanned the gaping hole in what remained of the window. It
was ragged and cracked; surviving slabs of thick glass threatened to fall into the square. "Did you see it happen?"

She shook her head. "I was upstairs," she repeated.

"And I was next door," interrupted her well-prepared friend.

"So you can't be sure what did it," he reproved them. "Can you?"

Slocombe approached the window cautiously. "What *could* have done it?" he asked with a puzzled frown. He peered at the ground. "Did somebody throw something?"

"More like an explosion?" Maggs suggested excitedly. "A bomb, maybe?" She looked from Slocombe to Den and back again. "Don't you think?"

Two or three onlookers had followed the threesome down the alley, and were listening in. A man guffawed at Maggs's words.

"Did *anyone* see – or hear – anything?" Den pleaded, looking at each in turn.

Blank looks. It was half past eleven on a sunny Saturday morning in a popular and picturesque village. Surely someone had been in the teashop?

"Wasn't there anybody in the shop?"

"We were closed," the TV-watcher explained. "We only open at tea-time. We're a teashop, you see."

"Right," said Den slowly, glancing at his comrades. "Makes sense, I suppose."

"We have to compromise," the woman went on. "You might have noticed Amanda's coffee shop, just a little way down the street on the other side? The one with the awning? She opens in the mornings."

Everyone did their best to peer through the interior of the shop and out into the street beyond, where a striped awning was just visible through the open door.

"Who does lunches?" Maggs put in eagerly.

"The Goose and Goslings. Down by the river," came the prompt reply.

Slocombe hummed thoughtfully until Maggs jabbed an elbow into him. An awkwardness was developing, with Den reluctant to leave the scene of an apparent misdemeanor. Maggs was looking at him narrowly, head cocked, obviously wanting to know whether he intended to reveal his official status. With a slight shake of the head, he gave his response. "You need to get someone to remove all the glass," he told the two women. "It could fall on someone and hurt them. It should all be boarded up. People need to be kept away until then." He turned to the shuffling onlookers, and flapped his arms at them. "That's it, people. Nothing to see. Go and enjoy yourselves."

The same man guffawed again.

Missing her cue by a substantial margin, a strangled cry emerged from within the teashop. "That's Cynthia," said the woman without the broom. "I thought she was out."

The cry was repeated, more urgently this time, suggestive of a distressed shock that could only get worse. Den leapt forwards as if this was what he'd been waiting for all along. Maggs and her colleague followed closely. At the door, Den turned again to the dismissed gathering. "Please do go away," he said, and shut the door firmly behind his friends and the two original women. Maggs helpfully darted through the shop and closed the front door.

"Adrian!" came a traumatized voice. "What's happened to you?"

Den's professional expertise was permitted full rein. He crouched over a prostrate figure in a shadowy corner. To Maggs, peering under Den's arm, it looked for all the world like a very big matchstick – one end was covered in red stuff, and the rest tapered away insignificantly. Pools of the red stuff had collected on the floor, which Den did his best to avoid. Gradually all those present began to notice spatters, splashes, of blood on almost every surface in the tea-room; walls close to the thing on the floor, in particular.

"How does she know it's Adrian?" Maggs muttered. "How does she know it's a person at all?"

"Process of elimination, I should think," said Slocombe, pushing his sleeves up in an instinctive preparation for action. "It's not a cow, or a collection of old rags. It bleeds, therefore it is – or was – a living creature. Two arms and two legs, look." They both jostled for a better view. A disobedient crowd of sightseers was still hovering outside, the gaping hole that had been the rear window giving them a reasonable glimpse of the proceedings.

Den knew when he was required to reveal himself. He put his hand out to Slocombe. "Phone," he commanded. Then he swept the room with his glance. "Detective Sergeant Cooper," he introduced himself, with a little duck of the chin. "I'm afraid we have a fatality here. Would you all please move away, and be sure you don't touch anything."

"I'll do it, shall I?" said Maggs, pushing out her chest, and snatching the phone.

"No," Den said. "You don't know the right number."

"Not 999?"

"That takes too long. I'll get directly to the control room." He fiddled with the tiny buttons in the gloomy corner, and waited seventy-five seconds for his call to be answered. When he tersely explained the situation, he was told he should have called 999. By short-circuiting the process, he'd caused all sorts of difficulties.

"Pity we haven't got the van," Slocombe said to Maggs. "We could have done the removal."

She commiserated with a *tsk* and quick shake of her head. "Can't win 'em all," she observed. "And it's hardly on our patch. It'll be a Plymouth hospital from here, won't it?"

The undertaker shrugged. "Maybe. But South Devon's geography's too much for me. More likely Exeter, shouldn't wonder."

Den was struggling to remember the protocol for encountering a sudden death when in some other's force's area. Certain basic rules pertained, however, and these he strove to enforce. Slocombe and Maggs, in the meantime, were unwilling to leave the entire arena to their friend.

"Are you *sure* he's dead?" Drew asked in an undertone. "That looks like fresh blood to me. Shouldn't you be trying some first aid?"

Den rubbed his fingertips together, dislodging flakes and splashes of drying blood. "He's dead," he said grimly. "I felt his neck for a pulse."

"His neck seems to have taken the brunt of it," Slocombe remarked. "Nasty."

"Very badly gashed," Den agreed. "But it's the face that really got in the way. Most people have a nose, for starters." Cynthia and the other two women all heard him, and squealed in unison. Den and Slocombe both had the grace to look uncomfortable.

"It's horrendous," Maggs summed up, with a sidelong glance at the victim. "His face has been practically *shredded*."

"Must have been the flying glass," Slocombe suggested.

Den shook his head in slow motion, eyeing them both with a superior air. "The glass all flew *outwards*," he reminded them. "There's nothing on this side of the window." His glance fell on Maggs. "Better take her outside," he advised his friend. "She's gone a funny colour."

Maggs rallied. "If I wasn't so black, you'd say I was pale," she quipped.

"I thought you were immune to this sort of thing?" Slocombe accused her.

"They smell different when they're fresh," she blustered. "And you must admit this isn't very nice."

"It's quite mysterious," Slocombe said thoughtfully, making no move to take her outside. "What on earth could have happened?"

The police detective gave the entire premises a careful visual inspection. The front door had been open, he recalled, onto the village street. Blinds were pulled down over the large front window, obscuring most of the bright sunlight. The siren of a remarkably prompt police car could be heard a mile away.

Two uniformed female constables materialized three minutes later, treating Den with reluctant respect. "Police doctor's on his way," one said briskly. "Now, what have we got here?"

"No obvious signs of an attack," Den began clumsily.

"You mean – apart from a bloke whose face has been sliced off," argued the brisk WPC. She seemed to be nearly forty, and caught by surprise at the day's temperature. Her hair was damp on her forehead.

"I mean – no weapon, no sounds of a fight, nobody seen acting suspiciously," Den elaborated.

"It could have been an accident," Maggs asserted stoutly. "That's what he was trying to say. Some sort of explosion. Gas, I should think."

"We didn't *hear* an explosion," Slocombe reminded her.

The Cynthia woman was weeping with ever-increasing volume. Whoever Adrian was, it appeared that she cared for him considerably more than anyone else present did. "I think she can identify him," Den said helpfully.

"It's *Adrian*," she screamed. "He's my boyfriend. Oh, Jesus – look at him. They said they'd get him – but he only popped out for a minute." She wailed afresh. "How on earth could anyone do this to him? He was only out of my sight for a moment." She glared at Den. "Why don't you *do* something?"

"Boyfriend," Maggs muttered. "Hmmm."

"Shut up," Slocombe told her. "I thought you were going outside."

"That was ages ago. I'm fine now," she boasted.

Den was trying to pacify Cynthia, who was now on the brink of hysterics.

A brief hiatus ensued, while a ring of people stood looking down at the floor, backing away as the thickening blood trickled very slowly towards them over the tiled floor.

"How long before the photographer and forensics get here?" Den asked. "We can't touch anything."

"Quite a while," the stout constable admitted. "We were passing and heard the call. Everyone else'll be coming from Exeter. Nearly an hour, with all the traffic."

"Names and addresses?" Den suggested. "Statements? Outside?"

"It'll need an incident room won't it?" Maggs asked. "If it's a murder, there has to be an incident room."

"All right, everybody," responded the constable. "Can we have you all outside, please?"

Maggs left slowly, squinting back at the broken window. The sun was still blazing down on the street. The volume of day trippers had apparently increased. The kite-flyers had given up, but the buzzing remote-controlled motors seemed to be louder than before.

Slocombe hovered on the edge of the group. "You always manage to look like a butler," Maggs told him. "Even in casual gear. It's the way you stand there, waiting for someone to ask you something."

"It's the undertaker training," he nodded, unperturbed.

"It's spooky," she accused. "You should try to loosen up."

"I'm perfectly loose," he assured her. "It's your problem, not mine."

She pursed her lips. "So what do you think happened to poor old Adrian?"

"I've no idea," he admitted. "None of it makes any sense."

"Are we sure he was cut by flying glass? Maybe somebody dragged him in from outside, after the window landed on him? Before we got there? That's the simple answer."

"So simple it's stupid," he waved the idea away. "There'd be a lot of smeared blood, outside and in – and a trail through the doorway."

"The front door was open," she remembered. "Hey, Den – don't forget the front door was open."

Den inclined his head in acknowledgment. "It was," he told the two WPCs. "Wide open onto the street. But the teashop was closed. Nobody was inside."

"Why was the door open if the place was closed?" asked the quieter, thinner constable. "Wouldn't people have gone in?"

Maggs looked over the officer's shoulder at the door. "There's a CLOSED sign on the window," she noticed. "They'd probably have seen that."

Everybody considered this, and most shook their heads. "If it was open, people would go in," Slocombe stated. "That's human nature."

"So Adrian had probably just come in," Maggs suggested. "Leaving it open behind him. Maybe someone was chasing him?"

Den cleared his throat. "I need everyone's names and addresses. And where you were during the past hour. And whether you knew the deceased."

"Steady on!" Maggs hissed at him. "Remember it's not your patch."

Much earlier than expected, the police doctor showed up. It was a middle-aged woman, who might easily have been first cousin to the dominant WPC.

"You were quick!" said Maggs admiringly.

The doctor cocked her head sideways. "And who might you be?" she enquired coldly.

Maggs stepped backwards, chin held high, and refused to answer. "A friend of mine," Den supplied through gritted teeth. "Not that it's any business of yours. Your job is to examine the body."

The doctor sniffed. "I don't believe I know who *you* are, either," she said. "I like to know who I'm dealing with."

"Your business is with the poor bastard in there –" Den flapped an arm. "And good luck to you."

"Let's leave them to it," Slocombe suggested restlessly. "We can answer questions later, if they want us to. I'm nearly ready for some lunch."

"Eeergghhh," said Maggs. "Doesn't *anything* put you off your food?"

"Hardly anything," he admitted.

"Yeah, go on," Den encouraged them. "I'll catch you up in a bit. What did that woman say the lunch place was called?"

"Something to do with birds and rivers," Maggs managed. "We'll find it. The trick'll be to follow everybody else."

They set off, both reluctant and relieved to abandon the grisly scene. "What on earth could have done it?" Slocombe repeated. "Something sharp, slashing – like a whole cluster of knives. All those small deep cuts, gouged into him . . ."

"You should have been in Forensics," Maggs told him. "Not nearly enough mysteries for you in undertaking."

"Oh, I don't do too badly," he smirked.

"Watch out!" she cried suddenly. Coming towards them at head level was a buzzing model airplane, controlled by some invisible individual. Slocombe sidestepped swiftly, and the toy flew on oblivious, arcing gracefully, and rising to the tops of the trees across the park.

Maggs stood stock still, as if turned to stone. Then she slowly scanned the open field before them. "It isn't all cars and kites," she said slowly. "Look."

Three people were immediately visible clutching small boxes and gazing raptly into the sky. One gave them a cheerful unapologetic wave – evidently the owner of the plane that had just missed them.

"Don't suppose it was him, then," said Maggs thoughtfully.

"Don't suppose it was any of them," Slocombe responded. "But it shouldn't be too difficult to track down who it was. Not now we know how it was done." He made a graphic swooping gesture. "In through the front door, and out through the back window – without stopping to open it. Must have had some power behind it. You'd think it would have stalled."

"It did," Maggs realized, remembering the scampering small boys and the sharp toy they'd been carrying, at the entrance to the alley.

THE TROUBLE
AND STRIFE

CATHERINE AIRD

Detective Inspector Sloan sighed deeply and started to explain all over again to the woman sitting in front of him that people may go missing of their own accord at any time if they so wished. What they called it these days was "dropping out" but he didn't suppose that the aggressive woman before him would want him to use the term about her daughter.

"Not my Susan," declared Mrs Briggs firmly, "whatever you're going to try to tell me about it being a free country."

"Anyone," stated the policeman, who hadn't been going to say anything about it being a free country. He also forbore to explain that Susan Cavendish wasn't "her" Susan any more but had apparently been a married woman in her own right for nearly three years now. She should have been her own woman long ago.

"She's not been in touch for a full month," said Mrs Briggs, ignoring this, "and that's not right, is it?"

"She doesn't have to be in touch if she doesn't want to be," repeated Sloan patiently. "She is, after all, of full age."

"And I may say, officer, she is also an Englishwoman born in wedlock and had her feet on dry land when I last saw her," Mrs Briggs completed the adage tartly, "but she's still missing."

"Which she has every right to be if she so wishes," pointed out the detective inspector. With a mother like Mrs Briggs he might very well have opted to go missing himself.

"And that's never happened before," insisted Susan's mother, ignoring this last remark of his, too. "They used to come in to see me every weekend without fail. Susan did my shopping while that no-good husband of hers did any odd-jobs about the house I needed doing."

"I see." Sloan had known a good few sons-in-law who never did a hand's turn in their wife's mother's house but this didn't seem the moment to say so.

"And I'm just not satisfied that she's all right," said Mrs Briggs belligerently. "So I'm reporting her missing here and now, whatever you say."

"Was your daughter all right when you last saw her?" parried Sloan.

"It depends what you mean by all right," responded Mrs Briggs. "Physically she was as fit as the butcher's dog . . ."

"That's something," put in Detective Constable Crosby from the sidelines.

Mrs Briggs favoured him with a baleful stare and turned back to Sloan. "But she wasn't happy in herself even though she said the divorce was working its way through – and not before time, too, if you ask me . . ."

"Divorce?" said Sloan, the policeman in him automatically pricking up his ears.

"She'd decided to leave him at last," said Mrs Briggs. "Nasty piece of work, I always said, that Christopher Cavendish, for all that he's done well at his job."

"And what was that?" enquired Sloan, pulling a piece of paper towards him.

"He was one of those computer people," she said, sniffing. "You know – the sort who sit at home all day in front of a screen and call it working. How does anyone know whether you're working or not, that's what I want to know?"

"I dare say the usual yardsticks apply," murmured Sloan.

"Come again?"

"The making of money," said Sloan smoothly.

"He did that," she admitted grudgingly. "They had a lovely

old house, though a bit on the small side if they'd wanted to start a family . . ."

"Ah, I was going to ask about—"

"Which mercifully, the way things have turned out, they hadn't done." She sniffed. "Susan wanted a baby – don't ask me why. Nothing but trouble, children. I was always telling her that."

Detective Inspector Sloan made a note.

"Of course, half of the house will be my Susan's when they settle up – half of everything, come to that – so she won't come out of it too badly." She glared at Sloan. "If she's all right, that is."

"Tell me, have you approached the husband –" Sloan paused and looked down at his notes "– yes, he is the husband still, isn't he, if the divorce hasn't come through yet? – about where she might be? He at least might have some idea, even if they have parted, as you say they have."

"That's the trouble," Mrs Briggs said instantly. "I don't know where he is either."

"So the husband is missing, too, is he?" asked Sloan with interest.

"Well, I never," remarked Detective Constable Crosby.

Mrs Briggs bridled. "I wouldn't know about him being missing but the house has been sold – I do know that – and he's gone too, but where I don't know. Good riddance for Susan, if you ask me." She gave a self-satisfied smirk. "I always said she should never have married him in the first place. If I told her that once, I told her so a dozen times."

"Not good enough?" put in Detective Constable Crosby helpfully. He was still a bachelor himself.

"Not by a long chalk," said Mrs Briggs, taking a deep breath preparatory to enlarging on this at length.

Detective Inspector Sloan forestalled her. "And have you made enquiries at her place of work?"

"In a manner of speaking," conceded Mrs Briggs. "Not that I got very far."

"How come?" asked Detective Constable Crosby, in whom his superiors had so far failed to instil any proper sense of formality when dealing with members of the public.

"Susan worked for a temping agency in Berebury and they say that someone just rang in one day to say she wouldn't be available for work any more."

"Someone?" pounced Sloan.

"They couldn't swear it was her," said Mrs Briggs. "In fact, they couldn't even be sure that it was a woman who had rung." She suddenly became a little more human and admitted, "That's when I began to get really worried."

"I see, madam." He did, too. "You say their marital home has been sold . . ."

"The estate agent's sale board has come down and Wetherspoons cleared the furniture at the end of last week." She pursed her lips. "Sid Wetherspoon wouldn't tell me where they were taking it. Commercially sensitive information, he called it."

Detective Inspector Sloan made a note. He'd have a word with the estate agents and the removal people himself.

"And their solicitors won't tell me either," she went on in aggrieved tones. "Client confidentiality was what they said."

"Quite so," murmured Sloan.

"There was something else . . ."

"What was that, madam?"

"All Susan's stuff was in that van that went along with Christopher."

"Not just his?" asked Constable Crosby, patently puzzled.

"No, and I do know that because I watched it go." She snorted gently. "It was just as well she wasn't pregnant after all . . ."

"After all . . . ?" prompted Sloan, leaving aside for the time being the more germane matter of all the furniture going from the house together.

"She'd wanted a baby at first but one didn't come along," said Mrs Briggs. "And, before you ask, the doctor wouldn't tell me anything either. Said he'd be struck off the Register or something like that. Excuses," she said richly, "all of them."

"That'd be because of that chap Hippocrates," put in Crosby. "He's the one the doctors swear by." He frowned. "Funny that, since he wasn't a Christian."

"At least," said Mrs Briggs, ignoring this, "there being no

baby on the way will have made the divorce simpler, which is something to be thankful for."

"Quite so," said Detective Inspector Sloan, rising to his feet. "Well, thank you, Mrs Briggs. We'll be looking into the matter for you . . ."

"Then there's the question of her car . . ." said the woman, not making a move. "That's worrying, too."

Detective Constable Crosby's face brightened. "Do you know the number?"

"Course I do," she came back at him on the instant. "And the make."

"What's so worrying about her car?" asked Detective Inspector Sloan quickly.

"She sold it before she disappeared. At least," she said meaningfully, "someone did. Took it into that big dealers down by the river and sold it . . ."

"For cash or a trade-in?" asked Crosby.

"Cash," said Mrs Briggs promptly.

"How do you know that?" said Sloan.

"I saw it in their showroom." She twisted her lips. "Besides, car dealers don't have funny ideas about what's commercially sensitive information."

"Except the real second-hand value," muttered Crosby. "They'll never tell you that about any car you're trading in."

"That I wouldn't know, never having been a driver myself," she said, reminded of another grievance. "At least their old house was on an easy bus route for me. It suited me nicely being where it was – I could get there whenever I wanted."

"And what car does your son-in-law drive, madam?" enquired Sloan as casually as he could. These days owners of cars and their addresses could be traced by police authorities with the speed of light.

"Christopher?" she said scornfully. "Oh, he didn't have a car. Only Susan did. Said he didn't need one, working from home like he did." She screwed up her face. "And anyway he'd got some potty idea about not adding to the world's pollution problems. What he thinks he could do about global warming beats me."

"I think," said Detective Inspector Sloan a trifle portentously, "you'd better leave things as they are at present, madam. We'll be in touch in . . . er . . . in due course."

"I'm sure I hope so," said Mrs Briggs, "but if you ask me, he's made away with her and made off with all the money."

"Have you any particular basis for making these allegations, madam?" asked Sloan wearily. He was beginning to feel quite sorry for both her daughter and her son-in-law.

"I thought you'd never ask," she said acidly.

"Well?"

Mrs Briggs dived into her handbag, retrieved a glossy sheet of paper and waved it before his eyes. "This."

"The estate agent's sale particulars of their house?" said Sloan.

"That's right," she said.

"What about it?"

"Read it," she commanded. "Especially the bit about the garage."

" 'Detached garage, brick with slate roof,' " he quoted, " 'well-equipped with work-bench, tool cupboard and two electrical points.' " He lifted his gaze. "Sounds very nice. What's wrong with it?"

"There's something missing from the description," she said stubbornly.

"What?" asked Sloan.

"Inspection pit," she said. "There always used to be one there and it isn't mentioned in this."

"And you think—" began Crosby incautiously.

"Yes," she said. "I do."

Detective Inspector Sloan got rid of Mrs Briggs by falling back on an age-old police formula comprised of thanking her for coming in and promising to keep in touch with her to let her know how their enquiries were progressing.

He was nothing like as circumspect when talking to his Superintendent. "I don't like it, sir. I've had a look at it and the inspection pit in the garage at the Cavendishes' old home has obviously been filled in very recently . . ."

"Go on," said Superintendent Leeyes gruffly.

"The estate agents say that they paid the cheque from the sale of the house direct to the bank as agreed. It was made out to both Christopher and Susan Cavendish and their instructions were that it was to go into the couple's joint account there."

"Which said joint account could still be functioning," said the superintendent heavily, "if either had power to draw on it."

"Exactly, sir." He cleared his throat. "In fact, since then all the withdrawals have been made by Christopher Cavendish."

"I don't like it," said Leeyes.

"I also had a word with Sid Wetherspoon, the removals man," continued Sloan. "He took all the furniture over to a house right out in the country behind Almstone but Christopher Cavendish had asked him particularly not to disclose where it was to anyone . . . he stressed that bit very heavily to Sid. Said there was woman trouble and he was sure Sid – man to man – would understand."

"Well, then . . ." said Leeyes.

"Very nice place, actually, sir, that house, but empty except for the furniture that Sid had delivered there."

"The neighbours?" Superintendent Leeyes always insisted that inquisitive neighbours were worth their weight in gold to an overworked police force.

"The woman next door had seen a man and a young woman arrive there a week or so ago. She'd offered them the proverbial cup of tea over the garden fence but they said they had a plane to catch and wouldn't be back until they'd had a long holiday."

"That's a good one," snorted Leeyes.

"The neighbour said the pair were collected by hire car and haven't been seen since."

The Superintendent tapped his desk with his pencil. "I don't like it at all, Sloan. I'm afraid that in the first place you're going to have to open up that inspection pit."

"That's what I thought, too, sir."

"Then get a warrant . . ."

It was half an hour before the spades of the sweating diggers who were working in the garage struck anything.

"It's metal, from the sound of it," called out Detective Constable Crosby.

"Keep going," commanded Sloan.

"Looks like a small strong-box," said Crosby, while his fellow constable scraped away the mixture of sand and aggregate that was covering a square metal edge.

"A little water and cement in there," observed Sloan, "and that lot would have set into concrete overnight."

"Perhaps it was something he meant to do," said Crosby, straightening up. "And didn't get round to." The constable himself was a great procrastinator.

"Criminals usually make mistakes," said Sloan. "Can you get a grip on it?"

In the event the metal box came out quite easily.

"It's not even locked," said Crosby, surprised and somehow disappointed.

Detective Inspector Sloan lifted the lid. The box contained nothing but a plastic bag. Inside it was a conventional "Change of Address" card of the variety bought at any stationers' shop. The details had been completed with a waterproof pen and spelled out the address of a house.

"But that's where Sid Wetherspoon delivered the furniture," said Crosby.

"It is indeed," agreed Sloan. "Read on, Crosby."

The detective constable peered over Sloan's shoulder and read out aloud " 'To Whom it Might Concern' . . . I don't get it, sir. Who does it concern?"

"Us," said Sloan pithily. "Keep going."

"It says 'Strictly Confidential'," said Crosby.

Detective Inspector Sloan tapped the card. "Don't forget this last message."

At the bottom of the card was written "Important. We don't want Mum to know where we are until after the baby's arrived."

"Christopher Cavendish was right when he told Sid Wetherspoon that he'd got woman trouble, sir," explained Sloan to Superintendent Leeyes later. "He had. We just thought it was the wrong woman, that's all."

BROTHERLY LOVE
An Angel Tale

MIKE RIPLEY

"Who's an ageing hippy?"

"You are. I thought they'd died out in the last century."

"Say that again," I snarled, "and I'll defenestrate you, if that's the correct term for someone who carries their teeth in their top pocket."

"Okay, okay, calm down. Watch the blood pressure, Angel."

"Then you watch your lip. Just remember, I don't have to be doing this."

"I know. And we appreciate it."

At last the royal "we" had appeared. I'd wondered how long it would be.

Technically, he was right about the last century. It was the first year of the new millennium, that no-man's-land between 1999 (year of religious fanatics and mega-huge newspaper supplements on who had done what and who was going to do what) and – at last – Stanley Kubrick's *2001*. The newspapers were getting ready for that one, too, offering prizes to anyone who could name another film with Keir Dullea.

People had gone ape-shit over the New Year, as you might expect, and I can't say I had a quiet time myself.

The "in" Christmas gift had been a checkbook, even for people who hadn't written a check for ages, because the date lines had all been reprinted 20—. The Jazz Warriors were top of the charts all over Europe, and the newest House release had an electronic drumbeat of 190 beats per minute. Ail this (except the checkbooks) made my New Year's resolution an early retirement from the music scene. The old B-flat trumpet was upended for the last time on New Year's Eve. That was it, no more jazz for me, I said. "No heart in it anymore?" asked the few friends who noticed. No, too bloody difficult; though I never said it.

I was even sticking to my job (well, four nights a week) as meeter and greeter at the Ben Fuji's Whisky and Sushi Bar in Threadneedle Street. I did it originally just for a weekend as a favor to Keiko, the daughter of the owner, who was called neither Ben nor Fuji, who had got me out of a tight spot in a night club in Chancery Lane (now there was a sign of the times!) one evening by proving to three argumentative out-of-towners that she really did have a black belt in karate.

To be honest, I quite liked the job. I knew enough about sushi without actually eating any, to blag my way through, and with a copy of Sir Michael Jackson's *Guide to Whisky* (29th edition) under my desk in the entrance hall at Ben Fuji's, I could always come up with a nugget about the 350+ whiskies the place stocked.

And business was booming, especially now we were starting the Golf World Cup, hosted in England for the first time. Since the anti-Japanese measures passed by the U.S. Senate in the mid-nineties and the subsequent boycott of anything involving the Japanese, the Americans were not taking part. Consequently, England were joint favorites with the Japanese, although we had Scotland in our qualifying group, which meant the odds were still generous. The World Cup, said to draw the largest television audience in the world, meant a large screen in the bar, showing golf (edited highlights in a window to the top right of the screen showing live action) twelve hours a day with video back-up facility if an act of God stopped play. The sponsors had ensured nothing else would.

It also meant lots of package-tour golfers, many of them

Japanese, flocking into and through London, and Ben Fuji's was well and truly on their "must visit" lists. Knowing that the big prize money was put up by the Japanese these days, we also had a regular clientele of British and European golfers, many of them including a visit as part of their preparation for entering the Japanese Open.

Keiko would teach them Japanese food and manners, and I would tell them about Japanese drinking habits, then take their photographs on my Nikon Instanto and get their autographs. (To sell later if they made it.)

It was mostly a load of bull, as Ben Fuji's was hardly a traditional Japanese restaurant. The basement had originally been a "Japanese Room" with paper walls and floor mats. That had given way to a Nintendo virtual-reality golf driving range, which was far more profitable. In any case, European labor laws now prevented waitresses from serving men on their knees.

Basically, my job was vetting – and being nice to – the non-Japanese clientele. No rough stuff was required. Keiko and a couple of the waiters were more than capable of handling that, and one of the sushi chefs could pin a fly to the wall at thirty feet if the mood took him. The official job description was a sort of junior maitre d'. The subtext was more subtle. After their experience in America, every Japanese business preferred a domestic front man, however limited his powers.

So there I was, the acceptable face of sushi in Threadneedle Street.

Not that what happened had anything to do with Ben Fuji's being a sushi and Scotch bar. It was just that I was working there the night Sam "Sinister" Dexter decided to call in and get drunk.

I had actually met Sam Dexter once before, though he wouldn't remember.

It had been at a press party to mark the engagement of rock 'n' roll legend Rory D. to that season's hot starlet from the Royal Shakespeare Company (sponsored, that year, by Brahma beer from Brazil – "where the nuts come from"). Rory D., or Rory Dee to be more accurate but less commercial, had played in a heavy metal band I knew called Astral Reich a few years before, and so I claimed lifelong friendship in order to get at the free booze and canapés. To be honest, I was going through a bad patch at the time, and I would have adopted Rory if it had got me into a free lunch.

I was standing at one of the buffet bars, balancing two plates and two glasses (all mine, though it looked like I was waiting for someone) and talking to a couple of Rory's roadies when he swayed across the room and aimed at a waitress clutching a tray of drinks.

I recognized him from the picture above his byline in the newspapers and also the two or three times I'd caught him on a late-night TV show. With twenty-six channels now, *anyone* can get on, but Dexter – "Sinister" to the media world – was usually good for some choice titbits of scandal. Ironically, he could get away with hints and innuendos on TV, which he would never dare print, even as "alleged" rumors, in his newspaper columns since the latest tightening up of the Privacy Charter Act (1993).

"C'mon, darling," he boomed as he reached the waitress. "Stop resting your tits on that tray and bung me some booze. I'm Sam Dexter and famous with it, and I don't intend paying for my drink."

"Why change the habits of a lunchtime," I muttered and the roadies sniggered in agreement.

Dexter made no sign that he'd heard me, and our paths didn't cross for the rest of the party. But three days later he used the line in one of his columns as if he'd said it about Rory D.

Isn't it amazing how long you can hold a grudge?

When Dexter came into Ben Fuji's that night, he didn't notice me. He staggered up to my desk and breathed secondhand alcohol at me and spoke to me, but he didn't *notice* me. I was not there to be noticed. I was there to serve.

"Table for one, my son. At the sushi bar'll do if you've nothing else, but don't cram me in like a fuckin' sardine. Give me two seats and some elbow room, the most disgusting thing on your menu, four portions – four, mind you – of that horse-radish sauce shit you serve and let me work my way through the whisky list. Is that clear? Like me to run any of it by you again?"

He rocked back a little too confidently on his heels and

produced a packet of cigarettes and a disposable lighter. The cigarettes were American and a brand I hadn't seen since they banned advertising cigarettes altogether.

He lit up and ignored me, pretending to examine some of the prints on the wall. I wondered whether he was expecting me to ask "Smoking or nonsmoking?," but I assumed he knew that no Japanese restaurant was nonsmoking. As just about everywhere else in London was, it was actually good for business.

"Table for one, sir, right this way," I said, turning my back on him and leading him into the restaurant.

I held a menu to my chest, and as I caught Keiko's eye, I upended it, showing her three fingers of my right hand. That was our agreed warning sign for a "potentially difficult customer."

As I was doing it, Dexter breathed in my ear: "Do the *geishas* come in the service charge, or do I have to negotiate privately?"

I added the fourth finger to the hand code: *We've got a right bastard here.*

Keiko, all neat in a black two-piece suit, skirt one inch below the knee as was proper and, as it happens, fashionable, made her own code sign to me (two specks of imaginary dust flicked off her sleeve) which meant she wanted me in the kitchen, pronto.

Actually, she wanted to talk to me in the kitchen, and no matter how many times I'd deliberately misunderstood her that way, she never laughed. This, after all, was business.

"Okay, Tenshi, who's your friend?" she opened as soon as the curtain hissed behind us. She called me "Angel" in Japanese because it is my name.

"No friend of mine, though beings lower down the food chain might claim an affinity with him," I said, keeping a watchful eye on Mr. Iishi, the sushi chef, who was sharpening his eighth knife of the evening.

"Speak English," snapped Keiko, "that's what we pay you for."

"He's a shit, Grade A."

"Then why didn't you bump him?"

"He's also a journalist, a notorious one and *your* standing orders say I have to be nice to journalists. It's part of your public relations policy. You know, Rule One: Keep smiling, but don't turn your back."

Keiko looked at me over the top of her glasses and shook her head slowly. I don't know why she blamed me for her headaches, though I've noticed other people do, too.

"Keep an eye on him, eh, Tenshi. Let me know if the boys have to deal with him." She straightened her skirt to go back into the restaurant, then remembered the monitor.

Ben Fuji's had video cameras hidden in four strategic points, with two monitors, one in the kitchen and one in the manager's office, which for all intents and purposes, was Keiko's, where there was a VCR. You'd never guess where the equipment was made.

The kitchen monitor showed Dexter sitting at his table, two glasses of whisky and one of iced water in front of him. He was scanning the other diners and leering at the waitresses, all dressed in kimonos and clogs, making them easy, slow-moving targets. Dexter wasn't quite ready to start groping yet, though. He kept looking at the menu and narrowing his eyes. He'd obviously had a long day, and I didn't think he'd spent it at the opticians.

He also did something else. Every few seconds his left hand would swoop near, sometimes onto, the brown envelope jutting out of his jacket pocket. It was the action of a man who thinks he left his wallet in another coat and needs reassuring.

There wasn't time to watch him further. Above the monitor a green light flashed on which meant someone had trodden on the sensors under the doormat outside the entrance. More customers, so I had to get back to my desk. (I'm sure they only have the sensor there to check up on me.)

"Try and get the boys to serve him," I told Keiko, "and get the chef to hurry it up. Tell the girls to keep clear and not to be cheeky. And don't refuse him any alcohol."

"If you say so, but I hope you know what you're doing," she said primly.

I thought I did, up to that point.

Three of them were lurking in the entrance as I made it back behind my desk, and the first thing that struck me was how young they were. One was early twenties, but the other two must have been teenagers, especially the one hanging behind at the back with his jacket collar turned up.

The one who looked old enough to vote (though few people did that these days) approached me, his right hand in his pocket, his left tweaking his nose. Interesting body language. He was a policeman – and wouldn't you know it, they *are* getting younger.

"Do you have a bar?" he asked in a London accent, but a posh one.

"Certainly, sir, but it's for diners only. Will that be a table for three?" I could behave myself when it was called for.

"Er . . . the bar is in the restaurant?" he fumbled.

"Yes, quite correct."

"There isn't a separate bar?"

"No, only in the restaurant. We have a restaurant licence. People eat here. Occasionally."

He stopped tweaking his nose at that and wanted to say something, but held himself back. One of the younger lads behind him whispered something I couldn't catch.

"Do you mind if I just have a quick look around the restaurant before we decide . . ."

I'd had enough of this.

"Is there a problem, officer?"

That stopped him for a second, then basic instinct took over. "How did you . . .?"

"The Doc Martens," I said smugly. "Nobody else wears them these days."

He looked down at his shoes, then mentally kicked himself for doing so. They always do, though; it never fails. I could have added that the Marks & Spencer's suit one size too big to cover the gun in the belt holster was also a dead giveaway, but you can go too far.

He recovered well. He held up a finger and said, "'Ang on a minute," then turned to his two young companions, and they went into a huddle.

Then he came back to me, and he had a Warrant Card in his hand.

"Is there anywhere we could have a word?"

"Downstairs." I pointed to the stairs knowing that the virtual-reality driving range was unoccupied. "I'll get cover and join you in one minute."

He looked relieved and said, "Thanks" almost as if he meant it.

I stuck my head into the restaurant and made eye contact with Keiko, then jerked my head toward the entrance. She acted like she hadn't seen me, but I knew she had.

Without making it obvious, I clocked Dexter, who now had four whisky glasses in front of him and was perusing the whisky list for more.

When Keiko joined me, I explained that we had some more out-of-the-ordinary customers, one of whom was a senior policeman, and I would happily put myself on the line dealing with them to avoid any confrontation with the management. That usually worked, and it did again. Keiko said she would get Hiroshi, who had good English (in fact, better than mine when he wanted to), to man the desk, and I could sort out the police downstairs, which she was sure would take all my charm, diplomacy, and skill *and no more than ten minutes*.

"You'd better call me Tom," said the policeman.

"Oh yeah? And they're Dick and Harry?"

I nodded toward the two lads who were examining the virtual-reality gear like it was Christmas.

The young copper was staring at me.

"That's Gordon and Henry," he said, as if reading it off a card. "I'm looking after them."

I couldn't keep a straight face.

"Come off it, Tom. I've read *Thomas the Tank Engine*."

Then I stopped. I suddenly realized he hadn't.

"You know, Gordon the stuck-up Blue Engine and Henry the wimpy Green Engine with the sad expression . . . Thomas – Tom – Gordon and . . ."

He blushed then, and turned a killer look on the two teenagers he was "looking after."

"They thought up the names, didn't they?" I asked softly.

"Yes, but that's not important. Look, I need – we need – to know about the movements of somebody upstairs in the restaurant. We need to keep an eye on him without being seen. Can you help?"

"Is this official?"

"Semi-official," he said carefully.

"Then glad to help, officer. Detective Sergeant, wasn't it? Sorry, but I didn't get a chance to examine your Warrant Card very closely."

"It's real, that's all you need to know."

"Fine by me, Tom. Can you tell me what this is about?"

"No."

"I have my employers to think about."

"No."

"Very well, we at Ben Fuji's are always anxious to cooperate with the law and will do so respectfully and diplomatically. Oi! Harry!"

The younger of the two youths looked up from the VR helmet he was examining like a rabbit caught in headlights.

"What's your father do these days?" I shouted as if doing a stand-up routine.

"He's still King," he answered.

Then he bit his tongue.

"Gordon – that really is his name – is a friend from school, one of the few I can trust," he told me. "Thomas is actually Sergeant Dave Thomas."

"Your bodyguard."

"Yes, and I don't want to get him into trouble. I'm not really supposed to be out with just one. I'm afraid Gordon and I rather conned him into accompanying us into the Forbidden Zone."

"London?"

"Yes. We're almost out-of-towners now."

"So why the expedition?"

He gave me another once-over (the fifth by my reckoning) before answering.

"My brother, my elder brother," he started, as if he had lots to choose from, "does not pick his friends as well as I do.

"One of them has talked to the press about a party brother-dear attended last month where there was some silliness involving a swimming pool and various naked ladies in compromising positions."

"Nobody invited me," I said before I could stop myself. "Sorry. Go on."

"Worse still, someone had a video camera and recorded some of the . . . er . . ."

"Juicy bits?"

"Yes. Juicy bits. God, that sounds disgusting."

He *was* young.

"Anyway, this so-called friend has sold the tape to an absolute shit."

"Sam Dexter."

"Why, yes. How did you know?"

"I recognized him from your description."

He smiled at that, something he rarely did, if the newspapers were to be believed.

"Does your brother know?" I prompted.

"No, and he wouldn't know what to do if he did. Anyway, he's on tour at the moment."

He said it as if he were talking about a second-rate rock band doing one-night stands around the Midlands.

"So what did you have in mind?"

"Well, Plan A was to stop my brother's dippy friend from selling the tape. God knows, he doesn't need the money; just doing it for the mischief. But we were too late. He'd done the dirty deed by the time we got there. Fortunately, Dexter had gone straight to the local pub to celebrate."

"Does he know what's on the tape?"

"Yes. He insisted on a viewing before buying."

"Can I ask how much?"

"Thirty thousand quid, he said, and he felt pretty shitty when I called it thirty thousand pieces of silver," he said proudly.

I'll bet. I could feel lower than toenail dirt for that sort of money.

"So you followed Dexter?"

"Well, Thomas – Dave – did, at least into the first three pubs. Then he took a cab here. He has the tape in his pocket. I saw it."

So did I, in a brown envelope.

"And just how were you going to relieve him of it?" I asked gently.

"We never actually got down to detail on Plan B," he said seriously. "Gordon thought we should borrow Dave's gun and mug him, but I don't think Dave will go along with that. So, really, we haven't got a plan. We just need to keep an eye on Dexter and wait our chance. Would you help us do that?"

How could I refuse?

"I tell you what; you stay here and I'll check out Dexter. There's no way you can show your face in the restaurant without him seeing you, and if he thinks you're after him, it will just convince him he's on to something big."

"Good plan. Thanks. How can I repay you?"

"I'll think of something."

I didn't have to go far to get a situation report on Sinister Dexter. Keiko was waiting by my desk.

"He is a pig, that man. He is griping everyone. Not only my girls, but customers, too!"

"I think you mean 'groping,'" I said calmly.

"Whatever. Get rid of him, while he can still stand."

Now I only usually listen to about forty percent of what Keiko says, but as she once bested me in a nine-hour sake drinking session, I do respect her views on male alcohol consumption.

"How pissed is he?" I asked seriously.

"Weaving in the wind. Another three or four scotches and he'll start griping the men."

I knew it was worth listening.

"Keiko, you've got it. I want you to keep him here and keep the table next to him free."

"No problem, I wouldn't put anyone there."

"Good thinking. Now tell one of the waiters to drop something or spill something on Dexter's table. Then we want lots of profuse apologies and take him the bottle – the bottle, mind you – of the Tobermory Malt, the twelve-year-old."

Well, that's what it said on the bottle, but I know it to be a single malt that had gone overproof and now clocked in nearer sixty percent than forty percent alcohol.

"Give him the bottle . . . ?" Keiko started, but she was talking to my back as I headed for the office.

"Glenda?"

"Perhaps. Who wants to know?"

"Angel."

"Darling! Long time no . . . well, no anything, really. Whad-deryerwant?"

"I want you to seduce somebody in a Japanese restaurant and pick his pocket and within the next hour."

"Seems reasonable. Have I time to put my face on?"

"Got any money on you?"

"Not a cent, but Sergeant Dave has." Henry smiled.

"Has he £250?" I asked, swapping my dinner jacket (Keiko had insisted) for my leather bomber.

"I'll ask."

Henry and Sergeant Dave went into conference. Gordon was fully plugged into the VR machine, whapping balls down a fairway somewhere.

"He wants to know what you want it for," Henry came back.

"I'm hiring somebody to pick Dexter's pocket and get that tape for you."

"In that case, I'll get the cash."

No questions, no arguments. Who says breeding doesn't tell?

"You didn't have to come," I told them for the tenth time.

"Listen, Angel, if that's your name, I'm going to have enough trouble accounting for £250 without receipts as it is. If you just drove off into the night with it, I'd be back on traffic duty."

"You have a point, Sergeant."

"Plus" – Thomas put his face up to the open glass partition – "I'm not supposed to be farther than five feet from his nibs even when he's peeing. Where the hell are we anyway?"

"The Barbican."

"Do people still live here?"

Now if "Henry" had said that, it would have made headlines. Instead he chimed up with: "This is a taxi, isn't it?"

"It was," I said over my shoulder.

"A Fairway."

"Do they still make them?"

"No."

"Is it old?"

"About twelve years. You still see them around."

Ordinary mortals do, anyway.

"It's not a real one, though. I mean a licensed Hackney Carriage?"

"No, it's delicensed," I answered patiently. After all, the kid still probably went train spotting.

"He's called Armstrong Two," I said. There was a half minute of silence from the back.

"Why Armstrong *Two*? What happened to *One*?"

Bright lad.

"That's a long story."

The one advantage Armstrong Two had over Armstrong One – apart from being in one piece – was the mobile phone fitted in a dashboard mounting. I used it to call Glenda when we were close.

"Be outside and ready to jump in exactly two minutes," I told her when we were five minutes away.

"You've got to be kidding, Angel, I'm nowhere near *dressed* even."

"Good, that'll speed things up."

"Oooh – you smooth-talking fucker, you."

I hung up and pulled Armstrong over to the curb, got out and, walked to the boot where I keep various emergency-only items.

I moved round to the nearside passenger door and opened it.

"Take off your jacket," I said to Henry. "And put these on."

I handed him a sweatshirt three sizes too big for him (advertising a now bankrupt chilli-to-go and carwash in Bangor, Maine) and a baseball cap (adjustable – one size fits all) plugging the Romford Spartacists, which was a gridiron football team, not a political movement.

Henry complied with enthusiasm.

"This is so Glenda won't recognize me, isn't it?" he chirped, crumpling a suit jacket that probably cost half an Armstrong.

"That's right, and just hope she doesn't."

He looked at me quizzically.

"Trust me on this one," I said.

"Do you *know* who you've got in here?" Glenda hissed out of the side of her mouth. As she was sitting in the rumble seat behind mine, I could hear her perfectly well without her spitting in my ear.

"Shut up and forget it," I hissed back.

In my mirror I saw Sergeant Dave Thomas reach for his wallet.

"Payment on results," I said loudly. "That's the usual way, isn't it Glenda?"

She straightened up in her seat and made a futile effort to drag her short skirt down a centimeter. If she'd succeeded that would have made it only seven inches above the knee.

"Haven't had any complaints so far, Angel," said Glenda.

Henry, Thomas, Gordon, and I were in the manager's office looking at the restaurant on the video monitor. Glenda was out there doing her stuff, and it was Academy Award-winning stuff.

Keiko had done her bit, organizing a minor accident, groveling apologies, and then a free (or at least to-be-paid-for-later) bottle of the Tobermory head-banger. And Dexter had gone along like he'd read the script. If his pupils hadn't been so dilated, there would have been a glint in them saying he was going to finish the bottle just to show them. Whoever "they" were.

Glenda had tick-tocked her buttocks into a chair at the table next to him, fluffed up her auburn curls, smoothed her skirt, and picked up a menu. Dexter was at her like a shark coming out of Lent.

He persuaded her to try a whisky as an aperitif. Then as an alternative to sake. Then just for the hell of it. Then to finish the bottle.

Glenda, who could drink me under the table and carry me home (and, indeed, has) matched him drink for drink and then – master stroke – ordered champagne. Even without sound, we could feel Dexter say, "And why not?"

When I lip-read Glenda describing the basement room with its virtual-reality golf range (about which I'd briefed her) and then pantomime that she needed to use the toilet, I knew he was hooked. Glenda stood, played with the hem of her skirt and the string of large (fake) amber beads balanced on her bosom, fell back a pace, and allowed herself to be steadied by Dexter's outstretched, sweaty hand.

"Nice touch, that," I said, admiring a professional when I see one.

I realized no one was listening; they were all looking at the monitor as if they'd never seen anything like this before. Then Henry looked at me, dead serious.

"You're getting a kick out of this," he said, deadpan. "And I've been wondering why, because there's nothing in it for you. In fact, you haven't even asked for anything. You're helping us just for the hell of it, just to stir things up. You don't really care one way or the other, do you? You don't have problems like this, do you? You're like one of the old hippies who just drift through life in your battered old delicensed taxicab, just to be a rebel, thinking it all a bit of a bad joke."

The kid was getting too close for comfort.

"Who's an ageing hippy?" I snapped.

It got triple x-rated (as they say now on TV) pretty quickly once Glenda and Sinister made it to the virtual-reality room.

The VR driving ranges had semicircular control panels raised on small platforms like a conductor's rostrum. They contained all the electronic gizmos needed to run the ranges and to protect them from the helmeted VR golfers; they were leather padded.

Glenda realized the erotic potential of the podia immediately, and as Dexter bent over to examine the virtual-reality helmet, Glenda goosed him something rotten.

"I say!" said Gordon, glued to the screen.

"Ignore him," whispered Henry. "He's very young in many ways."

"I'd forgotten he was here," I said, fiddling with the VCR controls.

Dexter couldn't quite believe it either. He swung round and walked into Glenda's open arms. Glenda backed him up against

a podium and planted a smacker on his lips, her hands dis-
appearing inside his jacket. Without unplugging her lips, she
slipped his jacket off and held it with her left hand while her
right went to his groin.

Sergeant Thomas and the green-and-blue engines were
watching her right hand, as was Dexter. I was watching her
left as she freed him from the jacket and then hitched it round
until she was near the pocket with the envelope. Dexter's hands
and mind were fully occupied in trying to push up her skirt.
That short, leather skirt, which had flown up like a Venetian
blind in the restaurant, now seemed to be glued to her long,
high-heeled legs.

Just as Glenda's red fingernails closed around the envelope,
Dexter decided the skirt problem needed a better perspective,
and so he took an unsteady step backward.

The problem was he kept going, the back of his thighs hitting
the edge of the podium and tipping him backward. Glenda,
probably thinking he had realized she was doing a lift, dropped
the jacket and removed her support from his back. He toppled
over, hit the floorboards and bounced slightly before coming to
rest. I hoped the alcohol had acted as enough of a muscle
relaxant to prevent serious damage.

Glenda looked down at him in amazement from the control
panel. She stamped one of her high heels so effectively the four
of us jerked back from the monitor, as if we'd heard it. Then she
pulled off the curly auburn wig and flung it over Dexter's face.

"Bloody hell," said an aristocratic voice. "She's a man!"

"Welcome to the world, Harry."

I had to introduce him to Keiko and the staff; that became part
of the deal though they were sworn to secrecy. We did it in the
kitchen so the punters couldn't see, and it went down well all
round. He said he knew their emperor and what a jolly nice
bloke he was. They said they didn't but, of course, they'd take
his word for it.

Then we paid off Glenda, and I offered to drive her home, but
she said she never finished her dinner and sushi was *so* erotic . . .
On Henry's instruction, Sergeant Thomas put enough cash
behind the bar to ensure she wouldn't go hungry.

It was my idea to pile Dexter into the back of Armstrong. Sergeant Thomas (and Henry) knew he lived in Finchley, and a Euro driving license in his wallet confirmed the address and that he had enough cash to pay even my exorbitant rates. (I also took the trouble to remove £90 for his meal and one of these days I must remember to pay it into Ben Fuji's.)

"If he wakes up," I said, pulling on my leather bomber jacket and smoothing my hair flat with hair gel (hair gel was back in a big way), "I'll just play the aggrieved musher."

"Pardon?" asked Gordon politely.

"Cabbie. Ferryman. Hackney Carriage operative. Hatless Chauffeur."

"Oh," he said vaguely. It was way past his bedtime.

I took Henry to one side as I closed Armstrong's boot. The street was deserted, but he had turned up the collar of his jacket, and he still wore the sweatshirt and hat I had given him.

"You want these back," he said, starting to peel off his jacket.

"No, no. Keep them. I'll add them to the bill."

He fixed me with his eyes. I'd read somewhere they'd been trained to do that.

"There will be a bill?"

Sergeant Thomas hovered close behind him, so I dropped my voice.

"We ageing hippies aren't into money, man. Can you dig that?"

He smiled and for once the newspapers were right, he didn't smile enough.

"You've got the tape?"

He patted the inside pocket of his coat.

"And you'll turn it over to your brother?"

He waited five careful seconds before answering.

"I'll bring it to his attention."

They were taught not to tell lies as well.

"Are there any copies?"

"No." He was confident. "There wasn't time."

"Good. Then this is the one we put in the envelope in Sinister's pocket."

"What's that?" he stared open-eyed at the cassette I offered him.

"I taped the scene in the basement, right up to Glenda revealing her . . . er . . . credentials."

"Christ, he'll have a heart attack," he said gleefully, grabbing it. "I hope he doesn't watch it before he gives it to his editor."

Then he flashed a look at me.

"Are there any copies?"

Good thinking, kid, you're coming on.

"No. But Dexter doesn't know that."

Henry's face bisected.

"Way to go, Angel. You used to say things like that, didn't you?"

He put the new cassette into Dexter's brown envelope.

"May I do the honors?" He indicated the slumped figure of Dexter, snoring loudly, stretched across Armstrong's backseat.

"Be my guest."

He turned, then stopped and offered his hand. I wasn't sure whether I should bow or not. So I didn't.

"Thank you, Angel, if that's your name. I still don't understand why you've helped us, but I'm grateful, and if there is ever anything I can—"

"Don't worry, I'll call."

He looked puzzled.

"I know where you live," I explained.

He smiled again and pulled me closer as we shook.

"You know, I was going to ask you for Glenda's phone number for my uncle," he whispered. Then he squeezed my hand. "I still might."

It was my turn to grin.

Sergeant Thomas hadn't finished with me, though. As Henry put the new tape onto Dexter's comatose person, Thomas took me to one side as only policemen can.

"I don't have to remind you, sir, that—"

"No you don't; it's okay."

"And I hope you'll give me your address so that—"

"No way, Mr. Tank Engine. You'll just have to trust me."

He sized me up.

"Well, we have to trust somebody, I suppose."

"That's the spirit, Sergeant. And should I ever have my

collar felt, you won't mind if I mention your name, will you? Of course, I won't say how we met."

Mr. Nice Policeman was in danger of giving way to Mr. Nasty. There's a Jekyll and Hyde gene in all of them.

"So that's your price, is it?"

"Partly, Dave, partly. And I may never call it in. I may not have to, seeing as how you've already noted my registration number and will no doubt put it through the police computer tomorrow."

Even in the streetlight he blushed.

"Don't worry, Dave, always C.Y.A. – cover your arse. That's all I'm doing."

"So what else do you get out of it? Come on, I want to know."

"Well, Sergeant, look at it this way. You like young Henry, don't you?" He nodded. "And he's going to go far, isn't he?"

"I . . . er . . ."

"Put it this way: If you were a betting man, would you put money on *his* being the face we see on our stamps in a few years' time?"

"Possibly."

"So would I. And I'll be able to say I had him in the back of the cab once."

AN ACQUAINTANCE
WITH MR COLLINS

SARAH CAUDWELL

The train has reached Reading, and I still have not decided whether to say anything to Selena concerning the late Mr Collins. It is hardly probable that anything can be proved; it is even possible that there is nothing to prove; and unwarranted investigation might cause undeserved distress. Murder, on the other hand, is a practice not to be encouraged.

I could almost wish that I had not, finding myself with an hour or so to spare before a dinner engagement in central London, chosen to pass it in the Corkscrew. Had I spent it in some other hostelry, I should now be returning to Oxford with a mind untroubled by any more disquieting burden than my responsibilities as Tutor in Legal History at St George's College. It is idle, however, to regret my decision. It was to the Corkscrew that I directed my steps, and indeed in the hope that I might find there one or two of my young friends in Lincoln's Inn.

I am well enough known there, it seems, for the barman to remember who I am and in whose company I am most often to be found.

"If you're looking for some of your friends, Professor Tamar," he said as he handed me my glass of Nierstein, "you'll find Miss Jardine right at the back there." He gestured towards the dimly lit interior.

Selena was sitting alone at one of the little oak tables, in an attitude less carefree than one expects of a young barrister in the middle of the summer vacation: her blonde head was bent over a set of papers, which she was examining with the critical expression of a Persian cat having doubts about the freshness of its fish. Reflecting, however, that in the flickering candlelight she could not in fact be attempting to read them, and that in deliberate search of solitude she would hardly have come to the Corkscrew, I did not hesitate to join her.

She greeted me with every sign of pleasure, and invited me to tell her the latest news from Oxford; but I soon perceived, having accepted the invitation, that her attention was elsewhere.

"My dear Selena," I said gently, "the story I have been telling you about the curious personal habits of our new Dean was told to the Bursar, in the strictest confidence, only this morning, and may well not be common knowledge until the middle of next week. It seems a pity to waste it on an unappreciative audience."

She looked apologetic.

"I'm sorry, Hilary. I'm afraid I'm still thinking of something I was dealing with this afternoon. I happened to be the only Junior left in Chambers – the others are all on holiday – and the senior partner in Pitkin and Shoon came in in rather a dither, wanting advice in conference as a matter of urgency. I'm told he's quite a good commercial lawyer, but he candidly admits to being completely at sea over anything with a Chancery flavour. So whenever a trust or a will or anything like that comes his way, he pops into Lincoln's Inn to get the advice of Counsel. And since the sums involved are generally large enough to justify what might otherwise seem an extravagance, one wouldn't like to discourage him."

I nodded, well understanding that a solicitor such as Mr Pitkin would be cherished by the Chancery Bar like the most golden of geese.

"He's inclined to fuss about things that don't really present any problem, so I thought I'd be able to put his mind at rest quite easily about whatever it was that was worrying him. The trouble is, I wasn't, and I can't help wondering . . . It might help to clear my mind if I could talk it over with someone. If you'd care to hear about it . . .?"

"My dear Selena," I said, "I should be honoured. I must remind you, however, that I am an historian rather than a lawyer – on any intricate point of law, I fear that my views will be of but little value."

"Oh," said Selena, "there's nothing difficult about the law. The law's quite clear, I can advise on it in two sentences. But the sequence of events, you see, is rather unusual, and in certain circumstances might be thought slightly . . . sinister."

The matter on which Mr Pitkin had required advice was the estate, amounting in value to something between three and four million pounds sterling, of his late client Mr Albert Barnsley. Having acted for Mr Barnsley for many years in connection with various commercial enterprises, he was familiar with the details of his background and private life. He had related these to Selena at greater length than she could at first believe necessary for the purpose of her advising on the devolution of the estate.

The late Mr Barnsley (Mr Pitkin had told her) was what is termed a self-made man. Born in Yorkshire, the son of poor but respectable parents, he had left school at the age of sixteen, and after completing his national service had obtained employment in quite a humble capacity with a local manufacturing company. By the age of forty he had risen to the position of managing director – a sign, as I supposed, that he possessed all those qualities of drive, initiative and enterprise which I am told are required for success in the world of commerce and industry.

"Yes," said Selena, thoughtfully sipping her wine. "Yes, I suppose he must have had those qualities. And others, perhaps, which moralists don't seem to value so highly – the ability to make himself agreeable, for example, in particular to women. His progress was not impeded, at any rate, by the fact that he had married the chairman's daughter."

"Perhaps," I said, "she was anxious to be married, and he was her only suitor."

"Far from it, apparently. According to Mr Pitkin, Isabel was a strikingly attractive woman who could have married anyone she wanted, but she set her heart on Albert Barnsley. Her father, as you might expect, was something less than delighted. But Isabel talked him round in the end, and he gave the young couple his blessing and a rather elegant house to live in. Mind you, he didn't take any more chances than he could help – he put the house in trust for Isabel and any children she might have, and when he died he left his estate on the same trusts."

"So Barnsley did not in fact benefit from his wife's wealth?"

"Not directly, no, apart from living in the house, but that's not quite the point. I don't say that being the chairman's son-in-law would mean he could rise without merit, but it would tend to mean, don't you think, that there was less danger of his merits going unrecognized? And after her father died, of course, Isabel's trust fund included quite a substantial holding in the company, and her husband could always rely on the trustees to support his decisions. Quite apart from that, Isabel was very skilful at dealing with the other major shareholders – after all, she'd known most of them since she was a child. She was a woman of considerable charm and personality, wholeheartedly devoted to her husband's interests, and there doesn't seem to be much doubt that she contributed very significantly to his success."

"Were there any children?"

"One daughter – Amanda, described by Mr Pitkin as something of a tomboy. The sort of girl, he says, who'd rather have a bicycle for her birthday than a new dress. Actually it sounds as if she'd probably have got both, being an object of total adoration on the part of her parents. Her father in particular was enormously proud of her. People used to ask him sometimes if he wouldn't rather have had a son, and he used to say that Amanda was a son as well as a daughter – she could do anything a boy could do, he said, and do it a damn sight better. But I'm talking of five or six years ago, when Amanda was in her mid-teens. After that things changed."

Under Mr Barnsley's management the company had flourished, expanded and in due course been taken over by a larger company. The takeover was not one which he had any reason to resist: his personal shareholding was by now substantial, and the price offered – as well as increasing the value of the funds held in trust for his wife and daughter – was sufficient to make him, as Selena put it, seriously rich.

The terms agreed for the takeover included his appointment to a senior position in the company making the acquisition: he was an active and energetic man, still in his forties, and the prospect of retirement held no charms for him. Though his new responsibilities required his presence in London during the working week, he had no wish to sever his connections with his home town or to uproot his family. He accordingly acquired a small bachelor flat in central London and returned at weekends to the house in Yorkshire.

"That is to say," said Selena, "he began by doing so. But after a while the weekends in Yorkshire became less frequent, and eventually ceased altogether. You will not find it difficult, I imagine, to guess the reason."

"I suppose," I said, "that he had formed an attachment to some young woman in London – what is termed, I believe, a popsie."

"I think," said Selena, "that the current expression is bimbo. Though in the present case that perhaps gives a slightly misleading impression. Natalie wasn't at all the sort of girl who dresses up in mink and mascara and gets her picture in the Sunday newspapers. There wasn't anything glamorous or sophisticated about her – she was just a typist in Barnsley's office. She was from the same part of the world that he was, and it was her first job in London – I suppose in a way that gave them something in common, and perhaps made him feel protective towards her. She was young, of course – about twenty-two – and reasonably pretty, but nothing remarkable. That's Mr Pitkin's view, at any rate – he found her rather colourless, especially by comparison with Isabel."

It occurred to me that it might have been the contrast with Isabel that Barnsley had found attractive. It was clear that his wife had given him a great deal; but if it is more blessed to give than receive, then plainly Natalie offered him ampler scope for beatitude.

"No doubt," said Selena. "But as you will have gathered, she wasn't the kind of girl who wanted to be given jewellery or dinners at the Savoy or anything like that. It's rather a pity really, because with a little luck and discretion Barnsley could have had that sort of affair without upsetting anyone, and they would all have lived happily ever after. But Natalie was the domesticated sort, and wanted to be married. And he couldn't give her that quite so easily."

Because Isabel declined to divorce him. Mr Pitkin, having reluctantly and with embarrassment accepted instructions to negotiate with her on Mr Barnsley's behalf, had found her implacable. There was nothing, she said, to negotiate about: she did not want anything from her husband that he was now able to offer her; and she saw no reason to make things easy for him. If she ever found herself in a position, by raising her little finger, to save him from a painful and lingering death, she hoped (she said) that she would still have the common humanity to raise it; but to be candid, she felt some doubt on the matter. Mr Pitkin had perhaps been slightly shocked at the depth of her bitterness.

"Though it seems to me," said Selena, "to be quite understandable. It must be peculiarly disconcerting, don't you think, to be left for someone entirely different from oneself? Not just like going into one's bank and being told there's no money in one's account when one thought there was, but like going in and being told one's never had an account there at all. A feeling that all along one must somehow have completely misunderstood the situation."

I asked what Amanda's attitude had been.

"Extreme hostility towards her father. It was, you may think, very natural and proper that she should take her mother's side, but I gather it went a good deal further than that. She seems to have felt a sense of personal betrayal."

I thought that too was understandable. When a man forms an attachment to a woman young enough to be his daughter, I suppose that his daughter may feel as deeply injured as his wife; and for Amanda, as for Isabel, it must have been peculiarly wounding that he seemed to love his mistress for qualities precisely opposite to those which he had seemed to value in herself.

"At first," continued Selena, "she simply refused to see him or speak to him. But eventually she found that an inadequate way of expressing her feelings, and she wrote him a letter. Mr

Pitkin still has a copy of it on his file, but he said rather primly that he couldn't ask a lady like myself to read it. I don't actually suppose that Amanda Barnsley at the age of seventeen knew any expressions which are unfamiliar to me after several years in Lincoln's Inn, but one wouldn't wish to shatter Mr Pitkin's illusions. It was clearly in the crudest and most offensive terms that Amanda could think of, particularly in its references to Natalie, and was evidently designed to enrage her father beyond all endurance."

"And did it succeed?"

"Oh, admirably. Within an hour of receiving it Mr Barnsley was storming up and down the offices of Pitkin and Shoon demanding a new will, the main purpose of which was to ensure that Amanda could not in any circumstances inherit a penny of his estate. Poor Mr Pitkin tried to calm him down and persuade him not to act with undue haste, but of course it wasn't the least bit of use. So Mr Pitkin, following his usual practice, came along to Lincoln's Inn to have the will drafted by Counsel, and it was executed by Mr Barnsley three days later. The effect of it was that the whole estate would go to Natalie, provided she survived him by a period of twenty-eight days, but if she didn't then to various charities. Not, of course, because he especially wanted to benefit the charities, but to make sure that there couldn't in any circumstances be an intestacy, under which Amanda or her mother might benefit as his next-of-kin."

"Did Amanda know that she had been disinherited?"

"Oh yes – her father straightaway wrote a letter to Isabel, telling her in detail exactly what he'd done. His letter, I regret to say, was not in conciliatory terms – it made various disagreeable comments on what he called Isabel's vindictiveness in preventing him from marrying the woman he loved and referred to Amanda as "your hell-cat of a daughter". It was written, I need hardly say, without the advice or approval of poor Mr Pitkin. Isabel didn't answer it, and there was no further communication between them for a period of some three years. Perhaps, before I go on with the story, you would care for another glass of wine?"

I wondered, while Selena made her ways towards the bar, how she would justify the epithet "unusual". The events she had recounted, though no doubt uniquely distressing to the principals, seemed to me thus far to be all too regrettably commonplace. I recalled, however, that she had also used the word "sinister"; and that Mr Barnsley was dead.

Returning to our table with replenished glasses, Selena resumed her story.

"In the spring of this year Mr Pitkin received a letter from Isabel. She had not written direct to her husband, she said, for fear that he might not open her letter, or if he did that he might have the embarrassment of doing so 'in the presence of someone else'. But there were matters which she felt they should now discuss, and she did not think that her husband would regret seeing her. She would be most grateful if Mr Pitkin would arrange a meeting.

"I have the impression that poor Mr Pitkin was rather alarmed to hear from her. Though, as I have said, he admired her personality and charm, I think that he was also rather frightened of her, and he was by no means sure that she didn't mean to make trouble of some kind.

"Mr Barnsley himself evidently shared these misgivings, and was more than half-inclined to refuse to see her. But she seemed to be hinting that she might now be prepared to agree to a divorce, and that was enough to persuade him. It would have been another two years before a divorce could take place without her consent, and Natalie was still very unhappy about what she saw as the insecurity of her position.

"He seems to have hoped at first that he would be supported by the presence of his solicitor, but Mr Pitkin very prudently said it was out of the question, since Isabel had asked for a private meeting. Besides, if her husband were accompanied by his legal adviser and she were not, it might look as if they were trying to browbeat her.

"So a week later Mr Barnsley summoned up the fortitude and resolve which had made him a captain of British industry and set forth alone and unprotected to have tea with his wife at the Ritz Hotel. He thought, Mr Pitkin tells me, that the Ritz would be the safest place to meet her – meaning, as I understand it, the least likely place for a woman such as Isabel to make a scene."

She wanted, it seemed, to talk to him about their daughter.

Amanda was now twenty, reading English at a provincial university and specializing in the nineteenth-century novel – she had formed a great passion for the Brontës. Her academic progress was satisfactory, and she was perfectly well behaved – almost unnaturally so, perhaps, for someone who had been such a lively and exuberant schoolgirl. Of recent months, however, she had seemed to be out of spirits, and during the Easter vacation had shown such signs of depression as to cause her mother serious concern.

Isabel had questioned her; Amanda had denied that anything was wrong; too anxious to be tactful, Isabel had persisted. Amanda had at last admitted the cause of her dejection: in spite of everything, she still found it unbearable to be estranged from her father. The admission was made with many tears, as evidencing an unforgivable disloyalty to her mother.

Isabel had been dismayed. The bitterness which she had at first felt towards her husband had faded (she said) into an amiable indifference; it had not occurred to her that her daughter's feelings towards him were more intense, and that the girl was still tormented by conflicting loyalties.

It was (said Isabel) a piece of heart-breaking nonsense: when all she minded about was making Amanda happy, she turned out to be making her miserable. If Amanda wanted to be reconciled with her father, then let them be reconciled; if the fact of his still being married to Isabel was in some way an impediment, then let there, by all means, be a divorce.

"Which meant, as I understand it," said Selena, "that her consent to a divorce was conditional on Barnsley making friends with Amanda again. This account of Amanda's feelings is all based, of course, on what Isabel told him – you may perhaps choose to take a more cynical view of her motives."

I remarked that one might expect a study of the Victorian novelists to have reminded her of the practical as well as the spiritual advantages of being on good terms with any relative of substantial fortune.

"Trollope," said Selena with evident approval, "is always very sensible about that sort of thing – I'm not quite sure about the Brontës. But be that as it may, Mr Barnsley was quite content to accept Isabel's account of things at its face value. It wasn't only that he was pleased about the divorce – he was really very touched to think that his daughter still cared so much about him. After all, it was a long time since the offensive letter, and until she was seventeen he'd idolized her. He told Mr Pitkin to put in hand the arrangements for the divorce, and wrote in affectionate terms to Amanda to arrange a meeting."

"Was it," I asked, "a successful reunion?"

"Evidently, since shortly afterwards he mentioned to Mr Pitkin that once the business of the divorce was dealt with he would have to do something about changing his will."

"Did he indicate what he had in mind?"

"He still wanted to leave the bulk of his estate to Natalie, but to give a sufficient share to Amanda to show his affection for her – about a fifth was what he had in mind. Well, with both parties consenting and no arguments about property or children, the divorce went through pretty quickly, and he made arrangements to marry Natalie as soon as the decree was made absolute.

"Mr Pitkin admits to having felt a certain apprehensiveness about the occasion. It was going to be a very quiet wedding in a registry office, with a small reception afterwards, but it was also going to be the first time that Amanda and Natalie had met each other, and he felt Mr Barnsley's view that they would get on like a house on fire might be a little over-optimistic. He remembered Amanda's letter, and he didn't quite trust her not to do something outrageous to show her disapproval. He also had the impression that Natalie was becoming a trifle jealous of Barnsley's renewed affection for his daughter, and might have some difficulty in concealing it.

"But as it turned out his misgivings were quite unfounded. Amanda wore a suitably pretty and feminine dress and was charming to everyone. She and Natalie shook hands, and Natalie said she hoped they would be great friends, and Amanda said she hoped so too, and then they had what Mr Pitkin calls a very nice little conversation about how Amanda was getting on with her studies. So that by the time Mr Barnsley and his bride left to go on their honeymoon, which they planned to spend driving round the Lake District, Mr Pitkin feels able to assure me that everyone was getting on splendidly.

"The only slight embarrassment was the fault of Mr Barnsley

himself – he judged it a suitable moment to remind Mr Pitkin, in the hearing of both Natalie and Amanda, that he wanted a new will drawn up. It wasn't, in the circumstances, an entirely tactful remark. But no one else took any particular notice, and Mr Pitkin simply assured him that a draft would be ready for his approval on his return to London.

"As it would have been, no doubt, if Mr Barnsley had ever returned from his honeymoon."

She fell silent, while at the tables round us there continued the cheerful clinking of glasses and the noise of eager gossip about rumours of scandal in the City. I thought of Mr Barnsley setting forth with his unsophisticated young bride, and reflected that those who lack glamour are not necessarily without avarice.

I asked how it had happened.

"There was an accident with the car. Barnsley and Natalie were both killed instantly."

"Both?" It was not the contingency that I had envisaged.

"Oh yes," said Selena, "both. Something was wrong with the steering, apparently. Well, things sometimes do go wrong with cars, of course. But it was quite a new car, and supposed to have been thoroughly tested, so the local police were just a little puzzled about it. Enough so, at any rate, to ask Mr Pitkin, very discreetly, who would benefit under Mr Barnsley's will. But he gave them a copy of the will made three years before, and when they saw that the beneficiaries, in the events which had occurred, were a dozen highly respectable national charities, they didn't pursue the matter. There are limits to what even the most aggressive fund-raisers will do to secure a charitable bequest."

She paused and sipped her wine, regarding me over her glass with an expression of pellucid innocence. I have known her too long, however, to be deceived by it, and I had detected in her voice a certain sardonic quality: I concluded that I was overlooking some point of critical importance. After a moment's thought I realized what it was, for the rule in question is one of respectable antiquity.

"Surely," I said, "unless there has been any recent legislation on the matter of which I am unaware, the effect of Mr Barnsley's marriage—?"

"Quite so," said Selena. "As you very rightly say, Hilary, and as Mr Pitkin discovered for the first time this morning, when he instructed his Probate assistant to deal with the formalities of proving the will, the effect of the marriage was to revoke it. I'm afraid a great many people get married without fully understanding the legal consequences, and in particular without realizing that when they say "I do" they are revoking any will they may previously have made. But there is no doubt, of course, that that is the position under English law. So Mr Barnsley died intestate."

"I fear," I said, "that I have a somewhat hazy recollection of the modern intestacy rules. Does that mean that his estate will pass to Natalie's next-of-kin? There is a presumption, I seem to remember, where two persons die together in an accident, that the younger survived the older?"

"That's the general rule, but actually it doesn't apply on an intestacy if the people concerned are husband and wife. In those circumstances neither estate takes any benefit from the other. But even if Natalie had survived her husband by a short period, her next-of-kin would take relatively little – the widow's statutory legacy, which is a trifling sum by comparison with the value of the estate, and half the income arising from the estate during the period of survival."

"In that case," I said, finding myself curiously reluctant to reach this conclusion, "I suppose that the whole estate goes to his daughter?"

"Who, if her father had died before his marriage, would have taken nothing, and if he had lived to make another will would have taken a comparatively small share of it. Yes. She is, as Mr Pitkin was careful to tell me, entirely ignorant of legal matters and will be even more astonished than he was to learn that that is the case. So naturally he didn't want to give her such momentous news until he'd had it confirmed by Chancery Counsel, and that, he said, was why he'd come to see me. But the question that was really troubling him, you see, was one he couldn't bring himself to ask, and which it would have been outside my competence to answer. That is to say, ought he to mention to the police how very advantageously things have turned out from the point of view of Miss Amanda Barnsley?"

It now for the first time occurred to me that I possessed an item of knowledge of possible relevance to the events she had described. Uncertain whether or not I should mention it, and having had no time to weigh the consequences of doing so, I remained silent.

Selena leant back in her chair and gave a sigh, as if telling the story had eased her mind.

"Well," she said, "it's lucky that Amanda's reading a nice harmless subject like English literature. If she'd happened to be reading law it might all look rather sinister. But non-lawyers don't usually know that a will is revoked by marriage, and I wouldn't think, would you, that it's the sort of information she'd be likely to come across by accident?"

The hour of my engagement being at hand, I was able to take my leave of her without making any direct answer. During dinner I put the matter from my mind, thinking that during the journey back to Oxford I would be able to reach a decision. But the train has passed Didcot, and I remain undecided.

It seems extraordinary and slightly absurd that I should find myself in such a quandary on account of an item of knowledge which is not, after all, in any way private or peculiar to myself. Indeed, if the work of the late Mr Wilkie Collins were held in the esteem it deserves, the plot of his admirable novel *No Name*, in which the revocation by marriage of her father's will deprives the heroine of her inheritance, would no doubt be known to everyone having any pretension to being properly educated. As it is, however, I suppose that relatively few people have any acquaintance with it – unless they are studying English literature, and specializing in the nineteenth-century novel.

COME AGAIN?

DONALD E WESTLAKE

The fact that the state of Florida would give the odious Boy Cartwright a driver's license only shows that the state of Florida isn't as smart as it thinks it is. The vile Boy, execrable expatriate Englishman, handed this document across the rental-car counter at Gulfport-Biloxi Regional Airport and the gullible clerk there responded by giving him the keys to something called a Taurus, a kind of space capsule sans relief tube, which turned out on examination in the ghastly sunlight to be the same whorehouse red as the rental clerk's lipstick. Boy tossed his disreputable canvas ditty bag onto this machine's backseat, the Valium and champagne bottles within chattering comfortably together, and drove north.

This was not the sort of assignment the despicable Boy was used to. As by far the most shameless and tasteless, and therefore by far the best, reporter on the staff of the *Weekly Galaxy*, a supermarket tabloid that gives new meaning to the term degenerate, the debased Boy Cartwright was used to commanding teams of reporters on assignments at the very peak of the tabloid Alp: celebrity adultery, UFO sightings, sports heroes awash in recreational drugs. The Return of Laurena Layla – or, more accurately, her nonreturn, as it would ultimately prove – was a distinct comedown for Boy. Not an event, but the mere anniversary of an event. And not in Los Angeles or Las Vegas or

Miami or any of the other centers of debauchery of the American celebrity world, but in Marmelay, Mississippi, in the muggiest, mildewiest, kudzuest nasal bowel of the Deep South, barely north of Biloxi and the Gulf, a town surrounded mostly by De Soto National Forest, named for a reprobate the *Weekly Galaxy* would have loved if he'd only been born four hundred and fifty years later.

There were two reasons why Boy had drawn this bottom-feeder assignment, all alone in America, the first being that he was in somewhat bad odor at the *Galaxy* at the moment, having not only failed to steal the private psychiatric records of sultry sci-fi-pic star Tanya Shonya from the Montana sanitarium where the auburn-tressed beauty was recovering from her latest doomed love affair, but having also, in the process, inadvertently blown the cover of another *Galaxy* staffer, Don Grove, a member of Boy's usual team, who had already been ensconced in that same sanitarium as a grief counselor. Don even now remained immured in a Montana quod among a lot of Caucasian cowboys, while the *Galaxy*'s lawyers negotiated reasonably with the state authorities, and Boy got stuck with Laurena Layla.

But that wasn't the only reason for this assignment. Twenty-two years earlier, when Boy Cartwright was freshly at the *Galaxy*, a whelp reporter (the *Galaxy* did not have cubs) with just enough experience on scabrous British tabloids to make him prime *Galaxy* material, just as despicable in those days but not yet as decayed, he had covered the trial of Laurena Layla, then a twenty-seven-year-old beauty, mistress of the Golden Church of Sha-Kay, a con that had taken millions from the credulous, which is, after all, what the credulous are for.

The core of the Golden Church of Sha-Kay had been the Gatherings, a sort of cross between a mass séance and a Rolling Stones world tour, which had taken place in stadiums and arenas wherever in rural America the boobs lay thick on the ground. With much use of swirling smoke and whirling robes, these Gatherings had featured music, blessings, visions, apocalyptic announcements, and a well-trained devoted staff, devoted to squeezing every buck possible from the attending faithful.

Also, for those gentlemen of discernment whose wealth *far* exceeded their brains, there had been private sessions attainable with Laurena Layla herself, from which strong men were known to have emerged goggle-eyed, begging for oysters.

What had drawn the younger but no less awful Boy Cartwright to Laurena Layla the first time was an ambitious Indiana D.A. with big eyes for the governorship (never got it) who, finding Laurena Layla in full frontal operation within his jurisdiction, had caused her to be arrested and put on trial as the con artist (and artiste) she was. The combination of sex, fame, and courtroom was as powerful an aphrodisiac for the *Galaxy* and its readers then as ever, so Boy, at that time a mere stripling in some other editor's crew, was among those dispatched to Muncie by Massa (Bruno DeMassi), then owner and publisher of the rag.

Boy's English accent, raffish charm, and suave indifference to putdowns had made him a natural to be assigned to make contact with the defendant herself, which he had been pleased to do, winning the lady over with bogus ID from the *Manchester Guardian*. His success had been so instantaneous and so total that he had bedded L.L. twice, the second time because neither of them could quite believe the first.

In the event, L.L. was found innocent, justice being blind, while Boy was unmasked as the scurrilous Galaxyite he in fact was, and he was sent packing with a flea in his ear and a high-heel print on his bum. However, she didn't come off at all badly in the *Galaxy*'s coverage of her trial and general notoriety, and in fact a bit later she sent him the briefest of thank-you notes with no return address.

That was not the last time Boy saw Laurena Layla, however. Two years after Muncie it was, and the memory of the all-night freight train whistles there was at last beginning to fade, when Laurena Layla hit the news again for an entirely different reason: She died. A distraught fan, a depressingly overweight woman with a home permanent, stabbed L.L. three times with a five-and-dime steak knife, all the thrusts fatal but fortunately none of them disfiguring; L.L. made a lovely corpse.

Which was lucky indeed, because it was Boy's assignment on

that occasion to get the body in the box. Whenever a celebrity went down, it was *Galaxy* tradition to get, by hook or by crook (usually by crook), a photo of the recently departed lying in his or her casket during the final viewing. This photo would then appear, as large as physically possible, on the front page of the following week's *Galaxy*, in full if waxen color.

Attention, shoppers: Next to the cash register is an intimation of mortality, yours, cheap. See? Even people smarter, richer, prettier, and better smelling than you die, sooner or later; isn't that news worth a buck or two?

Getting the body in the box that time had been only moderately difficult. Though the Golden Church of Sha-Kay headquarters in Marmelay – a sort of great gilded banana split of a building with a cross and a spire and a carillon and loudspeakers and floodlights and television broadcasting equipment on top – was well guarded by cult staff members, it had been child's play to Mickey Finn a staffer of the right size and heft, via a doctored Dr Pepper, borrow the fellow's golden robe, and slip into the Temple of Revelation during a staff shift change.

Briefly alone in the dusky room with the late L.L., Boy had paused above the well-remembered face and form, now inert as it had never been in life, supine there in the open gilded casket on its waist-high bier, amid golden candles, far too much incense, and a piped-in celestial choir oozing out what sounded suspiciously like "Camptown Races" at half speed. Camera in right hand, he had reached out his left to adjust the shoulder of that golden gown to reveal just a bit more cleavage, just especially for all those necrophiles out there in Galaxyland, then it was *pop* goes the picture and Boy was, so far as he knew, done with the lovely late lady forever.

But no. It seemed that, among the effects Laurena Layla had left behind, amid the marked decks, shaved dice, plastic finger-nails, and John B. Anderson buttons, was a last will and testament, in which the lady had promised her followers a second act: "I shall Die untimely," she wrote (which everybody believes, of course), "but it shall not be a real Death. I shall Travel in that Other World, seeking Wisdom and the Way, and twenty years after my Departure, to the Day, I shall return to this Plane of Existence to share with You the Knowledge I have gained."

Twenty years. Tomorrow, the second Thursday in May, would be the twentieth anniversary of Laurena Layla's dusting, and an astonishing number of mouth-breathers really did expect her to appear among them, robes, smiles, cleavage, Wisdom, and all. Most if not all of those faithful were also faithful *Galaxy* readers, naturally, so here was Boy, pasty-faced, skeptical, sphacelated, Valium-enhanced, champagne-maintained, and withal utterly pleased with himself, even though this assignment was a bit of a comedown.

Here was the normally moribund crossroads of Marmelay, a town that had never quite recovered from the economic shock when the slave auction left, but today doing its best to make up all at once for a hundred and fifty years of hind teat. The three nearby motels had all quadrupled their rates, the two local diners had printed new menus, and the five taverns in the area were charging as though they'd just heard Prohibition was coming back. Many of the Sha-Kay faithful did their traveling in RVs, but they still had to eat, and the local grocers knew very well what *that* meant: move the decimal point one position to the right on every item in the store. The locals were staying home for a couple days.

Boy traveled this time as himself, a rare occurrence, though he had come prepared with the usual array of false identification just in case. He was also traveling solo, without even a photographer, since it wasn't expected he'd require a particularly large crew to record a nonevent: "Not appearing today in her Temple of Revelation in the charmingly sleepy village of Marmelay, Mississippi . . ."

So it was the truth Boy told the clerk at the Lest Ye Forget Motel, unnatural though that felt: "Boy Cartwright. The *Weekly Galaxy* made one's reservation, some days ago."

"You're a foreigner," the lad in the oversize raspberry jacket with the motel chain's logo on its lapel told him, and pointed at Boy as though Boy didn't already know where he was. "You're French!"

"Got it in one, dear," Boy agreed. "Just winged in from jolly old Paris to observe the festivities."

"Laurena Layla, you mean," the lad told him, solemn and excited all at once. Nodding, he said, "She's coming back, you know."

"So one has heard."

"Coming back tomorrow," the lad said, and sighed. "Eight o'clock tomorrow night."

"I believe that is the zshedule," Boy acknowledged, thinking how this youth could not have been born yet when Laurena Layla got herself perforated. How folly endures!

"Wish I could see it," the lad went on, "but the tickets is long gone. Long gone."

"Ah, tickets," Boy agreed. "Such valuable little things, at times. But as to one's room . . ."

"Oh, sure," the lad said, but then looked doubtful. "Was that a single room all by yourself?"

"For preference."

"For this time only," the lad informed him, speaking as by rote, "the management could give you a very special rate, if you was to move in with a family. Not a big family."

"Oh, but, dear," Boy said, "one has moved *out* from one's family. Too late to alter that, I'm afraid."

"So it's just a room by yourself," the lad said, and shrugged and said, "I'm supposed to ask, is all."

"And you did it very well," Boy assured him, then flinched as the lad abruptly reached under the counter between them, but then all he came up with was some sort of pamphlet or brochure. Offering this, he said, "You want a battlefield map?"

"Battlefield?" Boy's yellow spine shriveled. "Are there public disorders about?"

"Oh, not anymore," the lad promised, and pointed variously outward, saying, "Macunshah, Honey Ridge, Polk's Ferry, they're all just around here."

"Ah," Boy said, recollecting the local dogma, and now understanding the motel's name. "Your Civil War, you mean."

"The War Between the States," the lad promptly corrected him. He knew *that* much.

"Well, yes," Boy agreed. "One has heard it wasn't actually that civil."

★ ★ ★

In the event, Boy did share his room with a small family after all. In a local pub – *taa*-vin, in regional parlance – he ran across twins who'd been ten years old when their mother, having seen on TV the news of Laurena Layla's demise, had offed herself with a shotgun in an effort to follow her pastoress to that better world. (It had also seemed a good opportunity for her to get away from their father.) The twins, Ruby Mae and Ruby Jean, were thirty now, bouncing healthy girls, who had come to Marmelay on the off chance Mama would be coming back as well, presumably with her head restored. They were excited as all get-out at meeting an actual reporter from the *Weekly Galaxy*, their favorite and perhaps only reading, and there he was an Englishman, too! They just loved his accent, and he loved theirs.

"It's one P.M.," said the musical if impersonal voice in his ear.

Boy awoke, startled and enraged, to find himself holding a telephone to his head. Acid sunlight burned at the closed blinds covering the window. "Who the hell cares?" he snarled into the mouthpiece, which responded with a rendition of "Dixie" on steel drum.

Appalled, realizing he was in conversation with a *machine*, Boy slammed down the phone, looked around the room, which had been transmogrified overnight into a laundry's sorting area, and saw that he was alone. The twins had romped off somewhere, perhaps to buy their mother a welcome-home pair of cuddly slippers.

Just as well; Boy was feeling a bit shopworn this morning. Afternoon. And that had been the wake-up call he must have requested in an optimistic moment late last night. Most optimistic moments occur late at night, in fact; realism requires daylight.

Up close, the banana-split Temple of Revelation appeared to have been served on a Bakelite plate, which was actually the shiny blacktop parking area, an ebony halo broadly encircling the temple and now rapidly filling with RVs, tour buses, pickup trucks, and all the other transportations of choice of life's also-rans.

And they were arriving, in their droves. Whole families, in their Sunday best. Sweethearts, hand in hand. Retired oldsters, grinning shyly, made a bit slow and ponderous by today's early-bird special. Solitaries, some nervous and guarded in hoods and jackets too warm for the weather, others gaudily on the prowl, in sequins and vinyl. Folks walked by in clothing covered with words, everything from bowling teams and volunteer fire departments to commercial sports organizations and multinational corporations that had never given these people a penny. Men in denim, women in cotton, children in polyester. Oh, if Currier and Ives were alive in this moment!

Boy and the rental Taurus circled the blacktop, slaloming slowly among the clusters of people walking from their vehicles toward the admission gates. Show or no show, miracle or nix, revelation or fuggedabahdid, every one of them would fork over their ten bucks at the temple gate, eight for seniors, seven for children under six. Inside, there would be more opportunities for donations, gifts, love offerings, and so on, but all of that was optional. The ten-spot at the entrance was mandatory.

Everyone here was looking for a sign, in a way, and so was Boy, but the sign he sought would say something like VIP or PRESS or AUTHORIZED PERSONNEL ONLY. And yes, there it was: MEDIA. How modern.

The media, in fact, were sparse in the roped-off section of parking lot around to the side of the banana split, where a second entrance spared the chosen few from consorting with the rabble. Flashing his *Galaxy* ID at the golden-robed guardian of the MEDIA section, driving in, Boy counted two TV relay trucks, both local, plus perhaps half a dozen rentals like his own. Leaving the Taurus, Boy humped onto his shoulder the small canvas bag containing his tape recorder, disposable camera, and a folder of the tear sheets of his earlier coverage of Laurena Layla, plus her truncated note of gratitude, and hiked through the horrible humidity and searing sun to the blessed shade of the VIP entrance.

It took two golden-robers to verify his ID at this point, and then he was directed to jess go awn in an keep tuh the leff. He did so, and found himself in the same curving charcoal-gray dim-lit corridor he'd traversed just twenty years ago when he'd gotten the body in the box. Ah, memory.

Partway round, he was met by another fellow in a golden robe, next to a broad black closed metal door. "Press?" this fellow asked.

"Absolutely."

"Yes, sir," the fellow said, drew the door open, and ushered him in.

With the opening of the door, crowd noises became audible. Boy stepped through and found himself in a large opera box midway down the left side of the great oval hall that was the primary interior space of the temple. Raised above auditorium level, the box gave a fine view of the large echoing interior with its rows of golden plush seats, wide aisles, maroon carpets and walls, battalions of lights filling the high black ceiling, and the deep stage at the far end where L.L. used to give her sermons and where her choir and her dancer-acolytes once swirled their robes. The sect had continued all these years without its foundress, but not, Boy believed, as successfully as before.

The stage looked now as though set for some minimalist production of *King Lear:* bare, half-lit, wooden floor uncovered, gray back wall unlit, nothing visible except one large golden armchair in the exact center of the stage. The chair wasn't particularly illuminated, but Boy had no doubt it would be, if and when.

Below, the hall was more than half full, with the believers still streaming in. Sharing the box with Boy were the expected two camera crews and the expected scruffy journalists, the only oddity being that more of the journalists were female than male: four scruffy women and, with Boy, three scruffy men. Boy recognized a couple of his competitors and nodded distantly; they returned the favor. None of them was an ace like himself.

Ah, well. If only he'd succeeded in that Montana sanitarium. If only Don Grove were not now in a Montana pokey. If only Boy Cartwright didn't have to be present for this nothingness.

The con artists who ran Sha-Kay these days would no doubt produce some sort of light show, probably broadcast some old audiotapes of Laurena Layla, edited to sound as though she were addressing the rubes this very minute rather than more than twenty years ago. At the end of the day the suckers would wander off, very well fleeced and reasonably well satisfied, while the fleecers would have the admissions money, fifty or sixty thousand, plus whatever else they'd managed to pluck during the show.

Plus, of course, TV. This nonevent would be broadcast live on the Sha-Kay cable station, with a phone number prominent for the receipt of donations, all major credit cards accepted.

No, all of these people would be all right, but what about poor Boy Cartwright? Where was his *story*? "The nonappearance today in Marm—"

And there she was.

It was done well, Boy had to admit that. No floating down into view from above the stage, no thunderclaps and puffs of smoke while she emerged from a trapdoor behind the golden chair, no fanfare at all. She was simply *there*, striding in her shimmering golden robe down the wide central aisle from the rear of the hall, flanked by a pair of burly guardians to keep the faithful at bay, moving with the same self-confidence as always. Most of the people in the hall, including Boy, only became aware of her with the amplified sound of her first "Hosannas!"

That had always been her greeting to her flock, and here it was again. "Hosannas! Hosannas!" spoken firmly as she nodded to the attendees on both sides, her words miked to speakers throughout the hall that boomed them back as though her voice came from everywhere in the building at once.

It was the same voice. That was the first thing Boy caught. It was exactly the same voice he'd heard saying any number of things twenty years ago, *hosannas!* among them as well as *oh yes!* and *more more!*

She's lip-synching, he thought, to an old tape, but then he realized it was also the same body, sinuous within that robe. Yes, it was, long and lithe, the same body he well remembered. The same walk, almost a model's but earthier. The same pitch to the head, set of the shoulders, small hand gesture that wasn't quite a wave. And, hard to tell from up here, but it certainly looked like the same face.

But not twenty years older. The same age, or very close to the same age, twenty-seven, that Laurena Layla had been when the fan had given her that bad review. The same age, and in every other respect, so far as Boy could tell from this distance, the same woman.

It's a hologram, he told himself, but a hologram could not reach out to pat the shoulder of a dear old lady on the aisle, as this one now did, causing the dear old lady to faint dead away on the instant.

She's real, Boy thought. She's returned, by God.

A chill ran up his back as she ran lightly up the central stairs to the stage, the hairs rose on his neck, and he remembered all too clearly not the body in the box but the body two years before that, as alive as quicksilver.

She stopped, turned to face her people. Her smile was faintly sad, as it had always been. She spread her hands in a gesture that welcomed without quite embracing, as she always had. "Hosannas," she said, more quietly, and the thousands below thundered, "Hosannas!"

Boy stared. Gray sweat beaded on his gray forehead. His follicles itched, his clothing cramped him, his bones were gnarled and wretched.

"I have been away," Laurena Layla said, and smiled. "And now I have returned."

As the crowd screamed in delight, Boy took hold of himself – metaphorically. You are here, my lad, he reminded himself, because you do not believe in this crap. You do not believe in any of the crap. If you start coming all over goose bumps every time somebody rises from the dead, of what use will you be, old thing, to the dear old *Weekly Galaxy*?

Onstage, she, whoever she was, whatever she was, had gone into an old routine, feel-good mysticism, the basic tenets of Sha-Kay, but now delivered with the assurance of one who's been there and done that. The faithful gawped, the TV crews focused, the second-string stringers from the other tabs wrote furiously in their notebooks or extended their tape recorders toward the stage as though the voice were coming from there, and Boy decided it was time to get a little closer.

Everyone was mesmerized by the woman on the stage, or

whatever that was on the stage. Unnoticed, Boy stepped backward and through the doorway to the hall.

Where the golden guardian remained, unfortunately. "Sir," he said, frowning, "were you going to leave already?"

"Just a little reconnoiter, dear," Boy assured him.

"I'm not supposed to let anybody past this point," the guardian explained, looking serious about it.

This was why Boy never went on duty without arming himself with, in his left trouser pocket, folded hundred-dollar bills. It was automatic now to slide hand in and C-note out, the while murmuring, "Just need a quieter location, dear. Those TV cameras foul my recorder."

The reason employees are so easy to suborn is that they're employees. They're only here in the first place because they're being paid for their time. Whatever the enterprise may be, they aren't connected to it by passion or ownership or any other compelling link. Under the circumstances, what is a bribe but another kind of wage?

Still, we all of us have an ass to protect. Hand hovering over the proffered bill, the guardian nevertheless said, "I don't want to get in any trouble here."

"Nothing to do with you, old thing," Boy assured him. "I came round the other way."

The bill disappeared, and then so did Boy, following the long curved hall toward the stage. More and more of the temple layout he remembered as he moved along. Farther along this hallway he would find that faintly sepulchral room where the body had been on display, placed there because crowd control would have been so much iffier out in the main auditorium.

That last time, Boy had had no reason to proceed past the viewing room, which in more normal circumstances would have been some kind of offstage prep area or greenroom, but he knew it couldn't be far from there to the stage. Would he be closer then to *her*?

The likeness was so uncanny, dammit. Or perhaps it was so canny. In any event, this Laurena Layla, when close to people, kept moving, and when she stopped to speak she kept a distance from everyone else. Could she not be observed up close for long? If not, why not?

Though as Boy came around the curving hallway his left hand was already in his pocket, fondling another century, there was no guard on duty at the closed greenroom door; a surprise, but never question good fortune. In case the undoubted sentry was merely briefly away to answer mother's call, he hastened the last few yards, even though the brisk motion made his brain-walnut chafe uncomfortably against the shell of his skull.

The black door in the charcoal-gray wall opened soundlessly to his touch. He slipped through; he pulled the door shut behind him.

Well. It did look different without a coffin in the middle. Now it was merely a staging area, dim-lit, with the props and materials of cultish magic neatly shelved or stacked or hung, waiting for the next Call. A broad but low-ceilinged room, its irregular shape was probably caused by the architectural requirements of the stage and temple that surrounded it. That shape, with corners and crannies in odd shadowed places, had added to the eeriness when Boy and his Hasselblad had been in here twenty years ago, but now it all seemed quite benign, merely a kind of surrealistic locker room.

There. The closed door opposite, across the empty black floor. That was the route Boy had not taken last time, when the viewers of the remains had been herded through the main temple and over the stage, past many opportunities to show their sorrow and their continued devotion in a shall we say tangible way, before they were piloted past the dear departed, out the door Boy had just come in, and down the long hall to what at this moment had been converted into the VIP entrance.

After a quick glance left and right, reassuring himself he was alone and all the stray dim corners were empty, he crossed to that far door, cracked it just a jot, and peered one-eyed out at what looked like any backstage. Half a dozen technicians moved about. A hugely complex lightboard stretched away on the right, and beyond it yawned the stage, with Laurena Layla – or whoever – in profile out there, continuing her spiel.

She looked shorter from here, no doubt the effect of the high-ceilinged stage and all those lights. The golden chair still stood invitingly behind her, but she remained on her feet, pacing in front of the chair as she delivered her pitch.

How would it all end? Would she sit in the chair at last, then disappear in a puff of smoke? A trapdoor, then, which would make her devilish hard to intercept.

But Boy didn't think so. He thought they'd be likelier to repeat the understated eloquence of that arrival, that L.L. would simply walk off the stage as she'd simply walked onto it, disappear from public view, and come . . . here.

She would not be alone, he was sure of that. Determinedly alone onstage, once free of the suckers' gaze, she would surely be surrounded by her . . . acolytes? handlers?

Boy had his story now. Well, no, he didn't *have* it, but he knew what it was: the interview with the returned L.L. The *Galaxy* had treated any number of seers and mystics and time travelers and alien abductees with po-faced solemnity over the years, so surely this Layla would understand she was in safe hands when she was in the hands – as he certainly hoped she soon would be – of Boy Cartwright. The question was how to make her see his journal's usefulness to her before her people gave him the boot.

The old clippings; the thank-you note. Waggle those in front of her face, they'd at least slow down the proceedings long enough to give him an opportunity to swathe her in his moth-eaten charm. It had worked before.

His move at this point was to hide himself, somewhere in this room. This was where he was sure she would travel next, so he should conceal himself in here, watch how the scam proceeded, await his opportunity. *Snick*, he shut the stageward door, and, clutching his canvas bag between flaccid arm and trembling ribs, with its valuable cargo of clippings and thank-yous, he turned to suss the place out.

Any number of hiding places beckoned to him, shady nooks at the fringes of the room. Off to the right, in a cranny that was out of the way but not out of sight of either door, stood two long coatracks on wheels, the kind hosts set up for parties, these both bowed beneath the weight of many golden robes. Don one? At the very least, insert himself among them.

As he hurried toward that darkly gold-gleaming niche, a great crowd-roar arose behind him, triumphant yet respectful, gleeful yet awed. Just in time, he thought, and plunged among the robes.

Dark in here, and musty. Boy wriggled backward, looking for a position where he could see yet not be seen, and his heel hit the body.

He knew it, in that first instant. What his heel had backed into was not a sports bag full of laundry, not a sleeping cat, not a rolled-up futon. A body.

Boy squinched backward, wriggling his bum through the golden robes, while the crowd noise outside reached its crescendo and fell away. He found it agony to make this overworked body kneel, but Boy managed, clutching to many robes as he did so, listening to his knees do their firecracker imitations. Down at mezzanine level, he sagged onto his haunches while he pushed robe hems out of the way, enough to see . . .

Well. *This* one won't be coming back. In this dimness, the large stain across the back of the golden robe on the figure huddled on the floor looked black, but Boy knew that, in the light, it would be a gaudier hue. He felt no need to touch it, he knew what it was.

And who. The missing sentry.

I am not alone in here, Boy thought, and as he thought so he was not; the stageward door opened and voices entered, male and female.

Boy cringed. Not the best location, this, on one's knees at the side of a recently plucked corpse. Hands joining knees on the floor, he crawled away from the body through the robes until he could see the room.

Half a dozen people, all berobed, had crowded in, Laurena unmistakable among them, beautiful, imperious, and a bit sullen. The others, male and female, excited, chattered at her, but she paid them no attention, moving in a boneless undulation toward a small makeup table directly across the room from where Boy slunk. They followed, still relieving their tension with chatter, and she waved a slender forearm of dismissal without looking back.

"Leave her alone now."

This was said clearly through the babble by an older woman,

silver-haired and bronze-faced in her golden robe, who stood behind the still-moving Laurena, faced the others, and said, "She needs to rest."

They all agreed, verbally and at length, while the older woman made shooing motions and Laurena sank into a sinuous recline on the stool at the makeup table. Boy, alert for any eruption at all from anywhere, trying to watch the action in front of him while still keeping an eye on every other nook and cranny in the entire room – a hopeless task – watched and waited and wondered when he could make his presence, and his news, known.

The older woman was at last succeeding in her efforts to clear the area. The others backed off, calling final praises and exhortations over their shoulders, oozing out of the room like a film in reverse that shows the smoke go back in the bottle. Boy gathered his limbs beneath him for the Herculean task of becoming once more upright, and the older woman said, "You were magnificent."

Laurena reached a languid arm forward to switch on the makeup lights, in which she gazed upon her astonishingly beautiful and pallid face, gleaming in the dim gray mirror. "What are they to me?" she asked, either to herself or the older woman.

"Your life," the older woman told her. "From now on."

Outside, the faithful had erupted into song, loud and clamorous. It probably wasn't, but it certainly sounded like a speeded-up version of "We Shall Overcome."

Laurena closed her striking eyes and shook her head, "Leave me," she said.

Boy was astonished. An actual human being had said, "Leave me," just like a character in a vampire film. Perhaps this Laurena *was* from the beyond.

In any event, the line didn't work. Rather than leave her, the older woman said, "This next part is vital."

"I know, I know."

"You'll be just as wonderful, I know you will."

"Why wouldn't I be?" Laurena asked her. "I've trained for it long enough."

"Rest," the older woman urged. "I'll come back for you in

fifteen minutes." And with that, at last, she was gone, leaving Laurena semi-alone, the raucous chorus surging when the door was open.

Boy lunged upward, grabbing for handholds among the robes, knees exploding like bags full of water. His first sentences were already clear in his mind, but as he staggered from concealment, hand up as though hailing a cab, movement flashed from off to his left.

Boy looked, and lunging from another hiding place, between himself and the stageward door, heaved a woman, middle-aged, depressingly overweight, in a home permanent, brandishing a stained steak knife from the five-and-ten like a homicidal whale.

Good God! Have they *both* come back? Is there hope for Ruby Mae and Ruby Jean's mom after all?

Laurena's makeup mirror was positioned so that it was the whale she saw in it first, not Boy. Turning, not afraid, still imperious, she leveled her remote gaze on the madwoman and said, "What are you?"

"You *know* who I am!" snarled the madwoman, answering the wrong question. "I'm here to finish what my mother started!"

And in that instant Boy knew everything. He knew that the roused chorus in the temple auditorium meant that cries for help would go for naught. He knew that escape past the madwoman out that door toward the stage was impossible. He knew that he himself could make a dash for the opposite door, the one by which he'd entered, but that Laurena, by the makeup table, would never make it.

But he knew even more. He knew the scam.

However, what he *didn't* know was what to do about it. Where, in all this, was poor Boy's story? Should he zip out the door, report the murders, have *that* scoop? Should he remain here, rescue the maiden without risk to himself and in hope of the usual reward, have *that* scoop (and reward)? (The "without risk to himself" part tended to make that plan Plan B.)

How old was she, *that* was the question, the most important question of all. Answer that one first.

"Dears, dears, dears," he announced in his plummiest voice,

swanning forward like the emcee in *Cabaret*, "play nice, now, don't fight."

They both gaped at him. Like a tyro at the game arcade, the madwoman didn't know what to do when faced with two simultaneous targets. She hung there, flat-footed, one Suppho-se'd shin before the other, knife arm raised, looking now mostly like a reconstructed dinosaur at the museum, while Laurena gave him a stare of cool disbelief and said, "And who are *you*?"

"Oh, but, dear, you must remember me," Boy told her, talking very fast indeed to keep everybody off balance. "Dear old Boy, from the *Galaxy*, I still have your thank-you note, I've treasured it always, I brought it with me in my little bag here." Deciding it would be dangerous to reach into the bag – it might trigger some unfortunate response from the dinosaur – he hurtled on, saying, "Of course, dear Laurena, one had to see you again, after all this time, *report* our meeting, tell the world we—"

The penny dropped at last, and now she *was* shocked. "You're a *reporter*?"

"Oh, you do remember!" Boy exulted. "One *knew* you would!"

"You can't stop me!" the madwoman honked, as though she hadn't been stopped already.

But of course she could reactivate herself, couldn't she? Boy told her, "One did not have the pleasure of meeting your mother, dear, I'm sorry to say, but one did see her in custody and at the trial, and she certainly was forceful."

Whoops; wrong word. "And so am I!" cried the madwoman, and lumbered again toward Laurena.

"No no, wait wait wait!" cried Boy. "I wanted to ask you about your mother." As the madwoman had now halved the distance between herself and the shrinking Laurena, Boy felt an increasing urgency as he said, "I *wrote* about her, you know, in the *Weekly Galaxy*, you must have seen it."

That stopped her. Blinking at Boy, actually taking him in for the first time, a reluctant awe coming into her face and voice, she said, "The *Weekly Galaxy*?"

"Boy Cartwright, at your service," he announced with a smile and a bow he'd borrowed from Errol Flynn, who would not have recognized it. "And as a reporter," he assured her, "I assure you I am not here to alter the situation, but simply to observe. Madam, I will not stand in your way."

Laurena gawked at him. "You won't?"

"Good," the madwoman said, hefted her knife, and thudded another step forward.

"But *first*," Boy went hurriedly on, "I do so want to interview Laurena. Very briefly, I promise you."

They both blinked at him. The madwoman said, "Interview?"

"Two or three questions, no more, and I'm out of your way forever."

"But—" Laurena said.

Taking the madwoman's baffled silence for consent, Boy turned to Laurena. "The silver-haired party was your grandmother," he said.

Managing to find reserves of haughtiness somewhere within, Laurena froze him with a glare: "I am not giving *interviews*."

"Oh, but, dear," Boy said, with a meaningful head nod toward the madwoman, "*this* exclusive interview you will grant, I just know you will, and I must begin, I'm sorry to say, with a personal question. Personal to *me*. I need to know how old you are. You *are* over twenty-one, aren't you?"

"What? Of course I—"

"Honest Injun?" Boy pressed. "One is not a bartender, dear, one has other reasons to need to know. I would guess you to be twenty-five? Twenty-six?" The change in her eyes told him he'd guessed right. "Ah, good," he said with honest relief.

"That's right," the madwoman said.

They both turned to her, having very nearly forgotten her for a few seconds, and she said, "People don't get older in heaven, do they?"

"No, they do not," Boy agreed.

Laurena said, "What *difference* does it make?"

"Well, if you were twenty-one, you see," he explained, "you'd be *my* daughter, which would very much complicate the situation."

"I have no idea what you're talking about," Laurena said, which meant, of course, that she had every idea what he was talking about.

Now he did dare a quick dip into his bag, and before the madwoman could react he'd brought out and shown her his audiocassette recorder. "Tools of the trade, dear," he explained. "No interview without the tape to back it up."

Laurena finally began to show signs of stress, saying, "What are you *doing*? She's got a knife, she's going to *kill* me!"

"Again, darling, yes," Boy said, switching on the machine, aiming it at her. "Just so soon as I leave, at the end of the interview." Because now at last he knew what his story was, he smiled upon her with as much fondness as if she *had* been his daughter – interesting quandary *that* would have been, in several ways – and said, "Of course, in your answers, you might remove our friend's *reason* for wanting to kill you all over again."

Growling, the madwoman bawled, "Nobody's going to stop me! I'm here to finish what my mother started!"

"Yes, of course, you are, dear," Boy agreed. "But what if your mother *did* finish the job?"

The madwoman frowned. "What do you mean? There's Laurena Layla right there!"

"Well, let's ask her about that," Boy suggested, and turned attention, face, and recorder to the young woman. "I must leave very soon," he pointed out. "I only hope, before I go, you will have said those words that will reassure this lovely lady that her mother did not fail, her mother is a success, she can be proud of her mother forever. Can't she, dear?"

Laurena stared helplessly from one to the other. It was clear she couldn't figure out which was the frying pan, which the fire.

To help her, Boy turned back to the madwoman. "You *do* trust the *Galaxy*, don't you?"

"Of course!"

"Whatever this dear child says to us," Boy promised, "you will read in the *Galaxy*. Trust me on this."

"I do," the madwoman said with great solemnity.

Turning to the other, Boy said, "Dear, five million readers are waiting to hear. How was it done? Who are you? Time's getting short, dear."

Laurena struggled to wrap her self-assurance around herself. "You won't leave," she said. "You couldn't."

"Too bad," Boy said with a shrug. "However, the story works just as well the other way." Turning, he took a step toward the hall door as the madwoman took a step forward.

"Wait!" cried the former Laurena Layla.

CRY WOLF

HILARY BONNER

This morning, deep beneath the surface of the Indian Ocean, I watched a pair of six-feet-long Silvertip sharks glide right past me and felt no fear. I just could not believe their beauty. But then, there's a lot about life I can't believe nowadays.

I can't believe how happy I am for a start.

I have always craved adventure. My husband John would merely have regarded my solo trip to the Maldives to learn to dive at the age of 52 as proof of menopausal madness. John was a tax inspector and, perhaps because of his job, he was a very self-contained man. He certainly never wished to share his inner-most thoughts, and neither did he wish to listen to mine. I quickly gave up telling him my dreams. But I never gave up on the dreams. Indeed I used to fill my days with them when John was at work.

Books, music, TV, and video films, all transported me inside my head to other better worlds, to exotic places I never expected to visit where I fell in love with wildly exciting men and embarked on extraordinary adventures. Occasionally, once John had departed in our neat little car, I would walk to Taunton bus station from our neat little house on the outskirts of the town and take the first bus anywhere. Once I went all the way to Plymouth and, untroubled by the minor handicap of never having stepped aboard a boat in my life, stood on the Hoe where Drake played bowls as the Armada approached, imagining what it would be like to sail off around the globe.

I only just got home in time to get dinner on the table by six o'clock sharp. John was a man of routine. I didn't work because that would have got in the way, and we lived so modestly that his income was more than sufficient. We didn't take holidays because he saw no point in them. We didn't have children because he probably saw no point in them either. We hadn't discussed it. It just didn't happen, which as our sex life more or less ended after our first year of marriage was not perhaps a great surprise.

Only by escaping into fantasy worlds did I survive. Unfortunately sometimes my fantasies and reality seemed to become mixed up.

The first time this happened was about a year before John was due to retire.

"I've seen a man selling drugs to children on my street corner," I told the desk clerk at Taunton Police Station. His plump face displayed mild surprise when I gave my address, but I was none the less ushered into an interview room where a bright-eyed young constable called Perkins questioned me thoroughly, and I gave a full description of the perpetrator of the crime.

"Shortish, about 5 ft 6, early 20s, cropped blond hair, a scar down his left cheek and I heard someone call him Jacky."

"We should be able to get somewhere with that, madam," said PC Perkins respectfully. "Thank you very much."

"And I've got the registration number of his motorbike," I added.

But a couple of days later PC Perkins called to tell me that I had given him the number of a hearse owned by a local funeral director.

"I'm terribly sorry, Constable, I must have made a mistake," I confessed.

"Never mind, madam. We may well get this Jacky anyway."

I didn't hear any more though. However, a few months later I had to contact the police again. This time I dialled 999.

"There's a burglary happening next door, right now!" I told the operator dramatically.

A police squad car arrived commendably swiftly and two officers emerged, one uniformed, one wearing an anonymous mid-grey suit. I watched from the back bedroom window as they looked all around Number 31, peering through windows and eventually ringing the doorbell.

After a bit the one in the suit, a thin man with a world-weary sort of face, ambled across the communal lawn to my house. I opened the kitchen door before he knocked.

"I want you to tell me exactly what you saw, Mrs Drinkwater," Detective Sergeant Willis instructed.

"Of course," I replied and gave my evidence fluently. I watched *The Bill*. Regularly. And all the other TV crime dramas. I watched a lot of TV. I knew exactly what was required of a witness.

"I first noticed a white Transit van parked outside Number 31 just after my neighbours the Robsons left for work," I told him. "It was still there half an hour later so I stood by the window and watched for a while. Then two men came out of the house, one black, 6 ft tall, athletic-looking, mid-30s, wearing blue jeans and a brown leather jacket, the other white, about ten years older, couple of inches shorter, heavy build, greying hair and a goatee beard. They were carrying large suitcases. They loaded them into the rear of the van and went back into the house, coming out again carrying a TV set each. That was when I called the police. I watched them go in and out several more times, but they drove off just before you got here. I have the registration number of the van, by the way."

DS Willis looked impressed. But when he returned later that day he was stern.

"Mrs Drinkwater, your neighbours have now checked their home and confirmed that there has been no burglary and no break-in."

"I can only tell you what I saw," I replied lamely.

"Or what you imagined you saw," he muttered. "Oh, and by the way, the registration number you gave me is of a gold Bentley belonging to a company called Somerset Wedding Cars."

I expressed suitable astonishment.

"Wasting police time is a serious offence, Mrs Drinkwater,"

DS Willis said, shaking his head in a particularly weary fashion. "Look, don't do it again, will you?"

"Oh, no, Sergeant, of course not," I said, wondering vaguely if he knew of the earlier drug dealer incident. I kept my word too – well, until six months later when I really had to dial 999 again.

"I've just seen a schoolgirl being abducted," I cried. "Two men dragged her into a Range Rover outside Sainsbury's. They headed off in the direction of the motorway. I have the registration number . . ."

That evening, while John was eating his dinner, DS Willis came around with a uniformed sergeant. It seemed there had been no reports of a missing schoolgirl and the registration number I had supplied was of a Taunton Deane Council refuge collection truck.

"I am afraid we are going to have to arrest you, Mrs Drinkwater," said DS Willis.

John, of course, was horrified. He had known nothing of any of it.

"What on earth am I going to say at work?" he began. "Look, my wife must be ill . . ."

"Well, I wouldn't disagree with that, sir . . ."

"I'll get medical treatment for her; nothing like this will ever happen again. I retire next month. I'll watch her like a hawk."

DS Willis looked me up and down despairingly. I knew well enough what he saw. A dotty middle-aged women of average height and build who may once have been pretty, but it was hard to tell any more.

They let me off with a caution. And John did watch me like a hawk, barely leaving my side. He even accompanied me to the doctor's surgery. I had expected his retirement to drive me barmier than I may already have been. It did. His presence was stifling.

Then, four months after he stopped work, it happened.

Naturally I phoned the police.

"Three men have kidnapped my husband," I said. "They were talking to each other in Russian, I'm sure; perhaps they were Russian Mafia. They bundled him into a black stretch limousine with tinted windows. I have the registration number . . ."

It was DS Willis again who came round.

"The registration number you gave us is of an Aston Martin owned by the Prince of Wales," he said with a sigh. "I'd better speak to your husband, don't you think, madam?"

"But I told you, he's been kidnapped by the Russian Mafia . . ."

This time I was taken to Taunton Police Station and charged with wasting police time. The charges were dropped, however, after a police psychiatrist reported on my disturbed mental state and I agreed to see him on a regular basis.

The police lost interest in me very quickly then even though they eventually had to accept that John had disappeared. I hadn't seen him since the day I reported his kidnap, and neither had anyone else. However, nobody seemed to care.

"Your husband is a grown man and a free agent, Mrs Drink-water," said DS Willis.

"But he hasn't been in contact with anyone, has he? Not just me, not anyone . . ."

"Mrs Drinkwater, you've told us yourself, your husband has no close family apart from you. If he wants to leave home and start a new life that's entirely up to him."

DS Willis's tone of voice made it quite clear that if he were married to me that's what he'd do. Smartish!

So I just set about getting on with my own life. I found I had few problems. The house was in both our names. John had arranged for his pension to be paid into our joint bank account. His savings were in both names too – and they were not inconsiderable, after all we had spent so little. It was all very convenient.

After a while a bank statement arrived which showed that exactly half of John's monthly pension had been taken with his debit card from a central London cash-point. The next month the same amount was also removed.

"Very fair, that," said DS Willis when I told him the news. "Settles it, too."

He informed me the police would be closing the case – their belief now confirmed, no doubt, that my husband had merely had enough of his dotty wife and left her.

Which of course had always been my intention.

I knew well enough that next of kin were always prime suspects in a missing person or murder inquiry. Indeed, the police did go through the motions of searching our house, although not very thoroughly.

They certainly didn't notice that the garage was about two feet shorter inside than out. I had found it quite easy to build that breeze-block wall. I had become rather good at DIY over the years. John never liked paying out money to builders and decorators.

It hadn't been difficult either to dispose of my husband nor to load him into our barrow and wheel him into the integral garage. John was not a big man and I had always been strong.

I knew the drugs the doctor had helpfully prescribed for my supposed mental condition were a potentially lethal cocktail and I had saved them up specially. John noticed nothing amiss with the extra spicy curry I cooked one night for supper. In fact his death seemed quite peaceful. I was pleased about that. I had no desire to cause him pain.

He wasn't a bad man, after all. Just achingly dull. I had coped when he was working and I could disappear into my daytime fantasy worlds. But when he announced that he would be retiring at 60, a full five years earlier than I had expected, I went into a kind of shock, realizing with devastating clarity that I simply would not be able to stand having him round me all day. That was when I began to make my own retirement plans.

I couldn't have him killing my dreams, could I? The sensible alternative seemed to be to kill him. And it all went so awfully well. I know what you must be thinking. Have I no conscience? Apparently not. I feel no guilt.

I realize it is quite likely that one day the false wall to my garage and the body hidden beyond it will be discovered. But the terrible truth is that living with danger and uncertainty has added the spice to my life I have always longed for.

As I bask in warm sunshine on the bleached white beach of a paradise island, watching dolphins jumping just outside the lagoon, I relish being at the centre of an adventure beyond even the wildest of my dreams.

And, you know, whatever happens, I'll never be sorry . . .

"IT'S CLEVER, BUT IS IT ART?"*

M J TROW

The throng had thinned out a little after lunch and the pair were able to be more selective. Before, it had been a matter of edging past, touching titfers, smiling politely and gulping at the champagne before a careless elbow took its toll.

"What about that one, Mr Livingstone?" the younger man asked, slurring the words from the left corner of his mouth.

Mr Livingstone raised his pince-nez that dangled, after the style of Alma-Tadema, on a chain around his neck. He looked at the old lady his companion had pointed out. There was something about her bearing, something in what she was wearing . . . No. He shook his head.

"Let's peruse the Rubens, Daniel," he said loudly and whisked the young man away. He caught him sharply in the shin as they turned into the Upper Gallery.

"You're reading that programme upside down, man," he hissed, twisting his lips into a smile for the benefit of the passers-by, alarmed by the terseness of his remark. After all this *was* the National Gallery. And it *was* celebrating its sixtieth

* From "The Conundrum of the Workshops" by Rudyard Kipling 1890.

birthday. It was a shrine. A dedication to God and the Nation. Even whispers had to be delivered in hushed tones.

"How about that one then?" Daniel had caught sight of another elderly female, crouching beneath a vast canvas of cherubim and seraphim.

Mr Livingstone raised the pince-nez again. "Hmm," he nodded. "This one has distinct possibilities. Are you ready?"

Daniel nodded, a little too enthusiastically perhaps for Livingstone's taste. He squeezed him into a corner, covering his mouth with the programme, "Now, one last time; tell me again."

"I am Lord de Lancey, looking for a painting to buy. Money is no object. You are . . . who is it today, governor?"

"Stop that governor nonsense, Solomon. You're not in your ghastly East End tenement now. I've spent a fortune putting you through Miss MacNeill's School for Speech and Haute Couture. Any more of it and I'll be asking her for my ten shillings back. Today I am Hercules Brabazon Brabazon. I specialise in still life. Which is precisely what you'll be if you muck this up. Got it?"

"Indubitably," Solomon's shady Cockney vanished into the velvet tones of Eton and Trinity. For ten shillings, Miss MacNeill had really done a magnificent job.

"Right," hissed Livingstone, "Here goes," and he broke away from the young man, "No, no, sir, I cannot prostitute myself . . ." and he collided with the old lady. "Madam, forgive me. I must apologise."

"Come, come, sir." Solomon was with him, gripping his elbow, "You may be Hercules Hercules Brabazon, a struggling artist. You may be starving in a garret in . . ." his eyes glazed over as his words failed him. Livingstone pulled an excruciated face, sucking in his lips as though he had just swallowed a lemon –

"Tite Street. But I, Lord de Lancey, cannot possibly . . ."

Livingstone hit him with the chain of his pince-nez. The old lady had moved away from the bizarre pair.

"Pathetic!" snarled Livingstone, "All the finesse of a dray horse. Take it slower, man. You may as well carry a placard on your head with the legend 'I am a confidence trickster.' Now, look as if you're vaguely interested in art and leave the choice of target entirely to me."

"Very good, Mr Livingstone," and Lord de Lancey retired once more behind the unprepossessing facade of Daniel Solomon, part-time sharper's assistant and sometime glimmer of Shadwell parish. And behind the upside down programme.

But he didn't stay quiet for long.

"Oh, my stars!" he flattened himself against a particularly nasty sunset of Alfred Clint's and clutched his top hat nervously.

"What the Devil's the matter?" Livingstone asked him.

"Esclap," Solomon croaked.

"What? None of your gutter cant here. Speak English."

"The law." He'd turned quite pale.

"Solomon, you've turned quite pale. Get a grip on yourself, man," Livingstone's eyes flashed around the murmuring ensemble, drifting like cattle on the cud, lowing contentedly before the canvasses.

"There," Solomon said, "the bloke in the bowler and the Donegal."

"Ah, of course," Livingstone viewed his quarry through the pince-nez, "I should have known. No dress sense at all. Who is he?"

"Name of Lestrade," Solomon whispered. "A Miltonian from the Yard."

"A detective from Scotland Yard, eh?" Livingstone was quietly chewing the chain of the pince-nez. "What rank?"

"Er . . . Inspector. Look at those eyes. Shifty. That rat-like face. Ferrety. That nose . . ."

"Yes," Livingstone frowned. "Where's the end of it?"

"Bitten off, they say," hissed Solomon. "What's he doing here? He's on to us."

Livingstone twirled gracefully on one heel so that he stood between his man and Lestrade, "Not possible, Daniel," he said calmly. "Look at me. In the face, man. Now watch my lips, 'Not possible'."

He had his back to the Yard man, staring icily at Solomon the whole time. "Now, there are two men with him. Right?"

Solomon's left eye crept cautiously upward over Livingstone's right shoulder. He nodded.

"Do you know them?"

Solomon shook his head.

"The secret of a truly great artist like myself is observation. The tall one. The one with the curly blond hair and blue eyes. You've known more of the boys-out-of-blue than I have. Does he look like a policeman?"

"Well, I . . ."

"Of course he doesn't. Look at his clothes, man. His bearing. Eton, I'd say. And probably the Guards."

"Which Guards?" Solomon asked mindlessly, waves of panic running through him.

"*The* Guards," a horrified Livingstone told him.

"What about the other one?" Solomon quivered. "The little one. Was he in the Ghurkas?"

"Please," Livingstone was brittle. "Spare me your working-class wit. That is Mr Edward Lutyens. Second to Ruskin he is the most revered art critic in the country. But, unlike Ruskin, he probably knows that even married ladies have pubic hair."

"Aaargh!" a strangled cry from a married lady nearby told them that they had lost another quarry.

"Damn!" Livingstone snarled.

"What say we get out of here, Mr Livingstone?" Solomon hoped.

"What say you stop your knees knocking and act like a man? You say this Lestrade knows you?"

Solomon nodded, swallowing, "Felt my collar a couple of years back."

"What for?"

"Because the bastard enjoys it," Solomon's whisper had become falsetto.

Livingstone patted his arm, "There, there, my dear fellow. Down, down, thou climbing sorrow. We've got to face him."

"What?"

"What did he arrest you for?"

"Well, I wasn't exactly arrested . . ."

"Questioned, then?"

"Knobbing," Solomon looked a little sheepish.

Livingstone instinctively took a pace backward, careful to keep his back tightly against Huskisson's "Fairies".

"It's a fairground game," he assured him. "Under and Over."

Livingstone looked relieved, "All right," he said. "Now, remember. You are Lord de Lancey. Third son of the Marquess of Uffington. Educated at Eton and Trinity. Ask this Lestrade if you've met before. Give him one of your cards."

Solomon's jaw and programme dropped simultaneously, "Are you mad?" he hissed.

"Do it, Daniel," Livingstone said through clenched teeth. "The art world has turned its back on me once too often. Today, it starts paying up in earnest."

"No, look, couldn't we stick with the women? What about her over there? That one with the horse face and the awful frock?"

"That is Kate Greenaway, Daniel," Livingstone told him. "She doesn't sponsor poor artists. She *is* one. Now leave the subject to me please. Go on, man. The place will be shutting soon."

And Solomon drew himself up to his full height and with his knees knocking and his heart thumping crossed the floor of the gallery to the trio of spectators who were admiring the Tissot.

"Bless you," said Lestrade as he arrived.

"Ain't we met, sir? By Jove, I know that face!"

Livingstone curled up in a corner. Solomon sounded like a Regency Buck only eighty years too late.

"Er . . ." the Inspector's eyes narrowed.

"Eton, was it?" Solomon suggested.

"No," said Lestrade.

"Trinity, then," Solomon persisted.

"No, I don't believe."

"This is Inspector Sholto Lestrade," said the tall, blond curly man. "I am Harry Bandicoot. This is Mr Edward Lutyens. You have the advantage of us, sir."

Lestrade looked at his big companion. It was a common situation. Most people had the advantage of Harry Bandicoot.

"My card," Solomon flipped it adeptly from his waistcoat pocket, "de Lancey. Lord. Son of the Marquess of Effingham, don't you know."

"Really?" said Lestrade.

"Inspector?" Solomon was in full flight. "On the buses, are you?"

"No, the police," Bandicoot leapt in with his usual subtlety.

"Really? Peeler, eh?"

Livingstone was about to crawl away, his partner rumbled, when he heard sounds of merriment from the floor. He saw Lestrade tip his bowler, Bandicoot shake Solomon's hand. Even the acerbic Lutyens was smiling. Good God, had Solomon actually pulled it off? And as he turned, Livingstone's joy was complete. There stood a large old lady, arguably the wrong side of sixty, awash with make-up that gave her a deathly pallor. Her jewels would have shamed any Maharajah and she was alone and she was patently a suitable case for treatment.

She craned forward with her lorgnette to examine one of Richard Dadd's later works and sighed, "I'm very much in two minds about this painting!"

He was interrupted in his approach to the dowager by a beaming, triumphant Daniel Solomon, whose Lord de Lancey had clearly, bearing in mind Lutyens's presence, been a critical success.

"Well?" Livingstone sidled behind one of Landseer's bronze mastiffs.

"Very," grinned Solomon.

"I mean, how did they take it?"

"Lestrade didn't know me from Adam," he said.

"You see. I told you. All you need is nerve, Danny boy. What of the others?"

"The blond one is obviously an idiot. Lutyens was too absorbed in his paintings."

Livingstone noticed that Solomon's vowels were better, his consonants sharper than erstwhile. The de Lancey persona had stayed. Well, that was to the good. Chance to deflate the cocky young puppy after the dowager was safely bagged.

"The blond one's here taking advantage of the Gallery's celebrations to buy a painting for his wife. It's her birthday and he wants to surprise her."

"Why does he need a Scotland Yard Inspector?" Livingstone was prepared to play Devil's Advocate for a while. He didn't want to rattle his young protégé, but at the same time, he couldn't risk walking into a trap.

"They're friends," Solomon told him, "Lestrade's off duty."

"Do they ever sleep?" Livingstone wondered aloud.

"Trust me," it was the young man's turn to pat shoulders. "The arm of the law isn't as long as all that. You were right, Livingstone . . . er . . . Mr Livingstone. You persuaded me there was nothing to worry about. And there isn't. Now, what about that one over there?"

Livingstone raised his eyes heavenwards, "That's Lady Butler, Daniel. She's painted more soldiers than Catherine the Great got through. Fear not, I've made my choice."

In another part of the Gallery, Inspector Sholto Lestrade pressed what was left of his nose against a particularly turgid canvas. He craned first this way, then that.

"Is this the right way up, Mr Lutyens?" he asked.

"Of, course," the expert replied. "It's by J.M.W. Turner."

"Ah," Lestrade nodded sagely. That seemed to say it all.

"You know, Sholto," Harry Bandicoot was doing his best to look knowledgeable. "That de Lancey fellow. He's only a few years my junior, wouldn't you say?"

"Hum? What of it, Harry?" Lestrade turned away a little unnerved by one of Baron Leighton's twenty-foot nudes.

"Well, he told us he was at Eton. I don't remember anyone by that name."

"There, there, Harry." Lestrade patted his friend's arm. "You were probably too busy with all that Cocklid and Sissero to notice. Good Lord, is this *the* Thomas Hardy, Mr Lutyens?"

Lutyens raised a tolerant eyebrow, "Well, it's *a* Thomas Hardy, certainly, Mr Lestrade."

"What do you think Letitia would like, Harry?" Lestrade asked.

"Well, I must confess, Sholto, I'm no great shakes when it comes to art. That's why I asked Mr Lutyens along. He knows what I like."

"Perhaps this Conder?" Lutyens suggested as they reached the next canvas.

"Yes, yes, very nice," Bandicoot mused, "I do believe I've met his wife, you know. Anna."

"Whatever you choose, Mr Bandicoot," Lutyens said. "Please not a Millais. I always found him fundamentally philistine."

"Of course," Bandicoot nodded sagely. "Er . . . what about this?" He consulted his programme.

"Holman Hunt? Better, but still a crude and rudimentary colourist without taste or sensibility."

Lestrade had wondered into the far corner. A canvas of mournful tombstones caught his eye. It was his own fault. He had pressed too closely to see the title, not quite believing it and the ornate plaster frame had fetched him a nasty one as he stooped. And after all that, he *had* read it correctly – "The Churchyard" by Thomas Churchyard.

"There are an awful lot of von Hurkomers," he heard Bandicoot say and felt very much inclined to agree.

Livingstone was ready now, the subject framed by his pince-nez. Solomon, buoyed by his wool-putting over the dark eyes of Lestrade, was ready too. He nodded and the gambit began.

"Call yourself an artist?" Solomon asked imperiously. "You are a rank amateur, sir. Be off with you."

"Please, sir," Livingstone cringed, showing just enough frayed cuff for effect. "If you would but look at my work . . ."

"Gross ineptitude. Utter rubbish, patent balderdash. You can't hoodwink a de Lancey, sir. Not a son of the Marquess of Uppingham, anyway," and Solomon spun on his hired heel and strode away. Then, suddenly remembering his lines, "What did you say your name was, by the way?"

"Brabazon. Hercules Brabazon."

"Yes, well . . . be off with you, Brabazon. I've no time for starving artists, no matter how brilliant they may be. I've only your word for it that you're a genius." And this time he felt for good.

Livingstone hung his head and pulled the tatty crumpled sketch dejectedly from his waistcoat pocket.

"My poor man," a voice made him turn. The bait had been cast on the waters and the hook was being nibbled. "Forgive

me, I couldn't help overhearing . . . Did that . . . er . . .
gentlemen call you Hercules Brabazon?"

"He did, Madam," Livingstone inclined his head.

"Not Hercules *Brabazon* Brabazon?"

"The same."

"The famous artist!" The dowager clapped her gloved hands
together in delight.

"Famous, madam?" Livingstone laughed bitterly. "You are
too kind, though, I fear, incorrect."

"But surely, you are well hung in all the major galleries?"

"I do have one small still life in Gallery Three, dear lady.
But, alas, it does not pay the rent."

"The rent? Have you fallen on hard times, Mr Brabazon?"

"Rather, Madam, I have never left them, Mrs . . . er . . .?"

"Oh, forgive me. How unutterably rude," she held out her
hand for Livingstone to kiss. "I am Lady Throckmorton."

She paused for effect.

"Of the Northamptonshire Throckmortons."

Livingstone kissed the hand elegantly and all but raked the
gems from their gold housings with his teeth.

"Why, Mr Brabazon, what have you got there?"

"Oh, a sketch. Nothing, I assure you."

"May I see?"

For a while he feigned coyness, but eventually capitulated.

"Oh, very well, if you must."

She unfolded it carefully and caught her breath, "This is
exquisite," she said. "Those grapes, that dead . . . thing. So
lifelike."

"A mere trifle," he told her.

She looked more closely with the lorgnette. "So it is." Then
she saw the worn cuffs, the inferior gloves, the grubby collar.

"Mr Brabazon, I must buy this instantly."

"But . . . ? Oh, no, dear lady. It is not for sale."

"Surely. Shall we say five pounds?" She rummaged in her
handbag, then checked herself. "What am I thinking of? Shall
we say twenty?"

"No, no, that is far too generous. Oh well, if you press it upon
me," and he snatched the notes from her hand. "This will help
towards the rent. And indeed, it will go some way towards the

doctor's bills. As for the pawnbroker . . ." he sighed and turned away.

"Doctor? Are you unwell, Mr Brabazon?"

"I? No, I am fine, Lady Throckmorton. Apart from the astigmatism," he squeezed his eyes delicately and hobbled away from her. "And the assegai at Majuba Hill."

"Majuba Hill?" Lady Throckmorton quizzed him. "But I thought we were fighting the Boers there?"

"Indeed, madam, we were," Livingstone's mind was racing. Had he overplayed his hand? "But the sneaky curs had a contingent of native levies with them. Some cowardly black skewered me as I was sketching the contours of the hill for General Colley."

"Tsk, tsk," Livingstone sensed he had renewed his grip. "The doctor's bills are for dear little Effie. She is three today and has the fever. If only I could retrieve my brushes and my palette . . ."

"Mr Brabazon," Lady Throckmorton held up her hand. "You must say no more. I had no idea that our artists were struggling in this way. I am myself a Patroness of the Arts – oh, in a small way, of course. You must allow me to visit your studio and purchase a vast quantity of your works."

"Madam, I cannot allow it."

"Not?" she looked heartbroken under her rouge. "Tell me it isn't so."

"I have no studio, madam. Oh, I had one for a while of course. But I had to abandon it – the rent was so extortionate. I am currently living under . . ." his voice tailed away.

"Under . . ." she pressed him.

"Under the arches at Charing Cross."

She caught her breath, "But that place is notorious, Mr Brabazon, as a thieves' kitchen. Only the other day, His Grace the Bishop was condemning it in his sermon."

"Indeed, indeed," Livingstone crushed his testicles surreptitiously until his eyes welled with tears, "I fear it is so. At least we know the hour of the day – and the night – I and my thirteen children – by the arrival and departure of the trains."

"And Mrs Brabazon?" Lady Throckmorton's eyes were equally wet, though not for the same reason.

"Alas," he turned to face the nearest Landseer. "The cholera took her two years ago."

"You poor, poor man," she clutched his arm with a power rare in a woman her age. "Here," she ferreted again in her bag. "This is my town address. Please call this evening. Shall we say seven?"

"But I fear, Lady Throckmorton, that I have had to sell all my canvasses. I have nothing to offer."

"Talent, Mr Brabazon. You have years of creation ahead of you. If I can play my humble part in ensuring that that talent is not lost to the world."

"Er . . . how humble?" Livingstone ventured, hoping the leer of gold would not pierce the pince-nez façade of abjection.

"Ah," Lady Throckmorton's face fell. "I regret I can only let you have a cheque for £100 at the moment."

"One hundred?" Livingstone stepped back, clutching his heart, "I have no words, dear lady . . ."

"But should you call at seven, I will by arrangement with my bank, be able to furnish you with . . . shall we say £5000?"

"£5000," Livingstone repeated dumbly.

"All right, then," smiled Lady Throckmorton. "We shall say it. A bientôt, Mr Brabazon."

"Indeed dear lady," and Livingstone was still staring at his knees in the lowness of his bow as the dowager swept from the Gallery.

"Rather a change all this, eh, Sholto?" Bandicoot said.

"What is, Harry?" Lestrade asked.

"Soaking up the culture, I mean. Rather a far cry from skullduggery at the Yard?"

"Ah, yes. It's hard to imagine any crime being committed within these walls. Except for that Turner fellow of course."

"What do you make of this Archer Shee, Mr Bandicoot?" Lutyens asked.

"Bless you," Lestrade and Bandicoot chorused.

"Three thousand pounds?" Solomon was beside himself.

"As I live and breathe," Livingstone settled back in the snug of the Coal Hole. "At seven tonight."

"This is the last time we drink here, then, governor," the

younger man swigged his ale, "I've got to hand it to you. Half inching that bit of scribble from that Brabazon bloke was inspired. Can you draw, by the way?"

"How dare you?" Livingstone bridled. He was glad now he had short-changed his underling.

Solomon glossed over the affront in his complacency. "This is retirement then, Mr Livingstone?" he asked, puffing on his cigar contentedly.

"It may very well be, Daniel," Livingstone quaffed his pint.

"And the best part of it was fooling that idiot Lestrade. He didn't have a clue who I was."

Livingstone gathered up his hat and coat. "I have a tryst to keep. At Lady Throckmorton's. See you tomorrow at the usual place?"

"Tomorrow at the Dock and Doris," Solomon raised his glass. "It's been a pleasure working with you, Mr Brabazon."

"And with you, Lord de Lancey."

Livingstone was shown into an oak-panelled library by a flunkey with greying hair and an ill-fitting waxed moustache. The man looked vaguely familiar.

"I will tell Lady Throckmorton that you are here, sir," he said and left.

When the doors opened again, the dowager entered. Livingstone rushed to kiss her hand. This time she wore no gloves and he was surprised at the smoothness of her fingers.

"Madame," he said.

"Mr Brabazon," she gestured to him to sit, "I think we said £4000, did we not?"

"Er . . . I think we said £5000," he corrected her and chuckled, squirming a little on the cushions.

She smiled at him sweetly, "Of course," she said, "how remiss." She crossed to a table and drew out a cheque, signing it with a flourish. Livingstone crossed to her, his fingers wriggling at his sides.

"Dear lady," he signed, as the paper reached his grasp. "Dear lady."

"Dearer than you know, Mr Brabazon," a voice broke the magic of the moment.

Livingstone shot from the lady's side to confront a rather rat-faced man with a Donegal and bowler. He appeared to have mislaid the tip of his nose.

"Have you met Inspector Lestrade, Mr Brabazon?" Lady Throckmorton asked. Her voice sounded suddenly younger, her step was lighter. She smiled sweetly at Livingstone and took off her grey wig, shaking free the long, golden curls.

"How is dear Effie this evening?" Lestrade asked him.

"Er . . ."

"And the arches. Comfortable enough for you? Oh, and the thirteen children?"

"I . . ."

"You know, for a man with an assegai wound, Mr Brabazon, you crossed the floor a moment ago with astonishing speed."

"Ah . . ."

"Letitia," Lestrade crossed to the ex-dowager. "By the way, have you met Mrs Bandicoot? I think we'd better return this sketch to Hercules Brabazon. Carefully wearing gloves, of curse. Unlike you were when you helped yourself from the man's studio the other day, Mr Livingstone. I think Sergeant Collins at the Yard will have a field day with your dabs all over it."

"How did you know?" Livingstone sneered.

"As someone I once knew apparently never said, it was elementary. You see, Mr Lutyens, who was with us at the National, happens to know the *real* Hercules Brabazon by sight. Which wouldn't have mattered at all, of course, had Lady Throckmorton been the *real* Lady Throckmorton. We've been watching you for some time. Merely waiting for confirmation, so to speak, I'm afraid you've fleeced your last old lady, Mr Livingstone."

"Lady . . . whoever you are. I appeal to you . . ."

"Not in the slightest, I'm afraid, Mr Livingstone," Letitia countered.

"You see, it's all over, Mr Livingstone," Lestrade poured himself a brandy. "The gentleman who showed you in, did he look familiar to you?"

"Why, yes. He did," Livingstone admitted, "I couldn't place him."

Lestrade clicked his tongue, "I really must see him about that. But he is getting better. Slowly. Walter!"

The door opened and the flunkey entered.

"This is Sergeant Dew," he said. "He's been following you since you left the National – a little too obviously, I fear." Dew scowled. It was back to the drawing board for him. "You live rather well for a man with thirteen children. You've never been married in your life. And the closest you've come to the arches are some you tried to draw before you were thrown out of Mr Prinsep's Art School at the age of twenty-two."

"That's a damnable lie!" roared Livingstone. "I could have been a great artist. A legend!"

"Of course," Lestrade quaffed his glass. "If you'd had any talent at all."

The door crashed back to reveal a tall blond man carrying an unconscious dark one over his shoulder.

"Ah, Harry," Lestrade said, pouring them all a drink, "I see you've run into Lord de Lancey."

"Indeed," Bandicoot grinned. "And the way he went down after a single right hook, Sholto. I told you he wasn't at Eton."

"Sergeant Dew informed us of your whereabouts. In case you split up – as you did after the Coal Hole, I wanted Harry to be there, just in case. Walter, be so good as to take charge of Mr Livingstone and get some lads to fetch his assistant, will you? I'll see you at Bow Street later. Let's see," he counted silently on his fingers. "That's er . . . fourteen counts of false pretences, ditto of obtaining money under same, eighteen of theft, etcetera, etcetera. I'll leave the paperwork to you, Walter."

"Thank you, sir."

"Mr Livingstone," Letitia raised her glass. "A toast before you go. 'Ars gratia artis.'"

"'Ars gratia artis,'" Bandicoot took up the cry.

Lestrade demurred. His Latin wasn't what it was. But he was a little shocked by Letitia. Surely that meant something rather rude?

ONE FOR THE MONET

DAVID STUART DAVIES

I walked out into the midnight drizzle leaving the smoky claustrophobic atmosphere of the Velvet Cage. As the door swung behind me I could still hear the shrill notes of Tommy Parker's virile trumpet attacking the St Louis Blues. There was a blackout and yet the streets were far from quiet. Some soldiers on leave, slightly the worse for wear, staggered past me, noisy in their contentment. They were pursued by a couple of late night ladies who were trying in vain to attract their attention. Rain and the blackout were bad for business.

I'd had too much whisky, lost more than I could afford at the roulette wheel and was ready for my bed. As I wandered into Tottenham Court Road in the vain hope of finding a taxi to take me home, I became aware that I was being followed. The footsteps behind me were slightly out of time with mine, producing a surreal echo. I sobered up quickly and moved to the pavement's edge before spinning round to face my shadow. I found myself staring into the muzzle of a Luger pistol.

"Mr Hawke, we wish to engage your services." The owner of the pistol was short and stocky, wore a dark belted raincoat and a large-brimmed fedora which was pulled down in order to hide his face. The voice was Germanic.

"Your approach is a little unconventional but as long as you wield that pistol your wish is my command."

"You are a detective? A private detective."

"That's what it says on my card."

"We do business."

"Sure. Why don't you come round to my office in the morning: Kingsgate Court, off—"

"Tonight, my friend, before it is too late." So saying, he whistled shrilly and about a hundred yards down the road in the direction of Cambridge Circus a car engine started up and two bright moonlike headlights arced into life.

"We take a little ride," said my Germanic friend.

"Great. If you're going past Regent's Park you could drop me off at my place. It really is way past my bedtime."

Herr Gangster did not respond to this pleasantry. He merely waved the gun aggressively, indicating that I should get into the car which had now pulled up by the side of us.

Let me introduce myself. I'm Johnny Hawke or Johnny One-Eye as my intimates call me because – well you're not dumb, you can guess why. This eye-patch isn't for show. Accident with a gun while training to join the fray in 1939. Invalided out of army on to the civilian scrapheap. Fell into detective work through a series of "accidents", which would take too long to explain here and besides you want to know what why I've been abducted by a Luger-toting Kraut.

I was bundled into the back of the car and told to lie down. It's easy to obey orders like that when you have a gun poking into your lumbar region. As we drove away, I tried to figure what this was all about. If these guys were German spies, what use could I be to them? Do they know something I don't? Well, of course they do, dummy, I told myself. For one thing, they know where you're going.

The journey was short. We didn't leave the heart of London, although I guessed we'd gone south of the river. The car jerked to a halt and I was invited to step out. We seemed to be in a yard behind a large warehouse. Blackout or no blackout, a single shaded lamp threw down a small pool of light and illuminated a metal door which opened at our approach. A burly man with bristles instead of hair appeared and grinned in greeting. "Good lads. The boss said you'd be 'ere about now."

"And so we are," remarked my German friend, who strangely had lost all trace of accent. I was led into a small room in which two men sat drinking whisky from teacups. One man, fat, in a dark suit and a lurid tie that could curdle milk at a hundred paces stood up and flashed a grin at me, revealing a row of teeth dotted with gold fillings. His mouth was probably worth more than all my worldly goods put together. I knew him. Sammy Levine, one of the black market gang bosses; he ruled the roost south of the river. We had run into each on a few occasions in the past. Usually in courtroom four of the Old Bailey.

He held out his hand. I ignored it and took a Craven A from my cigarette case and lit up. "What is this cloak-and-dagger nonsense all about?" I said, attempting to cover my irritation with affected nonchalance.

"Cloak-and-dagger!" He wheezed a laugh. "I like, it Johnny. I like it." His girth wobbled with further merriment. With an audience full of Sammy Levines I could make it big at the London Palladium.

"And how come Herr Hitler here suddenly sounds like a Home Counties vicar?"

More laughter – this time they all joined in.

"Well, you've had your joke, folks, so if you'll excuse me I have an appointment with a mattress." I made to leave but my two abductors, losing their grins, took a step forwards.

"No one is going anywhere yet," snarled the Home Counties vicar in a very unclerical manner.

"Sit down, Johnny. Have a snifter of whisky, unruffle your feathers a bit," grinned my host.

I did just that and waited.

"I gotta job for you, Johnny," said Sammy Levine at length. "Legit work, I need not add."

"A job? You want to engage me . . ."

"Indeed I do. As a private dickie I hear that you're the best."

"I have an office . . ."

"Not my style, Johnny. I don't want no punks to know I'm visiting private dickies. Besides, I like a little cloak-and-dagger, to use your words." My words obviously amused him because he wheezed with merriment again.

"And my German abductor . . .?"

"Arthur. One of my boys. An actor when he can get work. He was in movies before the war – bit parts but he once had a scene with George Formby."

"Turned out nice again," Arthur grinned in a close approximation to the film star whom I hated the most. "It does me good to try out accents, keeps my hand in."

I turned to Sammy. "You have a job?"

"I do." Sammy poured me another drink. "OK, boys, scram. Leave the private dickie and me alone."

Like well-trained children, they left in single file.

"Before we go any further, you must know that I do not work outside the law. I don't play cards under the table."

"You insult me," he said in a tone that told me that I had done nothing of the kind. "I told you this is legit."

"Then why not go to the police?"

"And have my mother turn in her grave – if she were dead yet. Coming to a private dickie is bad enough."

"Shoot the dice, then, let me see your spots."

"Hey, you sound like one of those gangster geezers with the bent fedoras in the movies."

"In your company I feel like one. So what's the problem? It's late and I would like to lie down in my own bed before sunrise."

"Some bastard stole somethin' from me."

"Money?"

A giant shake of the head.

"Not money but my Monet."

There's something funny about this whisky, I thought. It's playing tricks with my hearing. "Again," I said cupping my hands to my ears.

"Someone has stolen my Monet – my lovely painting."

"Monet as in Claude Monet, the French Impressionist."

"Yeah, that's the guy. Had a lovely way with shadows."

"And how on earth did you come to own a Monet?"

Sammy smiled and rubbed his nose. "One does favours for certain geezers as we travel along life's highway and sometimes they express their gratitude in the most unusual ways – if you see what I mean."

I did see what he meant. Stolen goods is what he meant. And this is what Mr Sammy Levine called "legit".

"All I'm asking is for you to get it back for me. One stolen item returned. Don't really matter what it is. Technically it's mine, was in my gaff and someone pinched it."

"Someone. Any idea who?"

"Of course I have. Steve Blakeway, the geezer from over the river who's being trying to muscle in on my patch for months. He'd do anything to rock my boat."

"You have any proof, any facts to support this idea?"

"Course not. I just feel it in my waters."

"And it's high tide."

"You bet."

"Where did this painting disappear from?"

"My gaff. The family home."

Somehow I found it difficult to picture Sammy Levine with a family.

"A nice little villa in Pimlico. I live there for the moment with my ma."

"For the moment?"

"I'm getting married next spring." He suddenly dug his paw-like hand into his inside pocket and withdrew a glossy postcard-sized photograph. "This is the lucky lady. Susie. She's a looker, ain't she?"

She certainly was a looker: blonde, bright-eyed and, from what I could tell from the photo, well upholstered. She was also about twenty-five years younger than Sammy who, I reckoned, had pedalled well past the fifty mark. But apart from her looks, there was something else about the girl that aroused my interest. I knew her. Knew her as Lena Fortune, a singer. In fact I had seen her not many hours before in the Velvet Cage. She'd sung a few numbers with Tommy Parker's Quartet and then spent a fair amount of time smooching round the double bass player, leaving streaks of red lipstick all over his face. Not the actions, I reckoned, of a devoted fiancée, but I was not about to tell Sammy that. He who destroys the dreams of a fat gangster is likely to end up in a box.

"I'll need to visit the scene of the crime and see if I can work out how the theft took place."

"No problem – except how the theft really did take place. There are no signs round the place. No windows smashed, no telltale muddy footprints. I reckon even Sherlock Holmes would have been baffled."

"Great."

"I'll tell ma you'll be around tomorrow morning."

"After lunch, Sammy. I need my beauty sleep and it's after one a.m. now."

He nodded sympathetically and then scribbled down two addresses on a scrap of paper. "That's my gaff and this is where Steve Blakeway hangs out. I reckon if you took a shufty in his front room you'd find my Monet dangling over his fireplace."

I shrugged my shoulders in response. "I'll do what I can."

"Better than what you can, Mr One-Eye, better. I'll reserve a table at the Velvet Cage for midnight tomorrow night. One of your favourite spots, I gather. You can report back to me then and I'll introduce you to Susie, Susie Brook – she'll be singing there under her stage name: Lena Fortune."

A night for surprises.

The Home Counties vicar ran me home, talking to me now in the thick brogue of an Ulster peat-cutter. It was three in the morning when I fell into my pit but sleep did not come easily. I was very unhappy to be involved with this case. It was not one I would have chosen to take, if there had been any choice in the matter. I realized I had better get Mr Levine's Monet back or I would probably become intimately acquainted with the mud on the bottom of the River Thames.

Detective Sergeant David Llewellyn took three inches off the top of his pint before I had sat down. "It's been a dry morning," he said by way of explanation.

I smiled and said nothing.

"Go on, then, Johnny, fire away. You don't drag a man away from his desk at the Yard just to buy him a pint out of the goodness of your heart. You want something in return."

"You make me sound so calculating."

"I've always been a good judge of character." He grinned and wiped away the froth from his lips. "Not a bad pint, man. A second would go down a treat."

I ordered another beer for David and a whisky chaser for me.

We were in the Punch and Judy Inn, about a handcuff's throw from Scotland Yard. I liked to think of Detective Sergeant Llewellyn as my mole at the Yard. In the past I've tipped him off about certain nefarious activities I'd got wind of and in return he wasn't averse to throwing some information my way, if there was a pint or three included.

"Steve Blakeway," he said pulling his face. "The blighter's got form all right but he's been lying low for a while. The word is that he's got a new lady in his life and she likes things on the level. Never know, she might make a new man of him."

"What's she like? Not blonde carrying a couple of 38s?"

David grinned and shook his head. "Never seen her but, if she is, I wish I had. If you want a ganders I believe they hang out at that new roadhouse off the Islington High Street."

If there is a posh part of Pimlico, Oakham Grove was certainly it. Neat hedges, trimmed lawns and houses with names instead of numbers. Sammy Levine's gaff was The Lodge. Mrs Levine, Sammy's mum, who had been expecting me, let me in. She was like a junior version of Sammy in a dress. Her thinning hair was dyed the colour of wilting beetroot and the make-up had been applied with care . . . several times. There was so much powder on that ancient face she looked as though she'd dunked her phizzog in a bag of self-raising flour.

She made me wipe my feet twice before allowing me to enter. "I'm very houseproud you know. If one has beautiful things one must keep them beautiful."

I nodded in agreement.

"My son told me to expect you. From the insurance company, aren't you?"

"Something like that," I muttered.

"So you want to see where the painting was?"

She led me into a room off the hallway which appeared to be an office – Sammy's office I surmised, but everything was so tidy, the woodwork sparkling, the books and papers arranged so neatly that it was clear that no one actually worked in here. Even the coal of the unlit fire in the grate appeared to have been polished.

It was over the fireplace that I saw a rectangular shadow where the picture had hung.

"I know, I know," said Mrs Levine, in some distress. "It looks awful, doesn't it? I've tried household soda on it but it won't budge. There's nothing else for it: the walls will have to be painted."

"Unless the picture turns up."

Mrs Levine looked flabbergasted at this suggestion. "Well, yes, I suppose," she said at length.

I asked her to describe the painting.

Her mouth turned down as though she had eaten something with a very unpleasant taste. "I couldn't see what Sammy saw in it in the first place. It was called *Bathers by the Bridge*. A real murky-looking thing. Couldn't tell if they were bathers or just big reeds sticking up."

Mrs Levine was not an art connoisseur, then.

I examined the room and as Sammy had affirmed there were no signs of entry despite there being a large widow facing the lawn at the back of the house. In fact the window catches had been painted over and were undisturbed. It was true: Sherlock Holmes would have been baffled by this caper and so I would have been if one thing I'd sensed here hadn't triggered something off in my brain much later. As I leant against the windowpane, my hands on the mahogany sill, I heard a shrill cry behind me.

"Careful. You'll leave greasy marks." No sooner had I moved back than Mrs Levine, with the speed of a whirling dervish, had produced a yellow duster and tin of polish and was burnishing the contaminated woodwork.

I left, my hostess seeing me off the premises still clutching her duster and polish. No doubt she would have the room fumigated once I was out of sight.

The roadhouse off the Islington Road was called the Pink Flamingo – what else? – and it was rather a posh affair. Here was I in my pinstripe double-breasted elbowing my way to the bar through a sea of penguin suits and ladies in shiny dresses that redefined the word tight. I have a good eye for barmen. There were four on duty and fully occupied, despite the fact that the little hand had not reached ten yet. I refused to be

served by a tall young man with a harassed expression and a
scalp of exploding black hair and waited until I could attract the
attention of the senior member of the serving troop, a ginger-
haired fellow who affected a lugubrious grin which is, I know, a
contradiction in terms. But you should have seen him. Somewhere a circus was waiting.

I ordered a dry martini and told Ginger Nut to have one too.
In gratitude, he showed me his teeth. They belonged in a circus
too. As I handed over my money, I beckoned him nearer.
"Looking for a Steve Blakeway and his lady friend. Got a
package for them. Can you point them out?"

My question reaffirmed to Ginger Nut that there were really
no kind strangers in the world. He frowned and cynicism
returned to his weary eyes. Everything had a price, it seemed.
There was no such thing as a free drink. You always had to
provide some service in return.

He pointed to a corner table where a handsome young man
was chatting merrily to a pretty young woman. They were, in
the words of romantic fiction, lost in a world of their own. The
woman was blonde and curvaceous – but she was not Susie
Brook or her singing alter ego, Lena Fortune.

I gave Ginger Nut a broad grin and a mock salute and left the
bar. I observed the lovebirds for some minutes. They seemed
comfortable and engrossed in each other's company. It seemed
such a pity to intrude.

But I did.

I slid in beside Steve. I thought this was the safer option.

"Sorry to interrupt the party, Steve, but I wonder if you
could answer me a question?"

The gooey, cootchie-coo expression vanished from Steve's
swarthy features. "Who the hell are you?"

"A friend, I assure you. I'm on an errand for . . ." At this
point I leant forwards and whispered a name in his ear. It was
the name of the blackest villain in London's gangland – a
monster shark in the pool where Sammy Levine and Steve
Blakeway were mere minnows. At the mention of the name,
Steve's body stiffened and his eyes narrowed.

"What is it, Stevie, baby?" his paramour asked in a voice
borrowed from a cartoon mouse.

"Nothin' sweetheart," he replied, his eyes not leaving mine. "You take a trip to powder your nose while I have a quick business chat with this fellow here."

Sweetheart pouted, her thick pink lips pushing forwards like the end of an effeminate sink plunger. "I'm always powdering my nose when your business pals come round. It's a wonder I've got a nose left."

She was obviously a literal girl. A five-pound note crackled in Steve's hand and he slipped it to his lady love. "See if you can get yourself a nice cocktail on the way."

"Oh, Stevie, thank you." The eyes brightened and the elastic candy lips parted in a broad smile. With a giggle she left us alone.

Steve returned his attention to me. "So tell me what can I do for Mr—"

I held up my hand before he got to the name I'd just whispered. The one I'd lied about. "Please, Steve, not in public," I said. "You know how sensitive this gentleman is about his moniker being bandied about among the hoi polloi."

"Are they here too?"

"You never know. And coppers too. So no names, eh?"

Steve ran a finger around the inside of his collar. I'd got him nervous, which is what I wanted.

"Know anything about art, Steve?"

"Art who? You mean the geezer that copped it for the Brixton mail robbery?"

"Art as in paintings."

Steve did not have to think long on this one. He shook his head. "Nah."

"Specialist stuff."

"Certainly is. I can't tell the difference between a kid's scribble and Michael what's 'is face . . . Italian."

"Angelo. Michelangelo."

"Think so." His face denied the statement.

"You see the certain individual who we will not name has employed me to find a painting that's floating around on the black market. And, being a wise chappie who keeps his finger on the pulse and his ear to the ground, he thought you might have got wind of it."

"Is it by Michael what's 'is face?"

"No. It's a French Impressionist painting. *Bathers by the River*, it's called. By an artist called Monet."

Steve grinned, his eyes twinkling with merriment. "Nude bathers are they. Tarts with no clothes on, eh? Ah, so that's what this is all about. Why didn't you say? All that talk about French whatsits. Well you can tell Mr . . . y'know that I can let him have stacks of the stuff, genuine smutter. Pin-sharp photos of some lovely ladies – all shapes and sizes, all starkers, give or take a suspender belt or two. What's his preference?"

"I'm sorry to disappoint you, Steve, but I was serious about the painting. My employer is very desirous of getting his hands on it and prepared to pay or do anything – and I do mean anything."

Steve nodded and repeated the nervous tic with his forefinger and collar. "I'd love to help but I ain't seen no painting with or without nude birds on it. I wish I had. I'd like to do y'know who a favour."

He meant it too. Quite clearly Steve Blakeway was a dead end.

Then I got my break.

As I rose to leave Steve's girlfriend tottered back with a cocktail glass filled with the most amazing concoction. The drink was in three striped layers of green, yellow and red.

"What the hell's that?" asked Steve.

Sweetheart beamed. "Donny the barman made it specially for me. He called it a Traffic Light Surprise."

Steve chuckled. "It looks lethal. Better take care not to spill it on the table; one drop and it'll probably strip the varnish."

Of course it would! I wished them happy drinking and bid them goodnight.

One of the detective's most essential tools is not your disguise kit, or fingerprint powder or a magnifying glass. It's a stout and powerful torch. Well, that's what I've always found. It illuminates what you want in the dark, which is particularly useful to me, having only one good peeper, and is handy as a club, should the occasion arise. On this occasion that occasion did not arise. I expect you're thinking I went a-burgling Mr Steve Blakemore's gaff to see if I could find a Monet stashed away somewhere. But no. After talking to him, I was sure he knew nothing of Sammy's painting. I ruled him right out of the frame. No, I was coming closer to home.

The popular conception of a detective's life is all glamour and excitement. Well, it does have its moments, I must admit, but generally it's routine grind with the odd grubby little chore to perform now and then. As on this occasion. Rummaging around in someone's dustbin does not fit into my category of glamour – but needs must. And the experience was in a sense rewarding, though not very cheering.

I stood outside the Velvet Cage and lit a Craven A, enjoying both the smoke and the cool night air. I was tired but relaxed. In an hour I reckoned I could get drunk, having relieved myself of the burden of an unwanted case. I hoped to be richer, too, although Sammy had never discussed money and I thought it politic not to raise the issue last night.

"Oh, Monsieur, are you not going into the club tonight?"

The French voice came from behind me, along with the strong smell of Gauloise. I turned and faced the owner of the voice: a short and stocky fellow, wearing a dark belted raincoat and a large-brimmed fedora, which was pulled down to hide his face. It was Arthur, my abductor.

"Trying a new one tonight." I pointed to my throat.

"Certainment," he grinned.

"Very Charles Boyer."

"Merci, mon ami. Shall we entree?"

As the doors opened, I could feel the heat of the club waft towards me as though desperate to escape the stifling smoky atmosphere within. It was an atmosphere I liked, the foggy, jazzy, boozy world of the club where one can slip into veiled anonymity and soak up the pleasure. My world.

Miss Lena Fortune was in the middle of a smoochy version of "Embraceable You". She really had a good voice and with the dress she was wearing you could almost see where it came from. My French companion led me to a booth at the far side of the bandstand. There in all his plentitudinous glory sat Sammy Levine, a cigar emerging from his mouth as though it had been nailed there. He was accompanied by the bristle-headed fellow from the night before. "I knew you wouldn't let me down," he said, beckoning me to sit beside him. "No talk now till Susie's through."

Frenchie slid in beside me like I was the meat in a very dubious sandwich. So we sat in silence and waited until Lena/ Susie finished her set. After "Embraceable You" she went up tempo with "Blue Moon" and finished on "I Only Have Eyes For You". I'll say it again: she was good. There was a lovely timbre to her voice, raspy and yet smooth. I liked her style: melodic understated sex. As is the case in joints like the Velvet Cage, the applause was perfunctory, but that's part of the British character. After all, we can't be seen to be enjoying ourselves too much. Before she left the stand she went over to the bass player threw her arms around him and planted a big sloppy kiss on his mug.

Brazen girl, I thought and my thought must have registered on my mush because Sammy smiled knowingly at me through the blue net of cigar smoke that hung before his face.

"You call yourself a detective, Johnny, huh?"

I said nothing and waited.

"What d'you think's going on here? That my beloved's two-timing me, playing me for a dummy? Get your mind out of the gutter, Mr Private Dickie. The guy's her brother, for Christ's sake. He got his call-up papers this week. He's off to Catterick on Monday. He'll be fighting the Hun in a month's time." He waved a finger at me as though I was a naughty child he'd caught with his hand in the sweetie jar. "In your line of work, I thought the last thing you should do is jump to conclusions."

"It's down towards the bottom of the list anyway," I said.

My embarrassment was curtailed by the arrival of Lena/ Susie.

"You were terrific," grinned Sammy, removing the cigar briefly to give her a kiss on the cheek.

"You always say that."

He shrugged. "You're always terrific."

They both laughed.

"Listen sweetie, get lost for ten minutes, eh? I've got a little business with this gentleman here and then the night's ours. OK?"

She grinned. She was used to this. "Sure." She kissed him again and evaporated into the blue gloom.

"And that goes for you fellas also."

Our two companions did not need a second prompt. They also slipped behind the veil of cigarette smoke and disappeared.

Sammy Levine turned to me. His face was serious. "Now, Johnny, you have good news, I hope."

"I have bad news."

"What do you mean? You've made no progress? You don't know who stole my painting? I told you it's that jumped-up punk, Blakeway."

I shook my head. "No one stole your painting. Blakeway wouldn't know a Monet if it sat in his lap."

"You're losing me here. What d'you mean no one stole my painting?"

"Just that. It's not been stolen."

Sammy's face grew red and he began to chew his cigar. "Don't play the wise guy with me, One-Eye. If the thing hadn't been stolen, it would be still on my wall now."

"It hasn't been stolen. It has been moved."

Sammy snatched the cigar from his mouth and threw it on the table with some force.

"Moved. Stolen. What's the difference?"

"No crime has been committed."

"Who moved it?"

This was the moment I was not looking forward to.

"Your mother."

Sammy did not know how to react to this statement. His face, like a rubber mask, stretched into a series of emotions ranging from anger to incredulity, amusement and worry.

"My mother," he said eventually. "My mother 'moved' my painting."

I nodded.

"Where to?"

"The dustbin."

Sammy lurched forwards and grabbed my lapels. "That's

enough, Mr Comedian. You either talk straight or you won't be able to explain to the dentist why you need a new set of teeth."

"Sure," I said quietly.

He let me go and pulled out another cigar. "Now, clearly, plainly and in English tell me what you're on about."

"I will, Sammy. But don't interrupt or stub your cigar in my face. Hear me out, OK?"

He nodded. "OK."

"The problem lies with your mother's over-zealous nature when it comes to the house."

"She likes things nice," said Sammy breaking his word already. I reckoned that I'd better keep my eye on that cigar.

"Indeed, she does like things nice. Too nice at times. She was not overfond of the Monet, was she? To her it was just a grubby old painting."

"Yeah." Sammy grinned.

"That's it, my friend: grubby. To her it let down your immaculate office. Ruined the effect. Every time she went in, her eyes were drawn to that grimy little picture, the one where you couldn't even see the bathers properly. So . . . so she decided to clean it. To brighten it up."

Sammy's features froze but his eyes signalled that he was somewhat ahead of me.

"She tried to clean it with turpentine. She didn't realize that the paint would run and smear – reduce it to a mess. The picture dissolved with only a few drops. Less than a minute of her enthusiastic rubbing and it was ruined – just a murky blur. Hey presto – now you see a painting – now you don't."

"Oh, my . . . Oh, my God."

"What could she do? She hadn't the nerve to tell you what had happened, so she took it down, removed it, and let you think it was stolen."

At last, Sammy was speechless.

"In panic, she broke it up – your Monet – and dumped it in the dustbin. It's still there. But a torn, bleary canvas is not much use to anyone, is it?"

"I can't believe it." But it was obvious that Sammy Levine could believe it. He knew his mum. In fact, he knew his mum even better now.

"Don't be hard on her, eh?"

He shook his head, his Adam's apple vibrating madly while a tear squeezed itself out of his left eye. "Poor mum."

"Mystery solved, Sammy," I said quietly, patting him on the shoulder. "Now, there is the question of my fee."

With my wallet somewhat fatter than it was than when I'd entered, I left the Velvet Cage some five minutes later. On the pavement outside I saw Susie/Lena in a passionate embrace with the bass player. As I passed, they broke from their clinch.

"Loving sister you got there," I said.

"And you're one naïve bastard," grinned Lena/Susie.

I flicked my cigarette into the gutter and made my way home.

WHO KILLED
PYRAMUS?

AMY MYERS

"Aphrodite!"

I stopped short. There was almost a "coo" in Father's voice.

"Dearest Queen of Beauty," Mighty Zeus added for good measure. "Laughter-loving goddess of love—"

All was explained. There was only one reason Father would have left his palace at morning nectar time to pursue me into the Graces' fitting-room. (They're the gown-makers up here on Mount Olympus.) Normally I would be summoned by his ghastly side-kick, my half-brother Hermes. Someone once told me the Romans call him Mercury – just right for that poisonous snake. Back to Father. The Great Thunderer was positively beaming – or at least trying his best. I could just see the twitch of his lips bursting upwards through the undergrowth of his Mighty Thundering Beard. That settled it. Upward turn of lips meant other parts of Father's anatomy were following the same path.

From my position of absolute power in matters to do with the latter (or almost), I could afford to beam too. Submissively, of course. One doesn't tempt the Fates, even though they too are related to Father.

"Mighty Father, Great Lord of Olympus," I began brightly, "what delight to see you."

"It occurred to me –" Father twiddled his robes, as though he hadn't a care in the heavens " – that I might borrow that magic girdle of yours this afternoon. I met this maiden called Thisbe."

I thought quickly. To borrow my girdle was to ensure success in romance. Not that there's much of that in Father's case; he doesn't believe in long courtships. He turns himself into a bull or a swan, a couple of snorts or quacks, and the maiden is no more.

"Father!" I looked shocked. "Don't you know there's a war on? How could you be thinking of love at such a time?"

"It's been on for years," he pointed out pathetically.

"But surely you should put duty first."

"You started it."

Father is always one to spot a flaw. It was he who first pinpointed Achilles' heel. Just because I rewarded Prince Paris of Troy for judging me to be the most beautiful of three goddesses by granting him Greek Helen, how could I know a ten-year war between the Greeks and the Trojans would result? Everyone makes mistakes.

"Hand me that girdle – " Father's beam had disappeared, " – and I don't want a fake one this time."

I giggled. It had been quite funny to see Father disguised as a panda and lumbering in vain after that flying nymph. He glared at me, and changing the giggle to a cough, I whipped off my girdle from the diaphanous gown that clad my wondrous body. After all, I could do with an afternoon off from Father's all-seeing eye. Aeneas, my mortal son, had decided to waddle out from Troy to take part in the war that afternoon, and he's so dim he needs a mother's eye on him. Unfortunately we gods are forbidden by Father to take any hand in the destiny of the war – officially. Unofficially he knows very well the whole war is run by the infighting on Olympus. When Father is off on his "missions", however, his all-seeing eye is closed.

"Glad you see it my way, Aphro." Father hesitated, then actually blushed. "Thisbe's a nice little thing. Lives in Babylon."

Babylon? Good. Father would be away for hours and hours. "Does she know you're coming?" I asked innocently.

"Not exactly. She's expecting Pyramus, a callow youth who

lives next door. Parents don't approve, so they'll see it my way too."

"How do they meet, then?"

"They make love through a wall," Father explained.

"Pardon?" I thought I knew every conceivable position – and quite a few that aren't – but this was a new one on me.

"The parents forbade them to meet, so they find a tiny hole in the wall to talk through. Only big enough to *talk*," Father added meaningfully.

"Don't tell me. You're going to disguise yourself as Pyramus."

Father was highly indignant. "He's got spots. Anyway, I believe in playing fair."

First I'd heard of it, but I let it pass. "So how will you make yourself known this time?" That's the delicate way of putting it. Usually his anatomy does it for him.

"A lion."

I goggled. "That's meant to endear a delicate maiden to you?"

Father bristled – good practice for intending lionizers. "Hercules says they can be very cuddly."

I sighed. The Olympian committee rooms had been arguing over that gentleman for months. Should he or should he not be promoted to be a god? Mighty Ox-Eyed Hera (my stepmother and Zeus's nagging consort) loathes Hercules, and on one of her mean days (which is most) practised her skills of hypnosis on him, ordering him to kill his entire family. As a result he was sentenced to hard labour – twelve of them in fact. The first was to fight a lion, which has given him an obsession about them ever since. Hera was hopping mad when he survived all twelve ordeals. Father couldn't openly display his pleasure, but the rest of us cheered and put him up for promotion.

Unfortunately Zeus now thinks of Hercules as his chief adviser on earthly matters, but Hercules, good chap though he is, is as thick as two cedar trunks, and I don't mean just physically. And as a result Father was going to open his lion's mouth and expect Thisbe to jump right in.

*　　*　　*

"Aphrodite!"

Hermes was squawking by my bed of pain – he's the only male on Olympus whom the sight of my naked body leaves cold. Guess why.

"What the Hades do you want? I'm ill," I groaned. I, goddess of love, had been wounded in battle. The afternoon had been disastrous. I merely swooped into the field of battle to save my son from this brute of a man – delightful in other contexts, I'm sure – who had meanly hit poor Aeneas with a rock. When I tried, as any mother would, to protect Aeneas, Diomedes actually chased me with a spear, knowing quite well who I was. Fighting with the gods is against all the rules. The Graces had run up a lovely little dress for me to wear into battle, and it was supposed to be impregnable. Was it Hades. They can sing for their money. The spear pierced my wrist so badly the ichor ran out. I promptly dropped Aeneas, and Apollo, who's a good sort, took care of him, while Iris, Hera's messenger, drove me home in Ares' chariot – and I know what currency *he'll* demand in payment. My mother Dione kissed the wound better, but it was still hurting during the night. I'd put in for a hearing in the Family Judgment Room, since it was quite obvious that one of my own loving family put the idea into Diomedes' head. However, I didn't expect to be summoned in the middle of the night.

To my surprise, Father was alone at the adjoining bar, drinking a stiff nectar. He looked almost scared. Had mighty Ox-Eyed Hera found out about his little fling? No, it must be more than that. Usually he blustered and thundered, and let the Greeks (her favourites) win the next round in the war, and there was no more said.

"Dead," he almost babbled as he saw me.

"No, no, I'm alive," I reassured him, glad that news of my wound had shaken him so.

"*She's* dead, *he's* dead."

"Who?" I asked blankly.

"Pyramus."

"That's good, isn't it?" I was puzzled. Nothing Father likes better than a clear field.

"Thisbe is too."

Not so good. One dead lover is sad, but it happens. Two dead lovers and both gods and mortals get upset and start asking questions, which if Father is involved is awkward. That means work for me. "Tell me," I said softly, nobly ignoring the stab of pain from my peerless wrist.

Father couldn't wait to oblige. "I arrived at the wall in Babylon a little late – and that blasted Pyramus was already there lisping sweet nothings through the wall. All mouth and no follow-up, or so I'd thought, but he seemed to be persuading my Thisbe that they should both run away that evening and meet under a white mulberry tree at the Tomb of Ninus outside the city, where they could plight more than their troth. I knew what the cad had in mind."

"So did you."

"Yes, but I'm Mighty Zeus, king of the heavens, not a pimply boy. It's a privilege for her."

"So it is," I murmured.

He picked up the sarcasm. "Any more lip from you, my girl, and I'll have a reshuffle. You'll find yourself goddess of knitting."

I maintained my dignity. Father's main idea behind any reshuffle is to get someone other than Ox-Eyed Hera in his bed as consort. If he excludes all his daughters, however, there are precious few candidates left.

"So I thought I'd wait till the evening," Father continued. "I thought Thisbe might like to see a nice cuddly lion around when she arrived. I'd chase Pyramus off, and have Thisbe to myself. The problem was there was already a real lion hanging around, and the minute it saw me it decided to have a go at me. We had a battle round and round the mulberry tree, and then I saw Thisbe coming up. I wasn't exactly looking cuddly at the time and there was a lot of lion's blood around, so she screamed and ran into the cave. I lost no time in running in to comfort her; when we came out, she was very comforted – but there was Pyramus lying dead on the ground. I thought the real lion had had a go at him, and I'd get the blame, since he'd now scarpered. I decided I'd get the Hades out of there."

"Like any self-respecting lion—"

"Watch it, Aphrodite." Father scowled. "Then I realized my

dilemma. I was in Babylonian territory, and I could see Queen Semiramis hunting in the forest. You know how she fancies she's a goddess. She'd smell a rat – or rather a lion – as soon as she heard about all this. There'd be a political scandal. So I went back to see if I'd left any – er – clues."

"My girdle!" I got it in one. "You'd dropped it." I was furious.

"In the heat of the moment," he said apologetically. "It had gone by the time I got back."

"*Gone*?" I shrieked. What would happen to the world if the power of love was left to just anyone?

"I found poor little Thisbe dead too. She'd obviously impaled herself on Pyramus's sword. Then Semiramis swept in, all glitter and hunting gear, and a little later the fathers of Pyramus and Thisbe too. I was still a lion, but she recognized me straightaway and more or less accused me of killing them. Oh, and she was wearing your *cestus*."

Upstart! We get them all the time now. I could see why Father was worried, however, and not only Father. We were both in trouble. Semiramis was a lower-ranking goddess than us, of course, and Father's supreme position has so far been unchallenged in Babylon. But she's an ambitious and dangerous lady, and likes to call herself the Great Mother Goddess of Babylon. She's always pestering me for new lovers, and it was some time before I cottoned on that she slaughtered them all after she'd had her wicked way with them.

On the other hand, she had control of my *cestus* at the moment. I had to tread carefully, or I'd be in for a wigging from Cronus, one of the Titans who used to rule the world. He's Zeus's father, and is long since forcibly retired from power, but he is called in occasionally to sort out squabbles.

"Murder," Father added gloomily. "She's going for the big one."

This was getting worse. We gods are in charge of life and death, but we take our Titanic Oath very seriously. We are not allowed to sanction a death if it is for our own pleasure, although there's a grey area about what happens if we do it to spite one another.

"She argued that Thisbe killed herself with the sword when

she saw Pyramus dead, but that Pyramus was murdered. No true lion could be to blame either because he was killed by his own sword plunged into his side. That meant suicide was out, according to blasted Queen Semiramis – who the Hades does she think she is? *Me*? – because suicides aim for the chest or stomach. But it *looked*, she said, as if Pyramus had found Thisbe's bloodied veil and assumed a real lion had eaten her. Either way, I'm in the frame."

"Perhaps Thisbe did it." I wasn't at my best in the middle of the night, wound or no wound.

"She was underneath a lion all the time," Father pointed out. "Me."

"True." Then my wits returned. "Father, *what* bloodied veil?"

Father cleared his throat. "That's the point. Semiramis couldn't know, but Pyramus didn't see the veil."

"*What* veil?"

"The one I put there after they were both dead, when I realized I might get mixed up in it. It was soaked in her blood, so I whipped it off Thisbe and dropped it some way away."

I was aghast. There were political issues to be considered. If Father was accused of this unlawful killing, it could provide a handle for the Titans, now safely chained up, to claim back supreme power. And what would happen to *me* then, as Zeus's daughter? I could spend the rest of eternity imprisoned in Tartarus. Fear sharpens thinking.

"Are you sure it was Pyramus's sword that was used to kill him?"

"Yes, but Thisbe used it too, so it was at her side, not his." Zeus can think fast too when his own security is at stake.

"How do you know it *was* Pyramus's sword?"

"The ivory scabbard was empty, and the design matched the hilt."

"So whoever killed him didn't come prepared to kill him."

Father looked at me with new respect, and I felt a glow of filial pride. We were in this together.

For the first time one of Hermes' nasty little inventions came in handy. CloudBack wipes the slate clean and returns the world to where it was at a previous point in time. Father had frowned on it, but at Hermes' pleading he'd put it to the Olympian Assembly who had passed it, provided it did not interfere with life and death (King Hades saw to that, there'd be no one left for him to rule otherwise). We couldn't therefore go back to undo Pyramus and Thisbe's deaths, but we could return to the scene of the crime as it was when Father so ignobly left it. Unfortunately Aurora had just announced Dawn, and when Ox-Eyed Hera lumbered forth from bed for morning nectar she insisted on coming with us to Babylon. Our family sticks together in public; it's in private the fun begins.

Somehow Hera must have guessed the reason for this jaunt. We don't get on, and she never asks for the use of my girdle, since she knows which side her ambrosia's buttered on. Anyway, the girdle wouldn't meet round her waist.

We decided to remain invisible for a while, till we summed up the situation. It was not only a sad moonlit scene, but a horrific one. Even the great white mulberry tree had been splashed with blood, and the bodies of the two lovers in the middle of the glade were lying in pools of it. I am used to unhappy endings, but I was moved by this sight. Pyramus was a handsome young man, whatever Mighty Zeus said, and the girl had been a beauty, long dark hair spread out over Pyramus's body. She was half-lying across it, and blood was still trickling from her body over him, though his was drying fast. At least Father's story added up in that respect.

A group of guards stood at a respectful distance, and two elderly men – the fathers, presumably – were sobbing by their children's sides. But my eyes were riveted on Semiramis – and my girdle tied carelessly round the waist of her smart gold hunting outfit. The usual long Babylonian tunic had slits up to her thighs, revealing smart boots, and a gold cap lined with leather adorned her head. There was no doubt she was majestically beautiful, but it was a cold beauty, not like my own warm loveliness.

I steeled myself to do a quick recce of the bodies while Hera shrieked and heaved in Zeus's reluctant arms. I had to admit Semiramis was probably right about it being murder, even though she didn't have the benefit of knowing about the veil. The wound was indeed in the side but when I braced myself to

pick up one of Pyramus's bloodied hands I could see no
lacerations to indicate any attempt to prevent the sword reaching him. But how, I wondered, did someone get close enough to
get the sword out of the scabbard? He couldn't have fallen
asleep – or could he? I noticed a brick lying by his side, and
when I smoothed his hair away I knew the answer. Someone
had clobbered him first with the brick, and then struck with the
sword to make sure of it. This seemed a little unsatisfactory as
an explanation, but it was the only one.

I noticed that the grass around the bodies was smeared with
blood in addition to the pools around the bodies, as though one
or the other had been dragged, or dragged itself. No matter,
save that it suggested that Pyramus (probably from the position
of it) had recovered from the brick and that the sword had not
killed him outright. Had he dragged himself towards Thisbe,
told her of his murderer? There was food for thought here, and
it wasn't ambrosia.

Meanwhile Semiramis seemed uncommonly disturbed over
the scene before her, which considering the routine way she
despatched her own rejects to Hades seemed very altruistic
indeed.

"Stand forth, Nebu, stand forth, Gordea," she commanded.

The two fathers tore themselves away from their children's
remains to obey the summons.

"Ah, great queen," Nebu sighed, "would I had let them
wed."

"Indeed," Gordea joined in. "We are justly punished for our
blindness."

"I have cheering news for you," Semiramis assured them.
"The gods have decreed at my suggestion –" I heard Father
growl at my side "– that the white mulberry tree now splashed
with blood shall bear red berries in memory of your children."

The fathers appeared overcome with this generosity – so
typical of a minor goddess to waste time on inessentials. Father
was still snorting, but had the sense to keep quiet.

Hera, on the other hand, was wobbling with mirth.

"What's so funny?" I asked coldly. She doesn't normally
giggle when she's caught Father red-handed. In this case, I
hoped the red hands didn't apply.

"She's wearing your girdle."

"Not for long, she won't," I snarled.

"Justice will be done," Semiramis informed us. "Nebu, Gordea, who killed Pyramus?"

"A lion," cried Gordea and Nabu together, a shade too eagerly.

A nasty smile crossed Semiramis's face. "I meant, which of you two. You both had reason – Nebu in anger at his disobedience, Gordea at his presumption in aspiring to your daughter's hand."

"It wasn't her hand he wanted," muttered Father.

"It was him." Nebu and Gordea again cried out in unison, pointing at each other.

"Oh, wickedness, great queen," Nebu then said eagerly. "Kill my own son? Never. Anyway I was at home when the news was brought, whereas Gordea—"

"Is innocent," Gordea cried. "Kill my dear neighbour's son? Why, I was at home too when the news came. That villain and I came here together."

"Liar," shouted Nebu. "We met in the forest."

"Who else had reason to wish them dead?" thundered Semiramis, practising for promotion to Olympus.

"The lion." Nebu and Gordea were once more in accord.

"With a sword?" enquired the queen, doing quite well for a junior deity. Indeed, very well, for she was sniffing the air, and not only for roses. I should explain that we gods have a sixth sense that can sometimes reveal when other gods are present.

"Stand forth, god, whoever you are!" she ordered.

I dug Father in the ribs. "You'll have to do it."

I must say he put on a grand show, appearing in all his majesty, not as a lion. Even Semiramis was taken aback at the dramatic result of her summons, especially when Hera and I materialized as well to display unanimity. Father appearing with his rolls of thunder out of a cloud in a suddenly darkened sky (Apollo always obliges) is a magnificent sight, and even Semiramis blenched.

"Who dare call *me*, Great Mighty Zeus, lord of the Heavens?"

"Who is this whore?" Hera was putting on a good show too. Biding her time to faint with horror, no doubt.

Semiramis awarded him the merest bow, indicating she was in charge. Hera did not receive one, only a glance that promised an interesting exchange of views at some less fraught time. "Great Zeus, what knowest thou of this tragedy?"

"I happened to be thundering over . . ." Father began carelessly.

"Tell the *truth*," I hissed at him.

"I was the lion," he roared out. "Does thou think now the lion killed these poor young people? Would the goddess of love be at my side even now, were it so?"

"Ah, yes." Semiramis smirked at me. "Could this be great Aphrodite's girdle?" She performed a slinky wriggle to display *my* property.

"It could, and I'll have it back," I said sweetly, stretching out my hand.

"Not so fast, lady – goddess," she added after a deliberate pause. "What was your girdle doing in this place of death? Touch of the rough stuff, was it?" Her speciality, of course.

"My girdle aids young lovers," I said piously. "It has been defiled in this place of death."

"I'll say," Semiramis declared mockingly. "Could it be that Great Zeus borrowed your girdle, then killed Pyramus, so that he could enjoy Thisbe at his will?"

"No," thundered Zeus, as a great screech came from Hera. She had decided it was time to faint, and the Mighty Queen of Heaven hit the ground with a mighty thud. I left her there and had another prowl around the scene of the crime. Oddly enough, it was Semiramis, rival Queen of Heaven, who came to her aid.

"Do not fear, Great Queen. We will seek justice from the Fates. If Zeus has broken the rules of Olympus and killed for his own pleasure, he must be deposed, and another monarch appointed. Perhaps a woman."

"Me, please," Hera said eagerly. I told you she was dim.

Mighty Father was in the middle of an apoplectic fit, it appeared, and about to summon his entire armoury of thunderbolts. I had some fast thinking to do. I did it.

"Stay thy hand, Mighty Zeus. There is one more candidate for the murder of poor Pyramus."

"Who?" sneered Semiramis.

"You."

That stopped her. "Were you not first on the scene, are you not renowned for the dexterity with which you dispose of lovers?" I projected my best goddess proclamation voice. "How do you do it, by the way?" I often wondered. Being a goddess she was immune from discovery through the Earth Vision Room, through which we gods keep an eye on what's going on below us. "Did you set your sights on poor Pyramus and then, when he fell in love with Thisbe, decide to kill him in revenge? Hades hath no fury like a goddess scorned?"

I'd shaken her, but she rallied. "How?" she sneered.

"Did Pyramus stand by while you removed his sword and stabbed him? Or did you clobber him with that brick first?"

"See my hands, great Aphrodite." She held them out. "Are they rough with brick dust, are they bloodied?"

I was bound to admit they were not – and yet there had been something strange going on. "You claim divinity, Semiramis?"

"I do."

"Then colourless ichor runs in your veins, not blood. It would not show on your hands."

"But it was never there!" she shrieked, falling to her knees. "You don't understand."

"Perhaps I would if you gave me that girdle back," I sighed. "Then you can explain what I don't understand."

Sulking, she handed it over. Now I could concentrate on getting Father out of his difficulty.

"When I first arrived here, Pyramus was dying, and there was no sign of Thisbe. I admit I had rather fancied him, but there was no saving him and I was furious with him for preferring that chit of a girl to me. He'd dragged himself over the grass, muttering that he could hear Thisbe somewhere."

"It was rather loud," Father whispered for my ears only.

"Did he happen to mention whether he'd killed himself or whether he was murdered and, if so, who did it?" I didn't trust this woman an inch.

"Thisbe. Murder, Thisbe, was all he said."

Father saw an opening. "So Thisbe killed him," he roared.

"I suppose she could have done, Mighty Zeus."

"No, she couldn't." I was furious with Father. "She had an alibi, remember?"

Hera's eyes glittered. There'd be thunder on Olympus tonight.

"So you, Great Semiramis, arrived to find Pyramus, who had scorned your arms, *alive*, killed him and left him for Thisbe to discover," I continued. "Then you staged surprise when you returned later."

"No, I did not. And what gives you the right to say so?"

"I do." Mighty Zeus, once out of his own orbit, is hardly streetwise, so he was happy merely to come in as back-up. "There's nothing you like more than finishing off young men."

"Yes, but only after—"

"Who could prove that?" I murmured, enjoying the sight of Great Semiramis falling to her knees.

"I'm innocent," she howled.

"I know." I did my own wriggle to show my girdle was once more back in its rightful place. I was centre-stage. My big moment had come.

There was a moment's pause while everyone took in my declaration. Father was furious, so was Hera, and Nebu and Gordea suddenly realized they were back on the suspect list.

"Which one of them do you accuse?" Semiramis asked eagerly, rapidly recovering her poise.

"Neither."

"Me?" Father thundered.

"No," I said more hastily.

"Who, then?"

"The wall did it."

"The *wall*!" Hera alternately trumpeted and snorted with laughter, and Zeus looked as if he was going to lock me in his special place for barking-mad gods. Semiramis, however, realized it was in her interests to humour me.

"Which wall, Wise Goddess?"

"The party wall between Nebu and Gordea's gardens, with the chink through which their children courted."

Hera lost what little control she had left. "It walked here," she howled. "It must have been jealous, when it heard Pyramus and Thisbe arrange their tryst. Then it threw one of its bricks at Pyramus and—"

"Then stabbed him with his own sword." Tittering, Semiramis changed sides rapidly, reckoning a queen of heaven outweighed a mere goddess of love.

"When you've quite finished laughing," I said coldly, "I will show you your wall. I think we'll find it hiding behind the Tomb of Ninus."

More paroxysms of laughter. I floated diaphanously round the tomb – it pays to scout round the scene of the crime.

"Come forth, wall," I ordered in my grandest voice, facing the tomb.

Slowly a long wall ten foot high snaked round the corner of the tomb and presented itself before me. I turned round to the goggling company. "See?"

"Witch," shouted Semiramis viciously.

"Insults will get you nowhere on Olympus," I replied sweetly. I turned to the wall again. "I order you to demetamorphose." I could sniff a god around as well as Semiramis. Better, for she looked flabbergasted.

The wall crumbled, and a young man stood there. No ordinary young man either. He was *very* handsome, and moreover it was someone Semiramis recognized. So did I. It was Tammuz, the Babylonian lookalike for Adonis, who spends half the year on earth as a mortal, and half in Hades as a junior god. Just as Adonis chooses me as his mate during his active period, Tammuz chooses the goddess Ishtar – which is one of Semiramis's pseudonyms. And once she got over being flabbergasted, she began to put two and two together extremely quickly.

Suddenly the idea of the wall being the guilty party no longer seemed so amusing to her. It was rather a surprise to me too. I expect to find the god of fertile nature like Tammuz prancing over the fields, not locked up in a wall. He is described as the god of "the tender voice and shining eyes", and I could see the reason for it. In fact, since I was a long way from Adonis, he looked almost tempting. But self-preservation came first.

I glanced at Father, only to find he wasn't there. He had

obviously taken himself off when he saw the political situation getting out of control.

"Explain yourself, Tammuz," I ordered.

"My love," he choked, seeing the bodies on the ground. For a moment I could believe the tears in those dewy eyes genuine. "What has happened?"

Semiramis didn't bother with the niceties. "You double-dealing toad! Which one did you fancy, Pyramus or Thisbe?"

I immediately went off Tammuz. If there's one thing I do insist on in my lovers, it's an ability to make up one's mind on the important matters of life.

For the first time he took in her presence. "Darling Semiramis," he said belatedly.

"Great Queen of Heaven to you," she snarled.

"What about me?" Hera's bosom swelled at this takeover bid, and Semiramis hastily kow-towed. "I forget myself. Unfaithful lovers, you know how it is."

Hera didn't. She spends all her time reining in Father.

"You were chasing Thisbe, weren't you, Tammuz?" It was time I asserted my authority. "If you were after Pyramus, you wouldn't have killed him." (Or would he, if Pyramus turned him down?) "Could it be you thought the best way of keeping an eye on Thisbe was to fall on her out here, having eliminated Pyramus?"

The handsome face scowled. "No, she wasn't my type. Anyway, I wasn't here at the time. I've only just rolled up, wondering what was keeping them. They were dead when I got here."

"Then what is this brick doing here?" My master card. I picked it up, glad that I'd accompanied my dull husband, the god of fire, to the kilns when they baked the bricks for the Babylonian defences. "We are outside the city here, yet this is a brick from Babylon. The cement has been made from hot bitumen and you can see a bit of reed attached to it. I think if we examine the thirtieth brick course on this wall we will find a gap right where the layer of wattled reeds was laid."

Semiramis stalked to the wall out of which Tammuz had appeared. Mighty Zeus cautiously reappeared to be in at the kill.

"You are right," Semiramis agreed. "Tammuz is adjudged guilty." Her eyes gleamed.

"It's a plant," Tammuz snarled.

"It's not," remarked Hera, puzzled. "It's a brick."

Not a plant, but maybe Tammuz was a stool-pigeon. Maybe even Semiramis needed an excuse to bump off her lovers. There were delicate politics here, and I should have to discuss it with Father. He seemed to think so too. He ordered the guards to hold Tammuz and summoned Semiramis to a private discussion between gods. Hera of course insisted on being present, wringing every drop of satisfaction she could out of Father's predicament.

I was asked to adjudicate though Father was eager to pounce on Tammuz immediately. He would be.

Semiramis, I reluctantly conceded, was innocent of blame. Why, if she fancied Pyramus, would she employ Tammuz as hit-god? She'd enjoy doing it herself. Moreover, she was highly unlikely to have used a brick and a sword to kill him off. She'd call Pyramus to judgment and do it nice and legally.

"It was Tammuz," I concluded. "He dropped a brick to stun Pyramus while still inside the wall, which gave him time to hop out and kill him with the sword. Or nearly kill him, if Semiramis speaks the truth."

"I do, I do," she swore eagerly. "Can I have him now? His six-month mortal period is just beginning."

"Certainly," said Zeus graciously. "Aphrodite, you've done almost as well as I could have done," he beamed. "What can I do for you?"

I answered promptly. "Swing the judgment tomorrow in my favour. Let me have revenge on Diomedes for wounding a goddess." I'd look forward to that. I began to see that Semiramis and I might be sisters as well as goddesses under the skin.

Semiramis was about to return to claim possession of her victim, when it struck me that I wasn't entirely satisfied with the verdict. Why hadn't Tammuz dropped the whole wall on Pyramus and killed him that way? Why the sword too? Ah well, it was a small point.

Then I saw Hera grinning. *Grinning?* Why? Zeus was in the clear. So what . . . It's not often Hera can put one over on me but she nearly did this time. She was gloating. Why? There could be only one reason. One of her little tricks had worked. Feverishly I ran over the whole thing again – and then I realized. There was an element we'd all forgotten. "The second lion!" I exclaimed. "Did you smell anything, Father? Are you sure it was a real one?"

It took Mighty Zeus only five minutes to see my point, while we all stood there. "Another god!" he roared at last.

"Hera?" I asked smugly. "Was it you?"

"Queens of heaven do not cavort inside lions," she said with dignity. "Who would, save your father?"

"Hercules likes lions," I said slowly. "Remember his favourite of the twelve labours? What about it, Hera?"

Zeus went white. "You're right, Aphro. To think he had a good go at me. That's the last I hear about him coming on board the Olympus team. But you can't blame Hera. She doesn't like Hercules."

"No. But she likes giving him blackouts so he can kill folk, don't you, step-mummy? Suppose you found out about Father's – er – liking for Thisbe and set Hercules up? Hercules did the murder, and so Mighty Zeus would veto his promotion, and you'd have your revenge on my poor Father. Just because he likes an afternoon off now and then."

"I didn't," Hera shrieked. "Anyway, Hercules only did the sword bit—"

Like I said, she's dim.

Father glowed with this opportunity – all due to me – to bar Hera from his bed, and immediately granted me a revenge of my own choosing on Diomedes. I was just as quick to think up a nice lingering slow one for him. I'd let him survive the war; and just when he thought he was returning home to be a fat cat – he'd find a nice kettle of Poseidon's stinking fish awaiting him there. Now what should it be . . . I dragged my thoughts back to the murder in hand.

Semiramis had been entranced by all this bickering among the gods, but she looked very disappointed as she realized that her prey was off the hook. "What about Tammuz?" she wailed. "Can't I have him?"

"No," said Zeus curtly.

"He did use the brick."

"That didn't kill him."

"But he meant it to."

"True." Zeus ruminated. He's always fair if his own interests aren't affected. "Very well, Semiramis, you may take him."

She smiled beatifically. "May I wait till the end of his mortal period before sending him to Hades?"

Zeus glared, but she had him over one of Dionysius's barrels. She could spread the lion story around earth, sea, Olympus and Hades. Worse, she could refer it to Cronos.

"Yes."

"By the way," I asked politely, "as goddess of love, I have professional interest in technique. How do you dispose of your lovers?"

"I've built a special place in Babylon."

"What kind of place?" I asked curiously. One never knows when such information might come in handy.

"Hanging Gardens."

THE HAMPSTEAD VEGETABLE HEIST

MAT COWARD

"So, you're going to use a zucchini, right?"

"Zucchini, yah. Basically, I'm thinking, they can't do you for using a weapon, or going equipped, or whatever, if all you've got in your pocket is a vegetable, see?"

Toby lifted his Pernod-and-Perrier to his lips and kissed it. Then he put it down again. I picked up my pint of bitter, stuffed half of it down my throat, and slapped the glass back on the table. I've got nothing against people who don't drink, but what I can't stand is someone who doesn't drink properly. I mean, why come in a pub if you're not thirsty?

"A zucchini," I said, "that's what, a courgette?"

"Okay, right, a courgette, yah. Sorry, I should've said. I spent a lot of time in the States before, and they call them zucchini over there. A courgette, that's right."

"And, let me get this straight: this is because of your mortgage?"

"Please, please, don't even say that word! I mean, we're not talking *mortgage* here, we're talking *mega*-mortgage. This isn't just a *mortgage*, yah? This is The Mortgage That Ate The West."

I don't know what we're supposed to call these types now –

these people who used to be yuppies. I mean, they're certainly not Young and Upwardly Mobile Professionals any more, not since the crash, and the property collapse, and the never-ending recession. "Rapsids", perhaps: Rapidly Sinking Idiots who thought their luck would last for ever.

Toby's luck had run out later than some, and heavier than most. I think this was because, even by yuppie standards, he wasn't all that bright. I don't care how solid the property market looks, or how much the bank pays its Vice-Presidents (Securities); no one with a fully functioning brain takes on a half-a-million-pound mortgage at age twenty-seven.

Anyone who does, if you ask me, *deserves* to lose his home fourteen months later.

"Why are you telling me this, Toby? Not that it isn't very interesting, and everything, but if you want to stick up a betting shop with an American marrow, just go ahead and do it. I'll read about it in the local paper when you get sent down. What do you want from me, the name of a bent greengrocer?"

"I don't know," Toby pouted. "Some sympathy for the devil, maybe? A word of encouragement?"

He had to be kidding. Not that I disliked Toby Reynolds, the yuppie who fell to earth. In fact, as an example of his breed, he wasn't too bad. Word in the pub was, he'd even been heard to crack a joke once or twice – after he was laid off, obviously, not before.

But I first knew this place in the seventies, when Margaret Thatcher was just a crazy woman on the TV, there were no mobile phones or personal organizers, people didn't drink bottled French water in pubs, and estate agents didn't have swimming pools, or personalized licence plates on their Jaguars, until they were too old to enjoy them. I won't pretend they were great days, but at least the area had a bit of tone back then.

Look at a map, and it'll tell you that Hampstead is a suburb of North London. But maps can lie. Hampstead, as any local will tell you, usually unprompted, is a village. True, London is only a few minutes away by Tube, but in spirit it's on a different planet.

To succeed in the area known to jealous outsiders by its postal code, you only had to be one thing: a character. Same as any

English village, right? You could be rich (more millionaires per square inch than anywhere else in the country), or you could be poor (plenty of bedsits, full of Marxist students, gay runaways, and Irish poet-bricklayers). You could be a pop star, a librarian or a Zoroastrian priest. Just as long as you were interesting to know. That's the sort of place it is.

Or used to be, before the mid-eighties, when all the yups moved in, with their lookalike designer suits, and their coloured spectacle frames, and their one-track conversation – deals, deals, deals. And now, if the mysterious revolutions of the money markets were forcing them out again, I wasn't going to complain. Cheer maybe, declare a public holiday, but not complain.

"Well, Toby, me old son, I wish you all the luck. And if you get banged up, I'll send you a postcard of the Heath, to remind you of happier days." I stood up. A few of the serious darts players had arrived, and I was eager to get into the game.

"Yah, sure, mate. But just wait a second. There's more. I know how I can make certain I get away with the robbery, and at the same time pin it on Danny Royal." He smiled, smugly. "Why don't I buy you a drink, yah, while I run it by you?"

I looked at him more closely. Yeah, now I came to think of it . . .

I sat down. I can play darts any night. A chance to frame Danny Royal only comes along once in a lifetime.

I won't bore you with what there was between me and Danny, expect to say that it went back about a dozen years, and it involved a knife, a broken arm, a deposit on a studio flat that wasn't actually for rent, an innocent country boy, and a guy who got thrown out of the North London mafia for being too much of a scumbag.

Danny was definitely Old Hampstead – an interesting character, you had to give him that – but if I could hurt him by helping one of the despised yuppie invaders, then I didn't have to think twice about whose side I was on.

Besides: a man has a right to pay his mortgage, doesn't he?

Thus, on the morning of the Great Hampstead Bookie Blag, Toby and I met in a tarted-up coffee shop, just across the High

Street from the betting shop. The place used to be a pub, but yuppies don't use beer, so now it sold pseudo-American Danish pastries, and pseudo-European coffee. I was maliciously pleased to notice, at ten in the morning, that it was virtually empty.

As Toby sat down next to me, I spoke to him out of the side of my mouth: "You got da piece, Bugsy?"

"Oh, yah, sure," said my accomplice, loud as you like. "The zucchini's right here in this brown paper bag. You got yours?"

"Don't wave it all around, stupid," I screamed, very quietly.

"Why? It's only a vegetable. You can't be arrested for waving a vegetable around a café."

"It's a fruit, not a vegetable."

"Right. Sure." He looked puzzled. "That make a difference in law?"

"No difference at all. I just don't want my face associated with your face – or your fruit, or your brown paper bag – in the memory of any lurking witness. All right?"

"All right, yah. Sorry, mate. I wasn't thinking." He thought for a moment; I could see his ears turning pink. "You recognized me straight away."

"I was expecting you. Don't worry about that, you look just like him. His own mistress'd be fooled."

It was true. Of course, Toby was a good bit younger than Danny, but then Danny's body was as crooked as his character – it lied about his age. The false moustache looked fine (plenty of actors in Hampstead; and, actors being the sort of people they are, you can always find one that owes you a favour). The clothes were spot on: camelhair overcoat, smart denim shirt and leather tie, expensive black jeans. He'd do.

Then he really surprised me. "Listen . . ." he said, and paused to gulp some cold coffee. "Do you have any, y'know, moral qualms about any of this? Um, basically," he added.

I goggled, boggled, and burbled a bit. *Morals*? Wow, this poor lad hadn't just lost his yuppie job, he'd lost his entire yuppie code. His orientation was shot all to buggery.

"You mean the stick-up? Or the frame-up?"

"Well, y'know, like, both I suppose. I mean, this isn't really my sort of scene, right? I used to be in banking."

"Exactly," I said. "So whatever you do today can't be half as wicked as what you've been doing for the past ten years. Now get up. It's time to go." He got up, put on his dark glasses, and began walking towards the door. "Hey, Toby," I called after him.

"Yah?" He looked back expectantly, like a dog about to get a tickle on the tummy for luck.

"You forgot your bloody courgette!"

Moral qualms? Sure, I had qualms, a little squeamishness, but nothing I couldn't handle. The bookie's would be insured, there wasn't really a gun, so no one could get hurt, and as for Danny Royal . . . if law and order was a real thing, not just a phantom they conjure up at election time, he'd have been in solitary confinement since the age of six. Justice delayed is justice just the same.

Danny's office was located, very conveniently, above an off licence, a few doors down from the betting shop which my confederate, Toby, was about to rob with a zucchini in a paper bag. Quite why a villain needs an office, instead of, say, a low dive or a murky alley, I couldn't imagine.

But, hey – this is Hampstead. Hampstead smiles on style.

"Good morning, Danny. How's tricks?"

Danny was alone, as we'd been sure he would be so early – even so, I was relieved. We'd known he'd be in the office; he always was on weekday mornings, just like a regular business-man. He didn't look surprised to see me, which irritated me somewhat.

"What you doing here, boy?" He was concentrating on his paperwork now, he wasn't looking at me. He'd looked at me once already, and he didn't see any need to look at me again.

"I'm here to bring you a little gift, something I thought you'd like. Here, Danny – catch!" I chucked the paper bag at his head. A zucchini doesn't weigh much, but it makes you feel awfully silly if it bounces off your head when you're not expecting it.

The only man in the world that I really hated sprang out of his swivel chair, and screamed "What's your game, boy? Just exactly what is occurring, you grubby little—"

He was going to call me something rude, I knew he was, and

that's something that my mother particularly warned me about when I first moved to the big city. So I hit him, quite hard, on the right eye. I shouldn't have, of course, it wasn't in the script, but there comes a time in a man's life when improvisation is the only show in town. Know what I mean?

I was just wondering what was going to happen next, and thinking it probably wouldn't be anything particularly funny, and watching Danny Royal sprawl across his desk, howling, when the office door opened, and a tough-looking kid of about eighteen walked in.

I froze, like a string bean alone in a catering-size deep freeze. I knew this kid: he worked on a stall in the community market. More to the point, he knew me.

"So what was all that about?" the barrow boy asked me, as I hustled him out of the street door. "I was just coming up to pay my rent to the King Rat. Did you floor him?"

"Er – yeah. Listen, Nigel, it's very important that nobody finds out about this, you understand? Absolutely nobody. Not about the fight, not even that I was there. Okay? You with me, Nigel?" I was pretty sure he hadn't seen the zucchini in the bag, which had rolled under Royal's desk, but I didn't want anybody who could place me in the office, when the cops started asking questions. So I gave Nigel a brief, but tastefully dramatized version of my long-standing grudge against his landlord.

"Don't worry, mate, anyone who thumps that piece of filth is okay with me. You have any idea what rent he charges me and my girl for one room and a shared lav? It's disgusting, I'm telling you, it's diabolical!"

We parted in the street, with a heartfelt handshake. As I had hoped, Nigel was thoroughly outraged on my behalf. I'd not only silenced a potentially hostile witness, I'd made a friend for life.

I ran to the phone booth at the top of the hill, jabbed out three nines on the dial, and told the police that the man who'd just robbed a bookmaker's in Hampstead High Street, armed with a suspicious bulge in a paper bag, was a certain Danny Royal, known criminal. I'd heard him planning it in the pub the night before. No, I wasn't willing to give my name, he'd kill me if he knew I'd grassed him up. Just get there quickly. They wouldn't recover the money – that was with his accomplice – but I was sure he wouldn't have ditched the weapon yet. His address? Yeah, as a matter of fact, I did know his address . . .

Toby Reynolds, ex-banker, ex-yuppie, one-time stick-up merchant, is currently serving three years in Ford Open Prison. It's true what they say: the rich never do hard time. Not even when they're not rich any more. He got away from the bookie's with five thousand quid: enough to keep a chap like him in comfort for, ooh, at least three months . . . if he hadn't blown a good thousand of it in one night's champagne-quaffing with his old pals from the City. At a wine bar right here in Hampstead. Right on his own doorstep.

And if he hadn't, when deeply in his cups, snatched a courgette (sorry, *zucchini*) from a passing waiter's tray and proceeded to point it around the room, shouting "Bang! Bang! Give us all the dosh!", while standing on a table. I said he wasn't very bright, didn't I?

I still think he might have got away with it if the frame-up had worked out better. It wasn't a great plan, but the cops were hot to nail Danny Royal, and would have found a way of stitching him up somehow.

But when they got to his office, they found him unconscious, covered in blood, and badly in need of emergency treatment. By the time he was fit to answer questions, he had more lawyers hanging off him than IV drips, and all the police had was an anonymous tip-off, a six-inch fruit, and a brown paper bag. Not much of a lunch, even, and as evidence it didn't amount to – well, to a hill of beans.

Royal must have known it was Nigel the barrow boy who injured him so thoroughly. Nigel who, disgusted by my tale of treachery, and by his own experiences with the King Rat, and figuring me (correctly) for the largely non-violent type, had decided to do us all a favour. He'd gone back up to the office as soon as I was out of sight, and given Danny a very, very deep massage.

Royal must know, but I don't think there's much he can do about it. Times are changing. Danny still has his friends, but

Nigel comes from a big, close West Indian family, well endowed with big, close brothers, uncles, and cousins. And an even bigger, closer grandmother. I think he's safe. As safe as any of us are these days.

I think I'm safe as well. Toby the yup may not be very clever, and he may not be my kind of people, but he knows about keeping his gob shut. And, given the incredibly stupid nature of the offence, the cops weren't exactly looking to round up a gang of criminal masterminds.

Toby will be out before long, and I'm going to try and get him a job. Maybe in one of the local boozers. After all, he's one us now, kind of.

I see Nigel in this pub or that, about three or four times a week. The first dozen or so occasions, he would give me a conspiratorial wink and send over a drink with his compliments. That got embarrassing after a time, so now, when our paths cross, I try to get *my* conspiratorial wink and complimentary pint in first.

Well, why not? Like I always say, Hampstead is a village. This is how people behave in villages.

THE ELEVENTH LABOUR

DAVID WISHART

So there I was, in the barber's chair, next to Flatworm Lentulus.

Pure accident; me, I don't go a bomb on Market Square barbering, not in the morning, anyway. You meet altogether the wrong sort of people. A morning shave in the Square is an old and hallowed tradition for broad-stripers en route to a hard day's politicking at the Senate House, and it gives the bastards the opportunity to knife a few backs off the record but *coram populo* without the consul shouting "order". Definitely not my bag, especially not on a full stomach. Still, sometimes it happens, usually as the result of what Perilla would call a concatenation of circumstances. In this case the concatenation involved decorators, a good walking day in June and an early meeting with my Market Square banker. It also seemingly now involved Flatworm Lentulus; you get these flies even in jars of the best ointment.

Lentulus is an old school pal of mine and not overburdened with brains, hence the nickname: match the guy against your average flatworm and as far as intelligence goes the smart money'd be on the one without the sandals. Not that it had held him back, mind: having nothing between your ears to stop the breeze blowing through ain't no handicap in Rome, not if your middle name's Cornelius and your family's been supplying the city with consuls since Brutus kicked out the Tarquins. Lentulus's elder brother had been suffect consul a few years back, and it was only a matter of time before Flatworm got his own Axemen to play with. Currently, he was big in the city judge's office up the hill.

He was big everywhere else, too. When he sat down next to me the barber's chair creaked like someone had lowered a marble block onto it. And it wasn't Gallic wickerwork, neither.

"Hey, Marcus," he said. "Now there's a lucky thing. How's the lad?"

I opened the other eye. "Lucky" wasn't a term I'd've used myself. The advantage of barber shops is that you can let your mind drift while the guy holding the razor does the work. If he knows his job – and I don't mean the scraping part – he'll take the hint and leave you in peace. The Flatworms of this world, however, are another matter. Tact was never Flatworm's strong suit: he could probably have spelled it, given help, but exercising it was another matter. And as far as observation was concerned, forget it on both counts.

The razor was a nick short of my Adam's apple. I waited until it was safe. "Hi, Flatworm," I said.

"Still sleuthing, are you?" He held up his chin while my barber's mate tied the bib round his neck and began rubbing in the oil.

"Yeah. On and off."

"That's good." He grinned as Oily Horace worked on his bristles. "Because I might just have something for you."

Oh, hell. One of the reasons for the banker's appointment was that Perilla had arranged an extended trip up to her Aunt Marcia's place in the Alban Hills, and we'd be leaving in less than a month. The last thing I needed was a case shoving its hoof in, because the lady would go spare. Especially with Flatworm involved. She'd never actually met the guy, mind, but she'd seen his library in the country villa we'd borrowed from him the year before, and she'd formed certain totally justified conclusions.

"Talk to the Watch," I said.

"I have. The buggers aren't interested." Flatworm shrugged, and Oily Horace tutted. "No crime, no investigation."

Uh-huh. That didn't sound a too-unreasonable attitude to me. The Watch were stretched as it was, and there wasn't too much love lost between the guys at the sharp end and the city judge's office. "What's happened, pal?" I said. "You lost a sock in the wash?"

"No. Not me. My next-door neighbour. Guy called Luscus."

"*Luscus* has lost a sock in the wash?"

He frowned. Sarcasm's wasted on Flatworm: you may as well try tickling a hippo. "No socks, Corvinus. Bugger was jumped on in his own garden yesterday evening and locked in a shed."

"Is that so, now?" Well, at least it wasn't a corpse. "And?"

"That's it. That's all there is."

Jupiter! Real earth-shaking stuff! No wonder the local Watch had told Flatworm to go and play with his marbles. "No burglary? Nothing stolen?"

"Not as far as Luscus knows. There was a statuette, one of these little garden things." Lentulus turned sideways as Oily Horace trimmed a sideburn. "The guy had taken it off its pedestal and left it lying. But that's the lot."

"Valuable?"

"Nah. Luscus picked it up a couple of years back in an auction of seconds. Heavy and crude as hell, and not worth nicking." He waited while the razor slid past his ear. "Come on, Marcus, boy. You owe me one. And Luscus grows the best apples in Rome. If I can help him nail the bastard who did it come September he'll give me a prime basketful."

I sighed. That's the way the city works: *do ut des, manus manum lavat*, scratch my back, I'll scratch yours. Still, after I'd seen my banker I didn't have anything else planned anyway. And good apples were good apples. "Split them fifty-fifty?" I said.

"Deal. Tell him I sent you."

Luscus's place was one of a line of big houses on the Pincian Road facing Lucullus Gardens. I knocked, and the door slave opened up.

"The master at home?" I said.

"Not yet, sir, but we expect him any time." The guy was wearing a sharp lemon-coloured tunic. He took a look at my dusty sandals and sniffed. "The mistress is in, though, if you'd care to see her."

"Yeah. That'd be great."

He stepped back to let me past. "Who shall I say is calling?"

"Name's Corvinus. Marcus Valerius Corvinus. I'm a friend of Cornelius Lentulus's."

That got me a bit of interest, at least: forget aristocrats, the bought help are the biggest snobs in Rome. "If you'd care to wait, sir," he said, "I'll see if she's receiving."

"Fine. Uh . . . by the way, what's the mistress's name, pal?"

"Allia, sir."

While I was waiting I inspected the lobby's decor. Nice; pricey, too: the goddess Plenty hoisting a cornucopia and scattering fruit, although she seemed to have a special offer currently on apples. A minute or so later, the guy came back and led me through the house into the garden.

Allia was sitting in a wickerwork chair under the shade of the portico. The lady was a stunner: twenty-five, max, and a dead ringer for the Plenty in the lobby. Minus the cornucopia, naturally.

She held out her hand. "Valerius Corvinus," she said. We shook; soft hand, strong grip. "I'm sorry, Publius isn't back yet. He has business in town."

"That's okay." I glanced past her into the garden itself. It was a fair size, and beyond the formally laid-out flower beds within the arms of the portico it seemed to be mostly fruit trees. Apples again. "Your neighbour Cornelius Lentulus sent me. I understand your husband had an, uh, unpleasant experience yesterday evening."

"That's right." Was that a flicker? And of what? Guilt? Amusement? I couldn't be sure. "Very odd, and quite inexplicable. Cornelius Lentulus did tell you, I hope, that nothing was stolen and no damage done?'

"Yeah. Although he did mention a statuette."

"Pomona. Yes. She wasn't taken, though, just dropped beside the wall."

"You think I could have a look round, maybe?"

"Of course. I'll show you myself." She got up. "Publius was rather shaken, but he wasn't hurt. Not at all. Still, at his time of life it was, as you say, not a pleasant experience."

We went out into the garden proper. Beyond the portico, it was surrounded by walls high enough to screen all but the tops of next door's trees. "Who're the neighbours?" I asked.

"Your friend Lentulus is on the right. The house on the left belongs to a man called Caesius."

"Uhuh." That would be the garden with the trees. And there had been a slight trace of hesitation in her voice that set my ears twitching. "So. What happened, exactly?"

We were in the orchard section now, and I could see the shed: a solid little lean-to against the left-hand wall. Pomona as well; she'd been put back on her pedestal in the centre. Flatworm had been right: whatever our garden-creeping pal had been about, as a motive pinching the goddess of apples was a non-starter. She wasn't even bronze or marble, and she had cross eyes into the bargain. Whatever Luscus had paid for her, even as a second, he'd been robbed.

"Exactly, I'm not sure," Allia said. "You'd have to ask Publius for the details. All I know is he arrived home early and went straight out into the garden as usual. Then—"

"Straight out?" Most guys coming home from a sticky day in the city unlimber the mantle and change into a fresh lounging-tunic before setting in for the evening. Me, I add half a jug of wine, but that's by the way.

"Yes." She smiled. "Corvinus, to my husband his garden is more important than I am. He spends most of his free time out here fiddling with the trees."

"Uh . . . 'fiddling'?"

"That's what I'd call it. We don't have any children, and Publius makes up for it by breeding a new strain of apples. Or trying to."

"Yeah?" The mind boggled. "How does he do that, then?"

"I think the technical terms are budding and grafting. What the difference between them is, if any, I'm not altogether sure. Again, you'd have to ask him." She led me over to one of the smaller trees; I'm no expert, but I'd've said it couldn't be any older than five years. "That's his favourite baby. A friend on the Syrian governor's staff sent him it, and it's the only one of its kind in Rome. Possibly west of Ephesus."

I could've been wrong, because both her voice and her

expression were serious as hell, but I had the distinct feeling that beneath her decorously lowered eyelashes the lady was laughing, and that somehow the joke was on me. I was fingering a white, bare patch at the base of the lowest branch when she glanced over her shoulder.

"There's Publius now," she said. "I'll leave him to carry on with the tour."

I turned round. She'd given me the hint when she'd mentioned his time of life, sure, but even so I'd expected someone just a bit younger. The guy coming towards us was sixty if he was a day. He didn't look too pleased to see me, either.

Allia went up to him and kissed him on the cheek. "This is Marcus Valerius Corvinus, dear," she said "Lentulus sent him."

The frown relaxed slightly and the heavy grey eyebrows lifted. Not altogether, though; all I got was a brief nod and a sour twist of the lips. "The chef wants a word about the dinner," he said to Allia. "You'd better see to it."

The lady never even blinked. "Yes, of course," she said. "Nice meeting you, Corvinus."

I watched her disappear into the house. Then I noticed that Publius Luscus was watching me watching her and glowering. I stopped, which seemed a good idea.

"So," he said. "You're a friend of Lentulus's?"

"Uh . . . yeah." I came away from the tree. "He sent me round to see if I could make any sense of what happened to you yesterday."

Luscus grunted. "Allia give you the details?"

"No. I've only just arrived. She was showing me the, uh, scene of the crime."

Another grunt. "Bastard must've been hiding in the shrubbery. First thing I knew there's a cloak over my head and I'm being bundled into the toolshed there." He nodded towards the lean-to. It wasn't padlocked, but there was a bolt on the door that looked pretty solid. "Yelled myself hoarse before these deaf buggers of slaves let me out."

"You any idea who could've done it?" I said.

The brows came down again. "No. He came from behind. He was big, though. And young." He glanced back towards the house where, presumably, Allia was discussing chickpea rissoles with the chef. "Arms like a bloody gorilla's."

"How did he get out?"

"Over Caesius's wall."

"You sure of that?" Then, when I got the sour look again, I added: "Sir?"

"Nothing wrong with my ears, son. Couple of minutes after he bolted me in I heard him thumping about on the roof. There's a wheelbarrow at the side there – " he nodded towards the wall of the lean-to; sure enough, it was propped front-down against the masonry "– and he must've used that to get up. Once he was that high getting over the wall'd be easy."

"There isn't a back gate?"

"Locked. I've had problems before with the local boys in the autumn scrumping the fruit. Not just boys, either. Now I keep it padlocked all the year round. I've one key, my gardener has the other. There isn't a third."

"Where is he at the moment?"

"Down in Ostia arranging for a cartload of lime dressing. The shipment was supposed to arrive yesterday, but it must've been late because he isn't back yet."

"Uhuh." Well, that was clear enough. Me, I felt sorry for the kids. If this old bugger got his hands on them I'd bet they wouldn't sit down for a month. "Why did the guy take the statuette?" Or rather, *didn't* he take the statuette; that aspect of things had been bugging me. He couldn't've carried it while he was climbing, sure, but if he'd really wanted the thing it would've been easy enough to lift it onto the shed roof and then drop it over the wall the other side.

"God knows. I only paid a couple of silver pieces for it, and I wouldn't've done that if it hadn't been a Pomona."

"You've no idea what he was doing here, then? None at all?"

He glanced towards the house again then turned back to me. "No," he said shortly. "Mark my words, though, Corvinus, if the bugger comes round here again, or if I find out who he is, I'll do worse to him than lock him up."

I was going to ask why he should bother to come back at all when I noticed the green glint in Luscus's eye. Combined with the look towards the house and his behaviour to his wife, that could only mean one thing, even if he hadn't put it into words, and the circumstantial details fitted like a glove. Luscus, evidently, suspected more than he was saying. Yeah, well; I'd seen the lady myself, and it was a tenable theory. Better than tenable. Also, it would explain how the guy had got into the garden in the first place. "Uh . . . you had a word with your neighbour yet? What's his name – Caesius? If the guy went over his wall then he might've seen something. Or one of his slaves might, anyway."

That got me a stare that was pure marble, and went on and on until I began to sweat.

"We don't talk," he said finally.

"Is that so, now?"

"That is so. I wouldn't give that bastard the time of day."

"You, uh, care to tell me why?"

"No. It's none of your business."

Me, I know when to back off: hard-line stichomythia gets to be pretty wearing on the nerves after a while. "Right. Right," I said. "Just asking."

"And I'm just answering."

Friendly bugger; especially since I was supposed to be helping him and he knew it. A little of Publius Luscus went a long way, and as far as I was concerned I'd had enough to last me to the Festival. I wondered how his wife stood it. "Fine," I said. "I won't take up any more of your valuable time."

Maybe that got through and he felt himself that he'd gone a bit over the top because the glare slowly turned into what could almost be called a smile. If you were prepared to make allowances and had an imagination the breadth of Mars Field, that was. However, the sarky old codger was trying his best and I gave him the benefit of the doubt. "It's very good of you to take an interest, Valerius Corvinus," he said. "Find the man for me and I won't prove ungrateful."

I thought of mentioning Flatworm's basket of apples, then decided against it. If he was that down on scrumpers it might be a bad move.

I left.

*   *   *

I didn't go far, though, just next door: Luscus might not talk to his neighbour, but I didn't see why the ban should extend to me. Besides, a word with Caesius – or his gardener, for preference – was the obvious next step.

"The master's occupied in his study," the door slave told me. "If you'd care to see the young mistress, however, she's in the summer-house."

"Fine by me, pal," I said. "Lead on."

We went through the lobby: Plenty with a cornucopia again, including the apples. A different model, this time with a more pronounced nose and a wider mouth, but all the same . . .

Interesting, right?

The garden was more or less identical, too. The trees that I'd seen the tops of over the wall were apples. Dozens of them. For two guys who didn't get on, it would appear that Luscus and Caesius had a lot in common.

Caesia – Caesius's daughter – was ensconced in a small summer-house set against the party wall with Luscus's property. I couldn't be sure, but I'd've bet that if I'd climbed onto its roof and looked over and down I'd've seen Luscus's toolshed directly below me. Interesting again.

She might not have been a patch on Allia, but she wasn't bad: younger, no more than eighteen, and radiant. That's not a word I use much, but it fitted. The girl's nose wouldn't't've looked out of place on a trireme, sure, and her mouth was wider than the Tiber's at Ostia. All the same, neither of these things mattered because the kid *glowed*. You could see her practically catch the sun like a ball and throw it back.

"Yes?" she said.

"Uh . . . Marcus Valerius Corvinus. I came to see your father."

"He's busy at the moment." I wouldn't't've believed the girl could blush, not in her state, but she did. The door slave bowed and moved out of earshot, but I noticed that he still hung around by the ornamental sundial. Chaperone duties, no doubt. "What was it about?"

"You hear what happened next door yesterday evening? The attack on old Luscus?"

The blush deepened. "No," she said. "Or not directly, anyway. Luscus and Father don't talk."

"So I understand." There was a folding stool in the corner of the summer-house. I pulled it up and sat on it. "You like to tell me why?"

"It's silly. They both breed apples. Caesius says his are the best, Father disagrees." She shrugged. "As I said: silly."

"Uhuh." At least the Goddess Plenty was explained: I'd've recognized that nose anywhere. And the mouth. "So you don't have any contact?"

"Oh, yes. Allia's very nice. I talk to Allia, when her husband's out. She's quite sensible."

"Right." Well, "sensible" was one word for it; personally, I'd've plumped for "normal". "I was just going to ask your father . . ."

I stopped, because she wasn't listening any more. Her eyes had shifted to a point behind me, and locked. I turned round.

A guy was hovering in the portico; a young guy, early twenties, thick-set, arms like a gorilla. He glowered at us, then took to kicking his heels by one of the pillars.

Things went: *click!*

Or most things, anyway. Details were still a problem, but that I could handle. I turned back to the girl.

"Your fiancé?" I said.

The blush was back in spades. "Yes. As of about an hour ago."

"Uhuh. What's his name?"

"Viridius. Gaius Viridius."

"Good at climbing, yes?"

She gave me a long, hard look: the little lady might only be a couple of years past the dedication-of-toys stage, but she was no fool. "Yes," she said finally, and her eyes never left my face. Now there was that same half-laughing sparkle to them that I'd've betted had been in Allia's, if I'd been able to see it under the lashes. "He is, actually. Very good."

That capped it. I stood up. I was smiling too, now. "You want to show me the tree, lady?" I said. "Just for my own satisfaction."

She led me to it without a word. It was an apple, of course.

Whether the splinting under the bandage constituted a budding or a graft I didn't know, and it didn't really matter.

"Why didn't you just ask Allia direct?" I said. "She'd've got it for you without all this fuss. And she knows he took it." *Knows*, hell: she'd practically told me what had happened herself. Shown me, certainly. I'd bet a dozen of Caecuban to a frayed bootlace that the two little schemers had planned the thing between them.

Caesia just looked at me. "But that wouldn't've been good enough," she said. "Gaius had to do it on his own. That was Father's condition. And he didn't do any damage. Or any harm. He was very careful."

"What about Pomona?"

"Well, he had to provide *some* reason for being in Luscus's garden, didn't he, poor lamb? She was all he could think of at the time, and he did set her down very gently."

I had no answer to that. Instead, I looked over at Gaius. The kid was still glowering at me from next to the pillar, waiting for me to finish my business and go. Well, that was fair enough; no doubt he and Caesius had thrashed out the marriage settlement in the latter's study already, and I doubted if, now the bride-price had been paid, the devious old bastard would've been too hard on the youngster. Besides, three's a crowd, and I'd already overstayed my welcome.

"He'll find out, of course," I said. "Luscus, I mean. When he looks at the tree."

"Oh, Father won't care. He has what he wanted, and Luscus can do what he likes. It was only the one twig, after all, and as I say the whole thing's silly." She glanced at me under lowered lashes: Plenty without the cornucopia, Part Two, and the nose and the mouth didn't matter a bit. "Will you tell him directly? About Gaius?"

I grinned and shook my head. "No. I think, lady, that I'll just go home and forget the whole boiling."

Flatworm's half basket was no loss. I never had been all that fond of apples, anyway.

(*Author's note*: The eleventh labour of Hercules was to steal the golden apples of the Sun from the Garden of the Hesperides for

King Eurystheus of Tiryns. On that particular occasion the guardian dragon was killed and Hercules had Atlas do the job while he stood in for him – literally – as holder-up of the sky; but a myth is a myth.)

THE STOLEN
WHITE ELEPHANT

MARK TWAIN

The following curious history was related to me by a chance
railway acquaintance. He was a gentleman more than seventy
years of age, and his thoroughly good and gentle face and
earnest and sincere manner imprinted the unmistakable stamp
of truth upon every statement which fell from his lips. He said:

You know in what reverence the royal white elephant of Siam
is held by the people of that country. You know it is sacred to
kings, only kings may possess it, and that it is indeed in a
measure even superior to kings, since it receives not merely
honour but worship. Very well; five years ago, when the
troubles concerning the frontier line arose between Great
Britain and Siam, it was presently manifest that Siam had been
in the wrong. Therefore every reparation was quickly made,
and the British representative stated that he was satisfied and
the past should be forgotten. This greatly relieved the King of
Siam, and partly as a token of gratitude, but partly also,
perhaps, to wipe out any little remaining vestige of unpleasant-
ness which England might feel toward him, he wished to send
the Queen a present – the sole sure way of propitiating an
enemy, according to Oriental ideas. This present ought not only
to be a royal one, but transcendently royal. Wherefore, what

offering could be so meet as that of a white elephant? My position in the Indian Civil Service was such that I was deemed peculiarly worthy of the honour of conveying the present to Her Majesty. A ship was fitted out for me and my servants and the officers and attendants of the elephant, and in due time I arrived in New York harbour and placed my royal charge in admirable quarters in Jersey City. It was necessary to remain awhile in order to recruit the animal's health before resuming the voyage.

All went well during a fortnight – then my calamities began. The white elephant was stolen! I was called up at dead of night and informed of this fearful misfortune. For some moments I was beside myself with terror and anxiety; I was helpless. Then I grew calmer and collected my faculties. I soon saw my course – for indeed there was but the one course for an intelligent man to pursue. Late as it was, I flew to New York and got a policeman to conduct me to the headquarters of the detective force. Fortunately I arrived in time, though the chief of the force, the celebrated Inspector Blunt, was just on the point of leaving for his home. He was a man of middle size and compact frame, and when he was thinking deeply he had a way of knitting his brows and tapping his forehead reflectively with his finger, which impressed you at once with the conviction that you stood in the presence of a person of no common order. The very sight of him gave me confidence and made me hopeful. I stated my errand. It did not flurry him in the least; it had no more visible effect upon his iron self-possession than if I had told him somebody had stolen my dog. He motioned me to a seat, and said calmly:

"Allow me to think a moment, please."

So saying, he sat down at his office table and leaned his head upon his hand. Several clerks were at work at the other end of the room; the scratching of their pens was all the sound I heard during the next six or seven minutes. Meantime the Inspector sat there buried in thought. Finally he raised his head, and there was that in the firm lines of his face which showed me that his brain had done its work and his plan was made. Said he – and his voice was low and impressive:

"This is no ordinary case. Every step must be warily taken; each step must be made sure before the next is ventured. And secrecy must be observed – secrecy profound and absolute. Speak to no one about the matter, not even the reporters. I will take care of *them*; I will see that they get only what it may suit my ends to let them know." He touched a bell; a youth appeared. "Alaric, tell the reporters to remain for the present." The boy retired. "Now let us proceed to business – and systematically. Nothing can be accomplished in this trade of mine without strict and minute method."

He took a pen and some paper. "Now – name of the elephant?"

"Hassan Ben Ali Ben Selim Abdallah Mohammed Moisé Alhammal Jamsetjejeebhoy Dhuleep Sultan Ebu Bhudpoor."

"Very well. Given name?"

"Jumbo."

"Very well. Place of birth?"

"The capital city of Siam."

"Parents living?"

"No – dead."

"Had they any other issue besides this one?"

"None – he was an only child."

"Very well. These matters are sufficient under that head. Now please describe the elephant, and leave out no particular, however insignificant – that is, insignificant from *your* point of view. To men in my profession there *are* no insignificant particulars; they do not exist."

I described; he wrote. When I was done, he said:

"Now listen. If I have made any mistakes, correct me."

He read as follows:

Height, 19 feet; length, from apex of forehead to insertion of tail, 26 feet; length of trunk, 16 feet; length of tail, 6 feet; total length, including trunk and tail, 48 feet; length of tusks, 9½ feet; ears in keeping with these dimensions; footprint resembles the mark when one up-ends a barrel in the snow; colour of the elephant, a dull white; has a hole the size of a plate in each ear for the insertion of jewellery, and possesses the habit in a remarkable degree of squirting water upon spectators and of maltreating with his trunk not only such persons as he is acquainted with, but even

entire strangers; limps slightly with his right hind leg, and
has a small scar in his left armpit caused by a former boil;
had on, when stolen, a castle containing seats for fifteen
persons, and a gold-cloth saddle-blanket the size of an
ordinary carpet.

There were no mistakes. The Inspector touched the bell,
handed the description to Alaric, and said:

"Have fifty thousand copies of this printed at once and
mailed to every detective office and pawnbroker's shop on
the continent." Alaric retired. "There – so far, so good. Next,
I must have a photograph of the property."

I gave him one. He examined it critically, and said:

"It must do, since we can do no better; but he has his trunk
curled up and tucked into his mouth. That is unfortunate, and is
calculated to mislead, for of course he does not usually have it in
that position." He touched his bell.

"Alaric, have fifty thousand copies of this photograph made,
the first thing in the morning, and mail them with the descriptive circulars."

Alaric retired to execute his orders. The Inspector said:

"It will be necessary to offer a reward, of course. Now as to
the amount?"

"What sum would you suggest?"

"To *begin* with, I should say – well, twenty-five thousand
dollars. It is an intricate and difficult business; there are a
thousand avenues of escape and opportunities of concealment.
These thieves have friends and pals everywhere—"

"Bless me, do you know who they are?"

The wary face, practised in concealing the thoughts and
feelings within, gave me no token, nor yet the replying words,
so quietly uttered:

"Never mind about that. I may, and I may not. We generally
gather a pretty shrewd inkling of who our man is by the manner
of his work and the size of the game he goes after. We are not
dealing with a pickpocket or a hall thief, now, make up your
mind to that. This property was not 'lifted' by a novice. But, as
I was saying, considering the amount of travel which will have
to be done, and the diligence with which the thieves will cover

up their traces as they move along, twenty-five thousand may be too small a sum to offer, yet I think it worth-while to start with that."

So we determined upon that figure, as a beginning. Then this man, whom nothing escaped which could by any possibility be made to serve as a clue, said:

"There are cases in detective history to show that criminals have been detected through peculiarities in their appetites. Now, what does this elephant eat, and how much?"

"Well, as to *what* he eats – he will eat *anything*. He will eat a man, he will eat a Bible – he will eat anything *between* a man and a Bible."

"Good – very good indeed, but too general. Details are necessary – details are the only valuable things in our trade. Very well – as to men. At one meal – or, if you prefer, during one day – how many men will he eat, if fresh?"

"He would not care whether they were fresh or not; at a single meal he would eat five ordinary men."

"Very good; five men; we will put that down. What nationalities would he prefer?"

"He is indifferent about nationalities. He prefers acquaintances, but is not prejudiced against strangers."

"Very good. Now as to Bibles. How many Bibles would he eat at a meal?"

"He would eat an entire edition."

"It is hardly succinct enough. Do you mean the ordinary octavo, or the family illustrated?"

"I think he would be indifferent to illustrations; that is, I think he would not value illustrations above simple letter-press."

"No, you do not get my idea. I refer to bulk. The ordinary octavo Bible weighs about two pounds and a half while the great quarto with the illustrations weighs ten or twelve. How many Doré Bibles would he eat at a meal?"

"If you knew this elephant, you would not ask. He would take what they had."

"Well, put it in dollars and cents, then. We must get at it somehow. The Doré costs a hundred dollars a copy, Russia leather, bevelled."

"He would require about fifty thousand dollars' worth – say an edition of five hundred copies."

"Now, that is more exact. I will put that down. Very well; he likes men and Bibles; so far, so good. What else will he eat? I want particulars."

"He will leave Bibles to eat bricks, he will leave bricks to eat bottles, he will leave bottles to eat clothing, he will leave clothing to eat cats, he will leave cats to eat oysters, he will leave oysters to eat ham, he will leave ham to eat sugar, he will leave sugar to eat pie, he will leave pie to eat potatoes, he will leave potatoes to eat bran, he will leave bran to eat hay, he will leave hay to eat oats, he will leave oats to eat rice, for he was mainly raised on it. There is nothing whatever that he will not eat but European butter, and he would eat that if he could taste it."

"Very good. General quantity at a meal – say about—"

"Well, anywhere from a quarter to half a ton."

"And he drinks—"

"Everything that is fluid. Milk, water, whisky, molasses, castor oil, camphene, carbolic acid – it is no use to go into particulars; whatever fluid occurs to you set it down. He will drink anything that is fluid, except European coffee."

"Very good. As to quantity?"

"Put it down five to fifteen barrels – his thirst varies; his other appetites do not."

"These things are unusual. They ought to furnish quite good clues toward tracing him."

He touched the bell.

"Alaric, summon Captain Burns."

Burns appeared. Inspector Blunt unfolded the whole matter to him, detail by detail. Then he said in the clear, decisive tones of a man whose plans are clearly defined in his head, and who is accustomed to command:

"Captain Burns, detail Detective Jones, Davis, Halsey, Bates and Hackett to shadow the elephant."

"Yes, sir."

"Detail Detectives Moses, Dakin, Murphy, Rogers, Tupper, Higgins and Bartholomew to shadow the thieves."

"Yes, sir."

"Place a strong guard – a guard of thirty picked men, with a relief of thirty – over the place from whence the elephant was stolen, to keep strict watch there night and day, and allow none to approach – except reporters – without written authority from me."

"Yes, sir."

"Place detectives in plain clothes in the railway, steamship, and ferry depots, and upon all roadways leading out of Jersey City, with orders to search all suspicious persons."

"Yes, sir."

"Furnish all these men with photograph and accompanying description of the elephant, and instruct them to search all trains and outgoing ferry-boats and other vessels."

"Yes, sir."

"If the elephant should be found, let him be seized, and the information forwarded to me by telegraph."

"Yes, sir."

"Let me be informed at once if any clues should be found – footprints of the animal, or anything of that kind."

"Yes, sir."

"Get an order commanding the harbour police to patrol the frontages vigilantly."

"Yes, sir."

"Dispatch detectives in plain clothes over all the railways, north as far as Canada, west as far as Ohio, south as far as Washington."

"Yes, sir."

"Place experts in all the telegraph offices to listen to all messages; and let them require that all cipher dispatches be interpreted to them."

"Yes, sir."

"Let all these things be done with the utmost secrecy – mind, the most impenetrable secrecy."

"Yes, sir."

"Report to me promptly at the usual hour."

"Yes, sir."

"Go!"

"Yes, sir."

He was gone.

Inspector Blunt was silent and thoughtful a moment, while the fire in his eye cooled down and faded out. Then he turned to me and said in a placid voice:

"I am not given to boasting, it is not my habit; but – we shall find the elephant."

I shook him warmly by the hand and thanked him; and I *felt* my thanks, too. The more I had seen of the man the more I liked him, and the more I admired and marvelled over the mysterious wonders of his profession. Then we parted for the night, and I went home with a far happier heart than I had carried with me to his office.

Next morning it was all in the newspapers, in the minutest detail. It even had additions – consisting of Detective This, Detective That, and Detective The Other's "Theory" as to how the robbery was done, who the robbers were, and whither they had flown with their booty. There were eleven of these theories, and they covered all the possibilities; and this single fact shows what independent thinkers detectives are. No two theories were alike, or even much resembled each other, save in one striking particular, and in that one all the eleven theories were absolutely agreed. That was, that although the rear of the building was torn out and the only door remained locked, the elephant had not been removed through the rent, but by some other (un-discovered) outlet. All agreed that the robbers had made that rent only to mislead the detectives. That never would have occurred to me or to any other layman, perhaps, but it had not deceived the detectives for a moment. Thus, what I had supposed was the only thing that had no mystery about it was in fact the very thing I had gone furthest astray in. The eleven theories all named the supposed robbers, but no two named the same robbers; the total number of suspected persons was thirty-seven. The various newspaper accounts all closed with the most important opinion of all – that of Chief-Inspector Blunt. A portion of this statement read as follows:

The chief knows who the two principals are, namely, "Brick" Duffy and "Red" McFadden. Ten days before the robbery was achieved he was already aware that it was to be attempted, and had quietly proceeded to shadow these two noted villains; but unfortunately on the night in question their track was lost, and before it could be found again the bird was flown – that is, the elephant.

Duffy and McFadden are the boldest scoundrels in the profession; the chief has reason for believing that they are the men who stole the stove out of the detective headquarters on a bitter night last winter – in consequence of which the chief and every detective were in the hands of the physicians before morning, some with frozen feet, others with frozen fingers, ears, and other members.

When I read the first half of that I was more astonished than ever at the wonderful sagacity of this strange man. He not only saw everything in the present with a clear eye, but even the future could not be hidden from him. I was soon at his office, and said I could not help wishing he had had those men arrested, and so prevented the trouble, and loss; but his reply was simple and unanswerable:

"It is not our province to prevent crime, but to punish it. We cannot punish it until it is committed."

I remarked that the secrecy with which we had begun had been marred by the newspapers; not only all our facts but all our plans and purposes had been revealed; even all the suspected persons had been named; these would doubtless disguise themselves now, or go into hiding.

"Let them. They will find that when I am ready for them, my hand will descend upon them, in their secret places, as unerringly as the hand of fate. As to the newspapers, we *must* keep in with them. Fame, reputation, constant public mention – these are the detective's bread and butter. He must publish his facts, else he will be supposed to have none; he must publish his theory, for nothing is so strange or striking as a detective's theory, or brings him so much wondering respect; we must publish our plans, for these the journals insist upon having, and we could not deny them without offending. We must constantly show the public what we are doing, or they will believe we are doing nothing. It is much pleasanter to have a newspaper say: 'Inspector Blunt's ingenious and extraordinary theory is as follows,' than to have it say some harsh thing, or, worse still, some sarcastic one."

"I see the force of what you say. But I noticed that in one part of your remarks in the papers this morning, you refused to reveal your opinion upon a certain minor point."

"Yes, we always do that; it has a good effect. Besides, I had not formed any opinion on that point, anyway."

I deposited a considerable sum of money with the Inspector, to meet current expenses, and sat down to wait for news. We were expecting the telegrams to begin to arrive at any moment now. Meantime I re-read the newspapers and also our descriptive circular, and observed that our $25,000 reward seemed to be offered only to detectives. I said I thought it ought to be offered to anybody who would catch the elephant. The Inspector said:

"It is the detectives who will find the elephant, hence the reward will go to the right place. If other people found the animal, it would only be by watching the detectives and taking advantage of clues and indications stolen from them, and that would entitle the detectives to the reward, after all. The proper office of a reward is to stimulate the men who deliver up their time and their trained sagacities to this sort of work, and not to confer benefits upon chance citizens who stumble upon a capture without having earned the benefits by their own merits and labours."

This was reasonable enough, certainly. Now the telegraphic machine in the corner began to click, and the following dispatch was the result:

> Flower Station, N.Y.: 7.30 am
> Have got a clue. Found a succession of deep tracks across a farm near here. Followed them two miles east without result; think elephant went west. Shall now shadow him in that direction.
>
> Darley, Detective

"Darley's one of the best men on the force," said the Inspector. "We shall hear from him again before long."

Telegram No. 2 came.

Barker's, N.J.: 7.40 am

Just arrived. Glass factory broken open here during night
and eight hundred bottles taken. Only water in large
quantity near here is five miles distant. Shall strike for
there. Elephant will be thirsty. Bottles were empty.

Baker, Detective.

"That promises well, too," said the Inspector. "I told you the
creature's appetites would not be bad clues."
Telegram No. 3.

Taylorville, L.I.: 8.15 am

A haystack near here disappeared during night. Probably
eaten. Have got a clue, and am off.

Hubbard, Detective.

"How he does move around!" said the Inspector. "I knew we
had a difficult job on hand, but we shall catch him yet."

Flower Station, N.Y.: 9 am

Shadowed the tracks three miles westward. Large, deep,
and ragged. Have just met a farmer who says they are not
elephant tracks. Says they are holes where he dug up
saplings for shade-trees when ground was frozen last
winter. Give me orders how to proceed.

Darley, Detective.

"Aha! A confederate of the thieves! The thing grows warm,"
said the Inspector.
He dictated the following telegram to Darley:

Arrest the man and force him to name his pals. Continue
to follow the tracks – to the Pacific, if necessary.

Chief Blunt.

Next telegram:

Coney Point, Pa.: 8.45 am

Gas office broken open here during night and three

months' unpaid gas bills taken. Have got a clue and am away.

                                                    Murphy, Detective.

"Heavens!" said the Inspector, "would he eat gas bills?"

"Through ignorance – yes; but they cannot support life. At least, unassisted."

Now came this exciting telegram:

                                            Ironville, N.Y.: 9.30 am

Just arrived. This village in consternation. Elephant passed through here at five this morning. Some say he went east, some say west, some north, some south – but all say they did not wait to notice particularly. He killed a horse; have secured a piece of it for a clue. Killed it with his trunk; from style of blow, think he struck it left-handed. From position in which horse lies, think elephant travelled northward along line of Berkley railway. Has four and a half hours' start; but I move on his track at once.

                                                    Hawes, Detective.

I uttered exclamations of joy. The Inspector was as self-contained as a graven image. He calmly touched his bell.

"Alaric, send Captain Burns here."

Burns appeared.

"How many men are ready for instant orders?"

"Ninety-six, sir."

"Send them north at once. Let them concentrate along the line of the Berkley road north of Ironville."

"Yes, sir."

"Let them conduct their movements with the utmost secrecy. As fast as others are at liberty, hold them for orders."

"Yes, sir."

"Go!"

"Yes, sir."

Presently came another telegram.

                                        Sage Corners, N.Y.: 10.30

Just arrived. Elephant passed through here at 8.15. All

escaped from the town but a policeman. Apparently elephant did not strike at policeman, but at the lamp-post. Got both. I have secured a portion of the policeman as clue.

                                        Stumm, Detective.

"So the elephant has turned westward," said the Inspector. "However, he will not escape, for my men are scattered all over that region."

The next telegram said:

                                        Glover's, 11.15

Just arrived. Village deserted, except sick and aged. Elephant passed through three-quarters of an hour ago. The anti-temperance mass meeting was in session; he put his trunk in at a window and washed it out with water from cistern. Some swallowed it – since dead; several drowned. Detectives Cross and O'Shaughnessy were passing through town, but going south – so missed elephant. Whole region for many miles around in terror – people flying from their homes. Wherever they turn they meet elephant, and many are killed.

                                        Brant, Detective.

I could have shed tears, this havoc so distressed me. But the Inspector only said:

"You see – we are closing in on him. He feels our presence; he has turned eastward again."

Yet further troublous news was in store for us. The telegraph brought this:

                                        Hoganport, 12.19

Just arrived. Elephant passed through half an hour ago, creating wildest fright and excitement. Elephant raged around streets; two plumbers going by, killed one – other escaped. Regret general.

                                        O'Flaherty, Detective.

"Now he is right in the midst of my men," said the Inspector. "Nothing can save him."

A succession of telegrams came from detectives who were scattered through New Jersey and Pennsylvania, and who were following clues consisting of ravaged barns, factories, and Sunday-school libraries, with high hopes – hopes amounting to certainties, indeed. The Inspector said:

"I wish I could communicate with them and order them north, but that is impossible. A detective only visits a telegraph office to send his report; then he is off again, and you don't know where to put your hand on him."

Now came this dispatch:

> Bridgeport, Ct.: 12.15
> Barnum offers rate of $4,000 a year for exclusive privilege of using elephant as travelling advertising medium from now till detectives find him. Wants to paste circus-posters on him. Desires immediate answer.
>
> Boggs, Detective.

"That is perfectly absurd!" I exclaimed.

"Of course it is," said the Inspector. "Evidently Mr Barnum, who thinks he is so sharp, does not know me – but I know him."

Then he dictated this answer to the dispatch:

> Mr Barnum's offer declined. Make it $7,000 or nothing.
> Chief Blunt.

"There. We shall not have to wait long for an answer, Mr Barnum is not at home; he is in the telegraph office – it is his way when he has business on hand. Inside of three—"

> Done. – P. T. Barnum.

So interrupted the clicking telegraphic instrument. Before I could make a comment upon this extraordinary episode, the following dispatch carried my thoughts into another and very distressing channel:

Bolivia, N.Y.: 12.50

Elephant arrived here from the south and passed through toward the forest at 11.50, dispersing a funeral on the way, and diminishing the mourners by two. Citizens fired some small cannon-balls into him, and then fled. Detective Burke and I arrived ten minutes later, from the north, but mistook some excavations for footprints, and so lost a good deal of time; but at last we struck the right trail and followed it to the woods. We then got down on our hands and knees and continued to keep a sharp eye on the track, and so shadowed it into the brush. Burke was in advance. Unfortunately the animal had stopped to rest; therefore, Burke having his head down, intent upon the track, butted up against the elephant's hind legs before he was aware of his vicinity. Burke instantly rose to his feet, seized the tail, and exclaimed joyfully: "I claim the re—" but got no further, for a single blow of the huge trunk laid the brave fellow's fragments low in death. I fled rearward, and the elephant turned and shadowed me to the edge of the wood, making tremendous speed, and I should inevitably have been lost, but that the remains of the funeral providentially intervened again, and diverted his attention. I have just learned that nothing of that funeral is now left; but this is no loss, for there is an abundance of material for another. Meantime the elephant has disappeared again.

Mulrooney, Detective.

We heard no news except from the diligent and confident detectives scattered about New Jersey, Pennsylvania, Delaware and Virginia – who were all following fresh and encouraging clues – until shortly after 2 pm, when this telegram came:

Baxter Centre, 2.15

Elephant been here, plastered over with circus-bills, and broke up a revival, striking down and damaging many who were on the point of entering upon a better life. Citizens penned him up, and established a guard. When Detective Brown and I arrived, some time after, we entered enclosure and proceeded to identify elephant by photograph and description. All marks tallied exactly except one, which we could not see – the boil-scar under armpit. To make sure, Brown crept under to look, and was immediately brained – that is, head crushed and destroyed, though nothing issued from débris. All fled; so did elephant, striking right and left with much effect. Has escaped, but left bold blood-track from cannon-wounds. Rediscovery certain. He broke southward through a dense forest.

Brent, Detective.

That was the last telegram. At nightfall a fog shut down which was so dense that objects but three feet away could not be discerned. This lasted all night. The ferry boats and even the omnibuses had to stop running.

Next morning the papers were as full of detective theories as before; they had all our tragic facts in detail also, and a great many more which they had received from their telegraphic correspondents. Column after column was occupied, a third of its way down, with glaring head-lines, which it made my heart sick to read. Their general tone was like this:

THE WHITE ELEPHANT AT LARGE! HE MOVES UPON HIS FATAL MARCH! WHOLE VILLAGES DESERTED BY THEIR FRIGHT-STRICKEN OCCUPANTS! PALE TERROR GOES BEFORE HIM, DEATH AND DEVASTATION FOLLOW AFTER! AFTER THESE, THE DETECTIVES. BARNS DESTROYED, FACTORIES GUTTED, HARVESTS DEVOURED, PUBLIC ASSEMBLAGES DISPERSED, ACCOMPANIED BY SCENES OF CARNAGE IMPOSSIBLE TO DESCRIBE! THEORIES OF THIRTY-FOUR OF THE MOST DISTINGUISHED DETECTIVES ON THE FORCE! THEORY OF CHIEF BLUNT!

"There!" said Inspector Blunt, almost betrayed into excitement, "this is magnificent! This is the greatest windfall that any detective organization ever had. The fame of it will travel to the ends of the earth, and endure to the end of time, and my name with it."

But there was no joy for me. I felt as if I had committed all those red crimes, and that the elephant was only my irresponsible agent. And how the list had grown! In one place he had "interfered with an election and killed five repeaters". He had followed this act with the destruction of two poor fellows, named O'Donohue and McFlannigan, who had "found a refuge in the home of the oppressed of all lands only the day before, and were in the act of exercising for the first time the noble right of American citizens at the polls, when stricken down by the relentless hand of the Scourge of Siam". In another, he had "found a crazy sensation-preacher preparing his next season's heroic attacks on the dance, the theatre, and other things which can't strike back, and had stepped on him". And in still another place he had "killed a lightning-rod agent". And so the list went on, growing redder and redder, and more and more heart-breaking. Sixty persons had been killed, and two hundred and forty wounded. All the accounts bore just testimony to the activity and devotion of the detectives, and all closed with the remark that "three hundred thousand citizens and four detectives saw the dread creature, and two of the latter he destroyed".

I dreaded to hear the telegraphic instrument begin to click again. By-and-by the messages began to pour in, but I was happily disappointed in their nature. It was soon apparent that all trace of the elephant was lost. The fog had enabled him to search out a good hiding-place unobserved. Telegrams from the most absurdly distant points reported that a dim vast mass had been glimpsed there through the fog at such and such an hour, and was "undoubtedly the elephant". This dim vast mass had been glimpsed in New Haven, in New Jersey, in Pennsylvania, in interior New York, in Brooklyn, and even in the city of New York itself! But in all cases the dim vast mass had vanished quickly and left no trace. Every detective of the large force scattered over this huge extent of country sent his hourly report and each and every one of them had a clue, and was shadowing something, and was hot upon the heels of it.

But the day passed without other result.

The next day the same.

The next just the same.

The newspaper reports began to grow monotonous with facts that amounted to nothing, clues which led to nothing, and theories which had nearly exhausted the elements which surprise and delight and dazzle.

By advice of the Inspector, I doubled the reward.

Four more dull days followed. Then came a bitter blow to the poor, hard-working detectives – the journalists declined to print their theories, and coldly said, "Give us a rest."

Two weeks after the elephant's disappearance I raised the reward to $75,000 by the Inspector's advice. It was a great sum, but I felt that I would rather sacrifice my whole private fortune than lose my credit with my Government. Now that the detectives were in adversity, the newspapers turned upon them, and began to fling the most stinging sarcasms at them. This gave the minstrels an idea, and they dressed themselves as detectives and hunted the elephant on the stage in the most extravagant way. The caricaturists made pictures of detectives scanning the country with spy-glasses, while the elephant, at their backs, stole apples out of their pockets. And they made all sorts of ridiculous pictures of the detective badge – you have seen that badge printed in gold on the back of detective novels, no doubt – it is a wide-staring eye, with the legend, "WE NEVER SLEEP". When detectives called for a drink, the would-be facetious barkeeper resurrected an obsolete form of expression, and said, "Will you have an eye-opener?" All the air was thick with sarcasms.

But there was one man who moved calm, untouched, unaffected through it all. It was that heart of oak, the Chief Inspector. His brave eye never drooped, his serene confidence never wavered. He always said—

"Let them rail on; he laughs best who laughs last."

My admiration for the man grew into a species of worship. I was at his side always. His office had become an unpleasant place to me, and now became daily more and more so. Yet if he could endure it I meant to do so also; at least, as long as I could. So I came regularly, and stayed – the only outsider who seemed to be capable of it. Everybody wondered how I could; and often it seemed to me that I must desert, but at such times I looked into that calm and apparently unconscious face, and held my ground.

About three weeks after the elephant's disappearance I was

about to say, one morning, that I should *have* to strike my colours and retire, when the great detective arrested the thought by proposing one more superb and masterly move.

This was to compromise with the robbers. The fertility of this man's invention exceeded anything I have ever seen, and I have had a wide intercourse with the world's finest minds. He said he was confident he could compromise for $100,000 and recover the elephant. I said I believed I could scrape the amount together; but what would become of the poor detectives who had worked so faithfully? He said:

"In compromises they always get half."

This removed my only objection. So the Inspector wrote two notes, in this form:

Dear Madam: Your husband can make a large sum of money (and be entirely protected from the law) by making an immediate appointment with me.

Chief Blunt.

He sent one of these by his confidential messenger to the "reputed wife" of Brick Duffy, and the other to the "reputed wife" of Red McFadden.

Within the hour these offensive answers came:

Ye Owld fool: brick McDuffys bin ded 2 yere.

Bridget Mahoney.

Chief Bat: Red McFadden is hung and in heving 18 month. Any Ass but a detective knose that.

Mary O'Hooligan.

"I had long suspected these facts," said the Inspector; "this testimony proves the unerring accuracy of my instinct."

The moment one resource failed him he was ready with another. He immediately wrote an advertisement for the morning papers, and I kept a copy of it—

A. – xwblv. 242 N. Tjnd – fz328wmlg. Ozpo, –; 2 m.! ogw. Mum.

He said that if the thief was alive this would bring him to the usual rendezvous. He further explained that the usual rendezvous was a place where all business affairs between detectives and criminals were conducted. This meeting would take place at twelve the next night.

We could do nothing till then, and I lost no time in getting out of the office, and was grateful indeed for the privilege.

At eleven the next night I brought $100,000 in banknotes and put them into the chief's hands, and shortly afterward he took his leave, with the brave old undimmed confidence in his eye. An almost intolerable hour dragged to a close: then I heard his welcome tread, and rose gasping and tottered to meet him. How his fine eyes flamed with triumph! He said—

"We've compromised! The jokers will sing a different tune tomorrow! Follow me!"

He took a lighted candle and strode down into the vast vaulted basement where sixty detectives always slept, and where a score were now playing cards to while away the time. I followed close after him. He walked swiftly down to the dim remote end of the place, and just as I succumbed to the pangs of suffocation and was swooning away he stumbled and fell over the outlying members of a mighty object, and I heard him exclaim as he went down:

"Our noble profession is vindicated. Here is your elephant!"

I was carried to the office above and restored with carbolic acid. The whole detective force swarmed in, and such another season of triumphant rejoicing ensued as I had never witnessed before. The reporters were called, baskets of champagne were opened, toasts were drunk, the handshakings and congratulations were continuous and enthusiastic. Naturally the chief was the hero of the hour, and his happiness was so complete and had been so patiently and worthily and bravely won that it made me happy to see it, though I stood there a homeless beggar, my priceless charge dead, and my position in my country's service lost to me through what would always seem my fatally careless execution of a great trust. Many an eloquent eye testified its deep admiration for the chief, and many a detective's voice murmured, "Look at him – just the king of the profession – only give him a clue, it's all he wants, and there ain't anything hid that he can't find." The dividing of the

$50,000 made great pleasure; when it was finished the chief made a little speech while he put his share in his pocket, in which he said, "Enjoy it, boys, for you've earned it; and more than that – you've earned for the detective profession undying fame."

A telegram arrived, which read:

> Monroe, Mich.: 10 pm
> First time I've struck a telegraph office in over three weeks. Have followed those footprints, horseback, through the woods, a thousand miles to here, and they get stronger and bigger and fresher every day. Don't worry – inside of another week I'll have the elephant. This is dead sure.
>
> Darley, Detective.

The chief ordered three cheers for "Darley, one of the finest minds on the force," and then commanded that he be telegraphed to come home and receive his share of the reward.

So ended that marvellous episode of the stolen elephant. The newspapers were pleasant with praises once more, the next day, with one contemptible exception. This sheet said:

> Great is the detective! He may be a little slow in finding a little thing like a mislaid elephant – he may hunt him all day and sleep with his rotting carcase all night for three weeks, but he will find him at last – if he can get the man who mislaid him to show him the place!

Poor Hassan was lost to me for ever. The cannon-shots had wounded him fatally. He had crept to that unfriendly place in the fog; and there, surrounded by his enemies and in constant danger of detection, he had wasted away with hunger and suffering till death gave him peace.

The compromise cost me $100,000; my detective expenses were $42,000 more; I never applied for a place again under my Government; I am a ruined man and a wanderer in the earth – but my admiration for that man, whom I believe to be the greatest detective the world has ever produced, remains undimmed to this day, and will so remain unto the end.

BAMPOT CENTRAL

CHRISTOPHER BROOKMYRE

There was a six-foot iguana swaying purposefully into Parlabane's path as he walked down High Street. It had spotted him a few yards back and instinctively homed in on its prey, recognising that look in his eye and reacting without mercy. Some kind of sixth sense told cats which person in any given room most detested or was allergic to their species, so that they knew precisely whose lap to leap upon. A similar prescience had been visited upon spoilt Oxbridge undergrad hoorays in stupid costumes dispensing fliers for their dismal plays and revues. It was for this reason that a phenomenon such as the Fringe could never have thrived in Glasgow. In Edinburgh, most locals were stoically, if wearily, tolerant of such impositions; though in the west, dressing up as a giant lizard and deliberately getting in people's way would constitute reckless endangerment of the self.

"There's no getting past me, I'm afraid!" the iguana chirped brightly in a stagy, let's-be-friends, happy-cheery, go on, please stab me, you know it'll make you feel better tone of voice. "Not without taking one of these!" it continued, thrusting a handful of leaflets at him.

Parlabane had put on the wrong T-shirt that morning, forgetting that his errands would unavoidably take him through places residents knew well to avoid during the Festival (or to

give it its full name in the native tongue, the Fucking Festival).
He was wearing a plain white one, which was nice enough but
vitally lacked the legend "FUCK OFF – I LIVE HERE", as
was borne on several others at home. His August wardrobe, he
liked to call it.

"Keeble Kollege Krazees present: Whoops Checkov!" the
leaflet announced. "An hilarious pastiche of Russian Natural-
ism! Find out what Constantine really got up to with that
seagull!" Followed by the standard litany of made-up newspaper quotes.

"Come along tonight," solicited the iguana. "It might even
cheer you up a bit!"

Parlabane swallowed back a multitude of ripostes and summoned up further admirable self-control by keeping his hands
and feet to himself also. He breathed in, accepted a flyer and
walked on. Remain calm, he told himself. He was over the worst
of it now, having passed the Fringe Society office. North Bridge
was in sight.

It was his friend's son's birthday the next week, and the gift
Parlabane wanted to get him was only on sale in a small toy shop
on the High Street. If it had also been on sale at the end of a
tunnel of shite and broken glass, he'd have had to think long and
hard about which store to visit during this time of year; as it was
he'd had no such choice. The gift was a poseable male doll in a
miniature Celtic kilt. The intended recipient lived in Los
Angeles and would have no inkling of there being any significance to the costume, knowing only from Parlabane's attached
note that the doll was to be named Paranoid Tim and must be
subjected to every kind of abuse David's little mind could
dream up.

He looked down at the pavement, carpeted as it was in further
leaflet-litter, mostly advertising stand-up gigs by the A-list
London safe-comedy collective, the ones who had each been
bland enough to get their own Friday night series on Channel
Four. He wondered whether anyone doing stand-up these days
wasn't "a comedy genius", and daydreamed yet again about Bill
Hicks riding back into town on a black stallion and driving these
lager-ad auditions into the Forth to drown.

Maybe he should have just sent the kid a card and a cheque,

he thought, eyeing a nearby mime with murderous intent. But what the hell, he'd bought it now, and whatever he sent wouldn't spare him the next ordeal he had to face that day: a trip to the Post Office.

He picked up pace going down towards Princes Street, as the unpredictable crosswinds made North Bridge an inadvisable pitch for leafleting. The route was therefore comparatively free of obstacles, save for a gaggle of squawking Italian tourists staging some kind of sit-in protest at a bus-stop. Parlabane approached the St James shopping centre with a striding, let's-get-this-over-with gait, all the while attempting to take his mind off the coming horrors with another calming fantasy involving the three female flatmates from *Friends*. This time he was disembowelling them with a broadsword, the chainsaw decapitations having grown a little tired.

It was too simplistic to lay the blame at the feet of the Tories' Care in the Community policy. There had to be something deeper, to do with tides, leylines and lunar cycles, that explained why every large Post Office functioned as an urban bampot magnet, to which the deranged couldn't help but gravitate. From the merely befuddled to the malevolently sociopathic, they journeyed entranced each day, as though hypnotically drawn by the digitised queuing system. Parlabane remembered those Les Dawson ads a few years back: "It's amazing what you can pick up at the Post Office." Yeah. Like rabies. Or maybe anthrax.

He bought a self-assembly packing box at the stationery counter, then after ten minutes of being humiliated by an inert piece of cardboard, returned to purchase a roll of Sellotape and wrapped it noisily around the whole arrangement until Paranoid Tim was securely imprisoned. It looked bugger-all like a box, but the wee plastic bastard wasn't going to fall out, which was the main thing.

Then he joined the queue.

There were three English crusties immediately ahead of him, each boasting an ecologically diverse range of flora and fauna in their tangled dreads. They were accompanied by the statutory skinny dog on a string, and were sharing round a jumbo plastic bottle of Tesco own-brand cider and a damp-looking dowt. The dog wasn't offered a drag, but it looked like it had smoked a few in its time, and probably preferred untipped anyway.

Behind him there was a heavily pregnant young woman, looking tired and fanning herself with the brown envelope she was planning to post. And behind her were a couple of Morningside Ladies muttering about whichever Fringe show had been singled out for moral opprobrium (and a resultant box office boost) this year by Conservative Councillor Moira Knox. He'd got off lightly, in other words, and the queue wasn't even very long. The ordeal was almost over.

Except that at the Post Office, it's never over till it's over.

He caught a glimpse of a figure passing by on his right-hand side, skipping the queue and making directly for the counter. Parlabane was following the golden rule of PO survival – never look anyone in the face – but was nonetheless able to make out that the person was wearing a balaclava. His heart sank. It was the number one fashion accessory of the top-level numpties, especially in the height of summer, and this one looked hell-bent on maximum disruption.

Then from a few feet behind him he heard an explosion, and turned around to see fragments of ceiling tiles rain down upon the betweeded Morningsiders. Behind them was a man in a ski-mask holding a shotgun.

"RIGHT, NAE CUNT MOVE – THIS IS A ROBBERY!"

Parlabane turned again and saw that the balaclavaed figure at the counter was also holding a weapon.

Screams erupted as the people milling around the greetings cards and stationery section at the back animatedly ignored the gunman's entreaty and began pouring out through the swing-doors.

"I SAYS NAE CUNT MOVE!" he insisted, discharging another shot into the tiles, this time covering himself in polystyrene and plaster-dust. He wiped at his eyes with one hand and waved the shotgun with the other, running to the door to finally cut off the stream of evacuees.

"Lock the fuckin' door, Tommy, for fuck's sake," ordered the balaclava at the front counter.

"I'm daein' it, I'm daein' it," he screeched back. "An' dinnae use ma fuckin' name, Jyzer, ya fuckin' tube, ye."

"Well, whit ye cawin' me mine for, ya stupit cunt?"

Jesus Christ, thought Parlabane, watching the gunman on door-duty usher his captives back into the body of the kirk. It was true after all: the spirit of the Fringe affects the whole city. The worthy ethos of amateurism and improvisation had extended to armed robbery. Must have been Open Mic Night down at the local Nutters & Cutters, and first prize was lead role in a new performance-art version of *Dog Day Afternoon*.

From the voices he could tell they were young; but even if they had remained silent it still wouldn't have stretched his journalistic interpretative powers to deduce that they were pitifully inexperienced.

He rewound the action in his head, doing his Billy McNeil replay summary. Three seconds in, Mistake Number One: Discharging a shotgun into the ceiling to get everyone's attention, like simply the sight of the thing wasn't going to raise any eyebrows. There were several hundred people outside in the shopping mall, and a large police station two hundred yards away at the top of Leith walk.

Four seconds in, Mistake Number Two: Charging into the shop and leaving umpteen customers behind you, out of sight, with a clear exit out the front door, through which they rush in a hysterical panic.

Seven seconds in, Mistake Number Three: Blowing another hole in the roof, then turning your back on the remaining customers while you chase after extra hostages that you won't need.

Eight seconds in, Mistake Number Four: Telling everybody your first names.

Ten seconds in, Mistake Number Five: Finding yourself with at least ten customers plus staff as prisoners. One or two is usually plenty.

In a moment of inspiration, gunman Tommy began rearranging the queuing cordons and ordered everyone behind the rope.

"Stay there an' dinnae move, right?"

The customers were uniformly terrified, with the exception of Parlabane, who was just in far too bad a mood to entertain any emotions other than fury and hatred. Decadence is often born of boredom. Nihilism even more often born of a walk through the Old Town in mid-August.

"Wouldn't you prefer us to sit down?" he offered, figuring these guys were going to need all the help and advice they could get.

Tommy thought about it. He looked like he'd need to do his working on a separate sheet of paper, but he got there eventually.

"Eh, aye."

Jyzer was busy making Mistake Number Six, pointing his weapon at a young teller and ordering her colleagues to stay in their seats, where they could each press their panic buttons just in case the two resounding shotgun blasts hadn't been heard first-hand at Gayfield Square polis emporium.

"Jesus Christ," Parlabane sighed, the words slipping out before he could stop himself.

"Shut it, you," Tommy barked. "You got a problem, pal?"

Yes he did. He had a problem with the fact that the chances of these two eejits shooting someone through incompetence-generated panic were increasing by the second. He considered amelioration the wisest policy right then.

"Eh, no problem," he said. "But I was wondering . . . I mean, it's just an idea really, but maybe you should move the staff over here beside us, you know, so there's just one group of hostages to keep an eye on, and your china can get on with posting his airmail or whatever."

"Christ, mate," said one of the crusties, "why don't you offer them our bloody wallets as well while you're at it? I mean whose side are you on?"

"Fuckin' shut it, you," snapped Tommy. "An' it's no airmail, it's a fuckin' robbery, right?"

Parlabane held his hands up and shrugged. Whatever.

Jyzer, who by superiority of one synapse was the brains of the outfit, had cottoned on to Parlabane's thinking and gestured the other tellers to file out from behind the counter. Then he ordered Tommy to collect everybody's wallets, proving that he was broad-minded and open to suggestions from any of the hostages.

"Sheer fuckin' genius," Parlabane muttered to the crusty, who wouldn't meet his gaze.

Tommy backed away, eyes flitting back and forth between

the growing pile of wallets and purses and the front doors, outside which a crowd had gathered.

"Oh, I just knew something like this was going to happen," muttered one of the Morningsiders to her companion. "I just knew it."

"Me too, Morag, me too."

Parlabane had suffered enough.

"Well, it's a pity neither of you fucking clairvoyants thought to tip anyone off, then, isn't it?" he observed.

"Now, son, there's no need for that."

He looked away. This was the quintessence of British "respectability". There were two brainless arseholes holding them prisoner with shotguns, but they could still get upset about the "language" you used.

Jyzer's initially quiet dialogue with the remaining teller was beginning to gain in volume. Parlabane hadn't caught what Jyzer was asking for, but he wished to hell the stupid lassie would hurry up and give him it, especially as there were now two uniformed plods peering in the doors and hustling the onlookers back. He looked at his watch, figuring the Balaclava Brothers had a few more minutes before an armed response unit showed up to raise the stakes.

"Look, I ken ye're lyin', awright? We've had information. We ken they're in there. Insurance bonds, fae Scottish Widows. They come through here the last Monday o'every month. So fuckin' get them or I'll fuckin' blow ye away."

The girl had tears in her eyes and was struggling to keep her voice steady. "I swear to God, I've never heard of any . . . insurance bonds coming through here. In fact I don't think I've ever heard of insurance bonds full stop."

"Look, don't gie's it. Last Monday o' every month. Scottish Widows. It should say it on the parcel."

"But this isn't a sorting office. The only parcels coming through here are the ones folk are sending. They go straight in the slots over there, or in the basket through-by. Please, I'm not lying. You can come through and look."

"I fuckin' will an' aw," he said, walking around to the counter's access door. "An' if ye're lyin' I'll fuckin' mark ye, hen. I'll no be a minute, Tommy," he assured.

"Insurance bonds?" one of the tellers asked of a colleague.

"Naw, I've never heard of them either."

"Wouldnae come through here anyway, would they?" queried another.

"D'you think they've got the right place?"

"Fuckin' shut it, yous," Tommy ordered again. "We've had information. We ken whit we're daein' so sit nice an' it'll aw be by wi' soon, right?"

Parlabane sighed again. Insurance bonds. Jesus Christ almighty. It just got better and better.

"What's an insurance bond, Tommy?" he asked calmly.

"I tell't yous aw tae shut it, I ken whit insurance bonds are, right?"

Parlabane made a zipping gesture across his mouth. There was a suspicion growing inside his head. It had germinated early on in the proceedings, but the last few moments had poured on the Baby Bio and it was seriously starting to sprout.

They sat in silence, apart from the occasional yelp from the crusties' skinny dog. Tommy's eyes looked wide and jumpy through the holes in his ski mask.

"Fuck!" came a furious, low growl from the back office. "Fuckin' Jesus fuckin' *fuck*!"

The girl stumbled nervously out to join the hostage party, followed by Jyzer, whose woolly mask could not conceal that he was little at peace with himself.

"So, d'ye get them?" Tommy asked.

Jyzer took a slow breath to calm his rage. It didn't quite make it.

"Naw, I never fuckin' got them, ya stupit cunt. Fuckin' Scottish Widows must've changed the delivery day or somethin'."

"Aye, awright, dinnae take it oot on me."

"Well, stop askin' fuckin' stupit questions."

"But what are we gaunny dae?"

"Shut up, I'm tryin' tae think."

Parlabane looked to the front of the Post Office. One of the uniforms was pointing in and talking to someone out of sight down the mall. Three men in matching kevlar semmits filed into place in front of the sports shop opposite, taking up crouching positions and raising automatic rifles.

Parlabane swallowed. Not everyone was going to be home in time for tea, he feared.

"Giros!" Jyzer announced. He turned to the teller who had most recently joined the ranks of the illegally detained. "Giro money. Pensions nawrat. Hand it ower."

"I don't think that should be your number one priority right now," Parlabane said, pointing at the front window.

"Who asked . . . aw, fuck." Jyzer took a step back, like that extra two feet would put him out of a bullet's projectile range.

"This is the police," announced a hailer-enhanced screech. Whatever it said next was lost as Jyzer finally showed a spark of dynamism.

"Right," he stated. "Staun up, aw yous. An' line up across the shoap, facin' away fae the windae. That's it."

They got to their feet unsteadily, most of them turning their heads to cast an eye upon the assembly outside. Jyzer and Tommy stepped behind their human shield, out of the police marksmen's sights.

"Terrific," muttered one of the crusties. "Now we're the filling in a gun sandwich."

"Noo, go an' get us aw the cash in the shop," he commanded the teller, handing her the sports bag that already contained their wallet harvest.

"We have all exits covered," resumed the loud hailer. "Please put down your weapons, release your hostages and come out with your hands on your heads."

"Come on," said Parlabane tiredly. "Do what the man asked. He said please, after all."

"You think we're fuckin' stupit, don't ye?" Jyzer observed, accurately. "Smart-arsed cunt," he added, hitting a second bullseye.

"Well, maybe you'll prove me wrong by explaining how you were ever planning to get out of here, with or without your, ahem, Insurance Bonds."

"Stop windin' him up, mate," warned the crusty who had earlier proffered the highly constructive wallet suggestion.

"I'm not winding him up. I'm just curious to know the secrets of how true professionals work."

"Want me tae slap the cunt, Jyzer?" Tommy offered.

"Just keep the heid and keep your hauns on the gun, Tommy. Dinnae let him distract ye. He's up to somethin', this cunt."

A telephone started ringing on the other side of the counter as the teller returned with the sports bag, presumably now containing cash and very possibly a dye-charge, seeing as Jyzer had made Mistake Number Fuckknows by leaving her alone to fill the thing.

"Get that," Jyzer commanded. "No you," he added, as Tommy made to reach for the receiver.

"It's for you," the teller said. "The police."

He gestured to her to rejoin the human shield, taking hold of the bag as she passed, then picked up the phone. Tommy stayed in place, sweeping the gun back and forth along his line of vision like it was a searchlight. The crusties' skinny dog ambled lazily over to him, yawned once and began half-heartedly shagging his leg.

"Get tae fuck, ya wee shite," he hissed, kicking out at it to shake the thing off, his eye relaying between his prisoners and his foot. "Fuckin' dirty wee bastard."

"TOMMY!" Jyzer barked, placing a hand over the mouthpiece. "Will ye fuckin' keep it doon – I'm on the phone here."

"Aye, awright. Fuck's sake," whined Tommy, hurt.

Jyzer shook his head and took his hand off the blue plastic. "Sorry, what were ye sayin'?" he resumed. "Naw, naw. You listen. Fuckin' just shut it an' listen, ya polis cunt."

The Morningside contingent tutted in stereo either side of Parlabane.

"Before we even have this conversation, I want to be lookin' oot that front windae an' seein' *nae* polis, right. Nane. Get them away fae the front o' the shop then phone us back." He slammed down the handset with an obvious satisfaction. Parlabane suspected the sense of accomplishment would be short-lived, but was admittedly impressed at this first sign of Jyzer having any idea what he was doing. In fact, he had noted with some surprise that neither of the pair had shown much sign of panic at the arrival of the ARU, and started to wonder whether their grossly conspicuous entrance had been less of an obvious blunder than he had first assumed.

Jesus, these heid-the-baws couldn't have a *plan*, could they?

He looked back over his shoulder, Jyzer and Tommy peering between the arrayed hostages. The marksmen got to their feet and moved out of sight left and right, as if exiting a stage. Parlabane figured it a safe bet they'd be returning for the fifth act.

The phone rang again.

"Right. Very good. Well done. Noo here's what we want. Naw, naw, shut it. We aw ken what *you* want: you want the hostages oot an' us in the cells so's ye can boot fuck oot us. Well, the bad news is you cannae have baith, right? So there's gaunny have to be a wee compromise. You can have maist o' the hostages in exchange for a helicopter. We want it on the roof o' the St James Centre in hauf an 'oor. We'll be takin' wan hostage wi' us, an' we'll tell the pilot where we're gaun wance we're on board." He slammed the phone down again.

"A helicopter?" Parlabane asked. "What, has Fife no' got an extradition treaty?"

"Fuckin' shut it."

"Another rapier-like comeback."

"Right," Jyzer declared, suddenly pointing his shotgun at the pregnant woman. "Step forward missus, ye're comin' wi us."

"No her, Jyzer," Tommy dissented. "She's dead fat. She'll be slow."

"She's no fat, she's fuckin' pregnant, ya n' arse. The polis'll no mess aboot if we've got a gun tae a pregnant burd's heid."

The pregnant woman began to whimper, tears running from terrified eyes. She put a hand out and grabbed Parlabane's shoulder to steady herself.

"Not a good idea, guys," he stated.

The phone began ringing again.

"I thought I tell't you tae shut it," Jyzer said, thrusting the gun into Parlabane's face.

"Look at her," he demanded, staring into Jyzer's eyes. "She's ready to burst. Do you want her goin' into labour during your dramatic getaway?"

Jyzer looked at the woman, sweating, tearful, and imposingly up the stick.

"Know somethin'?" he declared. "You're absolutely right. We'll take you instead."

Parlabane, who was firmly of the belief that no good deed ever goes unpunished, had been expecting this. He shrugged, put his parcel down and took a step forward, trying not to dwell on the potential indignity of surviving several professional attempts on his life only to be plugged by some shambolic half-wit down the Post Office.

Bugger it. Just as long as getting killed there didn't mean you went to Post Office Hell.

Jyzer picked up the phone again while Tommy gestured Parlabane to walk ahead of him through to the area behind the counters. The skinny dog gave another yawn as they passed, then trotted over to Jyzer and began humping his shin, its pink tongue lolling out of the right-hand side of its mouth.

"Naw, naw. We'll let the last hostage go wance we've arrived at. AYIAH! Get tae fuck ya clatty wee cunt . . . naw, no you, officer. Dug was tryin' tae shag me leg."

Jyzer eyed the crusty who was holding the other end of the string. "Heh Swampy, that thing touches me again an' I splatter its baws aw ower this flair, awright? Naw, no you officer. Aye that's right, *aw* the hostages. Once we're up an' away, we cannae shoot them, right? So they're aw yours – but no' until we're up an' away. An' we're no comin' up until the chopper's there. If we come up the stairs an' there's fuck-all, it's gaunny be a fuckin' bloodbath, right? Cause ye'll no have gie'd us any choices – we'll have to shoot oor way oot. Noo, next time this phone rings it better be tae say wur transport's arrived."

He put the phone down again.

"Are we gettin' a helicopter, Jyzer?" Tommy asked.

"Don't be a fuckin' eejit, Tommy. They're just stringin' us alang, same as we're stringin' them alang. C'mon."

They backed into the passage leading to behind the counters, Tommy keeping a gun on Parlabane, Jyzer still training his on the hostages.

"Nane o' yous move," he called out, stopping at the door that led into the storeroom at the rear of the counters. "We'll be watchin'. Stay where yous are. You might no' see us, but we'll still see you. Dinnae try anythin'. Just cause ye cannae see us doesnae mean we're no there."

"I'm sure they bought that," Parlabane said, nodding, as they retreated into the storeroom. "I don't think it would have crossed their minds at all that you might not be watching them. I mean, if you'd overstated your case it might have raised suspicions, but . . ."

"Fuckin' shut it," grunted Jyzer, nicking back and popping his head round the door to check his prisoners weren't making a swift but orderly exit.

"More Wildean badinage. Do you mind if I write some of these comebacks down?"

"You'll no' sound so smart talkin' through a burst nose, smart cunt, so I'd fuckin' wrap it if I was you."

"And if you burst my nose you'll be leaving a nice fresh trail of blood along your escape route; that's if you fuckin' clowns have got an escape route."

"We've got mair ay a plan than *you* think, smart cunt."

"Course you have. You're fuckin' professionals. Tell me again about these insurance bonds . . ."

Jyzer back-handed Parlabane across the jaw, which was very much what he'd been hoping for. Unfortunately the blow came on the wrong side, so he had to execute a largely unconvincing 180-degree stumble before getting to his intended effect, which was to fall down heavily against the door so that it slammed loudly with his back propped hard against it.

Despite Parlabane's abysmally obvious pirouette, it still took Jyzer a few moments to suss the potential problem, by which time the sound of breaking glass was filling the air as the police broke into the front shop and began ushering the hostages out.

"Fuckin' cunt. Fuckin' cunt."

Jyzer kicked viciously at Parlabane until eventually he rolled clear, then threw the door open to see his prisoners fleeing and the armed cops kneeling down to take aim. He slammed it shut again and pushed a table up against it, then backed into the room, indicating to Parlabane to crawl over against the wall to his right. Jyzer knelt down a few feet away, the gun pointing halfway between his prisoner and the door, his eyes shuttling between both targets.

"We've still got a hostage in here," he shouted. "Any o' yous cunts tries this door and we'll do 'im, right? We still want that fuckin' helicopter."

"OK, OK, everybody stay calm," appealed a voice from the other side of the door. "Everybody just calm down. I'm pulling my marksmen back to outside the shop, so don't panic and do something we'll all regret."

"I wouldnae regret shootin' you, ya cunt," Jyzer hissed at Parlabane, who just smiled.

"Sorry, Jyzer, but in case you've no' worked it out, the *last* thing you can do is shoot me – I'm your only hostage. Soon as I'm out of the equation, it's you versus the bullets. That's unless you professionals can take out a team of trained marksmen with your stove-pipes there."

Frustration was writ large in Jyzer's eyes. He clearly wished he could blow Parlabane away, or at the very least, finally silence him with a telling oneliner. He settled for:

"Fuckin' shut it."

Then he called out to the cops. "We're aw calm in here. Yous keep calm an' aw. An' get on wi' gettin' that helicopter."

Tommy was hectically hunting through drawers and cupboards, having tried the handle on the only other door in the room.

"I cannae find the keys, Jyzer," he gasped in a loud whisper.

"Well they've got tae be here somewhere. Keep lookin'."

"Couldn't possibly be on the person of one of your erstwhile hostages?" Parlabane suggested.

"Aw fuck," Tommy sighed.

"Keep at it, Tommy, there'll be another set somewhere. Dinnae listen tae that cunt."

"What were you wanting from the stationery cupboard, anyway?" Parlabane asked. "Checking there's no, eh, insurance bonds mixed in wi' the dug-licence application forms?"

"Would ye fuckin' shut it aboot the bonds. They were meant tae be here. Scottish Widows changed the delivery. They're worth thousands. Nae ID needed. Good as money."

"That's right, they're transgotiable," Tommy contributed.

"Shut it, Tommy, that's no the word. Keep lookin'. An' as for you, bigmouth, that's no' any stationery cupboard. Behind that door's the thing that's gaunny make you eat every wan o' your smart-cunt words."

"What, proof that Madonna's got talent?"

"Naw. That door leads tae the underground railway. Belongs tae the Post Office, for sendin' stuff back and forward. Runs fae here doon tae the main sortin' depot at Brunswick Road, which is where we've got a motor waitin'. They'll still be coverin' the exits up here while we're poppin' up haufway doon Leith Walk. And wance we're there, you'll have outlived your usefulness, 'lived' bein' the main word. Aye, ye're no so smart, noo, are ye?"

Parlabane shook his head, squatting on the floor against the wall.

"Underground railway?" he asked, grinning.

"Aye."

"I've got two words for you, Jyzer: insurance bonds."

"An' I've got two words for you: fuckin' shut it. Tommy, have ye fun' thae keys yet?"

"Sorry Jyzer. I don't think there's a spare set."

"Fuck it," Jyzer said, getting to his feet. "You watch him, Tommy." Jyzer walked over to the locked door and pointed his shotgun at the metal handle.

"No, don't do that!" Parlabane shouted, too late.

Jyzer pulled his trigger and blasted the handle, then reeled away from the still-locked door, bent double and groaning.

"AAAAYAAA FUCKIN' BASTARD!" he screamed, falling to the floor, blood appearing from the dozens of tiny wounds where the pellets had ricocheted off the solid metal and back into his thighs, hands, wrists, abdomen and groin.

"STAY OOT!" Tommy shouted to the cops behind the door. "STAY OOT. The hostage is awright. Just a wee accident in here. Just everybody keep steady, right?"

"Let's hear the hostage," called the cop. "Let's hear his voice."

Tommy, looking increasingly like the least steady person on earth, waved the gun at Parlabane and nodded, prompting him to reply.

"I'm here," Parlabane shouted.

"You OK, sir?"

"Do you really want me to answer that?"

"I mean, are you hurt?"

"No. But Jyzer here just learned a valuable lesson about the magic of the movies."

"What?"

"That's enough," Tommy interrupted, scuttling over to check on his writhing companion. "What's the score wi' that helicopter?" he called.

"I think an air ambulance might be more appropriate," Parlabane said.

"Fuckin' shut it," Tommy hissed. It was the only part of Jyzer's role he had been so far able to assimilate.

"It's over, Tommy," Parlabane said quietly. "Your pal's in a bad way, there's polis everywhere, and I'm afraid you're three hundred miles from the nearest underground postal railway, which is in London."

"It's no'. There's wan here. We've had information."

"Is everybody OK in there?" asked the policeman.

"STAY OOT!" Tommy warned again, his voice starting to tremble. "The situation's no' changed. Stay oot."

Jyzer continued to moan in the corner, convulsed also by the occasional cough.

"There's no such things as insurance bonds, Tommy," Parlabane told him.

"Shut it. There is."

"Where did you get this 'information'?"

"That's ma business."

"Did you pay for it? Is someone on a percentage?"

"Naw. Aye. The second wan."

"Never done anything like this before, have you?"

Jyzer moaned again, eyes closed against the pain.

Tommy shook his head. He was starting to look scared, like he needed his Mammy to take him home.

"Somebody put you up to it? Somebody force you?"

"Naw," he said defensively. "We were offered this. Hand-picked. He gied us the information, an' we'd tae gie him forty percent o' the cally efterwards."

"You been inside before? Recently?"

"Aye. Oot six weeks. Baith ay us."

"And I take it you weren't inside for armed robbery."

He shook his head again.

Parlabane nodded. He reached into his pocket and pulled out his compact little mobile phone.

"Whit ye daein'? Put that doon."

"Just let me call the cops outside, OK? Save us shoutin' through the wall the whole time."

"Aye awright."

He dialled the number for Gayfield Square, explained the situation and asked to be patched through to the main man on-site.

"Are you sure you're all right, sir?" the cop in charge asked. "What's your name? Do you need us to get a message to someone?"

"I'm fine. My name's Jack Parlabane. Yes, *that* Jack Parlabane, and spare me the might-have-knowns. I didn't *try* to get myself into this, it just happened. Now, Tommy here's not quite ready to end this, I don't think. But I was wondering whether you might want to scale down the ARU involvement out there. I've got a feeling you'll be needing them elsewhere fairly imminently."

"Too late," the cop informed him. "Somebody hit the Royal Bank at the west end of George Street about fifteen minutes ago while we were scratching our arses back here. By the time any of our lot got there it was all in the past tense. We've been had."

"You're not the only ones."

"What was that?" Tommy asked.

"Bank robbery, Tommy," he told him. "A proper one. Carried out less than a mile from here while the police Armed Response Unit were holding their dicks outside a Post Office. Now who do you think could have been behind that? Same guy gave you 'the information', maybe?"

"But . . . but . . . we . . ."

"You were right about being hand-picked, Tommy. And you can both take some satisfaction from the fact that you carried out the plan exactly as intended. Unfortunately, you were intended to fuck up. What were the instructions? Grab the mysterious insurance bonds, create a hostage situation, keep the polis occupied, then escape via the magical underground railway? And were you given a specific date and time, perhaps?"

There was confusion in Tommy's eyes, but on the whole resignation was starting to replace defiance. Jyzer gave a last mournful splutter and passed out.

"Don't suppose you want to score a few points with the boys in blue by telling them who set you up so they can get on to his tail?"

"Mair than ma life's worth."

"Fair enough. But it's still over, Tommy. Jyzer needs medical attention. The wounds might be superficial, but then again they might not. Come on. Put the gun down."

Tommy looked across at the unconscious Jyzer surrounded by bloodstains on the beige carpet, then at the locked door, then back at his hostage.

"Ach, fuck it," he rasped angrily, knuckles whitening as he gripped the gun tighter.

Parlabane took an involuntary breath, his eyes locked on Tommy's.

"The cunt's name was McKay," he said with a sigh. "Erchie McKay. Met him inside. He got oot last month, same as us." Tommy put the shotgun down on the floor and slid it across to Parlabane. "Just make sure they catch the bastart."

At eight-thirty that evening, the nightly performance of *Whoops Checkov* was abandoned after a number of powerful stink-bombs were thrown through the door of the auditorium by an unidentified male. It was, the unidentified male admitted to the woman driving his getaway car, childish and puerile, but then so is much of the Fringe.